BAD BLOOD

"Whoever murdered your brother," Hanson mused, "was destroying records."

"Why? You can't bury science. You can't burn it. You can't kill it. Someone else will eventually observe the same phenomenon and the trouble starts over again. Scott and Amanda were scientists, for God's sake!"

"So what? Dr. Tremain, your brother and his friends were on to something, doing something, learning something that someone didn't approve of. And I think they were killed because of it."

ACCLAIM FOR *RAISING ABEL*

"Brilliant, riveting...a thought-provoking and enlightening novel."
—*Tampa Tribune*

"A fascinating tale."
—*Winston-Salem Journal*

...AND FOR *DARK INHERITANCE*

"A splendid page-turner...a remarkable achievement."
—*Baton Rouge Advocate*

more...

RAISING
ABEL

RAISING
ABEL

W. MICHAEL GEAR AND
KATHLEEN O'NEAL GEAR

WARNER BOOKS

An AOL Time Warner Company

WARNER BOOKS EDITION

Warner Books, Inc.,
1271 Avenue of the Americas
New York, NY 10020

Visit our Web site at www.twbookmark.com

 An AOL Time Warner Company

Printed in the United States of America

Originally published in hardcover by Warner Books

First Paperback Printing: June 2002

10 9 8 7 6 5 4 3 2 1

TO
JENNIFER AND KEN ROYCE—
SOUL MATES
AND
SPECIAL FRIENDS.

ACKNOWLEDGMENTS

We would like to thank Dale and Linda Lovin for their help and input. After years in the Bureau they were invaluable when it came to providing information on the emotional and technical implications of an FBI field investigation.

We have relied on the numerous works of our colleagues in the field of physical anthropology. In particular, the works of Olga Soffer, Chris Stringer, Milford Wolpoff, Erik Trinkaus, Yoel Rak, Ofer Bar-Yosef, Fred H. Smith, Rebecca Caan, Mark Stoneking, and many others. To these professionals, we say thank you for your hard work in the struggle to unravel the legacy of our prehistory.

We would like to acknowledge Katherine Cook for her hard work on the manuscript. At Warner Books, Betsy Mitchell and Frances Jalet-Miller provided thoughtful and cogent suggestions to improve the book. We really appreciate the job Deanna M. Hoak did on the copyedit. It is a pleasure to work with such talent. We sincerely appreciate the support our publisher, Jamie Raab, has given to our anthropological novels. And of course, we are eternally grateful to Anne Zafian, Norman Krause, and the field force. Without the salespeople and the hard working reps, these books would never make it to the retailers' shelves. Thank you all.

Finally, Dr. Diane L. France of France Casting, Fort Collins, Colorado; and facial reconstruction expert, Betty Pat Gatliff, of Skullpture, Norman, Oklahoma, must be commended for their help and enthusiasm in truly *Raising Abel* and for their creative expertise in crafting Umber in *Dark Inheritance*.

PROLOGUE

Yevgeny Tubor had no interest in altering the course of human history on that cold and cloudless mountain morning. Had he been asked, he would most assuredly have told the inquisitor that he had no wish to challenge either Allah's will or authority. A devout Muslim, he prayed five times a day, read the Qur'an, and followed the Prophet's teachings as a modest and unassuming man should. He always sought to obey his elders and fulfill his duty to his tribe, clan, and lineage. He did his best to provide for his family, worked hard, and loved his wife and children.

It was in pursuit of those goals that he did what he did that fateful morning. He had little concern that the Christians considered the year—1999—to be the turning of a millennium. To him, it wasn't the masculine finale of an exhausted age, but yet another day illuminated by a shining sun under a crystalline blue sky. Yevgeny didn't believe in the Christian calendar. His years were those of the Prophet.

Yevgeny wore rugged felt-lined boots, a warm goatskin coat, and a thick felt hat. Even in midsummer, here at the broken margins of the glacier, the temperature barely hovered above freezing, especially this close to the ice. The footing was treacherous. He had to pick his way over tumbled and cracked gray stone, grit-filled brown ice, and slick surfaces where meltwater refroze into a glazed sheet. A man could break a leg, be pinned by shifting rock, or worse, slip into one of the black fissures that led down to Shaitan knew where. Fall into one of those, and a man wouldn't be found for years, if ever.

The reason that Yevgeny and others from his village climbed up to the toe of the mighty glacier was as mercenary as any: money. Four years previously, a team of scientists from Europe and America had come to this remote place high in Tajikistan. From where he stood, Yevgeny could look eastward to the mountain divide that marked the spot where the boundaries of his country joined those of Kyrgyzstan and China.

The scientists had hired Akhbar, Yevgeny's maternal uncle, and his sons to guide them to this place. They had used their wiry little mountain ponies to pack the scientists' equipment up the steep, rocky trails. Before that, no one had ever come to this jumbled mess of piled rock, gravel, and ice. Why would they? Nothing grew here for the goats to eat. The scientists, however, had scrambled around, taking measurements, samples, and photographs of the glacier. They had climbed out onto the treacherous snow-packed surface and drilled holes, taking round cores of ice from deep inside.

Akhbar had been there when the first bones were found in the piled rubble below the glacier. Yevgeny had seen them after they had been packed down the steep slopes to the village. Big, brown, larger than anything he'd seen in his life. The scientists had identified them as coming from mammoth, saber-toothed tiger, and something called a woolly rhinoceros. The explanation, according to the scientists, was that animals had been chased off of the high meadows and onto the glacier, where they had fallen into the crevasses. Hearing that, and curious, men like Yevgeny had come to the glacier in search, and in the process had created a new source of income for villagers. Fossil bones could be sold. Some were smuggled across the border into China to be sold as dragon bones in the apothecary shops. Bigger, intact bones were sold to antiquities dealers who braved the chronic, if sporadic, civil war to transport them out to Europe, America, and Japan for resale. The unique specimens, however, were sold to the scientists, especially to Professor Pietor Ostienko at the University of Moscow.

Ostienko had special requirements. He wanted bones straight from the ice, as fresh as possible, and he paid very well for them. In American dollars. He had even provided specific and detailed instructions on how to care for the specimens and a toll-free number straight to his office in Moscow.

And so Yevgeny had come here, searching, hoping to find one of the bones to supplement his meager income. He placed each foot with care, his breath frosting in the rarefied air. Cold came welling out of the ice to his left. It seemed to eat straight through his coat, into his flesh, into his very bones. A deep cold, ancient and primordial. A cold left over from the days of giant animals and myths. The breath of Shaitan might have blown down from hell to create such a cold.

Yevgeny shivered and glanced nervously up at the dirt-smeared ice that towered over his head. The snowcapped heights contrasted with the incredible vault of sky, as blue as lapis. In the glacier's shadow, even the light seemed weakened by the cold.

"I must be half-witted," he murmured uneasily. Propping himself on a canted slab of stone, he cocked his head and heard the faint grinding of tons upon tons of dirty ice. The glacier constantly groaned and whispered. The old stories, recounted late at night around crackling fires, told of devils who inhabited the stygian cracks in the ice. Flitting back and forth like phantasmal bats, they would leap out and possess the unwary soul who ventured too close. Yevgeny could well believe it. That sense of being watched, of foreboding, deepened and crawled around between his heart and liver.

He turned, ready to start back, sure that coming here to the edge of the ice had been a mistake. Far better to look in the stony piles of moraine below the ice for fragments of dry bone.

His foot slipped out from under him, and in the mad scramble to save himself, he clawed at the rock, barely keeping his grip on the rounded stone. For an eternal instant, he stared at the shining flecks in the granite millimeters from his eyes. His feet kicked futilely, seeking to find a purchase.

Breathing deeply, he shuddered as a strange fear coursed along his tingling nerves. Praise be to Allah, that had been a close one. He craned his neck, peering down into the black fissure below. The ice had fractured, actually been twisted around an outcrop of granite. How far down it might go was anyone's guess. Clear to Sheol for all Yevgeny knew.

He pulled himself up by brute force until he could

clamber onto the slanted stone and swallowed hard. Yes, a close one indeed. Quite by accident, he glanced sideways at the ice—and froze. For a moment, an unearthly silence filled the world.

There, half entombed in the eternal cold, the remains of a human face stared back at him. Bits of flesh had been torn from the bone. Strands of pale hair had woven into the ice as if borne by water. The jaw was missing, but the exposed upper teeth seemed to leer. At that moment, the heavy ice groaned; it seemed to come from behind the yellowed incisors that had bitten through the ice. Yevgeny stifled a scream as he looked into the sunken and distorted eyes.

winter rains had turned snow and portions of land. Yes,
I knew just what Quinn by tradition he'd planted the
weight of his form and bone. For a moment, an unearthly
feeling filled the world.

I was half-conscious in the eternal cold, the remote
ski-run race. I knew I had to act, to let the hour seep
slowly into the upper side of the sleigh, I was on for the
race. I quietly swept the snow vanishing, but on an
ancient magic newly washed abroad. What time of the
hour—a moment, to sense I'd come home from behind the
yellow sign, and had come through the deep tunnel.
Once a moment, as I looked into the smoke and the
silence.

CHAPTER ONE

THE BUS LURCHED OVER A POTHOLE, AND AVI RAAD clung to the overhead strap with one hand as he scanned the June 6 *Ha'aretz* for the latest update on the curfew. Several of his Arab laboratory technicians hadn't come in for work that day. Every time a dispute boiled up between the Palestinians and Israelis, it compromised his laboratory. Couldn't the two nations get it through their blocky heads that culture, history, and passions aside, scientific experiments did not proceed on a political timetable?

Most of the paper was filled with stories about the big religious conference being held in Tel Aviv. Christians of every sect and denomination were arguing with Jews and Muslims of every faction and description over the preservation of holy sites. A plague on them all, especially that American maniac, Billy Barnes Brown, who called for a new "philosophical Crusade." Whatever that was.

Over the whining of the bus, he could hear the babble of voices, most of them in accented Hebrew. The odors of diesel exhaust, falafel, hummus, and freshly baked bread assailed his nose. He knew most of his fellow passengers by sight. The majority of them, like himself, worked at the university. Each morning and night he traveled this route to and from his office and laboratory at Tel Aviv University. The bus wound through the same packed streets with the closely parked automobiles, the white-washed houses, and the colorfully dressed people. Each night he smelled their suppers, clutched close on their laps or dangling from their hands in paper sacks. His stomach tightened in response to piqued hunger.

The bus honked at the stubborn traffic around the intersection and slowed. Avi twisted to see through the driver's windshield. A uniformed soldier tweeted a whistle and gestured traffic through the congestion as two other soldiers warily inspected a stalled black compact. Two nervous Palestinians stood to one side, hands held high. Such things had thankfully become less common with the coming of the "peace." Though the tenacious, be they Hamas or the zealots in Mea Shaarim, would cling to their hatred to the bitter end.

Avi winced at the thought, noticing two of the hard-eyed Hasidim who stood on the sidewalk. They muttered behind their hands as they watched the soldiers search the stalled car. Their hatred might have curled around them like smoke.

Under his breath, Avi said, "You are the real enemies of mankind. Blinded by your intolerance and 'Truth.' " Reflexively, he folded his copy of *Ha'aretz* and fingered the scar on the side of his head. They might have marked him long ago and maimed his arm, but not so many years would pass before they learned that he and his colleagues had, in turn, irrevocably changed their futures.

He sighed as the bus inched through the intersection and onward to his stop. His feet thumped on the rubber-matted metal as he stepped down to the warm sidewalk.

With his paper folded under his bad arm, he walked the half block to the entrance of his apartment building. Nodding to the doorman, he passed through the glass doors, retrieved his mail from the drop, and crossed the tiled lobby to the elevator.

Built in the 1980s, the structure was one of those glass, steel, and white concrete marvels the government had slapped up to ease overcrowding. Although the building was just two decades old, work crews constantly clattered about the twenty-two stories, patching plaster, bolting cracked concrete, and fixing water pipes. One of the peculiarities of the building's construction ensured that when the toilet was flushed, everyone on the surrounding four floors was able to share the experience as the pipes screamed and the sewage gurgled.

When the elevator lurched to an unsteady stop, Avi stepped out onto the fourteenth floor and walked down his familiar hallway. Two maintenance men were pushing a cart from the other direction. They slowed, nodded, and smiled, allowing him time to fish his key from his pocket and open his door. He ran a fingertip over the mezuzah on the frame and started into his apartment.

Two strong arms caught him from behind, shoving him forward. Before he could scream, a hand clapped over his mouth, and he was bulldozed across the room and driven face first into the thick couch that buttressed his wall. In panic, he thrashed, trying to break free. Twisting his head to the side, he bellowed in fear, but the thick cushions muffled his shout.

"Now, now," a male voice told him from just behind his ear. "Don't make this more difficult than it has to be." English! *American* English!

"Who are you?" Avi cried against the cushions. "What do you want?"

"Divine justice," the voice hissed. An instant later, a balled fist slammed into Avi's right kidney. As he arched and gasped, a length of duct tape was slapped over his mouth. Pain made him wince; Avi tried to battle back. The soft cushions hindered his movements. Another blow to the back of his head left him reeling, unable to resist as his hands and feet were bound.

He flopped to the floor, looking up in terror as one of the men, dressed in a maintenance uniform, pulled back and kicked him viciously in the side. The spear of pain doubled him, leaving him panting through his nostrils, the tape pulling and puffing on his mouth.

He had experienced such pain before, at another beating, when the zealots broke his arm, scarred his face, and left him moaning in the dirt just below his archaeological excavation.

"That's better, Professor." The man smiled grimly down at him and smacked a gloved fist into a cupped palm. He appeared to be in his late twenties, blond, blue-eyed, and much too athletic. His hair, what could be seen of it under a tightly fitting cap, looked close-cropped, almost military. The man stood about a meter seventy-five. The second intruder, shorter, in his mid-forties and perhaps a meter sixty in height, walked over to the bookshelf and pulled down a photo of Avi. In it, his face was bandaged; the Hebrew caption read, "Professor recovers in hospital from beating received at the hands of Yod party radicals."

"Should have taken the hint, Professor," the second man said. "Even if they were Pharisees, they were right.

You were sinning against God. In the years since they closed down that dig of yours, you've just spiraled deeper and deeper into sin."

"Whoo muff woooo?" The tape muffled his words.

"Warriors of God," the blond giant said, smiling grimly. "Come to send you off to your judgment, you dirty Jew. God is waiting, and he has a great deal to talk to you about. But first we're going to have to ask you some questions."

That accent. American, yes, but from the southern states if Avi was any judge. Why? Why were they here? His troubles had always been with the ultraorthodox Jews, Israel's own bigoted fundamentalists.

"So," the dark-haired man said, and smashed the framed photo on the table. "You thought you were smarter than God? You and the rest? Or did you think you could *be* gods?"

Then, with a shiver of fear, Avi knew. His breath caught in his throat as the tall blond slid a gleaming knife from his belt.

"Repent your sins, Jew! God is coming!" The blond leaned down.

Avi's scream strangled itself against the sticky tape.

The sun, rising above the treetops, cast morning light through narrow white-framed windows and onto the red-white-and-black Navajo rug that lay on the living room floor. Ceiling-high bookcases covered each wall and were filled with volumes necessary to the trade of an anthropological geneticist: anatomy, primatology, paleoanthropology, human genetics, and statistical analysis. Two large four-door file cabinets, both antiques, looked time-worn and battered, their brass fittings use-polished. An oak table, topped with a lace tablecloth, dominated the room; piles of Xeroxed journal articles had been pushed to the side to clear a space for two plates. An empty bottle of Chianti dominated the bit of virgin tablecloth; two wineglasses had been left, their rims touching intimately.

The slanting light illuminated dust motes on the still air and gleamed on the stereo as Dr. Scott Ferris leaned down, sorted through the discs, and selected Loreena McKennitt. Inserting the disc, he pressed the "play" button and as the gentle strains filled the room, stepped back through the arched doorway into the kitchen. The capresso machine hissed and buzzed as streams of French Roast dribbled into two reproduction Anasazi cups. He stared for a moment at the black-and-white designs, fondly remembering the trip to Santa Fe when they had bought them from a sidewalk vendor on the Plaza.

He rubbed the back of his neck as he looked out the kitchen window at the big cottonwood in his yard. Early June in Fort Collins was his favorite time of year in Colorado. This was the eighth: Finals were over, his grades were turned in to the department, and the university slowed into a mellow lethargy before summer session. For three months he would have nothing with which to occupy himself except the continuing research. Not only were reports coming in on the children, but Bryce Johnson had just about finished another gene sequence. With that in hand, Avi Raad could begin the laborious task of synthesizing the base pairs in his PCR machines.

People said that the tall and athletic Scott looked more

like a ski bum than a professor. He walked with a slight limp, the result of a dislocated knee. The way women watched him pass had never ceased to amuse him. Amanda always preened when she was with him, stepping a little straighter, giving a slight toss to her gleaming black hair. They made a pair, Amanda and he. His blue eyes would twinkle with amusement, and her dark eyes would flash in Mediterranean jealousy. After all these years they still played that little game, though Amanda knew that he'd never consider another woman in his life. Careers and half the country might separate them, but mind, soul, and spirit, they were joined as no man and woman on earth.

This morning he wore a loosely belted terry-cloth robe with the Harvard escutcheon on the left breast as he lifted the brimming cups from the machine. He placed the coffees on the silver tray Ostienko had sent them from Russia and hummed in time to McKennitt's music as he half waltzed down the hallway to the bedroom.

Amanda lay under the twisted sheet, one bare leg and arm exposed. Her thick black hair made swirls across the pillow. He smiled at the profile she presented: something like a Greek goddess in relief. The sheet might have been sculpted of marble by Phidias himself.

"Good morning, lover," Scott said gently as he set the tray beside the bed and bent to kiss her cheek.

She murmured and stirred, stretching in a most feline manner. She almost purred as he teased her with the coffee cup, wafting the aroma past her nostrils.

"What time is it?" she asked, voice sultry with sleep.

"Seven-forty. Your flight doesn't leave for another five

hours. That's time for coffee, breakfast, and me. And not necessarily in that order."

She cracked an eye open, giving him a suspicious glance. "What makes you think I'd want you? I hate sex first thing in the morning."

"Okay. But we don't get to see each other for another what . . . two months?"

"That's a point." She took the coffee cup from his hand, cradling it as she sat up, the sheet falling to puddle in her lap. She gave him a wry if sleepy smile when his gaze fastened on her bare chest. "Don't strain your eyes that way. And drooling isn't considered flattering."

He chuckled and seated himself beside her. "I was just overcome. Males, as you know, are visually stimulated."

"And women, as you know, can be melted by a good cup of coffee and rapt male attention. The dilation of your pupils gave you away. Sex is starting to sound better." She sipped her coffee appreciatively, then added, "Assuming, that is, that you have anything left after last night. Males, as you are well aware, find performance to be a problem as they age."

He had opened his mouth in retort when the phone on the bedside stand gave off its warbling ring. Scott grunted, reaching with one hand to snag the receiver. "Hello?"

"Scott?" The accent betrayed the caller.

"Pietor?"

"Da! I think there is problem. Two men. They come to find me."

"I don't understand."

"You know Avi is dead?"

"What?" Scott felt something grow cold inside him.

"Da! I learn last night. He is killed. The laboratory . . . it is burned. Israelis think terrorism. Now, with two men following me, I think it is something else. I think project is compromised. Someone knows, Scott."

"Pietor, you're sure you're not being a little paranoid?"

"This is Russia. We have history. You do not. You call paranoia mental disorder; we call it selective advantage. I learned in good old days. Same reflexes are telling me this is not good. First Avi, and now two men are watching me? No, old friend. Someone is wishing to stop us. Be careful."

"Pietor?"

"I will be in touch. For time being, I use old escape route. See you soon."

"Pietor? Wait, I—" The dial tone indicated the connection had been cut.

"What was that all about?" Amanda was watching him through sloe eyes, fully awake now.

"Pietor. He said Avi's dead and two men were after him."

"Avi's dead?" Amanda asked, disbelieving. "Dead how?"

"I don't know." Scott frowned. "Let's see, it's a quarter to eight here; that would be three P.M. in Tel Aviv."

"It's Saturday. Avi would be at home." Her face had turned serious.

Scott dialed the international code and punched in Avi's number from memory. The familiar but foreign beeping told him that it was ringing in Avi's apartment. It rang and rang.

"Not there." He hung up and tried the lab, where to his

surprise, not even the answering machine picked up. Hanging up, he rose, stepped over the wadded blankets they'd kicked off the foot of the bed, and awakened his computer. Logging on, he checked his e-mail, found several communications about the children, but nothing from Avi or Pietor. Accessing the world news, he clicked on Israel, and after two reports on the peace process and the recent religious meetings, there it was: WORLD-RENOWNED GENETICIST FEARED MURDERED. HAMAS SUSPECT.

"Son of a bitch," Scott whispered, cold fingers of dread playing along his spine. Amanda had come to read over his shoulder, strands of her black hair tickling his ear.

"I don't believe it!" She shook her head. "His body was found in his burned lab? What do they mean the fire was accelerated with thermite? That's like phosphorus or something isn't it?"

"It burns really hot." Scott's vision seemed to waver. "This can't be happening."

As the article downloaded, a photo image of a blackened and gutted building formed. Fire hoses were snaked over the smoking mess, rescue workers picking through the debris. From the background, Scott could recognize the familiar university buildings behind the lab. In the foreground he could see the remains of centrifuges, electrophoresis tables, the big scanning electron microscopes, and the refrigeration unit, all covered with the fallen wreckage of the burned roof.

"Oh, my God." Amanda sank down, her hands on his shoulders. "We knew they would be upset, but Scott, not like this."

"They're not supposed to know," he said softly, a welling emptiness spreading inside him. "We need years, Amanda. Time to prepare them—not just the kids, but the world as a whole."

"God, Scott, you're not thinking of calling the police, are you? You're not going to tell anyone? They'd call you a lunatic!"

He shook his head. "Wait, think! Damn it, Amanda, we don't know for sure what's happened. This could be . . . maybe . . . well, just an accident, you know?"

She nodded. "That's right. Maybe it was Hamas? Or the Mea Shaarim people. They attacked him once before. A fertility clinic is still a target, even in Israel. It doesn't have to be related to the project." She sounded like she was trying to convince herself.

"Even if it was," he whispered hoarsely, "they shouldn't react this way. Dear God, Amanda, what kind of beings are we? Humans, I mean. Are we really that afraid?"

Her large dark eyes were on his, answering in a way words could not. In addition, she said, "Are you forgetting why we got into this in the first place? Are you forgetting why you walk with a limp, Scott? How you got that scar on your forehead? You know the power of blind faith over the human mind. It led to Crusades, to Inquisitions, to genocide and holocaust. Why couldn't it lead to this?" She pointed at the screen where Avi's face—an image taken from an old *Time* magazine article—had formed beside the burned clinic.

"We need more time." Scott's voice was pleading. "Meanwhile, we've got to be careful. Hide the records. We've got to pull the plug and scatter the—"

"Scott," she said, slipping around beside him to stare

into his half-panicked eyes. "Relax. The point I'm making is that we should be careful. Israel is a volatile place. Until we have proof that this is related to the project, we assume this is an accident—which it might well be. That means we stick to the original timetable. We publish the articles over the next couple of years like we had planned. We continue to document how they develop, and then we slowly disseminate that information so that it doesn't come as a huge shock to anyone. *We stick to the plan!*"

"So you're going to fly back to Ohio, even after hearing about Avi?"

"I paid too much for those tickets. They're nonrefundable." She paused. "Sure you don't want to come? It would give us time to come to grips with what happened to Avi. A jazz festival would make a great change of pace for you. Allow us to think."

He shook his head, aware that grief over Avi was going to come welling up from the depths and overwhelm him. But not yet. For the moment, he had a mountain of new data to analyze. He owed that to Avi, who had dedicated his life and soul to the project. It was more important now than it had ever been.

"I love you," Amanda whispered, lacing her arms around his neck. "Come on. Let's go back to bed. I just need you to hold me. Sometimes in life, that's the rarest gift of all. Just to be held when your heart is breaking."

He nodded as she overcame his resistance and pulled him to his feet. The computer monitor continued to display the blackened ruins of the lab and Avi's gentle-eyed face.

CHAPTER TWO

❖

LATE ON THE NIGHT OF JUNE 9, SCOTT FERRIS ROLLED back on the throttle and used two fingers on the front brake lever. As the bright red Ducati slowed, his boot tapped the shifter lever, dropping the machine into third gear. With a glance into the mirror, Scott wheeled off the dark highway and into the lighted parking lot of a convenience store. The road behind him remained dark, thankfully empty under the midnight mountain sky.

The Ducati's engine settled into that off-canter burble of an idle, and he shifted to neutral. The clutch made its characteristic rattling as Scott lowered the sidestand and killed the engine. In the silence that followed, his hearing echoed from helmet roar and the rich thunder of the Ducati's exhaust.

He looked up at the night sky, frosted as it was with a billion stars. The sky was so clear here in the high country. He stepped off the machine, unlatched his helmet, and propped it on the handlebar. Walking to the illuminated pay phone came as a relief, his leather pants chafing from the long ride. The Ducati ate into a man's butt after a couple of hours. Tonight was no exception.

As his tingling extremities enjoyed the freedom of standing, he tapped in his phone card number and then Amanda's home number.

On the third ring, her answering machine said,

"You've reached Dr. Alexander's residence. Please leave your name and number along with a short message, and I will get back to you as soon as I can. Thank you."

At the beep, Scott said, "Amanda? Scott. Listen, I've been worried—"

"Scott?" her sleep-muddled voice interrupted. "It's the middle of the night. I'm supposed to leave for Cincinnati in what . . . four hours? What's wrong?"

"I don't know. Maybe it's the hours I've been keeping. Maybe it's that Avi's really dead and Ostienko's disappeared, but I've been getting more and more nervous. I could have sworn that someone had been in my office. Then, this morning, I saw two guys sitting in a van outside. Just sitting there, watching. They were probably waiting for someone in the building. I'm just going nuts. But it got me thinking. So, I've taken a precaution. I put a copy of the basic research someplace safe."

"Where?"

"The condo. I think I showed you where Sis used to hide her dope."

"Scott, that's paranoid."

"Ostienko said that it can be a selective advantage."

"Where are you?"

"That little convenience store outside of Ward on the Peak-to-Peak Highway. Remember? I bought you a soda here about a year ago. I remembered the phone."

"It's . . . good grief, Scott, it's after two A.M. here, so it's after midnight there."

He nodded out at the night, seeing the gleaming Ducati under the store lights. "Yeah, I know. I thought I saw that same white van when I pulled out of town. It stayed with

me, three cars back as I headed south on I-25. I took the
Berthoud exit, and sure enough there it was, about a half
mile back. It followed me all the way to Lyons, so I
blitzed my way around a string of cars and ground off the
pegs taking the back road to I-70. One thing about a
Ducati ST4: On a twisty mountain road, there's no way
anything with four wheels is going to keep up with you."

"Scott, I'm worried about you."

"Yeah, well, if we're going berserk because of guilty
consciences, it will all pass. If there's really someone after
us, well . . ."

"You're thinking like you're in a movie, Scott. This is
the real world. We've done nothing illegal. We've
planned this all out so that an old wrong is made right and
no one gets hurt. We've covered this ground over and
over and over again. We're doing the right thing. It isn't
a matter of us acting irresponsibly. We've begun laying
the groundwork, publishing articles on methodology. All
we need is time to educate people, and in the end, a hundred years from now, it will be so normal no one will
think twice about it."

"Maybe we should tell Bryce. Let him know what he's
really been doing."

"Why?"

"So he can have time to think about it. To prepare himself."

"Scott, we agreed a long time ago. The fewer who really knew—"

"Just consider it. If people have found out, if they are
going to accelerate the timetable, Bryce is going to have
to know."

"I'll consider it. In the meantime, be patient. If anyone comes around asking questions, we'll rethink it."

"Yeah," he whispered, hearing the breeze through the night-blackened fir and lodgepole pine. The scent of conifers carried on the cool air. High in the sky, a climbing jet blinked against stars. "All we need is time. Time for us, the kids . . . hell, for the whole human species." He paused. "Tell me, Amanda, how does it feel to know that we're no longer alone?"

"As good as it did when I gave birth, Scott. Now, I'm going to sleep. I want you to ride safely on your way home. I love you and don't want you wrapped around a rock or tree on some sharp corner." A pause. "It will work out, my love. You just have to trust me on this."

"I love you," he said wistfully.

"Love you, too," she answered. "Good night."

He listened as she hung up, then replaced the receiver. His breath misted in the chill high-country air. The stars still shone down in a dusting of light against the blackness. He walked over to the Ducati and pulled his helmet on. No, he had no regrets, and someone had to pull humanity's proverbial head out of the sand. If that meant paying a price, then he would pay it, and gladly. He, Amanda, Avi, and Ostienko—they'd known the risks from the beginning. It just had to be done. For the future and the past, and for all of humanity, if not just for himself and his bad knee.

At the stab of the button, the Ducati roared to life. Snugging his helmet strap, Scott flipped up the stand, tapped the bike in gear, and let out the clutch. The rear wheel spun a couple of times on the gravel, then hooked up and catapulted him onto the narrow strip of blacktop.

The echo of the exhaust was lost in the trees as he chased the headlight's white cone into the night.

Rain left the streets of Manchester, New Hampshire, shining under the streetlights on that dark tenth of June. Drops spattered the windshield of Dr. Bryce Johnson's Dodge Durango. The worn wipers smeared more water than they squeegeed from the glass.

On his way home from his genetics lab at the University of New Hampshire, Bryce hummed along to the strains of Puccini's *Tosca.* The music had reached the crescendo in the second act: for Bryce's money, the high point of the opera. As the string of traffic slowed to a stop in a succession of brightening brake lights, Tosca dramatically plunged her knife into Scarpia's heart.

"Die, you bastard!" Bryce thumped the steering wheel, braking to a stop. Maria Callas sang out, *"Questo è i bacio di Tosca."*

"The kiss of Tosca!" Bryce chortled as Giuseppe di Stefano cried out, *"Aiuto!"*

"No help for you, you slimy pond scum."

The light changed to green. Traffic began creeping forward. Bryce accelerated. "Yeah, strangle on your own blood." Matching his voice to Tosca's, Bryce sang, *"Muori! Muori! Muori!"*

Scarpia's death rattle filled the Durango's plush interior. As the violins muted, Bryce imagined Tosca placing burning candles to either side of Scarpia's head and finally lowering the crucifix to his bloody chest.

Lightning flashed in the night sky, casting the trees in

eerie white and illuminating the strip mall at the junction of Dunbarton and Hill Road. It gleamed on the water-shiny cars and sparkled in the cascading raindrops.

Bryce signaled and took the right onto Hill Road before merging left. Humming along with the music, he took the left into his subdivision and followed the winding streets past tree-cloaked houses, parked cars, and the trash cans lining the curb—his nightly ritual passage through suburbia.

Pulling into his driveway, Bryce turned off the wipers and headlights and then the ignition before the gentle strains of the third act could begin. In the silence he could hear only the metallic pattering of rain on the Durango's roof. He reached into the passenger seat and picked up his briefcase with its precious notes from the day's research.

He closed the door behind him and pushed the remote button on the key fob that locked his Durango and set the security system, then dashed across the space to his side door before unlocking it and stepping into the warm, dry retreat of his house.

He'd been lucky to find the little split-level ranch. Just one of those blessed breaks he seemed to get. Well, lucky in everything but women. A divorce settlement sale on the market for a year, the house had been the major bone of contention between the previous owners until the judge decreed that it be sold—at whatever cost—and quickly! Bryce had waltzed in with a solid down payment and picked up the property for a good twenty grand below its appraised value. Were it any consolation, he wasn't the only one with woman problems.

He crossed the kitchen and dropped his briefcase on

the table. Walking into the dining room, he punched the answering machine button. The mechanical voice told him, *"You have two messages."*

The machine whirred. Then Candi's melodic voice informed him, *"Hi. Uh . . . Bryce? Listen, I've done a lot of thinking since last week. Look, this just isn't going to work. I thought I'd . . . well, I'm going to be seeing someone else."* A pause. *"I just can't keep sharing you with your research. You're a sweet guy. But you're just not . . . I mean, I need someone who's there! Who doesn't forget."*

He grimaced. They had fought two days ago when he'd spaced the special dinner she had made for their six-month anniversary.

"That's all. I just wanted to tell you that there were no hard feelings. I tried the lab. They said you were busy. Story of my life, right? Otherwise I'd have told you in person. Look, don't call me, okay. I mean, there's nothing left to say."

He stood foolishly, staring at the little plastic box with its unforgiving tape. The instant desire to smash the emotionless machine faded as the tape clicked and John Gerrolds said, *"Hey. We missed you at the meeting. I just thought you might want to know that we're having a target match Saturday at the range. Second thing, your dues are three months in arrears, and the gun club is going to drop you from the membership list. This is your last warning, buddy. Pony up."* Click.

"That was your final message," the machine intoned.

"Yeah, right. Hell of a day." He turned and walked back into the kitchen. For the moment, he stared at the briefcase where it lay, rain-spotted, on the table. Was there some reason, some divine justice, that he couldn't keep a girlfriend for more than a few months?

He took a bottle of Sam Adams from the refrigerator and retrieved the remains of the noodle casserole that Candi had made for him. At least she'd been a dynamite cook. He placed the bowl in the microwave and punched the timer button for five minutes before seating himself at the table. As the microwave hummed, he glanced over at the sink, where dishes were piled high—evidence that Candi hadn't been in the house for at least a week. Dishes had never been one of his strong points. The mute dishwasher seemed to glare balefully at him from where it lurked, neglected, under the countertop.

To hell with women. And to hell with dishwashers, too. They were nothing but trouble. He sighed and took a swig from the beer. He needed to establish himself. He was still only an assistant professor of anthropology at the University of New Hampshire. Once he had tenure locked up, then he could worry about a life to go along with his career. Damn it, he was well on the way down the "publish or perish" track. Three articles in major journals in the last year and a half wasn't bad. Not only that, but the research just kept expanding. The raw data Scott and Amanda were sending him drew him like a moth to a burning taper. New gene sequences and potential combinations, as if the very keys of humanity, were jangling from the tips of their fingers.

The microwave dinged. He stood, rummaging through the cabinet for his last clean plate. The thing about women, he thought as he spooned out steaming casserole, was that they really weren't hard to find. Not when a man had red-gold hair, an athletic build, and a good face. It seemed like all he had to do was go for a cup of coffee and some woman was talking to him, telling him he had a nice smile, or his hazel eyes sparkled, or some such.

He had demolished most of the casserole when the phone rang.

"Candi?" He jumped from the chair, charged into the dining room, and scooped up the handset. "Hello?"

"It's Scott." The voice sounded tense.

"Yeah, what's up? Hey, did you get your copy of *AJPA* yet? We're the first article—"

"Shut up! Listen!" Scott swallowed hard on the other end. *"Look, I can't go into details, but something's happened. I can't get hold of Amanda. I just get her damn machine. I think we're in trouble. Big trouble."*

"What trouble? I don't understand."

"You wouldn't. I've lied to you! Lied to a lot of people. But someone has found out. Someone was in my office. I'm being followed, and I—"

"Followed by who?"

"Listen to me, will you? The research. It's not *theoretical. It's* real. *It has been for over four years now! No matter what happens,* don't *call the police! Don't do anything but disappear, you got that?"*

"Scott, you're not making any sense!"

"There are people out there who will try and stop us, no matter the price. You got that? I want you to collect everything. Remember the peach brandy?"

Bryce frowned. "Well, yeah, that was at—"

"Shut up! Meet me there. Call Amanda. Find her. Tell her that people know. Tell her Ostienko was right. Tell her to leave her house, get the hell out of Athens, and meet me

*where we drank peach brandy. Key's in the foramen mag-
num. Got that? Repeat it."*

"Meet you where we drank peach brandy. The key is
in the foramen magnum. Why don't I just tell her to meet
us—"

*"People are being killed over this, pal. Avi's dead. You
got that? Dead!"* A pause. *"Look, if you've ever done
anything for me, do this. Pack up and leave. Tonight.
Take cash. Don't tell anyone where you're going. Don't
use credit cards."*

"Scott, this isn't making any sense."

"Trust me! I'll tell you about it when I see you."

"Scott, I—"

*"Hey, pal . . . if I don't get there, I want you to know
that I love you. And, well . . . I'm sorry I—"*

In the background, Bryce heard a voice—male, muffled—saying, *"Dr. Ferris?"*

A frightened Scott Ferris asked, *"Who are you? How
the hell did you get into my—"* Someone grunted, and the
phone clattered as if dropped. Bryce could hear what
sounded like a struggle: the hollow thumpings, as if flesh
were being abused, and grunts of pain.

A moment later, a man's deep voice asked, *"Hello?
Who is this, please?"*

Heart pounding, Bryce hung up. For a moment all he
could do was stare at the phone, suddenly, inexplicably
afraid. The research was real? His brain tried to race
through the implications.

A prank! It had to be. But in all of his life, he'd never
known Scott to be a prankster. Earnest, yes, and in his
profession, dedicated to the point of being driven. One of

his favorite sayings was, "Sometimes it takes an extremist to stamp out fanatics."

Bryce hurried down the hallway to his bedroom and pulled out his suitcase. As he threw clothes into the nylon bag, the implications began to seep in. The research was *real?* How real?

That deep male voice, so deadly calm, echoed in his brain, *"Hello? Who is this, please?"*

His gut churned as he pulled open the bottom drawer of the dresser and lifted his black nylon pistol case from beneath his underwear.

CHAPTER THREE

Mother is scared. He watches her with his big blue eyes. She is hurrying, and he hates it when she does that. The sound of her pants make a shush-zip sound with each step of her long legs.

He wants to suck his thumb. That always reassures him, but Mother has told him time and time again that thumb sucking is for babies. And he is four now. Almost five. Next year he is supposed to go to school.

Mother is taking clothes from her closet. He walks closer, carefully noting the red dress, the three pairs of *blue jeans, the brown corduroy pants. She takes four T-shirts, two white blouses, her three brassieres, and four sets of pink panties.*

"Muvver, whass wong?"

"We've got to go on a trip, honey." She slows, fear bright in her blue eyes. He reads her expression, and the fear in his own small body grows. It's an uncomfortable feeling, making his insides want to go to the bathroom. Making him want to run off on his stubby little legs and hide.

"We be oohkay?" he asks, concentrating so the words don't slur.

"Yes, baby." But fright lies deep in her voice. His hearing, better than hers, detects the tension, and his fear heightens. His sense of smell picks up the slight change of her odor—more metallic, like the smell of a copper penny.

The trouble had started with the phone call. From across the room he had heard a male voice, flat, changed by the phone. "Becky," it said. "We're in trouble. You've got to leave. Avi's dead. Someone knows . . . everything."

At that, his mother's spine had stiffened. "Scott? You're not serious?"

"I just heard. Avi's been murdered. Someone has been in my house. They've been through my papers. I think I've had someone watching me for the last couple of days. Just play it safe, huh? Go to the bank. Collect the envelope. It will tell you what to do. I can't talk now. Just do as I say."

And the phone had clicked as the man hung up.

Mother had stood for a moment, a terrible look on

her face. Then she used a finger to clear the connection, dialed a number, and said, "Celia? It's Becky. Scott just called. We're found out. Someone killed Avi. Call the others. We've got to run."

After that, she called several other women, her voice almost shrill. He had only seen Mother like that once before, when she and Aunt Eu had gotten into a fight over the phone. It had been late at night, when he was supposed to be in bed. Mother's voice had been shrill that time, too. And then Mother had said, "You've become such a bigot. I . . . I hate you." And she had slammed the phone down and sunk onto the kitchen floor, where she held her head in her hands and cried.

In complete panic, Abel had hidden in the dark, horrified and paralyzed. But the next morning Mother had been fine, smiling, patting him on the head. She had made French toast for him, with lots of cinnamon. Then, a week later, Aunt Eunice had come and talked with Mother. They had talked about him. About Aunt Eu having a boy like him. Maybe they could be playmates. It had been later when the shouting started. He had run and hid, clutching his buffalo for security.

As he watches Mother pack, he tenses his fingers, feeling the muscles in his arms swell. He is strong. Much stronger than his playmates—the ones in preschool who no longer tease him and call him "freak" because of the funny way that he talks. Fear always does this, makes him tighten his muscles against the runny feeling inside.

Mother rushes past and into the bathroom. She pulls bottles from the medicine chest, tossing them into a *plastic sack. She takes her hair dryer, the box of tampons, the shampoo from the plastic-screened shower.*

He follows her into his room, tears starting to streak down his face. His vision grows hazy with silver. She takes his clothes out of the dresser and tosses them into the bag.

"I don't wanna go," he says, the wetness in his nose turning his talk even funnier.

Mother bends down, her fingers wiping the tears from his sloping cheeks. "It's all right, my little man. We have to go away for a while. That's all."

"Go see Aunt Eu?"

"No, dear. We don't want to drag her into this. Not now. Not after what she said to me the last time. The psychotic . . . Forget it. She has enough troubles of her own." Her blue eyes cloud for a moment; then she sniffs bravely and says, "No, it's you and me for a while, sweetie. I just need you to be tough."

She stands then and finishes the packing. He turns, carefully picking up his toys: "Chaser," the stuffed buffalo he sleeps with; the magic snowstorm from Park City; and the little blue truck that Aunt Eu bought him back in Ohio. These he places in his canvas bag from Sam Weller's bookstore downtown. Mother takes him there to buy new "Hank the Cowdog" books, and one time, the lady behind the cash register gave him the bag.

As Mother hurries past with his suitcase, he takes one last look around his room. Memories from Ohio are faint, shifting into the gray past. This has been his place. His bed, with its magic covers, protected him from the scary things in the night: the small, stick-thin shadow people that lurk under his bed, and the black-clawed things that hide in the dark corners of the closet.

He takes one last look at himself in the mirror, staring into his somber, large blue eyes. He still wishes that his nose were a little smaller, and that his face were a little flatter. More like Brian O'Neil's. Brian lives next door and is his best friend. They play together and go to the same preschool. Brian doesn't call him names anymore.

"Abel?" Mother calls, stopping to take the picture of her and Aunt Eu from the table. She looks at it and then places it facedown, back on the table. "Come on, sweetie. We've got to go."

Abel swallows hard, runs a hand over his delicate and pale hair, and shoulders his bag. He is halfway out the door before he runs back and grabs up his copies of "Hank the Cowdog." Wherever he and Mother are going, she will want to read to him as she has every night since he can remember.

As he runs out the door, he looks up, afraid. "Muvver? Was I bad? Iss tha' why we gotta go?"

For the briefest of instants, he sees a terrible panic on her face; then she smiles bravely, fighting tears, and says, "No, little man. You're the best boy in the whole world." She checks inside his bag, frowns, and takes out the little blue truck, saying, "I don't want you to have that." She leaves it on the step.

"But, Muvver, Aunt Eu—"

"I know. Just do this for me, Abel." Her hands tighten on the pink suitcase. He can see her knuckles turn moon white with the grip. "Everything is going to work out fine, baby. I promise."

Her tears come as she leads him toward the car, and he is more frightened than ever. He wonders if his little blue truck is already lonely.

The layout of the Mayflower Hotel bar could be likened to a boot. A divider ran down the leg; the heel created an angle, faced by windows; while the toe formed a narrow little alcove with a single table. As though a refugee from the thousand-dollar suits of the other patrons, Special Agent Joe Hanson, in his two-hundred-buck JC Penney gray wool-and-rayon special, sat wedged in the boot tip. He had positioned his chair both to monitor the bar's patrons and to look out the window with its brown curtains and little dingle-balls. This way he could keep an eye on the people walking along the sidewalk outside. It was the eleventh of June, muggy and hot in the city. He could be doing worse than sitting here drinking Coke and enjoying the air-conditioning.

The table was prized by individuals who, in this most public of places, desired a modicum of privacy. Not that the Mayflower bar had a reputation for such. After all, the little lounge had played host to most of Washington, D.C.'s, rich and famous, from Monica Lewinsky right on down to Cabinet members, ambassadors, and the occasional foreign head of state. Being situated across DeSales Street from the ABC studios—in addition to the hotel's stature in national lore—ensured that it was a place to see and be seen. Which, to Joe's amusement, was one of the reasons "Maria Mason" had chosen to contact him here.

The furtive and covert didn't meet in the Mayflower, with its walnut trim, polished brass, white-coated waiters, and ever-curious patrons.

Hunching down in the leather chair, Joe glanced at his watch; the five o'clock rush would just be hitting the streets. Activity in the bar would peak at roughly five-thirty. In anticipation, he had arrived an hour and a half earlier just to hold this table and the relative privacy it ensured. That, and a good agent covered his bases, forever leery of an ambush. No one had ever accused Joe Hanson of being a fool. He was working on his fourth glass of Coke, having overtipped the waiter enough to maintain his continued welcome.

When the hands of Joe's watch had moved to five-fifteen a woman pushed her way through the crush, eyes searching until she found his table. The noise level had risen to a dull roar, and in the press, her arrival could have been characterized as "invisible." She wore a conservative gray suit designed to deemphasize the fact that God had graced her with a forty-two inch bust on a petite body that fit comfortably into a size five. Her dyed brown hair had been pulled back and pinned at the nape of the neck. A black, patent-leather handbag was clutched before her. Joe guessed her age at mid-forties, well preserved, with a delicate face dominated by a slim, straight nose. Something about her set him on edge. As her gaze met his, a sudden intensity burned through her defensive gray eyes.

She slipped into the chair he had insistently denied the blue-suited Interior Department lawyer who stood behind his friends at the next table. Placing her purse on the gray-brown carpet next to her feet, she gave him a wary grin. "Mind if I lie when I say that it's good to see you, Agent Hanson?"

"Be my guest." He shifted, attention on the crowd behind her. Surveying the packed room, he couldn't detect any interest in Maria's arrival except from the frustrated, and still bipedal, lawyer.

"I'm sorry. That was supposed to be a joke. Something to ease my tension." She looked at him. "When you get a chance, flag the waiter down. I'd like an eighteen-year-old Macallan. Neat, if you don't mind."

"Hey, who do you think I am?"

"You're Special Agent Joe Hanson, Federal Bureau of Investigation. When I called yesterday and explained my problem, they switched me to you. You've got an expense account for greasing snitches. So, grease me."

"If I wasn't the serious sober public servant that I am, I might be tempted to think that was an unsubtle innuendo."

"Yeah, well, I feel about as subtle as a brick." She gave him a level stare, an infinity of invitation behind her gray eyes.

He signaled the white-coated waiter. When the man approached, Hanson shouted over the din, "Macallan. The eighteen, please. Neat, with a water back. And a refill for me."

The waiter, a dark-haired man, gave an immaculate nod and slipped gracefully into the press the way a mullet wiggled through swamp grass. Joe returned his attention to Maria, aware of the lingering, almost resigned invitation in her eyes.

He knew that look, knew the kind of woman who used

it with a man she'd just met. "Thanks for the interest. It's flattering for an old fart like me."

"You're not that old," she replied wearily. "If anything, I've got ten years on you."

The waiter appeared out of the crowd, artfully leaning to place a glass of amber liquid and a tumbler of water on the black marble before Maria. He settled Joe's Coke on a napkin and removed his empty glass before vanishing back into the crowd.

Joe cocked his head, watching her take a sip of the scotch and savor the taste as she ran it over her tongue. "God, that's good. You don't know how I miss it."

"Uh-huh."

She studied him for a moment. "Hell, I'm an alcoholic. What the fuck do you think took me to the church in the first place? I bought into it and it kept me sober for seven years."

"And then?"

Her smile turned crooked. "I got too high up in the church. Started learning things. When I figured out that the Crusade wasn't really about God, but about power, money, and control, I lost my ardor for religion."

"Why'd you come to us?"

"What do you know about Billy Barnes Brown?"

Hanson shifted uneasily. "He's the biggest thing on religious TV. He was a major player in that big multidenominational conference in Jerusalem last week. Has that big solid-glass cathedral outside of Atlanta with all the spires and prisms inside. What's he call his ministry?"

"The Apostolic Evangelical Church of the Salvation. Me, I work for a subsidiary called the 'Christian Creationist Crusade.' It's huge, international, and the biggest hypocritical scam in the world. Someday, Agent Hanson, someone's going to figure out just how rotten that whole racket is, and when they do, I don't want to get busted along with the rest for fraud, extortion, racketeering, and the rest of it. I'm just on the money-raising side of it, mind you. I don't have the foggiest idea what the political wing is doing. If I did, I'd probably be too scared to talk to you." She pointed a finger at him. "I have something I think you'd be interested in, but first, I've got to know: If I turn over my information, can you get me out? Keep me safe?"

"Yeah, well, we kind of have a track record to be proud of when it comes to that sort of thing."

"Maybe." She shook her head. "You might have done all right against the Mafia, but they don't have the resources that the church has."

"Right." He sipped his Coke. "Okay. You asked for a meeting; I'm here. You're drinking twenty-five-dollar scotch on my tab. You said you were just going to see if you thought you could trust me. I don't think I'm the only guy in D.C. who will buy expensive scotch for an attractive lady like you. So, that leaves me asking: What do you want with me when you probably need to talk to the guys in the white-collar crimes unit? They handle the RICO stuff. My bailiwick is putting the wraps on guys who like to wear white sheets, burn crosses, torch Black churches, and paint swastikas on Jewish graves."

She studied him carefully. "I told the lady on the phone I needed to talk to someone about hate crimes. Not fraud. If I give you some papers, can you protect me? Make sure that the church doesn't know the source?"

"What papers?"

"Correspondence. A packet I picked up by mistake in Atlanta."

"By mistake?" he prompted when she hesitated.

"All right, I thought it was . . . Hell, never mind *why* I took it; I just did, okay?" Her gaze slipped off to the side, and her hands knotted.

"Maybe you'd better tell me where and when you found these papers. If I've got to make a pitch to my supervisor for a major operation, he's going to want to know. Look, Maria, if you really want our help we have to know just what we're dealing with, understand? If this thing is as big—"

"I was fucking Billy, all right?" She glared at him. "He saw me at the office a couple of years back. Pulled the whole slick thing." She made a gesture. "Hey, it was a fast track to the top. Maybe once a month I'd get a call, pick up a ticket at the airport, and meet him at some fancy hotel in the Bahamas, or a penthouse in Miami for a couple of days of good booze and wild sex." Her eyes focused on the distance. "Fool that I was, I thought I meant something to him."

"Wait a minute, isn't he married? Him and what's her name?"

"Bobby Sue." Maria cocked an eyebrow. "Since when did *that* mean anything? Him, and his model marriage? Rumor is that she's got her own thing going with her publicist. It's just another prop, a sham to keep the dollars rolling in from the starry-eyed faithful who believe that crap he spouts on Sunday mornings."

"So, in Atlanta you found out you were a slot machine, huh?"

She nodded, eyes downcast.

"And, being pissed, you picked up an envelope that you shouldn't have, something to get back at him with."

Another nod as she tucked brown hair behind her ears, exposing gold hoop earrings.

"And now you've figured out that it's too hot to handle?"

"He'll kill me if he finds out."

Joe leaned forward, hands laced. "You called me on Monday. This is Tuesday. How long have you had the packet? How much time has he had to figure out that it was you who took it?"

"I flew back on Sunday." She looked cowed. "He spends that entire day at the cathedral. If he discovered it was missing, it would have been Monday morning at the earliest."

"Did you have a fight? Anything that would point him in your direction sooner rather than later? Does he know you want to hurt him?"

Her mouth seemed to shrink. "I don't think so. Hell, I'm not sure he even thinks of me as a person. He . . . he had two of us there this weekend. Him and that blond slut that he calls an executive secretary. The one that went with him to Jerusalem. Can you imagine? The three of us in the same bed? I'd heard of such things." She shook her head. "Never thought I'd be part of it."

"Where was this?"

"His mansion south of Atlanta."

Joe studied her, seeing the guilt and self-disgust, reading that she'd swallowed her pride and played along. She was avoiding his eyes, watching the white-paneled ceiling with its big walnut beams.

"You're not the first. But let's get down to why you

called me. Just what's in this packet of papers you stole from old Billy Barnes Brown that would interest me?"

"I'm not sure." She frowned. "It's a list. Handwritten. Some of the names are Ph.D.s, professors from around the world. And there are women. At first I didn't think much of it, and then, Sunday night, sitting in the airport in Atlanta, you know those CNN news monitors?" At his nod, she continued, "This Israeli anthropologist. Avi Raad? He was the first name on the list. They showed the Israeli police investigating his murder. They said he was tortured to death, his apartment ransacked, and his laboratory at Tel Aviv University had been burned. Not just set on fire, but burned with thermite."

"It could be a coincidence." From what he had heard, the Israelis considered it a Hamas hit, but were still a little unclear on the motives.

Maria was shaking her head, eyes focused on infinity. "His name had a line drawn through it. There were two other names crossed out, too."

Joe leaned back. "Let me get this straight. You found a list of names in Billy Barnes Brown's bedroom—"

"Not his bedroom, his personal office. It's just down the hall. They were still passed out on the bed. I was trying to drown the memory. Looking for another bottle of bourbon. I don't know why I picked that envelope up. I just did."

"Right, okay. In his office. You picked up a list of names that you think are targets of Billy Barnes Brown's Crusade? What's the motive? Why jeopardize an international religious organization to whack a bunch of professors?"

Maria's gray eyes turned desperate. "I don't know!

This Avi Raad is dead, all right? I'm scared. I want out. Taken away. He's going to kill me!"

"Hey, it's cool. Settle down." Joe made appeasing gestures with his hands. "You got this list with you?"

She shook her head. "It's someplace safe. You promise me that you can make me disappear, keep me alive, and I'll turn it over."

He nodded, doing his best to look reassuring. "You know, people could consider this a setup. Revenge for a spurned love affair. A good attorney could make it look like you cooked this up out of spite. You ready for that?"

She took a deep breath, the action thinning her nostrils. "If those three scientists are dead, do you really think I could have done that? And the list. You have ways of lifting fingerprints and things, don't you? Matching the kind of paper? Police things?"

He nodded, granting her the benefit of the doubt. "All right, Maria, I'll take your word for it. If you've really got the goods, we'll make you disappear." He was already considering the bureaucratic nightmare looming ahead of him. His boss, Jack Ramsey, would approve it on Joe's word, but from there on up it was anyone's guess. Witness protection involved a literal mountain of paper, including forms, requisitions, reports out the ass, and rubber stamps all the way up to the director's.

She seemed to deflate with sudden relief.

"Do you remember any of the other names?" Joe pulled out his notebook.

"Yes. The ones with the lines drawn through them were Avi Raad, Scott Ferris, and Amanda Alexander. The next name was some Russian I've never heard of. Then came someone called Bryce Johnson. And there are others. Twenty-five in all."

"Wasn't there anything else? Addresses? Notations?"

"Ferris was in Colorado. Raad in Tel Aviv. Alexander, someplace in Ohio. Athens, I think. Johnson in . . . let me see, I think it's New Jersey. It's all on the list."

"All right, the sooner we get it, the better for all of us." He lifted an inquiring eyebrow. "Do you want to do this now? I can go with you, make sure. . . ."

She shook her head. "I've got things to do. I need to close my bank account. Do something with my cat. I—"

"If this is as serious as you believe, I don't want you going home. Not until we set up some protection. Let me make some calls and—"

"No!" she said firmly. "I'll be fine. I have things to do. *Personal* things. Tomorrow. At noon? Where should I meet you?"

"My office. Just walk in the front door. We'll be expecting you. We'll take things from there." He gave her his card, circling the address for the Washington Metro Field Office. "One other thing, Maria: I need your real name and address."

Her lips tightened; then she reluctantly admitted, "Elizabeth Ann Carter. I live over in Fairfax."

"Right." Joe grunted. "What does the Christian Creationist Crusade do?"

"We try to ban the teaching of evolution in public schools." She tossed off the last of her scotch. "It's a great hot-button issue, one that generates a pile of money for the church."

"Give me your street address and phone." As he wrote down 11256 West Osceola and her phone number, he added, "My number is on the card. If you need *anything* you call me. Got it? The switchboard will put you through to me."

She took the card with her left hand and nodded thoughtfully. The long, slim fingers on her right kept rotating the empty scotch glass, and she lifted it again, as if for another drink, hardly realizing it was empty.

"In the meantime," Joe said firmly, "don't call anyone. Not friends, family, no one. We'll take care of all those things later."

She nodded, a curious fatigue in her gray eyes. "As much as I'd like another scotch, Joe, I've got to be going. I'll see you tomorrow, and we'll see what can be saved of my fucked-up life."

She picked up her purse, stood, and nodded to him before pushing through the crowd. Even before she'd pressed between two suited businessmen, the Interior Department lawyer was looking enviously at the chair.

Joe jerked his head in assent. The chair was quickly slid to the next table. For a long moment, he looked down at his notes, an uneasy feeling crawling around his gut.

If Elizabeth could be believed, Billy Barnes Brown, the shining icon of the Christian Right, was going around murdering . . . what? Anthropologists? For teaching evolution?

Just bring the goods with you tomorrow, Elizabeth. And then we'll see. Tomorrow morning, early, he'd drive by, just to verify that she really lived at that address on West Osceola.

CHAPTER FOUR

THE RINGING DROVE BRYCE BERSERK. AFTER THE TENTH ring, the operator said, *"I'm sorry, sir, but your party doesn't appear to be answering. Thank you for using AT and T. Can I be of further assistance?"*

"No, thank you." Bryce hung up, his fingers still caressing the dark gray plastic of the receiver. He took a deep breath. Around him the clatter and chatter of the McDonald's restaurant created a familiar din. His change dropped musically into the receptacle; he drew it out with a finger before slipping it into his pocket.

Neither Amanda nor Scott had picked up. What did that mean?

Bryce ran his hand over his face, skin feeling like a latex mask. He had driven all night and phoned them across half of New York. His resolve had wavered as the morning of the twelfth waxed, to leave him here, at a roadside fast-food joint in Wheeling, West Virginia. He had alternately been desperate that this might be some sort of joke, and then equally certain that the grim, half-fanatical side of Scott Ferris' personality had landed him in some disastrous set of circumstances.

Amanda would have all the answers. If something terrible had happened, she would know. If it was a joke, she would have enough compassion to tell him before he drove clear across the country. Amanda was like that, intensely serious, considerate, and thoughtful in comparison to Scott's sometimes bulldog determination.

A joke? It had better be. Though what he'd do to get even with Scott for missing a night's sleep and screwing up his schedule at UNH would take some serious thinking. Stunts like this could wreck a friendship.

He chewed on his lip for a moment, then dialed the one eight hundred number for his phone service. Moments later he was talking to the answering machine in his department.

"Hi, this is Bryce. Listen, Dorothy, I need to have one of the graduate students, maybe Mary or Pat, cover my classes for the next couple of days. Something's come up, and I've been called out of town on an emergency. I'll keep in touch."

He hung up, rubbed his stubble-coated face, and walked over to the counter where he ordered up McDonald's version of breakfast. After he made his way to a table, he studied the map. Depending on traffic and roadwork, he should be at Amanda's by midafternoon. There, at least, he'd finally have real answers.

A sick sense of despair filled Joe Hanson's gut as he turned onto West Osceola and slowed. Fire trucks, patrol cars, and a throng of onlookers jammed the street. Finding no place to park, he pulled into a driveway, put the Taurus in park, and stepped out as the homeowner, a woman in her fifties wearing a sweatshirt and faded jeans, immediately turned his direction, shouting, "You can't park here!"

Joe slipped his ID from his pocket, letting her read the plastic-coated card. "I won't be long. I promise. And I'd sure appreciate it. You're not leaving anytime soon are you?"

She gave him a nervous glance. "No, I'm not. Yeah, it's okay." As he started toward the fire trucks, he heard her say to a neighbor, "What's the FBI want with Lizzy?"

His ID allowed him to pass through the police line, and he picked his way across fire hoses and past randomly parked patrol cars. Two referrals brought him to the officer in charge, a Corporal Pete Lzerski. Lzerski might have passed thirty, barely, and wore a neatly pressed uniform. The words "university grad" could have been rubber-stamped on his forehead.

Joe identified himself, seeing curiosity in Lzerski's mellow brown eyes. "I take it that's what's left of 11256 West Osceola?"

"That's it." Lzerski cocked his head, looking at the card Joe had handed him. "I don't usually have federal cooperation in an apparent arson, Agent Hanson."

Joe turned, sucking unhappily on his lower lip. "Yeah, well, it's a little more complicated than that. You wouldn't know where Elizabeth Carter is, would you? This was the address she gave me."

"She told you correctly. Or, I should say that according to the county clerk's office, she holds the deed to the property. We can't tell you if the body we pulled out of there is her. Not until the medical examiner takes a look."

Joe felt his stomach flip as he studied the smoking wreckage. "Son of a bitch. Arson, huh?"

"If you don't mind, sir, what's your involvement in this?"

"Elizabeth Carter was supposed to bring information to my office today. I just drove by on my way in. One of those bad hunches that seems to have paid off."

"What was she bringing you?"

"Nothing that's any good now, Corporal. Her 'instant credibility' just went up in smoke."

Lzerski gave him a level stare. "Anything you'd care to share with me? Something that might make my investigation a little easier?"

Studying the smoking ruin, Joe mentally reconstructed the floor plan of a three-room bungalow. From the looks of things, the fire had started in the front room, engulfing the walls and ceiling. By the time the firefighters had arrived, they'd managed to save only the rear corners of the house.

"Looks like it went up real fast," Joe offered.

"Lots of accelerant. Gallons of it. Enough to blow fragments of the picture window into the yard across the street. The explosion woke the neighbors at two-thirty-five this morning."

"If what she told me is correct, you're going to find that she worked for the Christian Creationist Crusade. Some kind of secretarial work. What you may not be able to find out is that she claimed she was Billy Barnes Brown's special squeeze. At least, until last weekend when she decided she didn't like the intricacies of a ménage à trois. She took something . . . what she called a 'hit list.' A bunch of scientists, or something. That's what she was bringing to the field office this afternoon."

"Did you get any of that on tape?" Lzerski asked cautiously.

"Get real. It was an initial contact. I didn't have the

first idea of what she was all about." *But, by God, I wish I had!*

"What else?" Lzerski was looking at him as if he were the oracle at Delphi.

"That's it. End of story. Now you know just about as much about Elizabeth Carter as I do. Your turn. What happened here?"

Lzerski placed his paperwork on the seat and led the way to the ruined lawn, now soaked and covered with ash, fragments of charred two-by-fours, and melted aluminum siding. Inside the ruin, crumbled drywall sagged from the remaining studs. Sections of the trusses that hadn't been completely incinerated lay beneath the smoldering remains of asphalt shingles. The hot-water heater and furnace leaned precariously together where a wall and part of the floor had collapsed. Another wobbling island of metal remained where the refrigerator, stove, and sink protruded from the destroyed kitchen. The place stank of fire, melted plastic, and the acrid cremation of an American household.

"Anyone see anything?" Hanson asked. Any notion that Elizabeth's "packet" might have survived vanished as he surveyed the devastation.

"We got one report of a light-colored van. Maybe a Chevy, but it could have been a Dodge. Late model, and by that, the informant thought from the last ten years or so. Other than that, no one saw anything after the explosion."

"I'd appreciate it if you could let me know what turns up. Sometimes people remember things later." He winced. "Where was Elizabeth?"

"She was found there," Lzerski pointed. "And not

much of her at that. She was in the center of the blaze, and like I said, they used a lot of gasoline. The investigator thinks it was ignited by some kind of time delay. They haven't found what yet, but they don't think the perp could pitch a match into that much gas and get out without being toasted himself."

"A perp? Then there's no chance Elizabeth could have done it to herself?"

"Nope." Lzerski shot a measuring sidelong look at Hanson. "Whoever did this isn't playing by normal rules, Agent Hanson. We've got a pretty good team here. Anyone less observant might not have noticed, but she was nailed to the floor."

Hanson turned on his heel. "What?"

"Yeah, nailed there. She was pretty well burned, but our guys are good at what they do. Now, it may not hold up after the autopsy, but for now, my people say that she was alive when the fire started. She just couldn't do anything about it because someone had nailed her wrists and ankles to the floor with big ten-penny spikes."

"Son of a bitch." Joe's stomach turned. Her face formed in his memory: an attractive, frightened woman, looking to him to keep her safe.

Corporal Lzerski shook his head. "Yeah, it's almost medieval, isn't it?"

Skip Manson was sitting in the passenger seat of the WQQQ television remote unit. He was in the process of reviewing his notes as Kahlid shot footage of the wreckage, the police, and the firefighters. Skip had been in the business long enough to know when he was being fed a line of bull. The information officer had only said that this was an arson/homicide. One victim, a woman, name being withheld pending notification of kin, had been located in the living room of the structure. Neighbors said she was Elizabeth Carter, a single woman who worked for some church foundation.

Skip chewed on the end of his pen as he considered. Drugs? Nine times out of ten, that's what these things turned out to be. He was starting to spin the story in his head, thinking up the tag line, when he saw the suited man walk across one of the neighbor's lawns to a Ford Taurus. The man glanced back, a pained look in his eyes, then spoke to the homeowner in whose drive he'd parked. He gave her a card, entered his car, and drove off.

Something about the man, about the way he'd walked, sent a tingle into Skip's antenna.

"Just about done," Kahlid said as he opened the back of the van and lowered his camera into a case jammed in amongst the electrical equipment.

"Yeah . . . wait a minute."

Skip put on his smile and crossed the street to where the woman stood with her arms crossed, a slightly shocked look on her face. She immediately shot Skip a reproving glance as he approached, saying, "I don't know what happened. I was asleep. I told that to the other cops that took my statement."

"I'm not a cop." Skip handed her one of his cards. "Skip Manson. I'm a journalist with—"

"I know you. From on TV!"

"Right." Skip turned and looked down that block to

the incinerated remains of the Carter house. "Hell of a thing. You don't think it was drugs, do you?"

She shook her head. "Not Lizzie."

"Oh, wasn't that guy who parked here with the DEA?"

The woman shook her head. "FBI." She held up the card. "Name's Joe Hanson. He's with . . ." She frowned. "Look here. It says 'Domestic Terrorism.' Can you imagine?" Then she looked back at the burned house where firefighters were rolling up hose. "Just what was Lizzie mixed up in?"

"I don't know," Skip replied thoughtfully. *But you can damn well bet I'm going to find out.*

The warm breeze blew down out of Boulder Canyon, across the slab-faced Flatirons and around Flagstaff Mountain. It seemed to caress the city of Boulder, Colorado. Buildings gleamed in the sunlight; heat mirages, like little wraiths, rose off the pavement. Tall pillars of cloud formed above the Rockies to the west. Later in the day, they would come spilling down over the Front Range with wind, lightning, and streamers of rain. For the moment, the city dreamed in the noonday sun.

Musicians played on the Pearl Street mall, their guitar cases open for donations. Robed acolytes strode along the hot cement: emissaries of the Naropa Institute. People filled the sidewalk cafés and sipped at gourmet coffees or microbrewed beer.

At the stoplight, Veronica Tremain glanced down the mall, smiling at the familiar sight. When the light changed she accelerated northward along Broadway. Her right hand caressed the polished wooden gearshift knob as she slipped the BMW into second, eyes on the traffic ahead of her. She took a right onto Mapleton. In front of the Catholic church, she wound through the balloon-infested maze of a Mexican wedding and gunned the engine as sloe-eyed young men flashed her smiles and clapped approbation. The city had painted curious white triangles on the speed bumps, and Veronica eased the Z3 coupe over them as she made her way the six blocks east to her house: a red brick, two-story Victorian that she had purchased after her separation from Ben the year before.

Veronica wheeled the BMW into the driveway and tapped the Z3's accelerator just to hear that throaty rumble of power before she turned off the ignition and propped her hands on the smooth wooden steering wheel.

Home. Damn. With a sigh she pulled the trunk release, opened the door, and stepped out. She took her suitcase and slammed the lid down. Her heels echoed as she took the walk to the front door. The mailbox was crammed full, and Ralph, her ex-hippie postman, had left several plastic bags at her door, anticipating the last day of her "vacation hold."

Veronica growled to herself, tired, rumpled, and perhaps a little jet-lagged. She hadn't slept on the flight from Hawaii to LAX, or on the leg to Denver International Airport. Instead, she had brooded over her homecoming and the contents that she guessed were in the big brown envelope she could see protruding from the blue plastic postal bag.

She unlocked her door and swung it open. Agile fingers tapped in the code to disarm the security system, and she dropped her suitcase onto the waxed hardwood floor.

She reached back to retrieve the sacks of mail and carried them inside, where she deposited them on the round antique table in the small parlor. Through the arched entrance to the living room, she could see the light blinking on the answering machine. In the delight of Hawaii, she had forgotten to call for messages. People were probably wondering where she was.

Veronica stepped to the hall closet and studied herself in the full-length mirror. She blinked at the fatigue staring back at her. Her long black hair had been pulled back severely and clipped into a ponytail that hung to her waist. Red rimmed her blue eyes. A faint trace of tan had replaced the sunburn that came of five days of lounging, golf, and snorkeling at Turtle Bay.

She hadn't planned the trip. Mary, her mother, had shown up at the door the day after graduation, suitcase in hand, shoved an envelope-clad ticket at her, and said, "Come on, Ronnie. You've got the degree. You are now Veronica Ferris Tremain, Ph.D. You're a bona fide physical anthropologist, the finest that the University of Colorado has ever turned out. Let's go celebrate."

"But, Mom . . ."

"Mom, nothing. You've worked like a dog this last year. It's my present to you." Mary had cocked her head, an eyebrow lifted. "You wouldn't want me to waste the cost of a ticket, now would you? The rooms are nonrefundable."

"Why didn't you warn me?"

"Because you'd have found a way around it. Scott got a trip. You get a trip. Besides, you can use the break."

How many years had passed since she'd done anything that spontaneous? For those wondrous five days, she had forgotten about the envelope and what it contained. For those marvelous five days, she had been free to laugh, to ignore, and even to forget.

As her father had said, the circle always came full around. Turtle Bay faded, and she stared at herself, clear-eyed, aware of the hollows under her cheeks, of the defeat in the set of her pale lips. She took a breath, noticing how the white blouse conformed to her high breasts, how the jeans clung to her narrow waist and accented her hips. Not bad for twenty-nine—and officially free. She still looked damned attractive, and she'd been more than aware of the men watching her in Hawaii. So, she'd stayed close to her mother, being coolly polite when men had introduced themselves; and, bless her heart, Mary had understood and played along.

When had things changed between them? Could that really have been her mother? The one she had despised, fought with, and almost killed herself to annoy? At what point in their rocky past had their relationship mutated into one of intuitive understanding? Had it been after Dad's death? Had she been so concerned with herself that she hadn't noticed?

Veronica turned toward the table and poured out the mail. The large manila envelope mocked her from where it lay partially buried by the phone, utility, and gas bills. She could see THEODOR BENNET, APPLEBY, AND GROSSET, ATTNYS AT LAW on the return address. In an effort to delay the inevitable, she picked up the plastic-wrapped copy of the *American Journal of Physical Anthropology* and scanned the table of contents to see if Scott's latest article had been printed. There it was: "A New Application of Polymerase Chain Reaction in the Reproduction of

Prehistoric Tissue Culturing," by Scott Ferris, Amanda Alexander, and Bryce Johnson.

She smiled, dropping it flat on the table. Good for Scott. Always the golden boy, the proverbial champion at the front of the race. She glanced across the living room to the framed news photo. Years ago she had clipped it from *USA Today*. Blood streaked down the side of Scott's head as he fought with a group of people dressed in fringes, beadwork, and jeans. Some carried placards, others axes. The photo had been taken just moments before one of the Native American activists had knocked Scott cold with an ax handle. After that, they'd stomped on his body as they battered down the door to the Harvard physical anthropology lab. They'd stomped on him again as they carried out most of the osteological collection. Yep, always the hero, Scott.

She fingered the rest of the mail and came to the manila envelope. As if all the fatigue in the world had fallen upon her she lifted it, slipped a fingernail under the seal, and ripped it open.

There it was, in neat black and white, all the signatures, seals, and stamps duly placed and affixed. Everything was now final. She stared at Ben's familiar script where he'd signed on his line. After a long moment, she slapped the paper down on the table and leaned her head back to stare at the white ceiling.

"Damn, Veronica, what a mess you've made out of your life." It was hard to believe that Ben had been one of the lesser mistakes.

She passed the answering machine on the way to the kitchen and noticed thirty-two messages. Thirty-two? Cripes, she'd only been gone for a week! She had just opened the refrigerator door and removed a bottle of cranberry juice when the phone rang.

After two long airplane rides, the snarled traffic on the drive from DIA to Boulder, and opening her final divorce papers, the last thing she could possibly countenance was talking with anyone. Hell with it, she was headed to bed. She'd call them back.

The machine clicked on, saying, "This is Doctor Veronica Tremain. I am currently unavailable. Please leave a message on the machine, and I will get back to you as soon as possible."

A click and a whir, then, *"Yeah, Doctor Tremain. This is Lieutenant Arthur Davidson of the Fort Collins Police Department. It's one-fifteen on the afternoon of the twelfth. Look, I still haven't been able to get a hold of you, or your mother. It's been two days now, and I really need to talk to you. I've even—"*

Veronica picked up the receiver, saying, "Yes, Lieutenant? This is Veronica Tremain. How can I help you?" A nervous tension began to build in her gut: a conditioned response from the bad old days of her wild youth and her dealings with the police.

"Doctor Tremain," the voice said in relief. "Good. You're home. Safe. I can't tell you—"

"Safe? Of course. Mother and I just went to Hawaii. We didn't think we needed to check in with the Fort Collins police to do that."

"No, uh, I suppose not. Why haven't you returned my calls?"

"I *just* got in the door!"

"You say your mother was with you?"

"Yes." The tension in her gut had turned to butterflies. "Listen, Lieutenant, what's this all about?"

"I'm sorry to be the one to tell you, ma'am, but your brother, Scott Ferris . . ."

"Yes?"

"I'm afraid he's dead, ma'am." The voice sounded so frank, so matter-of-fact.

"I don't understand." Dead? Scott was only thirty-eight. Healthy as a horse. He skied, hiked, rode his bike to class every day. His cholesterol was 130. He . . . A fist seemed to tighten in her throat.

"Ms. Tremain, your brother is dead. We suspect foul play. We'll have someone from the Boulder P.D. there to see you as soon as possible. Do you know the current whereabouts of your mother?"

"Heading home," she croaked, unsure when her will to speak had eroded. "We just got off the plane from Hawaii. United. Flight 2387. She's just about there by now." *Foul play?* She shook her head. This was impossible. "Who'd want to kill Scott?"

Lieutenant Davidson answered, "We don't know that yet, Ms. Tremain."

Through the parlor window she could see one of the black Boulder police cars pulling up outside.

"Dear God," she whispered.

The Durango coasted as Bryce slowed on Sycamore Street. The yellow tape looked garish against the ruined lawn and the charred remains of Amanda Alexander's house. Midday sunlight gleamed on the blackened wreck-age.

Through sleepless, red-rimmed eyes, Bryce stared at the place. In another life he had walked up that concrete sidewalk to the two-story frame house tucked under the majestic beech tree. He had slept in Amanda's guest bed-room, back there, on the northwest corner. All that re-mained were the skeletonized walls. In what was now the wreckage of the main room, he had eaten pizza, en-veloped by the overstuffed chair, the remains of which were a mass of blackened springs under the rubble of the fallen roof.

Scott and Amanda had sat side by side on the couch, laughing, excited as they talked about coding alus, hap-lotypes, and the exotica of human genetics. Thinking back, Bryce could recall the hidden communication that had passed between Amanda and Scott. How easy it had been at the time to lay it to the intimacy of two lovers. Easier now to understand that it had been some deeper conspiracy.

Why didn't they tell me? Why didn't they trust me?

He accelerated and drove slowly down the block. A blankness filled his mind. A hollow, gaping emptiness. Had this really happened to him? Could his life have sud-denly been turned upside down? Why?

In the confusion, a spark of anger flared to battle with his fear and disbelief. No wonder Amanda hadn't an-swered his calls. Bryce glanced at the cell phone lying on the seat.

Damn it, what do I do now? If he went to the police, what did he tell them? That someone had used his re-search? For what? No, first and foremost, he needed proof. For the moment, no one knew where he was. Nor could anyone find him if he was smart. If he used his head.

At the Kroger's store on the busy street that fronted Amanda's neighborhood, he bought a copy of the paper for the twelfth of June and found the story just below the fold. In harsh black and white the reporter laid it out: Amanda Alexander, professor of anthropology, had evidently been overcome in a house fire and was found burned to death in her bed. From the preliminary investigation by the fire marshal, the fire resulted from substandard wiring, having started in a broom closet.

Sitting in the seat of his Durango, oblivious of the parking lot and the shoppers around him, Bryce stared sightlessly at the paper. This couldn't be happening. Substandard wiring? No way!

CHAPTER FIVE

IN THE WASHINGTON METRO FIELD OFFICE, JOE HANSON sat in his little cubicle, blank gaze fixed on the file cabinet across from him. The computer terminal glared at him, the cursor blinking at the end of his final sentence. He'd finished his report, the infamous FD-302; made the phone calls; and now had nothing to do but wait—and re-play every single event in the preceding twenty-four hours.

Elizabeth Carter's haunted gray-eyed stare lingered in his mind. How the hell did a woman end up like that, defining herself by the men in her life? She had been ready to climb straight into his bed. If he'd said yes to her invitation, maybe taken her out to supper, she might still be alive, and her list—the one valuable enough that Billy Boy had snuffed her—might be in his hands.

Then again, it might not. He was a professional; he didn't mess with women on a case. Had she agreed to leave with him, he would have escorted her safely home. And the bad guys, if there were more than one, would still have torched her later that night.

Stop it, Joe. You're quarterbacking Sunday's game from the safety of Monday morning.

The phone at his elbow bleated.

"Special Agent Hanson." He propped the receiver against his cheek.

"Joe? This is Bob Dole, Denver Field Office. We met at Quantico a couple of years back at the antiterrorism seminar. We got your lead. Sorry to take so long, but it's been a little busy here this morning. You requested information on a Scott Ferris? Some kind of scientist?"

"That's right. I can use anything you can find out. The guy might be an anthropologist, or something related. I don't have an address or—"

"Forget it, pal. He's all over the news here. Assuming it's the same Scott Ferris, he's a—or was—an anthropologist up at Colorado State. Three days ago the Fort Collins Fire Department responded to a call. When they got there, Ferris' house was a fireball. Seems he was assaulted; some think it might even be torture. Somebody dumped him on his living room floor, piled his books on top, and doused the whole thing with gasoline. Fort Collins P.D. is handling it. I'll fax everything we've got and pipe the lead on to the Fort Collins residency."

"Yeah, right. Thanks, Bob." Hanson remembered him: tall, balding, and constantly irritated that his name was the same as the politician's. "I appreciate this. I need to talk to my supervisor, and I'll get back to you. This thing is starting to come together . . . and it's looking real nasty."

After he hung up the phone, he leaned back and stared up at the square fluorescent light panels hung in the acoustical ceiling. Around him, he could hear the familiar office sounds: the humming of the copy machine, the electronic warble of the phones, and muted conversations. Someone laughed.

Scott Ferris was burned to death three days ago! A cold streak ran down his back, the hair prickling at the nape of his neck. His chair squeaked as he leaned forward and began adding the latest information to his report. Ferris was dead, Avi Raad was dead, and dollars to donuts he was going to hear that Amanda Alexander had recently been cooked, too.

The fax buzzed and began to slowly spit out pages. One by one he picked them up, reading photocopies of the articles in the *Denver Post*, the *Fort Collins Coloradoan*, and the *Rocky Mountain News*. Adding to his notes and his report, he printed the whole thing and picked up the phone to dial the Cincinnati Field Office. After he asked for Felix Smith's extension, the switchboard put him on hold. He was sitting there, waiting, when Mitch Ensley leaned into his cubicle and said, "Boss wants to see you now."

Mitch was the sort of agent who would have left J. Edgar Hoover twirling in his grave. Hoover had insisted on handsome, dapperly dressed, and steel-nerved young white agents. With skin like coal, an unkempt suit, and a proverbial nervous twitch, Mitch was anything but. Instead he relied on unfettered brainpower and a dogged tenacity that finished cases, even if it took years. He had that unique personality that just made people want to talk to him.

"Be right there." Hanson collected his papers and stuffed them into a folder. As he passed the secretary's desk, he said, "Betty, if Cincinnati calls, patch them through to the supervisor's office, will you?"

At her nod, he followed Mitch down the hall.

Jackson Ramsey was having a delightfully dull day. He read the latest in the stack of reports and memos. He was a trim man, one who earned his promotions through hard work, dedication to the job, and ruthless energy. Unlike so many, Ramsey had won his appointment by efficiency—an unusual fact, this being Washington and just down the street from Headquarters, not to mention the seats of the executive and legislative branches of government. No one had ever accused Jack Ramsey of being a political appointee. He had spent his time on the street, going in on point and slapping cuffs on bad guys.

"Hey, boss."

Ramsey looked up from behind a battered metal desk. The mental alarms went off as he took in Hanson's expression. When Joe looked that way, something bad had happened. The file of papers in the agent's hand were clutched so tightly that the knuckles were white.

Ramsey took a breath and set the report to one side. "You look like hell, Joe. Did you meet with that Maria woman? What happened?"

Hanson stepped in, nodded to Mitch, who followed, and closed the door behind him. He dropped the report on Ramsey's desk and seated himself in one of the fabric office chairs. Mitch took the one to the left before fishing out a toothpick to chew on.

Ramsey picked up Joe's report, scanning it, aware that the two agents stared aimlessly at the soccer trophies, the family photos, and the meritorious service awards on the office wall behind him. The trophies belonged to Ramsey's son, Matt, his pride and joy.

Ramsey grunted to himself as he read about Elizabeth Carter, her meeting with Joe, and subsequent murder. He grunted again when he reached the faxed articles on Scott Ferris' death provided by the Denver Field Office. As he read about Avi Raad's murder, he was silent, engrossed. Closing the folder, he leaned back and fingered his thick chin, questioning eyes on Hanson.

"I think we've got a problem," Hanson said. "If you can believe that where there's smoke there's fire, I've got toasted corpses."

"No idea where this list is?" Ramsey thumped a thick finger on the report as he leveled sober blue eyes on Hanson.

"No, Jack, I don't." Hanson leaned back in the chair.

"I've been playing this over and over in my head. I can think of a hundred reasons for doing everything differently, starting at the Mayflower the other night."

"You did fine, Joe. Given what we had at the time, she wasn't credible." Ramsey's brow furrowed. "If it is Billy Barnes Brown who's behind this, your case just went hot. Other than this, how's your sheet looking?"

"We've just about finished with the Reubenstein case. Baltimore P.D. has the guy that threw the firebomb. Chances are he's going to plea-bargain rather than take a chance on a jury. The militia thing that BATF was so worked up about last week appears to be a bunch of guys and three women who just wanted to own and shoot rifles. There's nothing there. They bought semiauto guns legally and formed a club. Nothing political outside of membership in the NRA and a belief in the Second Amendment."

Ramsey nodded, turning his eyes back to the report again. Hanson was a good man. Solid. He'd had his problems and worked his way through them. If this went big . . . "Do you want this one, Joe?"

Hanson stiffened. "Jack, something's really wrong here. Somebody nailed my contact to the floor and charred her well-done. This guy in Colorado that Elizabeth mentioned was crisped, too. That's not coincidence."

Ramsey caught the phone on its first ring. "Ramsey here." He listened to the agent on the other end. "Who?" He nodded. "Yeah, he's here." He handed the phone to Hanson.

"Cincinnati?" Joe asked.

At Ramsey's nod, Hanson indicated the phone, and

Ramsey pushed the speaker-phone button. Hanson took the receiver. "This is Joe Hanson."

"Special Agent Hanson? This is Agent Beth Sennet. We picked up your lead on Amanda Alexander. We have some bad news for you. If she was a geneticist at the university in Athens, she's dead. Apparently she burned to death in a house fire."

Ramsey straightened as Joe shot him an "I told you so" look.

"When?" Joe asked.

"The Athens fire marshal's report states that the fire apparently started in a closet. Dr. Alexander apparently died in bed, probably from smoke inhalation. The house burned down around her at about two-thirty A.M."

"We would appreciate it if you could send anything you have along to us. It might tie into similar cases here and in Colorado."

"Can do. We'll notify the Athens residency and see what they can add. Are you the agent in charge?"

At Ramsey's nod, Joe said, "Yes, Beth."

"We'll be in touch. If you need anything, let us know."

Joe handed the receiver back to Ramsey and settled himself into the chair. Mitch wiggled the sodden toothpick from side to side with his lips. A frown lined his round face. Artfully talking past the toothpick, he asked, "What was that last name you had?"

"Bryce Johnson," Joe answered mechanically. "Somewhere in New Jersey. I sent a lead out to Trenton and Newark. Nothing's come back yet. On a hunch, I called several of the big universities. No Bryce Johnson on staff."

Ramsey swiveled in his chair and kicked his short legs

out. "Any chance that this list could show up? Maybe mailed in by someone else? A third party? Did you think Elizabeth was sharp enough to cover herself like that?"

Joe shook his head. "My gut says no. Just based on intuition, Jack, I'd say that she was the kind to stick it in the cookie jar and call it safe. But who knows."

"It'd be a godsend if it showed up in the mail," Mitch said absently.

"Those were the only four names she mentioned?" Ramsey prodded. "You're absolutely one hundred percent positive about that?"

"Yeah, Jack." Hanson cracked his knuckles. "She said there were twenty-five names. I didn't want to get too pushy, and to be honest, she didn't look like she remembered any more. I had the distinct feeling that she was wishing she'd never set eyes on that damn list, let alone lifted it."

Ramsey jerked a nod. If this really was Billy Barnes Brown and his politically powerful church, they were about to kick a hole in an ants' nest of trouble. "All right, Joe. Get your stuff together. We're going down the street to Headquarters. It's time we let the Bureau know what we've got."

"What if Billy Barnes Brown really is behind all this?" Mitch asked.

Ramsey picked up his "trophy" pen—the one Larry King had given him during an interview. Rolling it between his fingers, he said, "All we really know is that this Elizabeth Carter *said* he was behind it. We know that she's dead, and we've got a string of arson homicides that seem connected, at least in modus operandi. The rest, gentlemen, is up to us. If someone, Billy Barnes Brown or whoever, is killing people for an ideological reason, then we'd better figure it out."

Mitch tilted his head and made a face, as if his ear were bothering him. "Billy Barnes Brown. He's a big wheel. Coming up to have dinner with the president next week. You know, that big P.R. thing about reaching out to the 'Right'?"

"If he's behind it, we'll get him eventually," Joe muttered. He had a preoccupied look, one that reeked of self-castigation.

"We'd better," Ramsey murmured. "In the meantime I want you two to find the linchpin that holds this whole thing together. If it is Billy Barnes Brown, he's not risking his ass just to kill a bunch of anthropologists. No, there's something behind this, and as soon as we know, we can catch the son of a bitch."

Scott's body—or what was left of it—lay on a stainless steel gurney. Bits of charred flesh had flaked off, speckling the polished steel. The rounded vault of the skull had popped apart as the brain boiled within. Sunken pits remained in the orbits that had once held his sparkling eyes. Discolored, heat-cracked teeth were visible where the lips had peeled back and burned off.

This . . . *specimen*. This pile of charred flesh and bone, centered on the gleaming steel, surrounded by white antiseptic walls, couldn't be Scott. Not the Scott that Veronica knew. No, Scott pulsed with life, with that knowing smile. Scott looked out at the world through serious blue eyes. Thick dark hair curled on his head, not this vitreous mass of ash over the exploded skull.

Her teeth ached as she clamped them together. The muscles in her arms cramped from knotting her fists. Impossible. This couldn't happen. This reality simply would not fit into Veronica's cosmology.

"You're sure it's Scott?" she asked unsteadily. Lieutenant Davidson shifted behind her, the soles of his shoes grating on the cement floor. She could feel his gaze on the back of her neck.

Bill Boship, the county coroner, said, "Yes. Pretty sure." He stood to one side, wearing a green smock over his suit. "We have ways. Blood type, stature, apparent age, and the X rays we took of the teeth match his dental records. So does the steel pin in his right leg. You see, Ms. Tremain, the human body is as individualistic as a fingerprint. With our—"

"I know that!" She blinked at the silvering of her vision as tears tried to creep past her weary defenses. "My Ph.D. is in physical anthropology, Mr. Boship. Just like my brother's." She swallowed hard, remembering Scott's proud eyes. How he'd walked up to her after graduation, saying, "Nice going, kid! I'm so proud!" And he'd plucked her up and hugged her, almost to the point of pain.

The ash-coated orbits in the charred skull seemed to probe her, the gaze questioning. Heat-blued teeth gleamed in the white light where the cocked jaw hung at an angle—as if caught in a scream. The skin of the cheeks had crisped and flaked away.

"I'm sorry," Boship's voice remained professionally atonal. "In answer to your question, yes, we're sure."

In her disbelief, she tried to overlay Scott's face onto the blackened skull. The facial height, the slope of the frontal bone, the browridges . . .

Then she noticed the odd angle of the right arm. The humeral diaphysis—the shaft of the upper arm—had been crushed. Fire-blued splinters of bone protruded from the blackened flesh. She pointed. "I don't understand. That looks like a compound fracture. How else could the bone protrude?"

"That's a problem," Boship replied uneasily. "From the radiographs, the arm was broken before he died. Then, somehow twisted. You can't see it, the way the body is positioned, but the left arm is the same."

"What?" She turned, heart pounding. "How could that happen?" The bones of the arms and legs spalled in a fire, scalloped by the boiling marrow. They didn't splinter.

Forcing herself closer, she could see that the legs, looking so odd, had been twisted, the feet pointing the wrong way. A gaping hole could be seen where something had pierced the top of the foot; broken tarsals were visible inside the charred wound. She couldn't be sure, but the wrists looked similarly damaged.

"What happened to his wrists and feet?"

Boship glanced at Davidson, some unspoken communication passing between them.

"We don't know. Do you have any idea, Ms. Tremain?" Davidson's voice almost sounded like a challenge.

"No. A puncture of some kind." She could feel a desperate fear begin to crawl through her. She stepped over to where Lieutenant Davidson stood, his back braced against the wall, arms crossed.

He looked to be in his forties, with close-cropped black hair, a trimmed mustache, and long face with penetrating brown eyes. He wore a green wool sport coat and brown Dockers pants. The pocket of his white shirt was studded with pens and a small flashlight.

"Why would anyone do this?" she pleaded.

His normally cool gaze wavered for an instant, and he took a deep breath. "We don't know, Ms. Tremain. I've been here for almost twenty years now. We've never seen anything like this before."

"Robbery?" She shook her head. "Scott didn't have anything worth stealing. I mean, well, his skis and stuff. He always bought the best equipment. He didn't have cash on hand. It's all property, stocks, and investments. Nothing that anyone could fence."

Davidson shifted, clearly uneasy. "As far as we can tell, robbery wasn't a motive. Your brother had almost two hundred dollars in his wallet. The arson team determined that the usual things—TV, stereo system, computer, his two shotguns—were all in the house when it burned. The only oddity was the books. Your brother had a lot of them."

"Yes. His library filled the whole living room. Mostly journals. Physical anthropology and genetics. *Science*, that sort of thing. He was one of the leaders in the field."

"Yeah, well, that's one of the curious things." Davidson pulled at his ear. "All the books were piled onto the living room floor. Even file folders out of his desk drawers. Your brother was buried under the pile, and the whole thing was doused with gasoline. A lot of it. Then someone struck a match."

She staggered, blinking, trying to comprehend.

"Ms. Tremain," Davidson asked gently, "did your brother have enemies? Did he tell you about any threatening phone calls? Any hint that someone wanted to intimidate him? Cause him any harm?"

"No. I mean, he didn't mention anything like that." She swallowed hard. "And he would have. We were close."

"I see." The way he said it, he didn't really.

"He raised me," Veronica said hotly. "Dad . . . well, he didn't have time. He wasn't around. Scott was. He was ten years older than I was. He was the one who was always there. He came to my school plays. Took me to the mall, that sort of thing."

"And your mother?"

She ground her jaws. "Mom was there . . . sometimes. Other times, well . . ." She shook her head wearily. "What are you after, Lieutenant?"

"Anything you might want to tell me," he said evenly. Then, as if relenting, "Look, Ms. Tremain, we've got a homicide here that's unlike anything we've ever had in this city. Your brother was tortured and murdered in a very nasty way. We'll know more when the autopsy and the lab work is completed. But in the meantime, we've checked with the neighbors. No one saw or heard anything. No one in your brother's department was aware of any threats. As best we can figure, he lived for his research, had no enemies, and didn't irritate people." One eye seemed to narrow. "We're a little short on motive and suspects right now. And . . . call it a gut instinct, but this looks like a professional job, not just a burglary gone wrong."

"Jesus," she whispered, stepping away, trying to collect herself without looking at Scott's mangled body. "I've got to sit down. I'm not feeling well."

She took Davidson's arm, letting him lead her out to the hallway and down to a small office, where he offered her a metal folding chair. He perched on a paper-strewn Formica desk, his long face intent. A fluorescent light cast a white glow on the scratched walls and streaked linoleum. The brown rubber floor trim had come loose in one corner, and the trash can was overflowing. The Veronica reflected in the mirror behind the desk looked physically ill, pale, her composure shattered.

"Coffee?" he asked.

She shook her head, then sank into the chair. Leaning forward, she placed her head in her hands. "This isn't real."

"We're already checking," Davidson continued, "but is there any insurance? An inheritance, perhaps? Did he have a will?"

"I don't know about insurance. When Mom goes, he'd get half of her estate. I'd get the other half. There's the house up on Lookout Mountain, his interest in the condo in Frisco, a lot of stocks and bonds. Dad was an investment banker."

"I see."

She looked up at the tone, too emotionally drained to kindle the response his implication deserved. The words just slipped out. "God, you're a miserable person."

For the first time, Davidson smiled thinly. "I'm sorry, Ms. Tremain. In a case like this, we have to ask hard questions. Like I said, we're short on motive and possible suspects, and in a homicide investigation, I'm not paid to be a nice man. I need all the help I can get to figure this thing out."

She tried to think past the growing horror. "It's usually family, isn't it? That or a close friend. Someone who'd have a stake in Scott's death."

The neutral expression in his brown eyes didn't change.

She felt something tear inside her. "I wouldn't kill my brother, Lieutenant. Mother wouldn't . . . couldn't. He was her favorite. We don't have any reason."

The tears came welling from deep inside. This time she couldn't stop them, couldn't do anything but sit there in misery and hate herself, and the world, and the hard-eyed cop who watched her in silence.

She fumbled for her purse, found a tissue, and blew her nose. A painful knot had formed under her tongue, and her head ached.

Davidson's impervious shell cracked. "I'm sorry, Ms. Tremain. We're baffled. You're his sister, and in the course of the investigation, we pulled up your file. You've had a colorful youth: shoplifting, breaking and entering, alcohol and maybe some drugs, time on the streets as a runaway. What we'd call a troubled youth. But, with Dad's money and a fancy lawyer, you avoided paying any consequences. Look at it from our perspective: You hung out with some rough characters. Two of them are doing hard time at the pen in Canyon City. Maybe putting together a hit wasn't such a tough thing for a bright woman."

Horror left her mute.

"Do you know anything about your brother's death?"

She shook her head, stunned. "No. We were in Hawaii. Mother and me."

"Did your brother have a wife? Children? Any special friends? Anyone else he was close to?"

"Amanda." Her voice sounded scratchy. "God, who's going to tell Amanda?"

"Who is Amanda?"

"Amanda Alexander." Veronica stared dully at the shredded tissue in her hand. "I guess you'd call her a girl-friend. They lived together for a while back at Harvard. They had a child, but never married. Just saw each other whenever they could. Shared a room at professional meetings. They spent hours on the phone together. She's an anthropological geneticist like he is. It's just that in academia a department will usually hire only one profes-sor in a given specialty. They couldn't get jobs together."

Davidson was writing in a small notebook. "Where is Amanda?"

"Ohio. She's an associate professor there." Veronica sniffed. "Dear God, this is going to break her heart."

"Anyone else you can think of?"

She managed a dry chuckle. "If you're going to track down colleagues, Scott was pretty popular. He was a whiz kid when it came to genetics. He got along well pro-fessionally. Corresponded with half the anthropologists in the field."

"You're an anthropologist yourself." Davidson frowned. "Tell me, could someone, one of them, have done this? Professional jealousy? Some academic rivalry gone wrong?"

"Scott didn't fight with colleagues. He thought that these little feuds that people like Wolpoff and Stringer get into were silly. He never let his findings get personal with other researchers; he just published the data and let the chips fall where they might. The only people he didn't get along with . . ." She stiffened, fist tightening on the soggy tissue.

"Yes?" Davidson cocked his head, attentive.

The image flashed of Scott, blood running down the side of his head. "They beat him senseless. Put him in the hospital. He was weeks getting over it."

"Who? Who beat him?"

"They called themselves the National First Nations Liberation Front. They broke into the Harvard P.A. lab."

"The what?"

"The laboratory of physical anthropology. Scott tried to stop them, but they beat him up. Kicked him, broke some ribs. They stomped on his knee hard enough to give him a permanent limp. Then they battered down the door and took all the skeletal material they found in the lab." She looked up. "You know, for reburial? The trouble is, they got three Native American skeletons all right, but they took a Neandertal skull cast, two *Homo erectus* skulls, several skeletons from Pitcairn Island, some Carolina Biological specimens from India, two chimpanzees, and an orangutan."

Davidson was scribbling madly. "I'm sure there was a police report."

"There was. And articles in *Time* and *Newsweek*, as well as in *USA Today*. It was six years ago."

"Did your brother say anything about it—later, I mean? Recently?"

She wadded the tissue. "He never forgot. It changed him. I was an undergraduate when it happened. He said that fact couldn't be stopped. That sometimes extreme measures were necessary to . . . How did he put it? 'To

make the glazed-eyed acolytes of ignorance accept reality.'
Then he added with a smile, 'Fait accompli.' "

"What's that mean?"

"I don't know. He just smiled and said that one day I'd
understand. That anthropology was in for the most dynamic change since Boucher de Perthes picked up that
first hand ax. That the veil on the past was about to be
pulled back—no, ripped away! Those were his words.
We'd answer all the questions and silence the skeptics
once and for all. He always remained cryptic about it."

"Hmm," Davidson grunted.

A knock came at the door; a uniformed cop leaned in.
"Mrs. Ferris is here, Lieutenant."

Veronica stood on weak legs, glad that her brain had
begun to function again. "Lieutenant, you will *not* show
Scott's body to my mother. You will not question her unless
in the presence of our attorney. His name is Theodor Bennet.
I think I'd better call him now."

Davidson nodded. "You can use the phone here on the
desk, Ms. Tremain. Dial nine to get out." He fished in his
jacket with his left hand and produced a small tape
recorder from his pocket. His gaze fixed on her expression
as he thumbed off the "record" button. The machine made
an audible click in the still room.

CHAPTER SIX

Abel is glad that they are leaving the squalid little motel. He is tired of this place and of the smells that Mother doesn't seem to smell. The beds are hard and lumpy, and the one he has been sleeping in carries the old musty scent of vomit. The smell is in the pillow, and he can't get away from it. He desperately wishes he would have remembered to bring his own pillow. He left it on his bed at home, and Mother refuses to go back and get it. He worries about his little blue truck that Aunt Eu gave him. Instead, he hugs Chaser, his stuffed brown buffalo. Chaser's warm curly fur reassures him, and the gleaming black eyes share secrets that only Abel knows.

It is with relief that he follows Mother out into the warm Utah morning. The sun is streaking down over the Wasatch Mountains and gleaming on the Honda's windshield as Mother places her pink suitcase in the trunk. Then Abel goes through the ritual of being belted into his car seat in the back of the Honda. The familiar smell of the upholstery is a relief after the motel.

"Ready, Abel?" Mother asks as she starts the car.

"Weady."

Today the bank is open. He looks back through the rear window, squirming in his car seat to watch as they pull out of the terrible motel. The TV didn't work so

*well, and it didn't have his favorite channels. He misses
the reruns of Babylon 5. His favorite character is
G'Kar, because there is something about him, about the
way he looks, that makes Abel feel good. As if, one
day, he will be like G'Kar: brave, smart, and part of
the war council.*

He has never been to the bank before and watches as
Mother winds her way through the broad streets and
past the familiar sights of Salt Lake City. He points out
the buildings as they pass, saying the names: "Salll
Palace. Templlll Squarrr. Deltaaa Buildinnn. Shil-
drenss Mooseeum."

Mother pulls the Honda into a space in the bank's
parking lot. The sun beats down hot through the back
window. Summer has always bothered him. His pale
skin burns easily, and Mother always protects him with
creams and makes him wear long sleeves that are hot on
his stocky, round body.

Mother reaches over to unlock his restraint. Together they walk across the parking lot, and he looks
longingly at the towering range of the Wasatch Mountains rising to the east. One hand in Mother's, he points
at them with his free hand. "Cool thewe."

"Yes, sweetie, it's cool there." Mother nods, still uneasy. She looks around warily, as if afraid of something.
He has tried to understand, to learn the danger, but she
will not talk about it. The harder she tries to make believe that nothing is wrong, the more his stomach hurts.

The bank is huge. The lobby is big and grand, made
of polished stone, and most of all, wonderfully cool
after the heat outside. He tries to keep up, nearly running to keep from being dragged along by Mother. He

can't help but stare around, seeing, thinking about the way the big lobby is laid out and how the desks are placed around it. This place smells of people, paper, and the hot plastic smell of computers.

Mother takes him down a corridor to a glassed-in office. She leads him in and talks to the lady. From her purse, she takes out her driver's license, then signs forms. While she does this, he runs his fingers over the tall glass walls, feels the smoothness, and wonders at the brass rivets in the arm of the leather chair. The air carries the odor of a great many people. Someone who sat there not too long ago peed his pants. He can barely scent the trace of urine.

"Abel? Coming, sweetheart?" He looks up, smiling, aware that the lady behind the desk is giving him that puzzled look. Mostly he has grown accustomed to it, but somewhere, deep inside, it still bothers him. No one ever looks at Brian O'Neil like that.

Mother leads him across the hallway, and they pass through a thick steel door with big round pins sticking out of it. "Saafffe," he says, pointing.

"It's a vault, sweetie," Mother says, as she hands her papers to a man in uniform.

"Faalt," he tries, attempting to keep the sound out of his nose.

While the guard reads the papers she gave him, Mother reaches down, placing her fingers so as to squeeze his lower lip up against his teeth. "Now try."

"Vaalt."

"That's it, kiddo. Vee as in vault."

He pinches his lower lip up against his teeth with his stubby fingers. "Vaalt."

"Speech impediment?" the uniformed guard asks.

"Afraid so. But we make progress, day after day."

"Box 2612, ma'am. Do you need help?"

"No, thank you. Come on, Abel."

He resists the impulse to reach out and touch the guard's gun and obediently follows Mother deeper into the vault with its shining silver drawers. What could fill so many drawers? Mother is muttering numbers under her breath, before saying, "Here it is."

He watches as she inserts the key, turns it, and opens the door. Inside is a metal box, which she pulls out. As she takes it to a little cubicle, he raises himself on tiptoe to peer inside the square hole. Wonderful things could be kept there, like butterflies, balls, his Matchbox toys, and candy.

He doesn't see what Mother took from the box, but she is back, easing him out of the way, sliding the long metal box into the hole. "Want to slam the door?" she asks.

"Yess!" Eagerly he grabs the thick door with his pudgy fist and swings it closed. It takes two tries to press it hard enough to make the locks click.

"Tough-looking little guy," the guard says as Mother leads him out of the vault.

"He's all of that and more," Mother assures him before they head back the way they came.

At a bend in the hallway, he tugs hard on Mother's hand, pointing. "Thaa way!"

She cocks her head. "You sure?"

"Yes! Fowwow mee." He leads her back the way they came, out through the lobby and into the hot June sun.

The Fort Collins Marriott's in-house lounge was called Shay's. The step-up floor overlooked the lobby. A fake gas fireplace and Southwestern pastels gave the place a certain upscale Western atmosphere, although the fabric artwork detracted from the effect. For the moment, Veronica sat across from her mother, trying to relax, to find some sense of equilibrium in this mess.

They had spent most of the evening in the police department, but Mary, as usual, looked immaculate. Her silvered hair was pinned back. A black, form-fitting Armani dress appeared only slightly worse for the day's wear. Mary's wedding ring, a gaudy mass of sparkling diamonds, caught the light as she tapped her fingers on the tabletop. Her nails, of course, looked newly manicured.

The Fort Collins police had asked, but not insisted, that they stay in town. They still shared the need to remain close to Scott and the reality of his death. Besides, Veronica wouldn't have been able to face the drive back to Boulder. The problems had only begun to cascade down upon them. God alone knew what they were going to do about Scott's estate. She had no idea which insurance company would have covered his house, his life, or any of the particulars of his personal business.

And then there was the investigation. Veronica hadn't been surprised that Boship turned down her request to attend the autopsy. They didn't usually allow civilians—especially those who were potential suspects—to be present. At Theodor Bennet's request, however, Boship did consent to allow an assistant to videotape the procedure. That, in due time, she would be able to see.

She looked across the table to where her mother slouched in the bentwood wicker chair. Two half-empty glasses of bourbon rested between them on the green table. Mary had a wounded posture, as if she'd been squeezed out, left an empty husk. The hollow stare was dry-eyed, that of a woman completely cried out. Her cheeks were puffed and shadowed. The diamonds on her wedding ring prismed the light as she fingered the tumbler of Jack Daniel's.

"It's not real," Mary said, the usual perfect pitch of her voice off. "It won't be real for a couple of days." She closed her eyes and inhaled through her thin straight nose. "Dear God, it was bad enough when your father died. But this?"

Veronica could see Mary's control starting to fray. If that happened, Mary would collapse into a sobbing wreck. "Mother, we don't know everything yet. We'll get through this. Just like we always have."

Mary swallowed hard, nodded, and reestablished the iron control that had been her perpetual strength and her greatest character flaw. Her jaw muscles twitched. "I just keep asking, why? Why did this happen? Who would do this to Scott? For the life of me . . ." Her thin fingers tightened on the glass.

"They'll find out, Mother." Veronica reached across the table to lay her fingers on the back of her mother's hand. The skin had turned delicate with age, loosening over the petite bones. "What happened to Scott happened for a reason. When the police figure that out, they'll find the person who did this. Then, Mother, we'll have our day when they strap the son of a bitch into the chair down in Canyon City and fry his brains out."

"But what reason, honey?" Mary's watery blue eyes centered on Veronica. "You knew Scott better than I did. You were close to him. What did he tell you? What could it be?" She hesitated. "Drugs?"

"Not Scott, Mom. Never drugs. He might have smoked some grass back when he was an undergraduate, but he valued his mind too much." She sighed. "I don't know. I keep running everything over and over in my head. Things he said, offhand comments, that sort of thing. The problem is, I keep coming up empty. I can't think of anything, Mother. The only thing he lived for was his research."

"And . . . the Indian thing?" Mary reached for her crocodile handbag—a souvenir from Fremantle, Australia—and retrieved a hankie. "He changed after that, you know."

"Well, sure, Mom. God knows, he was beaten half to death. I think that's when he really grew up. When he figured out that the world could bite back."

"Tell me, Ronnie, do you think those people did this? That they came back to finish what they started?"

Veronica leaned back, tapping her long fingernails on the side of her glass. "I don't think so. I mean . . . I'm not certain, but it doesn't seem right. After that incident, Scott didn't go back to working with skeletal material. Like he used to say, 'genetics is safer.' " She paused, remembering his solemn-eyed stare as he stated, *"Just wait, Sis. Using genetics we can roll a stone into their garden that they can never roll out."*

He had turned into the proverbial Cheshire Cat after that and had given her an irritating big-brother smirk that she'd alternately loved and hated through the years.

Once, she and Ben had driven up for a spaghetti dinner at Scott's. Amanda had flown in from Boston to celebrate her new position at Ohio. She was eight months pregnant, consequences of a slipup in birth control during a journey she and Scott had made to Tel Aviv to consult with Avi about some research. Candlelight illuminated the dining room table, flickering on the sauce-stained plates. They had demolished the first bottle of Chianti and were well into the second when Scott raised a glass: "To Sis! Congratulations on being accepted into grad school! And, even more congratulations for picking paleo-anthropology as your specialty."

"Why not anthropological genetics?" she had asked snidely. "What's the matter, Bro? Tired of me dogging your tracks?"

Ben had laughed at that, but then Ben had always chided her for wanting to be too much like her brother. Amanda had watched from the side, radiating a warm smile. She seemed to glow, although she had abstained from the wine.

"No." Scott had turned inward for a moment, seeing something at a remote distance. "Things have changed, Ronnie. Something's happened. It's going to revolutionize anthropology. In fact, with it, some of us are going to change the world."

"Uh, how is that?" Ben had asked, a thorny edge to his voice.

Scott's eyes had cleared at the tone, and he smiled secretively as he picked up his glass and sipped the red wine. "Well, Ben, sometimes the only way you can get the attention of the ignorant and benighted is to beat them over the head with a two-by-four." His smile had widened, but his eyes hadn't wavered. "And this time, I'm going to swing it. You just watch. There's no room in the world for liturgical fanatics, no matter what their tribe or denomination."

"Scott," Amanda had interrupted with a subtle warning in her voice. He had glanced at her, grinned like an elfin boy, and shrugged.

"Better be a really big club," Veronica had muttered, feeling the effects of the wine.

"The biggest," Scott had assured, eyes locked with Amanda's and sharing some private communication.

"So? Tell. You don't keep secrets from me. Is Amanda in on this?"

His lips had twitched as Amanda laughed and placed a hand to her stomach. "Of course," he said. "She's my alter ego. And that's all I'm going to tell you. Give it up, Sis."

"Hell no! What are you up to?"

"Nothing! Forget it." Then he'd looked at Ben, grinned, and said, "So, Ben, how's the world of cardiac medicine? Had any fascinating cases lately?"

Ben, being stroked, dove into the conversation with the same gusto that he had when he sawed a sternum apart and sliced up the pericardium.

Gone. All of it. Ben divorced. Scott dead. The pretty lace curtains, the walnut dining table, the candles—all burned and turned to ash. Only the memory remained.

"Ronnie?" Mary's voice intruded, and Veronica realized she was staring aimlessly at the plastic chandelier lights.

"Sorry, Mom. I was just remembering."

"Anything pertinent? Anything I should know?"

"No, Mom. It was five years ago. Dinner at Scott's one night." She shook her head. "Amanda. My God. I've got to call Amanda. What in hell was I thinking of?"

"Your brother's death."

"Will you be all right? There's a phone just down the hallway."

Mary made a shooing motion with her hand, her unfocused eyes on the empty glass before her. Veronica hadn't even seen her finish the drink.

Veronica stood, taking her purse, pawing through the contents as she walked down the wide white hall. The collection of pay phones clustered in a special recess across from the elevator bay. Finding her address book, Veronica opened it to the first page and noted the number. She entered her phone card and punched in the numbers with a resolution that numbed her soul.

What on earth am I going to tell her? How do I say this? "Hello, Amanda? Your lover is dead?" She winced, a sick feeling in her stomach as the phone rang, and rang, and rang.

Bryce Johnson slipped behind a white Toyota and shot anxious glances around the Motel 8 parking lot. The security lights cast cones of yellow over the silent vehicles and washed up on the row of rooms with their dark windows and solid doors. His watch told him the time was 2:30 A.M. He had picked the darkest part of the lot, hearing occasional traffic whooshing across the Interstate 70 overpass no more than two hundred yards away. Between him and the highway stood a chain-link fence, a patch of weeds, and the off-ramp.

He used a screwdriver and wrench to loosen the nuts and screws holding the yellow New Mexico license plate. Each clink seemed to echo like a gunshot. Damn it, how could anyone but the deaf miss hearing him?

For a moment, he considered replacing the tags with his New Hampshire plates. But, no. They'd tie him to the Toyota's travel route. It was better this way. And besides, were this all to prove a mistake, he could replace his original plates.

Assuming I'm not just stark raving nuts!

If the police were looking for him, they would have broadcast a description of his laser-blue Durango and his plates. If they weren't, maybe changing plates was a sign of paranoia. Not knowing was a torture in itself. No matter what the paper said, someone had burned Amanda's house and murdered her. That didn't sound like the way the government would handle genetic research gone awry, but who knew where this went? What it entailed?

Bryce stepped around to the front in open view of anyone looking out of a motel window and crouched by the bumper. He inserted the screwdriver in the slotted head. It didn't give. He twisted harder, pushing on the blade; it slipped and clattered with a dreadful metal racket. He froze, heart racing, waiting for a cry, a sudden light.

After an agonizing minute he gulped air into his fevered lungs. His hands shook, making his hold on the tools difficult as he turned back to the recalcitrant plate. Grunting with effort, Bryce twisted. The screw gave. Using the wrench to hold the backing nut, he spun the screw loose. The nut rolled away under the Toyota.

His heart felt as if it would explode while he recovered his tools. Rising, he forced himself into an easy walk despite the desire to dash for his Durango where it was parked four spaces away. Bolting the New Mexico plates to the mounting bracket, he could breathe easier. A door slammed somewhere, and he almost cried out. Bryce spun around; nothing had changed. No movement caught his eye. The parking lot was still in the cold yellow light. Maybe it had been on the other side of the motel? Maybe his imagination had just tripped over a distant noise?

He waited, hearing only the sounds of the night, then forced himself to his work. *Is this smart? Putting the plates on now? What if the Toyota's owner comes out before I do? What if he notices his plates are gone?*

Sure, he answered himself, *and you don't think a man bolting license plates on in the parking lot in broad daylight wouldn't be noticed?* He'd just have to take the risk that the Toyota owner wasn't an early riser and, pending that, an observant one.

God, the number of things that a man on the run had to worry about!

When he finished, he slipped the room key from his pocket and crossed the parking lot. Entering his motel room, he stood for a moment, watching through a slit in the curtain, making certain that no one walked out to inspect his work.

Only then did he flop onto the bed and stare at the night-shadowed ceiling. His breathing and heart rate slowly returned to normal.

Dear God, how did this happen to me? The answers eluded him. What had Scott and Amanda done to him? How? All he had provided was the statistical expertise.

His genius, if you could call it that, came from the unique ability to model how genes worked, what percentages of genetic combinations could be expected in succeeding generations.

The research is real! I lied. I'm sorry. Scott's voice came back to haunt him. *Avi's dead!* Bryce winced at the thought.

"God, Scott. What did you do? Why didn't you and Amanda trust me? Maybe this never would have happened."

Who were the men in Scott's house? At least two of them. One to pick up the phone, the other to subdue Scott. If not the police . . . who?

He tossed and turned, struggling to get some sleep before his six-thirty wake-up call. His fingers curled around the polymer grip of his pistol. The Heckler & Koch USP .45 might have been his only friend in the world.

The cottonwood tree brought the extent of the tragedy home to Veronica. It drooped over the blackened wreckage, its leaves curled and dying where the searing flames had raced through on their violent quest for the night sky. Soot had painted the gray bark in gentle strokes as it wrapped tenderly around branches split by boiling sap. The roots, gnarled and bunched in the grass, looked as if they'd knotted against tremendous pain.

The sight wounded Veronica's heart. She and Theodor Bennet stood on the sidewalk before the yellow police tape. Somehow she had forced herself to come here, to look where three days ago, her brother had been burned to death. She had crossed her arms; the wooden expression on her face masked the turmoil within. *Scott. Dear God, Scott. How did this happen?*

She didn't remember reaching out, her fingers opened as if to grab a part of him. Instead she stared at her hand where it clasped the empty air and wondered how it had moved without her knowledge.

She would never touch him again.

Desultory traffic continued to pass up and down Loomis Street as if nothing had happened. Normal people continued to live their lives, heedless of the terrible grief and tragedy that had enfolded Scott Ferris and his family.

The ruination of the house had tumbled down on the foundation—splintered and burned wood, jumbles of black wreckage. She could see the scorched hulk of the once-racy red Ducati where Scott had left it parked inside the gutted back porch. The sight of it, as much as anything else, brought the extent of the tragedy home.

Theodor Bennet shook his head. "I'm so sorry, Ronnie."

"Yeah, me too, Theo. Even looking at it, I still can't believe. I'm so glad we didn't bring Mother."

A bear of a man, Theodor Bennet stood six-feet three, his body wide and thick. When he walked into a room he cut an imposing figure, not just from his size, but from the calculated intelligence in his brown eyes. Square-cut and rugged, his face brooked no interference, and the sense of self-security he exuded brought instant respect. On this day, he wore a black silk suit, white shirt, and conservative blue tie. Gleaming black shoes covered his feet, and a black felt fedora had been pulled in a slant across his thick, wiry gray hair.

Gazing through sober brown eyes, he surveyed the ruin. "I can't imagine why this would happen to Scott."

"Just bad luck, Theo. We haven't been batting a winning streak since Dad keeled over." She chuckled humorlessly. "Maybe we never have."

"How's that, Ronnie?"

"Oh, sometimes I think this family's jinxed. I mean, I look back, and what did I have as a kid? Dad might just as well have been dead. I only saw him on holidays, and then it was usually as a prop for a business dinner. You know, he hired a psychologist once to find out what to get me for Christmas. I was fourteen that year, and as far as Dad was concerned, I might have been !Kung for all he knew of how I lived, who I was."

"What's a Kong?"

"!Kung. An ethnic band of San tribesmen in southern Africa. Never mind. It's just that Scott was the only person in my life outside of my friends who was real. He was the one who kept me together." She shook her head. "But for him—and you—I'd have ended up badly, Theo. I was headed for it."

Scott's voice filled her, that calm reassuring tone telling her, *"It's all right, Sis. Calm down. Now, what's your trouble? How can I help?"* In her head, she answered, *"Be alive for me, Bro. Breathe again. Live again."* But here, faced with the horrifying reality of his last moments, she could feel him slipping away. Vanishing into the sky like those tongues of fire that had marked his terrible death. Had the dying tree felt his essence passing along with the flames? Had part of

Scott seared those steaming leaves? Helped to boil the green fluids from the ruptured cells?

"You were just a young girl desperate for attention, Ronnie. I'm glad Scott was there for you." Theo's expression lengthened. "And no matter what you thought of your father, he did his best for you, for Mary and Scott. Despite your other troubles, you never have had to want for anything."

"Only a father," Veronica countered. "Sorry, Theo. Some wounds just scab over; they never really heal." After a moment, she added, "And I don't think Mom is going to recover from this. It was bad enough when Dad died. But Scott was the reason she lived. This—the way he died . . . It's tearing her apart."

"I'll do anything I can to help."

She gestured. "What about all this? I mean, who takes responsibility? They're not just going to leave this mess sitting here while we wait for probate, are they? And there's insurance, safety deposit boxes, death certificates, all that stuff. I don't even know where to start."

"I'll handle that." He gave her a kindly look. "I have people who can run down that information. And, about the house, what do you want to do with it when the police are done?"

"Bulldoze it," she whispered. "Sell the lot. Don't you think?" For a long moment, she just stared, thinking back, remembering the day Scott had moved in. He and Amanda had carried in boxes of books, and the few pieces of furniture that Scott had accumulated from antique stores in Massachusetts, Vermont, and New Hampshire. Veronica had been in her senior year then, enamored with the question of Neandertals and why they disappeared some twenty-five thousand years ago. It had been a warm day, like this one. Full of sunshine and future. Scott and Amanda had been so in love, so excited.

"The best thing is," Scott had said, *"the vet school here has one of the world's best embryo transplant centers. It's amazing; unlike humans, who are pretty primitive, cattle have extraordinarily complicated reproductive systems."*

She shook her head. How like Scott. The whole world was a marvelous puzzle. What perverse twist of fate led a man like that to be tortured and murdered and left here in the smoldering ruins of his home? Had it been his dreams?

"Do you have any idea what this is all about?" Theo glanced at her with those powerful eyes.

"No, Theo. I swear." She paused and shook her head. "You'd think it would be me, wouldn't you? I was the one who was always in trouble." She swallowed hard. "So, what about Lieutenant Snake? Why is he being so hard on me and Mom?"

Theo shoved his hands into his pockets, scuffing at a patch of soot on the sidewalk. He glanced down Loomis Street at the old elms, the eighty-year-old houses, and the automobiles parked along the shaded curbs. "They're worried, Ronnie. This sort of thing doesn't happen in Fort Collins, any more than the JonBenet thing could have happened in Boulder. Experience indicates that the culprit is most likely family, friends, or in this case, criminal partners. The problem is, Scott wasn't into criminal activity. He didn't deal drugs, didn't fence stolen goods, wasn't into any kind of vice. The police are turning the

Anthropology Department upside down as we speak. You know your brother. Are they going to find anything?"

She shook her head. "Scott didn't have a criminal bone in his body. His passion was his work. He didn't even teach that much. He brought in grant money. Biotech, mostly. He wouldn't have been involved in anything like fraud or extortion."

"That's what has the Fort Collins police worried, Ronnie. They don't want to leave anything this high profile unsolved. No, this smacks of something criminal. This kind of death is meant as a message. But from whom, and saying what?" His probing gaze turned to her. "What was Scott into that anyone would want to kill him like this? Ronnie, seriously, I can't help if I don't know."

"I *don't* know, Theo!" She shook her head. "I honestly don't know." Her fists knotted, tears forming as she looked at the charred end of her brother's life. "And it's driving me half insane!"

CHAPTER SEVEN

IF I'M SUCH A SMART GUY, WHY DIDN'T I THINK OF THIS before?" Bryce muttered irritably as he inched along in the St. Louis rush hour. The humid afternoon heat that June 13 roasted the idling traffic that waited in predatory rows, jamming the Mark Twain Expressway, or, as he knew it, I-70 westbound. Overhead the jets came winging in, flaps and gear down, thundering as they glided toward Lambert–Saint Louis International Airport.

In the last fifteen minutes, Bryce had covered a daunting three-tenths of a mile from Exit 240 to Exit 239. As he picked up his cell phone, he enviously watched a car accelerate onto the empty ramp on his right. The big green highway sign said the exit led to North Hanley Road. For an instant, he wondered where that might take him, and then nixed the notion as he punched out the numbers on his cell phone.

At the ring, a computer voice said, *"What state, please?"*

"Colorado."

"What city, please?"

"Fort Collins."

"What listing, please?"

"The *Fort Collins Coloradoan.*"

"One moment."

God! Imagine having to listen to that same intonation all day long. It could drive someone to cut off his head so he didn't have to listen to the memory for the rest of his life.

Another computer voice intoned the number. Bryce scribbled on a piece of scrap paper. He slipped the clutch and let the Durango ease another couple of car lengths forward and didn't even growl as a white-and-red taxi wheeled over, forcing its way into his lane.

Inputting the number, Bryce thumbed the "send" button and listened to the distant ringing. As if it were the malignancy of fate, he had to wade through another computer system to reach a real human reporter.

"Hello, uh, my name's Hanley. Uh, Hanley North," he composed from the big green road sign. "I'm doing a little research, and I was wondering if you had covered any stories about a Professor Scott Ferris recently? He's at Colorado State—"

"You're joking, right?"

"No. I'm serious. I'm in New Mexico." He thought of his stolen license plates. "We were just wondering if you had any recent information on Dr. Ferris? Maybe an assault, or—"

"It's the biggest story we've had in this town since the Big Thompson flood. I didn't cover it myself, but the common knowledge is that Ferris was beaten, his legs and arms broken, and then he was burned to death."

Silence.

"Who'd you say you were with, Mr. Hanley?"

Bryce tapped the "end" button and stared woodenly forward, hardly aware of the Durango's air-conditioning as it fought the summer sun burning through the slanting windshield.

What in hell am I going to do now? Where am I going to go? Just who can I trust?

Veronica listened to the maddening ringing of Amanda's phone. After eight rings she returned the receiver to the cradle, lay back on the bed, and stared up at the ceiling of her hotel room. The white-spackled drywall held no answers. Amanda had an answering machine. Why hadn't it picked up the call?

Dear God, not Amanda, too. Veronica placed a hand over her eyes. In the shadow of her palm she recalled Amanda, her olive complexion echoing her Greek ancestry. She had had a tough life. Her family had come from Toledo, steel people or some such. Amanda's father had died when she was a girl: a boating accident on Lake Erie. The insurance money had propelled Amanda and her mother into the world of the affluent and bought Amanda's way into Harvard. Meanwhile, the mother, Dorothea, had remarried. Number two had made poor investments with Dorothea's money, then died of a heart attack. Dorothea had found herself destitute, face-to-face with poverty. She had been doing close to one hundred when she drove her Chevy Lumina into a highway bridge abutment several weeks later. The life insurance had seen Amanda through school.

Scott had been the only family Amanda had left outside of some cousins.

Scott. There he was again. Filling her memories, that invincible strength of his reaching out of the past.

"Just be strong, Sis. You're the tough one out of the bunch."

In the silence of her hotel room, Veronica said, "Yeah, Scott. Sure I am. I feel like broken glass."

The haunting image of Scott's face morphed into the corpse's as it lay on the stainless steel gurney. The cold memory of splintered bones protruding from fire-blackened limbs filled her. His arms had been broken and then twisted before they had piled his books on top of him and set him on fire. What kind of human monster could do such things? Why, in the name of God, had they wanted to hurt him that way?

Questions . . .

Somewhere outside, a motorcycle blatted out its authority to the world and slowly faded away into the muted sounds of traffic. A V twin. Probably a Harley. She knew that sound from her days with Ben and his fast bikes and sleek sports cars. She closed her eyes and fought the desperate urge to call him, to hear his voice. As much as she despised him, she'd give anything to have him here, holding her, soothing her wounded soul.

She shot a glance at the smooth plastic telephone on the nightstand. Involuntarily, she had already reached out, her fingers on the cold plastic.

The thought hit her: *God, Ronnie, you're a bitch of a mess. You'd even crawl to Ben . . . For what? A little peace of mind? A hug?* And . . . what? Know that by the next night he'd be slipping some other woman's dress off? Her fingers knotted, and she pulled her arm back.

She had never felt so alone, so vulnerable and fragile. Not even in the old days when she'd gone wild. Looking back, she could sense the truth of Theo's words: anything for attention. Now she just wanted reassurance. Wanted someone, anyone—even Ben—to tell her it would be all right.

But it wouldn't be. Scott was dead. Dead. Dead.

She jumped when the phone jangled. Pulling her long black hair back, she asked, "Hello?"

"Dr. Tremain?" a male voice asked.

"Yes?"

"Uh, I'm Special Agent Joe Hanson, ma'am. Federal

Bureau of Investigation. I've just come from talking to Lieutenant Davidson. You know him, I believe?"

"Yeah, I know him." She couldn't help the hostility in her voice. "What's this about?"

"I'm sorry to bother you, but would you mind taking a moment to talk to me?"

"Yes." She winced at the hard tone in her voice. "I'm sorry. I mean, yes, what can I do to help you?"

"I'm down in the lobby. If you don't mind, could you come down? I'd really like to ask you some questions."

In the lobby? She closed her eyes, forcing calm into her tense body. "Give me a minute. I'll be right down."

She hung up, splashed some water onto her face, brushed her hair, and collected her purse. Shit! The FBI? An uneasy tingle ran through her. Damn it, she should have told him no, not without Theo's presence.

As she closed the door behind her, she swore that she'd tell him nothing. Insist that Theo be there.

He was standing beside the registration desk, a middle-aged man with a square face and oddly weary eyes. He wore a brown sport coat, slacks, and a pale blue shirt with a matching tie. A leather briefcase hung from his left hand.

"Dr. Tremain?" He offered his hand. "I'm Joe Hanson." Next came the plastic-coated ID contained in a leather holder. Then he handed her a business card.

"Hello, Mr. Hanson." She held herself erect, taking the card cautiously. "I think I should tell you, I would like to have my attorney present for any interrogation."

A faint smile crooked his mouth. "Sure, if you wish, but I really don't think that's necessary." A pause while he read her wary expression. "Davidson's been a little hard on you, huh?"

"He could have taught Torquemada new tricks."

His competent glance took in her faded Levi's, the rumpled white blouse. Then he studied her eyes, reading the anger, confusion, fear, and fatigue. "I think you can relax for the moment. I just checked, the coffee shop is empty. Maybe I could spring for a cup of coffee and we could find a booth back out of the way."

"I'll drink your coffee, but I refuse to say anything until my attorney—"

"I said relax. As far as I'm concerned, you're not a suspect."

"I'm not?" she said weakly as she followed him into the café.

He turned, an eyebrow lifted. "Not unless you were responsible for your brother's death. You weren't, were you?"

"No."

"Good. If you were, it would really complicate my case." He nodded to the hostess and pointed to the booth in the far corner by the window. "Could we have that one?"

"It's nonsmoking." The young woman smiled with that plastic grace all good hostesses could adopt at will.

Hanson shot Veronica an inquisitive glance and at her negation, said, "That'll be fine."

At the table, Hanson asked, "Anything besides coffee?"

"No, coffee's fine." Veronica slid into the booth, watching Hanson warily as he seated himself on the bench opposite her, wincing as if his back hurt and setting his briefcase to one side. From the pocket of his sport coat, he removed a black leather notebook and retrieved a pen from his shirt pocket. Then he yawned. "Excuse me. Long flight on little sleep. It's still June thirteenth, isn't it?"

"It is. Long flight? Where did you come from?"

"D.C." He rubbed the end of his nose. "Normally, this would have been handled by the Fort Collins residency. Our guys here are in court. Not only that, but this has turned into a high-profile case. We've tripped over a lot of red flags. The Bureau's a big beast, but once it gets stung, it can motivate a lot of resources."

"Then I take it you're a resource?" She read the card he'd given her, stopped short, and looked up. "What's this mean? 'Domestic Terrorism'? You don't think Scott was involved in a militia or something, do you?"

"No. My particular bailiwick is what you'd call 'hate crimes.' That falls into my squad's jurisdiction. Believe it or not, I was in D.C. last night at nine. Since then, I've flown to Denver, checked in at the field office, driven up here, got acquainted with the local residency, debriefed Davidson, and found you." A self-conscious smile bent his lips. "I'm too young to feel this old."

"Then change professions," she told him coolly.

Hanson shot a look across the room where the hostess had retreated for the coffeepot. "Dr. Tremain, are you a Christian?"

"Well, I . . . uh, suppose so. After a fashion. I mean, as an anthropologist, I can tell you that growing up in American culture leaves everyone steeped in the tradition."

"How often do you go to church?"

"I don't. Excuse me, but what does this have to do

with Scott? He didn't go to church either." She gave him a level stare as the waitress brought the cups, poured them full, and asked if they had decided on anything else. They both shook their heads. "In fact, if anything, Scott hated the idea of churches. All the trouble he ever had was because of someone's idea of religious truth."

"I see," Joe said, watching the waitress retreat. He looked back at Veronica and asked, "Your mother? Does she go to church?"

Veronica laughed at that. "Not hardly."

Hanson reached into his briefcase, flipped through some papers, and placed one in front of her. "Dr. Tremain, are you familiar with any of these names?"

She picked up the paper, reading the four names. "Scott, of course, is my brother. Amanda is Scott's S.O. Avi—"

"Excuse me, 'S.O.'?"

She glanced at Hanson. "Significant other. Girlfriend doesn't exactly do it. Neither does lover, colleague, or anything else. They have an odd relationship. More than lovers, less than spouses. Their careers were the most important thing for both of them. Amanda even gave up her child for adoption to save her career. I've desperately been trying to call her all day."

He grunted and indicated the paper. "And the other two?"

"Avi corresponds with Scott. They coauthor papers. They're both anthropological geneticists. The same with Bryce." She picked up her coffee, sipping the hot liquid. "You see, Scott, Amanda, and Bryce are the brain trust of experimental anthropological genetics. Avi and his team are more hands-on, working with practical problems like removing thalassemia, Tay-Sachs, and PKU from gene pools. Practicing genetic therapy . . . those sorts of things."

"You lost me. Thassalemia sounds like a country somewhere near Greece . . . and didn't Tie Sacks play baseball?"

"Thalassemia is a series of genetic blood diseases, a biological response to malaria. Tay-Sachs is a degeneration of the nervous system which occurs with high frequency among Ashkenazi Jews. PKU stands for phenylketonuria, a genetic metabolic disorder that leads to mental retardation."

Hanson grunted again, his pen scratching out notes in the little leather book. "And Bryce Johnson, he's somewhere in New Jersey?"

"New Hampshire," she corrected. "Manchester. He's with the university, assistant professor of anthropological—"

Hanson raised a hand to stop her as he pulled a cell phone from his pocket, stabbed a button with a thick finger, and placed it against his ear. He was looking into Veronica's eyes as he said, "Mitch? Hanson here. Bryce Johnson's at the university in Manchester, New Hampshire. Not New Jersey." A pause. "Right. Let me know what happens." A pause. "Yeah, I'm with Dr. Tremain right now. She might be able to help." A pause. "Yeah, right. Take care, partner." He thumbed the "end" button and replaced the phone into his inside pocket. As he did so, Veronica caught the barest glimpse of his shoulder holster.

"Want to tell me what's going on?" She braced her elbows on the table, staring at him across the rim of her white coffee cup.

"I'm hoping our people can get to Bryce Johnson." Hanson's eyes had narrowed. "There is no easy way to tell you this, Dr. Tremain, but Amanda Alexander, Avi Raad, and at least one other woman are dead. In each case, there are similarities to the way that your brother was killed. Each one, with the exception of Ms. Alexander—and we're not sure about her—was tortured and burned." His expression tensed. "All but Ms. Alexander were nailed to the floor."

Veronica lowered the coffee cup; some spilled onto the table. From a distance, she heard herself say, "Nailed to the . . ." The odd punctures in Scott's wrists and feet suddenly made a horrible sense. "And Amanda . . . dead?"

" 'Fraid so."

"That's why the answering machine didn't pick up at Amanda's."

Hanson's pen poised over his notebook. "The phone company just hasn't disconnected the line yet."

He gave her a moment, allowing her to absorb the news; then, gently, he asked, "Dr. Tremain, do you have the faintest idea what this is about, why these people are being murdered? Why they're being nailed to the floor and burned?"

"No." Her voice sounded small and distant. "None of it makes any sense." *They nailed Scott to the floor?* She tightened her grip on the coffee cup, eyes locked on the way the color drained from her fingers.

"Did your brother ever mention Billy Barnes Brown? The Apostolic Evangelical Church of the Salvation? Maybe the Christian Creationist Crusade?"

She frowned, mind reeling. "Not that I recall. I mean, not in particular. As an anthropologist, I can tell you that we're always aware of people like that. For the most part, we go about our business, which is science instead of politics. Oh sure, we have symposia, sessions, at the professional meetings. They serve as a heads-up as to what's coming. That and we do community outreach to send physical anthropologists to public schools for fair time. That sort of thing."

"And you?" he asked. "Are you involved in the same kind of research that your brother was?"

She shook her head, trying to grasp the immensity of the situation. *Amanda and Avi dead? Why?* "I specialized in paleoanthropology. You know, fossils and human evolution. My thesis was on Neandertal cranial metrics, uh, the dimensions of the skull. My dissertation was on Neandertal and modern human origins. The problems and contradictions between the osteological, archaeological, and genetic data."

"The missing link?"

"I'm afraid, Mr. Hanson, that you're a little out of date. We don't have any missing links anymore. The problem these days is that we have too many links to fit into the same chain, and the links we have don't match the chain size."

"I see." But he clearly didn't. "Then, you don't think that your own life could be in danger?"

She frowned. "Why should it be?"

"We think there may be a hit list. Maybe as many as twenty-five people. Can you provide me with a list of names? People doing the same kind of work as your brother was?"

"I suppose. Yes. It's as easy as canvassing the bibliographic information in the literature. And Scott kept all of his . . . They burned it."

"Uh-huh," Hanson mused, scratching his chin. "Destroying the records."

"Why? I mean, you can't just bury science. You can't burn it. You can't kill it. As long as it's based on reproducible results, someone else will eventually observe the same phenomenon and the trouble starts over again."

"My guess is that your brother and his friends were doing something that someone didn't approve of."

"Scott and Amanda were *scientists* for God's sake!"

"So what? In my line of work, I deal with a lot of people who don't like what other people are doing because it threatens them, or they're paranoid, or they need a whipping boy—someone to torture because of their own inadequacies or fears. Dr. Tremain, your brother and his friends were onto something, doing something, learning something, and I think they were killed because of it. For all I know, you might be into it, too."

She gaped at him. "What the hell could be so threatening about human evolution?"

"I hope that wasn't a serious question?" His lips thinned to a bland line. "A lot of people consider it heresy."

She clenched a fist. "We don't live in the Middle Ages anymore. We don't burn witches at the stake."

At his sharpening expression, she froze. "My God, you don't mean . . ."

"It's not your God that I'm worried about, Dr. Tremain, but somebody else's."

Joe Hanson paused thoughtfully as he thumbed through the faxed pages Mitch had forwarded from Washington. He sat behind one of the institutional metal desks at the Fort Collins residency. An aluminum-framed window behind him gave a view of Fort Collins' rooftops, trees, and the afternoon traffic.

The Fort Collins residency had its offices high in the concrete "prison-style" Federal Building. Built in the seventies, the gray Goliath hulked over Howes Street. While the ground floor was dominated by the post office, assorted federal agencies had the upper floors. The windows were set back in recessed casements that created a brooding atmosphere on the outside.

From the papers Mitch had forwarded, his people in Washington had fixed their attention on Billy Barnes Brown. Mitch had turned the squad's resources to research, pulling in everything it could on Brown's life, his activities, and his church.

Joe noted the section on biography, scanning the pages. On impulse, he reached across the desk and picked up the phone. He dialed Ramsey's office number. Checking his watch, he figured he'd just catch his supervisor before the afternoon briefing.

"Joe Hanson for Ramsey," he said when Betty, the secretary, answered.

"One minute, Joe."

He swiveled in the chair, looking out at the thick green carpet of trees that covered the older section of Fort Collins. From here he would have been able to see the flames the night Scott Ferris was murdered.

The phone clicked. *"Joe?"* Ramsey asked.

"Hi, boss. Just checking in. I'm in Fort Collins at the residency. I've talked to the police, to the coroner, and to Ferris' sister. The police here don't have a clue, and I don't think they're going to find one, either. Jack, each of the murdered scientists is involved in something called 'anthropological genetics.' Doing things with human DNA. Given what you've found, does that ring any bells?"

Ramsey paused; Hanson knew he was taking notes. *"No, Joe. Not yet. But you might want to know that we sent an inquiry to the State Department. They're very interested in Avi Raad. Elections are coming up in Israel. Two things are critical. One, the latest implementation of the peace plan is fraying around the edges. If Raad was taken out by a Hamas hit squad, it could have serious repercussions. An escalation of terrorism. Two, if Raad was taken out by the extreme Right, it could mean an escalation by more radical ultraorthodox Jews."*

"I don't get that." Joe frowned.

"Apparently Israelis have their own problems with their version of the religious Right. A group of radical rabbis stopped an excavation that Raad was working on a couple of years ago. Something dealing with Neanderthals. I guess they have a lot of sites in Israel. It got ugly, and Raad was stoned and kicked. The beating put him in the hospital, left him scarred and with only partial use of one arm."

"Hold it." Joe pulled out his own notebook to jot down notes. "Something similar happened to Ferris. At Harvard. His sister was telling me about it."

"You think there's a connection?"

"Between ultraorthodox Jews and Billy Barnes Brown? I'd be skeptical. But then, there's a lot in this case that's not making sense yet."

"Uh-huh." Ramsey hesitated. *"We've got bad news for you. Bryce Johnson has disappeared."*

"As in . . ."

"Vanished. Gone. Not at home and nobody knows his whereabouts." Ramsey sighed. *"The one thing that's nice is that we've got Johnson's phone log. The last call he took came from a 970 prefix. Directory assistance informs us that it came from Colorado . . . from Scott Ferris' phone the night he died."*

"Son of a bitch. What time?" Hanson was staring out at the sky. Two crows flapped past, diving and dodging. The mountains looked green and cool beyond the tree-lined city.

"Eight-thirty that night. They talked for less than a minute. No one has seen Johnson since."

"So, was it a warning call from Ferris? Or a message from the killers?" Hanson drew a big question mark in his notebook.

"What did you glean from the crime scene? Anything that helps us?"

"Outside of the fact that someone tortured Ferris before they nailed him to the floor and burned him to death, nothing. None of the neighbors saw or heard anything until the fire at about three in the morning. Ferris lived in an old house that's in the student district a few blocks from the university. Lots of traffic, parties, that sort of thing. The locks weren't jimmied, no one saw anyone strange hanging around casing the joint, no tire tracks on the lawn, nothing. I called Lzerski before I picked up the fax Mitch sent. He's got a big fat zero, too. If you ask me, Jack, we're dealing with professionals here."

"We're ahead of you. We've started to put feelers out in all the usual places. See who's been hired recently. Who has these kinds of skills. And, you've got another problem. The paperwork came in on Amanda Alexander. Her house was burning about an hour after Carter's. Alexander wasn't tortured like Carter, Raad, and Ferris. The M.E. who looked over the body found nothing inconsistent with an accidental death."

"So, you're saying that it's a statistical fluke? Amanda Alexander just happens to go up in smoke the night after her boyfriend is bent, mutilated, and stapled to the floor, then turned into a crispy critter?"

"I'm saying there's something different in the way she died. If it's a related homicide, we have at least two killers working simultaneously. It's something we have to understand."

In the pensive silence, Hanson's gaze absently followed a light plane as it droned across the sky. Finally, he said, "Something else doesn't make sense, boss. About Brown, I mean. What would motivate Billy Barnes Brown to take these kinds of chances? He's putting himself, his church, everything at risk to kill a bunch of anthropologists. I don't know much about him, but I never thought he was a complete idiot. This is all going to come out. He's smart enough to realize that."

"If it is Billy Barnes Brown. We've only got Elizabeth Carter's word on that."

"Killing her like they did made that a pretty solid bet, Jack."

"Or someone wants us to think Brown is responsible

for the killings. So they coerced Elizabeth Carter to meet with you, drop the names, and then killed her to solidify her story."

"My gut told me she was telling the truth."

"Your gut, Special Agent Hanson, will have a hell of a lot less impact on a jury than it will on a chicken-salad sandwich."

"I know, I know." Hanson paused. "I don't suppose that the Athens, Ohio, P. D. came up with anything on Amanda Alexander?"

"Oddly, they did. She reported a burglary the day she was killed."

"And?"

"And not much." Papers could be heard rustling. *"Here we go. She had been in Cincinnati for a music festival. That was on the tenth. When she returned home at about two P.M. on the eleventh, she discovered that her answering machine had been taken. The police could discover no sign of breaking and entering. The only missing property was a Panasonic answering machine. The perps had even plugged the phone jack back into the wall."* A pause. *"Here's a note on the bottom of the report. The investigating officer, a guy named Dade, speculated that maybe the lady hadn't even owned an answering machine."*

Hanson frowned. "Ferris' sister said she did."

"I see. And how did you come by that tidbit?"

Hanson related the gist of his conversation with Veronica. Then he added, "So, Amanda Alexander arrives home, and her answering machine is missing. She calls the cops, they take a report, and that night she's murdered. Why?"

"Evidently a message she wasn't supposed to get."

"Why not just take the tape?"

"Maybe she had one of these new solid-state machines. They don't use tapes, Joe. It's all kept in a memory card." A pause. *"Ask the sister. She might know what kind of machine we were dealing with."*

"In point of fact, Mr. Supervisor, sir, I will. I have to meet the young lady over at the university. We're going to take a look at Professor Ferris' office. Fort Collins P.D. went through it, but said it was untouched. I thought maybe Veronica might see something they didn't know they were looking for."

"Then perhaps you should get to work, Special Agent."

CHAPTER EIGHT

H*e loves this place. The roar of the river is enchanting. The odors are pungent, wet, and muddy; the rocks, too, have their own smells, as do the plants. The scent of moss and damp earth fill him with delight as he jumps from rock to rock. He takes the time to scramble down and stare into the shadowed cracks where the rocks are piled onto each other. He fights the urge to*

taste the lichens. Mother doesn't like him to put things in his mouth.

Above him the sky is patched with clouds, and the mountains rise high, dotted with conifers and summer-green brush. Here the air is cooler, and he can jump and run, scrambling up and down the steep embankment.

"Hey! Not too close to the water!" Mother calls from above, her voice carrying over the river's roar.

He stops for a moment, glancing up to where she is setting out the picnic lunch. The wind is wrong for him to smell the rich aroma of fried chicken.

His attention is drawn back to the river, where brown water surges and leaps. Like giant flexing muscles, it tenses, bulges up, and crashes down, only to rise again. White spray and foam make the endless roar. He crawls down, finding a stone about the size of a football. This he strains to pull free. His muscles bunch, and the big rock peels out of the soil. Abel positions himself and lifts the heavy weight above his long head. Grunting, he flings it out, watching it spiral in the air before slamming down into the brown water. The splash is fulfilling.

"You gonna eat?" Mother calls down to him.

"Yesss." He whoops with pleasure and leaps from rock to rock until he has climbed the short distance to where Mother has opened the box of chicken. It appears golden-brown in the sunlight. She has set the plastic bowls of mashed potatoes, gravy, and coleslaw on a paper towel.

For the first time, Mother's blue eyes have relaxed. She wears a white T-shirt, blue jeans, and white tennis *shoes. She has dressed him in a long-sleeved shirt and hands him a hat to protect his head while they eat.*

"You see splassshh?" he asks. "I frow a big wock. Wight out thewe." He points before settling down beside her on the fragrant grass.

"I saw," she tells him with a smile. "Keep that up, and you're going to be a weight lifter."

"Stwong," he insists, patting his arm. "Like G'Kar."

He takes the chicken thigh she hands him and settles onto his bottom in the grass. The smell is wonderful, and his mouth waters as he bites into the warm meat. As he chews, he smells the breeze, picking out the mixed odors of auto exhaust, pine trees, spring flowers, and river. "I wike it heaww."

" 'Like,' " Mother insists. "Swallow your food. There, that's it. Now, remember, the tongue touching the back of the front teeth and close off your nose. Think about it, Abel. Concentrate and say it right."

He gulps the succulent meat, wipes his lips, and frowns. "I llllike it heawwwrrr."

"Took a while to get the r sound right, didn't it?"

He screws his face up, struggling to get the muscles of his mouth to the proper tension and says, "R is a harrd letterrr."

She laughs, the sound spontaneous and happy as she claps her hands. "Good boy! Abel, that was great." As he grins at her, the sparkle slowly fades from her eyes. "I love you so much, little man."

"I wuv you." He makes a face. "I lllluv you, Muvver."

She reaches out, ruffling his silky pale hair. "I know,

sweetie." And then the haunted pain creeps back into her eyes. *"No matter what, baby, I want you to know how proud I am of you."*

He hesitates, the fear growing in his belly again. *"We okay?"*

She nods, glancing up at the rocky slopes around them. *"I think so, kiddo. Things are just a little spooky right now."*

"We go home nowww?"

"Not yet, baby. We have to go to the mountains for a while. We're going to meet a man there, and he'll tell us what to do."

"What man?"

"Someone you knew a long time ago." She looks really sad.

He reaches out, placing his hand on hers. His skin is white against her tan. *"I make you feel better."*

She hauls him up then, pulls him close, and presses him against her. *"You always do. God, what would I do without you?"*

The BMW growled, sounding happy and healthy as she tapped the throttle. Reluctantly she turned off the ignition and sat for a moment, allowing the sudden silence to possess her. Originally she had wanted a more sedate vehicle. Leave it to Ben to insist that if she were getting a BMW, it had to be the Z3 coupe.

"It's got real style, Ronnie. Not only that, it oozes

charisma," he'd exclaimed. *"Of course, it isn't quite like my Viper, but you're going to love it."*

The fact of the matter was, she did. She'd fought to keep the little car through the long and tedious divorce proceedings, and had won. Now, here, just outside the Social Sciences building on the Colorado State University campus, the car provided a sense of security. Within it she was safe, invulnerable from the emotional wringer that she would face when she opened the door, stepped out, and crossed the parking lot.

She waited, feeling the temperature rise as the sun heated the interior. Her mind continued to reel, emotions packed behind crumbling walls of resistance. Since the moment she'd picked up the phone in her Boulder house, the reality of Scott's death had been crashing down upon her. Through denial, disbelief, and willpower, she had avoided the terrible grief she knew was coming. Her iron control had allowed her to deal with Mary, to send Mary home to plan Scott's funeral, a duty that would keep her mother occupied and distracted.

At home and out of sight, Mother can at least break down and bawl. I can't. She stared stolidly forward, seeing her hands where they gripped the polished wooden steering wheel.

Only after the heat grew fierce in the BMW's interior did she reluctantly open the door. The afternoon sun slanted down from the west, scorching the campus in bright light. Her heels rapped on the asphalt as she crossed to the huge square bulk of the building, opened the doors on the southeast corner, and climbed the flight of concrete stairs to the second floor.

The long hallway, familiar from the times she had vis-

ited Scott, brought the ache back to her heart. Special
Agent Hanson stood in the doorway to the Anthropology
office and saw her from the corner of his eye. He waved
and said something to the office's occupants.

Veronica stopped in front of Scott's door, looking up at
the laminated brown plastic sign that said "S. F. Ferris."
The wooden door remained the last portal to Scott's life.
This would have been his final stop on the way home to
assault, torture, and a hideous death. The length of yellow
plastic tape was emblazoned with "Police Line Do Not
Cross." The notion of a ribbon on a perverted birthday
present entered her mind.

Hanson came striding down the hallway. Behind him,
Lieutenant Davidson appeared and followed. Veronica
felt her hackles rise and, when Hanson was close, asked,
"What's *he* doing here?"

Hanson's craggy face reflected faint amusement.
"Oddly enough, we're on the lieutenant's turf here. He's
still in charge of investigating a homicide. But for a more
practical reason, he's been here before. He was the first
person in your brother's office after his death. The lieutenant can tell us what his crime scene team did when
they were here."

"Hello, Lieutenant," she greeted coldly and resisted
the impulse to ask him if he'd pulled the wings off any
butterflies today.

"Ms. Tremain," he returned soberly and reached past
her with a key to unlock the door. He entered and motioned Veronica and Hanson inside.

Veronica stopped short in the office and surveyed the
small room. The white cinder block walls, the onion-colored

heater under the plate glass window, the desk, the bookcase, all looked normal enough.

Only the faint white powder, for fingerprints she assumed, seemed out of place at first. It dusted the phone,
the doorknob, the top of the desk, and the drawer handles.

The framed photographs drew her like a magnet: Scott
and Amanda against the sun-drenched ruins of Masada.
Scott, Amanda, and Bryce at the New York meetings of
the American Association of Physical Anthropology. Another shot of Scott, Dad, and Mary taken on Mom and
Dad's last anniversary before a stroke turned Frank Ferris into an invalid; a second killed him three weeks later.
Then, last but not least, a picture of Scott and her at the
summit of Trailridge Road up in Rocky Mountain National Park. She'd been a sophomore. The instance for
that trip had been her breakup with Randy Jenson, her
first "real" boyfriend. The others, of her youth, had
mostly been trash she had insisted on associating with to
provoke dismay among her parents and her parole officers.

"Something important there?" Davidson asked, indicating her interest in the photo.

"Scott was interviewing for the position here at Colorado State. I was heartbroken over an old boyfriend.
Scott took me for a long drive and let me get all the rant-
ing and raving out of my system. He set the camera on the
rock wall . . . took that photo with the automatic timer."

The welling sense of grief began to press in on her.
She shook herself, turned, looked up at the bookshelf.
Something just wasn't . . . "The bookshelf. All those
empty places. The last time I was here, there were volumes there. I'd swear it."

"When was that?"

"About three months ago. Scott bought me dinner after my defense."

"Your defense?" he looked puzzled.

"Of my dissertation." She bit her lower lip, frowning, concentrating on reconstructing that day. "It had been snowing. A March storm. I left early to get here. Scott was late. Working at the lab. He didn't think I'd be early, and I waited for about a half an hour outside the door."

"Anything else not right?" Hanson asked, watching her intently. Davidson's face remained expressionless, but he was taking notes.

"I remember the heater making a ticking sound. But that was normal. Scott hugged me, opened the door, and asked how I was doing. I told him about my defense, about the questions I was asked. He asked about the divorce. How it was going." She walked over and placed a hand on the veneer table. "There's nothing here."

"There wasn't when we came in," Davidson told her.

"This isn't like Scott. This was his worktable. Always a clutter. He put his journals here, in order, so that when he wrote a paper he could cite each of the sources. And the note cards, the outline of the ideas he was working on, they'd be here. He called it a constructive clutter. That way he'd be able to reach right into the—" She pointed, stopping short, staring in disbelief.

"Yes, what?" Hanson asked, sensing her dismay.

Veronica swallowed hard. "The file cabinet. A two-drawer filing cabinet. He kept his articles there. His correspondence, that sort of thing."

Davidson crossed his arms. "We checked. There's no file cabinet on the department inventory."

She shook her head. "It wasn't department property. It was *his* file cabinet. One that he and Amanda found in some antique store in New England. A wooden one. Oak, maybe. It was right there between the table and the heater."

"Son of a bitch." Hanson turned, stepping over to the door to inspect the lock. "This wouldn't be much for a pro to get past."

A cold shiver was tracing its way down Veronica's back. The killers had stood right here. They'd come, invaded this place, and taken away Scott's work. Looking closely, she thought she could see faint scrapes on the linoleum where the file cabinet had been dragged out.

"Someone must have seen something," Davidson said with finality.

"It's summer session," Veronica responded woodenly. "Don't count on it. Even if they did, so what? Maintenance and housekeeping are in and out of buildings like this all night. Who'd notice another truck?"

"Campus police?" Davidson shrugged. "You never can tell. We'll ask around."

Joe Hanson placed his hands on his hips. "You said Scott was late, that he came from the lab. What lab?"

"Rupert Goldman's. He runs the embryo transplant studies in conjunction with the animal sciences department and the vet school." She pointed. "It'll be in the Rolodex on Scott's desk.

As Davidson bent to the cards, Hanson gazed thoughtfully at her. "Did Amanda Alexander have one of those classy digital answering machines?"

The question seemed to come from left field. "I . . . well, I just don't know. Maybe. She liked trendy things like that."

Jackson Ramsey tried not to wilt as he stepped out of the funky and featureless Dodge that GSA, or General Services Administration, had provided. Atlanta registered 101 degrees, and the humidity was hanging right in there at 99 percent. It was the thirteenth of June in the South, for God's sake. What did he expect? As sweat began to pop out of his pores, he wondered: If the humidity rose by another percentage point, did that mean they'd all be underwater? Just how did the scientists determine that kind of thing?

He squinted in the sunlight as Bill Weber, from the Atlanta Field Office, closed the driver's door and stepped around to join him. In a climate like this, people had to be nuts to wear suits. He looked down at his once neatly pressed gray blazer, conservative tie, and creased pants. This lunacy was a holdover from the Hoover days. Nothing else would explain it.

The sun stood at midday, blasting a hot white light through the dripping air. Green trees clotted the horizon, held at bay by manicured lawns that lined the paved drive on which they'd entered the grounds. Before them, a white-pillared building harkened back to a different America, one of order and pleasant predictability. The place didn't quite look like a Southern plantation, but something more like the 1950s, when everything was good about America. Could you call architecture like this "Colonial-Romanesque?"

"Ready?" Weber asked.

"Let's go do it." Ramsey reached for his briefcase and closed the car door. He walked up the hot white concrete toward the big double doors under the gabled porch. A discreet sign told them they were entering the headquarters of the Apostolic Evangelical Church of the Salvation.

Inside, a wave of cold air nearly knocked Ramsey over. Something about the South, he'd noticed, especially in Texas and Georgia, made them want to overcompensate for the climate. He knew better than to complain to Weber, who had once told him that he'd had a great-grandfather who had been killed by Sherman just north of here in 1864.

The foyer had neat white walls, waxed woodwork, and columns that rose to the ceiling twenty feet overhead. He could see his reflection in the polished gray marble under his feet. As he and Weber walked to the ornate maple desk twenty feet beyond the door, his steps echoed with a preternatural ring.

"Could I he'p y'all?" the dainty receptionist asked, a vacuous smile on her face. Ramsey kept his expression neutral. She had to have been chosen for this job out of a lineup of stereotypes. Thin-faced, with overcoifed yellow-blond hair, she wore a white frilly dress and way too much makeup.

"Special Agents Ramsey and Weber to see Mr. Brown, please." He provided his credentials. "We have an appointment."

She stared up at him with slightly glassy blue eyes,

picked up the phone, and through a ritual smile, said, "Marshall? There's two FBI agents to see the Reverend."

She listened for a moment, then hung up the phone, turning the smile on Ramsey. "It'll just be a minute," she told him in her thick Southern accent. "If y'all would just wait in th' receivin' room?" She extended an arm, her hand making a curious swirling gesture that waved them off to the doorway to the right of the desk.

"Thank you." Ramsey returned her plastic smile with one of his own and led Weber into the room. Here, another twenty-foot ceiling arched over walls decorated with poster-sized photos of Reverend Billy Barnes Brown. In some he was haranguing a microphone, sweat on his thin face, the fire of God in his gleaming blue eyes. In others, he was smiling down while holding the hands of grateful if decidedly ill patients in hospital beds. Ramsey particularly liked the one of Brown in an inner-city playground. There, he squatted on a broken teeter-totter, heedless of his expensive silk suit. Children were posed around him, staring at the camera with large and hollow eyes, their toothy grins reflecting a skeptical hope despite the trash at their feet.

Weber studied the photos, one by one, and gave Ramsey a sidelong glance that spoke volumes.

"Gentlemen?" a man in a red blazer with a patch on the breast asked. He looked to be about thirty-five, athletic, with close-cropped red hair. The air of importance with which he carried himself identified him as building security. "This way, please."

The route, Ramsey noted wryly, took them down long hallways studded with pictures of the Reverend. In some he was baptizing, in others, swinging a hammer to build a house. Between the pictures, Ramsey could glance in doorways and see cadres of secretaries pecking away at word processors, talking on telephones, and hustling papers back and forth.

At the end of the hall the security guard tapped a code into the lock and admitted them into an elevator. He tapped another code into the keypad that served instead of buttons. The elevator rose while the guard stood "at ease" saying nothing. Ex-military? He seemed to take his role seriously. Weber was masking a smile. Yeah, Bill knew. Barnes was demonstrating his power. Letting the Fibbies know that they were entering the lair of the alpha male.

Their guard stepped out and led them down a plushly carpeted hallway decorated with what Ramsey assumed were expensive oil paintings and antiques. It might have been a hallway at Monticello that ended in a carved walnut door. The guard opened the golden knob and stepped to one side as the door swung soundlessly open.

Ramsey, followed by Weber, stepped into a bright, airy, high-ceilinged office. White-framed French windows gave the place a quaint and delicate atmosphere, as did the powder-blue walls. Victorian furniture, upholstered in white, had been placed tastefully around the room. Even the carpet, an expensive weave, was spotlessly white.

Billy Barnes Brown rose from behind a hulking battleship of a desk and crossed the open floor, his hand out. "Gentlemen, welcome. Agent Ramsey? I hope your flight was all right."

"It was." Ramsey took the man's hand, shaking it firmly, meeting those quick blue eyes, the honest expression. "This is Special Agent Bill Weber, Atlanta Field Office."

"Agent Weber, welcome." Brown turned his charismatic smile on Weber and offered his hearty handshake. Then he said, "Your director and I are old friends. As a favor to him, I am most anxious to be of help to you. Assuming that I can. Come, let's sit; it's a bit less formal than me perching myself behind that big desk."

He led the way to a corner of the room where two ornate French couches faced each other over a small marble-topped table. A porcelain coffeepot, three cups, decorative cream and sugar decanters, and spoons rested on a silver tray that would have been worth a month's salary had Ramsey bought it in an antique store in Annapolis.

Brown indicated that Ramsey and Weber take one couch while he took the opposite. Once seated he told them, "I took the liberty of having coffee made. It's an Arabica blend, hand roasted by a special friend of mine." He was already pouring. "Sugar? Cream?"

"No, just black," Ramsey told him, while Weber opted for cream and sugar.

Cup in hand, Brown leaned forward, a frank expression on his narrow face. "Now, gentlemen, how can I help you?"

Ramsey sipped the coffee, pronounced it excellent, and studied Brown. "How long did you know Elizabeth Carter?"

Brown's lips twitched; his gaze remained level. "About three years." He gave Ramsey a sad smile. "I'm not going to play games with you, Agent Ramsey. If you don't know, I assume you will eventually find out. Liz and I were very close. When we could ... we spent weekends together."

"Lovers?" Ramsey prodded.

Brown nodded, a sober expression on his face. "I don't ask you to understand, Agent Ramsey, but I would ask for your discretion. I married Bobby Sue when I was eighteen and she was barely seventeen. We married to escape our parents. I made promises to her that I still keep. She is bound to me in holy matrimony." He smiled again. "That we fell out of love years ago might be a tragedy, but it does not justify breaking a promise that we made before God."

"And adultery?" Weber asked. "I seem to recall that it came up once or twice in Sunday school."

Brown nodded. "A fair observation, Agent Weber. I have no answer to give you except that I dance precariously from the sharp horn of one dilemma to another. In the end, sir, my reasons and justifications will be weighed, my heart inspected, and final judgment rendered by my Lord, Jesus Christ. I tell you only because a woman I have been involved with has been brutally murdered." His eyes seemed to narrow, the twitch at the corner of his lips visible. "Because of that, I will help you in any way I can to bring the culprits to justice."

"She called our office," Ramsey said evenly. He went on to relate the essence of Joe's report, watching as Brown nodded, his blue eyes thoughtful.

For a long moment after Ramsey finished, Brown stared down at the porcelain coffeepot. He seemed completely composed, lost in thought, not the least agitated. Finally he said, "Agent Ramsey, I give you my word as a minister of the Gospel and a man of God: I *never* composed any list of anthropologists. I have no involvement in the death and torture of anyone. Not of Avi Raad, or Elizabeth, or this Scott Ferris, or . . . What was the woman's name?"

"Amanda Alexander." Weber's voice was wooden.

"Or of her, either." He glanced up, meeting Ramsey's eyes. "I do not believe in evolution." He pronounced it *evil*-ution. "I think it is misguided at best, Satanic at worst. It belies the special qualities of the human soul bestowed upon us by our Lord at the Creation. I think it is the worst brain-rot our children can be filled with, not counting the insidious evil spawned by Hollywood and these video gamers. We have glorified violence and Satanic worship. It becomes easier to do if you can teach our children that they are nothing more than animals."

"And this list that Ms. Carter claims to have picked up from your office?" Ramsey asked.

He shook his head absently, a confused look in his eyes. "I *never* compiled any list, Agent Ramsey. I have no idea where Liz might have come up with it." He took a deep breath, a pained expression on his face. "I think as you look into her life, Agent Ramsey, you are going to find that Elizabeth Carter had some serious problems. She had been poorly used by men, her father in particular. That last night we spent together, I told her that I was unsure if we should continue our relationship. While I do not drink to excess, on occasion she did. One of the reasons she came to the church was because of her alcoholism. When I awakened the next morning, she was gone . . . as was the contents of an entire decanter of bourbon."

"How large a decanter?" Weber asked.

"Large," Brown answered. "It's cut crystal, made in Ireland, and holds at least a liter. In that state, I have no idea what Liz might have thought, seen, imagined, or contemplated."

"She told our agent that a third woman was with you that night." Ramsey waited for any reaction.

"My executive secretary dropped by three times that night. We had just returned from Jerusalem, as you no doubt know. I had made commitments to several of the attendees at the conference. Mrs. Campbell was tying up loose ends, asking for signatures, that sort of thing. Since she has come into my employ, Mrs. Campbell has become a close friend." Brown steepled his fingers and said delicately, "It might be that Liz resented that fact. It may have contributed to her delusions. Mrs. Campbell and I did leave Liz alone for a while. We did some work in my office."

"The one down the hall from your bedroom?" Ramsey asked, remembering Joe's notes.

"That's right."

"Ms. Carter told my agent that she found the list there. Could your secretary have left it on your desk?"

"I can't tell you, Agent Ramsey." For the first time, Ramsey thought he saw the faintest dilation of Brown's pupil. Or was that just the bright sunlight on the white carpet?

"You were in Jerusalem at the same time that Dr. Avi Raad was murdered in Tel Aviv," Weber said neutrally. "Coincidence?"

Brown smiled, amused. "Agent Weber, I will give you a copy of my schedule for those five days. Believe me, every spare moment was packed. And, but for a couple of hours of sleep each night, I was never alone or out of earshot of the press, for that matter. Had I stopped to murder a man, I would have had six reporters there to help me."

"So . . ." Ramsey pursed his lips. "You have no idea why Elizabeth Carter would implicate you in these murders?"

He looked genuinely perplexed. "I was going to terminate our relationship. I had doubts about Liz's stability. I knew she was back in the bottle, and well, I was about—"

A knock came at the door. A moment later an attractive blond woman stepped in. She wore a form-fitting peach skirt that reached to just below the knee. Her white blouse was conservative, but did little to camouflage a high and full bust. When her blue eyes fixed on Brown's, Ramsey could see a sparkle of anticipation that almost seemed electric.

"Excuse me, Reverend." She crossed the room with a firm composure. The woman almost dripped a sensual magnetism. Or was it just pheromones from her delicate perfume?

When she handed Brown a sheaf of papers, Ramsey would have sworn that he saw an electrical spark pass between them. Carpet static, no doubt, but the look in Brown's eyes betrayed more than a little shock. He seemed to warm, his expression softening with anticipation.

"I'm sorry to interrupt, but accounting needs a signature on these vouchers. They're for the missionary group leaving for Rwanda. Jacobs can't release travel funds without the signature, and they've a plane to catch at four."

"Gentlemen," Brown said, rising, "may I present my executive secretary, Mrs. Campbell. Eunice, this is Special Agent Ramsey and Special Agent Weber. They're here about Liz Carter."

"My pleasure." She jerked a curt nod and glanced sidelong at Ramsey with the sort of stare she'd have given a bug.

Brown took the documents, a line forming on his brow as he thumbed through the papers. As if coming to himself, he looked up. "Gentlemen? If you wouldn't mind, could we postpone this until later? In the meantime, if I can be of any help, please, feel free to call on me. Mrs. Campbell can make the appointment." He smiled. "She has my full confidence."

Rising, Ramsey shook hands again, trying to read the man behind the expression. He drew yet another blank. "Thank you, Reverend. We'll be in touch."

At the door he looked back, past Weber's shoulder. Brown was already back at his desk, attention centered on the papers. The Campbell woman had turned and was watching him, a probing curiosity in her blue eyes. Her hip was cocked suggestively in the peach skirt. A slim white hand was positioned in a singularly provocative way on the desk, as if caressing it.

"Life in the cloth is hell," Weber muttered as he stepped through the door. The red-blazered security man stood in his "at-ease" posture. He didn't even give them a nod as he led them back through the maze to the doorway and out into the muggy Atlanta heat.

Skip Manson swung his leg as he perched with one cheek on the news desk. Leo Schwartz, the WQQQ station manager, stood with his arms crossed, one quizzical eyebrow raised. Leo stood close to six feet, with a bald head bordered by short gray hair. Fifty years of cigars, bourbon, and eighty-hour weeks had etched lines into his long face. Now he studied Skip through thoughtful eyes. Kahlid leaned back in an office chair with the look of an idle spectator. The cameraman wore faded jeans and a loose white shirt.

"How does it line out?" Leo asked.

"Weird," Skip answered. "My source inside the P.D. tells me that Elizabeth Carter was nailed to the floor before they set her place on fire. Estimates are that they doused her with about ten gallons of gasoline."

"Jesus."

"Yeah, and that's not all." Skip gave Leo a satisfied smile. "The FBI's Domestic Terrorism squad is involved. I've placed a couple of calls to the Washington Field Office where this guy Hanson works. I keep getting the secretarial brush-off."

"What else?"

Skip reached behind him and handed over a series of newspaper articles. As Leo took them and started to finger through them, Skip added, "I don't know if I'm the only reporter in this whole country to notice this, but it's the same M.O."

Leo looked up. "And did this Scott Ferris know Elizabeth Carter?"

Skip shrugged. "How much would you be willing to fork out to find out?"

Leo sucked on his lips for a moment as he stared into the distance of the newsroom. "Two gruesome murders, one in Fairfax, one in Fort Collins, both victims maimed and burned, and the FBI's Domestic Terrorism guys are involved?" He shrugged. "It could be chance. Just one of those coincidence things. No one else has reported a link between Ferris and Carter."

"Just think about it, boss. I've got a hunch about this one."

Schwartz slipped the clippings back to Skip. "Get me something else and I'll turn you loose."

Skip grinned, gave Kahlid the high sign, and said, "You can bet on it, boss."

Rupert Goldman's office was located in the Animal Reproduction building in the Foothills Campus, a ten-minute drive from the main Colorado State University campus.

Joe Hanson shot a cautious glance at Veronica Tremain as they waited in the hallway outside Goldman's office. The tension in her face had begun to worry him. He knew that glassy-eyed, pinched expression. The pressure had to be incredible. Her brother had been killed in a hideous manner, one that she was more than equipped to fully understand. While still in initial shock, Davidson had raked her over the coals. She hadn't had the time even to begin to deal with the grief. The kid was struggling to keep it all together when she wanted to shatter into a thousand pieces.

She still looked good despite the dark hollows under her haunted eyes. Her hair gleamed in the fluorescent light, raven black with bluish tints when the sun hit it just right. She had the kind of high full breasts that men dreamed of, and her thin waist and rounded hips did wondrous things to a snug-fitting pair of jeans.

You're too old for her, Joe. A man nearing his forties shouldn't be having thoughts about women in their midtwenties. *And she's business. You know the rules. You don't go messing around with women who are part of an investigation.*

Of course, if he'd broken that golden rule with Elizabeth Carter, this whole damn thing might be wrapped up by now. He hadn't, and it wasn't, and all the reasons he'd never have crossed the lines with Elizabeth were the same here and now. Besides, Veronica Tremain needed time to bury her brother, to come to terms with the way he'd died.

Joe brought his thoughts back to the hallway where he stood. Linoleum floor, institutional walls, and featureless wooden doors were illuminated by square fluorescent light boxes hung in acoustical panels. The walls had been posted with brightly colored bills and fliers advertising rides to different parts of the country—share the gas. Horses for sale. Livestock shows. Scholarship opportunities and guest lectures by visiting scholars.

He glanced at Davidson, catching the officer as he studied Veronica Tremain with hooded eyes and an obvious interest. While he could sympathize, the guy had been a nerd. They were standing several paces away, and

Joe couldn't help but whisper, "Too bad she's a suspect, huh?"

Davidson grunted, his gaze turning wary as he shot Hanson a sidelong glance. "Yeah." He shrugged, voice low. "It's looking more and more like she's not the perp. After this is all wrapped up, who knows?"

"A word of brotherly advice, Art. She's told me several times that she thinks you're a little lower on the evolutionary ladder than pond scum." He gave the man a thin smile. "And believe me, the good doctor knows a hell of a lot about evolution."

At the look in Davidson's eyes Hanson turned away, half wondering what had prompted him to say it. He would have liked to believe it was a form of paternal protective instinct. The lieutenant was a fucking bulldog. Not that bulldogs didn't make good cops, but sometimes when they got their teeth into something, they couldn't see clear to bite the real bad guy when he passed by.

A man rounded the far corner and approached them in a swinging gait. He carried a ring of keys that rattled with each step. In his mid-fifties, with a thoughtful face like Columbo's, his white hair was short-cropped. Wrinkles matted the tan polo shirt, open at the collar; and the brown Dockers looked like they'd never met an iron. His leather loafers were soundless on the linoleum floor. Inquisitive blue eyes met Hanson's, and the man nodded, greeting them in a melodious voice. "Special Agent Hanson, I suppose. Lieutenant Davidson. Good to meet you. I'm Rupert Goldman."

Hanson turned as Veronica walked over. "Dr. Goldman, this is Dr. Tremain. Scott Ferris' sister."

Goldman shook hands, taking extra time with Veronica. "I'm sorry to meet you in these circumstances. I can't believe this could have happened to Scott. I'm still in shock. Is there anything I can do?"

Veronica withdrew her hand from his. "No. But it's kind of you to offer."

Goldman nodded, clearly unsure what to say. "Scott told me a great deal about you. Just finishing your doctorate, I hear. Physical anthropology. Going to follow in Scott's footsteps?"

She smiled, the action forced. "No. My specialty is somewhat different. Paleoanthropology."

"Dr. Goldman"—Hanson flashed his ID and handed over a business card—"could you tell us just what Dr. Ferris did in your lab?"

"Come on in. My office is more comfortable." Goldman stepped past, jangling his keys as he opened the door. He led the way into a book-lined office and flipped on the lights. A computer screen stared at them in blank gray. Piles of paper cluttered the desk. The trash bin was overflowing, and venetian blinds were lowered at half mast against what had no doubt been morning sunlight; their side of the building now lay in afternoon shade.

Goldman removed a slide carousel from one chair and a cardboard box full of photocopied academic articles from another one. "Excuse the mess," he said absently. "I'm presenting a paper in two weeks. Papers are better if you write them the night before you deliver them, but the slides and graphics take a little more time." He stepped behind his desk, hands spread, and lowered himself into the worn office chair. "I apologize, but I only have the two chairs."

"I'm happy to stand," Davidson replied lightly, a smile barely bending his lips.

"You were going to tell us about Scott Ferris' work in your laboratory," Hanson prompted. "Will it bother you if I take notes?"

"Heavens no." Goldman shook his head. "I'm a professor, after all. I'm not sure I can talk eloquently unless someone is scribbling at the same time. Conditioned response, I think."

Veronica's eyes had lost focus. "Scott took the position here at Colorado State partially because you have one of the foremost embryo transplant centers in the country. I can understand that he was interested in reproduction, but why not in a medical school?"

Goldman frowned slightly. "Let me give you a little bit of background. I'm assuming, Dr. Tremain, that you're familiar with the human reproductive system?"

"I am." Veronica leaned forward in the chair; her blue eyes fastened on Goldman.

"Then you know that the human reproductive system is relatively primitive."

"Huh?" Davidson asked. "Primitive? How?"

"Women have a bicornate uterus," Veronica said. "Unlike cattle, where the reproductive system is a great deal more evolved—specialized, as it were."

"That's right," Goldman agreed. "That's not to say that the human system doesn't work. Obviously, we're here. But then, so is the duck-billed platypus. Primitive doesn't mean that it doesn't work, just that other systems, like those in cattle and horses, are more complex . . . um, sophisticated. They present a different group of problems to the researcher."

"So, why did Scott Ferris want to work with your lab?" Hanson cocked his head. "What do cows have that a human would be interested in?"

"Complexity." Goldman leaned back. "If you can successfully transplant embryos in bovids, cervids, and equids, you can transplant them in anything. Scott came here to learn procedures. How they might apply to humans. He wanted the hands-on experience of working with embryos. You can't do that sort of research on people. You hit an ethical wall. For the moment, we *can* work on animals, and to be honest, if humanity ever begins to seriously work on reducing its genetic load, the work we're doing here, and in Australia and Scotland, will provide the human model."

"What's a genetic load?" Hanson asked.

"The number and frequencies of deleterious genes in our population," Veronica said woodenly. "Remember the thalassemia, the Tay-Sachs, and PKU?"

"I remember." Hanson shifted in his seat. "Then, I take it, you're light-years ahead of similar research in humans?"

"That's correct." Goldman rubbed his hands together. "Our interest here is agricultural. Increasing productivity. Think of it like this: If you have a perfect cow, one that has a potential carcass yield of seventy percent, or a magnificent bull, you can't reproduce that animal. No matter how you breed them, the F_1 generation will always contain only fifty percent of those genetics."

"Eff what?"

"The F_1 is the first successive generation of offspring," Veronica told him. "F_1 would be your children; F_2, your grandchildren; and so on down the generations."

"By the very nature of reproduction, the genes are mixed and matched," Goldman continued. "Evolution created the different species so that they would produce constant variation. Now, to bring this back to agriculture, if you produce an outstanding animal, one that has better economic value than his fellows, it would be cost-effective to create a whole herd of them. Duplicates, clones, like the famous Dolly, the sheep in Scotland. Let's say you own a feedlot, and you have this marvelous bull. He has the potential to augment carcass yield—that is, the amount of meat in relation to bone, skin, internal organs, and so forth. Let's say that animal can give an extra ten percent over the average run-of-the-mill slaughter steer. It would behoove you to clone that animal, create an entire herd of duplicates. For every one hundred head in your feedlot, it would be the equivalent of running ten extra head, but without having to raise them from calves, feed them, and pay the vet bills."

"More from less," Davidson summarized. "That's what Ferris was into? Reproducing humans that way? Like cloning John Elway to breed better quarterbacks?"

Goldman's smile turned plastic. "No. Not at all. Like I said, our interest is agricultural. His interest was how reproduction worked. How embryos could be created, manipulated, transplanted from one organism to another, and how human reproductive biology differed from that in other species."

"Sounds spooky to me," Davidson growled. "What possible use would it be to humans if you didn't want to make copies?"

"A great deal, Lieutenant." Goldman leaned back. "Especially in cases where fertility problems are at issue. Sterility is on the rise. We are dumping contaminants into the environment every day. Many of these molecules act on the human system in the same way that estrogen does. In fact, we call them estrogenizing molecules. Plastics, the kind you drink out of; dish soap; even the urine passed by women is full of it. Dealing with it is going to be a long-term problem, but, in the meantime, let's say you were sterile. You and your wife wish to have a child, but you can't produce viable sperm. What if I told you you could have a child anyway? We'd take one of your wife's eggs, and one of your germ cells, what we call a gamete. When that cell divided through a process we call meiosis, we would insert your half with her half, create a zygote, and implant it in her womb. In that case, the science would offer you a normal life."

"And the child would be just like a normal child." Hanson nodded his understanding. "Half and half, right?"

"Correct. Just like regular sexual reproduction the way God intended." Goldman lifted an eyebrow. "Unfortunately, despite what you'd believe from the monster movies, the scare TV, and this damned tabloid journalism, that's what drives most of this research in humans. It just runs into a storm of controversy over the potentials, not the actual goals."

Veronica frowned. "How much of this kind of work was Scott doing?"

"A little bit of everything. He wanted hands-on experience, so he helped us flush oocytes; learned how to use a micropipette; learned to locate, remove, and splice genes. He spent his time at the microscope like the other students, and then he took those results back and applied them to human evolution and potential cures for genetic disorders."

"Just how difficult would this be?" Hanson asked. "I mean, could he have done any of these things to people?"

Goldman chuckled. "Was he the proverbial mad scientist? No. I'm afraid not. Oh, to be sure, he had the knowledge and the skills. He could have. But he didn't. It takes a well-equipped laboratory, Agent Hanson, and willing subjects." His smile widened. "One of the rites of passage my female graduate students are fond of is taking the junior male students and offering to impregnate them: to implant an embryo onto the exterior small intestinal wall. In theory, there's no reason why it wouldn't develop. The parental blood supply is there for nourishment. It would have to be born C-section, of course."

"But no takers," Veronica asked wryly.

"Not to date, and I'm afraid I'd have to put my foot down. We *don't* work with human material in *any* form in this laboratory." Goldman's expression cooled. "Is that why you think . . . I mean, that Scott . . ." He shook his head, eyes concentrated someplace distant while a deep frown etched his face. "I can tell you for a fact that Scott never worked on human tissue in the lab. I would have known. And besides, we don't have the facilities here for it even had Scott wanted to."

"Did he ever receive any threats?" Hanson asked. "Malicious mail, phone calls, anything that might have indicated someone wanted to intimidate him?"

"No, I can't remember anything like that." Goldman frowned. "Well, he didn't have too much sympathy for scientific ignorance. He really hated those silly papers, the ones at the grocery store checkout that sensationalize faces on Mars, chimpanzees mating with humans, and aliens. He called them 'the opiates of the unwashed masses' and 'the greatest threat to human intellectual freedom since the Inquisition.' "

Hanson tapped his pen on his notebook in the silence that followed. "Let me turn that around. Did you ever hear him threaten anyone?"

Goldman studied his desk with a pensive frown. "In relation to his work maybe. You might possibly say that."

"How?" Veronica demanded.

"Oh, it was late one night. In fact, we were working on one of Scott's projects. He wanted to know if we could create a viable embryo from a frozen specimen taken from a slaughtered animal. In essence, reproduce that animal. That way if a prize animal were struck by lightning, broke a leg, died of bloat, or whatever, a rancher could take a tissue sample and a lab could reproduce it. We were working with cryopreserved, differentiated bovine cells—"

"You lost me again," Hanson interrupted, writing rapidly. "What's a differentiated cell?"

"Higher organisms have two kinds of cells, Agent Hanson. Differentiated somatic . . . uh, call them body cells: muscle cells, bone cells, nerve cells, skin cells, all the rest. Those provide a given function within the organism. The second kind are gametes: the cells dedicated to reproduction. They turn into sperm in males or eggs in females. As in the example I gave to the lieutenant earlier, we have trouble with differentiated cells when we use them for reproduction."

"Not their specialization," Hanson guessed.

"Right. You see, the trick is to culture the cells and put them in a state of stasis where you know what the status of the chromosomes is. By means of microsurgery the nucleus is removed and placed in an anucleated ovum at the right stage of suspended second meiosis."

"What?" Davidson looked blankly at Goldman.

"In simple terms," Veronica explained, "you take the nucleus from the adult cell and use it to replace the nucleus in an egg cell."

"Right," Goldman said as he gave Davidson a worried look. "But, you see, the trick is doing it from a frozen specimen. People have been using adult cells ever since Wilmut and Campbell cloned Dolly back in the nineties."

"How can you do that?" Davidson asked. He crossed his arms, obviously unconvinced about the utility of such research.

"By the chemical environment we place it in," Goldman replied. "That gets pretty technical. Different nodes, uh, the sections of DNA that control the transcription sequence, have to be stimulated by a protein environment. Think of it like this: DNA is something like a computer program. Each cell carries the *entire* program for an animal. Most differentiated cells are running at the end of that program. Our job is to place the nuclear DNA, the initial program, into a new computer, and essentially reboot the system."

"That's what Scott was doing?"

"For the most part, yes." Goldman cocked his head. "But it's not inherently sinister. Here, let me show you." He spun in his chair, taking a picture of three cows and two bulls from the bookcase behind him. "For the last couple of years we've become pretty good at reproducing genetically identical lines of stock. By changing the genes, inserting the Y or X chromosomes, we've created breeding strains that are exact duplicates down to the—"

"Get back to that night," Hanson prompted.

Veronica reached for the picture, frowning as she looked down at the identically spotted cattle.

"We had recovered a fibroblast—a connective tissue cell—from a sebaceous gland in a hair follicle. Scott suspected, correctly, that due to the oil content, it might not have been as badly damaged by lysing."

"What?" Davidson asked.

Irritated, Veronica said, "Water is a bipolar molecule. When it freezes, it lines up, takes up more volume, and breaks the cells. Now, be quiet and let Dr. Goldman finish."

"Right," Goldman said. "We identified a fibroblast in 'Go' state." He glanced at Davidson. "That's a cell that's more or less dormant. That's important because you don't want chromosomal replication to have been initiated. Otherwise you end up with too many chromosomes in your clone and it's nonviable."

"But you managed to recover the nuclear DNA intact?" Veronica had straightened.

"Yes." Goldman preened. "But I'm not going to tell you how. Our paper on that is coming out in *Science* next month. Suffice it to say, we implanted the recovered nucleus into an empty egg, and mitosis"—at Davidson's frown he added—"cell division and replication, was taking place. Not only had it divided, but we had what appeared to be a viable blastocyte. Um, a blastocyte is an early embryo."

"Then," Veronica said, "if you had implanted it, it would have grown?"

"I would have expected that, yes. The genome activated, meaning the DNA was working, synthesizing transcribing RNA and directing the synthesis of protein."

Hanson cleared his throat. "The science is fine, Doc, but what about that night? I'm here on a murder investigation, not to scoop your *Science* article."

Goldman frowned. "Scott had this look of incredible excitement. I'll never forget, he said, 'This is the key. With it we can finally blast those medieval zealots into the twenty-first century.' "

Goldman made a gesture. "I asked him what on earth he was talking about. And he said, 'You know, there are people alive today who still want to believe the world's flat. They think that God literally fashioned us from a ball of mud six thousand years ago. I mean they really truly *believe* that crap. And I'm just the guy to slap them across the mouth with reality.' "

Davidson asked, "So, just who is he slapping? The Flat Earth Society? That's a joke, isn't it?"

Goldman shrugged. "I assume he meant *them*. You know, the people who buy those silly tabloids and think science is the Devil's work."

"I don't get it," Veronica said. "Scott was an anthropologist. What did he care about dead cows?"

"The process is the same whether it's a cow or a mouse or a human. Cellular cycles work the same in all of us. He was learning how the reproductive system worked and how his precious genes are transmitted from generation to generation."

"When was that?" Davidson asked.

"About five years ago."

"And that's all he worked with? Just cows?" Hanson asked.

"Oh, people sent him different specimens. He was working with colleagues in labs all around the world. They would ask him to sequence segments of DNA."

"Human?" Hanson asked.

"I told you"—Goldman looked suddenly nervous—"we don't work on human tissue."

"How can you be sure?" Veronica asked. "I mean, we're talking about cells here."

"Because I watched over his shoulder." Goldman leaned back, a faint sheen on his skin. "It's *my* lab. I run it. And, on top of that, I knew Scott Ferris. I've never known a man so methodical and dedicated to flawless and immaculate work in the laboratory." Goldman smiled in sudden relief. "Besides, you'd need a human female volunteer to carry the embryo to term. To work on humans would take equipment that we don't have here." He lifted an eyebrow. "And what? Do you expect me to believe that Scott was sneaking around, kidnapping young coeds, dragging them in here at midnight and inserting creative embryos into their uteruses? Get real."

"Why would anyone care about a cow? Surely, you're not talking about a golden calf here?" Hanson scowled down at his notes.

"No." Goldman leaned back. "As a matter of fact, we're talking about a registered Angus. And, outside of a couple of tunnel-visioned ranchers I know, no one worships them."

CHAPTER NINE

THE LITTLE TABLE IN TGIFRIDAY'S HAD BEEN PLACED before the wood-framed window, looking out into the B terminal at Atlanta's Hartsfield airport. People passed in twos and threes, accented by occasional solo businessmen who rounded the stairs, briefcases and travel totes in their hands. Behind Jackson Ramsey's back he could hear the bartender as he worked the handles on the taps, took orders from the barmaids, and ran credit cards through the reader. This was the ritual of American commerce. Cash registers were the plastic-framed altars attended to by the white-shirted acolytes with name tags on their breasts.

"What's that look?" Weber asked, inquiry in his eyes as he sipped at a glass of red beer.

Ramsey sipped his own and answered, "Guess I've got religion on my mind today."

Weber grunted, checking his watch. "You've got thirty minutes until your flight. What do you think, Jack? How did you read that meeting?"

"Billy Barnes Brown is one slick customer any way you look at it. If he's up to his neck in this thing, he's got an iron control like I've never seen."

"My gut says he's hiding something." Weber hunched forward on the tall chair, eyes on the passengers passing beyond the restaurant window. "Something about that guy . . ."

"It's your Baptist upbringing, Bill. You can't stand it that a preacher is screwing around on his wife. Where were you raised?"

"Across the line. Alabama. Little town about a half hour south of Birmingham."

"You go to church still, don't you?"

Weber nodded, a tight-lipped expression on his face. "It's just that he seemed so up front about it. Not even a trace of remorse that he was banging one of the church's employees."

"Not only that, but did you see his face when Mrs. Campbell came in? I thought the boy was going to sit up and pant. Call me dense if she's not squeezing his bean." And, as Brown had intimated, that indeed might have motivated Liz Carter to do something rash. So, she was jealous? That still didn't explain how she got nailed to her floor and burned.

Weber said, "Why do I get the impression I'm in the wrong business? I've got two nasty divorces behind me, and I spend my evenings alone with the TV. He seems to slip from one gorgeous dish to another, and no one cares that he's married!"

"Well, one thing's sure. If there's a linchpin here, it's that list that Carter claimed to have. He didn't so much as flinch when I brought it up."

"Maybe it didn't exist. No one's seen it, right?"

Ramsey grunted, then added, "Maybe not, but the Carter woman gave Ramsey the names of three dead people and one who's missing. She didn't just pull them out of the phone book."

"And Brown was in Jerusalem when Raad was done."

"That he was. I'll have some of our guys check his

schedule. I mean, damn! It's almost too coincidental." He screwed his face into a grimace. "That's why I don't like it. Bill, something's not right about this. It's nothing I can put my finger on, but something about that visit just doesn't wash. There's a problem there, and we're not seeing it."

"You caught on to the game he played? That little stroll down the Billy Barnes Brown photo hall of fame? The no-neck security guy? That clever descent to our level so that we could talk man-to-man?" He shook his head. "I hate to be manipulated, Jack."

"Me, too." He sipped his beer, considering. "On the other hand, a guy like Brown doesn't build an empire like that by being a fool. I think he's a dead-eyed ace when it comes to psychology and manipulation. He's an actor of the first caliber. A powerful man who knows how to utilize his resources."

"So, what do you want us to do? Turn him upside down?"

Ramsey frowned. "I'm not sure, Bill. Less sure now than when I flew down here. Here's the conundrum: If Billy's behind the murders, is he betting that we'll eliminate him because he's the too-obvious suspect doing the much-too-obvious thing? Is he betting that—as we have just seen—we'll think he's way too smart a guy to ever kill an opponent in such a ham-handed way?"

Bill mused on that for a moment. "You know what they tell you in the Academy? When you start chasing your epistemological tail, it's generally because you're short on motive. And that, my friend, is just what you're into here. You can't evaluate Brown until you know why he'd want to do Ferris, Raad, Alexander, and Joe's girl in D.C."

"Yeah." Ramsey grinned crookedly. "So, go ahead, turn Brown upside down. I have a hunch he was telling us about half of the truth. I'd give six month's pay to know which half."

The litany of town names progressed: Grinell, Campus, Oakley, Mingo, Colby, Levant, Brewster, Edson, Goodland. Sunset had come at Mingo, at least, what he could see of it. Towering thunderheads filled the sky, each backlit until they seemed haloed above the dusk-green land.

Mingo? Bryce pondered. What sort of a name was that? What kind of people lived there? How different were they from the ordinary sort of people he had grown up with in Center Harbor, New Hampshire? Western Kansas seemed like a different universe as the Durango purred its way into the storm-blocked night.

His fear had receded, leaving an unhappy futility to gnaw at him. That afternoon, in Hays, he had used a pay phone to call his father in Florida.

"Bryce? Where are you? I've had a call from the FBI. They wanted to know where you were. They said you needed to call them immediately. The fellow's name is Joe Hanson." A pause. *"Bryce, damn it! What kind of trouble are you in?"*

The breath might have been squeezed out of him.

"Bryce? Are you there? For God's sake, boy, tell me what's wrong. We can work it out."

"Dad?" His voice had seemed to come from some-where distant. "I'm fine. I just wanted you to know that I'm all right. Call Mom for me, please? Tell her I'm okay. Best to you and Kathie."

He had hung up the phone, remembering from some-where that it took thirty seconds to trace a phone call. Re-membering from some other corner of his brain that with modern electronics, it was instantaneous.

"The FBI?" he had wondered as he hurried back to the laser-blue Durango. "God damn you, Scott. What did you do?"

He couldn't afford another mistake. He glanced suspi-ciously at the cell phone on the seat. Could they trace that? Did they have some way of telling which satellite the signal bounced off?

For the first time he began to regret having bought the Durango. The stylish vehicle wasn't the sort that blended in, not with the dazzling paint and rakish body lines.

"Yeah, right," he shouted at the Kansas night. "How was I supposed to know I was going to be a fugitive?" He was too damn young to drive an Oldsmobile.

He made a disgusted sound and checked the speedometer. He'd set the cruise control for sixty-nine. A perfect speed for not drawing attention. In the headlights, the infinite gray slab of interstate spun out of the dark-ness, the white lines racing toward him like slow tracers to flash beneath the curve of the fender.

A gust of wind shook the Durango, and another of the endless eighteen-wheelers came ghosting up behind him, its powerful diesel dopplering into a muted roar as the big rig bored its way westward. Bryce flashed his lights as the long vehicle passed. The heavy aluminum trailer swayed in another gust of side wind, and the trucker signaled before pulling into the right lane. He then flashed his taillights in a thank-you.

To the south, lightning strobed through the thunderhead, illuminating the huge cloud like a Japanese lantern.

Giant raindrops peppered the windshield. Bryce turned on the wipers and tapped the brakes to cancel the cruise control.

Scott better have left me some answers. That single thought possessed him. What if he arrived at the condo and . . . nothing?

What did he do next? Call the FBI? Sure, and tell them what? "Hello, I'm apparently a fugitive from justice. I don't know what the hell I did, but Scott and Avi and Amanda are dead. I don't know if you killed them or someone else did, but here I am. Come get me."

Could it be espionage? Had Scott been peddling secrets to someone? The Mossad? Was Avi Raad an Israeli cutout? Had Scott been another Jonathan Pollard?

Get off it! Since when would Scott have had any access to military or political secrets?

Scott and Amanda both traveled. It seemed like half of the time they were off to one part of the world or another delivering papers, attending symposia on human genetics, paleoanthropology, or biotechnology. Suppose, just suppose, that someone gave them the information and they were the couriers?

He frowned, blinked against the gritty fatigue in his eyes, and sipped cold Burger King coffee from a Styrofoam cup. That was crazy. No one used couriers anymore. In the information age, all anyone had to do was scan a sensitive document and send it clear around the globe as an e-mail.

It couldn't be drugs. Scott hated them and the dealers who supplied them on the street. *"If I could be king for a day,"* Scott had once told him, *"I'd kill them all! Those sons of bitches snared my little sister with that shit!"*

No, it couldn't have been drugs. Not with that look of absolute loathing in his eyes. They had been sitting in a trendy little bar on Massachusetts, a couple of blocks east of the university in Cambridge. Scott had already sucked down half a pitcher of beer, and Amanda had been particularly solicitous. It had taken Bryce about fifteen minutes of cautious prodding to pick the scab off and discover the source: a phone call from Scott's mother about his wayward little sister.

Bryce made a face and tensed his arms and shoulders, fighting fatigue. The Durango purred through the stormy night, water hissing from the wheels. The lights of Goodland glowed against the rain. The wipers charged and retreated across the glass, a metronome of monotony.

Ronnie, now, there was a character. After years of Veronica stories, Bryce had built a three-dimensional image of Scott's hell-raising little sister. He had been ready for purple hair, razor-blade earrings, black lipstick, and vocabulary that consisted of, "Hey, wow! Like cool, you know?"

Instead, he'd been shocked to meet an articulate beauty with a probing blue-eyed stare that seemed to pry its way right into a person's soul. He would have fallen in love with her that day at the condo if she hadn't spent most of her time talking about this guy, Ben, in his last year of medical school at the University of Denver. After all, what did a starving graduate student in physical anthropology have to offer a stunning package like Veronica Ferris when the competition was a handsome, dashing, soon-to-be-rich heart surgeon?

Bryce tapped the padded-leather steering wheel. She was—or should be—freshly divorced. Did he dare call her? Could she have the slightest notion of what this was all about?

No, pal, just leave her alone. She's probably a wreck anyway. Scott had been her lifeline. Without him and his gentle guidance, she'd have destroyed herself.

Funny thing, wasn't it? Scott had saved his sister, but in the process, how many other people, himself included, had he destroyed?

A bolt of lightning arced across the sky; actinic light cast blue shadows for the briefest of instants. Two seconds later the crack-bang seemed to split the world.

The FBI? Sweet Jesus, I'm in real trouble.

Veronica watched as Special Agent Hanson toyed with his orange juice, his thick fingers slowly turning the glass. He sat across from her, his body slumped sideways in the bentwood chair at the Marriott hotel lounge. A shriveled red maraschino cherry canted among the ice cubes in his drink.

Veronica had opted for a double Glenlivet, neat, with a water back. The amber liquid sat untouched in front of her. The plate of nachos that Hanson had ordered for an appetizer hadn't arrived yet. He kept glancing uneasily at the scotch in her glass.

"Yes, Special Agent?" Veronica lifted an eyebrow.

"The scotch," he muttered. "It wasn't so long ago, I bought scotch for a lady."

"And?"

He shrugged. "The next morning she was dead." He made a face, obviously trying to mask his feelings. "There are times I hate this job."

"Yes?" She hesitated. "And the standard line is . . ."

He gave her a blank stare.

Veronica said dryly, "Well, if this were a movie or a novel, this is the point where you're supposed to tell me how you're a lonely guy, driven by a mission to right wrongs, and in spite of all your personal angst, you soldier on, misunderstood, living alone in your little apartment, your only passion being the reality that you're the final line between criminal chaos and the collapse of decent society."

He threw his head back and laughed. "Me and Sam Spade, huh?"

"You mean the stereotype is wrong?"

"Sometimes. I got into it because I thought it would be exciting. It was. It is. And sometimes it's really boring. It's also a pain in the ass. You'd be surprised at the paperwork, the bureaucratic nightmares, the intransigence within the agency, the petty politics, and general bullshit."

"Who's the dead woman?"

"Murdered," he corrected soberly. "Just one of those things. She came forth with information. The bad guys got her before she could come in. No one's fault really, except for the people who killed her. She was just . . ."

"Go on."

"You know, sometimes this job depresses me. I get really tired of human nature. The pettiness, the bigotry and hatred. And sometimes, like in her case, basically good people can get screwed up. Who knows where it started? With a man somewhere. Maybe her father? A husband or boyfriend? Somebody started her down the road that led to someone nailing her to the floor and setting her on fire with gasoline."

"Jesus! Just like Scott?" Veronica straightened. "You bought her a scotch, you say?"

"It was an initial contact. I didn't know what she had, how important she would turn out to be." His gaze focused on something in the past. "The world is full of ifs, Dr. Tremain. Part of being a professional is realizing that you can't anticipate them all. Not and maintain any kind of equilibrium or sanity."

She studied him, reading his thoughtful expression. "Is that why you only drink orange juice?"

An amused smile curled the corner of his mouth. "I don't drink. A very good friend of mine told me that every human being is born with a certain number of drinks billed to his account. I finished mine off early."

"You're single I suppose?"

He nodded again. "It's the irregular hours. She was one of those people who planned everything. A good woman who got too many phone calls telling her, 'Honey, I'm going to be late.' " His right shoulder rose in its expressive shrug. "A person can't just tell himself, 'I'll check that lead in the morning. My shift is up.' By morning, the lead is cold, the case is blown."

"You sound like you've come to terms with it."

He gestured. "Yeah. Like I said, I like my job. I get a

real kick out of the chase. It's better when the guys I'm after are proven guilty and locked away. And I keep score. I'll get the guys that got Elizabeth, and Scott, and Amanda."

She appreciated the certainty in his eyes. "Earlier, when we met the first time, you asked me about a church. Is that who you think did this?"

"No comment, Dr. Tremain."

"I see." She paused. "I take it there's a reason you won't tell me?"

"We don't give out information on potential suspects in big cases. Not that I don't trust you, but it's bad form. The only place that an agent spills his guts to a pretty woman like you is in the movies. Then you become an amateur sleuth, and amidst exploding automobiles and wild shoot-outs with HK machine guns, you solve the case and kill the bad guy when the entire Federal Bureau of Investigation can't."

"You mean it doesn't work that way in the real world?"

"Nope. And real machine guns run out of ammunition in a big hurry. Figure it like this, if a machine pistol has a rate of six hundred and fifty rounds per minute, and the clip holds twenty, how long will it shoot?"

"Uh, let's see . . ." She started to do the math.

Hanson apparently didn't want to wait. "The pistol shoots a hair over ten rounds per second. That's one-thousand-one, one-thousand-two, and you're out of ammo."

"Why make a gun that only shoots for two seconds?"

"Because in an extreme circumstance that's about how long it takes a man with a fully automatic pistol to clear a room or a hallway." He smiled. "It just doesn't make very good film."

"I see." She picked up her scotch and sipped.

At that moment the cocktail waitress arrived with a tray containing a heaping pile of nachos. She laid out napkins, forks, and two plates before setting the tray on the middle of the table. "Can I get you anything else?"

"No, that's fine for now," Veronica said. As the woman walked back to the blond-wood bar, Veronica opened the tab and scribbled down her room number and the tip.

"Hey!" Hanson pointed, his mouth full of corn chips. "Thass mine!"

"Sorry, Special Agent. Given your track record when it comes to buying scotch for women, I'm not taking any chances."

He considered her for a moment and nodded before scooping another chip through the melted cheddar.

"Why did you want to buy me a drink?" She placed her hands before her, fingers interlaced on the wood-trimmed tabletop. "If it were a movie . . ."

He shook his head, grinned, and washed the nachos down with orange juice. "Sorry. Attractive as you are, you're business, not pleasure."

"Gee, thanks. I've never had anyone tell me that in such a flattering manner before."

A twinkle lay behind his eyes as he picked up another chip. "All right, so drink your drink, eat some nachos, and tell me what you really heard in that meeting with Goldman this afternoon. You're the one with a Ph.D. in anthropology. What does all this genetic stuff have to do with Scott Ferris being tortured and killed?"

"I asked myself that the whole way back from Goldman's office." She finally reached out and picked up a chip with a lighter coating of cheese. "If Scott was killed because of his genetic research, why not kill Goldman and his colleagues, too? I mean, they're the ones who are running the lab. What kind of threat are cloned cattle anyway?"

"Maybe his research is a dead end?" Hanson narrowed an eye. "What I mean is, Scott wasn't killed because of his science. Maybe he discovered something else, maybe about someone? Maybe he told Amanda Alexander and Avi Raad?"

"Told them what?" She paused, trying to understand this new direction.

"Did Scott ever tell you anything about anyone? Maybe a Christian leader? Any hint that he might have some information, some kind of dirt . . . perhaps damaging to his character? A nasty little secret about someone like Billy Barnes Brown? The Apostolic Evangelical Church of the Salvation? Maybe the Christian Creationist Crusade?"

"No. Scott thought they were all deluded fanatics, sort of social sheep that they'd let themselves be swindled intellectually and monetarily. He wouldn't have anything to do with 'fundamentalist' anything. He despised them. These people—not Christians, mind you, but Indians—beat him up at Harvard. Put him in the hospital for weeks."

"But he didn't give you a specific reference?"

"No." She chewed thoughtfully while he watched her expression. "I'm serious, Special Agent Hanson, I—"

"Call me Joe."

"Sure, Joe, Scott did call me on occasion and bad-mouth the Creationists. We'd talk, you know, about what he was working on . . . what I was working on. He'd say that something or another would rock the Creationists back on their heels when it finally came out. Or he'd wonder what their reaction would be."

"Did he ever single out any group? Mention them specially?"

She shook her head. "If he did, it didn't stick. It's not like he had a vendetta against Billy Brown or his church. He devoutly believed in tolerance—that the scientific method would win out in the end. I'm sorry, Joe, but if he had any kind of compromising information on anyone, he never told me."

"Who might he have told?"

"Amanda." She swallowed hard. "He didn't keep anything secret from her."

Hanson nodded, not mentioning the obvious. After a time, he said, "So, if Scott's research is a bust, a dead end, why were he and Avi Raad, and Amanda, killed in the same fashion? Tortured and burned?"

"And Bryce?" she asked, heart quickening.

"Still missing. I checked in just before I came over here. From the report, his office has been cleaned out. Every paper, every file, his computer, everything, gone. One of the graduate students saw a truck late one night. Didn't think anything of it. Just a moving company. Two men, both large and muscular, were wheeling a file cabinet out." He paused, cataloging her reaction. "His house was burned to the ground that very night."

"But no body."

He shook his head slowly. "He left a message for his secretary two days before the arson that he wouldn't be in. That he needed a graduate student to cover his classes. It's as if Bryce Johnson just dropped off the face of the earth. His car is missing. It's a '99 Dodge Durango. Blue. Outside of that, we don't have any leads beyond the fact that on the night Scott was killed, he placed a call to Bryce."

Veronica froze, a chip halfway to her mouth. "Scott called him? About what?"

"We're good, Dr. Tremain. Just not that good. All we have are the phone records."

She centered her gaze on the table, wondering what that meant.

"Any ideas?" Hanson asked gently.

"It could have been coincidence. They had just authored an article in *AJPA*. Uh, given your blank look, you don't read the *American Journal of Physical Anthropology*. I don't blame you—some of it is a little heavy. Scott and Bryce were best friends. Met at Harvard." She smiled, remembering Bryce: handsome, intelligent, with that special glint in his eyes when he looked at her. If she hadn't already been involved with Ben . . .

"That looks like a direct hit," Joe observed.

"Excuse me?"

"I take it that you know Dr. Johnson." Hanson had withdrawn the inevitable notebook. "Tell me about him."

She wondered where to start. "Let's see, I met him five, no six years ago. Scott and Amanda brought him home during Christmas break. He was just finishing his thesis and diving into his Ph.D. work. I remember Scott saying, 'Sis, this guy is going to knock 'em dead and rewrite our understanding of human evolution.' That was back when the controversy was really boiling up over the statistical functions people were performing on mitochondrial and Y chromosomal DNA."

"Right. Whatever that means." Hanson gave her a reproving look. "Does everything in anthropology come at the expense of a fifty-cent word?"

"No. The really good stuff comes in buck-twenty-five words. Anyway, the three of them spent most of their time up at the condo, skiing. I went one day, and, well, you know, Scott and Amanda made one pair, Bryce and I another." She smiled, remembering the interest in his eyes, how he'd treated her royally. "Problem was, I'd just met Ben. I was still at the starry-eyed stage with him. Now, looking back, I wonder . . ."

"Were you and Bryce Johnson close? By that, I mean did you communicate? Would he have given you any idea where he might have disappeared to?"

She shook her head. "Sorry. The last time I saw him was two years ago at the American Association of Physical Anthropology meetings. We had dinner. He asked about my dissertation. I told him I was divorcing Ben. He told me he had just been given a temporary position at New Hampshire. That was important to him. His mother was up at a little place called Center Harbor. It's on some lake with a buck-fifty name. He said there was this really neat white ship that they cruised up and down the lake on. He said that it was incredibly romantic in the summer under a full moon."

"You remember all that?"

"Hey, Special Agent Hanson, he's an attractive man. He was paying attention to a woman with a freshly broken heart. Unlike so many, he was an absolute gentleman about it." She wrinkled her nose. "Maybe it's because I was Scott's little sister. But I'd like to believe otherwise."

"Has he been in contact since?"

"A couple of letters. A postcard from Rome on one of his trips to Tel Aviv."

"Whoa. What was he doing in Tel Aviv?" Hanson had perked up.

"How should I know? He didn't write that. Just that he was on his way. It was a postcard. 'Hi! Wish you were here!' That sort of thing. People don't usually say anything important on postcards."

Hanson sighed and dipped into the nachos again. "No, I guess not." He chewed thoughtfully and glanced at his watch. "Did Bryce and Scott ever fight?"

"They were friends, Joe. They squabbled; then they made up. They liked each other."

"Any trouble between them over Amanda?"

"Get real. If you're looking for a love triangle gone wrong, Amanda and Bryce weren't a potential mix." She arched an eyebrow. "If you think Bryce hired a hit, forget it. His only source of income is his salary. I thought you people did background checks."

He laughed at that. "Yeah, we know what was in his bank account the night he left." A pause. "How'd he afford Harvard?"

"Full-ride scholarship based on brainpower, a ninety-ninth percentile placement on the GRE, a four-point-five GPA as an undergraduate, research assistantships, teaching assistantships, and a couple of articles in the refereed journals. He also worked part-time as a lab assistant to the medical examiner in the Suffolk County Coroner's Office. For a while he was a candidate, or whatever they call them, for the U.S. Olympic Pistol Team. He couldn't do it because of the cost and the time taken from his studies."

"Bright boy."

"Yeah, he could outshine the sun." She took a nacho chip and chewed thoughtfully, remembering his red-blond hair, the way his New England accent mutated simple words like barn into "bawn."

"Anything else?"

"Joe, you've just about wrung me dry. I've racked my brains, and I keep coming up with stuff I've already told you."

She cocked her head. "Mind if I ask a personal question?"

He gave her a crooked smile. "Go ahead."

"Deep down, what's your intuitive sense? Was Scott doing something illegal?"

"Deep down? My gut says no, not illegal, but it may have been something that people with certain convictions might have thought immoral."

She considered that, remembering the determination in Scott's eyes when he talked about the religiously deluded.

"Dr. Tremain," Hanson said after wiping up the last of the nachos, "I really want to thank you for all of your help. We've got people working on that bibliography you gave us. You've been invaluable."

"That sounds oddly final."

"Didn't mean to." He studied her thoughtfully. "I've got appointments tomorrow morning with the professors in Scott's department. Davidson already talked to them, and I have his notes. I'll see if I can shake anything else out of them before I head back to Washington." He shook his head. "I don't know. It just seems like we're missing something here."

After a long silence, Veronica asked, "Joe, about this church. Do you have anything that ties them to Scott's death?"

He gave her a measuring appraisal. "Officially, I'm telling you 'No comment.' If I were talking to Mitch, my companion in crime, I'd say I've got nothing that would stand up in court. All I have is a dead woman's allegation." A pause. "But it's early in the game. And, I think it's a big game. Something is going to break, and when it does, I'm going to snare the people who did this."

"I'll go with you tomorrow, see if I can . . . What?"

He was shaking his head, knowing eyes on hers. "I want you to go home, Dr. Tremain. You have my card. If anything comes to you, as it often does in cases like these, you call me. Even if it seems trivial. On my end, I promise, if I have any questions about the scientific stuff, I'll call you."

She just stared at him, slightly in disbelief. "That's all?"

"For the time being. Like we were talking before, this is the real world, not the movies where I drag you along as screen candy to help solve the crime. Besides, my boss, Ramsey, would fire me if I did." He smiled and stood up. "Thanks, Doc. For everything. Oh, and for the nachos, too. Next time it's my treat. I'll be in touch."

With a sinking sensation, she watched him walk across the carpet, step down to the main lobby, and stride purposefully for the door.

CHAPTER TEN

◆

He climbs the steps, carrying his canvas bag that contains his precious buffalo, the snowstorm, and his books. This place is wonderful, cool, with scented winds blowing down from the tree-covered mountains. In the distance, snowcapped peaks seem to scrub the very sky itself.

The steps are made of wood, varnished so the grain can be seen, and covered with a scratchy surface like sand stuck to plastic. He wants to reach down and rub the tip of his finger across it, but instead, dutifully carries his bag up behind Mother. On the second floor, she stops and sets the suitcase down. He hears the key clatter in the lock and she turns it, easing the heavy door open.

In that instant, he stops, his heart leaping. There, above the door, is a huge white skull staring down at him. On the creature's head are giant, branching horns. He stares into the empty eyes and at the long snout.

"Whaa that?" He barely feels his mouth drop open, attention fixed on the beast.

"That's a deer, Abel. Come on. It's been long dead and won't hurt you. Think of it as . . . as a kind of guardian, huh?"

He nerves himself to creep forward, then scoots

through the door before the monster beast can leap down and get him.

Inside, the room is cool, carpeted, with comfortable-looking furniture. He lowers his bag to the floor and pulls out his buffalo. Tucking it under an arm, he follows Mother across the room, staring at the books, the TV, the fireplace, and placing it all in his head.

There on the shelf to one side of the fireplace is a big metal buffalo, bronze in color, its back arched and its tail curled as if snapping. For a moment Abel stares, clutching Chaser and his bag. The bronze buffalo seems to glare at him, saying something Abel can't hear.

"Chasuw, wook! Buffawo." He holds Chaser so that he can see the bronze buffalo. Abel cocks his head, trying to understand what the bronze buffalo is saying to him.

"Sweetie? Come see," Mother calls.

His shoes clump onto the shining vinyl flooring in the kitchen, and he passes a counter, a refrigerator, and a white stove. Ahead of him is a table, and beyond it, a marvelous view of the lake. Wonderful blue water laps at the shoreline far below them. From here he can look down onto the trees. Out on the lake motorboats drone across the water, casting white spray and V-shaped wakes behind them.

"Jesus," Mother whispers. "Is this some place, or what?"

"Somepwace," he answers automatically, and remembers the huge monster beast above the front door. Do deer really grow that big? How had the whitened bones ended up there? He glances uneasily over his shoulder just to make sure the beast hasn't sneaked in

*the door when he wasn't looking. What had the heavy
metal buffalo been trying to tell him?*

*"All right, kiddo, it looks like we're home for a
while. Take a look upstairs. According to the plans
we're supposed to wait here for further instructions."*

*"Home?" he mouths uncertainly. "Heaww?
Where's my piwwow?"*

"That's 'pillow,' sweetie. Try it again."

"Pilllloowww."

*"That's a good boy." She reaches down to pat his
shoulder. "Let's get unpacked. We'll get settled, go and
do a little shopping, and what the heck, I see a dock
down there. Do you want to go fishing?"*

"Fishshing?"

"It's fun."

*He looks over his shoulder and remembers the
gleaming white skull hanging outside above the door.
But here, inside, with the metal buffalo, it should be
safe.*

The low-pressure system had been born in the Cana-
dian Rockies and had rolled down across Alberta, Montana, and Wyoming, bringing chilly temperatures and rain
to the Colorado Front Range.

Veronica chose to follow U.S. 287 south through
Loveland, Berthoud, and Longmont, where she caught
the diagonal for Boulder. It was the morning of the fourteenth. Scott had been dead for four days. She was going
home. Rain spattered her windshield and tattooed the

Z3's roof. Under the sleek water-beaded hood, the stout six cylinder rumbled with a brassy arrogance.

She passed occasional farmlands that still held out against the successfully wealthy who craved an ever in-creasing number of five-acre tracts on which to place a five-thousand-square-foot house for themselves, their two children, the sport-ute, two dogs, and maybe a horse or two.

To the west, low gray clouds hid the massive uplift of the Front Range. Wisps seemed to be torn from the bot-tom of the overcast; stringers of mist curled in the falling rain.

Her cell phone rang. Reaching the slim unit from her purse in the passenger seat, she flipped the cover open and asked, "Hello?"

"Ronnie?" Theo's gravelly voice asked.

"Hi, Theo. What's up?"

"I've started looking into Scott's estate." He paused uncertainly. *"Ronnie, did you know he was in debt up to his eyebrows?"*

She frowned, checking her mirror, signaling, and ac-celerating to pass a U-Haul truck. "That doesn't make sense, Theo. How on earth could he be in debt? He should be comfortable on his dividends and interest alone."

"It's gone, Ronnie. The stocks, the investments, the property, all of it. He even had two mortgages on the Fort Collins house. The only things he had clear title to were his motorcycle and that ratty old pickup he insisted on driving."

A sudden stillness swept through her. "Wait a minute,

Theo. You're telling me that Scott managed to blow over a million dollars in assets in the last seven years?"

"More than that, I'm afraid. I talked to Clarence."

"What did our charming broker tell you?"

"That Scott has been selling consistently, much to Clarence's dismay. Scott's holdings were down to zero even before the market topped out. Clarence told me that Scott liquidated his holdings for cash. Adding it all up over the last six years it comes to close to two million three hundred thousand. Slice the government's twenty-eight percent in capital gains off the top, that's still a million six fifty and some change. I haven't been able to obtain his bank statements yet to determine the history of his activity, but you should know, he's got only a couple of thousand in his checking and savings combined. If he had any CDs I can't find them." The silence stretched before he asked, *"Ronnie, did you know about any of this?"*

"No, Theo. I mean . . . it's nuts! Why would he divest? Where did the money go? I mean, shit! What was he doing? Where did he put it?"

"I was hoping you could tell me."

"Well, damn it, I can't! If he was divesting, he never mentioned it to me."

"Ronnie, answer me honestly now. Do you think he was paying someone off?"

"Blackmail? Theo . . . who on earth could have been blackmailing Scott? For what? You know Scott: Mr. Squeaky Clean. Now me, I'd be made for the part. But Scott? He always followed the rules, and it only pissed him off when someone else *didn't*!"

Theo's voice lowered. *"What about the child, Ronnie?"*

She considered that as a Chevy Suburban roared past and blew enough spray to overwhelm her wipers for the moment.

"I don't think so, Theo. I mean, what's to blackmail? Amanda had the child. They put it up for adoption. She and Scott made the decision together. They didn't try to hide it. And, even if they did, who cares if Amanda had a child out of wedlock?"

After a long silence, Theo sighed. *"I don't know. I'm grasping at straws here. Something's wrong, Ronnie. None of this makes any kind of sense. Scott was a smart man. We talked . . . well, when you were having difficulties. The Scott Ferris I knew would have come to me the second he had any kind of legal problems. He even consulted me about the adoption of that baby, though an attorney in Boston handled it. He knew me, knew the system. It's not like him to allow himself to be cleaned out over something rotten."*

"God, Theo, I can't help you. Honestly, I'm feeling like the proverbial rug has been pulled out from under me. If you're feeling lost, I'm even loster."

"Where are you?"

"Just coming into Boulder. In fact, the Jay Road light just turned red." She braked and pushed the clutch in, slowing to idle behind a line of traffic. "I'll be home in about fifteen if you need anything else, Theo. And I want to know before you tell Mom, all right? I don't want to worry her."

"Right. She's upset enough as it is. You know, Scott . . ."

"Yeah, it's all right, Theo. Scott was her favorite. I'll talk to you later."

She pressed the "end" button, flipped the phone

closed, and dropped it on the seat next to her purse. Shifting into first she accelerated through the light and followed 119 past the Celestial Seasonings building and the Lazy Dog sports bar. Passing the Coco's and the Kmart, she took a left at the light on Twenty-eighth and made her way home.

Slowing for the speed bumps, she eased the Z3 across humps of asphalt and pulled into her drive. At the turn of the key, the rumbling exhaust went silent. Veronica sat in the quiet, preoccupied eyes on her comfortable Victorian with its big shady elms and delicate wooden trim.

She picked up her purse and tripped the trunk latch before stepping out and retrieving her suitcase from the rear. She hurried through the misty rain and onto the front porch. Fiddling with her keys she opened the door, tapped in the security code, and dropped her suitcase. Going back for the mail, she placed it onto the pile that was still unopened from her last return.

Her shoes clattered across the wooden floor when she kicked them off. Suitcase in hand, she padded down the hall to her bedroom. Returning to the living room, she grimaced at the blinking light on the answering machine. She hadn't taken the time to check messages after Davidson's call.

Picking up the phone, she dialed from memory. Mary answered on the third ring. "Hello, Mom? I'm home."

"Oh, dear, Ronnie. What more have you learned?" Her mother's voice sounded scratchy, the way it did when she had a cold. *My God, she's been crying.* Mary hadn't even done that after Dad's death. Rather, she'd been the perfect upper-class widow, a stately lady possessed of all the dignity in the world.

"Not much, Mom. I spent quite a bit of time with the FBI agent. He's pretty sure it wasn't anyone local. The best guess is that it's something tied to Scott and Amanda's work. Bryce's house—remember him?—well, it was burned, too, and his office at the university was cleaned out. Another researcher, Avi Raad, is also dead."

"Bryce? He was such a nice boy."

"Missing."

"Who would do this?" Mary's desperate voice trembled. *"Why, Ronnie?"*

Veronica ground her jaws. "They'll find them, Mother. The FBI is serious about this case. They don't send people out from Washington unless they're putting a major push behind it."

"I know." Mary sniffed. *"I . . . I've got to go, Honey. I'll call back later. When I . . . "*

"It's all right, Mom. I'm here. Go ahead and cry." Veronica's own grief came welling up, spurred by her mother's. How typical of them. They could only cry together, grieve together, while separated by the safe distance of the telephone.

After several minutes of sniffles and choking sobs, Mary said wearily, *"I'm better now, Ronnie. Thank you. Dear Lord God, I'm just so—"*

"I know, Mom. Me, too. It's like having a leg cut off, part of your heart torn out."

"I don't know what I'd do without you, Honey."

"You'd do just fine, Mom."

"No," she said woodenly. *"Not this time. This time, part of me was killed along with Scott."*

After hanging up, Veronica beat a hasty retreat to the bathroom for Kleenex and struggled to regain her own composure. For what seemed like an eternity, she bawled, allowing the deep-seated ache in her belly to expand and engulf her. Afterward she stared at her red-eyed reflection in the mirror, wondering why crying—the simple voiding of the lacrimal ducts—made a person's eyes swell up like that.

Come on, you don't have to prove Joe Hanson 100 percent right. You can deal with all the bullshit before you break down and wilt.

She stalked out of the bathroom with a purpose, found her notebook and a pen, and took a deep breath before pushing the "play" button on the answering machine.

The first four messages were from friends and colleagues congratulating her on her graduation. Then, message five began: *"Sis? Listen. I think something's really gone wrong. If anything happens to me, warn Amanda and Bryce. I've left messages on Amanda's machine, but she's off to some music thing. There's some important info where you used to hide your dope in the hills. If I'm just paranoid, you won't ever hear this 'cause I'll drive down and erase it before you get home."* He laughed. *"Of course, if you do hear it, you'll know that I'm fucked. Promise me, Sis, if you've never promised me anything before, find the info, keep cool, and stay out of it! All I can tell you now is that Cain's raised Abel."* A pause. *"Take care, Sis. Hope Hawaii was fantastic. I love you."*

Veronica stabbed the "playback" button, her vision silvering with tears. She played the message over and over, listening to Scott's voice talking to her from the grave.

"What's this?" Leo Schwartz asked as Skip Manson leaned into his office and flopped a smudgy-looking fax of a photograph on his desk. The WQQQ station manager looked irritable. He always did on days when he had to do the dog-and-pony show with the corporate suits when they came down from New York to discuss ratings, advertising, and worst of all, profits. Not only that, some moron had plugged a wrong electrical cable in the wrong plug and had fried the guts out of one of his fifty-thousand-dollar cameras in the newsroom.

Hanging in the doorway by one hand, Skip had a grim look about him, one of serious sobriety. He pointed with an impudent finger. "That's a fax of a photo that's running in the paper in Manchester, New Hampshire, tonight. It was a house. It belonged to one Bryce Johnson, Ph.D., an assistant professor of anthropology at the University of New Hampshire."

"So, who's Bryce Johnson, and why would I care?" Leo picked up the fax, squinting at the burned wreckage with fire trucks in the background. The place reminded him of the crisped insides of his camera.

"Next page, Leo."

Schwartz lifted the second sheet and frowned at a list of names and titles. "I don't get it."

"It's a bibliography, boss. I picked it up over at the library in Georgetown." Skip stepped into the room, an intensity in his eyes as he studied Leo. "Remember? We talked about the Elizabeth Carter fire? Ferris? Does this ring a bell?"

"Yeah, I told you to find a link."

"Bryce Johnson is one of Scott Ferris' coauthors. So is a fellow named Avi Raad and a Dr. Amanda Alexander—both deceased. Burned. Torched. Incinerated. You asked for a connection between Elizabeth Carter and Scott Ferris. Well, boss, I haven't found that yet, but—"

"My God," Leo whispered as he fingered through the rest of the pages Skip had tossed onto his desk. "What the hell is happening here?"

"Whatever it is, it's just breaking." Skip raised an eyebrow. "There's going to be a scramble for this one. I want to be in on the ground floor."

Leo nodded. "Whatever you need, take it and go." If Skip could break this, it would make next month's meeting with the suits just a little easier.

The Colorado Rockies rose in rugged majesty. Bryce had never seen them in summer, never understood how green they could be, their slopes mantled in thick stands of fir and lodgepole pine. The view on the descent from the Eisenhower Tunnel had stunned him, piercing his ragged fatigue and worry. What really surprised him was that it was raining on the east side, and when he broke out, it was into bright daylight on the west. Bryce signaled and took the Frisco exit off of I-70. As he slowed on the exit ramp, the vague notion that he'd made it crept through his tired brain.

He had been four days on the road; the constant tension every time he saw a patrol car, or when a vehicle followed him for too long a time, had eaten away the last of his reserves.

After the rain in Kansas and Colorado, the Durango's gleaming laser blue had faded, dampened by road grime. At the Flying J in Limon, he had carefully switched plates again. He had had time to think. To minimize risk, he didn't want to take plates from anyone traveling extensively on I-70. Rather, the best odds for misleading any possible pursuers would be to take plates from someone traveling ninety degrees from his route of travel. Luck had blessed him with a blue Durango from Montana.

He took a left under the underpass and glanced enviously at the Holiday Inn across from him. A Best Western lay to his right. The image of a nice quiet room, a comfortable bed, and hours of uninterrupted sleep filled his head like a narcotic. But if anyone was here, looking for him, they'd check the motels. His dwindling supply of cash made it even less viable.

He passed the crowded Safeway parking lot and made his way past the little malls with their Starbucks coffee shops, mountain bike rentals, ski shops, and real estate offices. Frisco looked completely different from when he had been here in winter. In early summer, with the aspens leafed out, verdant grass grew where snowbanks had been piled high beside the road. What was now a crystal-blue lake had been a white flat east of town, crisscrossed by snowmobile tracks.

He frowned, trying to remember. Which way was Scott's condo?

He took a right at the light, then a left into the parking lot behind the microbrewery. Finding a parking space, he pulled in and slipped the Durango into park before shutting off the ignition. He sat dully for a moment with hands propped on the wheel, trying to make his exhausted mind work.

Coming off the interstate, he remembered going straight. Climbing after they went through town. From the heights, the condo looked out over the lake. The ski area had been farther up the road in a place called Breckenridge. When they came back to town to eat at Annie's they'd turned at the light, as he had just now. And down main street had been the Moose bar where they'd drunk beer for the rest of the night. He remembered that because Veronica had irritated him by talking about her new boyfriend, Ben.

Yeah, it had to be up Highway 9, but how far? He frowned. The turnoff had been a narrow gap between two piles of snow. Part of a sign, the name of which he couldn't remember, had stuck partially out of the drift.

Locking the Durango, he stretched and walked across the parking lot to the brew-pub's corner entrance. The place was filled with high tables, and wooden chairs cluttered a tiled floor. A central bar dominated the corner of the ell; glasses were hung over ornate taps.

Bryce took a right behind the partition to the men's room and relieved himself of 150 miles of recycled coffee. Then he found the pay phone, flipped through the white pages to Frisco, and found Mary Ferris' phone number and address: 23 Eagle Lane.

Bryce sauntered over to prop his butt on a stool and leaned on the chrome-and-wood bar. When the young woman tending the taps—a twenty-something blond—walked over, he said, "Hey, I'm supposed to meet a friend of mine at his condo. Uh, he said I couldn't miss it, but I guess I did. Twenty-three Eagle Lane. Off Highway 9. You ever heard of it?"

She considered, a frown incising her too-wide forehead. "Yeah, I think so. It's about three miles out on the left. It's got a big wooden sign on the highway. Has an eagle carved in it. Each of the streets is Eagle something or other. Lane, Drive, Circle. You get the picture?"

"Hey, yeah, thanks."

"Can I get you anything? We've got a brand new wheat beer, fresh out of the keg."

"I'll be back. Thanks." He fought the urge to tip her, aware of his vanishing funds.

Back in the Durango, the sun through the windshield would have cooked eggs. So, what next? Smart: he had to play this smart. The exhaustion draping his brain made that difficult.

Scott had been pretty cagey: *"the place were we drank peach brandy."* Even if his assailants had heard, which they probably had, they wouldn't have the slightest idea what he was talking about. It could have been anywhere. *"Key's in the foramen magnum."* Only an anatomist would have understood that. Bryce definitely remembered the skull: a weather-bleached elk that Scott's father had killed someplace out in western Colorado a couple of years before his fatal stroke.

Bryce turned the key, hearing the reliable Durango purr to life, and slipped it into reverse. No, he couldn't just drive up to the place and trot to the front door. This would have to be done carefully. Somewhere, somehow, Scott would have left him a clue as to what this was all about.

He took a right onto Colorado 9, accelerating into traffic and merging when the four-lane narrowed to two. He kept his eyes on the housing developments, the condominiums and resorts, until he spotted the big wooden sign with the eagle. Through gaps in the pine and fir, he could see the slanting roofs and the stained wooden sides of the complex. The incredible blue of Dillon Reservoir sparkled in the light.

Bryce drove on, passing two more condo complexes. Then the highway curved southward away from the lake and up the valley toward Breckenridge. He took a left onto a dirt access road, turned around, and headed back in the direction of the condos. He passed the first development and made a right into the second, just up the road from the Eagle subdivision. Pulling into a parking space in the shade of a tall lodgepole pine, he turned off the engine, reclined his seat, and lay back.

In the silence, he could hear the muted roar of traffic on the highway and the sound of laughing children playing on a second-story deck to his right.

Before closing his eyes, he snugged the big black HK .45 into the crook of his arm. Night would come—and when it did, maybe Bryce Johnson could finally solve this whole damned mess.

The drive into D.C. from Dulles that night on the fourteenth of June proved uneventful. One of the nicer benefits of a 9 P.M. arrival was the light traffic on the main arteries into the city. Joe Hanson leaned back, his right hand propped on the wheel as he turned into the Washington Metro Field Office parking lot, got a nod from the attendant, and drove down the ramp to his spot. He slipped the Taurus into park, turned off the ignition, and collected his briefcase.

Passing through security, he took the stairs and made his way down the official corridors, heels tapping on the polished institutional floor. The burr of activity that accompanied the day shift had mellowed to the occasional jangle of a phone, the whirring of a printer, and the desultory conversation of the few agents on night duty.

To his surprise Jackson Ramsey's door was still open; the lights were on. Joe stopped, tapping lightly as he leaned in. Ramsey looked up from behind his desk, phone to ear, and gestured Hanson in.

"Yeah, right. Good work. Hanson just got here. I'll call you back. Right. Take care." Ramsey replaced the handset on the cradle and leaned back, stretching his powder-blue shirt, wrinkled now, and pulling his red-lined blue suspenders tight. "Hey, Joe. Whacha got?"

"Not much more." Hanson dropped into one of the fabric-covered chairs, set his briefcase to one side, and rubbed the back of his neck as if the massage would stimulate his tired brain. He pulled out his notebook and related the information from Fort Collins. ". . . So, that's about as far as we can go there. Ferris was doing genetic research, but not on people. Did Billy Brown finger him, Alexander, and Avi Raad for a hit? Maybe. But we don't have any proof beyond Elizabeth Carter's word. If the proof existed, say a threatening letter, a record of a phone conversation, I haven't found it. Or else it's in the ashes in the Ferris or Alexander houses."

"Or in the missing files."

Joe nodded.

Ramsey worked his jaw back and forth, as if to clear his ears. "I went to Atlanta and saw the good Reverend." After he related the meeting, he grinned at Joe's inquiring gaze. "I don't know, Joe. The guy's smooth. Real smooth. My hunch is that he knows something, but I'm not sure that he's at the bottom of this."

Joe pursed his lips, thinking. "It's too pat. I mean, why would he? Sure, he's got a big money-making church, but why put it all on the line? It's too damn obvious."

"Sometimes people do crazy things, but, yeah, I'm skeptical, too," Ramsey said. "We've finally obtained Ferris' phone records. The night of his death he called Amanda Alexander five times. Apparently getting her answering machine. He called his sister once, Bryce Johnson once, and a Rebecca Armely once."

"Who?" Hanson leaned forward.

"Rebecca Armely. She's . . . or she was in Salt Lake City." Ramsey fished through the papers on his desk. "Okay, here we are. Rebecca Canton Armely, age twenty-seven. Born, Rebecca Jennifer Canton, Dayton, Ohio, 1975. Graduated high school, attended University of Ohio for her B.S. and finished with a master's degree in '99 in physical therapy from Harvard. Married one John Armely, of Boston, in June of '99, divorced from same, August of 2001. Rebecca was granted exclusive custody of their single child. Parents are both deceased. She's got one older sister. And the child was adopted in 1999—a boy, Abel Armely, currently age four. She and Abel relocated from Boston to Salt Lake in September of 2000. Has worked as a physical therapist for a local HMO, no record, no arrests, nothing."

"Who is she?" Hanson leaned back frowning.

"Boston, you said? As in where Alexander, Ferris, and Johnson went to school? She wouldn't have studied anthropology with them, would she?"

"Bingo! She minored in anthropology." Ramsey lifted an eyebrow. "Have you ever thought about becoming a cop? You're good at this."

"Bite a fart, boss." Hanson took the paper that Ramsey handed across the desk. The photocopy was of a legal document, official with the Massachusetts state seal. "Adoption papers for . . ." He whistled. "Son of a bitch."

"Yep. It appears that little Abel was Amanda Alexander's child."

Hanson leaned back, tapping his teeth with the corner of the document. "Veronica said something about that. It didn't register at the time."

"So, be a guru, Joe. Tell me where Rebecca has disappeared to." He handed over another photo—one lifted from the Utah DMV computer. He hated driver's license photos, but for the moment it was the best they could do. She appeared to be an attractive blond woman, narrow of face, her expression dominated by serious blue eyes. "You didn't see her in Fort Collins, did you?"

Joe shook his head. "Not that I would recognize." He gave Ramsey a leery expression. "Has her apartment been torched?"

"Nope. We've had a team on the place since we tagged her number. No one's been close to it. The folks in the building say that Becky was a quiet neighbor, dedicated to her son. Dated occasionally, but no overnighters. They said the boy was a little odd, different somehow, and had a speech impediment."

"Any pictures of the kid?"

"None. The only photo they found was of her and the sister. She packed efficiently. Most of her clothes are gone, along with the boy's. But the fridge is full, as if she just walked out the door. She's been missing since the night of Ferris' phone call. Hasn't showed up at work. This wasn't a planned trip. We've talked to her employer, her landlord, and some of the neighbors, but she hasn't been in touch with any of them. It's as if she and the boy just dropped off the face of the earth."

Hanson checked his notebook. "Okay, let's put this in perspective. Avi Raad is killed on June sixth. On June tenth, Ferris is killed. He calls Johnson and Armely. They split. The next day, June eleventh, Amanda Alexander returns home, reports her answering machine is stolen, and is killed that night or early that next morning. On the same day, I sit down with Elizabeth Carter, and on the morning of the twelfth, she is nailed to the floor and burned alive. On the thirteenth, Johnson's office is cleaned out and his home is burned." He looked up. "One hit squad? Or two?"

Ramsey picked up his prize "Larry King" pen, rolling it back and forth. "If it's one, it's a sloppy way to run a railroad. But Carter and Alexander—if related—would mean two. No matter, these guys are traveling. What keeps them from screwing up? Being seen by the neighbors? Missing a hit? You just don't make something like this up as you go along."

"Nope. Not unless a great deal of planning went into it before the operation started."

"We're checking the airlines, seeing if we get a hit on people flying from Denver, to Athens, to D.C., and then to Manchester."

Hanson leaned forward, replacing the papers on the desk, a fragment of an idea slipping around the back of his tired brain. "Something tipped Ferris. He had time to call his friends and his sister. She was in Hawaii. Maybe Ferris hung up when he got the machine."

"Or he left a message. Come on, Joe, his mother and sister go to Hawaii—and he didn't know it? They only live a little way down the road, for God's sake. Why call her if he knew she was out of town?"

"You're right. But Veronica would have told me if she'd received a message from Scott. I'll call her, just to be sure." He waved it away. "Getting back to the point, something tipped Ferris off. And, yeah, I'm guessing that these guys are real professionals. They've done all the scouting, got equipment pre-positioned, trucks ready to go, uniforms, keys, whatever. Elizabeth said there was a list of names. Brown and his cronies could have been setting this up for months. Studying these people and their habits."

"*If* it's Brown."

"Right. Outside of your visit, what have you got?" Hanson allowed a hopeful expression to cross his face.

"He was in Jerusalem the day Raad was killed in Tel Aviv," Ramsey said guardedly. "We checked. He was visible the whole time, in conferences, with reporters. Outside of it being one hell of a coincidence, his story checks out. We went for the phone logs next. After getting the judge to cut the subpoena, we've started combing through it all. Do you have *any* idea how many calls the Apostolic Evangelical Church of the Salvation receives in a day?"

Hanson pursed his lips for a moment. "He's gonna

skunk you on the phone calls, chief. Maybe there will be a slipup, but if what we've seen is any indication, these guys are pros. If it was me, I'd use satellite phones under a pseudonym. NSA might, *might* be able to tag it, but if my guess is right, and we're dealing with talent, they won't."

"So?"

"So, it's a smaller database to track down the talent. How many people have the brains and skill to run an operation like this? We're not talking about Mafia hit men being drafted, but real professionals. Maybe ex-military, intelligence types, security analysts? Someone who has worked in the craft for a long enough time to know how to torture a man to death in his house so that the neighbors fifty feet away don't know anything's wrong. That's what they were doing: torturing these people for information before they nailed them to the floor and burned them."

"All but Alexander."

"Maybe."

"To learn what?"

"Elizabeth is easy. They wanted to know what she knew. They wanted the list back. She wasn't the kind to bite her lip and endure. She spilled everything she knew, and then they killed her."

"Then they know that we know." Ramsey stopped twiddling his celebrity pen.

"Sure they do, Jack." Hanson rubbed his hands together. "They're just betting that they're good enough that we can't prove it. Problem is . . . to date they're right."

CHAPTER ELEVEN

V ERONICA DOWNSHIFTED TO SECOND, MATCHED THE ratios, and let the Z3 take the corner. Her headlights illuminated the familiar sign and glared whitely on the conifers that blocked the other side of the drive. She braked, letting compression slow her on the downhill, made the corner around the mailboxes, and took the tight curve at the bottom of the slope faster than she should have, tires rasping on the pavement. She passed the first building, its sloping roof and wooden decks cast in yellow by the parking lot lights. The second building was mostly dark; a few of the windows were illuminated. The headlights played briefly on the wooden walls as she slung the BMW through the tight left to curve down to the third building. The tires squealed in protest as she neatly pulled into the parking slot and rolled to a stop. She set the brake and killed the engine.

God, keeping hours like these is going to kill me. How long had it been since she'd had a full night's sleep? Three days now since the flight in from Hawaii, and hours of despair since Davidson's phone call? Scott's message had tortured her, replaying in her mind. For nearly an hour she had paced from one end of her house to the other, checking the locks, making sure the windows were secure. Wishing, for the first time, that she had a big dog, or even a pistol. In the end, no matter how tired she felt, she couldn't stand the uncertainty. She had thrown her suitcase into the trunk and driven straight here.

She pushed the knob that cut the headlights and plucked her purse from the passenger seat. Stepping out into the cool night, she enjoyed the smell of the forest and the dampness of wet duff. God, had she ever been this tired?

Following the walk, she passed under white cones of light cast by the overhead floods. Her booted heels tapped out a cadence in the night. At the stairs, she paused, digging through her purse for the other set of keys, and then trudged wearily to the second floor. The wooden steps echoed hollowly under her feet.

Scott, please, tell me that the answers are here. She pulled the ring of keys out with a jangle, found the silver one, and inserted it into the lock. She turned it, hearing the tumblers click, and pushed the door open.

She stepped into darkness, pressing the heavy wooden door closed behind her. She locked it and flipped the light switch. The room remained black.

"Son of a . . ." A curious prickling ran up her spine. The faintest hint of an odor, something familiar but not quite right, hung in the air. She stopped, sniffing, a chill of warning like an unbidden current in the close air.

She stood for a moment, allowing her eyes to adjust to darkness. The dark bulk of the heavy leather couch hunched against the wall. The coffee table appeared as an inky rectangle against the gray carpet. To her right, stairs led to the upper story and the two bedrooms. On her left, the bookshelves and fireplace lay in shadow. She took a step, head cocked, listening, sensing something not right.

Step by step, she eased across the room, past the recliner and the breakfast bar to the kitchen, and flipped on the light. In the glare, everything looked in its place. The wall-to-ceiling bookcase, the furniture, the rugs and lamps. Even the Jackson original bronze of the bison rested in its place beside the fireplace.

Was it her imagination, or was that the faintest odor of . . . Yes, coffee. The pot was almost full, the little red light glowing.

The hall flooring behind the stairs creaked as if under a heavy foot. Sudden panic sent a shiver up her back. She could feel it; the eerie presence of another human being. Step by step, she backed toward the telephone where it hung in the wall-mounted cradle. Fighting the urge to fling herself at the door, she reached behind her, fingers groping for the smooth plastic. She backed another step, eyes searching the shadows.

Her fingers slipped off the surface; then she grasped the handset, almost puffing with relief. Images of Scott's charred body floated in her brain.

Another creak, this time behind her. She whirled, staring into the black muzzle of a pistol. A man was looking at her over the sights, his face unshaven, his hair curiously wet and plastered darkly to his head.

"I have to ask you to hang up the phone now," he said in a deadly earnest voice.

Bryce stared into her frightened blue eyes. The white dot of the HK's sights centered just above her heart.

"Ronnie!" he gasped, breathing deeply, lowering the

pistol. "Ronnie, it's me, Bryce Johnson. For God's sake, don't scream." His knees suddenly turned weak; he backed against the kitchen stove, fighting the trembling that began in his legs and crept into his arms.

"Bryce?" She stared at him in disbelief. "What are you doing here? *Why in hell are you here?*" She watched him wide-eyed, glanced down at his pistol, and then back at the phone, as if still longing to pick it up and dial nine-one-one.

"Scott called me," he said leadenly, the weight of the .45 somehow incongruous in his right hand. "The night he was killed. He told me to go where we drank peach brandy. You were here, Ronnie, remember? Right over there." He pointed at the glassed-in fireplace with his left hand. "The fire was crackling. Remember, Ronnie? The four of us were sitting on the rug, drinking that peach brandy we picked up at the liquor store in town." He rubbed his face with his left hand, feeling utterly foolish.

Veronica was watching him through deadly blue eyes, her mouth set as if weighing each of his words.

He muttered, "I must be losing my mind."

"Why are you here?" she repeated stubbornly. "Damn it, Bryce, what's this all about?"

"I *don't* know, Veronica!" He raised his hands, aware that she followed the movements of the pistol with growing fear. He shook his head and thrust the HK into his waistband. "Sorry. I've been under a great deal of pressure for the past four days. Seeing Amanda's—"

"You *saw* Amanda?"

He gave her a flat-eyed stare. "She's dead, Ronnie. I saw what was left of her house. Burned to the ground. The story in the paper said it was accidental. But it wasn't.

Scott asked me to warn her. I tried calling . . . and got nothing. I drove all night, and . . . and . . ." He swallowed hard, feeling a painful swelling under his tongue. He studied her distrustful face, asking, "What the hell is this all about, Veronica? What did Scott tell you?"

"You tell me." Hostility seemed to be boiling inside her.

He shook his head, utterly defeated. "I don't know. Scott told me he'd lied to me. What does that mean? Lied about what?"

"You know he's dead, don't you?"

Bryce nodded. "I called the Fort Collins paper. The Colorado something."

"The *Coloradoan*," she supplied. "He was killed the night he called you."

He could only muster the energy for another nod. "I heard them. He was on the phone to me when they . . . they . . ." He closed his eyes and took a deep breath. "I heard him try to scream. Heard them hitting him. Then this man picked up the phone and asked, 'Who is this, please?'" He met her hard eyes. "That was Scott's murderer talking to me."

She crossed her arms defensively. "Where did you put the stuff from your office?"

"What stuff? Scott told me to leave, to warn Amanda that Avi was dead, and then to meet him here. That's what I did."

"You didn't go back to your office?"

"No!" He straightened. "What is it, Veronica? Tell me."

"Someone cleaned out your office two days after you

disappeared. Bryce, they burned your house to the ground." Her steely glare didn't waver.

Bryce tried to comprehend. *Burned my house?* With effort, he stiffened his weak legs. *Dear God, what does Mom think?* He could imagine the panic in her mind and shook it off, trying to think.

"That would have been the day after I left Amanda's." He grimaced at the distrust and accusation in her eyes. Did she think that he . . . "Figure it out yourself, Ronnie. I got here this afternoon. It's four *hard* days' drive from New Hampshire."

"What kind of research were you doing?" If anything, her gaze had hardened.

"Computer work. Genetic probabilities and sequence mapping. Scott and Amanda would send me a nucleotide sequence, and I would input it on the mainframe. They wanted to know the possible combinations down to fifteen generations. That, and they would send me a sequence and ask me to cross-check it against the catalogue in the human genome. I'd take their data, cross it with mapped sections of known human chromosomes, and compare frequencies. Any discrepancies were to be flagged and reported back to them."

For the first time, her antagonism cracked. "Human genotypes?"

"Yes."

"You're sure?"

"Well, it sure as hell wasn't a pig's!"

"But Goldman said—"

"He's involved in this, too?" Bryce rubbed his wet hair back. He had just stepped out of the shower, feeling clean for the first time in days, when he had heard someone climbing the steps. Then had come the adrenal fear when the key grated in the lock and the door swung open. He had already unplugged the light in the main room so that no one would spot him going in or out. And now, the intruder turns out to be a very suspicious and hostile Ronnie? "Fucking hell, what am I involved in? Why the hell is the FBI chasing me? *What the hell did Scott do to me?*"

He stomped across the floor, no longer caring if she called the cops or not. In desperation, he dropped onto the overstuffed couch and rubbed his beard-shadowed cheeks.

Veronica hung her head, long black hair draping around her face in a mantle. "You're going to tell me, Bryce, that you can think of no reason anyone would want to kill you, or Scott, or Amanda, or Avi? I mean, people don't torture other people to death and burn them for no reason."

"Ronnie, I'll tell you this just once: I didn't do anything against the law. Nothing illegal to my knowledge. Nothing that I thought was illegal. I did research. Scott and Amanda provided me with DNA sequences, and I did my best to test them in an attempt to determine how genetic combinations would work out. I'm a computer hack, for Christ's sake. I told them what they'd get before they did the experiment in the lab."

"Then why did they clean out your office?"

"The only thing I can think of is that the Feds wanted Scott's data."

"The Feds?" She fixed that piercing stare on him.

He nodded. "I called Dad. He said that the FBI had been trying to find me. That just made me run harder."

She sighed. "Bryce, I've been working with them. If

you're really innocent, you'd better call Special Agent Hanson and tell him what you know."

He gave her a dull stare. "You're working with the FBI?"

She nodded, still reserved. "If you haven't been lying to me, you'd better call Agent Hanson. If you know anything that can lead them to Scott's killers, you'd better tell them"—her expression turned icy—"or, pistol or not, I'm going to be your worst nightmare, Bryce."

He took a deep breath. "You've got it." He paused. "I don't suppose that you just look in the phone book under Agent Hanson?"

She flipped a card out between two slender fingers. He reached out, took it, and walked to the phone. "That's a D.C. area code and . . . uh, it says 'Domestic Terrorism'?" He shot her a skeptical look, tapping the card. "Is this for real?"

"That's the man. It's after midnight in D.C. I'd use his home number."

Bryce lifted the receiver, listened for a dial tone, and punched in the numbers. The phone rang once, twice, three times, and then an answering machine clicked on. "Hi, this is Joe. You know the drill: Leave a message and I'll get back to you."

After the beep, Bryce said, "Hello, Agent Hanson. This is Bryce Johnson. I need to talk to you. I'm at . . ." He squinted, picking out the number on the phone and reading it off. "Call me when you get a chance."

He replaced the handset and shot a nervous look at Veronica. "All right, Ronnie. I called. Now, do you really think I'm still involved in this?"

She shook her head. "Bryce, I don't know what to believe anymore." A faint smile crooked her lips. "But if your life the past couple of days is anything like the shit reflected in your face, it's been about as horrible as mine."

"Yeah. Tons of laughs," he said bitterly. Then, as it sank in, he said, "I'm really sorry about Scott. No matter what this is all about, he was a good man. A good friend." He met her eyes. "And I know what a super brother he was to you. Yeah, I'll do anything I can to help nail the sons of bitches that did this to him and Amanda."

The glacial ice behind her blue eyes melted just the least little bit. "I appreciate that."

He shifted, suddenly aware of the vulnerable look in her eyes. He didn't remember her being this slim and poised. Her hair caught the light from the kitchen, gleaming and dark. Damn, she was more beautiful than he remembered. "So, how's Ben?"

She bit off a dry laugh and stepped past him, opening the refrigerator. "Well, let's see. It's Friday night, a little after ten. He's probably got her half smashed on good bourbon. He should have her home by eleven, and out of her bra by eleven-thirty. The panties should slide off five minutes later. After that"—she leaned her head back so the wealth of raven hair slid down her back—"it's anyone's guess how long she'll keep him up."

"Sorry to hear that." He stood and walked into the bathroom for his cup of coffee, afraid he'd end up staring at her. The black sweater she wore had rounded itself around her breasts and was tucked tightly into her Levi's, accenting her slim waist. "At the AAPA meetings, a couple of years back, you said you were getting a divorce. Is that still happening?"

"It's happened. Past tense." She twisted the top off a bottle of orange juice as he stepped into the room. "And you? Has, uh, what's her name got you on a short leash?"

He shook his head. "The last one was named Candi." He saw the look. "No, she was nothing at all like the name would imply. Actually, she was a homebody. Liked to cook, and was appalled by the idea of peignoirs, teddies, or any such feminine frills. In a manner of sad and singular coincidence, she called to tell me it was over the day Scott died." He stared down into the coffee. "Funny. Since then I haven't even given her a thought."

Veronica might have been staring at infinity again, hardly aware of him. He could see the thoughts spinning in her head.

"You know, you look like you could use a good night's sleep yourself."

She shot him a sidelong glance. "I could. And it's my house." The suspicion had returned. "By the way. How the hell did you get in here?"

"The elk skull. Scott told where the key was." He pointed at the front door. "Foramen magnum. The trick is to balance on the railing while you fish around for the wire."

She seemed to come to a conclusion. "You might be all right, but maybe you'd better go down and take a room at the Holiday Inn. I'd sleep better."

"Still don't know who to trust, huh?"

The cold glare was back. "Scott and Amanda are dead. What do you think?"

"I think if you'd feel better, I'll go out and sleep in my car."

"Why not the hotel?"

"Because, this boy's about flat broke. I took what I could get out of the ATM. I didn't have time to go to the bank for a travel loan."

She was chewing on that when the sound of feet could be heard on the wooden stairs. Bryce tensed, reached out, and pulled Veronica back into the shadowed bathroom behind the stairs. To his surprise, she didn't resist, and she barely flinched when he pulled the black Heckler & Koch .45 from his waistband.

Heart pumping, he struggled to take a breath. A band might have constricted around his throat. "Shhhh. If it's trouble, I want you to run to the back, slip out the sliding door, and get the hell away from here."

"It's a two-story drop from the deck," she told him. "The only way out is through the front door."

"Then drop flat and stay down."

He felt her nod as a key slid into the lock and the tumblers turned. As the door swung open, a woman's voice asked, "Did you leave the kitchen light on?"

"Nooo."

"You're sure?"

"Yesss. I tuwrn it offf," came the slurred response.

Bryce bit his lip and leaned forward to peek around the frame. A blond woman stood in the doorway, staring warily about the room. A little boy held her hand, his big blue eyes blinking as he looked around and pointed with his free hand. "There, Mother. Thass not you puwse."

The woman took a hesitant step into the room, pushing the little boy behind her, and calling out, "Hello? Amanda? Is that you? Scott? Are you here?"

Bryce swallowed hard and slipped the pistol into his

waistband again before stepping out. "It's all right, Becky. It's Bryce. Scott told me to come here."

She froze, eyes huge, like a deer in the headlights. Then she squinted, barely relaxing. "Bryce? What are you doing here?" Rebecca continued to watch warily, unwilling to step past the safety of the doorway and escape. "Scott told me to meet him here, but until he or Amanda arrives . . ."

Veronica stepped out from the hallway. "My brother, Scott Ferris, is dead. He was murdered in his house in Fort Collins. And, since this is my house, along with his, may I ask who you are, and what you are doing here?"

The blond woman braced herself with one hand on the doorjamb. "Scott . . . dead . . . ?" She swallowed hard. "Who?"

"They don't know." Veronica squared her shoulders. "I asked, who are you?"

Bryce said woodenly, "Her name is Rebecca Armely. We're old friends from Harvard. She's a close friend of Amanda's. And the boy is . . ."

As if in a trance, Veronica fixed her attention on the pale blond boy who peered past the woman's leg with frightened eyes. She said, "Yes, this is Abel. Scott's son."

The white garage door gleamed in the glow of the Taurus' headlights as Joe Hanson pulled into his driveway and slipped the car into park. His little house waited patiently, windows dark; the small lawn, as usual, looked parched. Virginia creeper clung tiredly to the walls, and the leaves had that wilted look. When he had bought the two-bedroom house in Fairfax, the idea of a lawn had appealed to him. The momentary fantasy had been based on images of himself decompressing from the stresses of the job by puttering in a small garden out back, mowing, watering, seeing something grow as a result of his efforts. Instead, he now felt the additional pressure to take care of it when he never had the time.

It hadn't been the first time he had fooled himself with false promises about making changes in his life. When he had passed his thirty-eighth birthday, he finally had come to the conclusion that he shouldn't try to jack himself around with bullshit that would never be. The honest truth was his life was his work. For as often as he spent time at home, a smart man would have bought a condo in the city.

Yawning, he turned off the lights, stepped out of the car, and reached into the backseat for his suitcase. Locking up, he walked along the concrete walk to the front door and sorted through his key ring. The white corners of envelopes stuck out from the black sheet-metal mailbox fastened to the wall. Opening the door, Joe slid his suitcase in on the wooden landing and fished the bills, fliers, and junk mail out of the box. Inside, he flicked on the light and closed the door. He walked through the living room, sorting the mail, and wondered how someone without a life—like himself—could get so many bills.

At the refrigerator, he took out a half-full bottle of cranberry juice, popped the top, and sniffed. Since nothing stung his nose, he assumed it to be safe and tilted the bottle back, chugging.

Returning to the dining room, he glanced at the answering machine with its message light blinking insistently. Damn it, here it was, way after midnight, and all he wanted to do was sleep. He made a face, walked over to the machine, and used a fingertip to punch the "replay" button. Sliding a pen from his pocket, he yawned again as the machine rewound and told him it was now the fifteenth of June.

"Hi, Uncle Joe. It's Betsy, your niece. Brad and I were wondering if you would be free this Fourth of July. I know, it's early, but with you, we have to plan ahead. Anyhow, we're having a barbecue at the place over on the East Shore, and wanted to know if you could escape your grisly job long enough to come socialize with family? The kids miss you. Please give me a call."

The kids missed him? Sure they did. They just knew that he always brought them something, special gifts that their mother wouldn't buy for them.

Then he heard, *"Special Agent Hanson? This is Skip Manson, WQQQ. I keep getting the brush-off at your office. In the next couple of days, we're going to be running a story linking the Carter, Ferris, Alexander murders. I'd really like the Bureau's comments before we do. If you would give me a call."* Joe made a face and shook his head. Well, damn it, it was inevitable, but how had the reporter found his home number?

The machine clicked to the third message: *"Sorry, wrong number."*

Joe waited through three of those, a different voice every time, one about every eight hours during the day.

"Hello, Agent Hanson. This is Bryce Johnson. I need to talk to you." Joe snapped to attention, writing as Johnson read out the phone number. After the machine clicked off, he added, "Call you, Bryce? You bet your ass I will."

He had just plucked the receiver from the cradle when two strong arms grabbed him from behind. He opened his mouth to bellow, but a thick hand slapped a length of duct tape across his lips. As he bunched himself to fling his attacker off balance, something stung his neck, and the injected liquid made a cool sensation in the muscles beneath his mastoid.

A blow to the side of the head dazed him, sending him staggering. Instinctively he reached for the .40-caliber Sig in his shoulder holster. Someone kicked his feet out from under him and he fell, crashing to the floor. The cool sensation had spread, rolling through his head like a wave, and in its wake, a hazy lethargy left his thoughts foggy and his muscles slothful. He blinked, groaned, tried to get his hands under him, and barely succeeded. When he managed to make it to hands and knees, one of the blurring figures stepped into his vision and used a foot to topple him face first onto the dusty wood of his dining room floor. Despite his blurring vision, the crepe soles of the man's shoes filled him with panic. No wonder he hadn't heard.

"Sorry, Special Agent Hanson"—the voice seemed to come from a great distance—"but you're not going to be calling anyone for a long . . . long . . ."

A gray curtain descended.

CHAPTER TWELVE

VERONICA LAY ON THE THICK LEATHER COUCH, A PAT-
terned Pendleton blanket covering her slim body with its
soft warmth. The refrigerator shut off abruptly to leave a
thick and tangible silence. Slivers of light illuminated the
room where the parking lot floods slipped past the
drapes.

She replayed the events of the day, thinking back to
the call she'd made to her answering machine: *"This is
Skip Manson, Mrs. Tremain. It's a little after eight p.m.
on the fourteenth. I'm a reporter with WQQQ. I was wondering if I could get together with you. I'd like to talk to
you about your brother. I've been reading some of his
publications, talking to some of his professional colleagues. If you could give me a call, I would really appreciate it. I'm here, in Denver, at the Hilton out by the
airport."* He had proceeded to leave a phone number that
Veronica ignored. Great! That was all she needed. Some
insipid reporter asking, "How do you feel about your
brother's murder?"

Why on earth had Scott dragged Rebecca and the little
boy into this? And Bryce? Here? She still had trouble understanding that.

The room seemed to hold its breath, stirred by memories of times past when she, Scott, and Amanda had sat by
the fire, laughing, sipping good wine or smooth brandy.

Of other times when she and a few friends had sneaked up here to drink, smoke, and snort themselves into a narcotic oblivion.

Had that really been her? So angry, alone, and fucked up?

Somehow she'd hung on, turned herself around, and put her life in order. Scott had been her beacon, leading her through the maze of self-imposed traps, the depression, and the withdrawal from booze and drugs. Drawn to the dark side by a need for rebellion and attention, she had been one of the lucky ones. Thankfully, she hadn't been born with an addictive personality, or she'd be dead or jailed by now.

Scott. He was watching her, as if seeing through the years, through death itself, his calm gaze probing, asking what she'd do next.

I don't know, Bro. I still haven't figured out what you got yourself into.

Rebecca had been unwilling to talk. Instead, she had taken the little boy and led him off to her room, saying she needed time to think, to consider.

Veronica hadn't had the energy to resist. Desperately tired, she had retreated here, to the couch, and wrapped the blanket around herself in the darkness, trying to think, to sleep, to come to some sort of conclusion about what this all meant.

Bryce, haggard himself, had retreated to one of the upstairs bedrooms and flopped onto the bed. She still didn't know what to make of him. How could he have been part of Scott and Amanda's research and not have known what they were doing?

She pinched her lower lip with her teeth and shot an uneasy glance at the kitchen, now cloaked in darkness.

"There's some important info where you used to hide your dope in the hills." If she interpreted correctly, Scott had hidden something in her old stash. She had had several hiding places—as all kids in trouble did—where she stashed her drugs, condoms, and other things she didn't want her parents to know about. She'd had several temporary caches around the condo, but the most ingenious was a recess behind the cabinet kickboard next to the stove where no one would think to look. How on earth had Scott known? To her knowledge, she'd never told him about it. Why should she? It was even a bitch to get into, necessitating a screwdriver to take the panel loose.

Veronica glanced at the darkened stairway to the upstairs bedrooms. The place was silent. Could she believe Bryce's claim that this was the first night's safety since his ordeal had begun? Could she trust him? His hazel eyes haunted her, looking oddly vulnerable. She'd seen his soul reflected there, wounded and wary, plagued by an uncertainty that had touched her. Damn, she really wanted him to be innocent of all this.

Why was that? What *had* she seen in those earnest eyes? What did she want to believe about him, and why? Just because he was handsome, articulate, and definitely male, or was it that he was a link to Scott, to the freshly dead past that she craved?

Well, you'd better figure it out, Ronnie. Your track record with men isn't anything to brag about, and this time, it could get you killed. Therefore, she promised herself she'd be cautious, refuse to take him at his word.

What about Rebecca? What did she know about her?

Only that the woman had been one of Amanda's fellow students at Harvard, and that she'd adopted Scott and Amanda's child.

The urge to rise, to creep over to the cabinet and check the space beneath, might have been a physical demand. But what if one of the others heard? She didn't dare retrieve whatever Scott had hidden and chance that the others, whatever their motives, might get their hands on it.

How well she remembered the look of desperation in Bryce's eyes when he'd scared her to death with that pistol. The man was frightened, and all she had was his word that he wasn't part of this madness.

It's late and you're tired, Ronnie. This is your two-o'clock-in-the-morning mind. Wait until you've slept to make decisions about anything.

That, she figured, was the first commonsense thing she'd done in days.

The battle to free her mind of the lurking images of Scott's charred body on the gurney, the broken bones and the gaping holes in his wrists and feet, the lingering odor of his burned house, and the grief in her mother's eyes proved impossible to win.

He opens his eyes to the night. The sound is a hollow, hoo, hoo, hoooo. He knows this sound, having heard it many times on PBS: owl. A square of white light is cast on the bedroom floor by the round face of the full moon. Beside him, his mother's breath purls in her throat. She breathes deeply, chest rising and falling, comforting him.

The owl hoots again, closer this time.

He moves carefully, inching away from Mother's

side, and swings his legs over the edge of the bed, only slightly worried about the shadow people who might live under there. The moonlight reflecting through the room should keep them at bay.

On bare feet he pads to the window and looks out at the night. Moonlight bathes the pointed tops of the trees, washing out the green color and casting stark shadows so that it might be a giant prickly blanket that covers the land. Beyond the trees he can just see the lake, the water sparkling with a thousand moonbeam eyes.

The owl hoots again, closer this time, but try as he might, he can't catch a glimpse of the night bird.

What would it be like to fly on silent wings through the darkness? He can see it in his mind's eye, the spear-topped trees passing below as his wings cleave the cool air. He knows that Owl sees as well in the dark as Abel does in the day. What could he see down there in the shadowed depths of the forest that isn't there in daylight? Shadows have always frightened and fascinated him. The forest, he has discovered, is a place of shadows, of great wonders and terrors.

Far across the lake he can see twinkling yellow lights from distant houses, and higher along the waist of the mountain, headlights on the cars driving across the interstate. He knows that highway. It would take him home, back to his familiar bed and his long-lost pillow.

He wonders if moonlight is shining into his little room in the apartment. If his toys, his pillow, and his magical blanket miss him as much as he misses them. Reflexively, he glances across at Chaser, lying on his side on the bed. At least he and Chaser are together.

The owl hoots again, more distant now. For a long time he stands, watching the moonlight.

His ears pick up a sound and immediately place it: Veronica has shifted on the couch downstairs. Even with another bedroom down the hall, she sleeps in the front room under the pretty blanket with its picture of a man wearing a coyote cape. She has told him this is Trickster, an Indian legend. The coyote eyes on the blanket fascinate him. Perhaps she sleeps there because the Trickster blanket is magical, like his blanket at home.

He hears her stand up and can't help but walk quietly to the door. He slowly rotates the knob, eases the door wide enough to squeeze through, and tiptoes to the top of the stairs. He can see Veronica standing quietly at the counter that separates the kitchen from the front room. Her head is tilted, as if listening. She looks up at him, but doesn't see him where he stands in the shadows.

For the first time, he realizes that shadows have another dimension. While they can hide things from him, so, too, can he use them to hide from other things. For the moment, the revelation is so stunning that he hardly notices when Veronica eases into the kitchen.

Step by step, Abel creeps down the stairs, his senses sharpening. An unfamiliar excitement builds as he slips from shadow to shadow, cataloging sounds. He can hear Bryce's snoring from behind one of the upstairs bedroom doors. The humming of the refrigerator might be the droning of bees. A semi truck travels past on the highway beyond the complex, and he hears the floor creak ever so faintly under Veronica's feet.

Mother doesn't see as well as he does in the darkness. He has known this for some time. Does Veronica see as well?

He watches, and sees her bump one of the kitchen chairs. The sound might be thunder, but no one hears it. Veronica says a bad word under her breath and takes another step. She opens a drawer and removes a screwdriver.

Abel ghosts into the darkness under the counter and huddles there, intrigued as Veronica stops at the counter to the left of the white stove. She bends down and uses the screwdriver to loosen a board underneath the cabinet. The screws make a squeaky sound as Veronica undoes them.

Veronica grasps the board and pulls it away from the cabinet bottom, muting the scraping sound with her other hand. She looks around—right at Abel—but she doesn't see him in the shadow.

He smiles. This is really fun! His heart is beating faster, and he fights the urge to giggle. That would give him away, and although Veronica was nice when she explained the Coyote Trickster to him, he still doesn't really trust her. She might get mad if she discovers him spying on her.

She takes a deep breath and lies flat on the floor, sticking her arm into the hole up to her shoulder. For a moment, Abel can't believe it. What is she doing?

With her bottom raised up, he can hear her labored breathing, and the sound of fingers feeling along rough wood.

"God, Scott," she whispers, "where is it?" She continues to fish under the cabinet with her arm. "Where I hid my stash, right? That's here."

In the end she makes a pained sigh and withdraws her arm. As quietly as possible, she bats the dust off of her sleeve and stares down at the black hole. Even in the dark, Abel can see the frown on her confused face.

As she carefully replaces the board on the cabinet, Abel retreats quietly to the shadow of the big reclining chair. For a long moment, she stares around the room, her face lined with thought.

Abel waits, watching as she flips her long black hair over her shoulder. "Damn it," she says softly, "if it's not under the cabinet, where would he have put it?" For a long time she stands; sometimes she shakes her head as she looks around the room.

Abel hides in the shadow as she walks back to the couch. The leather complains as she sinks onto it and wraps the blanket around herself. Abel hesitates, and hears a different sound. He stands up slowly, an anxious feeling in his breast. The muffled noises are Veronica crying under the cover of the blanket.

Abel can't decide if he should go to her, pat her, like Mother pats him, or leave her be. In the end, he retreats up the stairs to the landing. Indecision fills him, and he wonders if he should go and get Chaser. He could let her hug Chaser, and the buffalo would make her feel better.

Unable to find the resolve, he slips to the doorway and hurries to the bed. Mother still sleeps soundly. He takes Chaser, hugs him close, and whispers, "Wewonica. She's sad. Just wike me and you."

The clink of steel against glass shredded the last of the nightmares; the smell of coffee carried Veronica into the new day. She blinked an eye open to glance around the familiar furnishings of the Frisco condo. For the briefest of moments, she wondered if she was going to feel the piercing blast of a hangover when she sat up. Then she smiled wanly. Conditioned response. She wasn't used to waking up sober in this room.

She stretched, and the night's events came back to haunt her: the grief, the futile search for whatever Scott had left for her, and the empty fear afterward that Scott had been killed before he could reach the condo.

Better to have been hungover and wondering what the hell she'd done the night before than to have suffered through that sense of loss, frustration, and dashed hope. They had just led to nightmares that had left her shaken and in a cold sweat.

She raised her head and saw Rebecca Armely standing at the counter where she poured a cup from the coffeemaker. The odd little boy stood beside her, staring out through the sliding door to the back deck and the lake beyond. From the angle of the sun, it had to be close to eight o'clock.

Veronica took a deep breath, and Abel's head spun, cued by the faint sound as she sat up. His large blue eyes fixed on her. What an odd little boy. He pulled at his mother's pants and pointed. Rebecca cast a wary gaze at Veronica and asked, "Coffee?"

"Yeah, please." She yawned, a foul taste in her mouth.

"I overslept." Her bladder was full, and the soft couch had cramped her back.

Rebecca walked over with a cup of steaming black coffee. Abel remained where he was, watching as though she might be some terrible monster. Hell, for all she knew, she was. Children were beyond her comprehension, and while other teenage girls had been earning money baby-sitting, she had been drinking beer and seeing how much hell she could raise without getting caught.

Veronica took the cup and said, "Thanks."

Rebecca watched her for a moment, her thin face reserved, a thousand questions seething behind her light blue eyes. She was an attractive woman with a medium build, well-shaped bust, and broad hips. She wore her blond hair in a ponytail that hung halfway down her back. Mascara appeared to be the woman's only vanity.

Rebecca hesitated. "I'm still having trouble accepting that Scott's really dead."

"Me, too." Veronica paused. "But I've seen the body." She struggled to keep the lance of grief from slicing through her control.

"Who did it?"

"They don't know." Veronica sipped at the hot coffee in an attempt to avoid the descent into tears. "You said that Scott told you to come here?" At Rebecca's nod, she asked, "Why? Rebecca, please, no one seems to know what this is all about. Amanda, Avi, and Scott are dead. Something terrible is going on, and no one seems to be able to tell me what."

Rebecca's eyes flickered. "I don't really know."

Bitterly, Veronica said, "Yeah, thanks, I can tell."

"Look, I don't know you. Amanda told me stories

about Scott's wild sister. That's you, right? Why the hell should I tell you anything?"

"My brother and his girlfriend were tortured and then set on fire to burn to death," Veronica snapped. "The best guess as to why is because he was working on something. You were Amanda's friend. You adopted their child. If you're part of whatever they were doing, you're going to be next. Now, doesn't that sound like one hell of a good reason for cooperating?"

Rebecca considered, expression guarded. "Maybe. Or maybe I should load Abel into the car and just disappear."

"Were Scott and Amanda breaking the law? Was it something illegal? Drugs? Blackmail?"

Rebecca's lips thinned. "No. I'll put your mind to rest about that much, at least. I never knew Scott to do anything patently illegal. He might have skirted around the edges of ethics on occasion when it came to research, but I don't even think he cheated on his taxes. He wasn't that kind of a man."

Veronica stared at the woman over her coffee. "What kind of a man was he?"

"A crusader." Rebecca lifted a challenging eyebrow. "He and Mandy remade the world."

"She hated to be called Mandy."

Rebecca considered her for a moment, then admitted, "I know, but not everyone else did."

"Testing me?" Veronica glanced across the couch back. Abel continued to stare at her with unbroken focus. She lowered her voice. "Does he know that Scott and Amanda . . ."

Rebecca crossed her arms, look turning hostile. "We don't discuss them. Never have. He doesn't know.

Amanda's decision, not mine. It so happens that I agree with it. Please, don't bring it up. Abel has enough to worry about as it is."

Veronica nodded. "All right." She hesitated, glancing back at the silent boy with his big head and oddly jutting face, the nose so prominent. *Midfacial prognathism.* The technical term came tumbling out of her memory. "I never even saw him before the adoption."

Rebecca settled into the stuffed chair across from Veronica. "Did that bother you?"

"I was head-deep in graduate studies. No. But now, looking back, it's odd that he didn't send pictures. Mother was really upset."

Rebecca laced her fingers together over a knee. "Trust me. Scott and Amanda knew what they were doing."

"That's a bit cavalier, don't you think? It's my family."

"We're all related, Mrs. Tremain. Even if we have to go back two hundred thousand years to the last split in the family tree."

"Call me Veronica. I'm having trouble with your smug attitude. I don't like it when people are condescending about knowing more than I do."

Rebecca's brow lined. "Let me ask you something: How did you feel about the Swiss banks repaying money to the Holocaust victims a couple of years back?"

"I thought it was a little late in coming, why?"

"And Native American land claims? Should the Sioux be given the Black Hills?"

"I don't know enough about that, but if they really have a legal leg to stand on, maybe so."

"How far back in time should we go, Mrs. Tremain? Excuse me, Veronica?"

"I suppose that justice is justice. Why should the passage of time—"

"A thousand years?"

"Sure, if you can document—"

"Five thousand years?"

"That's getting a little far-fetched."

"So, we can ethically right wrongs back to five thousand years ago? Justice is finite?"

"You lost me."

"It's not a complicated question. How far back would you go to right an old wrong?"

Veronica sensed the trap, but couldn't fathom the nature of it. "I'm sure as hell not going to apologize to the chimpanzees because my ancestors lived on the eastern side of the Great Rift Valley, if that's what you're after."

The faintest twitch of a smile crossed her lips. "Even the most radical of us don't take matters to that extreme."

"So, that's what this is all about? Righting old wrongs?"

"By golly, Veronica, I think you've got it!" Rebecca stood and walked purposefully to the kitchen, where little Abel's serious gaze had fixed on the floor. Veronica's heart skipped. He was looking at the dust pattern there—dust left from where she'd groped so desperately in that narrow hollow.

"So, what's for breakfast, sweetie? Eggs and bacon?" Rebecca was smiling down at the boy.

"Yesss," Abel slurred. He clasped his hands and nodded, and obediently opened the refrigerator and began handing out the egg carton and a package of bacon.

"Make yourself at home," Veronica murmured under her breath as she stood. The little boy turned his head, as if he'd heard from clear across the room. She felt his stare as she ambled to the bathroom.

Squatting on the pot, she unrolled the TP and tried to make sense of Rebecca's argument. How long did the statute of limitations run for righting old wrongs? The allusion to Nazi gold being returned to Holocaust victims had been just that, hadn't it? An allusion?

How many times had Scott and Amanda traveled to Tel Aviv to visit with Avi Raad? Six or seven that she knew of for sure. Nazi gold? She made a face. That just didn't feel right. Scott would have said something, dropped a clue. Nothing in his conversations with her even hinted at political involvement in anything. He even avoided the catfights at the American Association of Physical Anthropology meetings. To her knowledge, he'd never so much as attended a business meeting. The best way to make him faint was to suggest that he chair the CSU anthropology department.

She stood, zipped her pants, flushed, and fumbled the medicine cabinet open. In the back she found her old toothbrush and paste. Then she washed her face and studied her reflection in the glass. Her eyes were so red-lined they looked like Ohio road maps. Retrieving a brush she worked on her knotted hair until it gleamed. Satisfied, she checked herself and stepped out for the next round with Rebecca.

The smell of eggs and bacon greeted her. "Can I do anything?"

"I think we're covered here." At the stove, Rebecca glanced over her shoulder.

Abel had busied himself with meticulously setting silverware on the bleached-wood kitchen table. He had to climb up on each chair in the process, but one by one he laid out the spoons, and then the forks, and finally the knives.

Despite his concentration, Veronica could sense his awareness of her: some sort of child's radar that kept him apprised of her every movement.

She finally bent down, saying, "Hello, Abel. How are you doing this morning?"

He stopped short, the last knife clutched in his chubby hand. Reserved, he studied her thoughtfully for a moment before saying, "I'm fine." He frowned, using one hand to pinch his lip, and articulated, "Vewonica."

"That's really good. Not many people can get my name right so quickly."

He gave her the briefest hint of a smile. "Thank you."

"Where do you live?" Veronica continued.

"Salt Lake," Rebecca answered. "After Scott's call, it took us a while to get here."

From the corner of her eye, Veronica watched Abel place the last knife and clamber agilely down from the chair. He seemed pretty stocky for a four-year-old, and agile on his feet. "How long have you been here?"

"A couple of days. We were getting a little cabin-fevered, so we went out and found a movie last night." Rebecca gave her a measuring glance. "Sorry to startle you, but we were expecting Scott and Amanda." After a pause, she tipped her head toward the stairs. "Have you known Dr. Johnson for long?"

"Years." She reached for her coffee cup. "Ironically, I first met him here. He was my brother's guest on a skiing trip."

"Scott and Amanda were fond of him. He and I, we

went out a few times. I think I was too serious for him. I know they valued his analysis of their data." She used a spatula to flip the eggs.

"Bryce says he doesn't know what this is all about either. Doesn't that sound strange, that he could be part of the team and not know what was about to happen?"

Rebecca shot her another of those maddening glances. "Mrs. Tre . . . Veronica, sometimes the fewer people who know about something, the better."

"Yeah? Well, in case you haven't heard, Mrs. Armely, Avi, Scott, Amanda, and some woman in Virginia are dead. Murdered over my brother's little project."

Rebecca turned, suddenly off guard, face pale. She swallowed hard. "What woman?"

Veronica crossed her arms, the coffee held in her right hand. "Someone involved with the D.C. branch of Billy Barnes Brown's church. Apparently she called the FBI to provide information about some people the church was interested in. They killed her for it." At the rising tension in the woman's face, Veronica paused. "Rebecca, I want to know what's going on, or I'll pick up the phone and call the FBI right now. I think they'd have some serious questions for you."

Rebecca might have been stone, the spatula clutched in her fist. Finally, Abel, looking worried, said, "Muvver?"

"It's all right, sweetie." But her eyes didn't leave Veronica's. She turned back to the eggs, her expression masking her thoughts. Without looking back, she said, "Billy Barnes Brown, you say? He's placed evolution right up at the top as Enemy Number One. God knows, I've dealt with his Christian Creationist Crusade before."

"So, Scott had a history with these people?"

"What? No, not that I know of." Rebecca scowled, as if trying to decide how much to say. "I first learned about them through my sister. She was abused as a child and was looking for something to fix her life. She's been involved with them for years . . . and I really crossed swords with them this last fall. They wanted to ban evolution from the classroom. I worked on a petition drive, went to school board meetings, that sort of thing." She seemed to come to a decision, turning to face Veronica. "I know I've sounded hard, but this thing with Amanda and Scott, it's almost beyond belief. We knew people would be upset, but murder?" She looked dazed.

"Upset about what?"

The pause lengthened. Veronica had opened her mouth to speak when Rebecca blurted, "Anthropological genetics. It's the Rosetta stone for human evolution, you know."

"What?"

"The code." Rebecca watched her intently. "That's what Scott and Amanda unlocked. That's why someone might have killed them. I mean, it's hard enough on the Creationists that we keep finding these fossils. They can't call them freaks of nature anymore. Biotech firms are building organisms from raw DNA. They can't say that God snapped his fingers and made animals out of clay. Or that selection doesn't work on gene pools."

"I thought that was obvious. What was Scott's angle?"

Rebecca scraped the eggs into a bowl. "What's the hottest question in biological anthropology today?"

"Modern human origins. I just finished my dissertation on the subject. One school of thought says that modern humans evolved in southern Africa about two hundred thousand years ago. They were us. Same light bone structure, same cranial shape and axial skeleton. These early moderns traveled, created works of art, exploited different environments, and supposedly displaced the Neandertals in Europe and the Archaics in Asia. The second school of thought is that human evolution happened multiregionally, that even though groups of humans were spread from Western Europe to Australia, they interbred enough that gene flow kept the populations from speciating. That modern humans evolved gradually across the entire world to end up as us."

"Scott and Amanda solved that." Rebecca placed bacon on a plate, then laid it on the table.

Veronica, having not eaten in twenty hours, felt her mouth watering. Apparently, so did Abel, who had turned his attention to the sizzling bacon.

"He forgot to tell me that, and it's my specialty. Do you want to enlighten me?" Veronica asked as Rebecca tore paper towels from the roll to use for napkins.

"Do you want to wake Johnson up?"

"Let him sleep. After the drive he's had, and the ragged-out way he looked last night, he probably deserves it. Now, what about modern origins?"

"Replacement is a dead issue," Rebecca said simply. "That's going to piss a lot of people off. Not just the 'Out of Africa' people within anthropology, but out in the real world, too. The implications are a little unflattering."

Veronica smiled as she seated herself at the table. "Everything about anthropology is unflattering. Back in the 1800s, people didn't like to think they were closely related to apes. In the early twentieth century we wanted to believe that our wonderful brains evolved first. Then they debunked Piltdown man in the fifties and proved that we started out as small-brained apes. To lessen the egotistical blow, we decided these Australopithecine creatures were mighty hunters."

Abel had levered himself into a chair and was listening intently as he picked up his fork. Rebecca spooned eggs onto his plate. He kept glancing at Veronica.

"Man the hunter," Rebecca said.

"Turns out it was man the scavenger. We were beating the vultures off to process lion and hyena kills when we weren't dinner ourselves. That was an even worse blow to our inflated egos. Now we have possible evidence of cannibalism going back to six hundred thousand years ago with the Bodo skull from Ethiopia. How much more unflattering can you get?"

"We've still got a ways to fall," Rebecca said uneasily. "I think that's what someone feared. The final bit of information that was going to knock us forever off the pedestal was locked up in Scott and Amanda's research. Check their notes, Veronica."

"I can't. Everything in their houses was burned. Their notebooks and files were taken from the offices. There's no paper trail left."

Rebecca's resolve wavered. "All of the notes?"

Veronica nodded, fighting the temptation to glance at the cabinet bottom. Was that what Scott had tried to leave there?

"Mmmm. Good," Abel said as he chewed. "Hungwee, Muvver."

Rebecca smiled, her expression positively maternal.

"So, what's the big deal? What did they discover, Rebecca?"

With aplomb, she said, "I don't know."

Veronica met her steely gaze with one of her own, saying firmly, "I think you do."

Rebecca leaned forward on her elbows. "I don't much care what you think. I've told you all I'm going to for the time being. If you decide to call the FBI, I will tell them exactly what I told you. After that, they will have to let me go, and I swear, you will never see me or Abel again."

Veronica narrowed an eye. "What's your objective in all this?"

Without batting an eye, she said, "The uncompromised safety of my son's life."

"And you think you're at risk?"

Without the slightest hesitation, Rebecca said, "They'd kill us in an instant."

CHAPTER THIRTEEN

SICKNESS OVERLOADED JOE HANSON'S SENSES. HE HAD never felt this way, not even after the benders he'd taken with a bottle of cheap rum. Waves of nausea rolled through him; his body seemed to burn and prickle, the fire starting in his bones and radiating through his tense muscles. Thoughts drifted aimlessly around his head, things he could barely grasp before they slipped away into the hazy soup.

"He's coming around." The voice sounded disarticulated and far off.

When Joe tried to swallow, a terrible taste filled his mouth, and his tongue stuck in the back of his throat. The tickling sensation of impending vomit lurked just behind his uvula, making breathing difficult. *God, either puke or swallow! Get it over with!* But the feathery urge just hung there, stuck like an oversized pill.

"Joe?" a deep voice cast him loose from his thoughts. "Joe, can you hear me?"

Hanson fought a bitter battle to open his eyes and instantly regretted it; his vision was swimming and liquid. He blinked them closed again, content to suffer the misery in darkness.

"Joe, I know you can hear me."

"A little water," another voice, younger, with a deep Southern accent, said.

Joe recoiled when the tube touched his lips and cool water was squirted onto his tongue. Impulsively, he swallowed, and his body bucked as his stomach heaved. A bitter blast of bile filled his mouth; he choked, coughing and gasping for breath. The stuff burned his windpipe, throwing him into a more violent fit of coughing. Desperately, he sucked in air, blinking through tear-glazed eyes.

Despite his distress, he glimpsed a cement wall several feet in front of him. He lay on a concrete floor. A single yellow light threw shadows on the featureless surroundings. He tried to focus on the man who crouched to one side. The bare bulb in the ceiling cast a golden halo around his blond hair and left his face in shadow.

"That's better," the blond Southerner said. "He's almost with us."

"Joe?" The deep voice came from behind him. "We're going to give you water again. Concentrate now . . . and try to swallow it. It will make you feel a little better."

The blond man leaned forward, a plastic sport bottle in his hand. Joe felt the tube on his lips, and this time sucked greedily. A coolness washed down his throat, easing the dangling gag reflex behind his tongue.

Afterward, he gasped for air, trying to keep his vision focused on the undulating concrete floor where he lay. The cement felt so cool, oddly insubstantial, as though he might sink through it.

"Joe, try to talk." The deep voice sounded soothing. "We can't help you unless you talk to us."

"Whaaa . . ." His mouth didn't function.

"That's all right, Joe. Try again. It just takes a little time."

"Whaaat haaa . . ."

"What happened?"

"Yeahhhh."

"You had a little accident, Joe. We're here to help you. We know how sick you're feeling, and we can make it better. First, though, we need to know some things. Can you help us, Joe? Concentrate." A pause. "Concentrate hard."

Hanson clung to the words, fighting for clarity. "Yeah." It came with such effort.

"You're the case officer on the Elizabeth Carter murder."

"Yeah." If he could just keep the world from spinning. He knew that voice. Had heard it before. Familiar . . . but . . .

"We need to know. Who did it?"

"Don't . . . know. Think . . ." He struggled to find the answer, lost in the haze that clogged his brain. "Church."

"What church?"

"Billy Barnes Brown's."

"Are you positive?"

"Seems like." He swallowed hard, wishing his mouth didn't feel like poorly molded putty.

"Do you have any proof?" The deep voice seemed tender, concerned.

"No."

"It's just a hunch, then?"

"Yeah." He blinked. "Woman . . . told me."

"Elizabeth Carter."

"Yeah."

"What does your supervisor think?"

"Don't . . . know. Ramsey . . ." What was it about Ramsey? "No proof."

"Do you have any leads, Joe? Anything you could take to a judge?"

It took a moment to wrap his wobbling mind around that. "No."

"Based on what we have, would a judge swear out a warrant? Subpoena records?"

"No."

"A wiretap?"

"Tried." Grasping, he tried to make sense of why that worried him. "Got nothing."

"Do you have any solid evidence that would indicate the church is behind these murders?"

"We got . . . jack. Nothing."

"Joe, think hard. Why would Billy Barnes Brown kill Scott Ferris?" The deep voice echoed concern.

Why would he? This was a familiar question. "Don't know." He swallowed hard. "Genetics . . . evolution . . ."

"You think he'd kill over evolution?"

Hanson moaned, fighting the fog in his head. "Doesn't make sense."

"Why not?"

"Nothing to gain. Everything to lose." That seemed right. But something bothered him. If he could just catch it as it floated past. The thoughts in his head were like fish, darting, slippery. His flesh seemed to be melting.

"Does Ramsey think the church killed these people, Joe?"

He tried to form an answer. How did anyone second-guess Ramsey? "Don't know . . . what he thinks." For a moment, he wondered if his body had floated off the floor.

"Have you talked to Bryce Johnson?"

"No." He tried to move his arms, surprised that he couldn't feel them. "Missing." Something nagged at him. What? "Phone call." What about a phone call? "Something . . ." It lay just over the horizon, as if he could just reach out and . . .

"Joe, pay attention. This is important. Who do you think is working for the church? Think now."

Whatever he was about to discover vanished. "What?"

"A name, Joe. Who is Billy Brown's agent?"

"Agent?"

"The hit man?"

"Don't know." He tried to shake his head, but the muscles in his neck remained limp. "Team. Professionals."

"Does Ramsey believe this?"

"I . . . told him . . ."

The young blond man shifted, his hair still glowing in the silhouette from the overhead light. When he moved, golden streamers followed his head as if his movement smeared the light.

"Did Ramsey believe you?"

"Can't . . . say . . ."

"Think, Joe," the voice cooed sympathetically. "Given what the Bureau knows, do you think they can solve this?"

He fought the urge to speak, but his tongue rambled on with a mind of its own. "Not with what we have now."

The voice turned very deliberate. "Joe, what do you know about the children?"

He worked his lips, mind stumbling over the words. "Children?" Something floated out of the haze. "With Betsy and Brad. Fourth of July . . . picnic . . ."

"Thanks, Joe. You've been a great help. We want you to sleep now. You need to oxidize the chemicals in your body. When you're clean, we'll go for a little drive and leave you where Ramsey can find you."

The blond man straightened, and the bare lightbulb overhead seared white heat through Joe's brain. He clamped his eyes shut and groaned.

He could hear their feet grating on the cement as the two men walked away. A door clicked as it opened. The lights went out, leaving him in blissful darkness. Then the door clanged shut and he could hear a hasp being secured by a padlock.

In the silence, his body floated, then whirled about, as if being sucked down by a whirlpool.

The block-pattern all-terrain tires hummed on the pavement as the big Chevy Suburban merged with the traffic on the Dulles Access. To either side, trees shaded the cut grass and provided relief for the midmorning sun. The green contrasted with the white road and the endless procession of shining vehicles speeding westward toward Dulles International.

Ted "Leopard" Paxton squirmed uneasily as fingers of unease caressed the back of his neck. He'd been in deep before, but never this deep. What worried him the most was that everything was snowballing. And with Joe Hanson on ice, it all boiled down to him—his skill and knowledge—against the Bureau. His advantage lay in the fact that they didn't know who he was—that the huge bureaucracy was a fumbling, stumbling beast, and it seemed headed in the wrong direction. So long as he and Elias didn't make another mistake they could still do this. But now, after the Liz Carter thing, he wasn't so sure. He'd worked with psychopaths before; in fact, he'd sometimes wondered if he wasn't one himself. But nothing like Ron Elias. He cast an uneasy glance at the man in the passenger seat.

The dark sunglasses hid his pale blue eyes. Through the open window, wind whipped his short blond hair. He wore a black T-shirt that emphasized his muscular chest and powerful arms. Faded jeans hugged a narrow waist and athletic thighs. Smudged white sport shoes covered his feet. He appeared completely relaxed as he sat in the padded bucket seat and watched the world pass.

To still his worry, Paxton asked, "What do you think?"

The blond shrugged, his eyes on the greenery. "We're okay. For the moment."

"Yes. For the moment." Paxton kept an eye on the mirror, noting the relative positions of the traffic. Not that it mattered; if the Bureau was tailing them, they'd never spot them. The Bureau used as many as ten different cars, none remaining in contact with the suspect long enough to become conspicuous.

"If we're going to keep this from falling apart, we've got to slow down. The Carter woman was worrisome enough. Taking down Hanson is pushing it." Paxton turned his head. "You know that, don't you? If he isn't handled just right, it's going to be a red flag for Ramsey."

The blond man grunted. "As badly as Lizzie Carter might have damaged us, it's worth the risk to know that we contained it. Ramsey hasn't got squat. Before he can take this further, he needs to have something substantive. If we cover our tracks well enough, he hasn't got a thing to take to a judge or a grand jury."

"Why the *hell* did you nail her to the floor? Damn it, you gave them a pattern!" Paxton thumped the steering wheel with his fist.

Elias' mouth tightened into a thin line. "You just don't get it, do you? We're at war. She died that way because she's an agent of Satan."

"Wake the fuck up! It's the twenty-first century. This isn't the Inquisition."

"Don't use profanity." A pause. "Besides, you're getting paid." The blond man smiled sadly. "I'm sorry for you, Brother. You don't know. You never lost your soul before. They locked me away and siphoned off my soul. Do you know what that's like? All those scientists in their white coats. The drugs, every day, until I didn't know who I was . . . what I was. They took my soul away from me, Paxton." His voice broke. "You don't know what it was like, locked in that room, and every day, they fed me more of that shit, and I watched my soul . . . slip . . ." He shivered, his muscles knotting. In a whisper, he said, "God came to me. He saved me."

Paxton recognized that brittle look, the glazing of the eyes, and changed the subject. "We've been lucky, you know. Eventually a random event is going to fuck us."

"Satan is never random." The blond man lowered his head, staring at the road from under pale brows.

Paxton gave him another sidelong glance and made a distasteful face. "Let's just do the job, huh? I've already got a hell of a lot more than I bargained for."

The blond man turned unfocused eyes on him. "You didn't believe it at first. You were just here for the money. Tell me, did you believe it at first?"

"Nope. I believed the five hundred thousand in the bank." He exhaled wearily. "Elias, why did you come to me anyway?"

"Because you were one of them. You knew how they'd think, and no one else has your skills." The blond man smiled, the expression almost foolish. "But God will get you in the end."

"Yeah, right." Paxton returned his attention to the road. "Just so His checks keep clearing."

The blond man reached into the rear and snagged a nylon-clad case. Unzipping it, he withdrew a square aluminum box, its hasps locked with a combination padlock. He rotated the tumblers, opened the lid, and exposed a scoped Thompson Center Contender pistol where it lay in a cutout in the foam. The end of the barrel had been threaded for the fourteen-inch beer-can diameter suppressor that lay in its recess. The top of an ammunition box, labeled "300 Whisper," could be seen where it nestled in the foam.

Paxton asked, "Have you ever used that in a tactical situation before?"

"In Afghanistan, after the war. It's a jewel. Silent as a whisper, no supersonic crack . . . and deadly accurate out to two hundred yards. Unless you're within ten feet, and paying attention, you have no idea that anyone shot anything. One minute they're standing there, the next, they're with the Lord."

The blond grinned again before snapping the case shut, locking it, and reinserting it into the black nylon case.

"I hope this is worth the expense of a charter flight," Paxton growled under his breath.

Elias patted the nylon shrouded pistol case. "Since nine eleven do you know a better way to get a pistol cross country? You said it before. They'll be checking the airlines, screening the checked baggage—and you can bet I'm not declaring that pistol. Charters are safer, faster. You heard Hanson, they can't even guess at the resources we have available to us."

"Praise the Lord," Paxton said ironically. "Did you call our people in Colorado?"

The blond nodded. "The van will be waiting at the airport, gassed and ready to go. They'll leave a map in the front seat."

"So, what do you know about Frisco?"

"Ski town in winter, resort in summer. Bryce Johnson picked a nice place to die."

For the moment Abel can forget the constant worry. He enjoys this place. The sun is warm, and Mother has him covered with a light cotton shirt and a hat to shield his delicate skin. He continues exploring, casting cautious glances at Mother as he wanders along the lakeshore.

Mother is sitting on an old weathered gray log, her face lined and thoughtful. She told the people at the condominium that she needed to go for a walk, to think. And Abel is glad that she did. He doesn't know what to think of Veronica. She frightens him with her intense and speculative look. She keeps looking at the place where she took the boards apart the night before. Something about that place worries her. Bryce seems nice, but preoccupied and anxious.

For the moment, Abel closes his eyes and inhales the soothing aroma of trees and water. The pine needles crunch under his feet. He hears the shriek of the birds that Mother told him were stellar jays. He has trouble pronouncing the name. The jays have tall dark blue crests that flop when they jerk their heads.

Using a fingernail, he picks a flake of bark from the

trunk of a pine tree and sniffs it; the odor of pine refreshes before he places it in his mouth and chews. The bark softens on his tongue, spongy against his teeth.

He stares up as a squirrel leaps from branch to branch before stopping, staring down at him with its tail curled over its back. It lets out a long churrrrring sound that makes Abel laugh. He reaches up, grabs the lowest branch, and lifts himself effortlessly into the tree. Branch by branch he levers himself up. The squirrel churrs and yips at him and finally makes a long leap into the next tree, where it continues to scold him.

Plucking a cone from the swaying limb, Abel pegs it at the squirrel, and is satisfied to see the little creature beat a hasty retreat.

The wind whispers through the branches; the sound might be the tree singing. Abel feels the tree sway with the wind and giggles. Here, for the first time since the day at the river, he feels somehow safe and relaxed. Wouldn't it be nice to stay here, to live in the tree with the squirrels and jays? He glances down, the branches partially obscuring his view of Mother where she sits hunched on the log, her attention fixed on the lake and the white-capped mountains beyond.

If she sees him up here, it will worry her. She doesn't like him to climb things. Dropping hand by hand, he descends the tree, stopping to hang by one hand from the lowest branch. If she turns and sees him, it won't frighten her when he is this close to the ground.

Hanging feels great. He pulls himself up, chinning on the branch, and finally lets go to drop to the ground. Then he notices that his hands are sticky. Wiping them on his pants doesn't seem to do much good. The sticky *sap leaves smudges on his pants. This is bad. Mother doesn't like him getting dirty, but not much of the real world is clean. Mother doesn't seem to understand that it's not his fault. Dirt just seems to creep onto him when he's not looking, like up in the tree.*

He tastes the sap with his tongue, finding the pungent tang pleasant. The faintest of movements in the tree catches his eye. He can see things like that. Things Mother misses. His sharp eyes find the squirrel, upside down, high on the trunk of the next tree. Abel fights the urge to go and chase it. He is happier when he is chasing things.

Mother hasn't moved. This bothers him. Usually, she is constantly keeping track of him, keeping him out of trouble.

He glances along the lakeshore where the waves are curling and splashing on the rocks. The drone of the motorboats is constant, and down a ways, fishermen are sitting with poles over the side as their white boat putts slowly along.

He eases up to Mother, seeing the frown lines in her forehead. "You all wite?"

"Hey, baby, yes, I'm fine." She still stares out at the water with empty eyes.

He pinches his lip and says, "Vewonica make you sad?" Now his chin is sticky, too.

She laughs, but not with humor. "She's a piece of work, isn't she? Scott always said she was tough as nails. But, no, she didn't make me sad, Abel. I just need time to think . . . to figure out what we should do next. Everything is different."

"Scawwy." He tries rubbing the sap on his pants again. It doesn't help.

"Scary, yeah." She plucks at the log with absent fingers. "I can't believe Amanda is dead. And Scott. We knew there would be trouble—but not like this. Not people . . . friends . . . being killed."

At this, he is silent. The fear rises inside again, evil and black, worse than the monsters that used to hide in his closet at night. "Bad men come heaw?"

Mother shrugs. "I don't think so. How would they find us? We didn't tell anyone where we were going."

Her scared look worries him, and he tries to distract her. "I got sticky stuff on me." He holds his hands out.

She doesn't seem to see. Instead she asks, "What do you think of Veronica? Do you trust her?"

He doesn't know how to answer this. "I want to go home."

Mother laughs, but the strained sound of it unnerves him. "Abel, I don't think we can ever go back to Salt Lake again. That's the problem, sweetie. I've got to make money to buy us food, pay the rent, and keep us healthy. We thought that with a degree in physical therapy no one would associate me with an anthropological background. If they know my name, they'll be able to trace me."

"Be a waitwess?"

She arched an eyebrow. "I suppose it beats being dead, huh?"

He bites his tongue, then cautiously adds, "I wuv you anyway."

For the first time her smile isn't forced, and she reaches out to ruffle his hair, her fingers immediately *catching and pulling.* "What's this? Pine sap? Have you been in the . . . Oh, Abel, look at you! You're a mess!"

"Sowwy. I didn't climb very high, I pwomise."

Her expression wavers, and he is unsure whether she is going to be mad, or upset, or hurt, and then she sighs in resignation. "Well, come on. Let's go back to the house and see what will clean this up. Then we'll figure out what we're going to do for money for the rest of our lives." She takes his sticky hand in hers and starts to lead him back up the slope toward the buildings. "One thing's for sure, kiddo, waiting tables is a damn sight better than lying on a slab."

For the moment, he wonders what a slab is, and then the shrieking of the jays distracts him. As he passes the tree, the squirrel churrs at him in a final parting shot.

CHAPTER FOURTEEN

"I'M SORRY," THE DISEMBODIED VOICE ON THE PHONE assured Veronica. *"Special Agent Hanson hasn't checked in yet. I've paged him and tried his personal cell number. As soon as he calls in, I'll give him your message."*

"Wait. What about his partner, uh, Mitch? Is he there?"

"I'm sorry, Dr. Tremain. He's also out of the office."

"But you know where he is?"

"Ma'am, I can't give you that information."

"If nothing else, call Mitch and make sure that Joe is all right. And please, tell Joe that Dr. Johnson has been trying to get in touch with him."

A long silence stretched. *"I'll take your message to Agent Hanson's supervisor. You'll be at the number you gave me?"*

"Yes."

"I promise you, Dr. Tremain, we will follow up on this. Thank you for your call. I'm sure everything will work out all right. Agent Hanson is one of our best."

"I know." Veronica hung up the phone and turned to where Bryce was wolfing down eggs. The morning light sparkled in his reddish-gold hair.

"So?" he asked as he chewed.

"So they're checking." She crossed her arms and narrowed an eye as she studied the kitchen. She'd taken the first opportunity to wipe up the dust with a damp paper towel. To her relief, no one seemed to have noticed that the board had been removed and replaced. In the meantime, she'd poked into every drawer and cabinet in the place on the chance that Scott hadn't really known where she kept her stash back in the bad old days. And found nothing.

"I don't like this, Ronnie." He washed down the last of the toast with a swig of orange juice. A fleeting look of futility crossed his face. "I've never felt this impotent before. It's like everything is out of my control."

She smiled. "I've been here before. I mean, not like

this, but waiting, unsure, knowing that at any minute there could be a knock at the door and police would be standing there with an arrest warrant. It corrodes your peace of mind."

"Do I want to hear about this? My nerves are already shot."

She seated herself and fingered her empty coffee cup. "Let's just say that I hung out with some very interesting people as a teenager. Outside of controlled substances, does grand theft auto, breaking and entering, or burglary ring any bells? Not only that, I was learning to be a pretty good pickpocket."

Bryce's eyebrows shot up, and his sudden interest amused her. "You're kidding? Scott said wild, but he never told me that."

"Gee, I guess you'll never leave me alone in your house from now on. You'd worry the entire time that Grandma's silver wouldn't be there when you got back."

"As I understand it, I don't have a house anymore."

"Right. Sorry."

"You never got caught?" He sipped the last of the orange juice. She liked the way his hazel eyes caught the sunlight streaming in from the deck, and how it made the hairs on his muscular forearms glisten.

"Twice. Both times Theo, uh, the family lawyer, managed to find technical problems with the arrest. Both were thrown out on technicalities. Had my father not been rich enough to hire the best lawyer in Denver, they would have sent me off for a nasty little vacation."

"Why'd you do it?"

"For all the usual reasons that spoiled rich girls do

things." She quirked her lips. "How about you, Johnson. Did you ever get into trouble?"

He lowered his eyes sheepishly. "Well, let's see. I got a couple of parking tickets in college. Um, I shot rabbits out of season for the stew pot . . . but never got pinched for it. My cousin and I drank beer under-age a couple of times at the hunting cottage when Dad and the rest were out hunting. My biggest sin was keeping my target pistol in Massachusetts for a week in violation of their damned gun law."

"My God, and you had the nerve to steal license plates?"

"The nerve?" he cried. "I was a shaking, blathering basket case the whole time! If anyone would have called out, 'Stop! Thief!' I would have fainted on the spot." He grinned. "I guess I'm not the brave 'spit-in-the-eye-of-danger' kind of guy."

She rolled her coffee cup back and forth. "No one is. Even the tough bastards I used to hang around with. When I first met him, I thought Louie didn't have a frightened nerve in his body. Louie had told himself that he was tough and smart for long enough that he'd started to believe it. Then one night he stiffed a guy on a meth deal. It's a long story, but we ended up hiding in a trash Dumpster in an alley off the Sixteenth Street Mall in downtown Denver. The guy stood there, not five feet from us, a pistol in his hand. We could hear him cursing under his breath, swearing what he'd do to Louie when he caught him. Shit, we didn't move for hours after the guy left, and you know, when we crawled out Louie was wet from the crotch down and still shaking."

"That would do it, I suppose." He studied her thoughtfully. "This was your boyfriend?"

"Not after that night. He said he'd beat my face in with a pipe wrench if I ever told anyone he'd peed all over himself."

"You just told me."

"That's all right. I'm safe as long as Louie stays in the pen. If they ever spring him, promise me you'll never blab."

His brow furrowed. "It'll be tough. Louie and I usually don't keep secrets from each other, but, well, in your case, I'll make a special effort."

"What a prince."

He chuckled. She couldn't help but notice the boyish quality, the sparkle in his eyes. She could really come to like this unassuming man.

You're under a lot of stress, Ronnie. Forget it. He's not your type.

The sound of feet made Veronica turn as the door opened and Rebecca led Abel into the room. Beyond the doorway, sunlight gleamed off of the pines and the amber tones of building B uphill across the parking lot. The lot was empty but for her BMW and Rebecca's Honda Accord.

"Come on." Rebecca led Abel over to the sink.

"Have a nice walk?" Veronica tried to keep the edge out of her voice.

"Yes." Rebecca remained coolly reserved. Her attention focused on Abel, she pulled one of the chairs over to the sink and lifted Abel onto it. As she turned on the water, she said, "Give me your hands."

Veronica stood and stepped around. "What did he get

into?" But seeing the dark stains, she knew. "Pine sap. Forget the soap-and-water routine." She turned to the utility closet and rummaged behind the mops and brooms to find a square tin of Coleman lantern fuel. She screwed the top off and sniffed, nose reacting to the familiar odor of white gas.

"Gasoline?" Rebecca's face mirrored horror.

"Trust me." Veronica wet the corner of a dishrag and looked inquiringly at Abel. "Hey, sport, you've got sap in your hair, on your shoulders, everywhere. You must have gone all the way to the top."

"I cwimb good," he said in his nasal slur. "Squwwel cwimbed higher."

"Yeah," Veronica agreed, ignoring the distrust in Rebecca's eyes. She bent down and used the corner of the cloth to sponge at the black stains on his hands. "I used to chase them myself. Little boys and little girls don't make much of a threat to a squirrel."

"You cwimb?" Abel asked, his disconcerting blue gaze on her.

"Not so much these days. But as a kid I did." She winked slyly. "Mostly because my mom didn't want me to. She thought it was dangerous."

Abel started to nod his head and stopped, shooting a wary glance at Rebecca.

Veronica bit off a smile.

Rebecca evidently decided that Abel wouldn't melt like the wicked witch of the west and retreated to the stairs.

Veronica lowered her voice. "She's a pretty good mother. She takes real good care of you."

"Yesss." Abel looked up at her. "Awe you mad at heww?"

"No, why would you say that?"

"You wowwy her."

Veronica glanced sidelong to where Bryce watched from the table. "Yeah, well, Abel, some terrible things are happening. I think we're all a little worried."

"Did that man caww back?" he asked seriously.

"What man?" She saw Bryce stiffen.

"The one wiff the effbweye."

"That's FBI." Veronica tensed. "You heard us talking about that?"

He nodded, looking as if he'd said something he shouldn't.

"It's okay," Veronica soothed. "No, he hasn't called back. If he does, we'll let you know. Deal?"

He nodded, returning his attention to where she scrubbed at his hands.

Something about the shape of his head—long for a child's—and the projecting nose cued an elusive part of her memory. As if she'd seen him before, or someone like him. What was it about Abel that looked so familiar? Surely not his stocky little rugby player's body. If the kid kept growing like this, he'd be one hell of a defensive lineman.

"Now, about your hair," she said, frowning at the task, "this might pull a little."

"I'm bwave."

"Yeah, I'll bet you are." The delicacy of his hair surprised her. For the first time, she got a close look at it, so pale, almost a platinum blond. Something from her studies reminded her of the Finns and their almost silvered hair.

"Curious," she murmured to herself.

"What?" Abel asked, trying to keep from squirming as she used the cloth to rub at the mat of sap.

"Nothing. Well, genetics." She glanced at Bryce, who continued to watch with amused eyes. "Boy, I think you've got a lot of recessive genes." Amanda and Scott had both been darkly complected.

"My jeans are bwue." He indicated his OshKosh denims.

"Yep. Silly of me." She laughed when he looked up at her with his large eyes. Her efforts had eliminated the worst of the sap. "Okay, Abel. Run along upstairs and have your mother throw you in the shower. A good shampooing will take the rest of that off."

"Thank you." He was so serious. Then he asked in a conspiratorial voice. "Can I jump down?"

"Sure."

He grinned happily and launched himself into the air. For the briefest instant, Veronica worried that he'd kill himself, but he slammed into the kitchen floor with both feet, whooped, and charged for the stairs.

"Quite a kid," Bryce noted as Veronica screwed the top onto the Coleman fuel.

Abel's little feet hammered up the staircase as he shouted "Muvvuh! Time fow a showwa."

Veronica replaced the Coleman fuel and dropped the soiled rag into the hamper after she'd washed it out. "He's not normal."

Bryce considered her. "Normal how? What's normal? He's a kid."

She chewed her lip for a moment. "Nothing in his phenotype is Scott or Amanda. Was that what they were doing spending so much time in Avi's clinic in Tel Aviv? Trying to cure a genetic disorder? Whose was it? Scott's or Amanda's?"

"No towheads in the Ferris clan?"

"Not to my knowledge, but you know how a recessive trait can be hidden for generations. Amanda's ancestry was Greek. I used to admire that gorgeous olive skin of hers."

"Why? You're a lot more beautiful than Amanda." As soon as he said it, he reddened.

"Thanks." She couldn't help but smile. "I always thought I looked like Morticia Addams. And it's hell getting a tan without burning myself into the color of a radish."

Bryce seemed to have recovered. "We always wish for what we haven't got." He stood, collecting the plates and carrying them to the sink. As he washed, he asked, "So, what's the game plan? Somehow, I don't like just waiting here for Agent Hanson."

"Where would you be safer? Only the FBI knows you're here, and for some reason, they don't seem particularly interested." She glanced at the stairs, hearing the shower on the second floor. "In the meantime, what we do is partly up to Rebecca. Bryce, she knows what this is all about. She's up to her neck in it, and we're not letting her out of sight until she comes clean."

After rinsing the plates, he opened the dishwasher and slipped them in with the others. "Soap's under the sink?" At her nod, he opened the cabinet and found the box. Pouring it into the little cup in the door, he added, "Ronnie, she's probably scared to death. Put yourself in her position. She's a single mother with a child, and someone is killing her colleagues. We went out a couple of times in college. She comes from a real screwed-up family."

"You dated her?"

"We went out for drinks a couple of times. Just enough to know that nothing was going to happen. Knowing something of her background, I can tell you, that little boy is her life. She'd do anything for that kid to ensure he didn't have to go through the shit she did."

"She said her sister was abused." Veronica raised an eyebrow. "That might explain why Rebecca has that sense of armor around her. Like she won't let anyone inside."

Bryce warily admitted, "It was her father. And I don't think it was just her sister . . . if you get my drift. People react differently to abuse. It turned Becky as hard as nails and made her fiercely protective. I can guarantee you, she'd die before she let anyone hurt a hair on that boy's head. Look at it from her perspective: She doesn't know who to trust. Sure as hell not you or me. Does she go to the police? And tell them what? That she and Scott and Amanda did something that people are killing to stop? What does that do to the boy? What if it's something bad enough that Social Services declares her unfit and takes the kid away?"

She stared vacantly through the glass door at the blue waters of the lake.

Bryce rolled the tray into the dishwasher and shut the door before he pushed the "on" button. "Seriously, what would you do in her position?"

"Turn into a panicked introvert like she seems to be."

"Right." Bryce pulled Abel's chair over and seated himself backward so he could lean his crossed arms on the chair back. The rusty hair on his forearms looked soft to the touch. "And consider this: Amanda and Scott were no one's fools. They wouldn't have allowed just anyone to adopt their child. They knew Rebecca Armely a whole lot better than I did. They trusted her with the boy. Now, whatever I might think about Scott's judgment when it comes to this misapplied research, he knew people."

"Then what was it about Rebecca?"

"You've already seen that she's as protective as a mother bear with her cub." His hazel eyes held hers. "Maybe they knew that the child would have developmental difficulties. Like you said, he's not quite normal. She's a physical therapist and probably specialized in developmental disorders. She's got to be pretty sharp or they wouldn't have signed on the dotted line."

"What if I told you I graduated at the top of my class?" Rebecca called from the top of the stairs.

"I'd believe it." Bryce craned his neck.

Rebecca slowly descended the stairs, her hair swaying with each step. She turned her pinched expression their way. "All right, I'll take a chance. Bryce, I know that you worked with Scott and Amanda. They had their reasons for not telling you what was going on. As to you, Mrs. Tremain, I don't know what your angle is here. I know that your husband is a physician, and Scott didn't think a whole lot of him."

"I didn't either. We're divorced." Veronica held up her left hand, indicating the naked ring finger.

Rebecca's hostility faded somewhat. "I stepped out for towels. I couldn't help but overhear part of your conversation. Yes, Amanda and Scott had their reasons for picking me, and no, I'm not a fool. I need help, and maybe you can provide it, but I'm telling you right off that I will not tell you everything. You'll have to trust me that I have my reasons and that they are not selfish or petty. Eventually, you will know everything, but the time isn't right for that yet."

"I was part of this?" Bryce asked. "My research was instrumental?"

"It was."

"Why didn't they tell me?"

"To be honest, Bryce, you didn't need to know." She raised a hand, cutting off his hot reply. "It wasn't to spite you, or cheat you. They didn't tell you because they were trying to protect you, keep from ruining your career if it went wrong."

"I think it's gone pretty wrong," Veronica snapped.

"Not the way we thought." Rebecca cocked a hip defiantly. "We were worried about academic censure, not . . . not this."

"Genetic construction," Bryce said wearily. "What they had me doing wasn't theoretical at all, was it? They were really manipulating and modifying human genetic material."

Rebecca responded with a curt nod. "Good for you. Maybe your Ph.D. didn't turn your brain to mush like it does to so many. But, as our Creationist friends would like to remind you, genetics is only a theory."

Veronica whispered, "So, what do you need from us?"

"Money, Mrs. Tremain. Some way to make a living."

"What's wrong with what you were doing?"

"Come on, wake up. If they killed Scott and Amanda,

do you seriously think they wouldn't kill me just as quickly? They'll be looking for a physical therapist. Do you think I could get a job without references? Proof of my education?"

"Wait a minute." Bryce straightened. "Your mother. Melissa. She's rich, isn't she? Don't I remember hearing that she'd married a billionaire or some such thing?"

Rebecca's expression soured. "Mom's dead. My sister inherited."

"So? Wouldn't your sister help you out?"

"Bryce, after Mom's death, Eunice fell apart. I tried to have her committed for her own protection. I didn't approve of the holier-than-thou wackos she was associating with. She moved south and married some wealthy bigoted prick from down in Alabama or somewhere. He keeled over from a heart attack six months later. Sure, she's stinking rich, but she's a psychological time bomb. I'd rather crawl through broken glass than ask her for a dented penny."

"And I thought I had family trouble," Veronica muttered.

"Why you, Rebecca?" Bryce asked uncertainly. "What's your part in this?"

Rebecca drew herself to full height. "Where do you think they got the genetic material, Dr. Johnson? I'm their donor."

For Jackson Ramsey, life in the Bureau meant paperwork. Along with evaluations, he and his people read or compiled inter- and intra-office memos, yellow copies and blue copies, reports, and reviews of reports. Then they put up with the predominantly asinine directives from the Hoover Building over on Pennsylvania Avenue, the generally asinine directives from Quantico, and the particularly asinine directives from the Department of Justice. Finally came the quarterly evaluation on Domestic Terrorism.

The idea, part of the post nine-eleven reevaluation, as originally pitched from the seventh floor of the Hoover Building, was that each field office would produce a quarterly synthesis of potential domestic threats that would in turn be kicked over to Headquarters, with a second copy sent to Quantico for the shrinks to study.

Theoretically the synthesis would serve as a heads-up allowing the director and assistant director to decide which resources to allocate to the special agents in charge, or SACs, at different field offices so that events like Oklahoma City, Waco, and the World Trade Center disasters might be preempted.

Jack Ramsey hated the quarterly report. He and his staff spent two weeks out of each three months doing nothing but compiling the first draft, having the secretaries type it all up, and submitting it. Three days later, it would come back covered with FLYNs—"fucking little yellow notes"—and red pencil marks, and four or five pages of suggested revisions of wording, phrases, and entire sections. Another week was spent rewriting the draft so that if a congressional committee requested the damn thing, all the chiefs in suits over at "the Bureau" would have their soft tails protected by the bureaucratic equivalent of grammatical body armor.

Ramsey was absently tapping his famous "Larry

King" pen on his desk. The clock had just flicked over to five-fifteen when Betty leaned in the door, that long-suffering look on her face. "Boss, do you need anything else before I brave the traffic and head for home?"

"No, thanks, Betty."

She lifted an eyebrow. "Two things, Jack. First, that reporter, Skip Manson, called again. I shifted him to the information officer who told him 'No comment.' He's not going away. And second, Matt's playing soccer tonight at six-thirty. Paula wanted me to remind you. They're playing the team they're tied with for first. It's an important game."

"Right." He shot another glance at the digital clock. "I can probably squeeze another half hour into this before I have to drop everything. If traffic is really bad, I can be a little late." He paused. "Uh, there's nothing happening, is there? Secret Service isn't blocking anything?"

"Not today." Betty gave him that knowing look. "Be out of here at a quarter of six at the latest. Paula will have my ass if you don't." She started to leave, then hesitated, leaning back into the doorway. "I should tell you, Joe Hanson didn't show up today. He had a couple of calls. One of the women on that case he's working on. Joe's secretary came down with a migraine and mentioned it to me on her way out. I tried Mitch. He's in Manchester, New Hampshire, talking to the campus police at the university. He hasn't heard from Joe either."

Ramsey pursed his lips, frowning. Cocking one eye he said, "Joe's not like that. You tried his home?"

"*Nada.* Zip, zero, zilch. No response from his pager or his cell phone. I've left a pile of messages on his answering machine. Just thought you should know."

"Right. Thanks. Something probably came up and he hasn't had time to respond."

Betty continued to half hang in the door. "This woman, Dr. Tremain . . . she said she couldn't reach Joe either. Joe's secretary said the woman was adamant that we check into it. And some doctor wants to talk to him."

Ramsey placed his pen on the papers and leaned back. "I get the hint, Betty. Thanks. I'll check into it."

She gave him a relieved smile and disappeared from the doorway, calling, "Six-thirty! Remember."

Ramsey reached for the phone, punching in Joe's number. After four rings the answering machine responded with Joe's canned message. After the beep, Ramsey said, "Yeah, I know the drill. So do you. As soon as you get this, call me. If it's after hours, use the cell. I don't care what time of night it is. Just check in, okay."

He hung up, then rang the pager number, and then tried Joe's cell. After eight rings the recorded voice told him that his party was no longer in the service area, or had reached his destination.

"Yeah, fine." He hung up and dived into the report.

Jack Ramsey ducked out of the office at five till six and barely made the end of Matt's game after inching through traffic jammed up by a wreck on the Key Bridge.

He didn't think about Joe Hanson again until almost noon the next day.

CHAPTER FIFTEEN

FOR THE SECOND NIGHT IN A ROW, VERONICA TOSSED AND turned on the couch. She had wrapped her Pendleton blanket around her like a sheath. The thorny problem of Abel, Rebecca, her brother's death, and the missing package knotted in her brain like an old rope. Nevertheless, she had pretty much come to the conclusion that whatever her other secrets, Rebecca wasn't a murderess. If Bryce was involved, he was one cool character. It further irritated her that she liked him—and feared it would cloud a dispassionate and objective analysis of his part in Scott's death, be it direct or indirect.

After what seemed to be an eternity, Veronica finally crossed the threshold into sleep.

The jangling of the telephone brought her bolt upright.

"Son of a bitch." She unwrapped the blanket, stood, wobbled across the room and around the breakfast bar to where the phone hung in the kitchen. Placing the receiver against her ear, she said muzzily, "Yeah?"

She heard a man's deep voice say, "Bryce Johnson, please."

"Yeah, just a minute." She turned, hollering, "Bryce? Phone."

"Coming." He sounded grumpy, and within moments she could see his dark form feeling its way down the stairs. She stepped over and flicked on the kitchen light, then watched as Bryce squinted against the glare, crossed the room, and took the receiver from her.

"Hello?" His eyes were puffy, his hair standing on end. She couldn't help but notice that even for a bookworm professor, he was fit. His body was proportionately muscled, and red hair curled on his chest.

She caught the sudden stiffening, the widening of his eyes, as if he'd been stung by something. It took two tries before he slammed the phone back into the cradle and stepped backward, expression stunned.

"What? What is it?" Veronica's heart skipped.

Bryce shook his head, rubbing his hands as if they had something sticky on them. "It was him, the voice from that night when Scott called. I tell you, I *know* that voice. It's been in my nightmares."

"What voice?"

"The man who was in Scott's house the night he was killed. He took the phone from Scott . . . tried to talk to me." His finger pointed to the hanging telephone, the cord still swaying. "That was him. And he said he was Agent Joe Hanson, of the FBI, returning my call."

He clutches Chaser to his chest, comforted by the stuffed buffalo's curly fur. The ringing of the telephone pulls him from dreams of home, of Mother and Father before they fought and Daaa went away.

Daaa's final words: "Becky, I can't do this anymore. I'm not cut out for this. He's not right! I want my own children to raise. Born of my blood, and not some freak *that someone else pawned off because they couldn't handle the trouble."*

After that Daaa left and never came home again. Abel purses his lips and runs his stubby fingers across the buffalo's shaggy hump.

In the bed beside him, Mother sleeps soundly. If he concentrates, he can hear her heartbeat, smell her odor mixing with that of the bed: faint traces of perfume, soap, shampoo, and sweat.

He shifts and raises his head. The people downstairs are talking in soft voices, but he can hear them.

"I swear," the man says, "the only person I gave this number to was the machine that answered Joe Hanson's phone."

"That wasn't Hanson," the woman insists. "I know his voice, and that wasn't him."

"He's the FBI, for God's sake! How could someone else get his number?"

"I don't know," Veronica says, "but I'm going to find out."

Abel slips from the covers and pads carefully to the door. Placing his head against the wood, he hears the muffled clicks as a telephone number is punched in. He reaches up and gently turns the doorknob, easing it open before stepping into the hall. He could not do this without Chaser's reassuring warmth pressed to his chest. Buffalo are brave and fearless; Mother has told him so. Chaser will keep him safe.

He creeps to the top of the stairs and cocks his head. His acute hearing can barely detect the ringing of a distant telephone, and then Veronica turns slightly to look at the bare-chested man.

Her expression changes, and she says, "Hello? Agent Hanson, please."

Abel can't quite understand the words coming through the telephone. The woman has it pressed too tightly against her ear.

"Never mind who this is. I would like to speak to Agent Hanson, please . . . and you're not him."

Abel can tell that a long silence passes, and then he hears the man's deep voice saying, "Who is this, please?" as Veronica replaces the receiver on its cradle. Something about that voice sends a shiver down Abel's spine and he hugs Chaser.

Veronica turns, and he can see her worried expression. She gives Bryce a scared look. "Whoever that is, it's not Joe."

"So, what are we going to do?" Bryce has his arms crossed across his bare chest.

Veronica has that perplexed look. "Whoever it was is in Virginia . . . at Joe's house."

"I say we pack up and go, now, tonight."

She glances at the wall clock. "It's nearly three A.M. I say we get up early and roll out of here by seven. God, you can hardly drive here from Denver that quickly, let alone Washington D.C."

"Yeah," Bryce mutters. "It's probably just my nerves."

Watching the two of them, Abel can feel their growing fear. The last time a phone call came, he and Mother had to leave home. Will they have to leave here now? If they do, where will they go? He fights the urge to cry, trying to draw strength from Chaser. But the scared feeling gets worse, eating him like a monster.

Together he and Chaser start back down the hall. His stomach is so upset he can't sleep. He hears Bryce go to bed again, and Veronica's body makes faint squeaking sounds as she shifts on the couch downstairs.

Abel carefully climbs into bed. Mother is sleeping uneasily under the blankets. For a long time, he lies there, his fingers knotting in Chaser's fur. Everyone is afraid. Why? What has happened to make them all so scared?

He can hear the rumble of a car, the grating of tires on pavement. Who would be coming at this time of night? With Chaser tucked under his arm, he slips down the hallway and into Bryce's bedroom. Hugging Chaser tight for security, Abel walks to the window.

He arrives just in time to see a white van, its lights off, appear around the building up the hill. In the moonlight the van moves slowly to a parking space across the lot from Veronica's BMW. The taillights flash, and he can hear a clunk as it is shifted into park. A moment later the motor is turned off. Abel watches, and wonders why no one gets out of the white van. After what seems like a long time, a door clicks and a man dressed in black steps out. He carries a bag over his shoulder as he walks agilely toward the building.

Abel has to move from room to room to keep track of the man. He catches glimpses of him as he slips through the trees at the base of the building. In the rear, the man stops, studying the upper floors of the condo. Abel watches from the shadows behind the bathroom window. The man's hair is silver in the moonlight and cut close to his head like a swim cap. The glow makes *his face look pale, the eyes like charcoal, ghostly and scary.*

The man seems to see through the night, to stare into Abel's eyes. That connection is almost electric, sending a spike of fear through Abel's heart. Involuntarily, he steps back, swallowing hard and clutching Chaser to his chest.

For a moment, he loses sight of the man. When he steps back to the glass, the man is gone.

He finally makes his way back to the landing; Veronica is no longer awake. Feeling bad, he takes Chaser, and together, they go back to lie next to Mother. From the muted sounds she is making, her dreams are troubled.

Sleep does not come.

Bryce woke up feeling haggard, echoes of the man's voice playing in his head from the late-night phone call. He opened his eyes to slanting yellow light and yawned. He had slept in this little bedroom years before. Paintings of wildlife and mountains— original oils—hung from the walls. Knick-knacks and framed photos of the Ferris family rested on the dresser. He took a moment to pick up a studio family shot that had Scott, Veronica, Mary, and Frank posed against a blue background. Scott looked like the bright undergraduate that he'd been at the time. Veronica, who must have been in her early teens, stared out with angry blue eyes. She had been a knockout even then. What would she have said if someone had told her that both her father and brother would be so early dead?

He shuffled through his bag for his cleanest dirty clothes and walked down the hallway to the upstairs bathroom. The shower beat on his skin as he considered that photo of the young Veronica. How much of their lives would have been different if he'd met her that first year he had known Scott?

He kept catching himself watching her, wishing he could pull that marvelous body close and feel her against him as he reassured her, and in the process, himself. Could he do that? Would she let him?

How long had it been since she left Ben? Over a year, at least. Was that long enough for her to find her footing? From personal experience with Cathy, three years before, catching a woman on the rebound was easy. She was vulnerable and desperate for attention, consolation, and company; but it usually led to disaster.

He stared at himself in the mirror as he toweled off. *See this thing through first. Survive this, and then you can start exploring the possibilities of a relationship.*

As he walked down the stairs, he couldn't get her out of his mind. Confound it, he couldn't wait to see her, to be amazed that she was every bit as beautiful as he remembered from the night before. If not more. He had enjoyed sitting, watching her move about the kitchen: the sway of her hips, the streaming gloss of that black hair, and the curve of those luscious breasts under her shirt. He wanted to see her give him that intimate look that passed between a man and woman.

It's your gonads talking, boy. But he doubted it. When he fell in lust with a woman, it was the desire to spirit her off to the sack and peel her clothes off first thing. What he felt with Veronica was a need to hold her, to make the world right.

If she'd be interested.

When they had time.

After they could stop worrying about murder and missing FBI guys.

After secrets were uncovered, and burned bodies were buried.

Maybe his perpetual bad timing was congenital?

Veronica still slept on her couch, the blanket pulled up around her chin. He stopped and looked down at her face. The classic hollow of her cheek beckoned a finger to tenderly stroke it. Raven hair had spilled around the fabric pillow in a dark swirl. Her eyes were flicking back and forth under the lids, lost in a REM dream that he hoped was pleasant. As soon as she awakened, it would be to the memory of that ominous phone call and the knowledge that they had to leave and put as much distance between this place and them as possible.

He reached out, hesitated, and imagined himself patting her, telling her it would be all right in the end. Then he stepped carefully past the breakfast bar into the kitchen. Within minutes he had coffee perking, had pulled the last of the eggs from the refrigerator, and had started the remains of the bacon. He would wait and toast the bread last thing so that it would be hot when people buttered it.

"Wow! A domestic male."

He turned to see her, her hip cocked against the breakfast bar, hair tumbled in an unruly mass. She'd slept in her clothes; they were a wrinkled mess. Damn, she looked good.

"Hazards of the bachelor life. But don't push your luck. I can do gourmet, but only when I have the time to concentrate, and no preoccupation with research or a full schedule."

"I'll keep that in mind." She turned, and he was granted the delightful vision of her trim butt as she ambled toward the little bathroom under the stairs.

He heard the water go on in the shower and lowered the temperature on the eggs. Pouring the first cup of coffee, he walked to the sliding glass door and opened it. Cool air caressed his face. The lake sparkled a melodious blue. Distant peaks rose in jagged splendor, white against the cerulean sky. This would be a fairy tale but for the lingering reality that someone out there wanted to kill him.

Where had Veronica's Special Agent Hanson disappeared to? That thought preoccupied him as the jays rasped their hoarse calls in the trees below. A speedboat bashed across the water, two people kneeling on the seats as they sped past.

He heard the pipes squeak as Veronica turned off the water. She had called her mother yesterday and had talked for nearly an hour. He had stepped out here, to think, to grant her privacy, and to wonder about the perpetual fear in Rebecca Armely's blue eyes. The news of Scott's death had terrified her. Those fearful waters were building behind the dam of her resolve; how long before the concrete cracked and gave way to a rush of panic?

"Good mowning, Bwyce."

He turned to see Abel standing in the doorway behind him, a pair of white flannel pajamas on his stocky little body. His pudgy arms mashed the fuzzy buffalo to his chest.

"Who have you got there?"

"This is Chasuw. He's a buffawo. He's bwave."

Bryce leaned down, smiling, saying, "Hello, Chaser." To Abel he said, "Can I pet him?" At a nod, he reached out and patted the furry hump.

"He hewps me," the boy said with his nasal drawl.

What was it about Abel that drew the eye? He certainly wasn't retarded. In fact, the little boy showed remarkable mental agility, demonstrated excellent spatial relations, and possessed superb upper-body strength. The boy's memory for detail had been downright remarkable. He just had problems talking through that long nose. In addition, there was something about the way he walked, a powerful, peg-legged forward propulsion that hinted of rhinoceroslike determination rather than grace.

Abel stepped up to the edge of the railing and looked down, as if searching for something. The drop was a good two stories to the condo deck below.

"What are you looking for, Abel?"

"Man."

"You should be an anthropologist."

Veronica stepped into the kitchen, her hair wrapped in a towel. She had changed into a white turtleneck that accented her thin waist, broad shoulders, and symmetrical breasts. A woman who looked like her shouldn't do things like that to a man like him. Especially this early in the morning.

She poured a cup of coffee and walked to the phone. Lifting it from the cradle, she started pressing the number pad and stopped, a sour look on her face.

"What's up?" Bryce stepped into the kitchen.

"Phone's dead."

"Ah, technology."

She frowned and hung up. "That just cuts it."

"After hearing that voice on the phone last night, you're telling me we've got no phone service? I don't like it." Bryce glanced back to make sure that Abel wasn't climbing up onto the railing and stepped back into the kitchen. "Agent Hanson didn't show up like the cavalry. I say we pack up and fly like rockets."

"It happens on occasion up here. And just where did you have in mind to go to?"

He struggled to ignore the impact her tight sweater had on his hormones. "I don't know, but sitting still reminds me of being a bull's-eye target. The target is placed at a prescribed distance, and the shooter has plenty of time to determine the elevation and windage."

"Delightful metaphor."

"That's because I'm not clever enough to do a metafive."

Veronica arched an eyebrow. "A hereditary problem, no doubt. Let's try Mother's. She's got this incredibly huge house high on Lookout Mountain overlooking the Front Range. If Rebecca doesn't object, she can take Abel and set up house until the Feds figure this thing out. Mother needs the company. She's taking this hard. If she locks herself away in solitude, it'll kill her."

"You'd better call her first. Give her a little bit of warning. I remember your mother. Always immaculate. She wouldn't want us just dropping in. Something like a doily might be out of place on the counter."

"And she'll need to dress for the occasion." Traces of humor had supplanted her worry.

"Personally, I thought she was a great lady when I met her."

Veronica cocked an eyebrow. "Try living with perfection. Over time it has a certain abrasive quality."

They turned when Rebecca descended the stairs. She checked first thing to find Abel where he stood at the railing looking down. Then she walked to the coffeepot, poured a cup, and sniffed. "Marvelous. I might live after all." She looked haggard.

"Sleep well?" Bryce asked.

"Horrible. One nightmare after another." She gave them a flat-eyed look. "I heard you talking about going to Mary's?"

"It's a big house. Closer to Denver . . . and the police, if we need them." Veronica glanced uneasily at Bryce. "I'd rather be moving. Bryce is right. I'm starting to feel uneasy here. Besides, the phone's dead. By the time they send a truck to repair it, we could be at Mom's."

"It's such a pretty place," Bryce said regretfully. "Reminds me of home but with a bluer lake."

"Where's home?" Rebecca asked. "Don't I remember that it was Vermont, or somewhere?"

"New Hampshire. A place called Center Harbor. I grew up on Lake Winnipesaukee. Like this but with smaller mountains, more houses, and different forest."

"Breakfast ready?" Veronica nodded toward the pans.

"Anytime you are."

"Abel?" Rebecca called. "Bring Chaser and wash your hands. It's time to eat."

Then we'll be leaving, Bryce promised himself. *Not a moment too soon, either.*

Like a lazy snake, Ron Elias lay on his belly atop the sleeping bag he had unrolled in the back of the white van. A shiver crept along his spine. He hated being inside anything this cramped. Images came spidering out of his mind: nylon restraints, buckles, faceless white-coated men with needles. He swallowed hard and tightened his grip on the pistol butt. That made the difference. That and the job. This was God, testing him, making sure he was strong enough, that he deserved his soul.

The big Contender pistol rested on its butt, the barrel supported by a Harris bipod. The suppressor—a long black steel cylinder threaded onto the barrel—ruined the single-shot pistol's clean lines and made it look front-heavy. Using binoculars, he studied the second-story condo for signs of movement. He had seen silhouettes of people shifting behind the windows. Meticulously he re-traced every detail of the wood-sided walls, placing them in his memory. The van windows added a little distortion.

"Coffee?" Paxton asked from behind. "It's been two hours since dawn." He sat cross-legged behind the driver's seat, a set of headphones over his close-cropped dark hair. A bank of sophisticated eavesdropping equipment had been bolted to the van's side. With it, they had been able to patch through Hanson's home phone system to ensure that Johnson was in the residence and to intercept the unknown woman's call to Hanson. From time to time Paxton adjusted the dial on a cellular telephone monitoring system cased in a black polyurethane box. With the phone line cut it would be Johnson's only way to call for help.

"After I make the shot." Caffeine changed blood pressure, made the nerves jumpy, and affected a shooter's fine motor control. Elias shifted, pulling his knee out slightly to change the circulation in his leg.

Long years of training held him in good stead. Waiting was part of the game. Patience, the singular virtue of his occupation. Better this than the helter-skelter rushing they had been doing for the last couple of weeks. He didn't like traveling; it bothered his biorhythms.

They had known the plan would go awry. Implementation of an operation always anticipated every conceivable contingency. The targets had been carefully chosen, studied for months, and alternate scenarios planned for. The Jew had gone down perfectly. The Ferris hit had not unfolded as anticipated. They had been forced to act before Ferris hung up the phone. He still didn't know what had tipped the man, but God had been on their side. Ferris hadn't been so tough. After crushing his legs with a sledgehammer, they had stripped off his pants. With the sledge handle strapped to his foot, they had started turning. Sweat had popped from Ferris' forehead as he watched with bugging eyes. The man's flesh had twisted like a wet towel, bone splinters lancing through the skin. The tape on his mouth had muffled horrible screams.

The one thing Elias hadn't expected had been Paxton's reaction: that squeamish look, the nervous sweat forming on his skin like little pearls. The man didn't understand retribution or punishment for sins against God. That bothered Elias. Paxton had argued against nailing Ferris to the floor. If it had been good enough for Christ when he died to absolve mankind of its sins, it was certainly good enough for a Satanic beast like Ferris. He wished he could have been there for the Alexander job instead of leaving it to Paxton. Somehow, he was sure it hadn't been handled as appropriately. Damage control instead had sent him to Virginia, and Liz Carter. It had been his pleasure to introduce her to Hell.

Now they had Bryce Johnson: traced to this mountain condo by a telephone number. Confirmed by the call they had made from the hill before they drove in. He would die before he could ever reach the FBI. After that it was a simple process of moving from address to address as they mopped up the remaining obscenities.

He caught movement as the door opened. A blond woman stepped out, a pink suitcase hanging from her hand. She spoke over her shoulder to someone inside. Johnson, perhaps?

"Movement. A woman," Elias said, lowering his binoculars and caressing the grip of the pistol. He nudged the rear cargo doors with one hand; they parted just enough to allow a slit. Taking up a prone shooting position, he eased the suppressed muzzle through the opening and centered the telescopic sight on the woman.

Behind him, Paxton shifted, picking up his own binoculars. "Shit! You know who that is?"

"The woman from Salt Lake?"

"That's her. Son of a bitch. If we're lucky, we've got three for one."

"Maybe." Elias snugged his elbow and allowed his finger to caress the trigger. "If the kid's with her . . . and Johnson is in there."

"Bet on it." A pause. "How do you want to do this?"

Elias followed the woman through the Leupold scope's crosshairs. He could feel his heart rate slowing as old discipline settled in. "Wait," he whispered. "See what she does. Not out in the open."

"Right," Paxton whispered. "If she heads back . . ."

"Keep an eye on the door."

"Covered. I can see someone moving inside. An adult. Probably Johnson."

Elias studied the woman, noticing that she was attractive, with serious blue eyes and a nice body. Such a waste; but then Satan often distracted the righteous by wrapping obscenity in beauty.

He controlled his breathing as he eased the hammer back and tracked his target. The crosshairs centered on her chest. She was wearing a white T-shirt that conformed to her torso. Nice tits.

She stopped at the battered old Honda and opened the car door before placing the suitcase in the backseat. Then she turned and headed back toward the stairs. Elias watched her climb them on the way to the half-open door.

"I'll drop her in the doorway. Then I'll drop Johnson right on top of her when he comes to check. Done right, we'll have them all in one little pile, right there inside the door. Neat. Clean." And they had called him insane?

He could see her T-shirt where it molded the brassiere strap and rested the crosshairs on the snap in the middle of her back. His world faded into the sight picture as he took up the slack in the trigger, the breath balanced in his lungs.

CHAPTER SIXTEEN

Veronica reached for her black nylon bag, picked it up, and turned toward the door. Morning sunlight coming through the picture window had bathed the Jackson bronze of the buffalo in warm light. Odd that she would remember that later.

Rebecca filled the doorway, her foot swinging through the arc that would carry her across the threshold. The same morning light shone in her blond hair and outlined the white T-shirt's shoulders.

Rebecca's body made a loud popping sound, like someone had just clapped his hands hard. At the same instant, she jerked, a shock wave traveling through her gelatinlike breasts, up her neck, down her arms and legs. The front of her shirt leaped as a red hole exploded from her sternum. Simultaneously, the wooden wall across the room made a cracking sound.

Rebecca pitched forward, every joint loose, and smacked face first into the floor.

Veronica stared—her body robbed of movement. A horrible rattling sound came from Rebecca's open mouth. Her limbs twitched as though severed. She coughed, blood blowing out of her mouth and the small red hole in her back. A scarlet pool was spreading from under her chest.

"I thought I'd . . ." Bryce stopped halfway down the

stairs, stood frozen for a moment, cursed, and leaped for the landing. He darted across the room, slamming himself against the wall beside the doorjamb. Reaching out, he pulled Rebecca's body to one side. Bright crimson smeared the floor. In a lightning movement, he shot an arm out and slammed the door closed before launching himself at Veronica and bodily muscling her to the floor.

She panicked under the impact of his body, thrashing, kicking, fighting a scream.

"Hush!" Bryce ordered, clamping a hand over her mouth. "Stop it! Damn it! *They're trying to kill us!*"

She gasped, tearing her gaze from Rebecca's limp body to stare into Bryce's face, so close to hers.

"Easy," he whispered, removing his hand. "Easy, Ronnie. Take a deep breath. There. That's it. Control, now. Are you all right?"

She couldn't swallow. Her tongue stuck in her throat.

"Stay down. Don't move. Don't look at Rebecca. Just stay here and don't panic." He patted her, then crawled over to grasp Rebecca's wrist and look at the plate-sized bloodstain in the middle of her back. She heard his breath catch.

"Muvver?" Abel asked, halfway out of the bathroom, his wide eyes searching for anyone. Chaser was clutched against his chest; his canvas Sam Weller's bag hung from his hand.

Instinctively, Veronica scrambled across the room and pulled Abel back, attempting to shield him from the sight of his mother. In frenzied panic, she dashed into the bathroom behind the stairs. Abel had dropped his toys and was squirming powerfully, making frightened sounds. To her amazement, he managed to push away despite her adrenaline-charged muscles.

"Hush!" she hissed. "Abel. Don't move! Please, honey. Stay still."

"Muvver?"

"Shush! Quiet! Oh, God, Abel. Don't move. Just stay here safe, with me."

Bryce called in a strained voice, "I'll be right back. For God's sake, don't move!" His feet thundered on the stairway as he charged headlong up to his room.

Nine-one-one. She had to dial nine-one-one! From where she cowered on the bathroom floor, Abel sobbing in her arms, she could see the phone on the far wall. Could she make it, dash across that space and grab the phone off the hook?

"Abel," she whispered. "You've got to promise me, honey, that you'll stay right here. You've got to stay! Hear me?"

He nodded, blubbering with fright.

"Oh, God." Veronica fought the trembling in her frozen muscles. She released Abel, who scrambled over to huddle in the space between the wall and the toilet bowl. His fear-shot blue eyes were awash with tears. "I wan' Muvver," he moaned.

Veronica braced herself like a sprinter, hating the paralytic fear that sought to lock her muscles in place. The phone filled her tunneling vision. Now or never. She launched herself, flying across the floor, slamming into the wall with one hand as she plucked the phone off the cradle with the other.

Dropping, she scrambled into the recess of the breakfast bar and curled into a ball, her frantic fingers tapping out nine-one-one. When she jammed the phone to her ear, the dead silence shocked her. And then memory came tumbling back.

Cut? Shit! Angrily she shouted, "Damn you!" and cast the receiver away to clatter across the kitchen floor.

Bryce descended the stairs in three giant leaps, rebounded off the wall, and ducked low as he scrambled behind the couch. The black pistol filled his fist when he raised his head to look around. Veronica remained huddled under the breakfast bar, the dead phone rocking back and forth on the swaying cord.

Abel's horrified moans came from the bathroom.

She saw Bryce's frantic eyes search the room, running over Rebecca's corpse, the scattered toys, and the fireplace. His gaze fixed on the fireplace tools. Reaching an arm over the couch, he snagged the Pendleton blanket she had been sleeping under. Tucking it under his right arm, he crawled to the hearth and pulled down the poker. Wiggling along the floor like a snake, he made his way to the wall beside the picture window.

"What are you—"

"Shhhh!" He waved her back angrily with the pistol. Wadding the blanket, he wrapped it around the poker and extended it until the rounded mass hung in the lower corner of the window. Not even two seconds passed before the wall cracked and splintered; the blanket jumped as something smacked the couch.

Bryce dropped the poker as if it were electrified and scuttled along the wall like some oversized rodent. He motioned her toward the bathroom.

As hard as it had been to dash to the phone, that terrible trip back to the bathroom was harder.

Bryce slammed through the door, hot on her heels. He was shaking, sweat glistening on his pale flesh. Abel had stuffed himself as far behind the toilet bowl as he could manage.

"What's *happening* to us?" Veronica cried, grabbing desperately at his shirt. "Why are they doing this? God, Rebecca . . . God . . ."

"Stop it," he snapped, shaking her arm. "Listen to me! We've got to get out of here."

"Can't," she tried to say, but her jaw had begun to tremble uncontrollably.

"Veronica, listen," he said sternly. "Either we get out of here or we're dead. It's not going to take them long to find a way to kill us. Fire, explosion, I don't know what, but these guys are pros. Can we cut through a wall into the next unit? Go through the floor?"

"The trash chute," she cried, grabbing him. "I've done it. As a kid. It's a tin-lined shaft that drops down two floors to the trash Dumpster in the basement. There's a garage door down there so the trash guys can roll the Dumpster out."

"Will we fit?"

She nodded, finding sudden hope. "And maybe someone will hear it . . . call the cops."

"Take Abel. We've got to do this now." He ducked out the door, crossed the kitchen in a crouch, and jerked the cabinet door open.

Veronica swallowed hard, her throat dry and knotted. She reached out, calling, "Abel? Abel, honey. Come on, we've got to go."

He shook his head, struggling to wedge himself deeper into the niche. Driven by adrenaline, Veronica manually dragged him, kicking and clawing at the linoleum, from his hiding place.

He screamed in fear, and she tucked him tightly against her shoulder. "I know, sweetheart. I'm scared, too. But we've got to do this or they will kill us. Be brave for me, Abel. Brave like Chaser, okay?"

He managed to jerk a quick nod between sobs.

She started out the doorway; Abel cried, "Chassuw?" and pointed. The stuffed buffalo lay on its side near the corner of the couch.

The reason for what she did eluded her, but shielding Abel's view from Rebecca's body, she crabbed sideways, to grab up the buffalo. Abel clutched it tightly. Her black bag and purse lay a handsbreadth beyond. She snagged them, then ducked low and raced around the corner of the breakfast bar to where Bryce waited by the chute, pistol stuffed in his waistband, a question in his eyes.

"Last minute pickup." Veronica extended an arm to rip the dish towels from the rack beside the sink. "You'll need to brace your knees and elbows to break your fall. The chute drops forty feet into the machine room. The Dumpster is another four-foot drop beneath the chute. There's a garage door leading out back where the trash guys roll the Dumpster out once a week. And, I'll tell you now, the tinwork wasn't designed for our weight."

"I'll take my chances." He grunted tensely. "You and Abel first. Good luck."

"No, you. You're stronger. Someone has to catch Abel."

To her surprise he gave her a crooked smile and nodded before climbing into the chute.

"Brace your knees against the frame," she told him, and heard the tin warp resonantly.

"This is nuts," he told her as she showed him how to wrap the towel around his hands for a friction brake.

"Want to stay and get shot at?"

"Not on your life. Wish me luck."

She stared into his hazel eyes for a moment, sharing the desperation, her soul aching with gratitude for his courage. Then he settled himself, lower lip clamped in his teeth as he suddenly dropped out of sight, the tin banging and cracking rhythmically as he fell.

"Okay?" she asked, poking her head in to stare down the black shaft.

"Send me the kid," he called, voice strained.

Veronica turned, lifting her bag, and let it drop. Call it practice. Then she looked at Abel; he was staring at her with horrified eyes, tears like gleaming diamonds on his slanted cheeks.

She bent over the shaft. "Just a second." To Abel she said, "You don't move."

She had to do this. Damn it, the kid could really get hurt. Heart battering her ribs, she ducked low and sprinted around the breakfast bar, vaulted the couch, and slammed to the floor in the corner where the Pendleton blanket lay wadded. Clutching it, she bolted back the way she had come, flesh tingling for the sudden impact of a bullet. She slipped round the breakfast bar, almost fell, and tumbled down next to Abel.

"Here," she said, wrapping the thick wool around him. "This will keep you safe." She lifted him, arms straining at his weight. Meeting his eyes with hers, she stuffed him into the shaft. "Hang on to Chaser. Bryce will catch you. If you stick, wiggle and you'll fall free."

"No! I don't want . . ."

She let loose of him, hearing the tin bang as Abel wailed his way down.

"Got him!" Bryce called.

She grabbed her purse from the table and dropped it down the chute. Charged with fear, she swung her legs over the void and tucked her knees against the far wall where the framing supported the tin. She wrapped one of the towels around her hands and lowered herself, blocking her arms and knees. Turning loose, she tried to break her fall, the tin buckling and banging, each of the square frame sections battering her like baseball bats. She fell the final four feet into the steel Dumpster. Bryce's strong arms, and then plastic sacks full of garbage, broke her fall.

The first sensation: racking pain. The second: dim gray light from the square windows in the garage door, and the stench of moldy garbage.

"You all right?" Bryce asked as she stumbled to her feet.

"Damn, I'm too old for this shit anymore. How's Abel?"

"Okay." He levered himself over the edge of the Dumpster. "After that racket, I hope they didn't hear. Now what?" He stepped to the windowed garage door and stared out at the graveled drive.

She clambered over the rim and found Abel huddled in the blanket, his buffalo clutched to his chest. His blue eyes had a glazed look.

"My car's out front." Out where they could shoot her dead.

Bryce whispered, "Now or never." She noticed that he was limping as he reached down and picked up Abel. "When you open the door, we're running. Straight east into the trees. You have to go as fast as you can."

"Where are we going?"

"Next door," he told her laconically. "Your car might be out front, but my Durango is in the condo lot across the way."

She nodded, refusing to think, to consider the danger. Hanging her purse on her shoulder, she grabbed the handle of her nylon case. Twisting the latch, she threw her weight against the steel door and lifted.

Bryce ducked through, Abel cradled in his arms. He hobbled out into the morning. Veronica blinked in the glare and sprinted eastward toward the trees as fast as she could.

Somewhere, a shooter was drawing a bead.

CHAPTER SEVENTEEN

*B*ryce *is running hard. The world jerks with each step. Abel can feel the man's irregular stride, hear the soft*

grunts each time he lands on his right ankle. The amber-colored wooden walls are rushing past. He tries to look back, to catch a last glimpse in hopes that Mother will come running from the dark square they have just left.

Mother? Where is Mother? What happened to her? She has to be all right. She has to be. She will be all right. Abel knows it. It must be so.

Bryce is running fast. The building passes rapidly before Abel's eyes; the dark squares of windows are flashing past. Veronica runs in front of them, her long black hair streaming out behind her, shining in the sunlight.

They have cleared the corner, Bryce swinging onward in a limp as he hugs Abel close. He is panting, and Abel can feel the heat from his body. Across the gravel road, they are on grass. Then they duck into the trees, and Abel catches a last glimpse of the condo. He starts to cry again.

He wants Mother. He needs her to hug him close, to make everything okay again.

How did he get so empty?

Stabbing white pain lanced up Bryce's leg with each step. The thin Rocky Mountain air made him feel like he had run for ten miles. Laboring like bellows, his lungs burned. Abel's weight shocked him. What was a four-year-old kid supposed to weigh? The thick wool blanket had started to loosen, flapping around his legs.

To his surprise, the gut-chilling fear of a bullet—coupled with the too-vivid memory of Rebecca's ruptured body—proved a damned powerful stimulant. Frightened by his own body's vulnerability, he concentrated on Veronica's flying legs as she ran ahead of him.

Gulping air, Bryce had to keep reaching back to ensure the pistol was still in his belt. Lose that and he'd feel particularly naked—not that a .45 was much use against a sniper's rifle.

Veronica ducked a low branch, following a slightly worn trail through the duff. To Bryce's perception, they had been running for an eternity before they broke out into the neighboring building complex with its stone-clad walls, boxy fireplaces, and angled roofs.

The Durango sat where he had left it, still road grimy, but apparently unmolested.

"Veronica! That one." He pointed when she shot a look over her shoulder. Changing course, she ran to the door, yanking at the locked handle.

Gasping, his ankle on fire, he leaned against the side of the vehicle, fishing for his keys with his free hand. Abel was crying softly, his face buried in the shaggy hump of his stuffed buffalo.

Bryce found his keys, almost dropped them, and stabbed the button that unlocked the doors and turned off the security. Almost giddy with relief, he popped the door open, handing Abel into the backseat and slipping into the driver's. Veronica pitched her black bag into the rear beside Abel, who squirmed to escape the confines of the blanket with one hand, the other locked in the buffalo's fur.

The Durango purred to life, and Bryce shifted it into

reverse, hating the fact that he didn't let it idle for the pre-requisite thirty seconds to circulate the oil.

It took every ounce of restraint to keep from blasting out of the parking lot, swerving onto the road, and rock-eting as far as possible from the scene. Instead, he stopped at the stop sign, waited for a break in traffic, and accelerated to the legal speed.

Veronica had been peering anxiously back the way they had come, turning to ask, "What are you doing? Driving right back to them?"

He shot a quick glance down the drive as they passed the Eagle sign, and puffed out a relieved breath. "We've got to be smart. Got to think. Up the road toward Breck-enridge is a one-way trip. Back to town gives us a lot more choices."

"Yeah, like right to the police station." She crossed her arms, and he realized she was shaking, scared down to her bones.

"No, Ronnie." He put the pieces together as he spoke. "I didn't hear a shot. Did you? No report of a rifle?"

She looked at him, eyes panic-bright. "No. I mean, I don't think so. Just . . . just the sound of the bullet hit-ting." She frowned. "Both times."

"Veronica, think. *Damn* them! They waited until Re-becca had stepped into the doorway." He thumped the steering wheel with a fist. "That's what it was. I've seen this before. A drug hit in Boston. They shot the first guy in the doorway. When the second leaned over his friend, they shot him, too."

"You what? You've *seen* this before?"

"I worked for the Suffolk County coroner. I saw a lot of gunshot wounds." *Just not people I knew.* "These guys didn't panic, didn't make mistakes. When I came down the stairs, you were going to try and help her."

Veronica nodded, a sick expression on her face. "Dear God, I couldn't move. I was just frozen there. I couldn't believe it."

"That saved your life. He'd have shot you next." He fidgeted in the seat, powered by too much energy. "That shot at the blanket. He didn't shoot through the window. He shot through the wall where a man's chest would have been as he looked through the glass. This guy's smart, trained."

"How do you know that?" she asked crossly, every muscle flexed against the shakes.

His tongue caught in his throat as he thought about it. "He scouted the place. Determined the only way in was through the front. The rear of the building had a deck . . . and a long drop to the ground. He thought he had us trapped."

They rounded the gentle curve as the road widened into four lanes and entered Frisco. Veronica started, jumped up, and craned around in the seat to look behind them for pursuit. After a moment, she said, "Abel? Are you all right?"

"Muvver?" he sobbed.

"I'm sorry, Abel. I'm so sorry," she said gently and reached back between the seats to pat him reassuringly. To Bryce, she said, "We've got to go to the police. I mean, my God, there's a dead . . ." She bit her lip. "Rebecca needs to be tended to. Maybe they can arrest them."

"No. We can't." He frowned angrily, fear tingling within.

"What do you mean, no?" She was glaring at him.

"Think! Do you want to be the one to walk out of that police station door knowing that somewhere, within a half mile, some guy with a tuned rifle could be an ounce of trigger pressure away from blowing your head off?"

"We can't just drive away, Bryce."

He shook his head. "No. We call the FBI. They can alert the Frisco police, or the county sheriff, or whoever. I'd trust the FBI to keep us alive before I'd trust the local yokels here."

"What if you're wrong and we're busted before we get out of town?"

"Then I've just made another in a long line of mistakes." He shot a glance at the rearview mirror, keeping track of the cars that had followed them.

"Damn it!" Veronica rapped a fist against the drink console. "This can't be happening to me! To us!"

He continued past Main and out the strip. At the interstate he turned east, heading back to Denver—and immediately regretted it. Where the hell else would they expect him to go?

He glanced at her. In a moment she was going to lose it. He had to find something for her to . . . "Ronnie, call Hanson. Now. You've got to tell him what's happened."

Veronica swallowed hard, fumbled with her purse, and drew out the cell phone. That seemed to do the trick. She seemed more stable, given a purpose. Her slender finger pressed the keys and then the "send" button. "What does it say about your life when you know your FBI agent's number by heart. Shit! No signal."

"Hey," he said, reading the Dillon exit sign, seeing that Highway 9 also exited there. "Watch your language."

"Watch my language?" She glared at him, struggling with herself for control. "I didn't know you were the blushing type."

He jerked a nod toward the rear. "Little ears."

She seemed to wilt. "My God, what are we going to do?"

"Keep ourselves and the boy alive."

"You know, Joe told me the FBI was looking for you. How long before they pick us up?"

"I've switched a lot of plates on this thing." He glanced at the mirror as he slowed for the Dillon exit, stopped at the light, and took a left under the overpass. The way wound down into an emerald mountain valley as they headed northward toward someplace called Kremmling.

Veronica kept thumbing the "redial" button. "Damn! It's reading 'no service.' We should have stopped in Dillon, used a pay phone."

"It will keep. The local police wouldn't have taken those guys, anyway. We don't even know where they were shooting from. They could have dug a 'hide' last night, broken into one of the apartments across the way in the other building . . . anywhere. They could have been anywhere."

"What makes you so sure the deputies wouldn't have caught them?" He read her hostility for the pressure release that it was.

"Because you can't find a really good sniper unless you step on him."

"And *you* know this?"

"The Marine Corps snipers are the best in the business.

My cousin—the one I used to drink beer with—is serving in Kosovo. At the embassy."

At the tone in his voice, she remained silent, periodically bending down to press the "redial" button on her cell phone. The only other sound he could hear over the rush of the Durango was Abel crying in the backseat.

The green John Deere lawn tractor puttered happily along, the twin blades spewing an emerald haze from the mower vent. Ramsey actually enjoyed tackling this chore that most people considered tedious at best. Normally, Matt kept the lawn in shape, but today, for the first time since spring, Ramsey had taken the golden opportunity to enjoy an hour in the sun.

Time on the mower turned into quiet time. He had nothing to distract him but the patterns he left on the green lawn. He suspected that the psychiatric guys down at Quantico would have told him he enjoyed this because, for those rare instances when he was in the mower's yellow seat, he was finally and resolutely in control of the world, and any stray dandelion that doubted it would be blitzed into bits by a mere swerve of the wheel.

He and Paula had earned this place with its two-acre manicured lawn, the tall beech trees, and the two-story Colonial brick home. He, through the long years of dogged investigation, hard work, and tenacious dedication to the job. Paula's dues had been paid in endurance during the lonely years, through the phone calls when he said, "Honey, something's come up. I won't be home." During their married life, they had been uprooted time and again when he was reassigned to different field offices. Paula had taken those moves in stride. She had spent her time waiting up late, dreading the knock at the door and the sober-suited agents who would break the bad news. Fortunately, that knock had never come.

Then, three years ago, Jack Ramsey was promoted to supervisor of the Washington Field Office Domestic Terrorism squad—the best in the country, though the New York squad might have argued the finer points of that assessment. Finally, it had been Paula's turn, so he had taken her to the realtor's and said, "You pick."

She had opted for this place: a quiet, tree-filled neighborhood in Manassas Park. The schools were good, access to the city easy, and local amenities plentiful. The location caused a longer commute for Ramsey, but for the most part, with the hours he kept, he missed the worst of the traffic.

He had just made the turn around the crocus when he caught Paula in the corner of his eye. She had stepped out on the back porch, waving with one hand.

Ramsey raised the mower heads and turned toward the porch. He pushed the throttle forward and rumbled across the grass, executing a neat turn to parallel the rear patio slab. Throttling back to a putt-putt idle, he grinned up, saying, "Hey, gorgeous, miss me, or what?"

She smiled at that, but he could see the tension behind her gray eyes. "Sorry, as much as I'd like to keep you, Mitch is on the phone. He wants to talk to you."

Ramsey killed the engine and made a face. "If it's the quarterly report, I'm going to tell him that the real Jack Ramsey is living in Jamaica. I'm just the dumb doppelganger."

"Your words, not mine." She arched an eyebrow and turned back for the sliding door.

He stepped off the mower, walked into the cool dining room, and picked up the phone on the hutch, saying, "What's up?"

"Jack, I don't know . . . but I think we've got a problem."

"Nothing that involves flaking skin, I hope."

"The office just took a call from a woman named Veronica Tremain . . . uh, Scott Ferris' sister. She wanted Joe, but no one's seen him and he's not answering his phone. She says that someone just killed Rebecca Armely. Does that name ring any of your bells?"

"Yeah. Let me see. She adopted Amanda Alexander's child, right?"

"You got it. Her name turned up when I was in Ohio. She's on my list to be interviewed. I sent it on to Salt Lake a couple of days ago. They checked her place out and reported that she was gone. Hadn't been to work for about a week."

"Ferris called her the night he was killed."

Mitch paused. "I think we had better find Joe and sit down for a chat. Tremain asked us to notify the Frisco, Colorado, police department that Armely was dead in the family condo. She stressed that they shouldn't screw up the crime scene investigation, that ballistics would be important."

"She *what?*"

"I'm just reading the transcript from the recorded call, Jack. The switchboard transferred her to Hal. He was the only guy at a desk today. It's Saturday, boss. He tried to keep her talking, but she just gave it to him in a tense monotone. She said that they were on the run and she would call back. She wants to talk to Joe."

"Find him. Find her."

"Yeah, well, this was a cell call, and the reception was scratchy. She said she'd call back."

He thought for a moment. "Just where, exactly, is this Frisco?"

"Up in the hills west of Denver. Ski town."

"See if Denver can send someone from the ERT up there to meet with the local P.D. before they enter the scene. If this isn't a crank we want everything we can get from the scene. So far we've got squat."

"Right, boss."

"And *find* Joe!"

The Reverend Brown fingered the decorative handle of his coffee cup as he relaxed in the fabric-covered chair. The white tablecloth had been starched to give it a crisp appearance. The discreet murmur of conversation and the clinking of utensils and glass mixed with the faint strains of Vivaldi that drifted from the quartet playing in one corner of the dining room. Brown liked the Willard Hotel. He stayed here every time he was in Washington. Somehow the fact that in a previous incarnation it had sheltered Union officers gave the place a particular irony.

Thoughts shifted to last night, and he wondered if anyone suspected that he and his "executive secretary" had gone straight from the White House to the plush upstairs suite. She had been excited by his proximity to power.

He'd never known a woman could respond that way. The very thought of it stirred his manhood.

He glanced around thoughtfully. This wasn't the sort of meeting he could have brought Mrs. Campbell to. At the moment, she was out shopping, blasting her way through D.C. the same way she did through the expensive boutiques in Buckhead.

Ah, there! He rose as the tall white-haired man appeared in the doorway and spoke to the maitre d'. At the latter's nod the white-haired man spoke to the two suited men who followed him. Without a word, they turned, walking out of sight as the maitre d' led Judge Louis Harthow to Brown's table.

"Judge! Good of you to take a moment from your schedule to see me." Brown stood, clasping the judge's hand as the maitre d' held the visitor's chair.

"Not a problem, Reverend." The judge smiled, his age-lined face florid from the heat outside. When the waiter appeared, he said, "Oh, nothing for me. I've only got a couple of minutes."

Brown indicated his cup. "More coffee, please. Judge, you're sure you wouldn't like a glass of lemonade? I can recall when—"

"Yes, indeed. Good of you to remember. Just like old times, eh?" The judge smiled up at the waiter. "If you have it."

"We do, sir." The waiter, a trim man in his thirties, gracefully picked up the menu and departed.

"How's Bobby Sue?" the judge asked, his watery blue eyes vaguely out of focus over his political smile.

"You know the answer to that, Judge." Brown waved it away. "We're doing the same that you and Laura are.

She has her life; I have mine. We're both trapped in a relationship we can't get out of without drawing the press down on us and looking like fools. So, we make the best of it."

A frown lined the judge's face. "Sorry to hear that, Reverend. As sorry for you as for me. Laura has her work with autistic children. I have my life in the Bureau. When necessary, we dress up and attend the functions, each smiling, acting out our parts." Then he brightened. "I didn't get more than a chance to say hello last night at the reception. So, what did you think about dinner at the White House?"

"Staged, Judge. All glitz and empty speeches. There was a lot of handshaking, big smiles, and lots and lots of flashbulbs popping and good old Southern homilies. The president is something of a dolt, but I have to tell you, I was impressed by the first lady. In the end, his staff and my staff are supposed to interface, improve communications, and establish a dialog."

"Ah." The judge nodded in sympathy. "That's good for another couple of political appointments to a few more meaningless committees."

The lemonade arrived, and Reverend Brown watched the waiter set the glass down with meticulous grace, then refill his coffee. After the man asked if there was anything else, and then retreated, the judge narrowed an eye. "So, Reverend, why did you want to see me? I assume it wasn't for the sake of old times back in Tennessee."

Brown shifted his position, his face hardening. "Judge, what the hell are you trying to do to me?"

To Brown's surprise, Judge Harthow seemed taken

aback. "I beg your pardon? Billy, what are you talking about?"

"This thing with the burned anthropologists. I'd assumed you'd been briefed."

"Well, yes, about the basics. The Bureau is looking into it. Washington Field Office has the lead, I believe. The report's on my desk."

"And you haven't read it?"

"Why, no, Reverend. One of my aides gave me a verbal brief on Friday. Said that the investigation was just forming up, but it looked like some sort of conspiracy."

"The *conspiracy* is *my* church!" Brown struggled to keep his voice down. "*Your* Bureau is after me, Judge. Now, I can see by your expression that you're a little surprised by that bit of information. Well, I suggest you take a close look at what your little bulldogs have sunk their teeth into, because it's *my* ass!"

Harthow looked perplexed, his long pale face slack. "You? You did this? Burned these people?"

"No, Judge." Brown shook his head. "What kind of a simple idiot do you think I am? You *know* me. We go way back, you and I, to the days when you were a starving young lawyer in Chattanooga and I was preaching out of a tent and living on canned stew. My ministry made the difference when you ran for the state senate. I'd like to think my little chat with the governor helped your appointment to the bench."

"Right on both counts."

Brown flashed a smile of agreement. "I covered your ass; you covered mine. Now, do you think I'd risk everything I've built to murder a couple of anthropologists just because they want to spout some evolutionist babble?"

The judge's slack face slowly tightened. "I had no idea. What have my people done?"

"A couple of your agents dropped in last week. I made special accommodations to meet with them. I thought they had a legitimate reason. One of my employees, a lady with whom I had a relationship, was murdered."

"The informant," the judge guessed, racking his brain for the details.

"That's her. Liz Carter. And, Judge, I'm more than willing to answer any questions your people might have, but it has come to my attention that my phones have been bugged, and people are asking into my personal life. I will *not* be harassed by people with a political agenda."

"Your phones . . ." The judge shook his head, a grimace on his lips. "I had no idea." He sobered then, that eye narrowing in the manner he'd taught himself while on the bench. "Billy, do you give me your word you had nothing to do with this?"

Brown reached into his jacket and removed his pocket edition of the New Testament. "On my soul, Judge, and by my faith in the Lord Jesus Christ, I swear I did not murder, nor cause to be murdered, any of those people. So help me God."

The world has turned cold and mean. All Abel has left is Chaser. He holds him close. The curly soft fur is

warm against his hollow-feeling chest. Veronica and Bryce have tried to be kind. They bought him candy and have been talking to him all day. A terrible sorrow fills their eyes when they look at him. But they are strangers. He doesn't answer them, turning his head away.

Mother will come back. All he has to do is believe. If he believes hard enough, it will happen. It has to.

Once again, he is in a strange place. A motel. It is in a little Wyoming town: Baggs. The rooms are small, the bed hard and carrying odors of too many bodies. Adults, he has noticed, don't seem to mind the smells. When he mentions them, they look at him as if the stink isn't really there.

His stomach hurts. Everyone is worried, and their fear infects him like a bad cold. He wants to go home. He wants Mother. Most of all he wants for everything to be the way it was.

His books, the snowstorm, his canvas bag are all gone. Left on the floor. Where is Mother? What happened to her? Even when he closes his eyes, he can smell the warm blood; it hangs in the air, metallic.

Where did that smell come from? Why won't they take him back to Mother? She would hold him in her strong arms. She would make everything okay.

What would he do without Chaser? His arms ache as he crushes his buffalo close. Chaser . . . Chaser . . . He weeps softly into the buffalo's fur, wishing—wishing so hard his head begins to hurt.

When sleep finally comes, monsters and the blond-headed man steal through his nightmares.

The place was called the Drifter: a motel, restaurant, and bar on the east side of the road in Baggs, Wyoming, just across the state line. The room rate had been more than reasonable. Veronica bit her lip as she studied Bryce from the corner of her eye. He looked terrible, his face drawn from the pain in his ankle. He had it propped on a pillow, his boot and sock off. Swollen to twice its normal size, it hurt just to look at it. Immediately after checking in, Veronica had raided the ice machine and packed one of the thin washcloths with cubes to cut the swelling. Now she alternately worried about Bryce and the boy.

"How is he?" Bryce asked softly.

Veronica straightened from where she bent over the bed. Abel had finally gone to sleep, his chunky body curled around the stuffed buffalo, its black eyes shining in the light cast by the lamp. He looked so pathetic with the covers pulled up to his chin. Abel's eyes were puffy from crying.

"Poor little guy." She sighed wearily. "How can you be that young and understand that someone would kill your mother like that?"

Bryce eased himself into a different position, extending his hurt leg and wincing. Lines of worry mixed with pain. He stared vacantly at the blank TV screen, then shook his head. "Whoever these people are, they need to be hunted down and shot like vermin."

She paced back and forth between the beds. The small room had been furnished with a nightstand, a TV on a dresser, a chair, and a cramped bathroom. The room was on the ground floor, the Durango just outside.

In the parking lot, a truck rumbled to life and someone whooped. Saturday night in Baggs sounded lively. Oil-field workers, and some wayward tourists, and bearded men in Western dress made up the clientele. If ever there was a place where no one would think to look for them, Baggs, Wyoming, was certainly it.

Veronica stepped to the phone where it rested on the nightstand between the beds. "Move over."

Bryce scooted sideways, groaning and favoring his swollen ankle. They both had aches and bruises from the slide down the garbage chute. She couldn't wait to take a good look at the black-and-blue marks when she took her shower.

Picking up the phone, she punched in the numbers for her mother's, dreading this call she would have to make. No doubt the police had already called Mary about the shooting. She would be worried sick.

The phone rang once, twice, and then, on the third ring, Theo picked it up. "Ferris residence."

"Theo?"

"Veronica? Thank God. Where are you?"

"I can't say. Is Mom all right?" She kept her voice down, afraid to awaken Abel.

"We're worried sick. Mary called me the moment the FBI called. What happened? Where are you? Are you all right?"

"It's them, Theo. The ones who killed Scott. They shot Rebecca right in front of us. She was just stepping into the room, and, God . . . I heard the bullet hit her."

"All right. Settle down. Tell me what happened from the beginning."

Veronica closed her eyes, composing herself against

the building panic. Point by point, she related the events, ending by saying, "So, we ran. Picked a direction that we thought they couldn't anticipate, and drove all day."

"I see." She could hear him writing on the other end. "We've got to get you to come in. I've been on the phone to the FBI here in Denver. They want to get your statement. The same with the Summit County Sheriff's Office."

"We didn't do it." She swallowed hard. "Bryce says the ballistics will prove it."

"I know. I know." Theo sounded reassuring. "Veronica, what is this all about?"

"We don't know. Something about genetics research."

"You mentioned someone named Bryce? Who is he?"

"Bryce Johnson, one of Scott's colleagues." She explained about Scott's phone call to Bryce. About finding him at the condo.

"Just a minute."

She could hear Theo place a hand over the phone and could make out muffled conversation. Bryce was watching her warily. "I'm talking to my lawyer," she reassured him.

Theo said, "Veronica? There's an agent from the FBI here. She has been waiting, hoping you would call. I'm going to put her on another line. In the meantime, you mentioned Abel. Is he with you, too?"

"Yes. He's safe. But it's been terrible for him. He's asleep now, but pretty shook-up." She laughed, aware that it was panic-driven. "So are we."

The phone clicked, and a female voice said, "Ms. Tremain? I'm Special Agent Jennifer Jones."

"Where's Joe Hanson?"

"That was one of the questions we were going to ask you. Have you heard from him?"

"No. I've been leaving messages at his number in Washington. And when I call his home phone, all I get is some strange man who isn't Joe. Bryce thinks he's Scott's murderer."

"I see. We'll check into that. Where are you?"

"You're not tracing this call, are you?"

Theo said, "No. But as a precaution, Veronica, I've given them permission to place a tap on the line for your mother's protection."

A fist tightened around her heart.

"Can you tell me what happened at the condo?" Jennifer asked.

Veronica nodded, as if they could see it. Then she told the entire story again, trying to remember every detail.

"The trash chute?" Jennifer sounded relieved. "That was a smart move."

"You can't feel the aftereffects."

"I can guess. Ms. Tremain, you said that Bryce Johnson is with you?"

"And Scott's son, Abel."

"Why didn't you go to the police?"

"My client doesn't need to answer that question," Theo said.

"It's all right, Theo." Veronica rubbed her face. "We didn't think we would be safe. These people, the ones who killed Rebecca, Bryce says they're professionals. We didn't feel safe at the Frisco jail. It was the first place they would have expected us to go."

"I see. Are you willing to come in?"

"God, yes! Life as a moving target isn't all that it's cracked up to be."

Jennifer gave her a confident chuckle. "I'm glad you've kept your sense of humor. I'm assuming that you're still in the West somewhere. I'm here in Denver. Could you come here?"

"We could. But not to the field office. Bryce thinks these guys are pros, snipers. They could be waiting for us there."

"We have a safe house. No one but FBI personnel knows about it. They won't be able to find you there. Do you have a pen?"

Veronica searched around, rummaging through her purse. "Yes."

Jennifer rattled off a phone number and an address in Lakewood, a suburb of Denver.

Veronica repeated it as she scribbled on a deposit slip in her checkbook.

"Can you find it?"

"I think so."

Jennifer gave her directions, adding, "It's a cul-de-sac. That way we can control access. Watch who comes in and goes out."

"I think we can be there late tomorrow." She glanced at Abel. "Can you find some 'Hank the Cowdog' books? I think Abel would like that."

"From the bag in the condo?"

"Yes."

"We'll see if we can't bring the canvas bag."

"That will make someone very happy."

"I'll be there all day tomorrow, Ms. Tremain. Mr. Bennet will be there, too."

"And then what? Look, I really need to talk to Joe Hanson."

"I understand. As soon as he calls in, I'll give him the message. But, after that, we'll have to deal with events as they arise."

"Do you have any idea who these men are who are hunting us?"

"No, ma'am. Take no chances. Until we have you in our protection, you're at risk."

"Yeah, we've figured that out."

"Between now and then, is there anything you need?"

"Besides fire suits and bullet-proof vests? How about a change of clothes? Some for me, some for Bryce?"

"We'll deal with that tomorrow."

"All right." She paused. "Theo?"

"Here."

"Tell Mother that we're all right."

"Do you want to talk to her?"

She winced, taking the cowardly way out. How could she answer Mom's questions? "No, Theo. Please. I can't right now."

"I understand. I'll see you tomorrow with Agent Jones. In the meantime, be careful."

"Understatement of the year, Theo."

She hung up, feeling gutted. Bryce gave her a sober look. "Do you think they'll throw me in the pen for stealing those license plates?"

"Who knows? I just want this over with."

He grunted. "Will it ever be over, Ronnie? We're not going to be safe until we figure this thing out. They don't have any leads, do they?"

"Agent Jones didn't give me that impression."

He sighed. "Well, if I have to be running for my life, it's a hell of a lot more pleasant to do it with a beautiful woman."

She reached out and took his hand. "I haven't said thank you for catching me in the chute this morning. I could have really been hurt."

He smiled, a warmth in his hazel eyes. "I wouldn't want you hurt." With that, he eased off the bed, wincing as he put weight on his injured foot. "I'm headed for the john. In the meantime, make sure the door is locked . . . and prop the chair under the doorknob." He reached into his waistband, withdrawing the pistol and laying it on the bed. "If you need this, the safety is off. Point, and pull the trigger. Do you understand?" His eyes bored into hers.

She looked askance at the pistol, then nodded, the memory of Rebecca's bloody body clinging like cobwebs in her mind.

"If I get up in the middle of the night," Bryce said, "I'll call out so you don't blow a hole in me."

She bit her lip and nodded.

He gave her a grin; then he hobbled to the bathroom door and closed it behind him. She picked up the phone again, dialing her home number. At the answering machine's message prompt she punched in her code. Three messages from the reporter, Skip Manson, repeatedly asked her to give him a call. The other messages were from friends offering condolences. Feeling miserable, she hung up the phone and stared at the little boy sleeping on the bed beside her.

Someone was singing in the gravel parking lot. She double-checked the locked door and safety chain and propped the rickety chair under the knob.

Resettling herself on the bed, she glanced at Abel, trying to understand how a little boy would deal with the destruction of his world when she couldn't deal with it as an adult. She reached out with an absent hand and fingered his delicate hair. So soft, so fragile.

An errant thought of Ben crept into her head, a memory of his smile and the devilment in his eyes. Why on earth would she think of him? A pickup roared outside, and she heard the clatter of gravel as the driver raced out onto the highway and into the night.

Plumbing cycled, and a moment later Bryce hobbled out and lowered himself onto the bed. He looked exhausted.

She took her turn in the small bathroom and stepped out, crossing to the second bed. Abel hardly stirred when she scooted him over and slipped under the thin covers. She reached out, over the ominous presence of the pistol, and turned out the light.

Lying there in the darkness, an aching loneliness settled on her. Thoughts of Ben spiraled out of her memory. Why him? Bryce had saved her life that morning. But for him, and his quick thinking, she'd be a corpse now, a ragged red hole blown through her body. And Abel? Would they have killed him, too?

Probably.

Reaching out in the darkness, she traced the cool outline of the pistol with her fingertip. Her memory filled with the image of Rebecca's face, contorted in violent disbelief, blood bubbling from her gasping mouth.

Abel shifted, unconsciously wrapping his short arms around her. She pulled him close, driven by some deep primate instinct, and held him, thankful for the warmth of his little body. What kind of human would do this to a child? Hurt him, try to scar him for the rest of his life?

Sleepless, she lay in the darkness, listening to the sounds from the bar. Waiting for the rattle of a key in the lock, or the soft rasp of a shoe on the cement outside the window.

CHAPTER EIGHTEEN

In the dream, Mother is talking to him, holding him close to her breast, her fingers running through his hair. A part of him, deep down inside, is afraid. When he looks up, Mother's head is missing, and the blond man stares down at him, smiling.

Abel's fear lances through him, and a warm rush drains out around his legs.

He awakens, smelling urine. The warmth still trickles down around his thighs. He is ashamed. Mother will be upset with him when she finds out.

In the darkness, he can sense a warm presence. Mother? No, a different smell, Veronica's, filters past his nostrils. He is sleeping beside Veronica . . . in a motel. Mother is missing, back at the condo where the blond man can find her.

He stifles a sob, reaches out for Chaser, and wiggles off the bed. His wet pants turning cool, he looks around in the darkness, fearing each of the shadows where the blond man could be lying in wait. Shamed by the smell of his pants, he hugs Chaser and tries to crawl under the bed. A wooden box stops him.

With terror rising, he scuttles into the bathroom and finds the darkest shadow under the sink next to the cool porcelain toilet. He huddles there in the dark and presses Chaser close. It is cold and miserable. He tucks Chaser under his chin and whispers, "Muuver? Whewe awe you? Pwease?"

Aspirin barely cut the pain. Bryce had to hobble to the Durango braced on Veronica's shoulder.

The cool Wyoming air refreshed him as he thumbed the button on the key remote and opened the passenger door. Abel, his buffalo tucked to his chest, watched with big blue eyes. Sullenly, he crawled into the backseat, propping himself between Veronica's black bag and his buffalo.

"Muvver says I need a caw seat," he said woodenly.

Veronica leaned into the back while Bryce propped himself against the Durango's side. "Here, we'll just have to make do with the seat belt, Abel. When we get to Denver, we'll get you a proper car seat so that you can be safe."

Abel averted his eyes.

Veronica straightened and gave Bryce an anxious

look. "I'm worried about him. I found him curled around the back of the toilet, and he'd wet his pants in the night."

"Ronnie, give him a break. He's had his whole world destroyed." Bryce eased his long body into the passenger seat. He took a moment, looking around. The Drifter motel had been painted a reddish brown with white trim. Baggs, in the daylight, was unlike anything he'd ever seen before: the streets graveled, large cottonwoods casting shade in the morning sun, and the houses with a weathered look. The big four-wheel-drive pickups—apparently the preferred mode of transport here—were mud spattered, rugged looking vehicles. Each had a rack in the back window that held a rifle, or sometimes a coil of rope. Most sported a dog or two in the bed, and they, too, had a half-wild and sturdy air about them.

What did people do here? How did they live their lives, and how different were they from the New Hampshire communities where he had grown up?

Veronica settled behind the wheel and adjusted the driver's seat. She flipped her long black hair out of the way and started the Durango. He watched her slender hand as it gripped the shifter and she backed around, gravel popping under the tires.

They headed north, crossing the Little Snake, a rocky clear-water stream lined with cottonwoods and willows. Just out of town, Wyoming 789 passed emerald alfalfa fields on the east, while rugged sandstone ridges, their slopes dotted with junipers, rose on either side of the valley. Overhead, the sky stretched in an endless cumulus-speckled blue. Within miles, the fields gave way to sagebrush and greasewood flats.

Her expression sobered. "Bryce, tell me about Scott's

research. What were you doing? Don't give me the technical stuff, just the meat of it."

"In a nutshell? All right, I would take restriction sequences from Scott's data, compare them with existing data from the Human Genome Project, and identify nucleotide frequencies and expressions that were different from the reported norm. He wanted statistical probabilities of gene recombinations. Even highly technical projections of chromosome crossover during prophase one. I made models of how the bivalent chromatids could be expected to affect the distribution of gene frequencies through—"

At her caustic glance, he said, "All right, in the plainest English, Scott would map sections of DNA, and I would compare them with normal human values. That is, did the stuff he was finding match what had already been observed in the literature. If it didn't, we cataloged it, computed the possible mixing of genes and how they would be expressed down through generations."

"And you found a lot of differences?"

He grimaced when the Durango bumped over a bridge and pain shot up his ankle. "Not many, but more than we were used to seeing in human samples. Some were new. Less than one percent."

"Where were the samples from?"

"Scott told me some were from bonobos. They're the least studied of the great apes. Another specimen came from Asia. A bit of frozen tissue from a mummy."

"That explains the samples Goldman told us about. That must have been bonobo material. Whoa! Abel, quick, look out the window. See those animals? They're antelope!"

Bryce turned to look where she was pointing, seeing the tan-and-white antelope standing behind the right-of-way fence.

Abel leaped up and peered through the glass. He seemed to see them immediately, watching intently as they passed, then following them over the backseat. Bryce couldn't help but notice the intensity of his interest. Like a dog seeing a rabbit, Abel's entire being had focused on the antelope.

"Antewope." He repeated the word over and over in his nasal drawl. "Like deew," he told Chaser when he settled back into the seat. He had squirmed out of the seat belt. Well, sure, the chance of dying in a traffic accident couldn't be discounted, but when men with guns were trailing you, it didn't seem such a big deal.

"Okay." Veronica had returned to the problem. "So you've got the nucleotides cataloged; computing the generations does what?"

"It gives you a predictive model to determine the possibility of Founder Effect on a limited population." He tried to look innocent. "You do know what Founder Effect is, don't you, Doctor?"

"Don't be an ass. It's the gene frequency that results from a limited number of ancestors. Those few initial ancestors cause a population to be different. A limited breeding potential, if you will."

"Very good. You get an A today, and the right to buy me lunch."

"Starve, *Herr Professor*." She studied the narrow strip of asphalt as it wound its way northward through sage flats and greasewood bottoms. They passed a sign indicating "Dad," a cluster of collapsed buildings on a rutted dirt road that led off into the Wyoming desert. It looked like a cheery place.

"So, if Agent Hanson is correct," Veronica asked, "why does Billy Barnes Brown and his church care if you map ape and mummy genes? It can't be that he's concerned about inserting human genes into a population of apes. The pharmaceutical companies have been doing that for years."

"You've got me there, Ronnie." He braced an elbow on the armrest and considered. A sign indicating the Overland Trail flashed past. He looked out across the rolling sagebrush, following the faint dirt track toward the horizon.

"You sent me a postcard from Rome one time."

The statement came at him from left field. "Yeah, I was hoping that Ben was a passing fad." It just slipped out.

He couldn't read her expression when she said, "I assume your intentions wouldn't have been honorable."

"Not in the least." To change the subject he said, "I was on the way to Tel Aviv. I had a catalogue of potentially deleterious genes that I had identified from Scott and Amanda's data. Avi wanted to see if any matched those observed in patients of his. Things he could manipulate to reduce birth defects in his clinic."

"Smooth transition, Dr. Johnson. I might buy you lunch after all. Just how good was Avi's lab?"

"One of the best in the world." He paused. "Avi was a strange man. A weird mixture of optimistic pessimism. He had a love-hate relationship with humanity. He loved the wonder of life, and despised the reality of adult behavior. You should have seen him. When he was working around pregnant women and newborn babies, he positively glowed. When he watched the evening news, he'd say, "Vee should nuke zem all!"

"Was he good at what he did?"

"Probably the leader in his field. After he turned from archaeology he dove into genetics with a vengeance."

"Why didn't he like archaeology? Tired of pseudo-science and guess-and-by-golly interpretation?"

Bryce fingered his chin. "He and Scott had a lot in common. They were both beat up by religious freaks." He considered that. "Watching them, you would have thought they shared souls despite coming from different corners of the world and different cultures. Sometimes it was spooky, as if they didn't even need to speak to know what the other was thinking."

"Tell me about Avi's work."

"What's to tell? His thing was genetic disease. Of all modern human ailments, it's the easiest to cure. Instead of taking a chance on a baby being born with cleft palate, or Tay-Sachs, just fix the DNA before the zygote divides and a child that would have lived in misery will be born happy, healthy, and hale. The initial cost of the genetic surgery is a pittance compared to what society will fork out in specialized care and support to keep a dysfunctional person alive during his lifetime."

"How could Scott's work affect that?"

"By tagging deleterious genes, the ones that lead to developmental problems. That's why Avi flew me over there. To compare notes and findings. On the side, I had a new program that allowed me to do more with his computer data."

"Why not run it here? He could have faxed the data, couldn't he?"

"Security, my dear Doctor Watson. You've got to understand, there's money at the bottom of all this. Avi's clinic held the patent on a whole slew of genetic surgeries. He didn't want the data I was manipulating to fall into other hands. It's hard to patent a procedure if someone else claims it first. If you register it, you get to license it and sell it. Then you can afford to do more research to find more means of treatment that you can patent and license."

She considered that. "Grim, isn't it? Dollars are the bottom line to research?"

"The way of the world." He tried to stretch his throbbing leg and gritted his teeth.

She gave him a concerned look. "We better get you into a doctor soonest. It's not broken, is it?"

"No." He hoped he wasn't lying. "Probably just a bad sprain."

"You ran like the wind yesterday."

"Impending death can do that to you." He wished for more aspirin. "What would an American fundamentalist church have against an Israeli clinic fighting birth defects and dealing with fertility problems?"

"Religion does odd things to people. Come on, Bryce, think about it. How many times does a case make the news where the parents won't allow an operation that would save their child's life? Maybe, in Billy Barnes Brown's book, Avi crossed some line. Barnes might believe that it's God's will that those couples be denied children, or that babies be born with trisomy twenty-one."

"Some kind of God that is."

"They think it's punishment for original sin."

He thought about that. "It's not enough, Ronnie. Not to begin a campaign of terror and murder. And why us? Why not the other clinics in Switzerland, the U.S., Canada, and England?" He looked out at the aqua-colored sagebrush flashing past. "No, this is something that strikes at the very root of their faith. I can't believe it's entirely ideological either. Money and power have to be involved. Something that Scott, Amanda, and Avi were doing threatened them enough that they're willing to murder over it."

He tapped his fingers on the armrest. *If we can't figure it out, we will never be safe again.*

The miles rolled under the Durango's tires. Veronica fought a constant battle with fatigue and sipped at cold coffee from a Styrofoam cup in the Dodge's drink holder. They had stopped at Flying J, a couple of miles west of Rawlins, refueled, taken a bathroom break, and bought overcooked fried chicken. Bryce had barely made it from the vehicle to the men's room and back without collapsing, his face drawn and pale. His ankle seemed to be getting worse, but he had brushed it aside.

She had taken Abel into the women's room and given him an askance look as he dropped his drawers and climbed up on the seat.

For years she had shared the facilities with other women and their children. Surprised, she realized this was the first time she had ever gone through the maternal drill herself. She smiled cynically. *Twenty-nine years old, and a whole new world is unfolding around you.* Well, so be it. The fact of the matter was that this was Scott's child. Her nephew. Blood kin. That sudden knowledge sobered her.

She raised her head to glance into the mirror. In the rear seat, Abel lay curled around his buffalo and had fallen into a deep sleep. What on earth had urged the little boy to go to sleep behind the toilet in the middle of the night? Why wouldn't he talk? He just ignored them, staring off into the distance, looking broken.

Come on, Ronnie. You know the answer to that. His mother is dead on a slab somewhere. He's terrified.

Bryce, too, was sawing logs. He reclined in the passenger seat, his head lolled to the side. How could he sleep with the throbbing agony in his ankle?

"Your intentions weren't honorable?" she asked gently, and smiled. "Too bad you didn't push it." And she shook her head. As if, at the time, she'd have been completely recovered from smooth, sexy Ben Tremain and his slick ways.

That had to have been another crooked phase of her maturation process. From hoodlums to Ben, she'd craved the excitement, misleading herself the entire time by thinking men had to be daring, given to excess, to be exotic and romantic.

She tried to picture how Ben would have reacted at the condo. He would have collapsed into a pile of writhing jelly. Worse, his first instinct would have been to rush over and help Rebecca—where a bullet would have killed him on the spot.

He would have reacted just like I did. That brought a tingle of horror to her soul.

She studied Bryce, remembering that first time she had met him. Bryce had been in a white sweater, handsome enough, and reserved. He had talked to her, but almost shyly, and he hadn't been any great shakes on skis. She had literally cut circles around him, appalled by the number of times he fell down. His references to the "ski hills" in New Hampshire had amused her, too. She had thought his New England accent unmanly.

You were young then, she reminded herself—as if six years were an eternity.

"God, Ronnie," she whispered to herself. "Have you been a damned fool all of your life?" She sucked on her lips, frowning as another in the endless stream of semis roared past in the left lane.

She glanced south to stare longingly at the timbered mountains. How many years had it been since she had ridden up here with Ben? It had been a fast ride on a Kawasaki ZX-12R, powering around curves at the tires' traction limits. They had streaked past a Wyoming Highway Patrol car doing somewhere around 85 on a curve. Ben had opened the big Kawasaki up on the straight south of Riverside. The speedometer needle wavering at 150, they rocketed to the Colorado border faster than "Motorola overdrive." There they had picked up a leisurely and legal pace all the way to a cheeseburger at the Elk Horn Café in Walden.

So, what was the difference between bravery and "damn-fool stupid," as Scott would have said?

She glanced uneasily at the man in the seat beside her.

CHAPTER NINETEEN

Ramsey hated the seventh floor, the sanctum sanctorum of the Federal Bureau of Investigation. Worse, this was Sunday afternoon, and that added to his wariness. The seventh floor belonged to the "meat seats," as some of the field agents had started calling the upper-echelon bureaucrats and political appointees. Ramsey had always considered himself a cop. Being called into the rarefied air on the seventh floor of the Hoover Building on Pennsylvania Avenue left his hair prickling.

He absently tugged at his trousers to make them hang a little straighter and juggled his briefcase with his other hand. The elevator hummed and slowed, the light blinking onto the number seven. It stopped, swayed the slightest bit, and the doors opened to the reception area.

Ramsey checked in, and was directed to a small wood-paneled conference room. An expensive walnut table sat in the middle of the aggressively air-conditioned room. For a brief instant, Ramsey wondered if this was the room where Daniel Potts got the news that he was being sacked over Ruby Ridge. The thought didn't contribute to a sense of ease. Nice chairs were positioned around the table. Three dark televisions with a sophisticated electronics console covered one end of the room. Telephones and computers lined the wall to the right. At the other end, a small refrigerator and stainless steel coffee bar provided refreshments.

A young woman, perhaps twenty-five, stood at the coffee-maker, and the faint aroma of French Roast carried in the filtered air. She turned—a petite brunette with close-cropped hair, an upturned nose, and blue eyes—and glanced his direction. "Agent Ramsey?" she asked. "Coffee? Or maybe a soda?"

"Please, coffee." He checked his watch. Fifteen minutes early. He took the cup she offered and was directed to a chair at the table. From the plastic ID card, he noted that she was a technician.

"I'm Mary West," she introduced. "The others should be here soon. If you need anything, sing out."

"Thanks."

He placed his briefcase on the table and pulled out the chair, too charged to take a seat. Instead he wandered over to the communications system and studied it absently.

He turned when Tom Powell, director of the Criminal Investigations Division, and his assistant director, Karen Sues, entered the room, each with a notepad in hand. Powell was another of the "real agents"—a man who had spent time working cases and busting bad guys. He was tall, thin, and wiry, with graying hair. Karen Sues had made her reputation in white-collar crimes, chasing through mountains of bank records, financial transactions, and corporate structures to scotch money laundering. She had broken up more than one drug ring, and she provided the kind of goods to the Justice Department that had nailed down a perfect conviction record.

"Jack, good to see you again." Powell walked across the carpet to extend his hand.

"Hi, Tom. It's been a while since Baltimore." Ramsey referred to a raid they'd made on a suburban house that served as the nerve center for a drug ring. Their "dynamic entry" had netted the ringleaders without a shot being fired.

"Pleased to meet you, Jack." Sues offered her hand. "I've heard a lot about you. All of it good." She must have been in her forties, had a professional look, her short hair waved. Sober brown eyes studied him through thick glasses. She wore a conservative gray suit.

"Good work on that Ramirez case." Ramsey responded. "I had the good fortune to nail a couple of the guys in Miami." He glanced at Powell. "What's this all about?"

"The Ferris case has been bumped up to a higher profile. The director wants a heads-up on where we're at."

As if on cue, Louis Harthow stepped through the door. He had served as a federal judge in Tennessee, a big party donor before the White House picked him for the top-dog position at the Bureau. Tall, with white hair and a distinguished bearing, he wore an expensive suit and carried a leather-bound binder under his arm.

On his heels came Harry Benning, the assistant director, a portly man reputed to be a political climber. Benning had a reputation for having spent more time at parties than on investigations, and for reporting in sick when field operations were going down. He had artfully managed to sidestep any circumstance where snap decisions had to be made, and had avoided any situation where criticism might have been leveled against him. His field reports were notorious for having been literary masterpieces that said nothing, but made you feel good about them anyway. He, too, was immaculately dressed, a suit worth two grand over a starched white shirt, dark blue tie, and dark suspenders. His belly had grown along with his career.

"Good afternoon." Harthow crossed to offer his hand to Ramsey. "It's good to meet you, Jack. I've read your file. An outstanding career."

"Thank you, sir." Ramsey tried to take the judge's measure. Nothing betrayed itself behind his hooded blue eyes.

Fujiki and Axelrod entered last, each carrying a folder under one arm. They ran the Headquarters Division for Domestic Terrorism, and had been briefed the week before by Ramsey and Joe Hanson.

The technician saw to everyone's needs, providing bottled water for Judge Harthow. Ramsey noted that Benning waited until the director's decision to also choose bottled water.

"All right," Harthow said as he settled himself into the chair at the head of the table. "Let's see what we've got." He looked at Ramsey. "Where are we on this Ferris thing?"

Ramsey leaned forward in his seat, unsnapping the latches on his briefcase and withdrawing the file. He outlined the information that Joe Hanson and Mitch had provided. Detailing the case to date took him twenty minutes.

"So," Harthow said, leaning back in his chair and extending his feet, "does this strike you as the actions of a serial killer?"

Ramsey shook his head. "No, sir. We think it's a well-organized and financed operation. With the exception of Elizabeth Carter, these people have all been tied to some sort of anthropological research. We think they took the Carter woman down because she came to us."

"And that is your only tie to Billy Barnes Brown?" Harthow's eyes fixed on Ramsey's. "This woman's word?"

Ramsey shrugged. "That and her employment. Hanson talked to her, and the next morning she was dead."

"And where is Special Agent Hanson now?"

Ramsey felt heat under his collar. "We don't know, sir. He didn't show up for work on Friday, and he hasn't checked in since. Mitch Ensley is trying to find him as we speak. He's not at his home, and we don't know where else he could be. His family and friends haven't heard from him."

"I see." Harthow frowned. "You said that the Tremain woman is coming in today?"

"That's right. Bob Dole, the Denver SAC, is setting up a safe house. From the report I received this morning, Tremain talked to one of Bob's people in Denver and said she'd come in. She has Dr. Johnson and Rebecca Armely's child." Ramsey went on to explain the adoption of Amanda Alexander and Scott Ferris' little boy.

"What has Denver discovered about the Colorado shooting?" Benning asked.

"The Denver Evidence Response Team is on scene. The preliminary they gave me just before I came over here was that Rebecca Armely was shot in the back, severing her spinal column at about the seventh thoracic vertebra. The bullet took out the aorta, the heart, and exited through the lower sternum. They got the slug, a .30-caliber one-sixty-eight-grain boattail—probably a Sierra, but that's a guess for the moment. They have a second bullet hole in a wall below the window and think the slug is in the couch. The best assessment is that the shooter was outside, probably in the parking lot given the reconstructed trajectory.

"Tremain claims that they slid down the garbage chute to escape. Given the buckling of the tin, that seems to check out. The ERT doesn't think the scene was contrived. Ms. Armely's Honda and Dr. Tremain's BMW are still in the lot. Our people are going over both vehicles."

"Anything to connect them with the church?" Harthow asked.

"No, sir. As I've said, the only thing we have on that is Elizabeth Carter's word through Agent Hanson."

"And he's missing?" Benning asked, an irritated look on his face.

Ramsey said nothing.

"I'm bothered by this connection with the Reverend Brown." Harthow's expression had turned grave. "Under no circumstances do I want you, or any of your people, to mention any connection to the Reverend, or the church. You haven't, have you?"

Ramsey shook his head. "To date, the press has been a little slow on the uptake. They have mentioned FBI involvement in the Alexander and Ferris murders, but haven't tied them to the Carter hit yet."

" 'Hit'?" Benning asked, his face bland. "At this stage, I don't think we should be referring to her murder in those terms. It's a loaded phrase."

"Yes, sir."

Harthow tapped his long fingers on the tabletop. "I met with the Reverend yesterday, and listened to his concerns. I share them and have serious doubts about the implication of Reverend Brown's church in this affair. I first met him in Tennessee. He was a good man then, and he's a better one now. He has personally assured me that he has had nothing to do with this. I take him at his word."

He fixed them, one by one, as he looked around the table. "Let me tell you about the Reverend Brown that I know. He did a great deal of good; his ministry is active in most of the prisons. On Friday I was invited to dinner with him at the White House. He and the president were talking about a new outreach program for inner-city drug abusers. The church is going to fund employment. Nothing big, just picking up trash, cleaning graffiti, recycling programs, that sort of thing. The idea is to provide gainful employment and teach job skills to people who have never had the opportunity." Harthow fixed Ramsey with a steely gaze. "It's a win-win situation."

Tom Powell looked up from the notes he'd been taking. "And what if we do discover a connection?"

Harthow opened his hand. "Obviously, if something concrete turns up it will change the equation. Until that time, all we have is hearsay based on a missing agent. Isn't that right?"

Ramsey said nothing, but couldn't help grind his teeth.

"For the moment, people, I am directing you to remove this phone tap. I realize that everyone went through channels, and you thought you were doing your jobs. The Reverend has given me his word he's not involved, but since one of the victims was one of his people, he's willing to be of any assistance he can. You are to respect him for the man he is, not some drug-dealing hoodlum. Understood?"

"Yes, sir." The mantra was echoed around the table. Ramsey felt his ears burning.

"Meanwhile"—Benning slid a manila file several inches forward on the tabletop—"I've been reviewing Special Agent Hanson's file. He had some trouble a couple of years back. Almost flushed his career down the john before he claimed to have dried out. What are the chances that he's gone on a bender again?"

Ramsey stiffened. "I'd call that unlikely. Joe Hanson has been one of the best agents I've worked with. If he was back in the bottle, I'd have seen it."

"Twenty-five-dollar-a-glass scotch at the Mayflower? We checked his credit card charges and matched the receipt to the bar tab."

Ramsey shifted uncomfortably. "He was making an initial contact. He said that Elizabeth Carter ordered the scotch."

" 'He said,' " Harthow interjected. "I'm not doubting your agent, Jack. It's just that with a case this politically sensitive, we don't want to get caught in the proverbial wringer."

Powell glanced at Karen Sues, then said, "I think we should dedicate more resources to cracking this. We've got a mountain of material to sort through: the victims' phone calls; their travel, activities, and acquaintances; professional rivalries; interviewing family members; checking credit card use —"

"Let's not blow this out of proportion," Harthow replied stiffly. "If we open the throttles we could start a locomotive that we won't be able to stop. Until we have something concrete, and by that, I mean good hard evidence, I don't believe it would be wise to dedicate additional resources to this case." He looked around. "As it is, I see this thing chewing up a lot of budget. I know that you people in the field can become enamored of an investigation, but let's be honest, shall we? In the end, I have to justify our expenses to Congress. We're already into extra expenses with travel and man-days. I don't imagine this safe house in Denver is going to be cheap either. I'd like to see this woman and her friends brought in, debriefed, and cut loose just as quickly as possible, before the accountants start screaming."

"Yes, sir," Powell replied, expression neutral.

"What about the shooter?" Ramsey asked, feeling uneasy. "And the killings to date? With respect, sir. We're not dealing with Bubbas here. The killings have been professionally conducted. No evidence has been left at the scenes. The break-ins at the university offices were perfect. Not so much as a fingerprint or a jimmied lock. It's been antiseptic."

"Your point?" Benning asked. He had read the direction that Harthow's wind was blowing and was ready to bird-dog.

"The point," Bruce Fujiki replied, "is that politics and the budget aside, Ramsey's right. If it was a Bubba hit, or some sort of academic professional jealousy, someone would have slipped up somewhere and given us a solid piece of evidence. So far, every crime scene, including the one in Israel—and they've had a crack team on it—has been sterile."

"That's another thing," Harthow said. "The State Department considers Dr. Raad's death to have a high-probability connection with Hamas. I think we should respect their expertise here."

Powell and Sues had funny looks on their faces, but said nothing.

"If that is indeed the case," Fujiki said carefully, "I think it would argue strongly that we dedicate more resources to the case. If Hamas is involved—"

"But that is unlikely, isn't it?" Benning asked. "If I had to bet, I'd say that Hamas took Dr. Raad down, and someone here decided that copycat killings would be blamed on them."

Ramsey clamped his jaws in disbelief. *That's about the dumbest thing I've heard in years!* Harthow couldn't have it both ways. Hamas, and not Hamas.

Harthow checked his watch. "That will be it for today, ladies and gentlemen. Thank you all for taking time from your Sunday schedules to meet with us. I would appreciate daily updates."

"Yes, sir," Powell said as Harthow stood, smiled, and collected his folder. He strode toward the door the way a man did when he had a purpose. Benning, like a little beagle, trotted hot on his heels.

Ramsey and the others had stood as the bosses left. His adrenaline had risen, his muscles charged. He lowered his eyes to the folder on the table beside his briefcase, trying to make sense of it all.

Powell stepped around the table, meeting Ramsey's eyes. "Jack, you know more about this than anyone. Honestly, what have we got?"

Ramsey hesitated, trying to interpret Powell's expression. Hell, this guy had spent his time on the street. He knew how the world worked. The Tom Powell who had gone through the door first in Baltimore was this same guy. "All I've got are pieces, Tom. I don't know how they fit together yet, but my gut tells me it will make a really nasty picture."

Powell nodded, glancing at Karen Sues, sharing some secret communication; then he turned his attention back to Ramsey. "Your gut, huh? Aren't you the guy who says that guts work better on chicken-salad sandwiches?"

"That's me. But I've also been in this business long enough to know that something, somewhere, always cuts us a break if we've got the people in place to find it."

"People," Fujiki said quietly. "That might be the tough part." He glanced at Powell.

"For the moment," Powell said, "my hands are tied. Give me something solid, guys, and I'll see what I can do. In the meantime, I'll make some discreet calls and forward what you've got to date down to Quantico. You never know who might have 'spare time' on his hands and need a project."

Ramsey gave them a wry smile. There were times when the bureaucratic bullshit really frustrated him—and others when he was damn proud to be part of the finest law enforcement agency in the world.

"I'll find that piece," he promised, "no matter what it costs."

Those words would come back to haunt him.

CHAPTER TWENTY

TIME HAD NEVER PASSED SO SLOWLY. JOE HANSON STARED up at the cement ceiling. He lay on a metal cot, irritated that it had been screwed to the floor with thick expanding bolts. A single forty-watt bulb hung from the ceiling. The door, set into the concrete walls, sounded like solid steel when he thumped it with his knuckles, and the heavy knob defied every effort on his part when he tried to turn it.

A plastic bucket sat in the corner, noxious now with his waste. The water supply consisted of a gallon plastic jug. The only food had been from a brown paper bag filled with tins of sardines. Hanson hated sardines more than any other food in the world. Hunger had forced him to clamp his nose and swallow the salty oily swill.

Ventilation came from a can-sized hole out of reach near the roof. He had listened at the hole and heard nothing. Nor had anyone come when he shouted. He would have liked to look through it, but couldn't. He had thought about using the honey bucket to stand on, but the flimsy plastic wouldn't support his weight.

They had left him in his shirt, pants, and shoes, the latter without laces. He had no idea where his billfold, watch, gun, belt, keys, or other possessions had gone. He wasn't even really sure how he had come to be locked here. The last cogent memory had been arriving at his home. He vaguely remembered the answering machine telling him something. And then the nightmare memories of being sick, of talking to strangers . . . Well, were they real? Had he done that, or did his memory play tricks on him?

He had tried to escape, had stomped on the tin sardine lids, bending the lip back and forth until he had a thin sliver of metal to try and slip the lock with. It hadn't worked despite hours of endless trying.

So, here he lay, resting after his latest effort to build a reasonable knife out of sardine tins. He welcomed anyone to try. Without tools, and only the weight of his body, he ended up with flat blobs of soft metal. He had tried to undo the springs from the mattress, but his fingers weren't pliers. Nor could he take the welded bed frame apart to make a club.

The best he could have done was slit someone's wrist open with the edge of a tin. Now, if his assailants ever came back, all he'd have to do is get them to extend their wrists and allow him to saw until he severed arteries.

How credible was an unkempt agent brandishing a sardine can? "FBI! You're under arrest."

He burped, the heavy pungency of sardines in his nose. Maybe that was it: wait until they stepped in the door and belch. That ought to lay anyone out flat.

His training included close-quarter combat, and he had the requisite skills to take down a matched opponent. That option wasn't currently available.

He didn't know when he drifted off, but the click of the door brought him awake, and in an instant, he was on his feet.

The door had swung open, allowing him a glimpse of

another concrete room, this one with a table sitting in the middle of the floor.

"Joe?" a familiar voice said.

He stepped quickly to the side of the door, waiting, hoping that someone would step through.

"Joe, we don't want to hurt you. Step into the middle of your room and drop to your knees."

"What if I refuse?"

"We will close the door and leave you there. We don't have much time, and I can't tell you how long it will be before we get back this way. It could be two weeks, maybe a month. How is your water holding out? Do you have enough sardines to see you through? What happens if the light burns out?"

Yeah, well, that was a point.

"Joe, do you want to get out of there?"

"Actually, I was just growing used to the place. I think I'll change the colors, though. I've always been partial to baby blue."

"Step over to the middle of the room, Joe. Face the wall and drop to your knees. Cross your ankles. Place your hands behind your head. That's the only way. Or we'll lock the door again."

He hesitated, and figured, what the hell. He wasn't going to find out what this was all about in a bunker. He stepped to the center of the floor, lowered himself to his knees, and followed their directions. He hardly heard them until cuffs clicked on his wrists. Another set were slapped on his ankles. So much for the patented FBI kung-fu karate escape.

"Stand up, Joe."

Doing so was difficult. He had to prop himself and

scoot his feet under him. Standing, he turned, seeing the blond man and an older dark-haired man. Something about him . . . "I know you."

"It's been a while," the older man said. "Into the room, please. Don't make us hurt you." He carried a length of rubber hose in one hand. From the way it hung, it looked weighted.

Who was this guy? Joe shuffled into the second room on baby steps bounded by the length of chain on his ankles. The table was wooden, heavy, and a single chair rested beside it.

"Have a seat, Joe."

"It would be rude to take the only one. I think—" The rubber hose slammed across his shoulders, staggering him and flashing pain through his body.

"I'm not in the mood for repartee," the dark-haired man said flatly. "Sit."

Joe gasped and sat, then took a quick survey of the room. Just like the other, but larger. The place looked like a storeroom of some sort. The single lightbulb cast shadows as the two men moved to either side of him. The dark-haired man caressed the weighted hose.

"Okay, cut the crap," Joe said, tingles of worry in his gut. "What's this all about?"

"I'm not sure you'd understand." The dark-haired man hitched a seat on the corner of the table and studied Joe thoughtfully. "We're not in a particularly good mood, Joe. We've had some disappointments over the last couple of days. We wouldn't appreciate it if you disappointed us, too."

"I wouldn't think of it."

"Good." The older man nodded, and the blond man

reached for something that crackled. Stepping into view he carried a paper sack, the kind with twine handles. From the sack, he removed a bottle of expensive Macallan scotch. "Just to prove that there's no hard feelings, we're going to have a drink together."

The silent blond man withdrew two plastic cups.

"Gee, I hate to be a party pooper, guys, but I'm off the juice."

"Juice is good for you," the dark-haired man said as he broke the seal and twisted the cork from the bottle. Pouring a finger in the first plastic cup, he set it on the edge of the table. Pouring the second half full, he extended it toward Joe's lips.

Joe butted the cup with his head, spilling scotch.

Instantaneously, the rubber hose caught him across the top of his head, the painful rap bringing tears to his eyes and blurring his vision.

"That's not nice, Joe. We could have bought something cheap, but a good single malt, well, you should be more grateful."

Hanson gasped, feeling the lingering sting from the blow. "What if I don't drink?"

"We'll beat you into submission and use a tube. Either way, you're going to drink this bottle."

"Scotch . . . on top of sardines? You're a sadistic bastard."

"Drink."

"Why?"

"It's for your career, Joe." The dark-haired man leaned down, meeting his eyes. "Joe, think. You have a choice to make. You can leave here, your career in ruins, and have a nice life. You've still got family who care for you.

Betsy and the kids. You can still go to that Fourth of July picnic. Or, we can tie a plastic bag over your head and go out for a cup of coffee. When we come back in a couple of hours, it will be dark. We'll take you out back and bury you in the forest where no one will ever find you. Come on, Joe, this is a chance. We don't want to kill you. It would be inconvenient for us."

"Yeah, I can see concern dripping from your pores."

The cup was extended again, and Joe, playing for time, made a face as he sipped. The familiar taste of the liquor burned down his throat. At the same time, he tensed his arms and legs, straining against the handcuffs and the shackles. The pain kept him centered as the dark-haired man offered another drink.

"Why ruin my career?" he asked as the man poured another glassful.

"Because, like so many, you're a good agent, Joe. Just like I was."

Hanson squinted up against the light. "I thought I knew you."

"Five years ago. The Oakdale siege. You remember what happened?"

"Yeah, you were on point on a Critical Response Team. I remember Oakdale, the Bureau's other black eye, the one that didn't get any press. Some kind of wacky Christian family that set up in an apartment and proclaimed the end of the world. Claimed to have a bomb. Somebody shot a kid . . . a little girl."

"She was dressed in camys." The dark-haired man gave him a hollow look. "I came around a hall corner and she pointed a pistol at my head." He glanced away. "Plastic. A squirt gun."

Hanson remembered: Ted "Leopard" Paxton. An Army Intelligence officer with a great track record working for the military Special Operations Command. After retiring from SOCOM, he'd joined the FBI, worked for a couple of years training agents at Quantico, and wanted to gain field expertise. A computer and electronics expert, his students still raved about what he could do with surveillance gear, jammers, bugs, and computer systems. He'd turned in his resignation even before the little girl had been placed in a body bag.

"So, why are you here . . . trying to get me soused? Come on, Ted, what's this all about?"

"After the incident . . ." He looked away.

"They cleared you of responsibility."

"What do *they* know?" He shot Hanson an irritated look. "I'm working for the other side now."

"Killing people is God's work?" He could feel the warm haze spreading from his gut.

"You haven't read much history. Suffice it to say that when you've lost everything, God's agents pay better." He reached into his pocket to produce a stainless steel cigarette lighter, a fancy one emblazoned with a black shield. In the shield's center, a grinning white skull stared out, a slim arrow piercing it from side to side. From a vest pocket, he produced a package of Player cigarettes. Lighting one, he took a drag and exhaled.

"Hey, gimme one of them," Joe said brazenly. He'd never smoked in his life, but this was a way of prolonging the inevitable intake of alcohol.

Paxton lit a cigarette and set the lighter down before he passed it to Hanson. The smoke almost blinded him. He hated cigarettes more than he hated sardines. It took all of his effort not to cough as he sucked a little into his mouth.

"I think he needs to drink," the blond man said with a heavy Southern accent. "We don't have a lot of time."

"No, I suppose we don't." Paxton offered the glass again, and Hanson was forced to reach up and take the cigarette out of his mouth. They didn't have time?

"What's the hurry? And where am I, anyway?"

"In the arms of the Lord. Want to sing 'Onward Christian Soldiers?'" Paxton made him take another swallow. "Come on, Joe. You can do better than that. Swallow up. The old Joe Hanson could drink like a fish."

"My gills dried out. So, what? You get me sloshed and drop my sorry carcass on the Bureau doorstep? Just like that?"

"No, Joe." Something somber hung behind Paxton's dark eyes. "You're going to drive home. Just like nothing happened."

"Yeah, why don't I believe you?" He could feel the alcohol now. And Paxton just kept offering that cup of poison. Joe tried letting some leak out the side of his mouth, and Paxton withdrew the cup long enough to lift the weighted hose and smack it along the side of his head.

"Joe, we don't have time for foolishness. We're only doing this because unlike my pal, here, I don't think you're in league with Satan. If I believed him, we'd just kill you."

Lying bastard. He could hear it despite the ringing in his ears. He drank the next time the cup was offered. So, they wanted him drunk? He'd be drunk. He let the muscles of his neck relax, but the endless stream of scotch kept coming. The cigarette was out, and he shifted, stuffing it into the top of his pocket as Paxton refilled the glass.

"Enough," he muttered, aware that he didn't have to pretend. "I'll pass out. Stomach's close to empty, you know?"

Paxton leaned down. "You weigh close to one-seventy. Keep drinking. We'll tell you when you've had enough."

"Macallan," he mumbled, letting his head droop. "Good stuff."

"We thought it appropriate. A bit of symbolic synchronicity."

"You're the two who took out 'Lizabeth Carter?" He let his head loll sideways. "Why nail her to the floor?"

Paxton shook his head, offering the scotch. "Just drink, Joe."

Time was running out. The booze was going to numb his wits beyond any kind of reliable function. He lurched to his feet, Paxton stepping back reflexively. Hanson spun, tripping on his shackles, and fell sideways. He clutched at the table and crashed to the floor, hoping that Paxton hadn't seen the quick action.

"Sick," he told them. "I'm gonna puke." As he waited for the length of hose to strike him, he stuffed the palmed lighter into his pocket and moaned.

The blow didn't come.

"Is that enough?" the blond man asked.

"Half a bottle of eighty proof? I should think so. Let's give him about fifteen minutes to let what's left soak in. You go bring his car around, and I'll prop him up and top off his tank."

Joe felt hands grab the back of his neck and swing him around. Paxton was staring down at him, blocking his body with one knee as he tilted the bottle to Joe's lips and forced more of the amber liquid into his mouth. Rather than gag and choke on it, Joe drank, trying to spill as much as possible down the side of his mouth.

He knew this feeling, had been intimate with it for so many years. Then his stomach convulsed, and he threw up on Paxton's sleeve.

"Shit!"

"Sorry," he said, and turned to spit onto the floor.

When the blond man returned, he was wearing latex gloves and carrying Joe's possessions. Hanson felt the keys, coins, and beeper being placed in his pockets. The belt was threaded through the loops on his pants, and his shoes laced up. Finally, they slipped his watch onto his wrist.

Hanson had trouble focusing when the blond man threw him over a shoulder and walked out into the night. A large steel-walled church stood against a forest backdrop. Hanson could hear singing, see the lines of cars parked in the lot, lit by floods.

The blond bent down, opened the passenger door to the Taurus, and settled Hanson into the seat. Then the blond did something strange. He slipped a rainsuit over his clothing and tucked a shower cap onto his head before climbing into the driver's seat and starting the car.

"Gonna shoot me? That what the rainsuit's for? Worried about bloodstains on your clothes?"

"Shut up," the blond drawled.

Hanson had lost track of Paxton, but as the blond started the Taurus, turned on the lights, and drove into the night, headlights appeared, shining into the back window.

The blond drove like a madman, tires shrieking as he rounded corners, taking dirt shortcuts. "Y'all don't want to try and jump out, now," he said. "At this speed, it'd kill you."

"Yeah," Joe rasped, his stomach in turmoil. "Come on. Wha's the suit for? You gonna do me? Bang! Quick shot to the head?"

"It keeps fibers off the seat." The blond slung them, tires shrieking, around a corner before he turned up a snaking road. "The gloves won't leave prints."

"I'll still get you." Hanson frowned, feeling the world spinning. How could he drive when he couldn't even stand up?

The Taurus braked to a halt; Hanson pitched forward against the dash, fighting to hold on with his manacled hands.

"All right, Joe." The blond reached out to unlock the handcuffs and bent down to unshackle his feet. "Get in and drive. Home's that way." He pointed down the steep mountain road.

"Where . . . where am I?"

"The hills, western Virginia. Take that road back to Washington." The blond man popped the hood release and stepped out of the car. He quickly bent over the running engine and did something Joe couldn't see before he slammed the hood.

A big white Suburban had pulled up behind them.

"Go!" The blond man leaned down. "Climb into the driver's seat, and go!" He stuck a pistol into the window. "I'll count to five, and blow your head apart!"

Hanson took two tries to wiggle his body into the seat. He blinked, fought the urge to be sick, and slipped the

Taurus into gear. As the car began to move, a gunshot rang out, the muzzle flash yellow in the darkness. Reflexively, Hanson stomped the accelerator. The Taurus sped forward, heading down the long straightaway.

His heart was hammering, his vision blurry. The car continued to accelerate, even when he took his foot off the throttle. He stamped on the brakes; the car slowed, the engine struggling against inertia. He seemed to be winning the battle. The smell of burning brakes came rolling up from the floorboards. Then he was into a corner, across the centerline, swerving. Headlights flashed at him, and he cranked the wheel back, aware of trees rushing past his window.

The Taurus began to pick up speed, the brakes screaming, losing the battle between endless gasoline, gravity, and the thin layer of overheated pads.

A stone railing appeared on his left, the sort that highway engineers placed on scenic highways. Far out in the night, he caught a faint glimpse of lights in a valley far below. To his right, trees blurred where they grew out of the rocky mountainside.

A big black arrow filled the diamond-shaped yellow sign. Curve. Twenty-five miles an hour. The speedometer was climbing past sixty. Joe took the only option, cranking the wheel toward the hillside. The Taurus dropped into the ditch, bounced, and gyrated before crashing into the vegetation. The steering wheel twisted out of his hands, and then the world turned upside down.

Momentum and gravity hammered Hanson into the roof. He wasn't conscious when the Taurus crashed through the stone barrier and plunged down the rock-studded side of the mountain.

CHAPTER TWENTY-ONE

❖

ON THE LATE AFTERNOON OF THE NINETEENTH Veronica eased the Durango into the cul-de-sac on De France Drive. She pulled in at the right address: a white two-story house with natural-stone facing on the lower floors. Evergreen shrubs and a small tree gave it a perfect suburban camouflage. Immediately behind the house the base of Lookout Mountain rose into the night.

"We're here," Veronica said wearily. "Look at this place. Four hundred and fifty grand at a minimum. We're paying way too many taxes."

She glanced at Bryce. "How are you doing?"

He opened his door, and the dome light illuminated his ashen face. "I don't know if I can walk."

"Whewe awe we?" Abel asked from the backseat. His first words in hours.

"Home away from home, kiddo." Veronica stepped out and stretched her tired back muscles. Abel squirmed out behind her, his buffalo filling the crook of his right arm. He stared around with uneasy blue eyes, taking in the mountain, the blinking red lights of the radio towers, and the glowing white *M* on the mountain.

"What that?" He pointed.

"That's the symbol for the Colorado School of Mines. It's just over there." She pointed north. "In a town called Golden."

Abel's low forehead lined. Then, just as if a switch had been flipped, he turned off again, face blank.

A woman opened the front door and stepped out onto the cement porch. She walked quickly down the driveway, a smile on her face. She wore a midlength skirt, white blouse, and a loose wool jacket. "You must be Dr. Tremain. I'm Special Agent Jennifer Jones, Federal Bureau of Investigation." She offered her identification. "Did you have any trouble getting here?"

"Hello, Special Agent Jones." Veronica shook hands, gazing briefly at the plastic-coated picture ID. "Why is it that you are all 'special' agents?"

"Damn," Bryce said as he hit his foot against the door frame.

"Are you hurt?" Jones asked, stepping around the front of the Durango.

"Ankle," he muttered, and between Veronica and Jennifer was able to hop into the house. Abel followed uncertainly behind, holding his buffalo in an iron grip.

They maneuvered Bryce to a couch and lowered him. The living room boasted a glass-fronted fireplace, white walls, a drape-covered picture window, light blue carpeting, and comfortable-looking stuffed chairs.

"Nice place," Veronica said. A well-furnished dining room could be seen through the archway. The polished wood table and chairs looked Oriental—and expensive.

"Drug property seizure." Jones propped her hands on her hips and looked around. "Normally I spend my time in the back of a surveillance van. One of my better assignments was squatting beside a trash can in an alley downtown. I was supposed to be homeless. Hell . . . I was. At least for that three-week assignment."

She didn't look the part now, her tawny hair tied back, her blue eyes thoughtful. Veronica decided she was a striking woman.

"And who are you?" Jones leaned down toward Abel.

He scuttled behind Veronica's knee and peeked out warily, his thumb creeping up to his mouth for reassurance.

"This is Abel," Veronica introduced. "Rebecca's son. Abel, say hello to Agent Jones. She's here to take care of us."

Abel might have been mute. He curled his fingers into Veronica's pant leg and tightened his grip on his buffalo.

"It's okay, Abel." Jones gave him a big smile that he didn't seem to buy. "We'll take a few days to relax, and then we'll become great friends."

When Jones straightened, Veronica asked, "Where's Theo? I thought he'd be here."

"He had an 'emergency.' Something about another one of his clients. Someone named Hardesty." Jones shrugged. "We won't be discussing the case until he arrives."

"Right. Then . . . what next?"

"First, let's have you pull your vehicle into the garage, out of sight. Second, unpack. I'll show you where your rooms will be. Third, we'll have a doctor take a look at Dr. Johnson's ankle. Even from here it doesn't look good."

"You ought to feel it from my end," Bryce growled.

Abel stuck to Veronica like she was made of Velcro. He climbed in beside her when she started the Durango. He watched the garage door rise, attention rapt. When she eased into the garage, he craned his neck, trying to see everything, and then stood in the seat to watch the door close behind them.

"Pretty cool, huh?"

He nodded as he climbed out of the Durango and waited as she retrieved her black bag from the rear seat. When she stepped up into the kitchen, he was right behind her, his buffalo dangling by one horn.

The kitchen looked like something out of *Better Homes and Gardens*, too perfect to have been lived in by real people. Actual breathing humans spattered grease, spilled orange juice, and left smudges when they wiped up with soiled dishrags. Here, everything sparkled.

She followed Agent Jones through the dining room to a stairway with a polished walnut banister. A golden angel with a trumpet—apparently an antique—stood on the newel post. The stair steps were oak with a red Persian carpet runner down the middle. Ornate brass rods held the thick carpet in place.

Jones led her to an upstairs bedroom with draped windows. The white-walled room had an airy feel. A quilt-covered king bed with an ornate headboard filled one wall. Her one nylon bag hardly justified the walk-in closet. A dresser with a tall mirror sat beside an entertainment center that included a big-screen TV and stereo system. The bathroom, in understatement, could be called plush, with a black marble sink and a contour-molded toilet. The glass-enclosed slate-tiled shower sported golden knobs and a swan-shaped spray head.

Abel took this all in, his eyes fixing on things one at a time as if committing them to memory. The momentary notion came to her that he seemed to process information differently than most children, pausing and studying each new thing in his environment. He sniffed at things, as if he could smell them the way a dog did.

"This will be home," Jones told her. "The rules are: No phone calls without my approval. The drapes remain drawn at all times. You are not to go outside unless I have approved it, and even then, we'll have to wait for the right conditions. I'm here to keep you alive and safe. To do that, I need your help."

"You've got it."

"I need you to understand. You're not a prisoner, though after a while you may begin to feel like one. You, Dr. Johnson, and the boy are material witnesses in the death of Rebecca Armely . . . and possibly in the murders of your brother and Ms. Alexander. You are part of an on-going criminal investigation in which a party, or parties, may try and profit by your deaths. That is why you must understand that the rules in force here must be obeyed, even if they seem dumb and nonsensical. Believe me, we have reasons for everything we ask of you."

Veronica's deep-seated fatigue gave way to sober reality. "Yes, Agent Jones, I do understand."

She nodded, spreading her arms. "Well, in that case, make yourself at home. You look tired. But, before I leave to take care of Dr. Johnson, do you need anything? Food? Something to drink?"

"We stopped at a fast-food joint in Fort Collins." She glanced at the bed. "No, just a hot shower and a good night's sleep."

Jones bent down. "Abel? Come on, I have your room ready." She smiled. "I have a surprise there for you."

She started out, but Abel just clung to Veronica's leg. Sighing, she cast a longing gaze at the shower and, Abel hovering close behind, followed Jones down the hall to the next door. Here, a smaller bedroom with a double bed and draped windows had been prepared for Abel.

Jones stepped over to the bed and picked up a familiar Sam Weller's book bag.

"My bag!" Abel cried, breaking his silence. He rushed forward, eyes alight, and opened it to peek inside.

"I think it's all there." Jones winked at Veronica, and together they retreated to the hallway.

"I'll check on you in a bit," Veronica called, but Abel seemed not to hear, taking a glass globe from the bag and turning it. To Veronica's surprise, he watched, rapt, as snow swirled over a mountain scene.

"Shower time," Veronica said. "I'll take a peek at him before I go to sleep."

"He's a cutie," Jones replied as they walked back down the hall. "I've never heard a child talk with that nasal tone."

"He has trouble with *r*s and *l*s, too." Veronica paused at her door. "He's had a pretty tough couple of days." She hesitated. "Have you ever tried to tell a little boy that his mother is dead?"

Jones nodded. "Once. I know the feeling. Listen, I've got another patient downstairs." She lifted an inquiring eyebrow. "I assumed he'd want a room down the hall?"

Veronica nodded. "You assumed correctly." She stepped into her room and closed the door. Good for Jones. Professional and discreet. Veronica walked to the bathroom door, paused to pull off her boots, and shucked her blouse over her head. In front of the mirror she unsnapped her bra and slipped out of her jeans. She made a face at the bruises on her white skin—relics of the slide down the chute. Reaching into the glass-encased shrine, she turned on the hot water and fiddled with the cold until the temperature reached perfect. She was in the act of sliding her panties over her hips when she froze.

Abel stood in the bathroom door, his buffalo dangling from one hand, his canvas bag over his shoulder. His expression could only be called wounded.

"Abel!" she cried. "What are you doing here?"

"Scawed."

She could barely hear his voice. He looked miserable as he lowered his eyes.

"God, Abel. You don't just walk in on women in the shower."

His crestfallen expression crumpled into outright panic, tears welling in the corners of his eyes.

She felt like something she'd scrape off of her shoe. "It's okay, Abel. I'm a little tired. Just . . . just go wait. Uh, in there. On the bed. Pet your buffalo. I'll . . . I'll be there in a little while." He remained frozen in place, head down, his fingers clutching the buffalo as if it were a life raft. "Go on, Abel." She led him out; reluctantly, he followed.

She finished undressing and entered the shower, closing the glass door behind her. Stepping into the spray, she almost gasped as the warm fingers of water massaged her tired flesh. A new bar of soap lay on the holder. She might have been in religious ecstasy as she soaped herself and used the bottle of shampoo to wash her long black hair. For a simple eternity she stood, allowing the hot water to work its magic. Fifteen minutes later, she screwed the knobs closed.

She could see him through the glass. He hadn't made

a sound, or she hadn't heard him over the rush of the water, but Abel had huddled himself on the floor beside the shower door, his blue-eyed attention centered on Chaser's gleaming black eyes. He was talking softly to the buffalo, but Veronica couldn't make out the words.

Her heart melted at the sight. He looked so pitiful, crumpled into a ball like that, the buffalo his only friend in the world. She remembered how she had found him that morning, curled in the space behind the motel room toilet.

God, Veronica, what do you expect him to do? Just shoulder through as if he were a man? She bit her lip and cocked her head, wringing out the thick mass of her long black hair. He didn't look up when she pushed the shower door open and reached across for one of the luxurious maroon towels.

Wrapping her hair, she took the second towel and dried off, keeping a wary eye on Abel to see if he'd peek at her. At the young age of four and a half, such male proclivities apparently hadn't been aroused from his latent DNA. Trust to biology and time; they would.

She tucked the second towel around her breasts, then stepped out, looking down. "Abel? Are you okay?"

He said nothing, his nervous fingers curling through Chaser's thick fur.

She squatted down to reach his level and placed a finger under his chin to raise his listless eyes to hers. She could have lost herself in that vulnerable stare. "Abel, kiddo, you have to talk to me. I can't help unless you tell me what's wrong."

"I want Muvver," he mouthed the words. Then, "Scawed."

"It's been pretty tough, huh?" Veronica lowered her voice. "I'm sorry, Abel. God, how do I make you understand when I don't myself? We just have to go on. Your mother isn't coming back. She can't, although she loved you so very much."

His large eyes seemed to expand, taking in part of her soul. That pinched expression remained triste. Somehow, different and remote, it accented the protruding planes of his face.

"You're one very brave boy, Abel. Did you know that?" He avoided her eyes while his chubby fingers fumbled absently. His book bag lay beside him, and he reached for it, pulling the straps into his lap.

"Come on. Let's go put you to bed. I think Agent Jones—"

"Nooo," he drawled, a pleading in his eyes.

She hesitated, remembering how reassured she had felt in the motel room when she'd slept beside him. "Yeah, sure. You can stay with me."

His face was smeared with grease, and he'd gotten something sticky tangled in his hair. She pointed at the fancy Jacuzzi tub across from the shower. "But if you're staying with me, I insist that the men in my life be clean. Bath first . . . or you sleep in your own room."

She could see the indecision, and then he stood up, pulled his stained shirt over his head, peeled off his little red sneakers, and unabashedly took off his pants. He looked up at her, as if waiting for instructions.

It took her a moment to realize that he probably didn't know how to work the faucets.

"You have a doctorate in anthropology, Ronnie.

Women have been raising children for thousands of millennia. This can't be that difficult."

With the water running, Abel walked over to the toilet, studied the lid, and lifted it. Then he climbed up, almost slipped in, and seated himself. After he urinated and slid off the seat, he studied the toilet, found the handle—a depression molded into the fancy john's lines—and flushed. He stared with rapt fascination as the water in the bowl rushed around and sucked itself away in the siphon.

"He pees sitting down," she murmured to herself. It struck her that he'd urinated like that in every bathroom she had taken him into that day. Only then did it settle into her head that little boys, raised by women, didn't have any other role model.

All right, Ronnie, how are we going to deal with this? Simple as cake on Sunday: She'd tell Bryce, and he'd explain the realities of masculine nature to the little boy.

Abel trotted over to the big Jacuzzi, a frown lining his forehead. "Big," he said uncertainly. He glanced at her, a question in his eyes. "Dwown?"

"I won't let you drown." She fingered her chin. "Think of it like a swimming pool. Your very own private one."

He nodded, braced himself, and carefully backed into the tub. Seating himself in the water, he looked up at her, the patient question reflected in his expression.

Got it! Rebecca gave him his bath. She made a face of her own and reached for the soap. As she bent down to scrub the child, she wondered what this relationship was going to be like.

She rapidly discovered that wearing a towel around the house as a wrap was different than wearing one when you had to bend over a child and give him a bath. She ended up dressed before the process was completed. Nevertheless, they made it through the bath, and she extricated him from the tub. He was watching as the water drained away. Moving things seemed to fascinate him. She got him dried off and collected his clothes on the way back to the bedroom.

"No PJs," he said, looking up at her. She hated that look. It demanded answers, as if she just had them on tap the way a bar had beer.

"Nope," she replied. "No PJs." That problem went both ways. She slept naked. Last night she had slept in her clothes. She considered the big opulent king bed with its satin comforter and overstuffed pillows. Somehow, the idea of climbing into that in dirty clothes smacked of mortal sin.

She turned, pointing at his pile of clothes. "Put your underwear on."

He wiggled into his shorts.

That was better. She, herself, could manage in bra and panties. Somehow that made it all right until they could get clothes.

The ordeal wasn't over, she discovered as she turned off all the lights except the one on the nightstand. Abel crawled into the middle of the big bed, his buffalo and sack in his arms. He fished around in the sack and produced a little book, saying firmly, "Wead, pwease."

Veronica arched an eyebrow in a look that would have scorched Ben down to his toes. "It's late, kiddo. I'm half dead."

"Muvver always wead to me." He extended the book toward her.

She surrendered, figuring that five minutes wouldn't

hurt a thing. And if it made him sleep better, it might just be well spent.

"Whewe is Muvver?" the plaintive voice asked.

Veronica closed the book on her finger and met his confused eyes. "Abel, something terrible happened to her at the condo. She . . ." God, how did she say this?

"Is Muvver . . . Is she dead?"

Veronica nodded slowly, holding his eyes, willing him to understand. "Yes, Abel, she is. I'm so sorry."

He blinked. "Will she be aww wite?"

"No, Abel. She won't. Not ever again. Do you understand?" She swallowed hard, remembering the empty gaze in Rebecca's dead eyes. "Being dead is forever. She can't come back, no matter how much she loved you, and you loved her."

"Nevew?"

"Never."

His lips worked, and the frown lined his forehead. He didn't seem to understand, and then he pointed at the book. "Wead tiw Muvver comes back."

Unable to contradict the simple faith in his voice, she settled down with "Hank the Cowdog" and after the first few pages, couldn't help but laugh at Hank and Drover's dilemmas. Within the five minutes she had allotted herself, Abel drifted off.

Veronica put the book down and studied him. He lay on a pillow, his head turned toward the light. His mouth hung open, and she could see his white deciduous teeth and pink tongue. He looked so vulnerable, oddly cute despite his protruding face and that nose; the organ dominated his face. She could see blue veins through his

delicate white skin. What was it about him that kept prodding something buried deeply in her memory?

Maybe something to do with Scott? This was his child,
after all. Though Rebecca claimed she'd been the genetic
donor. Why didn't that make sense?

Bryce bit his lip and tried not to scream as the doctor,
a young man named Andersen, poked, prodded, and bent
his foot around. Sweat started to pop out on Bryce's forehead. Still, he had to be manful about this. Not only was
Veronica upstairs, but the pretty FBI agent, Jennifer
Jones, stood just behind the doctor, a frown lining her
forehead. It just wouldn't do to scream, wail, and blubber
in front of a tough G-lady like her.

He endured, squirming around on the couch and sinking his fingers into the thick cushions.

"Well," Andersen said, looking up through horn-rim
glasses, "it's not broken, though there may be some compression fracturing of the inferior fibular epiphyses. The
ligaments demonstrate distress, and the area around the
lateral malleolus exhibits considerable edema." He
picked up an aluminum clipboard and began jotting notes
with a Mont Blanc pen.

"That's Dr. Tremain's area of expertise. Unless it involves genetics or statistics, I speak English. What did
you say?"

"You have a bad sprain." Andersen stared up across the
rims of his glasses. "I'm going to put you in an air cast for
two weeks and prescribe a strong anti-inflammatory." His
displeased look turned toward Agent Jones. "I would be

happier if I could obtain a radiograph. Just to be sure that no spurs are loose and floating in the synovial fluid."

At her blank look Bryce said, "He wants to make sure no bone fragments are in the ankle-joint juice."

"And you only speak English," Andersen chided.

"Cryptology was a hobby of mine."

"Evidently, humor was not." Andersen stood and ripped a slip of paper from his notebook. To Jones, he said, "That should cover everything you'll need. If it doesn't improve within ten days, bring him by the clinic."

"Thank you, Doctor." She took the paper and led Andersen to the door. After she closed it behind him she turned, studying the scrawl. "It's really not a joke. Honestly, they can't write a lick. Look at this. I've seen graffiti on bridge abutments that made more sense."

Bryce leaned back into the thick cushion of the couch. God, he was tired. "How're Veronica and Abel?"

"Asleep." Jones walked over and looked down at him. "Like you should be. Are those painkillers Dr. Andersen gave you kicking in?"

"Not yet." Bryce gestured toward the door. "What do you do, keep him on retainer?"

She nodded. "I've worked with him before. The man has no sense of humor, but he's good at what he does. I think he likes the excitement of working with the FBI and never knowing who he's treating, or why they are where they are."

Bryce grunted.

Jones looked at the prescription. "I'm off to the nearest pharmacy. Do you want to climb the steps now, or wait until I return?"

"Now," he said, and yawned. "I might have dozed all day, but I didn't really sleep well."

She nodded, taking his arm and pulling him up. Together they hobbled up the stairway and down the hall to the room that would be Bryce's. The embarrassment of his predicament was tempered by the arm he had around the attractive agent's shoulders.

The place had a double bed, half bath, television, and bureau. The drapes were pulled, and the lamp on the nightstand cast a yellow glow over the room. It looked like heaven.

"Will you need anything else?" Jones asked.

He shook his head. "No. When do I get the third degree, thumbscrews, and electric shock treatment?"

"The what?"

"Interrogation. I hear you people have been after me for over a week now."

"Tomorrow. Get a good night's sleep, Dr. Johnson. You'll think better in the morning."

He smiled at her, wondering how he'd gotten lucky enough to be locked in a house with two beautiful women. "You're not what I pictured an FBI agent to be like."

"My husband would be glad to hear that."

"I'll bet you tell that to all the fugitives that cross your path."

"No, only the dangerous ones."

"That's flattering. Is Abel all right?"

She nodded. "Sleeping with Dr. Tremain."

"Good. I'll see you in the morning."

She indicated a black box on the nightstand. "If you need anything, press that. It shouldn't take more than twenty minutes for a round-trip to the pharmacy." She closed the door behind her when she left.

Bryce hobbled into the bathroom, used the facilities, and peeled out of his clothes. He eased himself onto the bed and arranged his leg so that his swollen ankle lay free of the covers. Satisfied, he reached over and turned out the light.

His head on the pillow, he tried to sleep. The image formed in his mind: Abel, snuggled up next to Veronica. He could imagine her warm body, the smell of her hair, almost feel her soft curves conforming to him.

Stop it, fool! He'd drive himself insane.

Images of her kept popping into his head. He could see the sunlight in her hair. His memory had engraved that little smile of hers, the one that lived at the corner of her full lips. Sometimes, when the circumstances were just right, he could see her soul mirrored in those wonderful blue eyes.

That led him to remember how she had looked in that turtleneck. How her hips swayed when she walked, and what it would be like to slide that fabric off of her smooth skin. His male hormones began to respond at the mere thought.

"Cut it out," he grumbled to himself, and masochistically lifted his leg and let his sprained ankle drop to the bed.

Yep, there was nothing like a spike of good old-fashioned pain to kill outright sensual lust for a woman. He tried to blink back the tears.

Immediately, the image of Abel cuddled in the hollow of Veronica's arm, just under those perfect breasts, formed in his head.

He thought about kicking the wall with his hurt foot.
It was going to be a very long night.

CHAPTER TWENTY-TWO

THE SMELLS ALWAYS BOTHERED JACKSON RAMSEY. ANTI-
septic chemicals, acrid preservatives, and maybe even the
smell of the people themselves, cold in death—they combined to knot in the back of his nose. The warp and weft
of mortality swirled around him. An image conjured itself
in his mind: that of a winding sheet, corrupted and gossamer, like cobwebs from an old cellar. No matter who
you were, one day you'd be laid out in a place like this.
Today the notion had been driven into his brain like a
cold steel spike.

The hallway could be classified as institutional: gray
walls, white linoleum floor with occasional black squares
to break the pattern. A black plastic kickboard trimmed
the sides. Overhead fluorescent lights cast everything in
soft white.

Stainless steel gurneys waited patiently, parallel
parked against the walls. Cold and mindless, they
mocked him, tools of the death trade, mindless of the

loads that were slipped from one to another and wheeled down these sterile odor-filled halls.

Mitch Ensley stood beside one of the featureless steel doors. He wore a dark blue suit, white shirt, and conservative tie. The toothpick in the corner of his mouth was little more than splinters. Ramsey tried to read the agent's weary expression, to see through to the grief and desperation that Mitch was hiding so well. Ensley and Hanson had been a team for almost six years now. They owed each other their lives. Mitch had been the strong crutch that Joe Hanson had leaned on to whip his alcoholism. God, the guy must be dying inside.

"Hi, Jack," Mitch greeted soberly and ran a nervous hand over his close-cropped peppercorn hair. "Glad you could make it this quickly."

Ramsey's gaze went to the door, and Mitch nodded. Ramsey stepped into the room: a standard autopsy lab with a battery of lights, hoses, magnifying lens, and the other exotica of dismemberment. The stainless steel table, grooved with drains, supported Joe Hanson's supine body. He looked oddly crooked, shoulders canted to the right. An effort had been made to lay the right arm straight, but the shortness of the limb and atypical bunching of the upper arm indicated it was broken.

"Son of a bitch." Ramsey stopped short. Joe's face had been bruised on the left side, the cheek crushed. His eyes were half open, staring sightlessly up into the overhead lights. The black hair that matted his waxy white chest gleamed as if oiled. His side bore the hematoma imprint of the steering wheel.

Ramsey shook his head, and through the other smells,

he caught the faint whiff of whiskey: sweet against the noxious reality of the morgue.

"This isn't Joe," Mitch said softly as he came to stand behind Ramsey.

Ramsey lifted an eyebrow, turning to meet Mitch's sober gaze. The stark illumination betrayed the faint wrinkles at the corners of Mitch's eyes; they shot chiaroscuro over his dark skin. "Looks like Joe to me."

"I mean, it's not like him to do this." Mitch's eyes narrowed, mouth hardening, as if struggling with something he couldn't quite lay a grip to. "Joe stopped drinking. I mean, cold turkey, boss. He was an alcoholic, sure. But this doesn't make sense. Sometimes alkys fall off the wagon, but why would Joe? The only time he ever got in trouble in the past was when he *wasn't* working."

"His witness was burned before his eyes. He didn't make a big thing of it, but I knew he took it hard."

Mitch shook his head with a greater obstinacy. "He wasn't some rookie straight out of the Academy, Jack. What happened to Elizabeth Carter was just one of those things—and Joe knew it. He was ready to find the sons of bitches who did it and take them down."

Ramsey turned his attention to the corpse. Outside of the bruises, Joe looked unnaturally pale, the blood having pooled in the low spots: the shoulders, the buttocks, the backs of the thighs. He avoided looking at the cruel blow to the side of Joe's head.

Mitch stepped beside him, pointing a dark finger at Joe's right wrist. "I'm not a forensic pathologist, Jack, but that's a ligature mark. From the width, a handcuff. You'll find a match on the left wrist. If you take a sharp look at the ankles, you'll see two more."

Ramsey bent down to stare at the hollow white flesh. Under the dark hairs, he could see the blue-black of bruise, and yes, it did look like the marks made when a suspect fought the cuffs. One, on the left shin above the ankle, had even cut the skin.

"Joe knew they were going to kill him," Mitch said evenly. "He didn't want us misled."

Ramsey straightened, pulling his cell from his pocket. He tapped in the coded number. On the fourth ring, a voice answered.

He got his SAC, Peter Wirthing, in the Washington Metro Field Office. "Peter? This is Ramsey. I'm at the Rappahannock County morgue. I want the ERT here ASAP. We need a complete autopsy, so send our best forensic medical examiner and a team to retrieve a vehicle. I need a work-up on Hanson's personal effects and car. I want to know everything . . . everything."

After confirmation he killed the connection and gave Joe Hanson a short nod. "We'll see, Joe." He looked at Mitch. "Personal effects?"

"His weapon and cell were in a black nylon bag in the backseat. At least they were when the car was turned over so they could use the Jaws machine to extract Joe's body. Two bottles of scotch were also found in the car. Joe was traveling downhill from Mount Marshall toward Front Royal at a high rate of speed. He nearly ran one car off the road, then apparently took the side of the hill rather than miss the curve."

"That car, did they report it?"

"Yeah, a Sarah Smith of fifty-five hundred Ames in Browntown. She was headed home when Joe came blasting down the mountain. She called the sheriff's office on

her mobile to report a drunk driver at twenty-one fifteen
hours. They had dispatched a car when a second call
came in at twenty-one twenty-three hours that someone
had had a wreck on the Mount Marshall road. They
didn't bring Joe down the mountain for another five
hours. We got the call at five-thirty this morning."

"We need his clothes, hands, hair, everything bagged."
Ramsey fingered his chin, looking into Hanson's slack
face, trying to see him as he was: alive, healthy, that calm
assurance in his expression. "I don't like this, Mitch."

"No, sir."

"Everyone who gets close to this investigation ends up
dead. From here on out, we're playing under new rules."

"How's that?" Mitch raised a quizzical eyebrow. "I
thought they plucked your feathers in that meeting yesterday. We going crossways with the director?"

"Take a hard look at Joe and tell me we're not. But,
discreetly, Mitch, discreetly."

"Jack." Mitch lowered his voice. "What have we got?
Huh? Joe's blood alcohol content is going to be right up
there around point two, point two-four, something like
that. If any attorney worth his salt sticks that in a jury's
hand, they'll hammer us flat with reasonable doubt."

"I know, Mitch, I know. Just find me one good solid
chunk of evidence. That's all I need."

A green-smocked young man walked into the room
carrying a black plastic sack full of clothing. "Here's the
personal effects you requested, Agent Ensley. As you requested, I wore gloves when I bagged them."

"Thanks, Sam. I appreciate that." He indicated a gurney at the side of the room. The technician placed the
plastic sack on the polished steel surface. "You might tell

the coroner we're having some of our people come in for the autopsy. We would also like to have some of them look at the car."

"That won't be a problem." Sam gave them a curious look. He probably didn't get many FBI agents in the building.

"That will be all. Thanks for everything you've done."

Sam nodded, leaving reluctantly.

Ramsey looked at his watch and took his notebook from his pocket. He flipped through the pages until he found a number, then punched it into his cell phone. After several seconds, he heard a sleepy voice answer, *"Special Agent Jones."*

"This is Jack Ramsey, Washington Metro Field Office. I'm just calling to see what the status is on Dr. Johnson, Dr. Tremain, and the boy."

"They got in last night and are still asleep. Johnson has a badly sprained ankle, but other than that they seem all right. They were pretty tired."

"Are you going to debrief them?"

"As soon as they are awake and we get some food into them. I've got a team coming at ten hundred MST. Anything in particular I can do for you, sir?"

"Keep them safe, Ms. Jones." Ramsey hesitated. "You might have your SAC give me a call. We've got a special situation here, and it might get a little close to the cuff. We need to keep a low profile on this one. If Dole could give me a call, I'm sure we can work things out."

"I see." A pause. *"I'm sure that I can do anything that needs to be done."* Another pause. *"Is there anything I should know?"*

Smart lady. "The case agent on the Ferris murder has been found dead, Ms. Jones. The circumstances are, well, shall we say, suspect. You and your team need to be aware that we are dealing with some very dangerous individuals. They seem to be particularly proficient at cleaning up loose ends. I think that the people in your custody are at considerable risk. Our perps are not your run-of-the-mill Bubbas."

"I understand, sir."

"I'll be on the horn to Dole. Maybe he can detail you some extra people."

"Yes, sir."

"If you need anything, or if anything breaks, give me a call." He rattled off his personal number.

"Yes, sir. Thank you, sir."

"I'll be in touch." Ramsey ended the call and thought for a moment. He tapped the button for Powell's office. "Tom? Ramsey. I'm at the Rappahannock County coroner's. Joe Hanson was killed in a car wreck last night. He's lying here on a table looking pretty sad."

"What happened?"

Ramsey outlined what he knew to date. "Tom. Something's fishy. You know it, and so do I. Mitch is here, and he doesn't buy the fact that Joe dove headfirst into a bottle."

A moment of silence passed. *"Hanson was a good man. If this ties into the Ferris murders . . ."*

"Yeah, the timing is sure coincidental, isn't it?"

"What are you thinking, Jack?"

"I want to go to Denver. Will you give Pete Wirthing a call? Maybe help him to find a way to authorize my travel voucher? He'd do it for me on his own, but if this gets really political, I don't want his butt in the wringer on my account."

"What's in Denver?"

"Johnson, Tremain, and Rebecca Armely's boy. Tom, we've got too many UNK-UNKs here." That was Bureau slang for too many unknowns.

The long pause stretched. *"If I'm going out on a limb, I'd really appreciate it if you didn't hand the director a sharpened saw."*

"Robert Dole is SAC in Denver. I'll have a discreet talk with him. He's been around for long enough to know how to trim a tree without breaking his neck."

"Go, Jack. This thing stinks. But you be damn careful."

"Yeah, I just wish someone would have said that to Joe Hanson."

"If I'm in the middle of this, I want a complete report. I'll talk to Peter so he'll know I'm in the loop."

"S.O.P., Tom. And thanks."

"Have a nice trip. If it looks like they took down one of ours, we'll land on them like a ton of bricks."

"I'll be in touch."

Ramsey ended the call and punched in his office number. When Betty answered, he said, "Betty? Could you run over to the SAC's office for a travel authorization, and then down to Travel and get me a ticket for an afternoon flight to Denver?"

That taken care of, he sighed and looked at Mitch. "If it's Billy Barnes Brown, he'd better be right about having a direct line to God. He's going to need all the help he can get."

In the darkness before morning, he awakens. He lies comfortably in the warm bed. This mattress is new. It smells of freshness. For a moment, he wonders where he is, thinks of Mother, and then remembers: Veronica says that Mother is dead. How can he believe that? She can't die. Not when he needs her.

Veronica said that Mother is never coming back. He tries to understand, one part of him sad, another part sure that Mother will find him again. He doesn't know what to believe.

Beside him, Veronica's deep breathing is rhythmic. Her smell isn't Mother's; it reminds him of the terrible things that have happened, that continue to happen.

Nightmares have tortured him through the long night. In one, he was huddled next to Mother's cold body while the blond-headed man leered at him from the shadows. Fear, like cold rain, had left him weak and trembling. In another, he was clinging to a branch in a high pine tree, and the blond-headed man reached out and started shaking the branch until Abel lost his grip. He screamed in fear, that sickening feeling of his stomach rising in the long fall. He jerked awake in the instant that his body hit the ground.

Now, in this strange place, fear coils inside him. He inches away from Veronica, stopping to finger her long black hair where it spills over the pillow in a gossamer web.

Veronica isn't like Mother. She doesn't have that same love in her eyes. She doesn't talk to him the same way. Her voice softens, but not into the coo that Mother talked to him with. Can he trust her? Or will she leave him?

His longing for Mother is a physical pain. How can she be dead? Why would God let this happen to him? Mother always told him that if he was good, God would take care of him. He looks up at the shadowed ceiling and wonders where God is and what he did wrong that God would let Mother die.

He reaches out and pulls Chaser close, unhappy that his buffalo has gotten so far away in the night. Tugging his buffalo along, he slips out of bed and walks over to the window to peek out past the drapes, half afraid the blond man will be out there, looking up in the moonlight.

But he sees no man. The mountain rises immediately behind the house. In the faint light before dawn, he looks at the bushes, grass, and rocks. He can sense them, imagine himself in their shadows, smell the grass, even through the window.

Movement. Two deer are browsing just beyond the chain-link fence in the backyard. They seem peaceful, and suddenly he wishes he could be them. Unafraid, beautiful, and serene. His vision narrows until the deer are all that he can see. They are free.

He wonders if he will ever be that way again.

"Mother?" he whispers. "Please, don't be dead. Come back."

A single tear creeps down his cheeks as he watches the deer. The silence in the house presses down on him, squeezing his broken heart. In fear, he tucks Chaser close and retreats to the bathroom, and the darkest cor-

*ner where evil can't find him. There he huddles, afraid
that even in the darkness he may not be safe. The
empty ache and loneliness build. His tears drop onto
Chaser's fur, where they are absorbed and vanish.*

Ramsey held a Styrofoam cup half full of cold coffee.
Joe's body lay supine on the table, his chest opened in a
classic Y incision. Something had changed for Ramsey.
This was no longer Joe Hanson. Just splayed meat.

The forensic examiner waited, leaning against the autopsy table next to the county coroner. Both wore gowns
and surgical masks. On occasion, they dictated notes into
small recorders they carried, but the actual cutting, the
fluid and tissue sampling, was being done by the FBI's
medical examiner. A courtesy to the Bureau since Hanson
had been one of their own.

A pale and shaken Mitch Ensley stood to Ramsey's
right, watching as the next phase of the investigation
began.

In the room's sterile light, FBI technicians laid Joe
Hanson's clothing out on the stainless steel table. Stating
their names, the place, the case number, and the nineteenth of June date, they had begun their analysis. They
worked in smocks, caps over their hair, plastic gloves on
their hands.

Joe's shoes were stained with blood, and one of the
technicians grunted. "Huh. This isn't right."

"What?" Ramsey asked, craning forward.

"The laces." The technician pointed with a pen tip.

"When laces are in shoes, they develop a polish where they run through the eyelets. Joe's are all out of sequence. Like the laces were relaced. And here, in the heel, we've got a piece of gravel. I'll have a geologist run down its origin."

"That will prove . . . ?"

"Maybe nothing." The technician bent back to the task, using a magnifying glass to study the soles. "I think I see fibers here. Most likely to match the floor mats in the Taurus. We'll take sticky-tape samples from the leather and soles and put them under the scope as a matter of course. We'll cross the blood, but it's probably Hanson's. He bled a lot in the wreck."

Ramsey sipped his cold coffee while the technician bagged the shoes. Too many things were coming up wrong. The autopsy had proven what Mitch suspected. Hanson had been restrained, probably from handcuffs. The bruises were deep—clear to the bone. His stomach contents had consisted of sardines and scotch. And not many of the former.

"Joe hated sardines," Mitch had said, his dark face grim. "He wouldn't eat the damn things. Not on a bet. Believe me, I spent enough time in the field with the guy. He said they made him want to throw up."

So, why had Hanson eaten a few sardines and drunk a bottle of scotch? From the stomach contents, and the blood alcohol level, it had to be close to a bottle. The guys from the lab said it was good stuff, too. Their WAG, or wild-assed guess, was that it was an expensive single malt. Probably Macallan, like the bottles recovered in the wrecked car.

"When Joe drank," Mitch had said, "it was any old rotgut. He wasn't a Macallan kind of guy."

The technician unrolled the pants, carefully searching the pant leg bottoms. "I've got weed seeds." He used tweezers to pluck at the fabric and carefully dropped the bits of seed into a bottle before labeling it. "We'll get someone from the Smithsonian to ID them."

That, too, may or may not help. Some weeds, like dandelions, grew everywhere. Other species were specialized to a certain soil, season, and environment.

The back pocket produced Joe's wallet, and using forceps, the tech went through it, cataloging credit cards, two pictures of smiling kids. Mitch said they were Betsy's little boys.

The left pants pocket produced a lighter and a half-smoked crumpled cigarette.

"Shit," Mitch said. "Joe didn't smoke." He made a face. "He hated cigarettes. His mother and father both smoked like chimneys. It killed them. Joe wouldn't even stay in the same car with a smoker."

"Take a sample," Ramsey said. "I want to know if he had nicotine in his lungs or blood."

The medical examiner nodded, turning back to the corpse. "Coming right up . . . but I can tell you by looking, this guy wasn't a smoker."

"Player cigarette," the tech noted, lifting the cigarette with forceps and studying it through a glass. "English brand. Now, where, do you suppose, did our guy find one of those?" He carefully bagged and labeled the specimen.

"What about the lighter?"

The technician used his forceps to pick up the steel

lighter. A black shield emblazoned with an arrow piercing a grinning skull covered one side. "Joe's?" he asked.

"Nope." Mitch squinted at the lighter. "It looks military, if you ask me. That's a unit emblem, if I'm not mistaken."

Ramsey's heart skipped. "I want that thing taken apart. Bless you, Joe, you may have just broken this thing wide open."

He glanced at his watch. "That cigarette and lighter might be the first solid lead we've found." He met Mitch's eyes. "I've got a plane to catch. The second you've got anything, call me. I'll be on the ground in Denver by eighteen-thirty our time."

"You've got it," Mitch said, his eyes narrowed as he glared at the lighter.

Ramsey tossed off the last of his coffee and stopped at the autopsy table. What remained of Joe Hanson would have curdled buttermilk. "Good work, Joe. You might have just hung the bastards."

CHAPTER TWENTY-THREE

BRYCE RECLINED ON THE OVERSTUFFED COUCH AND propped his leg on a pillow. The government's idea of a

living room, he decided, was a whole bunch nicer than
the little niche he had enjoyed in his Manchester house.
The entertainment center, with its computer, big-screen
television, stereo, and sound system beggared his little
Sony CD player and the Zenith tube he'd propped on a
box in his own home.

Not that it mattered. According to reports, everything
he'd owned had been turned to ashes. That included his
grandfather's old .30-.30 deer rifle, the photo albums that
recorded his life. His diplomas and keepsakes. The effect
could be likened to someone coming along behind and
erasing a portion of his life. Where he had been whole,
now a big hole gaped behind him.

Near his head a bottle of cold beer stood on a sandstone coaster within easy reach. The drapes, of course,
were pulled against the hot Rocky Mountain sun. Here, in
the house, the temperature stayed at a pleasant seventy-
two degrees.

Veronica had extended the leather recliner opposite
him. She still looked bushed, but her brows were lined.
Her long black hair had been braided, and at some time,
she had at least rinsed her long-suffering turtleneck.

Agent Jones had left an hour ago, taking their sizes
and disappearing into the mean streets of Denver to find
clothing for them. What he called interrogation, and what
Agent Jones called "an interview," was being delayed
until that evening. First off, Ronnie's lawyer was in court.
Second, some muckety-muck was coming from Washington to be present. Evidently the thumbscrews wouldn't
come out until then.

For the moment, Bryce enjoyed a curious game. He
watched Veronica, because to tell the truth, she was defi-

nitely worth watching. He had committed himself to learning every angle and curve of that marvelous body. His study would include each of her subtle expressions, the goal being to read the thoughts behind her classic face.

She, in turn, watched Abel, her frown deepening or fading depending on his actions.

Abel alternately squatted, sat, and squirmed around on the thick blue carpet, the TV remote in his hands. He, in his turn, watched the TV, alternating between PBS and the cartoon station.

The funny thing was, he couldn't seem to get a grasp on the way the remote worked. To change channels, he started at one and worked up to six, where the PBS station was, but when he went to the cartoons, he started at one again, rhythmically pushing the button to climb up into the twenties were he could find the cartoons.

"Abel?" Veronica asked as he started the routine over. "Why don't you just press the button up from six? You don't have to go all the way back to one."

He frowned. "Oh." He studied the remote, as if seeing it for the first time. "How?"

She leaned forward, the footrest sliding into the chair base. Bryce hid a smile when her knees cracked as she knelt down next to the boy. "Here, like this. See? You are at six. So you push in seven, eight, nine, ten . . . so on." The cartoon flashed on the screen. "Or, there's an even better way to do it. Here, you take the control and push the six. You know six, don't you?"

The frown ate into his sloped forehead. "Siss," he said, and pushed the button. When PBS appeared, he looked up as if to see a gleaming angel.

"That's right." Veronica showed him how to tap in a "twenty-two," but the number seemed beyond him. Resolutely, he pushed six, then climbed channel by channel through the stations to the cartoons. Then he pushed the six again. And did the whole process over.

Veronica glanced at Bryce. "Maybe twenty-two is a bit much for a four-year-old."

He nodded sagaciously, having already exhausted his knowledge of human child development by several light-years.

Veronica, however, had returned her attention to Abel. She reached out, tentatively running a finger across the top of his head.

Abel shot her a wary look, his blue eyes suddenly sober.

Veronica stood and walked from the room. She returned moments later with a stack of five glasses and squatted down next to him.

"Abel," she said, "I've got a game for you. Here, watch carefully." She set the glasses out in a precise triangle. "Can you make that shape with the glasses?"

"Yess."

She took the triangle apart and motioned for him to make it. Abel very carefully placed the glasses in the exact order that Veronica had laid them out.

"Okay." Veronica took one of the glasses. "Now, can you use one of the other glasses to make that same shape?"

Abel knotted his brow and looked at her like she was nuts. Then he reached out and took the remaining glasses back, laying out the pattern in exactly the same order, but with a new glass.

Using the glasses, Veronica made a rectangle, and took it down. Abel made the rectangle. Each time Veronica changed a glass, Abel rebuilt it exactly the same way, starting with the first glass and proceeding until he had constructed the pattern.

"What are you getting at?" Bryce asked softly.

"Something I noticed the first morning at the condo. I watched Abel place the silverware. Spoons first. Forks, and then knives. Each placed perfectly. This morning, he asked to help at breakfast and did it exactly the same way."

"So?"

"So, everything he does is the same. Patterned." A quizzical expression crossed her face. Abel stared up at her as if he didn't understand the problem.

"He's four and a half," Bryce reminded. "Isn't that how children learn?"

She chewed her lip for a moment, then shrugged. "Maybe."

"I hate it when you're cryptic."

She gave him an irritated look. "Abel? Let me feel your head, okay?"

"Watch it, kid," Bryce warned. "I took physical anthropology. Once they get to fingering your head they spend the rest of their lives trying to look under your skin."

Abel stoically allowed her to press here and there, and then she held his head just so between the palms of her hands.

Bryce watched those smooth hands and wished she'd hold his head that way.

"Something . . ." she started to say, then shook her head. "I don't know. He's so familiar."

"He's your brother's little boy."

"Only if Rebecca is lying about being the donor." She cocked her head. "And I never saw Scott as a little boy. He was ten years older than me. I was the unexpected result of a trip to the Riviera."

"I'll have to take you there sometime."

She gave him a mock look of disgust. "Why would I go with you?"

"Just a thought. The FBI might have a neat safe house there."

"Don't push your luck." She bent down and made a rectangle of the glasses, then placed the fifth in the exact center. "All right, Abel. Look at this very carefully. Do you see how it looks?"

He nodded, then glanced up at her, curiosity in his blue eyes.

She told him, "Go into the kitchen for a minute, and don't peek."

He jumped up and ran off in his stumpy-legged run. Bryce could hear him thump onto the linoleum. The kid had a gait that was different, more powerful than any child Bryce had ever watched. His feet hammered the ground like pistons.

Veronica took the glasses and rearranged them, turning the long axis of the rectangle ninety degrees. "Okay, Abel, come back and look."

He came charging out, practically sliding to a stop to look down at the glasses.

"What do you see?" Veronica raised an intent eyebrow.

"Diffewent."

"How?"

He pointed. "That tuwned wong."

"Can you fix it?"

He reached down and, one by one, moved the glasses back to their starting place, stating, "Thewe."

Veronica's face lined. "Okay, back to the kitchen."

After Abel charged off, she very carefully moved each glass exactly two inches to the right, calling, "Come look."

Abel raced back, an intent look on his locomotive-shaped face, and stared at the glasses. "Diffewent." And, before being instructed, he moved each glass precisely back where it had been.

"How did you do that?" Veronica asked.

He shrugged. "Spots on cawpet."

Bryce laughed, then stopped at the baffled look in Veronica's eyes. "So," he said, "he can't get the hang of the TV remote, but he's smart enough at four and a half to memorize the carpet pattern."

"He uses vision differently than other children," she said, a passion in her voice. "I don't have the tools. I'm missing something here. It's just out of reach, Bryce." She shook her head slowly, aware of Abel's rising anxiety. "Maybe I'm just tired." To Abel, she said, "It's okay, kiddo. You're doing just great."

Abel's large blue eyes took in her expression, reading beyond the smile.

Could Abel be the catalyst behind this entire mad situation? The notion froze Bryce for a moment. Abel seemed to sense his sudden unease, for those haunted eyes turned in Bryce's direction. That bulbous nose was working, as if he could smell a change in the air. Could the kid smell a change in mood? That didn't make any sense.

Bryce smiled, hiding his sudden suspicion, saying, "Hey, Abel, what kind of patterns can you make with those glasses? Can you do a circle?"

Abel frowned, looked down at the glasses, and shook his head.

"How about taking the glasses back to the kitchen?" Veronica asked. "Would you do that for me? And place them in the dishwasher like we did the breakfast dishes?"

Abel nodded, picking one up and trotting off to the kitchen. Bryce watched Abel make five trips to and from the kitchen. Then the boy scooped up the remote and went back to watching the television. But the joy had gone out of it.

Smart little guy—he picked up on stress just like an ordinary kid. But then, what should Bryce expect but that Scott and Amanda would have a bright child? Genes will out, and all that. And for some reason, he just couldn't make himself believe that the kid was Rebecca's. Something about that didn't sit right. Why would Amanda Alexander carry a child to term that was based on Rebecca's DNA?

He watched Abel's pensive expression, the way his stubby fingers caressed the black plastic remote and pushed the "channel up" button. In that moment, he struggled to see Scott or Amanda—some mixture of those two remarkable people combined—in this little towheaded boy.

And failed.

Then he struggled to see Rebecca Armely, with her firm chin, high cheeks, and narrow face.

And failed.

With the force of a thrown brick, he saw what he should have seen in the very first place. The answer was so simple. Any student in an introductory genetics class would have seen it. It was a textbook example.

Dear God, what is he?

CHAPTER TWENTY-FOUR

GOLDMAN ANSWERED THE PHONE ON THE THIRD RING.

"Dr. Goldman?" Veronica asked, glancing sidelong to where Jennifer Jones and Bryce watched from the kitchen breakfast bar. "This is Veronica Tremain."

"Yes, Veronica. How are you doing? What can I do for you?"

"We're interested in Scott's work. Could you tell me, was he cutting and splicing genes? Deleting and inserting new sections of DNA in his samples?"

"Of course. That's fairly routine these days. We have undergraduates doing that sort of procedure."

"Scott was doing this with cattle as well as the samples he brought in?"

"Oh, sure. Like I said, he was interested in the mechanics of the process. He thought that by understanding it, he could understand the forces working on human evolution."

"But, you're still sure that he didn't experiment on human genetic material."

"Positive. I helped Scott on some of the more difficult procedures. Using restriction polymerases to cut and delete sections and then to insert replacement DNA cultured by PCR, uh, that's polymerase chain reaction. With it, we can duplicate multiple copies of DNA strings . . . uh, gene sequences, if you will. Scott was quite good at it, a natural, as if he could sense the extent of the sequences."

She hesitated. "He worked on his own, though, didn't he?"

"I don't understand what you're—"

"He worked unsupervised, is what I'm saying. I mean, please, Dr. Goldman, he was a colleague. Another Ph.D. whose work, skill, and ability you trusted. You considered him a professional, didn't you?"

"Correct."

"I'm his sister, Doctor Goldman. I know Scott, how he worked. You weren't always looking over his shoulder, not in the way you led us to believe the other day in your office. I've been in enough labs to know that you had your own research, and you trusted Scott to do his, didn't you?"

A long silence.

"It's all right, Dr. Goldman." Veronica sighed. "This is just between you and me. I know for a fact that Scott was working with human tissue. That cat is out of the bag. I just need to know what kind. Did he tell you anything?"

A sigh. *"He told me he had a specimen—but he didn't say from where."* His voice dropped. *"He built a viable embryo from nuclear DNA obtained from that sample. He just wanted to know that it would work. Then we destroyed it. I was there. I saw it destroyed."*

"Why didn't you tell Agent Hanson that day?"

"Because he wouldn't have understood. Because it would have opened up a whole can of worms inapplicable to my lab and the work we do here. I can tell you that none of the embryos that Scott built were ever implanted."

"How do you know?"

"We couldn't have if we would have wanted to. We do cattle and horses, not people. We don't have the facilities here to work on humans. I mean, we don't even have an examining table, let alone a surgery. You'd need a clinic to do that sort of work."

"Okay, well, thank you, Doctor."

"Uh, have they made any progress on finding . . . you know, Scott's murderers?"

"I don't know, Dr. Goldman. If they get a break, I'll give you a call."

"Any time."

"Thanks." Veronica hung up the phone and considered his words.

"Illumination?" Bryce asked.

"Hardly." Veronica made a face. "Goldman told me that Scott did work on human samples. But he's positive that Scott destroyed them. Says that they couldn't have implanted them in any event. Unless a woman would have been amenable to being clamped in a head-catch like a cow."

"I used to go out with a girl like that. We called her Mad Mary. She ended up working for Smith & Wesson. In the handcuff division."

Veronica gave him a disgusted look and glanced at Abel, visible through the arched opening into the dining room. He sat on the floor, turning his snowstorm upside down and watching the white flakes settle. "Goldman is sure that Scott destroyed the embryos, and there was no way the CSU lab could have taken it any farther with humans. So, I guess whatever Scott was into, the little guy wasn't part of it."

She was aware of Bryce's intent look, and how his gaze darted away when she turned her attention on him. "What?"

Bryce hesitated, his expression a mask of indecision.

"Come on, spill it," she urged. "Damn, Bryce, we're all in this together."

"What precisely did Goldman say? That they *couldn't* have implanted a viable embryo, or that they didn't try?"

"He said it would take a clinic. And that . . . What? Jesus, Bryce, why are you looking at me like that?"

In a very precise voice, Bryce asked, "How many trips did Scott and Amanda take to see Avi in Tel Aviv? And just where, precisely, were they nine months before Amanda gave birth?"

For a moment, her eyes lost focus. "You think Abel . . ." She shook her head, refusing to believe. "No, I just can't believe it."

Bryce said gently, "I don't think he's Amanda's child. Your brother's either. And he's certainly *not* Rebecca

Armely's child. No matter what she claimed to be. I think that was a smoke screen. Her effort to protect the boy."

Veronica lifted an inquiring eyebrow. "Why would you think that?"

"Look at him," Bryce said firmly. "Look at the shape of his head, at that face. Rebecca had a delicate, upturned nose, a strong and pointed chin. Then look at his hair and coloring. Rebecca was an ash-blond. The kid's a pale blond—almost what you'd call 'platinum.' Your family tends to thick black hair, fine features. Amanda's heritage was Greek. Olive skinned, dark brown eyes."

"Scott had blue eyes." Veronica crossed her arms, unsure why the accusation disturbed her so. "And, as you should well know, blond hair in human populations is a recessive trait. It can be hidden for generations before it meets another recessive and expresses itself."

"Come on, Ronnie." Bryce waved it away. "You're too good a physical anthropologist for this. Hair color in humans is a multiple allelic trait. That kid's got hair like corn silk. Fine and wispy. And that color of blue in his eyes is unlike anything in your family. Admit it. Not only that, look at his body. At the way he's shaped. He's a little defensive lineman. You and Scott are tall, thin, gracile in build. So was Amanda. None of you are stocky. He's a *creation*, Ronnie. A being that Scott *built*. Maybe from scratch, maybe from bits and pieces, who knows, but that's why that boy is so important."

Veronica fixed her attention on Abel, ready to rebut . . . and couldn't.

You knew all this, didn't you? That subtle sense of wrongness had been triggered by Abel's physical appearance. The length ratio between his arms and legs was wrong. He was built like a little weight lifter, and his poorly proportioned head . . .

She swallowed hard, knowing what had been bothering her for so long. She knew intuitively that Rebecca had lied about being the genetic donor. Even by purposely ignoring the oddity of Amanda having a baby based on Rebecca's genetic code, a blockhead could tell with one look that this child shared none of Scott or Amanda's physical traits. But Amanda had carried that baby to full term. If not Scott's son, then whose? Why would Amanda carry another woman's child?

Agent Jones had stepped into the room, a notebook in her hands. She stopped short, immediately aware of the tension in the air.

"He's a creation, *Ronnie."* Bryce's words echoed in her head. When she looked back at Abel, Goldman's words haunted her. She felt the room spin, and clenched a fist to control the sudden beating of her heart.

"Ronnie? You look like you've just seen a ghost," Bryce said as she walked past him, stepped over to the couch, and knelt beside Abel and his snowstorm.

"What have you got there?" She struggled to hide her overwhelming fascination with the impossible.

"Snow," he told her seriously, his large round blue eyes meeting hers for a brief moment. "Cowd."

"You like cold better than hot, don't you?" she asked, studying the long shape of his head.

"Yess."

Jones was watching intently, a puzzled expression on her face.

She reached out, ruffling his hair, taking the opportunity to feel the contours of his head. The silky blond hair had a feathery feel. She could see the blue veins through his translucent skin. How delicate it looked. She ran the tip of her finger under his receding chin.

"Abel," she told him, her heart racing, "I want you to know, that no matter what, you have a place with me. I won't leave you alone. I promise."

A flicker of relief crossed his face.

Jennifer Jones continued to watch the interplay, aware of the impact, if not the import. "Would someone mind explaining what this is all about?"

Veronica stood and strode back into the kitchen on adrenaline-charged muscles. To Jones, she said, "I need to return to my house in Boulder. I need some things."

"No way," Jones answered firmly. "You don't set foot out of this house. Not for any reason."

"Then you'll need to send someone after my things. You can do that?"

"Is this important?" Jones asked.

Veronica smiled grimly. "If Bryce is right, and what I suspect turns out to be the case, it could explain everything. Scott and Avi's murders, the stolen notes, why Billy Barnes Brown would risk everything to kill so many people."

Agent Jones cocked her head, one eye narrowing. "Would you care to share your suspicions with me?"

"Not until I'm sure you won't consider me to be a half-baked lunatic." A notepad with pen lay next to the phone on the breakfast bar that separated the kitchen from the dining room. Veronica reached for them and began jotting notes. Bryce sidled up to stare over her shoulder, his eyebrows rising inquisitively.

Finishing, Veronica tore the paper from the pad and

handed it to Jones. "That's the list . . . with directions on where these things are in my house. I'll get you the key."

"This stuff is really that important?" Jones took the list, scanning the contents.

"I'll let you know after I have my equipment and the reference materials I've listed there."

Jones nodded. "I'll call someone in our Boulder residency. Assuming you don't have anything unusual in the way of security, our people will be in and out in less time than it will take you to walk back and find your keys."

"I always knew my tax dollars would come in handy."

"Hey," Jones said dryly, "we're the FBI."

"When I worked for the coroner in Boston," Bryce said laconically, "the Boston cops told me FBI stood for 'Fumbling Bumbling Incompetents.'"

"Jealousy on the part of the local yokels I assure you," Jones quipped. Then she picked up the phone, checked her notebook, and punched in a number.

As Jones read the list off to someone in the Boulder office, Bryce gave Veronica a curious look, then glanced at Abel. As usual, the boy had picked up on the growing tension and was watching them with that bewildered and frightened look.

"Whatever happens," Bryce told her levelly, "I'm with you." He nodded toward Abel. "And him, too."

She smiled. "Thanks, Bryce. But if I'm right, this could be as explosive as dynamite. You might want to wait until we see if—"

"I said I'm in, Ronnie. No matter what the consequences."

The house is quiet. Agent Jones is on the telephone in the kitchen, talking to someone as she takes notes. Bryce is asleep in the living room, his hurt foot propped on a pillow. Abel walks quietly, listening to the sounds of the house as the air-conditioning hums and the refrigerator rattles faintly. Sometimes wood pops, and the house creaks. He peers around the different rooms, tracing out the distances between the furniture and the way the walls are arranged.

He has it now, firmly in his head. He knows this place, all of the closets and hallways. He has even explored the cellar, smelling the musty odor of the cement and cool air.

He walks down the upstairs hallway and reaches up, turning the doorknob. He pushes the door open and steps inside, carefully closing the door behind him. He can smell her, hear her deep breathing.

On light feet, Abel crosses to the bed and peers over the mattress and rumpled sheets. Her hair, fragrant with the flowery smell of shampoo, is spread out over the pillow. He carefully takes his shoes off as Mother always told him to do, and climbs onto the bed. On hands and knees he crawls to her, and curls his body against hers.

In her sleep, she rearranges herself, one arm draping over his waist. He reaches out, pulling a long strand of her fragrant hair to him, and rubs it between his fingers.

Maybe, if he makes believe, she will turn into Mother. The visions cloud his thoughts. Sometimes he sees Mother as she was in the apartment: happy, alive, her eyes glowing with wonder when she looks at him and tells him how special he is. At other times, he sees her after the phone call, when they are packing to leave, and Mother's eyes have that glittering fear. Then he imagines her as she would have been on the condo floor: limp, eyes wide, frothy blood dripping from her mouth.

He bites back tears, wondering. Mother told him that she would keep him safe. And now, Veronica has told him the same thing. In his mind, he can see Veronica lying on the floor. Blood seeps through her long black hair. This same hair that he clutches so tightly.

"God? Keep Wewonica safe, pwease." He closes his eyes and hopes with all his might that the blond man will not come here and take her away.

CHAPTER TWENTY-FIVE

JACKSON RAMSEY STEPPED OUT OF THE JETWAY AT GATE B17 in the Denver International Airport. He paused on the gray carpet as people filed past him. Withdrawing his cell phone from his pocket, he punched in the number for

Mitch and waited for five rings before Special Agent Ensley's sonorous voice answered, *"This is Ensley."*

"Mitch? Ramsey. What's the latest?"

"You're going to love it. We've got the lighter pegged. It's a SOCOM escutcheon, all right. One of the elite units. These guys specialize in intelligence work, special reconnaissance, infiltration, electronic warfare, that kind of thing. They're good at penetrating secure environments and eavesdropping. The guys at Quantico took the lighter apart. They've got a couple of prints. If the lighter's owner was one of the guys in the unit, he's on file. We're working through our liaison at the Pentagon. They don't like allowing outsiders into their database. But, given the circumstances, we're getting their cooperation. As much as they dislike us in their database, they like the notion that one of their guys might have gone bad even less."

"I see."

"Yeah. We ought to have a make on the guy within a few hours. After that, we'll track his ass down and ask him a couple of pointed questions. You might want to know that the lab went over Joe's pants. They picked up spattered urine that contained feces."

"What?"

"Best guess is that Joe was held for a while in a place that didn't have a toilet. You get my drift?"

A coldness settled in Ramsey's gut. "Like in a basement or something."

"Yeah, they got cement dust off the sticky-tape samples from his shoes, but it's inconclusive."

Ramsey was thinking aloud. "Someplace where they would have taken his shoelaces off so that he didn't do something like make a garrote." He thought for a moment. "He wasn't wearing a tie, was he?"

"No, sir. Joe always wore a tie unless he was on a special job. If, however, they nabbed him at his house, he might have taken it off."

"Or they didn't give it back to him."

"Could be." A pause. *"His holster and piece were clean. The only prints we got were his. The ballistics lab says it hadn't been shot for weeks. Probably not since his last qualification. They're searching it by the square millimeter for fibers. We've got some results from Joe's hair. What appears to be cotton. Maybe from a pillow. You might want to know, Joe hadn't washed for a couple of days. He was a shower kind of guy. Being unwashed would be consistent if he'd been held for a while. There's one other thing."*

"That is?"

"Someone stuck needles into his neck and arm. It's been at least three days. We've got a guy in the lab who took a look at the likely places on the anatomy where such an injection might have been made. Trouble is, from the time of puncture to now, his body would have oxidized most of the chemicals. We're running samples of his blood for any residuals. They're taking a real hard look at his liver and adipose tissue, anywhere that a couple of molecules might have been preserved."

"Okay." He considered that, watching the people pass in the busy airport. Then he caught site of tall, balding, Bob Dole walking toward him. "My ride is here. Anything else?"

"Yeah, the cigarette. The guys at the lab say that it is

a Player cigarette. You don't just pick them up at a Seven-Eleven. We'll see where that takes us."

"What about the weed seeds?"

"Common enough. Some kind of mustard that mostly grows in the hills. Our best guess is that he was held someplace close to where the crash occurred. The lab boys say that from the blood alcohol content and what whiskey remained in his stomach, he probably died within about two hours of his first drink. We've drawn a circle around that area, and we'll have people hitting the trail at first light."

On a hunch, Ramsey said, "See if there's a church that has connections to Brown's. If there is, try and match the weed seeds."

"Got it."

"Dole's here." Ramsey nodded to the Denver SAC as he walked up. "I'm going to see the good Dr. Johnson. Maybe we'll finally get a handle on what's happening."

He punched the "end" button and shook hands with Dole. "Good to see you again, Bob. How're my witnesses doing?"

"Safe. We've got the place under surveillance." Dole was wearing a conservative gray suit and dark blue tie. Flecks of perspiration reflected on his forehead. He looked the way a special agent in charge was supposed to. "Come on, I'll run you out there."

Ramsey picked up his carry-on bag and followed Dole across the tiled concourse. Little brass fossils of dinosaurs and fish had been inset into the floor.

"Have a nice flight?" Dole asked.

"Cattle car. Their idea of food is getting more interesting with each flight. This time I got something that looked like a pita burrito."

"Want to stop for something real? They've got a good restaurant here. French, of all things. They're quick, too."

"Nope. Let's get to the bottom of this. I think things are about to fall into place."

He didn't see the dark-haired man who rose from one of the brushed stainless steel phone carrels in the middle of the concourse. Had he looked, he wouldn't have recognized Ted Paxton following in the press of passengers. The headset he wore could just as easily have been for a pocket walkman as a cellular telephone monitoring system.

The bag had been delivered to the De France Street house on June twentieth at five that afternoon: a black nylon satchel that felt reassuringly heavy as a young man in a suit and tie handed it over to Veronica in the front room. He appeared to be about thirty, handsome, with neat brown hair. Veronica appreciated the interest in his earnest eyes. He gave her a lady-killer smile: partly daring, definitely flattering, and all invitation.

"I hope that's everything." He raised an inquiring eyebrow.

"Have any trouble with the security system?" she asked, amused. Bryce had picked up on the agent's interest and had crossed his arms defensively.

"None at all," the young agent replied. "Uh, you might want to add a quality dead bolt to the back door, and your code is a bit simple."

"Simple?" she asked. "I thought one, two, three wouldn't occur to any rational thief."

"You should know that a reporter had your place staked out." He pulled a card out of his pocket and handed it to her. It read "Skip Manson, WQQQ News," and a Denver phone number had been scrawled on one side. "I brushed him off, told him I was your insurance agent."

"And he bought it?" Jones asked skeptically.

"I don't care if he did or didn't, but I briefed everyone to be on the lookout for him." He smiled at Veronica again, saying, "If there's anything else you need, just be sure to have Agent Jones call. She's got my number."

"I will. Thank you."

He hesitated, as if loath to leave. Then he nodded and opened the door before stepping out into the evening. Veronica caught a glimpse of slanting afternoon sunlight yellowing the houses across the street. Cabin fever had begun to set in. The door closed, blocking it from her view.

"You might at least check," Bryce said dryly. "He might have left a card. You know, just in case."

Agent Jones laughed and headed back toward the kitchen. Smells of spaghetti drifted out on steam-laced wings.

Veronica playfully punched Bryce in the ribs and walked back to the breakfast bar. Abel lay on the living room floor, attention rapt on the television—a science fiction show about a space station, the characters battling the shadow forces of darkness.

At the breakfast bar, Veronica opened the bag and withdrew a set of anthropological calipers, a beige refer-

ence book, a notebook, and dissecting kit. Several files in
manila folders followed.

"Looks like something left over from Torquemada's
little chamber of horrors." Bryce took the seat next to
hers. He picked up the spreading calipers and held them
sideways like insect jaws while he made snapping gestures. The tips clicked with metallic emptiness.

She gave him a disgusted look as she pulled a stainless
steel case from the bottom of the bag. She flipped it open
to check the rows of little plastic vials, each containing a
clear fluid. Several paper-wrapped lancets and test tubes
rested in the foam holder. A single syringe with plastic-
cased needles could be seen.

"Basic blood-typing kit?" Bryce mused.

"So . . . maybe you did take an anthropology course
once upon a time?"

"I pass out at the sight of blood."

"Yeah," she told him, remembering his resolve when
Rebecca's body lay sprawled on the floor. "And I'm the
wizard of Oz."

Bryce picked up the book, reading the title and frowning. "You've got to be kidding."

"What? That I'm the wizard of Oz?"

"No, I already knew that. I mean, the title of the
book."

"Hope I'm not right, okay?"

Bryce's gaze seemed to fasten on some interminable
distance. "Ostienko," he whispered. The frown deepened.
"No, it doesn't make sense."

"What?" She glanced at Agent Jones, who stood over
the stove, casting them surreptitious glances and apparently drinking in every word.

"He's one of Avi's good friends. They did a paper together on early modern humans in the Near East. Published it just after Avi was beat up by those ultraorthodox Jews at his dig north of Tel Aviv."

Veronica took a deep breath, forcing herself to remain calm. "I've met him. . . . Well, Scott introduced me at one of the meetings. I've heard him present papers at the AAPA. He's the leading Russian paleoanthropologist. As a youth, before the Communists lost it all, he was imprisoned for a while. Spoke out against the old Lysenkoism."

"What's Lysenkoism?" Jones asked, a wooden spoon in her hands.

"Trofim Lysenko dates back to the Stalinist years," Veronica said. "He was in charge of the Soviet Academy of Sciences. He didn't believe in Darwinian theory or modern genetics. His idea of evolution was that form followed function. For example, if you ran all of your life, your son would be born with longer legs. Since it came closer to the Marxist ideal, it was 'politically correct' in the fullest extent of the term. He insisted that Russian science mimic Marxist political theory, no matter what the data might have indicated. It set the study of biology in Russia back a century and a half.

"Ostienko was one of the young scientists who had access to Western data, to modern genetics. He spoke out in the last days before Gorbachev. They threw him into internal exile for it."

"Notice a pattern here?" Bryce asked. "Each of the principals, all dead, suffered because of someone's zealous beliefs."

"Scott despised intolerance," Veronica reminded

woodenly, unable to keep from glancing toward the front room. "And we don't know that Ostienko's dead."

"Lord help us, that's really what he was doing," Bryce murmured. "Giving the whole world the proof."

Veronica reminded, "Let's make sure first, all right?"

"What are you talking about?" Jennifer Jones took a step forward, her expression sharpening.

"Something impossible," Veronica said uneasily.

"What?" Jennifer demanded, unwilling to be put off.

Veronica lifted her calipers. "This will tell us. Just let me do some preliminary research. I think, with the results, I can explain this whole thing. Let me be sure before I spout off and lose all doubt about my sanity."

Jones pointed the spatula. "You tell me."

"As soon as I know for sure," Veronica promised.

From the living room, the sound of music and the final credits could be heard. Abel appeared, dressed in a T-shirt and new blue jeans. He wore small white sneakers: his FBI-provided ensemble. Their other clothes had been washed that day.

"G'Kaw!" he cried, one fist raised. "Be stwong, like G'Kaw!"

"You're that, all right." Veronica agreed. "Come on up here. G'Kar would like the game we're going to play. He'd be the first to step up and let me run the med lab."

Veronica watched as Abel nimbly climbed the chair. Again, she marveled at the boy's strength and agility. Normal children didn't exhibit that kind of development at his age.

Abel stood on the stool, looking skeptically at the calipers and blood kit.

"All right," Veronica said, "I need you to hold still. You be G'Kar, and I'll be the doctor."

"Wong clothes," Abel told her in his serious voice. "Got to be gween."

"We'll pretend, okay?"

"Okay."

She opened the notebook and flipped through pages of figures to a blank sheet. It had been divided into columns marked Glabella-Bregma, Inion-Bregma, Maximum Cranial Length, Maximum Cranial Width, Nasion-Prosthion Height, Nasion-Lambda Arc, and so forth. Some of the categories, like Basion-Bregma Height, she marked off by drawing a line through them.

"What's that?" Bryce asked.

"My dissertation notebook," she told him. "My raw data are here."

He grew pensive again as she picked up the spreading calipers.

Abel squirmed when she began running the blunt tips across the swell of his skull.

"Hold still."

"Cowd," he told her.

"You'd think I was a gynecologist. They'll warm up. I promise." She studied the calibration and wrote the number down in her book under "Maximum Cranial Width."

Next she placed one tip on the indent on the bridge of his nose and then ran the other around the back of his head, taking the greatest reading and jotting it down.

Abel endured, his expression shifting with each measurement, especially when she ran the little metric tape along the midline of his forehead and around to the protruding rear of his skull.

Agent Jones flipped her blond hair over her shoulder and watched, fascinated. "What are you doing?"

"Basic anthropometry," Bryce told her. "Anthropometry is a voodoo word that anthropologists use to cast numerical incantations and make the equivalent of human carpentry sound exotic."

"Peasant," Veronica muttered past the pen she clasped in her teeth as she measured the distance between the two external bony borders of Abel's eye sockets. "And you, you little munchkin, stop wiggling."

"Hungwy." Abel was looking for excuses to escape the ordeal.

"I'll measure your belly in a minute." Veronica wrote down the numbers. "What I'd give for an anthropometer rod. But when you normally work with bones, they just don't come in handy." Doing the next best thing, she guessed the location of his humeral head—the top of the upper arm—and measured the length down to his elbow, then the distance from the elbow to the outside point of the wrist. She tried the same thing with his leg, and figured the fudge factor would be acceptable for a gross estimation.

For height, she had him crawl down and stand against the wall. Then she measured his seated height from the floor to the top of his head.

Through it all, Agent Jones watched, keeping an eye on the bubbling sauce.

"Finished," Veronica told Abel. "Since I don't think I'm going to get the sliding calipers into your mouth to measure your teeth."

"Okay." Abel bounced up. "Eat now."

"Right," Veronica said, adding the last of the notations into her book. "Eat now."

Through supper, she ached to get at the figures, to compute the indices and compare them with those in the book. She still didn't have the data she'd need. The ones in the Trinkaus book were for adults, not subadults. She needed the Teshik-Tash data, but it was only available in Russian. Either the La Quina or Pech de l' Aze' data—reported in French—would have been applicable. She would have to make do with the Shanidar data. Not 100 percent applicable, but close enough to solve the riddle of Abel.

"Relax," Bryce told her, amusement in his eyes. "Don't wolf your food. Science is done better on a full belly." To Jennifer, he said, "Do you think we could get her a shovel before breakfast?"

Veronica narrowed an eye, then glanced at Abel, who clutched his fork in one fist. He had spaghetti sauce smeared over his prowlike face. He grinned in answer to her uplifted eyebrow. But within seconds, it faded, his thoughts turning inside again.

How could she blame him? He had a lot to live with. And, if her figures came out the way she hoped they wouldn't, his life wasn't going to get any easier.

Scott, damn you, what the hell were you thinking about?

It was at that moment that she caught the name "Scott Ferris" from the TV in the front room. On galvanized muscles, she leaped for the doorway in time to see file footage of Scott's burned house in Fort Collins.

"In the days after Scott Ferris' murder, his colleague, Amanda Alexander, also an anthropologist, was mur-

dered in a similar fashion." A camera panned across the remains of Amanda's house in Ohio. *"So, too, was the house of Dr. Bryce Johnson, a noted anthropologist and geneticist, burned in Manchester, New Hampshire."*

"My God," Bryce murmured as he stood beside her. "That's . . . I mean, that was my house?" The TV showed flattened and blackened ruins.

"Dr. Johnson remains missing," the reporter's voice droned on. *"The only missing piece of this puzzle is how Elizabeth Carter, a secretary in the Reverend Billy Barnes Brown's Evangelical Church of the Salvation, was tied to Ferris and his colleagues."* The camera showed another burned house, the subtitle stating "Fairfax, Virginia."

"So, what do we know?" A young man's face formed on the screen, the Denver skyline behind him. *"Someone is killing scientists, in particular, a group that centered around anthropologist Scott Ferris. We have few facts, but this we do know: Scott Ferris and his people found something . . . something that other people were willing to kill to protect."* After a pregnant pause, he added, *"Skip Manson, WQQQ News in Denver."*

The network talking head, looking duly grave, said, *"Thank you, Skip. We'll be following this story as it develops."*

Blanching, Bryce reached down and picked up the remote and killed the picture. "They're going to figure it out, Ronnie. Eventually, someone is going to break the news about Abel—and when they do, we're going to be in the middle of a hurricane."

CHAPTER TWENTY-SIX

❖

JACK RAMSEY STEPPED OUT OF DOLE'S CAR AND LOOKED around. The location couldn't be faulted for a safe house. Here, backed against the foot of the mountain, Ramsey could gaze over the lights of Denver. The radio towers up on Lookout Mountain blinked in a pattern of red lights. The dark bulk of Table Mountain rose to the north, like an opaque black monster squatting just inside the city's edge. High overhead, against the waxing night sky, a jet roared westward across the Rockies.

Ramsey closed the car door and gripped his briefcase. He followed Dole up the walk and waited as the SAC rang twice long, then once short. An attractive young blond woman answered the door.

"Hi, Jennifer," Dole greeted. "Everything all right?"

"Fine, sir. We just finished dinner. Come in."

Ramsey stepped into the living room, admiring the pale blue carpeting. The smell of Italian hung in the air, reminding him of his empty belly and the pita thing the airline had fed him. Of course, living on airline food had the definitive benefit of keeping a man's waistline under control. So did having one's stomach pumped. Neither was an idea contemplated with any glee by the sane and mentally balanced.

"What kind of security do we have?" Ramsey asked, turning his mind to business.

Dole answered, "I've placed a team at the turn-in at the end of the block to monitor traffic in and out of the cul-de-sac. Another agent is in the van conversion parked across the street." He shoved his thumbs into his belt. "No one can case the place without us tagging his plates and running it through the system. We're switching teams every eight hours."

Ramsey nodded. "Good. They'll eat up the overtime. God knows where we'll find the budget for it."

"You're a wizard at that sort of thing. Want to come to Denver?" Dole cocked his head. "Me, I'm a Montana boy in my roots. I'd just as soon be transferred to the Missoula residency. The fishing's better."

"What? And miss all the fun and excitement? You'd be half dead of boredom in a month."

"Are you kidding? Where did we nab the Unabomber? And remember the Freemen? Montana will be fun enough." Dole grinned. "Besides, I hate rush hour traffic."

Ramsey knew. D.C. had more than its share.

"I'll introduce you to Dr. Johnson, Dr. Tremain, and the boy." Jennifer turned, leading the way back into a dining room. There, a little blond boy was methodically removing the dinner plates, one by one, and carrying them to the dishwasher. At first glance, he just wasn't right. Something about the proportions of that big head and the thick trunk. Having raised a son of his own, Ramsey knew this kid, at age four, had to be as strong as a twelve-year-old.

The boy looked up, stopping in midstride to stare at Ramsey and Dole. Those remarkably large eyes—of the most incredible blue—reflected a deep-seated fear and distrust. For an instant, Ramsey wondered if the cerulean color came from contact lenses, then discounted it. Then, to his dismay, the kid raised his head, sniffing through that huge honker of a nose the way a dog would. It was just plain unsettling.

A man, his foot in a cast, sat at the table, studying them with alert hazel eyes. He looked fit, dressed in a sport shirt and new Levi's. A crooked smile bent his lips, and he said, "Now, unlike Agent Jones, you guys look like the FBI."

At the breakfast bar, a lithe, attractive woman worked at a calculator, barely wasting a glance on them. A silver clip at the nape of the neck restrained her long black hair; it fell to her belt in a gleaming black mass. She might have been a fashion model, with perfect cheekbones, a straight nose, and firm jaw. Frown lines incised her high forehead.

"Forgive Dr. Tremain, gentlemen." The hazel-eyed man raised himself and stumped forward on an air cast. "She's in the pursuit of science. An elusive quest at best, but for her, the game's afoot. Or, more accurately in this instance, askull." He offered a hand, correctly guessing that Ramsey was the principal. "Bryce Johnson. Glad to meet you."

"Special Agent Jackson Ramsey. This is Special Agent in Charge, Denver Field Office, Bob Dole."

"Pleased to meet you," Veronica told them after shaking hands. "Just a minute, please. I need to finish this."

As Johnson shook hands with the Denver SAC he mildly asked, "Dole? Like the politician?"

"I try to live that down. Actually, I'm a lot better looking." Dole smiled thinly. "And I don't need Viagra."

Ramsey said, "We've been looking for you, Dr. Johnson. We've got an entire list of questions that we're hoping you can answer."

Johnson's face tightened. "Interrogation time. Do I get a metal chair and bright light?"

"That depends." Ramsey tried to keep the tension out of his voice. The guy wasn't going to be an asshole, was he?

"It's okay." Johnson raised his hands. "First thing you should know, I can't stand pain, so I'll just go ahead and spill my guts. Have a seat. I think Jennifer's got coffee going back there."

Johnson levered himself into a chair as the little boy scurried around the table—as far from them as he could safely stay—and pulled the last of the plates before beating a hasty retreat to the kitchen.

"Dr. Tremain?" Ramsey asked. "Would you join us?"

She gave him an evaluative stare and lowered her calculator before stepping to the table. "Agent Ramsey, my attorney asked that I wait to make a statement until he could be present. He's hung up with a case."

"But you will be making a statement?" Ramsey cocked his head.

Tremain nodded. "Yes, I will." She indicated the papers before her. "It might be pretty interesting."

Ramsey placed his tape recorder on the table and took out his notebook, then turned to Johnson. "How about you, Dr. Johnson?"

"I don't know how much I can help you," Johnson began honestly. "I was the number cruncher for the team. Scott gave me data on DNA base pairs, and I ran the statistical manipulations—the probabilities, if you will—for how the different genes would combine down through the generations. That, and at other times, I was given raw data and asked to compare them with those cataloged by HUGO, the Human Genome Organisation. Since we're talking about millions of base pairs, sometimes it turned into a tedious process."

"What were these genes for?" Ramsey asked.

"Everything. The proteins that make up blood type, hair color, eye color, metabolic regulators, myriads of things. I reported my findings back to Scott, Amanda, and Avi. We were producing a series of papers, building on the results. Until I received a call from Scott Ferris, the night he was murdered, I thought it was all theoretical." His eyes had developed a thousand-yard stare. "Boy, was I wrong."

"Wrong how?" Ramsey asked.

"Scott and Amanda were building an organism." Bryce took a deep breath. "Not just any organism, but a human being."

"Let me get this straight." Ramsey looked up from his notebook. "You say they were making people? Genetically engineering a new kind of human? Frankenstein? Some sort of superhuman?"

"That's nuts!" Dole muttered. "They can't do that."

Johnson's brow furrowed. "That's a guess at this point. It will remain for us to actually do the research to prove that. But, for the moment, I think it's a reasonable working hypothesis that provides the rationale for murder, for Scott and Amanda's secrecy in this matter, and for the desperation of whoever . . . this church, or whatever, to stop it."

"A new type of human?" Ramsey repeated in disbelief. "Like in science fiction?"

The room was silent, only the hum of the air-conditioner fan audible. Johnson wove his fingers together, staring intently from face to face. "The notion of 'creating' a living human being from bits and pieces of DNA, of modifying the plan if you will, will be perceived by some people as treading upon God's domain."

"The Frankenstein story?" Ramsey sat stiffly, fighting disbelief.

"It's an old myth, Agent Ramsey. It plays on the deepest human fears and aspirations at the same time."

"Why?" Dole burst in. "I mean, why do this thing? Surely you knew it would create all kinds of trouble."

"*I* didn't do it!" Johnson snapped. "What I did was work with theoretical data. My goal in all this was to identify mutations, tag sequences that reflected genetic disease. My job was to model how frequencies recombined through time. *If* they really were building an organism, I didn't know about it."

"You couldn't tell?" Ramsey countered.

Johnson shook his head. "No. Keep in mind, DNA is DNA. It's made of the same base pairs no matter whether the organism it is retrieved from is green pond scum or a human being. The only difference is the number and order of adenine, thymine, cytosine and guanine base pairs, and how they are arranged into chromosomes."

"But you just said that pond scum and humans have differences, right?" Ramsey asked.

"Wouldn't you recognize human DNA?" Dole looked uneasy.

"Sure," Johnson replied. "I knew I was working with

human stuff. I thought we were cataloging the differences, the genetic variation between modern populations. That's part of what modern physical anthropology is all about. Tracing human variability, both phenotypic and genotypic."

"I thought that was done back in 2000 when the chromosomes were mapped." Dole looked confused.

"That's just the map," Bryce answered. "And it's a poor word to use. It tells us which region on the chromosome to look in to find certain genes, uh, DNA coding. Now, it doesn't tell us what that gene does, and even knowing its location, there can be different codes. Okay, here's an analogy: Imagine you've just mapped the human body. Now, if you want to study fingerprints, you know where to look, but, even though you can find the hand, you can't predict what the patterns are going to be until you actually record them. DNA is as individualistic as fingerprints."

"It's that complicated?" Dole asked.

Johnson smiled wearily. "It's a tedious job. You've got to understand, most of the DNA in your body is inactive. It's old or redundant information that's turned off."

At Ramsey's blank look, Johnson paused thoughtfully and said, "Think of DNA like an operator's manual for a Model T. Then, as new models roll off the assembly line, new instructions are added to the manual until you end up with a brand new F-150 straight off the lot. The manual still has instructions for crank-starting Model Ts as well as six-volt wiring diagrams for old 1940 pickups, and valve clearances for '61s, and all the rest. Over the years, a paragraph was deleted here, and there a typo changed a letter as the instructions were copied. The final book is huge, ten thousand pages, and with it, you can operate your brand-new pickup, but it still contains the old obsolete information. All that other stuff is there; we just don't access it because it doesn't have any relevance anymore."

"Our DNA is really like that?" Dole asked.

"Chock-full of old coding, yeah." Johnson nodded. "As a result, it makes it difficult to identify the source of the DNA segment unless you know which chromosome it comes from, and are familiar with the haplotypes . . . uh, the specific markers that act as signposts for a species, subspecies, population, or individual. I hit enough of them to know it was human or ape." He glanced back and forth, then said, "Trust me. If this ever comes up for peer review, my colleagues can corroborate my statement. All the notes are in my office."

"Not anymore," Ramsey said wearily. "Someone cleaned out your office. All of your notes are missing. And your house was burned." Ramsey narrowed an eye, reading the sudden realization in Johnson's expression.

The man took a deep breath, a flutter of anxiety giving way to bitter humor. "Well, then, ask the guys that are trying to kill us. Someone didn't want Scott infringing on the divine prerogative of Creation. Doing so was a little too dangerous and threatening for them."

He's telling the truth. That, or this guy is the slickest liar I've come across in the last twenty years. Ramsey nodded and jotted some notes into his book. "Did anyone ever contact you about your work? Threaten you? Did you receive any hate mail?"

"No, sir." Johnson slowly shook his head. "The first I knew about this was when Scott called that night." He related the contents of the phone call.

Ramsey perked up. "Would you know that voice if you heard it again?"

Johnson swallowed hard. "I *did* hear it again. At the condo, the day before Rebecca was killed. It happened after we tried to call Agent Hanson. The voice called us, claiming to be Joe Hanson."

That old familiar surge of excitement bubbled up in Ramsey's gut. "Stop, wait. Go back to the beginning. Tell it all, from the start to the finish. Every detail."

Dole bent down, making sure the tape recorder was running. Bryce Johnson started with a trip home on a rainy Manchester, New Hampshire, night. *Tosca* on the CD.

Ramsey smiled sardonically as Johnson told of stealing license plates, of the long, frightening trip to Colorado. Of meeting with Veronica and trying to call Joe Hanson.

The story of Rebecca Armely's shooting and the subsequent escape prompted Ramsey to ask, "You didn't see anyone?"

"No." Johnson's clear-eyed resolution left no doubt. "They waited until she had taken the suitcase to the car and walked back into the door. It was done as coolly as anything I ever saw working for the coroner in Boston. Veronica was a step away from her when I pulled her back. Played correctly, they could have killed us one after another as we went to help the dying."

Ramsey glanced at Dole. "That fits with what happened to Joe."

For the first time, Veronica Tremain looked up from her work. "What happened to Joe?"

"He was killed a few nights ago. A traffic accident."

Her jaw muscles bunched. For a moment, a terrible glitter lit her eyes. Softly, she said, "I'm sorry to hear that."

She seemed to wilt, the energy she had displayed poking at the calculator draining away. Her shoulders sagged, her head dropping. For a long moment she stared vacantly at the floor.

The cell phone in Ramsey's pocket rang. He pulled it out and flipped the cover open. "Ramsey."

Mitch's voice said, *"We got a line on him, Jack. Theodor Lance "Leopard" Paxton. Served with Delta Force from '86 to '94. Sterling record, several citations for bravery, valor, and initiative. Awarded the Bronze Star in Desert Storm for his work inside Iraq. You ready for this?"*

"What?"

"After his military service, he worked for us. For HRT. I just got off the horn to some of our guys. They say that from the very beginning he was bothered by what happened at Waco. Then he shot a kid during the Oakdale mess. Resigned that very night and disappeared."

Ramsey felt a coldness settle in his gut. "What else?"

"According to some of the people who used to work with him, he went to some sort of religious retreat in Georgia. Gonna offer his life to the Lord. No one's heard from him for about two years."

Silence.

"Jack? You there?"

"Billy Barnes Brown bases his operations in Georgia. Mitch, I want this Paxton. Bring him in, wring him out."

"Boss, if we bring Paxton in, he may not be the kind you can sweat, if you catch my drift."

"I do. Coordinate with the Atlanta Field Office. If you need SWAT, or any other resources, you use them. Remember the motto: 'No heroes.' This guy's an old pro. Probably a 'soldier of God,' and tougher than anyone we've got. Work under that assumption, and we'll keep people alive."

"Affirmative. I'll be in touch."

Ramsey killed the call and sat for a moment, putting the pieces together. A hollow had grown in the pit of his stomach. Paxton had been one of theirs. He remembered the Oakdale affair. Religious fanatics, a standoff that ended with a dead little girl. Paxton, drowning in guilt, had blamed himself.

"What's up?" Dole asked.

"If I'm not mistaken, we've got a holy war. Heretics burned at the stake. Joe Hanson told me that Elizabeth Carter had been nailed to the floor of her house. Like Jesus on the cross." He glanced at Bryce Johnson, meeting that intelligent hazel-eyed stare. "Correct me if I'm wrong, but doesn't Barnes' church run an outfit called Christian Creationist Crusade? It's one of his hot buttons. Maybe he didn't like it that your colleagues were about to meddle with human genetics."

"It doesn't sound like justification enough to commit murder," Jennifer Jones responded. She had been standing to one side, her arms crossed. "Come on, why kill Rebecca? She was just an innocent bystander."

"Maybe she was tainted." Ramsey narrowed an angry eye, thinking of Joe Hanson. "Maybe, according to their perspective, we all are. Guilty of usurping the throne of God."

"Why Joe?" Dole asked.

"He knew too much. Or they thought he did." Ramsey remembered the needle mark in Hanson's arm. Drugged for interrogation?

"Then, Jack," Dole said gravely, "from that perspective, we're all in jeopardy. Do these guys really think they can take on the entire Bureau?"

But for Joe pocketing that cigarette lighter, they'd have zip. These guys had been cool, professional. "Yeah, Bob. They do."

"Over what? Genetic research?" Dole looked at him askance.

"You still don't get it, do you?" Johnson said softly, glancing toward the living room. "That little boy in there, he's what this is all about."

"Huh?" Ramsey tried to keep the confusion out of his voice. "What's he got to do with this?"

"He's not my brother's biological son," Tremain said, her expression tight. "Or Amanda Alexander's either."

"Wait a minute," Ramsey countered. "I've seen the records. Amanda Alexander bore a little boy. Rebecca Armely adopted the child."

Tremain nodded, her long black hair catching the light. "She did. But that little boy wasn't conceived of her ovum. Or Scott's sperm. He was made, Mr. Ramsey. Created in a lab from disparate bits of DNA obtained from . . . Scott alone knew where. Avi did the in vitro fertilization, implanted the embryo into Amanda in Tel Aviv, and nine months later, Amanda bore the child." From her expression, each word wrenched her soul.

Bryce met Ramsey's disbelieving stare. "Now, Agent Ramsey, are you starting to understand the ethical, legal, moral, financial, and spiritual implications? The very future of the human species just landed in our laps like a ton of bricks . . . and people are already being murdered over it."

At that moment, Ramsey caught movement out of the corner of his eye. The little boy had crept to the edge of the kitchen doorway, a stuffed brown buffalo clutched to his chest. He was sniffing, as if smelling anxiety on the wind, and his eyes reflected a feral fear.

"In an increasingly bizarre twist of events, WQQQ News, in conjunction with our local ABC affiliate, has learned that several days ago a woman was murdered in the condominium belonging to the Scott Ferris family. The woman, whose name is currently being withheld by the Summit County Sheriff's Office, was apparently shot. The Summit County sheriff referred us to the Federal Bureau of Investigation." Skip gave the camera a cue, marking the place where the FBI spokesperson would say "No Comment" and proceeded. "WQQQ News has also learned that Special Agent Joseph A. Hanson of the FBI has been killed in a traffic accident. Special Agent Hanson was originally in charge of the Ferris-Carter case. Once again, the Federal Bureau of Investigation, replying by telephone from the Washington Metro Field Office has told us, 'No Comment.'"

Skip cocked his head slightly as he looked into the camera lens. "A great many questions remain tonight. What happened in that mountain condominium that led to a woman's death? Was that woman Dr. Veronica Tremain? Scott Ferris' sister, and yet another anthropologist? Did Special Agent Joe Hanson really die in a traffic accident, or is something more sinister involved here? And, finally, to what do we attribute the continuing stonewalling by the FBI? Ladies and gentlemen, it's time for answers." He paused for effect before adding, "Skip Manson, WQQQ News, reporting from Colorado."

"Cool!" Kahlid said, raising up from behind the camera. He grinned and tapped a pack of cigarettes on one palm before extracting one.

Skip turned, looking back at the condo with its yellow crime scene sticker. "God, this just keeps getting better and better," he murmured under his breath. "Hello Peabody!"

"Why did Scott do it?" Bryce asked. He remembered the shaken expression on Agent Ramsey's face as he began to understand the implications of an engineered human being. In that moment, the world had been suddenly and irrevocably changed. Each of the agents, Jones included, had turned shocked eyes toward Abel, who, understanding something had changed, but not what, had fled to Veronica's pant leg, where he hid his head and began to cry.

That had ended the interview. To their credit, Ramsey and Dole had demonstrated a compassion for the frightened little boy. The two agents had left an hour ago, promising to return in the morning. Dole had taken Ramsey to the Sheraton adjacent to the Denver Federal Center over on Union. Supposedly they had great government rates.

Jones had gone to bed, a sober and uneasy tension behind her eyes, especially when she looked at Abel. The revelation had disturbed all of them.

Now Bryce and Veronica sat on the couch in the darkened living room. The house had filled with quiet. A shaft of diffused light spilled down the carpeted stairs from the bedroom hallway and gave the room a faint illumination. Abel slept on the couch between them, curled around Chaser's body, his feet braced on Bryce's thigh. In the kitchen, the refrigerator fan kicked on.

"Why did Scott do it? I don't know." Veronica slowly shook her head and leaned it back, exposing her face to the shadowed ceiling.

Abel, perceptive as always, had cried himself to sleep, something inside him retreating to that central place where he hid in the presence of others. Would he sleep behind the toilet again tonight?

"My heart just aches for him," Veronica whispered, reaching out and running her fingers through the little boy's wispy hair. "It's not his fault that he was born."

Bryce reached out to pat Abel's leg. The boy squirmed, mumbled under his breath, and relaxed again. "We're missing something, Ronnie. Scott wasn't the kind to do something this irresponsible. This wasn't about showmanship, or grandstanding, or ego. Scott and Amanda weren't that sort of people." He frowned, suddenly unsure. "Were they?"

Veronica slowly shook her head. "I don't think so. Not that I'm such a great judge of character." She straightened her long legs, propping her feet on the coffee table. "Just look at my life. At the bipedal scum I hung around with as a teenager. Then there was Ben."

"I remember him as flashy, bright, and handsome. An ambitious man with brains." Bryce bit back the rest, that he'd disliked him on sight as a pretty boy, the type who had always had it handed to him on a shining golden platter.

"He uses people," Veronica said wearily. "After he got tired of me, he found other fields to plow. Flashy? Bright? Ben's all of that. There's something perverted in my character that I'm drawn to men like him. Lord knows what he'd have done when this broke." She rubbed her temples. "Sometimes I wonder how I manage."

"One day at a time," he soothed.

She turned her attention to him, studying his profile against the diffused light. "And then what? I mean, Scott's dead. Murdered and burned. His body's in the morgue. Even I have trouble understanding that it's final. Forever. Scott's not coming back. He won't be popping through that door tomorrow saying, 'Hey, Sis, what a great gig, huh?' " She swallowed hard. "And for the rest of my life, I'm going to be wondering about it. About how he died, how they muffled his screams as they broke his arms and twisted them. In my nightmares, I'll feel his flesh sear as they threw gasoline on him and lit a match." Her voice dropped. "Only it won't be a dream. It will be real because it actually happened to him."

Bryce reached across the sleeping boy and took her hand. "One day at a time," he repeated. "True wisdom is knowing what you have to do next, and doing it."

Her serious gaze met his. "They're still out there, Bryce. That's the worst of it. They got Joe Hanson and Rebecca. They're hunting us. It's different than I ever thought it would be. No one can prepare you for the fear that they might be lurking in the night. That the next second a bullet could blast through a window and your body will explode under the impact. Or worse, that they'll get away, and one day, a year from now, or two years, they'll be waiting in your house when you come home some dark night." She tightened her grip on his. "That you can never really be safe again."

"Well, let's see that they get caught, all right?"

She nodded, matching his grip with her own, as if by squeezing, she could kill the fear within her.

❖

Abel stirs when Veronica and Bryce rise from the couch. He feels Bryce's strong arms slipping under him. The veil of sleep is pierced, the dreams of death and blood shredding like tissue. In them, Aunt Eu was yelling at Mother, telling her she was damned. That God would get her for being bad. He blinks his eyes open.

He sways as Bryce lifts him effortlessly and says, "Hey, kid, you're a heavy one. Come on. It's time to take you to bed."

Abel yawns, reassured by the warm chest he lies against. Daa used to hold him like this. A very long time ago. Back before the problems. "Daa cawed me a monster."

"You're not, Abel. You're a wonderful little boy." Bryce smiles down at him, affection in his eyes. "I think you're a miracle."

"Chaser?" he asks.

"I've got him," Veronica says, her soft voice coming from behind.

Bryce carries him up the stairs, then to the room Abel shares with Veronica. Bryce pushes the door open with his elbow and flips on the light switch. The bright light makes Abel squint. Bryce swings him down and onto the soft bed. Abel rolls onto his side, pulling the pillow across to block the light. He can smell his familiar scent. Veronica places Chaser beside him, and he hugs his buffalo to his chest.

"If you have any trouble," Bryce says, "I'm just down the hall."

Through his slitted eyes, Abel watches Veronica from under the pillow. She stands close to Bryce, one hand on his arm, looking into his eyes. "Thanks," she says, "for listening to me."

"Anytime." A gentle concern fills Bryce's voice, and his expression is earnest, communicating something Abel can't quite interpret. He notices a slight change in their odors, and sniffs at the pungency.

"Good night," Veronica says.

"See you tomorrow." Bryce turns and closes the door behind him.

Veronica stands there, head tilted so that her long hair hangs to one side, her eyes on the door. Her fingers are laced in front of her, and she sighs. After a long time, she reaches out, and her slim finger caresses the light switch for a moment before she flicks it off.

In the darkness, Abel opens his eyes, waiting for them to adjust. He watches as Veronica undresses and steps into the bathroom. He hears water running, the sound of the toothbrush. She has forgotten to make Abel brush his teeth. He wonders if she will make him get up and do it, but after the water is turned off, and the toilet is flushed, she steps quietly to the bed and lowers herself beside him.

When her hand reaches over to pat his side, the feel of her brings a grateful reassurance to him. He is haunted by the way the FBI agents stared at him and how their odors changed; he knows fear when he smells it. They are afraid of him. Why? He doesn't want to hurt anyone.

For long minutes he lies there in the darkness, his fingers twining in Chaser's thick hump fur. He can sense Veronica's body growing limp, her breathing deepening. He cocks his head to the night and listens.

Something about the silence isn't right. What? He frowns. Carefully, so as not to wake Veronica, he slips over the side of the bed and pads to the window. He is just tall enough to raise his head up inside the drapes and peer out.

The night here isn't totally dark. Lights from the city below cast a glow across the grass, bushes, and stones of the mountainside behind the house. The deer aren't in their usual place. Where would they be? He waits, unmoving as the minutes pass. Surely the deer will come, won't they?

His quick eyes sense movement on the mountainside, a dark shadow. Abel waits, watching as the form creeps close to the back fence, hesitates, and skillfully vaults the chain link. Abel can hear the faintest clinking of the metal. The man is dressed in black, and his eyes are covered by a protruding tube. He crosses the grass with predatory grace, slipping up against the wall where Abel can no longer see him.

A slow fear has begun to build, and Abel swallows hard. This man wears a black cap over his head. Could it be the blond man?

Abel searches frantically, but he can't see down along the wall to where the man has disappeared. Racked by indecision, he wavers between waking Veronica and going back to bed, covering his head, and hoping that the covers and Chaser will keep him safe.

In the end, he remembers G'Kar, his hero, and creeps to the door, turning the knob. This is what his hero would do. Go and see, then, if there is danger, warn the others.

Shaking, Abel slips through the house on his bare feet. He stays to the shadows, understanding that he can see so much better than grown-ups. He sneaks from window to window, staring out at the back lawn.

The click-snap sound comes from the side of the house opposite the garage. Abel freezes, panic tensing his muscles, a cry stuck in his throat. He must move, or he will cower here, and the bad man, if that's who this is, will kill someone.

His muscles are trembling, and his mouth is dry, as if he were thirsty. The bright pounding of his heart and the tingle of fear paralyze him. He manages to scamper across to the next shadow, and then the next, finding that movement is easier once the first step has been taken.

Metal clinks again, and as Abel trots down the hall he can hear a faint hissing sound. He stops at the end of the hallway where Bryce's room is across from Jennifer's. The hissing sound is louder here.

Placing his ear to the wall, Abel realizes that the sound comes from lower down. He frowns, trying to understand what it means.

He wishes he had Chaser. But his buffalo lies abandoned on the bed. He must do this alone. Thinking about the way the house is built, he turns, sneaking to the stairway. His feet are padded by the thick carpet as he descends. He enters the kitchen, swallowing hard, and opens the door to the basement. Down there, it is pitch black. Even Abel has a hard time seeing, but he remembers. Step by step he goes down, hearing the faint hiss. He is halfway across the cool cement floor when he smells the pungent sweetness. He stops, and the odor rolls over him, making him wrinkle his nose.

CHAPTER TWENTY-SEVEN

"W E GOTTA GO SHEWIDAN." THE VOICE PIERCED VERON-
ica's dreams.

"Huh?" She rolled over, trying to fight her way
through the haze of sleep. "What?"

"We gotta go Shewidan," Abel insisted doggedly.

"Shewidan? What's that?" Veronica managed to blink herself awake. She lay in bed, the room dark. Abel appeared as a darker blotch perched on the bed in front of her.

"Shewidan. You know. Wamsey went there. We gotta go be safe."

"What are you talking about, Abel?"

"Blond man. He hewe."

"Who?"

"Blond man. Saw him that night at the condo. Befow he killed Muvver."

Veronica sat up, making a face, as if it would bring her muscles to life. "Wait a minute. Start at the beginning. You saw a blond man at the condo?"

"Yess."

"Why didn't you tell me?"

She could see his head slip to the side, looking away. He had his buffalo pressed to his chest.

"I dunno."

"You saw this blond man here? Where, Abel? Show me."

He reached out, took her hand with his, and pulled her. She let him lead her to the window, and she pulled the drapes to one side. "Thewe." He pointed out at the night. "He come acwoss fence. Then sneak awound to the side. I heaw him making sounds. Something stinks in the basement. Smells bad."

Veronica muttered under her breath. "All right. Let me get dressed. Turn on the lights and—"

"No!" Abel cried. "He see. I don't want you dead like Muvver."

At the fear in his voice, she agreed. "All right, Abel. But this had better be good. Let me get dressed and we'll—"

"Come now!" he almost cried, yanking desperately on her hand. Once again she was startled by the strength in his grip.

"All right . . . all right. If we run into Bryce out there while I'm walking around in a bra and panties, I'm going to paddle your bottom."

"No wites," he insisted.

"No lights," she agreed, allowing him to lead her out into the hallway, down the stairs, and through the kitchen. His sense of direction amazed her as he led her around the breakfast bar, to the basement stairs, and then down into the darkness. She felt her way with her feet, cursing herself for not flipping on the switch at the top of the stairs. She had descended a total of six steps when he said, "Smew that?"

She bent, sniffing, and caught the faintest odor. She took another couple of steps down, edging past him. The cloying pungency couldn't be mistaken. "Son of a bitch, gas!"

She turned, urging him up the stairs. "Hurry, Abel. We've got to wake Bryce and Jennifer. Get yourself dressed and packed. Run. This place could go up at any second."

She slammed her hip into the breakfast bar, and again against the dining room table as she made her way to the stairway in a mad dash. Feeling her way down the hallway, she flung Bryce's door open, fumbled her way to the bed, and called, "Bryce? We're in trouble! Wake up!"

"What?"

"The basement's filling with gas. It's a matter of time until the pilot light blows us into pieces. Abel says someone is outside. Get dressed. No lights. Meet me in the garage."

She turned, banged an elbow on the door frame, and grappled with the doorknob to Agent Jones' room. "Jennifer? We're in trouble! Wake up?"

"Huh?" a muzzy voice asked from the bed.

"Someone's outside with a gun, and the basement's filling with gas. Don't turn on the light. Get dressed and get to the garage."

Without waiting to see what Jones would do, she turned, felt her way to the hall and her room. Her heart was pounding like a frightened rabbit's. As she felt for her clothes, she stubbed her toe on the corner of the dresser. The rest turned into a blur as she pulled on her shirt and pants, forgot about her shoes, and grabbed up her nylon bag with its precious notes.

"Abel? Where are you?"

"Hewe!"

"Hurry! We've got to get to the garage."

She followed his dark shape into the hallway, hearing Jones talking on the cell phone. "I don't know. Dr. Tremain did. What? No, she says gas. I'll let you know."

"Hurry!" Veronica urged.

"You go on," Jones called. "Wait in the garage. The team outside is keeping an eye on things. You're sure there's gas in the basement?"

"Positive."

"Get yourself and the child into the garage." Jones was following, but turned off, and Veronica saw her start down the stairs, the glow of a flashlight illuminating the stairwell.

"Bryce?" Veronica almost tripped over the step that led down to the garage. The door was open, a darker rectangle in the gloom.

"Here." His voice came from the cool depths of the garage, and she heard the Durango's door open. The dome light illuminated her way to the passenger's seat.

"Abel? Get in the backseat. Hurry now. Have you got your buffalo?"

"Yess."

Veronica braced herself on the truck's fender. The metal slipped coolly under her fingertips. She watched Abel scrambling into the backseat, then slid into the passenger seat; she clutched her bag in her lap.

"What about Jennifer?" Bryce asked.

At that moment, the agent's dark form appeared in the doorway and called, "I'm opening the garage door. We can't take a chance on this. I want you to drive. No lights until you're three blocks away. My team will be on your tail for protection."

"What about you?" Bryce asked.

"I'll be fine. Now, go! Get clear. Stay safe. The chase team will take care of you."

Veronica closed her door, plunging them into darkness, and heard the garage door motor whine, the wheels clanking in their tracks. A starlit gap formed and widened behind them.

How much gas did it take? What was the right mixture before a pilot light flame ignited the whole thing? From the smell of it, a lot of gas had been pouring into the basement.

Bryce turned the key, and the engine roared to life. He slipped the transmission into reverse, telltale brake and back-up lights strobing the garage interior. He cut it closely enough that the luggage rack scraped the wiper on the door bottom as he rocketed backward into the street, stopped, and slammed the Durango into forward.

As acceleration pushed her into the seat, Veronica slouched, anticipating breaking glass, the spatting impact of a bullet.

Concussion—a giant fist out of the night—punched the Durango forward. Yellow light lit the street as a fireball rose into the sky. The Dodge pitched wildly, thrown forward by the detonation.

For an instant, Bryce fought for control. Veronica would have sworn they were up on one front tire. The Dodge reeled, almost rolled. Bryce muscled the wheel. The Durango sideswiped a parked car, and they rolled on around the curve.

Veronica climbed up in the seat, looking back. The rear window glittered in the gaudy light, shattered into a fine lacery of cracks. Through the slanting side window, she could see fire and debris twirling down in the hellish red light. A van conversion rocked on its side in the middle of the street. Where the house had been, only a burning crater remained.

"Sweet Jesus," Bryce murmured, craning his neck to see before the corner cut off the view.

Veronica slumped in the seat, trying to think. She turned, looking back to where Abel huddled in a ball, his buffalo clamped to his chest.

"Abel? Are you sure you saw the same man from the condo?"

Silence.

"Abel, I know you are scared, but tell me, did you see the same man from the condo?"

"Yess," he whimpered.

"I believe you," she stated, straightening. "How? My God, what have they done? Infiltrated the FBI?"

Bryce glanced at her, his face a mask of uncertainty as they pulled up for the red light at the Colfax intersection. Leave it to Bryce to stop. After what they had been through, she'd have run it.

Bryce asked, "What man? Who did Abel see?"

"He says he saw a blond man." Veronica looked over the backseat. "At the condo, right?"

"He killed Muvver. He was hewe, tonight. Wearing big gwasses. He cwimbed the fence. Then he sneaked around the house. I heawd him do something under Bwice's bedwoom. Something metal."

"Son of a bitch." Veronica bit her lip, trying to understand.

The light turned green. Bryce accelerated, taking Colfax toward the city. He glanced in the cracked mirror. "So, what next? I don't see any FBI car following. I think that was them on their side in the middle of the street."

Veronica mulled the different ideas in her head. Certainly they couldn't go to Mother's. Her place in Boulder was out of the question. Anyone searching for them would call every motel in the region asking if a Tremain or a Johnson was registered. She could ... "Hold it! There! That Mini-Mart store. I need to use that phone."

Bryce wheeled into the parking lot, and Veronica stepped out, wincing at the feel of the oily pavement under her bare feet. She pulled her purse from the black nylon bag and walked to the phone. Digging around, she found the right change and sighed thankfully when the exchange clicked and she received a dial tone. She entered the number from memory.

Five rings later, a gruff voice said, "Hello."

"Theo? It's Ronnie. We're in real trouble. Someone just blew up the FBI's safe house."

"What? Blew it up? Are you sure?"

She looked at the Durango, seeing the damage to the fender, the spiderwebbed glass in the back. Both taillights were broken out and the sheet metal bowed in. "I was there, damn it! You'll see it all on the morning news in a couple of hours. Gas explosion. Look, Theo, we're just starting to figure this out. We need a place to go. Someplace where no one can find us. I need a favor more than I've ever needed a favor in my life."

To Bryce's way of the thinking, the Brown Palace Hotel had to be one of the world's classiest operations. The desk clerk hadn't batted an eye when three bedraggled people had stepped in off the street to check in at four-fifteen A.M.

The journey to the hotel had been a masterpiece of ingenuity in itself. Theo Bennet had met them in the parking lot of an all-night diner on the corner of Speer and Colfax.

"Where we used to meet when I was a 'juvie.'" Veronica told Bryce later.

Bennet, wearing a pullover shirt, black slacks, and oxfords, had studied the Durango's damage and shook his head. "You're lucky you didn't get stopped getting here. Here, take my Caddy. I'll drink coffee inside until sunrise and drive your Durango home."

Bennet had made reservations for three at the Brown Palace, under his name and credit card.

"Thank you, sir," Bryce said, shaking the lawyer's hand. "I'll never forget this."

"You get used to it." A faint smile played about his lips. "Life around Ronnie is never anything but eventful." He leaned close. "But you might tell her that her shirt is on backwards and inside out before she checks into the hotel."

Bryce had forgotten that fact, too preoccupied with Ronnie's directions as they drove through downtown Denver's one-way streets to the historic hotel. Leaving Bennet's Cadillac with valet parking, Bryce accepted the little yellow receipt and hobbled painfully into the lobby. That's when he finally understood the meaning of real honest-to-God class.

How many places in the world could a limping and disheveled man with no luggage but a pistol case, a little boy with a stuffed buffalo, and a barefooted woman with her T-shirt on backward and inside out, check into a hotel without so much as a raised eyebrow?

With considerable aplomb, Bryce told the bellman that no, they didn't need help with luggage. He suspected that Abel—with his unusual strength—would have pulled the guy's kneecap off should he have attempted to carry Chaser up to the room. Veronica wouldn't let loose of her nylon bag with its notes, calipers, and research materials. For his part, Bryce wasn't about to let the man carry his nylon-cased HK up to the room.

As they crossed the lobby to the elevator, he marveled at the elegant interior. The nine floors were open to the lobby, row after row of brass-decorated railings rising toward a stained-glass roof high above. Pure, unadulterated, Victorian splendor.

When the tiger-striped brown elevator doors slipped closed behind them, Bryce asked, "Who thought of putting us here?"

Veronica pulled the unruly mass of her raven hair to one side. "It seemed like the only smart thing. If anyone calls the room, you are Theodor Bennet, with your wife and child."

"Wife?" Bryce gave her an inquisitive look.

"That's the story." She was tired enough, ragged enough, to have missed the innuendo.

"Right." He looked down at Abel. "Hi, Son."

Abel gazed up with his large, serious eyes. He just tucked Chaser more tightly to his chest.

The elevator opened; they crossed to the balcony and looked out over the railing.

"Wow," Bryce whispered. Abel pressed his face to the ornate grill and looked down at the lobby seven floors below. He fingered the casting curiously.

Veronica led them to the room and used the plastic key to open the door. Bryce followed her and Abel inside. Classical music played from the bedside radio, the sheets had been pulled back, and chocolates in gold foil rested beside the stacked pillows.

"Pick your poison." Veronica indicated the beds.

"Whichever," he replied.

"Right. Abel and I get the one closest to the bathroom." She turned, stepping up onto the tiled bathroom floor and shutting the door. After a moment, he heard her cry, "Son of a bitch!"

"What?" he asked, leaning next to the white wooden door. Abel watched uncertainly.

"My shirt's on backwards!"

"And inside out," he added.

"You're a real gem, Johnson. You could have told me."

"And had you change in the car? I'd have been distracted and run us off the road. Never wreck a lawyer's car. You might just as well kiss your future good-bye. It would be as dumb as opening your bank account to the IRS."

"I'll get you for this."

"Promise?"

He was standing a prudently safe distance away when she opened the bathroom door and stepped out wearing one of the hotel's white terry-cloth robes. Her hair was up, and she glowered at him as she crossed to the bed and slipped under the covers. She patted the space next to her, and Abel climbed up with his buffalo.

Bryce took the next shot at the bathroom and found another of the plush robes hanging from the back of the door.

When he stepped out, the room was dark, the music off. The room door opened under his grip, and he hung the Do Not Disturb sign outside before he locked up and limped to his bed. He made sure he could touch the HK .45 where it rested on the nightstand. Then he took the chair by the window and propped his swollen ankle on the foot of his bed. Had his air cast survived the explosion?

With one finger he raised the drape enough to look out

at the night. The city glowed in yellow light. Across from him stood an old stone church left over from Denver's frontier days, a beautiful building now dwarfed by skyscrapers.

"Do you think she's alive?" Veronica asked from her bed.

"I don't know. She was right behind us when I drove out. I'm hoping she made it to that vehicle before the explosion."

"If they could find us there . . ."

He nodded to the night. "We'll have to be very careful from here on out."

"I'm scared, Bryce."

He smiled at that. "Me, too. But we'll make it."

"You're a good man, Bryce Johnson. Solid."

He didn't respond, thinking about how close they had just come to death. Desperately hoping that Jennifer had survived, that yet another decent human being hadn't been killed. Hoping that Veronica and the boy wouldn't be next.

Ramsey paced, livid, as he crisscrossed the littered lawn in front of the De France street safe house, or what was left of it.

Robert Dole watched him with hooded eyes, expression pinched. He stood with his hands in his suit pockets, unwilling to speak until Ramsey's anger burned itself out.

"How?" Ramsey demanded yet again. "How could they know we were here?"

"*If* they knew," Dole reminded gently. "It's a gas explosion, Jack."

Fire trucks, police cars, and news trucks crowded the street behind them.

Ramsey couldn't help it: He drew back and kicked the hell out of a piece of shattered drywall that lay on the grass. Amidst the snaking fire hoses and bustle, no one seemed to notice.

"Jack," Dole continued, "we just don't know yet."

"Remind me, what have we got?"

"The guys in the van said they got a call from S.A. Jones at oh-three-ten. She said that Tremain reported that someone was outside, and the basement was full of gas. Jones was in contact with the agents in the van. According to them, she agreed that the basement smelled of gas. She evacuated the witnesses, and had set up the standard protocol when the place went up. The guys in the van were caught in the blast. One was knocked cold; the other has a broken arm. Special Agent Jones is at Saint Luke's. My latest update is that she's going to make it. They took a big splinter out of her chest, and she's got broken bones."

"And Johnson, Tremain, and the boy are gone? Vanished?"

Dole said nothing, jerking a bare nod. At that moment, one of the guys from the Denver ERT stood up from behind the wreckage of the back wall. He picked his way carefully across the lawn and stopped before Dole. A piece of twisted pipe lay in his hands.

"What have you got, Dewey?"

"Gas pipe, sir." Dewey, a thin man with a chocolate-brown complexion, held up the pipe. "I think this is it. The nut was unscrewed."

"You're sure?"

"Yes, sir. Uh, explosions rupture pipes, not fasteners. And, even if it did, it would have stripped the threads. We'll take it to the lab, but, sir, just from looking at it here, this brass has polish on it. Someone unscrewed it recently."

Ramsey knotted his fists, a thunderous frown incising his forehead. "We need to know, Dewey."

The man nodded, retreating and bearing his piece of pipe as if it were the Holy Grail.

"Who the hell are these people?" Dole wondered.

"Leopard Paxton, my people tell me, used to gather electronic intelligence. His specialty was infiltration and monitoring enemy communications, breaking into their systems. He was one of ours, Bob." He shot a half-lidded glance at Dole. *Monitoring? Infiltration?* "I think maybe we've been compromised. If that's the case, we may need to give this a little thought."

"Call Quantico?"

"Not yet. We still don't know how the hell they figured out that the house was about to blow. Suspicious, isn't it, that Tremain, Johnson, and the boy have vanished?" He turned on his heel. "Come on. Maybe Agent Jones is out of surgery. I need to know what happened here. In the meantime, put out an alert on Johnson, Tremain, and the kid. That blue Durango can't be that hard to locate." He smacked a fist into his palm. "Either they were part of this, or this happened specifically to kill them. Either way, I *want* those people, and I want them *now!*"

Abel hears the subtle knock on a door down the hall. It is muffled through the wood and walls of the hotel. A voice says, "Housekeeping."

After a moment, he can hear a door being opened and clicking shut.

Abel pulls his hand from his mouth, fighting the urge to suck on his thumb. Instead, he pats Chaser reassuringly and lifts his head. He remembers Veronica folding him into her arms after one of his nightmares, telling him, "Stay here, Abel. I don't want you sleeping behind the toilet. You saved our lives. You are the bravest little boy in the whole world. I'll keep you safe. I promise."

He had let her hold him until he drifted off to dreams of Mother, and fun times, and Brian O'Neil. Would he ever see Brian again?

Morning light sends a glow through the big window. He can hear the whisper of traffic from outside. The air-conditioner fan purrs in its cabinet below the window.

Bryce is sprawled flat on his back, his face slack, mouth open. Stubble coats his cheeks.

Abel turns and studies Veronica. Her face, too, is toward the light. He can see her eyes twitching under the lids. Mother's eyes used to move like that. At first it had scared him, but Mother told him later that it was dreams that made the eyes move.

He takes a long time, looking closely at Veronica's face, learning each of the shapes. He sees the faint speckles in her skin, the first hint of lines around the corners of her eyes. Her lashes are long, black, and delicate. He sees a bit of lint in her eyebrows and is tempted to pick it out, but that might wake her.

Since he has been with her, she has been kind to him. He feels the falling of his stomach and fights the descent into grief. He wonders where Mother went. How she could have died and left him. Veronica has treated him differently than Mother did: preoccupied, worried. So many times when he looks at her, he sees her concern for him. At other times, she is worried about him. That difference leaves him confused.

Unlike Mother, she believes him when he tells her things . . . like about the blond-headed man. Mother wouldn't have listened. Not like that. But Mother would have smiled at him, held him, and taken better care of him.

Still, he is glad that Veronica is his friend. And Bryce, too, with his black pistol lying on the stand beside his bed. Bryce and Veronica will keep him safe. Just like they did from the explosion last night.

The memory of it haunts him: that giant power that pitched the car around like a leaf; the loud snapping of the glass in the back; and the wild jolt when Bryce hit the other car.

Only after they had come here did the fear subside. Here, beside Veronica, he feels safe. Here, so high in the hotel, the blond man can't creep up and see him. With all these rooms, the blond man couldn't find them if he tried, could he?

Abel frowns, thinking about the strange glasses the blond man wore last night. What where they? Some-

thing to make him see better? But he hadn't worn them on the moonlit night at the condo.

If he ever finds me, he will kill me, just like he did Mother. A chill runs through his chest, and he reaches out to touch Chaser again. Why is he so afraid of death? Why does he feel so weak and scared?

Can't he be like Chaser? Buffalo are strong. He feels the strength imparted by that touch of the animal's fur. He is strong again. But with each memory of the blond man—and the clap of explosion that could nearly turn their car over—his fear grows. It is becoming harder and harder to be brave. He's so tired.

What will happen to them when he can't be brave any longer?

CHAPTER TWENTY-EIGHT

THE SENSATION OF WALKING—HOBBLING ACTUALLY— down the Sixteenth Street Mall surprised Bryce. He was alone, out in public, in a city where at least one man was stalking him with an intent to kill. A sick sense of vulnerability, of how fragile his thin layer of clothing was, had settled in his gut like a heavy, indigestible meal.

On the crowded mall with its suit-clad men and businesswomen, beggars, pedestrians, shoppers, and musicians, he couldn't shake the feeling that a bull's-eye had been drawn on the middle of his chest. He limped along warily, the scrap of paper folded in his hand.

He found a clothing store across from a Barnes and Noble bookstore, entered, and encountered a rather surly female clerk. She directed him upstairs to the women's shoe section. There, he picked out a pair of brown leather pumps, checked the size against the tracing he'd made of Veronica's foot, and recoiled at the price tag.

When it became apparent that he wasn't in the market for a two hundred dollar pair of women's shoes, he hit the cement for the walk to the Walgreen's three blocks down. There, in a bargain bin, he found canvas-top sneakers for five bucks a pair.

Retrieving his prize, he started back to the Brown Palace, ignoring the pain in his ankle and trying to walk normally. He couldn't help but wonder why everyone on the street didn't stare at him. The sensation prickled his skin. People passed him as if it were a normal day, not one immediately following an explosion that came within a breath of killing him.

That's when he saw the headlines on the June twenty-first edition of the *Denver Post*: FERRIS MURDER A CONSPIRACY?

He bent down, reading what he could above the fold. Mostly it was a recounting of the number of murders, their gruesome nature, and how Billy Barnes Brown's church might be involved.

He waited for the light, crossed Seventeenth Street,

passed the Native American art gallery, and smiled at the uniformed doorman who held the brass door for him.

At his floor, he walked to the room, tapped lightly on the door, and waited. The patter of little feet was followed by Abel's struggle with the door handle. Then Bryce ducked in, pausing long enough to ruffle Abel's hair and ask, "Miss me?"

"Yess." Abel smiled up at him. "Bettew now that you come back."

"Hey, it's the mean streets out there." Bryce stepped into the room, finding Veronica curled in the middle of the bed, wearing the white robe. Her long black hair draped artistically over her shoulder. When she looked up, an excitement filled her marvelous blue eyes. In that instant, he wished he had a camera.

"What?" she asked. "You look as if you've just seen a miracle. Did you get me shoes?"

He gave her a crooked smile. "Miracle is an understatement. You're beautiful this morning." He tossed her the package. "They'll get you by until we can find real walking gear."

She lifted an eyebrow, appraising him with a curious reserve, then pulled the black sneakers from the sack and jiggled the price tag with a finger.

"Nothing flashy like Ben would have bought you, but they'll do."

"Oh, I don't know. I might just keep these. Sometimes flashy things can become a pain in the ass." Her smile surprised him, as did the lowering of her voice when she said, "Thank you, Bryce."

He basked in the tingle. "No problem." Then he took a deep breath. "We're front-page news, but they don't seem to have connected the safe house explosion to the Ferris case yet."

"Great," she muttered; then a pensive look changed the cast of her expression. "Caught part of the news . . . they wonder if I was killed in the condo. Apparently they haven't identified . . ." She hesitated, biting her lip as she glanced at Abel. "Well, you know."

Bryce stretched and rolled his shoulders. "Isn't it nice to know that at least there's someone out there who's more in the dark than we are?"

"I'm hungwy," Abel's nasal voice interrupted.

"Right," Veronica said, taking a breath and unwinding her long legs from the bed. She stepped across to the hotel service folder, found room service, and started reading out the list of things for breakfast. Throughout the process, Bryce couldn't help but notice that she kept shooting him speculative glances, and something special lay behind those looks.

The office was paneled with walnut wainscoting below a velvet-patterned white wallpaper that gave the room a historical look. Even the light fixtures and dark wooden bookcases added to the sensation of having just stepped one hundred years into the past.

Jack Ramsey followed the secretary into the office and introduced himself, shaking Theodor Bennet's hand before he took one of the two leather chairs opposite the desk. "Thank you for seeing me on such short notice."

"Quite the contrary, I was about to call you. Dr.

Tremain is concerned about your agent, um, Ms. Jones. Is she all right?"

"Agent Jones is out of surgery. She's going to live. We don't know about the long-term damage, but the explosion drove a large splinter through her back and into her right lung. The other agents are recovering." Ramsey took out his notebook. "Where is Dr. Tremain?"

"Someplace safe." Bennet leaned back in an overstuffed chair, steepling his fingers before him. "After last night, she's a little wary of FBI protection."

"I have some questions I need to ask her about last night." Ramsey studied Bennet, trying to take the man's measure. This was one of Denver's most prominent attorneys, senior partner in one of the state's most prestigious firms. Within moments, any notion of trying to bulldog the man faded.

"My clients have provided me with an account of the events that transpired. Apparently the little boy sees very well in the dark. He hasn't been sleeping well. He told Dr. Tremain that he liked to look out the window at the deer that fed behind the house. Last night, the deer didn't come, but a man did. A blond-headed man, according to the little boy. The child claims to have seen this same man the night before his mother was killed in Frisco. Last night, the man was wearing what Abel called 'big glasses.' The fellow climbed the fence, and Abel heard him doing something that sounded like metal being rapped against metal. He said it came from under Dr. Johnson's bedroom. For that reason, Abel went downstairs to investigate. That's when he smelled something foul."

"The little boy did all of this?"

Bennet nodded, picking up a sheet of white paper and handing it across. "Those are the transcribed notes I took on the phone with Ronnie, uh, Dr. Tremain, about fifteen minutes ago. You may take a photocopy with you if you'd like."

"I'd like." Ramsey read the crisp lines. "This is the way it happened? It says here 'No lights.' What's that mean?"

"Apparently the little boy was traumatized when Ms. Armely was shot. He was afraid the blond-headed man was going to shoot through the windows." Bennet's gaze fixed Ramsey's. "Special Agent Ramsey, let's be candid with each other, shall we? Something very sinister is going on here. Scott's death wasn't a random act. Who are these people who are trying to kill Bryce, Veronica, and the boy? Why are they doing this? How, in God's name, did they find your safe house?"

Ramsey gave Bennet a wooden stare. "Honestly, sir, we don't know yet. We have some leads, but too many pieces of this thing are dangling. All I can tell you is that we're up against some very dangerous, very competent people. They seem to believe in what they're doing."

"They are murdering people, Agent Ramsey."

Powered by an adrenaline surge, Ramsey stood. Angrily, he paced back and forth, stopping for a moment to inspect the spines on the legal books covering one wall. "Yeah, I know they are. I also know that Scott Ferris and his people built a human being out of bits and pieces of DNA! We're supposed to have a moratorium on that sort of research. Didn't your Mr. Ferris give any thought to the ethics of creating a synthetic person?"

"We don't know that he did any such thing. So far as I

can ascertain, the boy isn't 'synthetic' is he, but real bone and blood? What I *saw* last night, Agent Ramsey, was one very frightened little blue-eyed boy holding a stuffed buffalo. He is not some grisly monster."

Ramsey shook his head slowly. "I like to consider myself to be an open-minded man. But this . . . I don't know. It's going to take some time. I'm still not sure that I believe that kid could have been made in a laboratory." He looked at Bennet. "What are the chances that this could be some kind of a snow job? A hoax that's gone wrong? It could be, couldn't it?"

Bennet gave him a weary stare. "I watched Scott Ferris grow up, sir. In many ways, he was like a son to me. I understand some of the research he's been doing. Not the intricacies, mind you, but the potentials. That boy is no hoax. Scott was attempting to do something important."

"You mean, irresponsible."

"No, I mean important." Bennet's serious expression didn't waver. "He wasn't the irresponsible kind. Believe me, he had a plan for all of this, and my suspicion is that had he not been killed, he and Amanda would have worked it out." Theo sighed. "Now, getting back to the reality of the situation, what happened last night?"

"I've got evidence that someone took apart the gas line that fed the house. They probably pushed the pipe through the collar in the foundation and pumped the basement full of gas. You're an attorney, so tell me: Without the wrench that did it, and no witnesses but a little boy who saw a blond man wearing big glasses, what are my chances in court?"

Bennet pursed his lips. "I see what you mean." He narrowed an eye, the bushy eyebrow puckering. "Agent Ramsey, are you tapping my phone?"

Ramsey started. "What?"

"Are you?"

"No!" Ramsey shook his head. "We don't have any reason to. I can guarantee you, if I did place a tap on an attorney's phone—especially one of your caliber—I'd be covered by a rock-solid warrant."

Bennet swiveled in his chair. "I had a case a couple of years back. Drugs, extortion, and some other things. At the time, it was deemed necessary to place a security system on my phone lines. Something activated that system this morning, Agent Ramsey. Now, I don't think you can trace the call back to Ronnie's cellular, at least not and locate her. But I highly resent—"

"It's *not* us. Maybe the press . . . No, it's not the sort of thing they'd . . ." Ramsey's frown deepened; then he suddenly smacked a fist into his palm.

"Yes?" Bennet asked.

"Sometimes the greatest gifts come from the most unusual places. Can I have the ERT, uh, the Evidence Response Team, take a look at your phone system here? Maybe, just maybe, they've been moving so fast, they've made a mistake."

Bennet considered. "I will have to talk to my partners. We have to protect the confidentiality of our clients. It wouldn't do—"

"You're too late," Ramsey said, waving him down. "You had better tell your partners to shut up right now. If the guy we suspect is behind this, you're already compromised." He started. "Did Dr. Tremain tell you where she was when she called?"

"By prior agreement, she did not." Bennet had straightened. "We were afraid you had tapped the lines trying to find her."

"No," Ramsey said, pacing faster now, his mind racing. "But if you're right, someone did. Look, we've got to assume they compromised your conversation with Dr. Tremain. Are you sure—positive—that her call couldn't be traced, that you didn't give away some clue as to their whereabouts?"

"Absolutely positive, Agent Ramsey."

Ramsey narrowed an eye, reading the lawyer's expression. "We've got to get them somewhere safe."

"They are safe."

"After that," Ramsey said, ignoring Theo, "we've got to put protection on you, Mr. Bennet."

"I hardly think—"

"I imagine Scott Ferris didn't either. Nor did Joe Hanson. But someone got what he wanted from both of those people. Like it or not, Mr. Bennet, we can't let them get to you."

Bennet looked like he'd swallowed something moldy.

Bryce wondered if there had ever been such a beautiful woman. He couldn't keep his gaze from straying her way. She was seated at the desk now, working on her figures. Frowning periodically, she leafed through the book the young FBI agent had brought her from Boulder.

Abel lay asleep on the foot of the bed, his head propped on his buffalo. His mouth hung open, large white teeth visible against the pink swell of his tongue. Being a hero had evidently been exhausting for the little guy.

Now Veronica turned, her critical eye on Abel, on the profile of his face.

"What?" Bryce asked.

"These data," she said, indicating the figures. "Abel isn't what we thought."

"You're telling me he's Amanda's kid?"

"Nope." She studied him, a curious swirl of emotion in her eyes. "Remember when you told him last night that he was a miracle?"

"Yeah."

"Well, he's a bigger miracle than we thought."

"I don't get it. I think a genetically engineered human is a pretty big miracle. Especially to have one as viable and smart as Abel seems to be. And his strength, my God. You've seen the things he can do. Like someone twice his age. He sees better, smells better, hears better . . ." Bryce shook his head. "Sometimes it scares me that Scott, Amanda, and Avi could pick so many traits that make a better human. I look at Abel and ask, 'Is that our future?' "

"Our past," Veronica corrected. At Bryce's dumb look, she said, "That big head? It has somewhere around fourteen hundred cc's of brain in it. That's about a third larger than a four-year-old should have."

"You're trying to tell me he's some sort of superhuman? That he's going to make us all obsolete? That he really *is* the future of humanity?"

"Past," she insisted doggedly. "That head of his, the indicies fall right into the middle of the Teshik-Tash and La Quina data set."

"The what?"

Veronica stood, flipping her long hair back. She stretched, and Bryce tried not to notice how it pressed her breasts against the fabric of the terry-cloth robe.

"I want you to understand, all humans have a range of variation. We're programmed to be individually different, but certain traits arise in given frequencies within populations. People have different phenotypes, meaning they look different from other humans, but the same for their group. Races, if you will."

"Right. So?"

She met his eyes. "We're agreed that Abel is at the core of this, right?"

"Yeah, so?"

"Scott and Amanda didn't make someone new. The Scott I knew wouldn't have done that. It would have been cruel and irresponsible. Abel isn't a constructed human, Bryce. He wasn't assembled out of some perverted recipe of human DNA to be some next-generation human."

"Then what is he? You said he was a Tish-Tash?"

"Teshik-Tash and La Quina were children who lived sixty thousand years ago in Asia and Europe, Bryce."

He gave her an askance look. "Run that by me again?"

Veronica settled herself in front of him and earnestly looked into his eyes, making sure he understood her. "I'm saying that Abel's skull, his body, has the same characteristics as people had sixty thousand years ago in Europe. The length-breadth ratio, the indices, are normal for those populations. The ratio of forearm length to upper arm length, which we call the brachial index, the length of the calf to thigh, which we call the crural index, falls within that mean." She tightened her grip.

"And there are other things. His midfacial prognathism. Yoel Rak compared that kind of face to a locomotive once. Look at it. It's like a prow, Bryce. And when you feel around, you can't find a canine fossa like modern humans have."

"Huh?"

"The hollow." She pressed a finger just under the corner of his nose. "Right there where the root of the canine tooth and the angle of the cheek meet. Abel doesn't have one. None of his people did."

Bryce shot a skeptical glance at the sleeping boy. "You're saying that Scott, Amanda, and Avi recreated a form of ancestral human by means of genetic manipulation? Some mixture of ape and human genes?"

She shook her head. "Not ape and human. You'd get something else, probably more like an Australopithecine, or a Habiline, or some form of *Homo erectus*. No, I . . ." Her expression strained. "Hell, I don't know. That's not my field. I'm a bone person. You'd know more about the effects of genes on phenotype."

"Wrong," he stated flatly. "I just did the math."

"Well, you must have done it very well, Bryce." She nodded. "Because right there, you have a living, breathing, fossil human sleeping on his own private buffalo."

"Ronnie, are you hearing what you're saying? That Scott and Amanda recreated a Tish-Tash—"

"Teshik-Tash."

"Right. Teshik-Tash. That they built a prehistoric human clone?" It was his turn to shake his head. "You can't do that, Ronnie. The genes are gone, the combinations lost. We can't do that sort of thing from fossil bone."

"Didn't you just coauthor an article on recovering genetic material from prehistoric DNA in the *American Journal of Physical Anthropology*?"

He frowned. "Yes, but Scott told me . . ." He experienced a sinking sensation.

"Yes?"

". . . That it was an archaeological sample from somewhere in Asia. From a high-altitude mummy." He took a deep breath, not knowing what to believe. Wondering if that, too, might have been part of Scott's plan. Solidifying the idea in the professional literature in preparation for eventually springing Abel on the world.

She stared decisively at him. "I don't care what you think they could or couldn't have done, the proof sits right there in that little boy. Scott figured out the genotype, the formula; you did, as you say, the math; Avi made the embryo; and it was implanted in Amanda. She gave birth, and Rebecca adopted it."

Bryce cocked his jaw. "That's nuts. You can't prove any of this."

She nodded soberly. "Bryce. It's my area of expertise. Abel doesn't have a protruding chin. Modern humans have a jutting chin. Abel doesn't. His chin recedes. I can prove this. All I need is to get that kid into an MRI machine, or take an X ray."

He looked into the fathomless depths of her blue eyes, uncomfortably aware that no doubts lurked down there in her soul. "I've never even heard of Teshik-Tash before."

She turned then. "No, you haven't. You know them by another name. In your language, you'd call that little boy there . . . *Homo sapiens neandertalensis*." She swallowed hard. "That's what they've done. They've dared Billy Barnes Brown—and all who place faith over science—to deny that evolution ever happened."

"You mean, Abel's—"

"A Neandertal boy. Right here in the beginning of the twenty-first century."

CHAPTER TWENTY-NINE

"ARE YOU SURE THIS IS A GOOD IDEA?" VERONICA ASKED as they walked from the desk to the Brown Palace's front door. Abel toddled along, his buffalo and his canvas bag clutched in his hands. Smart little guy that he was, he knew something else had gone wrong in his world. He was watching them with those wide blue eyes, a look of incipient terror on his face.

"Trust me," Bryce muttered. "Two hours ago, I'd have been happy to wait it out in the lap of luxury. But we made a mistake at the condo that I'm not going to make again. Especially if Abel's a Neanderthal."

"I need more comparative data." Her voice filled with frustration. "The only subadult Trinkaus evaluated was Shanidar Seven, and it was incomplete. His other work, on the Lagar Velho boy, described a hybrid. The skull was fragmentary, though."

They waited while the valet brought up Theo's Cadillac.

"What about Teshik-Tash?" Bryce asked.

"The report is in Russian by a fellow named Gremyatskij. You can't just find it at the local Barnes and Noble. At the physical anthropology lab in Boulder we have an old Carolina Biological cast of the La Quina child. That's who Abel reminded me of. I just couldn't make it all fit."

"Abel reminded you of a cast?" Bryce glanced down, meeting the little boy's eyes. He whispered conspiratorially, "She's a physical anthropologist. They're all a little weird."

Abel gave him a solemn doe-eyed look.

The Cadillac appeared from the guts of the parking garage across the street. The driver wheeled it out, cut a wide swath across the traffic, and held the door for Veronica. Abel climbed dutifully into the backseat, propping himself between his buffalo and his book sack.

Veronica said, "Thanks," and handed the valet a three-dollar tip. She adjusted the seat as Bryce climbed into the passenger seat. Putting the car into gear, she eased out into traffic before taking a left onto Seventeenth. "Okay, Dr. Johnson, you're the one who thought it was time to blow the joint. Where are we headed?"

Bryce had been chewing on his lip, making a face. "I don't know. Now that we think we know who Abel is—what he might be—I'd feel better as a moving target." He gestured to the traffic plugging Seventeenth Street. "Pick a direction. Any direction."

She gave him a twisted smile. "All right."

"I'm glad you're the one driving the lawyer's car. You never want to make a lawyer mad. You know, like with a scratch in the paint? They're an unpredictable life-form at best."

She laughed. "Yeah, I know. I think we need another car. I don't want to take a chance on Theo's." She gave him a challenging grin, "I don't know about you, but a Cadillac just isn't my style."

"Mine either. You're supposed to be sixty before a Cadillac starts to appeal to your sense of self-identity. It's something geriatric." He frowned, eyes on the traffic. "Abel can't be a Neanderthal." He looked over the back-seat. "Can you, little buddy?"

Veronica shifted her head to see him in the rearview mirror. His big blue eyes were fixed on Bryce. "No caw seat. Not safe."

Veronica shrugged wearily. "Half the world wants him dead, and he's worried about a car seat. I know of a Kmart on South Colorado Boulevard. Maybe we'd better get him one."

Bryce tapped his fingers rhythmically on the plush leather upholstery. "I still can't buy this. How could Scott and Amanda just cook up a Neanderthal?" He gave her a sidelong glance, eyes skeptical. "Sure, okay, I know what your indices suggest, but, darn it, Ronnie, he doesn't *look* like a Neanderthal."

"And what should a Neandertal look like, Dr. Johnson?"

"All the pictures I've ever seen have depicted black-haired, hulking, brown-eyed, stoop-shouldered brutes. Abel's skin is so pale he'd get a sunburn from a flashbulb. And look at that hair! Marilyn Monroe should have been so lucky! Not only that, but since when have Neanderthals had big blue eyes? The kid looks like a bug-eyed Norwegian."

"More like a Finn, actually." She paused, lips crooked. "So, tell me, Bryce, just how many Neandertals have you seen in the flesh?"

"Counting Abel? One."

She took Speer to First Avenue, passing in front of the Tattered Cover Bookstore, wondering if it would pay to stop, to peruse their anthropology section for Neandertal references. God knows, they had everything else in there.

"That's one more," she said, "than the people who drew those pictures had ever seen." Following First through Cherry Creek to Colorado Boulevard, she took a right, heading south. "Bryce, think about this: The only evidence we have are fossil bone, archaeological remains, and some teeth. No hair or eyes." She frowned. "But, it would make sense. They were cold adapted for over two hundred thousand years."

"Cold adapted?" Bryce glanced at her.

"That's right. They lived along the southern margins of the giant glaciers that covered Europe during the last ice age. Big, thick bodies don't radiate heat. It's called 'Bergmann's and Allen's Rules.' Big round bodies in cold country and thin long bodies in hot country. Inuit people are round and compact to retain warmth; Masai are tall, thin, and beanpole shaped to dissipate heat."

"And Abel?"

"The further north you go, the lighter people are complected. Pale skin allows the body to synthesize vitamin

D from limited sunlight. Abel doesn't like hot places or sunlight." She glanced back. "Isn't that right?"

Abel had gone into remote mode, talking in an inaudible voice to his buffalo. She caught the word "N'andertaw," pointedly aware that a living Neandertal was saying its name for the first time.

Veronica thumped the steering wheel. "What if modern *Homo sapiens* mingled with Neandertals? That's what Trinkaus' data from Portugal suggests. What if blond hair, blue eyes, and white skin are residual, the legacy of the Neandertals in our modern European populations? Remember what Rebecca said, that Scott and Amanda had solved the 'replacement' debate once and for all?"

"That leads me to another thought. We're assuming he's all Neanderthal," Bryce countered. "Maybe Scott and Amanda just picked certain archaic genes out of the modern gene pool."

She shot him a sour glance. "You know Scott better than that. He wouldn't have done this if he couldn't have recreated an original. What would the point be?"

Bryce was silent, thinking about it.

"Anything but a real respirating Neandertal would have been a trick, a sleight. They weren't into shams and hoaxes."

"No, never." Bryce looked miserable.

"You're the genetics expert. Where did they get the DNA? I thought mineralized bone, desiccated bone, anything over ten thousand years, and the DNA was so degraded that you couldn't use it."

"That's usually right." He concentrated on the back of the big Ford Expedition stopped at the light in front of them. "But Goodman reported on DNA taken from the Mezmaiskaya Neanderthals. That followed the mitochondrial DNA from the Feldhofer specimens. But those were just fragments of cellular DNA, not nuclear DNA. So, all right, suppose Avi recovered fragments from one of the Israeli specimens—say, Kebara, or Tabun. He sent it to Scott, who took the sample, augmented it through a PCR machine in Fort Collins, and filled in the blanks through DNA hybridization." He glanced at her. "You know what that is?"

She nodded. "You select a section of DNA from a given location on a chromosome and cut it with a restriction enzyme. Heat the strand and it separates. You do the same with another strand from a comparable location on a similar species' chromosome, and put the two halves from the different species together. As you lower the temperature, the two segments try and unite. Then you study how many base pairs don't match. That tells you the genetic distance between those species."

"Maybe that's what Scott and Amanda did."

"You don't look satisfied." Veronica accelerated across the I-25 viaduct. That Kmart had to be here somewhere.

"I'm not. They were out to make a point. Nuclear DNA is almost impossible to recover from thirty-thousand-year-old bone. It would be a miracle to find it preserved. It would be an even greater miracle to recover it, intact, from the fossil bone." Bryce was thumping the upholstery now. "But, if Scott was right, if the specimen I cataloged came from a high-altitude mummy?" He lifted an eyebrow. "Who found the mummy? Asia, Scott said. He never went to Asia, not that I know of."

"No," Veronica agreed. "He didn't. And if anyone else in the field had found mummified Neandertal remains, you can bet it would have been all over the profession. The press would have hopped right on it. CNN, *Time*, *Newsweek*—it would have been splattered everywhere."

"Assuming whoever found it reported it." Bryce's jaw had locked.

Veronica paused thoughtfully. "Do you know what the odds are that a paleoanthropologist would discover a mummified Neandertal . . . and *not* report it?"

"Astronomical."

"Right. Which leads us back to DNA hybridization with bits of nuclear DNA from fossil bone." She made a gesture on the steering wheel. "I don't know, maybe like Robert Broom did in the 1920s when he put pieces of Australopithecine together to get an idea of the skull before the 'Mrs. Ples' specimen was recovered from Sterkfontein."

"Nope. Wrong. You had it the first time. Scott and Amanda wouldn't have filled in the blanks with modern DNA. It would be a half-assed hybrid. They'd never make a halfway statement. It was all or nothing with them." He paused, then added, "Something's missing, Ronnie. We're not getting the whole picture here. And we're only guessing based on some measurements that you took. That's not the same as real proof."

She considered that, knowing he was right. Well, there was one way to find out. She flicked on the left-hand turn signal and pulled into the turn lane. When the light flashed yellow, she pulled a U-turn and headed back north.

"Now where are you going?" Bryce asked.

"To settle this once and for all." Her stomach had begun to flutter. She didn't want to do this. But, damn it, Bryce was right. A couple of measurements of the kid's head were just that. As some physical anthropologists had long been wont to say, indices were just numbers. The problem was in how you interpreted them.

Ten minutes later she pulled into the visitor's lot at the University Medical Center.

Bryce gave her a curious sidelong glance as she slipped the Cadillac into park and turned off the ignition. Her heart had begun to pound.

"Come on, guys. Let's put an end to this once and for all." She nerved herself for the encounter. Once, she thought she'd never have to so much as see his smiling face again. Now, she would have to not only see it, but smile at him as if she meant it. Did she have the courage for this? She'd rather spend a week with the stomach flu.

The interplay of Veronica's expressions fascinated Bryce as the elevator clicked its way upward. Her face might have been a mask, alternately reflecting revulsion, fear, anticipation, anger, and anxiety.

Abel, with his usual perspicacity, watched Ronnie with a wary apprehension that had grown into full-fledged angst. He clutched Bryce's hand in a crushing grip. In that moment, with the blood squeezed from his fingers, Bryce could well imagine the stocky little boy had a Neanderthal's strength. Chaser was stuffed in the crook of Abel's other arm, and from the protruding glass eyes, the grip was just as desperate.

The elevator dinged and the doors hissed back. They walked out onto the hospital's fourth floor, the hallway painted off-white and illuminated by ceiling squares of fluorescent light. Brown doors, inset in steel frames, lined the hallway. The tiled floor gleamed. Nurses in uniform passed, along with occasional doctors in green. The place had that smell, look, and feel that made Bryce's skin clammy.

Veronica led them to an office. The sign on the door identified DR. TREMAIN.

"You don't have to do this," Bryce said one last time.

The jaw muscles were jumping under her soft cheeks, a fire in her eyes. "Bryce, he's got the machines. Or at least access to them." She didn't knock, but pushed the door open.

Bryce glanced down at Abel and said in a low voice, "She's a tougher person than I am." And winked. Abel didn't react, looking more like he'd bolt for the door at the first loud noise. Smart kid, that Abel.

The room looked like a textbook example of a doctor's office. Medical books filled floor-to-ceiling shelving. Four huge file cabinets crowded one wall. Posters showing the locations of bones, muscles, nerves, and other body parts had been pasted to every open space. A three-pane aluminum-framed window cast light over a metal desk covered with piles of paper, a pen holder, coffee cup, calendar, and a note-jotted blotter. A picture of Ben Tremain standing in the open door of a long lean blue Dodge Viper was propped on one corner. On the other was an eight-by-ten color photo of a smiling Ben Tremain in bright yellow leathers astride a racy MV Augusta motorcycle, his helmet in hand.

"Just a minute," Tremain said, his head bent as he sat behind the desk writing furiously on the topmost paper in an open manila folder. He finished the sentence, glanced up—and froze, his eyes on Veronica.

Bryce tried to take his measure. The guy had to be thirty-five now, dark-haired, muscular, fit looking. He wore a physician's green smock. His close-cropped black hair, devilish brown eyes, and perfect nose balanced the strong jaw. The dimple in his chin, and the smile lines around his mobile mouth, would have worked like lode-stones for the female of the species. The first impression in Bryce's mind was that Ben Tremain could have doubled for an Italian sex-idol movie star.

Then a look of loathing hardened his features. "It's over, Ronnie. The papers are signed. I don't care what the cops are after you for, I'm out of it." He gave her a bitter smile. "If you're not out of here in the next second, I'm calling them to come and get you."

Bryce felt Abel's grip tighten further, if that were possible.

Veronica chuckled, and her eyebrow lifted. "God, Ben, it's nice to see you again. Given the shit I've been living for the last two weeks, I can't tell you the effect that the tone of true human compassion in your voice has on me. But I'm not here for help. At least, not the kind you're thinking." She turned, indicating Bryce. "Dr. Bryce Johnson, University of New Hampshire."

"Nice to meet you." Bryce tried to keep his voice professional, relieved that Tremain didn't stand or offer his hand.

"And this is Abel," Veronica introduced, half dragging Abel and his clutched buffalo forward.

Tremain glanced at the boy; then his gaze fixed, a slight frown marring his smooth forehead.

"Scott's dead," Veronica said pointedly. "If you've been reading the papers, or watching the news, you know that. The same people have killed Amanda and a woman named Rebecca, another of their colleagues. Currently, they are trying to kill us. Catch the news? The house out in Jeff Co.? We got out just before it went up. The FBI owned it. The technical term is a 'safe house,' so if you don't get off your damned high horse, I'll leave a note to our hunters explaining that you're in on this. They might dynamite your Viper."

Tremain's mouth had adopted a distasteful twist. "That's not for real, is it?" He glanced at Bryce, as if for assurance.

"We need to have some tests run." Bryce tried to remain professional.

Veronica added, "We need an MRI and X ray of the boy. A blood chemistry and DNA work-up would be very helpful. Abel may be the most special patient you've ever worked on, Ben. He's important enough that no matter what's between us, you've got to do it."

"I don't *have* to do anything, Ronnie." Tremain gripped his pen so hard his knuckles turned white.

"No"—she straightened—"but if the tests show what I think they will, you'll be glad that you did." She leaned forward, placing her hands on his desk. "How about it, Ben? You up for the challenge?"

In that instant, Bryce had the terrible desire to step forward, drag her back, and drive a fist through Tremain's haughty smirk. Instead, he bit his lip and tried to keep from glaring.

"What do you want me to test for?" Ben glanced again at Abel, seeing him through a physician's eyes.

"We don't think he's human," Veronica said levelly.

At that, Tremain broke out into guffaws.

"Come on, Ronnie." Bryce couldn't take it any longer. "We can find other labs that can do this. You don't need to stay here and have this—"

"No, wait!" Tremain lifted a hand. "I'll do it. Just for the pure pleasure of telling the guys at the first tee about it. Free of charge!" He laughed again, standing up. "Sure thing, Ronnie. I wouldn't miss this for the world!"

Bryce ground his teeth, battling the prehistoric male hormones that came frothing up from his limbic system as Tremain pushed past him, cavalierly taking Veronica's elbow in the process. She shot Bryce a warning glance at the last moment before his testosterone overloaded his good sense.

"Are you coming, Dr. Johnson?" Her voice betrayed icy control.

"Yeah," Bryce growled, aware of the HK's weight where it was stuffed into his belt beneath his light canvas windbreaker. For the first time he understood the urge to misuse a firearm. No, better to beat Ben Tremain to death with a hockey stick than give the gun grabbers another statistic. The physical exertion would provide more soul-fulfilling gratification.

"Come on, Abel. Let's go get you tested."

"Nooo," Abel whispered, tugging backward.

"Hey." Bryce bent down, lowering his voice. "You're not going to let that worthless piece of bipedal meat see that you're afraid, are you?"

"Don't wike him."

"I don't like him either, little buddy. But we have to prove we're better than he is. G'Kar could do it."

Abel didn't look like he bought it, but hand in hand, they followed Tremain and Veronica back toward the elevators.

Ben glanced back, noticing his limp. "Hurt foot?"

"A sprained ankle," Veronica told him. "Bryce got hurt rescuing us at the condo. Then he lost his cast when the safe house exploded."

Bryce smiled, shrugging, aware of Tremain's piercing gaze. "It only hurts when I walk on it."

"I'll see if I can't find a replacement before you go." Ben gave Bryce a speculative look, as if evaluating just how intimate he was with Veronica.

Bryce smiled placidly in return, and said, "Thanks, you never know when you'll have to catch another falling woman." If they had been dogs, their hair would have been on end and they'd have been taking turns peeing on the trash can next to the elevator.

With a ding, the light came on and the elevator door slipped open. Abel tugged Bryce off to the side, staying as far as he could from Tremain. The stuffed buffalo looked half crushed where Abel mashed it against his chest. Bryce figured the kid had sense. He glanced at Veronica, seeing the strain that she hid so well. But Ben Tremain only seemed to have eyes for her.

Yeah, well, buddy, you screw around on a woman like that, it always comes around to haunt you.

No matter what kind of data they needed, he couldn't shake the notion that coming here had been a bad mistake.

Each to his own, Leopard Paxton thought, as he sat patiently before the banks of computer equipment. He could spend hours like this, waiting, his mind idling in neutral until the sophisticated monitoring equipment was triggered. The majority of the day had been spent listening to the desultory talk coming out of the lawyer's office. The rest of the time, he had picked up bits and pieces of chatter off of the FBI's FM band: lots of talk about the explosion, about Special Agent Jones' condition and the status of the investigation. Despite his worst fears when they found the section of natural gas pipe, no one was talking like it was any kind of lead.

Paxton glanced over at Ron Elias, asleep on a rumpled sleeping bag in the air-conditioned rear of the van. Another screw-up. Not that Ron had done anything wrong. The plan had worked just like it was supposed to. Pump the basement full of gas, then wait for it to go up. The bedrooms were on the top floor. It was the middle of the night. How in the Lord's divine name had they escaped again?

In the conversation he'd overheard, Tremain had told the lawyer that the kid had warned her? That matched with the FBI communications he'd monitored the night of the explosion. The kid? Was he really Satan's spawn like Elias insisted? Nothing else would explain such luck.

Paxton made a face, knotting his mind around the problem. The next time it would have to be different, more direct, and they'd just have to accept the risks entailed.

But to do it that way wasn't smart. That bothered him.

Just like at Oakdale. They'd been in a hurry, trying to save the kids.

He paused while the FBI band crackled and a man checked in with the Denver F.O.

"Anything?" Elias asked from where he lay on the sleeping bag, one eye open to a slit. "I can't stand this waiting." He was getting jittery, that weird gleam in his eyes.

Paxton turned back to the monitoring equipment. "It will break for us, Ron. It always does." Damn it, he had half a million in the bank, and another 250 grand on tap for expenses. The client had promised another million after the spawn had been eliminated. After that they'd negotiate for the rest.

Paxton listened as Elias mumbled softly to himself. Was it worth it? The Bureau had tagged his ID. He felt once again for his missing lighter, and wondered how Joe Hanson had managed to snag it. His common sense told him to run. Now. His greed made him stay.

"Get thee behind me, Satan," Elias whispered, tossing and turning.

Paxton bit his lip, scanning the bands. Was that million worth the risks of continuing an operation with a madman? For God's sake, the client had sprung this guy out of an asylum!

And Leopard Paxton had started sleeping with one eye open. He wasn't sure anymore about Elias, about that look he got when he started talking about holy war.

CHAPTER THIRTY

Sᴋɪᴘ Mᴀɴsᴏɴ sɪᴘᴘᴇᴅ ᴀᴛ ʜɪs sᴄᴏᴛᴄʜ ᴀɴᴅ sᴛᴜᴅɪᴇᴅ ᴛʜᴇ man beside him. Since his story had gone worldwide, WQQQ's travel funds had moved him to the Adam's Mark in the middle of downtown Denver. And here, in the classy hotel lounge, yet another stroke of luck had fallen his way as a result of a little old-fashioned leg-work and the growing clout of a hot story.

Ben Tremain leaned back on the barstool and looked Skip up and down. "So, it pays well, being a reporter?"

"Not as well as heart surgery, Dr. Tremain." Skip no-ticed the man's glass was half empty and from old habit, lifted his finger to signal the bartender for another. The game had to be played carefully. It didn't do to let a source run dry; on the other hand, you didn't want to bla-tantly appear that you were getting him drunk either.

"I get by." Tremain smiled as if at some inside joke.

"I really appreciate you stopping by to see me." Skip smiled wistfully. "This whole story . . . I've never cov-ered anything like it. It's like a huge puzzle with half the pieces missing."

Tremain leaned forward, his eyes hawkish, intense. "What if I told you that I've got some of the pieces?"

Skip kept his expression neutral despite his quickening pulse. He made a bored gesture with his hand. "I came down here because you were married to Veronica. I was hoping I could get some background on her and Scott. You know, what sort of people they were."

Ben snorted, laughing as the bartender slid another scotch in front of him and retreated. "Background? Hell, I've got more than that."

"Really?" Skip set the hook, willing a bored look into his eyes. "Uh, do you want to enlighten me?"

"It'll cost you." Tremain said with complete aplomb.

"What?" Skip gave him a candid look of disbelief. "Let me get this straight. You want me to pay you for some background on Ferris and his sister? Get real! I can get that from old-fashioned research. You know, pounding the pavement? That's *not* the story, Dr. Tremain."

"I've got them." Ben smirked with an oozing superiority.

"Got them?" Skip could sense paydirt just under Tremain's smug exterior. "Your ex-wife is missing. Some think she was killed in that condo up at Frisco and I—"

"She's alive and well. Of course, the explosion at the FBI safe house in Lakewood came close to killing them yesterday. But, yeah, she's fine. She and that Bryce Johnson brought the kid by my office this afternoon."

"She did?" Skip clenched a fist where Tremain couldn't see it. Kid? What kid? Evidently, the confusion must have mirrored in his face because Tremain laughed and tossed off the last of his first scotch.

"Yeah, the kid." Tremain reached for the second glass and took a sip. "Damn! You didn't have a clue, did you?"

His cool blown, Skip asked, "What kid?"

"The one Scott Ferris and Amanda Alexander made." Ben stood up, taking his sport coat from the back of his seat. "That's what this story's about, Skip. It's the boy.

And if you'd like to run it, it'll cost you." Tremain pursed his lips, brow lined in thought. "Say five hundred thousand."

"Get real."

Tremain winked at him. "I am, Mr. Manson. This is the story of the millennium; either you run it, or someone else does." Tremain looked around the plush lounge. "Isn't that what's her name?"

"Yeah, Maureen Killdare from CBS." Skip made a face. "Look, I'll call my station manager, but I don't think—"

"You'd better." And at that Tremain flipped out a fifty to cover the drinks and called over his shoulder, "Just leave a message with my answering service. All you need to say is 'yes.'"

Tonight they are staying in the Denver Marriott, a big black glass tower in the middle of the city. Abel doesn't understand why they are moving from hotel to hotel. Each one is different, with its own smells; but here, at least, it is quiet, and he is even farther off the ground than last night at the Brown Palace. This hotel isn't as nice, doesn't have the feeling of friendly ghosts.

Veronica checked them in as the "Dermain" family, and hoped that the desk people wouldn't notice the difference between her credit card name and the registered name. If they did, Abel didn't notice it.

His afternoon had been terrible. He hadn't liked Ben, who looked at Veronica with mixed expressions.

One minute, he looked like he hated her. The next, his eyes softened, and Abel could sense Ben's collar heating, smell a curious musk coming off his body as he looked at Veronica with an odd hunger in his eyes.

Bryce had stayed silent, letting Veronica and Ben talk. But when Abel looked at him, it was to see a cool anger directed at Ben. Bryce really didn't like him. And if Bryce didn't, neither did Abel.

At first, Ben had been cold, a sly tone in his voice, but after they had walked down to the place called the X-Ray Room, he had started to change. They made Abel stand still in front of a square on a wall, and they left the room while the machine clicked. Then they made him turn and stand still again. Later, Veronica and Ben had looked at the filmy gray plastic sheet with its hazy forms. And both had grown excited.

Abel had looked, too, but only seen a fuzzy picture of his bones.

They had walked to the MRI lab, each of them silent, lost in their thoughts.

Abel was told to crawl onto a sliding bed and was given strict instructions not to move. He hadn't even been allowed to take Chaser with him. While Bryce made voices behind Chaser's head—as if he were talking through the buffalo about being brave—someone stuck a needle into Abel's arm. Then they shoved him into a white tunnel, and he lay there, trying so hard to be good and not move. It was loud, sounding like rocks rattling around his head.

Then Ben had pulled him out, but this time he wasn't talking, a funny look on his face. He treated Abel differently, and looked at him with curiosity-bright eyes. Then Ben led them to a small room, and Ben used a needle to draw blood while Veronica and Bryce told Abel how brave he was, and how if he didn't cry, they would take him for ice cream later.

Through it all, Abel noticed Bryce: His jaw clenched as he watched Ben, who watched Veronica whenever she was looking the other way. In the beginning, Veronica had talked to Ben in a stiff voice. By the time they were done, she was laughing with him. Ben spent a lot of time being real nice to Veronica, that odd musky odor growing. But Abel still didn't trust Ben.

Because when Ben wasn't sneaking looks at Veronica, he was casting puzzled glances at Abel. And, Abel decided, he didn't like being looked at by Ben Tremain.

Ben said, "I'll call you with the results as soon as they are in." And Abel thought Ben's smile would have sliced skin when he said, "Maybe we can get together to discuss the results."

"I'd like that, Ben," she'd answered.

Would she? Really? Abel hadn't understood. She'd had a strange smile as they left the hospital.

As Bryce and Veronica had promised, they took him out for ice cream and pizza. They also got him a safety seat for the back of the big Cadillac; then they drove here, downtown, to the big Marriott.

Abel rubs the bruise on his arm where they took his blood, and looks out the window. It is the middle of the night, and across from him, in the next building, a lady is working in one of the offices. She vacuums around desks and empties trash cans into a cart.

Abel can't even see down to the street. How high is the twenty-second floor? He tries to imagine.

He turns, letting the curtains fall back to cover the window, and rubs his sore arm. The word keeps rolling around in his mind: "Neanderthal." That's what Bryce calls it. Veronica tells him it's "Neandertal." She says that Abel doesn't need to worry about spelling it yet.

He steps over to the bed where Bryce sleeps, his mouth half open. Abel watches him for a long time. Bryce is different than most men. He winks at Abel, as if they are special friends. He doesn't make fun of the way he speaks. Unlike Daa, he hasn't called him a monster yet.

Sometimes Mother had men friends. They would go out for dinner, or to see a movie, but she never saw them for very long. Most of them, Abel didn't like because they would look at him with funny eyes and ask questions about him as if he weren't there. Things like, "What's wrong with him?"

Men come and men go. Daa went. It has been two years now. Daa never even calls. The other little boys he knew, like Brian O'Neil, they all had fathers who lived with them, or at least came to visit. Maybe Bryce could be like that. Maybe he could come and . . .

For the moment, Abel has forgotten that Mother is dead. That he will never live like that in Salt Lake City again. Will Bryce leave him, too?

He doesn't want to answer that question, so he steps across to the bed where Veronica sleeps and climbs up on the rumpled spread. He has promised Veronica that he won't sleep behind the toilet anymore. But he's worried. When he falls into a deep sleep, the monsters come, and he wets himself. He pulls Chaser to him and snuggles against Veronica's side.

"Not now, Ben," she mutters under her breath. "I'm too tired."

Abel turns his head, staring at her in the darkness. Why is she talking to Ben?

He hugs Chaser, and a horrible thought fills his head. What if Veronica goes to stay with Ben? If she does, Abel doesn't think Bryce will go with her. And if Bryce doesn't go, what will Abel do? Who will he stay with?

The idea is terrifying. He remembers the hungry look in Ben's eyes, and knows that he can never go there. Instead, he hugs Chaser and cries into the soft fur, wondering why Mother had to die. He is horrified by the warm wet spread of urine and hurries off the bed, afraid that Veronica will be mad, will take him to live with Ben.

He can't stand that, and crying, slips into the bathroom, and the darkness, and the safety of the shadows.

Bryce had found Abel asleep behind the toilet, reeking of urine. On the way from the elevator to breakfast, the boy had walked with his head down and had hardly answered the most direct of questions. In addition, it would have taken a crowbar and hydraulic jack to pry the stuffed buffalo out of his hands.

They had decided to take a chance on the Marriott restaurant, located in the hotel's first subfloor. An escalator led down from the lobby to the restaurant entrance. Across from it, a raised lounge had been set off by a brass railing. This morning only a single man in a business suit occupied it, a copy of *USA Today* in one hand, the other wrapped around a cup of cappuccino from the coffee bar upstairs.

"Three for breakfast," Veronica told the hostess. They were led into a large room with several raised galleries that blocked off the booths. Wall niches were filled with displays of grains, beans, and bottles of hot sauce. The effect was one of country goodness and the wealth of the harvest.

At the table, Bryce leaned over and pointed at the menu. "Abel, anything you want is yours. Fortunately, Veronica's bank account can bear any kind of damage we inflict on it."

She gave him a wry smile, and he noticed the haggard look in her eyes. A confusion lay there, something that had plagued her since the visit to the hospital yesterday.

Abel just stared emptily at the menu.

"You guys feeling all right?" Bryce asked, lowering his voice.

Abel shrugged, still silent and withdrawn. Veronica seemed to snap out of it long enough to frown at Abel and say, "You've got to pick something for breakfast." Then she looked her helplessness at Bryce, mouthing the words, "Now what?"

He winked at her, and as the waiter came by with coffee and orange juice, Bryce ordered Abel a big glass of orange juice.

"What did you and Chaser eat at home?" Bryce asked.

"Fwench toast," Abel whispered. "Muvver . . ." And he went silent, his mouth open.

Bryce met Veronica's pained stare, saying bluffly, "Well, French toast it is."

Abel didn't seem to hear.

"I'm worried about him," Veronica said in low tones.

"Yeah, me, too." Bryce straightened and sipped his coffee. "I'm headed for the buffet. Why don't you join me?" To Abel he said, "Kid, we're going to fill our plates. We'll be just over there. See? By the guy making omelets. You stay right here, take care of Chaser, and drink your orange juice."

Abel looked up with panicked eyes, slowly shaking his head. "No! Go wiff you!"

"Hush," Veronica told him, leaning down to his level. "We're just going over to get breakfast. You be brave. I'll watch you the entire time."

"Please?" Bryce asked, his soul wounded at the haunted look in the little boy's eyes. "I promise, no matter what, we'll be right back."

Abel's brow furrowed, his mouth twitching on the point of tears, but he nodded.

Bryce held the chair for Veronica and led her to the line. He kept glancing back at Abel, who watched them with an electric intensity.

"Something set him off," Veronica said, worry in her voice.

"Maybe he's afraid we'll take him back to the hospital. I don't think he liked Ben."

She shot him an inquisitive glance. "I don't think he was alone. By the way, you walk a lot better in your new air cast."

"I'm just waiting for the bill." Bryce decided to change the subject. "Ronnie, seriously, what about the boy? I mean, my God, he's legally Rebecca's son. We've got to give some thought to this. What do we do with him? Rebecca must have had family. Someone who's going to be asking about the boy."

She stopped short, expression tightening. "I hadn't even thought. Where was Rebecca from?"

"Ohio. Becky told me that her family started out in plastics. A factory or something up around Columbus. The father died, the mother inherited, remarried even more wealth, and she died. The older sister inherited everything. Nasty business that. Becky said her sister had flipped out—got religion and did lots of volunteer work. Prisons, institutions, that sort of thing for the church. She married some millionaire down south. Six months later, a heart attack took him. Meanwhile, Becky got her degree from Harvard and married a hometown guy. She adopted Abel and moved to Salt Lake for a couple of years. We didn't have much of a chance to talk at the condo, but Abel leads me to believe that the divorce wasn't nice."

"When are they ever?"

Bryce made a face. "Some of the guys who dated her back at Harvard said she had real trouble with sex. From the couple of times I went out with her, I can tell you she had trouble with relationships. Especially with men. All in line with what you'd expect from childhood sexual abuse. A nasty divorce doesn't surprise me. From what Abel tells me, his Daa didn't want anything to do with him then, so I'd guess he wouldn't want him now."

Veronica lifted her eyebrows. "What do we do? I mean, we're not, like, guilty of kidnapping or anything, are we?"

"Given the circumstances, I doubt it." He shrugged.

"At least Jack Ramsey didn't mention that particular charge the other night before the house blew up."

Veronica placed an order for an omelet doused in jalapeños, cheese, and red salsa. Then she said, "I think I'm going to have to prepare myself. I don't know when the little guy wheedled his way into my heart. I don't know how I'm going to give him up."

"So, like, do you always fall for Neanderthals, or is there a chance for an advanced version like me?"

"Order your breakfast."

He decided on ham and cheese, skipping the peppers that he thought would melt the top of his head off. The cook did a fancy job of preparation as they added bacon, sausage, toast, and hash browns to their plates. He even found French toast in a steamer and laid it on a separate plate for Abel. Through it all, Bryce kept glancing at the boy, waving and smiling at him. Abel just stared back with that fixed intensity like a puppy being left at the pound.

Veronica received her omelet and pressed the plate down onto the counter with both hands as she looked at Bryce. "This woman, this sister of Rebecca's, is she ready for this? Did Rebecca tell her who Abel is? What he is? Does she know that from here on out everyone in the world is going to be watching her ... watching him? I mean, damn, Bryce, Abel isn't going to have a normal childhood. Hell, half the lunatics in the world are already trying to kill him."

He nodded. "Yeah, I know, Ronnie. Wait until the press hears about this. You haven't seen anything yet. Talk shows, newspaper articles, reporters—they're all going to be waiting in line." He paused. "But, like I said, the last I heard, Becky and her sister weren't on speaking terms."

"What was the trouble?"

"She didn't like to talk about it. If your sister thought you were possessed would you use it as a topic of conversation?"

She pursed her lips, a fire in her eyes that he thought was damned attractive. After Bryce had received his omelet, he asked, "You ready to go back to the table, or are you going to try to push that plate clear through the counter?"

"I'm just pissed is all. I mean, what was Scott thinking? That you could reach back, pull a person out of time, and the world wouldn't notice?"

"No," Bryce told her reasonably. "I think the world was definitely supposed to notice." He led the way back to the table and noted the relief welling in Abel's eyes. "The thing is, I don't think he planned on being killed right off the bat. Scott wasn't some kind of nut. He was thorough, if anything. There had to be some sort of contingency plan, a way of minimizing the damage to Abel. He always thought things through. The problem is, we don't know what that plan was, and with him dead, we can't follow it."

At that moment, the cell phone in her purse rang. Bryce waited while she dug out the plastic phone and flipped the cover open, saying, "Hello?" A pause as the lines deepened in her forehead. "He's a little boy." Another pause. "I don't know, Ben." Silence. "Yeah. Okay. Sure. We can be there at . . . uh, with traffic, I'd say nine-thirty." The corners of her mouth tensed. "Sure. See you then." She pushed the "end" button and thrust the phone into her bag.

Bryce waited, noticing the tightening of Abel's expression.

"Ben's got news on the tests," she told them. "He wants to see us first thing."

Bryce took a deep breath. There were times when it was nigh onto impossible to maintain a professional equanimity, but he'd sure give it all he had.

Abel started to cry.

Ted Paxton stepped out of the van's passenger door and hurried across the asphalt parking lot to the Denny's on Union and Sixth Avenue. He pushed the door open, trotting to where Elias sat at the counter, his elbows propped, a cup of coffee in his hands. The place mat was covered with little blue Christian crosses that Elias had drawn with a ballpoint.

"Come on," Paxton said, reaching for his billfold before he flipped a ten out on the counter. "Tremain just got a call from her ex. They're on the way to his office. University Hospital. We got 'em!"

Elias was already on his feet, striding for the door with a cat-like grace.

"We do this smart," Paxton insisted as he closed the van doors. "Do you hear? We don't nail them to the floor. We don't make some weird statement. We take them, and dispose of them where no one will ever find them. I want it done by the book!"

Elias gave him a grin. "Sure, Brother. By the book, the

Good Book! So shall the angels of the Lord smite them hip and thigh!" And Elias threw his head back, laughing.

"I mean it," Paxton said nervously, aware that the glitter had solidified in his partner's eyes. "You're nuts, man."

Elias turned, a sober expression on his face. "You don't *ever* use those words with me. You got that, *Brother*?"

"Yeah, yeah, sure. Sorry." Paxton swallowed hard, a cold shiver working down his back.

"I am the wrath of the Lord," Elias insisted to himself, and began humming "Christian Soldiers," a smile of anticipation on his lips.

"Bathwoom," Abel said as they walked into the lobby of Ben's building at the University Medical Center. It was the first real statement the boy had made since breakfast. He'd been so listless that Bryce had had to physically pack him like dead meat down to the lobby when they checked out.

Veronica raised an eyebrow as Bryce said, "So, that orange juice has finally worked its way through, huh?"

Veronica placed a hand on his sleeve, dropping her voice. "Bryce, teach him how to pee, okay?"

"Huh?" He gave her a blank, hazel-eyed stare.

She gave him a singularly frustrated look and in desperation said, "Bryce, he was raised by Rebecca. He doesn't know about . . . well"—she gestured toward the men's room—"you'll see."

"Really?" His lips quirked. "You're sure you don't want to attend to it?"

She gave him a scathing glare. "Sure, and while I explain the realities of male biology, you go up and deal with Ben."

A gleam sparkled behind his eye. "With pleasure."

She shoved him toward the restroom. "I'll meet you upstairs. I trust you can find the way."

"Yeah, I know the way. I've got a right brain." Bryce said to Abel, "Come on, kid. It's time for a little Y-chromosomal bonding. Let's go learn how to beat our chests and brag about size."

Once in the door, Bryce led Abel to the stall and raised the lid. "There you go, buddy."

Abel gave him a puzzled look, stepped to the side and lowered the seat with a bang. Then he started to pull down his pants.

"Wait a minute," Bryce said. "Do you have to pee or potty? Uh, just water, right?"

Abel nodded, looking horrified.

"All right, little buddy. Welcome to the learning curve." Bryce tackled the problem of teaching Abel the rudiments of male biology. It was a first he figured he would never be able to brag about. As if he had anyone but Veronica to brag to. The "parent thing," a subject he'd never quite understood when socializing with others in his age group, was suddenly coming into focus.

He got Abel through the flushing phase and lifted him up at the sink to wash his hands. "All right, kiddo, let's get you cleaned up and we'll go see Ben."

"Nooo." The whisper came so softly he barely heard it.

"What's wrong, Abel?" He propped him on the sink and bent down to peer into those anxious eyes. "Come on, buddy, I can't fix it if you don't tell me what's wrong."

"Wewonica and Ben . . . I don't want you to go 'way."

"Ah," Bryce said knowingly. "I see. You think that Veronica's going to stay with Ben?"

At the hesitant nod, Bryce laced his fingers together. "She's not, little buddy. I'll see to it. I don't know how, but I'll figure some way to get her to stay with us." He squinted one eye. "Even if I have to drop Ben out of an upper-story window when she's not looking."

"Pwomise?"

"Yeah, I promise." Bryce reached out and bumped Abel's shoulder.

Abel seemed to relax.

"Okay, little buddy, let's get your hands washed. Then we'll go upstairs and figure out some way to impress Veronica with our male prowess. Give her the news that it's us or Ben, and she's got to make up her mind. You with me?"

"Yesss."

And that, Bryce thought, was about as brassy a lie as he'd told in days.

Veronica saw the confusion on Abel's face as he was led toward the men's room. Bryce's resigned expression didn't look much better. They made quite a team. She waited until they were out of sight before she broke a smile.

In the elevator, Veronica pressed the button for Ben's floor and took the moment to compose herself. She remembered the excitement in his voice that morning on the phone. *"Ronnie, who is he? What is he?"*

Leave it to Ben: He smelled an opportunity. The trouble was, she'd have to maintain control of the situation. Give Ben the slightest lead, and he'd have articles in the *Journal of the American Medical Association*, news conferences, papers at the next meetings, all to herald *his* discovery.

Her only defense would be to shorten his leash, threaten him with limited access to Abel. She would have to finally put her foot down, tell him . . .

God, listen to yourself, Ronnie! This is the same line you promised yourself before the divorce! She was tangling herself in Ben's sticky web again. The notion stunned her enough that she turned right instead of left when the elevator doors opened, walking away from Ben's office.

She took a deep breath, pausing at the nurse's station.

"Can I help you?" an older woman in uniform asked from behind the desk.

"No. Just needed a moment."

The woman nodded. Such statements weren't that unusual in a hospital. People were usually here for traumatic reasons.

Veronica turned back, walking toward Ben's office on wobbly legs. Just what was she doing here? Yes, they needed the proof of what Abel was, but she could have gone somewhere else to obtain it. Something else had made her run to Ben, something deep-seated that had spun out of the depths along with the fear and the fatigue.

No matter what she wanted to tell herself, the truth was that Ben did something for her, filled some need that she barely understood. Damn it, yesterday, she'd *wanted* to come here, as if to show off herself and her prize to him.

Now, she was committed. She *had* to see him. He had been so smooth yesterday, as if after those first few moments, everything had been forgotten. And when she'd looked into his eyes, that old longing had been there, the gleaming excitement that he had once had for her. Just like in the old days, that look had melted her.

"You're a basket case, Ronnie," she whispered under her breath . . . and saw the man. Tall, muscular, he leaned against the wall two doors down from Ben's office. He was watching her, and her soul skipped at that predatory look in his glittering eyes. His close-cropped blond hair caught the fluorescent light, giving it a silvered look.

Veronica nerved herself, forcing herself not to hurry, and on impulse, passed Ben's door, walking down two to Mary Olsen's, one of Ben's colleagues. Veronica knocked lightly, feeling the man's gaze burn into her back.

Her mouth had gone dry. She couldn't decide if she wanted Mary to answer, or not. After counting to ten, she made herself shrug, then walked to the end of the hall, pushed open the door to the stairs, and once out of sight, charged headlong down them.

She hadn't run like this since she was a teenager. Using her hands, she pushed off the walls on the landings. A misstep would send her tumbling, bruised at best, with broken bones at worst.

"Come on, Bryce, be there." Panting, she hit the crash bar on the first-floor door and burst into the hallway. Aware of the stares, she sprinted down the hall, past the elevators, to the men's room. Without a thought, she pushed the door open, calling, "Bryce? Abel? We've got to go!"

To her immense relief, they were standing at the sink, Abel supported by Bryce as he washed his hands. The man at the urinal turned to gape, his eyes wide with surprise.

"Bryce," she cried. "I'm not joking. I think we're in trouble."

He didn't even stop to turn off the water, but slung Abel over his shoulder with one hand and grabbed up the buffalo with the other, striding purposefully for the door. "What's up?"

"A man," she panted as he pushed past her. "He wasn't . . . right. Wrong somehow, scary."

"That's good enough for me," Bryce said. "You go out the door first. I'll follow two seconds later with Abel. Run for the Cadillac—and don't make any pretense of taking your time, all right?"

She swallowed hard and jerked a nod. They were already at the aluminum-framed door, and she strong-armed it, powered by adrenaline. Then she was out, running for all she was worth.

CHAPTER THIRTY-ONE

WHEN THE HOSPITAL DOOR SWUNG OPEN, VERONICA immediately ducked right, sprinting across the sidewalk, leaping off the curb, and crossing the drive. Instinct made her duck as she ran between a row of cars that choked the hospital parking lot. Sunlight sparkled on chrome and windshields. She could feel a sniper's crosshairs trying to settle on her dodging and weaving form.

Two rows over, Bryce was hobbling, bent over, Abel cradled in his arms. She clawed through her purse for the Cadillac's keys, and thumbed the button that unlocked the doors. The Caddy's lights flashed, indicating that the system was activated.

She ran the last few feet, ripped the driver's door open, and vaulted into the seat. The keys nearly slipped out of her fumbling fingers. She twisted them into the ignition, and the big engine roared to life. Bryce threw the passenger door open and slid into the seat, Abel still clutched in his arms.

"Hit it!" Bryce ordered, and Veronica floored the accelerator. In her panic, she almost ran over a woman and her daughter. They barely felt the speed bump as they rocketed toward the Colorado Boulevard exit.

"Call Ben," she told Bryce. "The phone's in my purse. You've got to warn him."

She took a chance, pitching the car into a hard right,

matching a small gap in the heavy northbound traffic. Horns blared behind her as tires screeched on the asphalt. Screw 'em; it wasn't her day to be a courteous driver. She took the next right, then a left. Winding through a residential neighborhood, she worked her way toward Martin Luther King Boulevard.

"What's the number?" Bryce flipped the phone open.

She recited from memory as the phone beeped under Bryce's fingers. Abel huddled next to him, tears streaking down his jutting cheeks.

"Ben?" Bryce asked after two rings. "Bryce. Listen, we had to leave. Ronnie spotted a man waiting outside your door. We think it's one of them." A pause. "Ben, listen to me! I'm serious. I want you to walk over and lock your door. Call security, have them come up and keep you safe until the police arrive. I'll call them next." A pause. "What? No, I'm *deadly* serious. I—" Bryce made a face. "Ben, *shut the fuck up!* This isn't one of your games. Call security!"

He pushed the "end" button, muttering, "Asshole." Then he punched in 911. After a moment, he said, "This is Bryce Johnson. I need to have the police sent to Dr. Ben Tremain's office at the University Medical Center. There may be an attempt on his life. This is not a prank— and you had better inform Agent Jack Ramsey of the FBI. He's available through the Denver Field Office." A pause. "No. I'm not going to stay on the line. I told you the problem. Handle it."

Bryce stabbed the "end" button, taking a deep breath. "Well, now what?"

Veronica recognized the sensations creeping along her nerves and muscles, the sick queasiness, the burning in her ears. She was coming down from the adrenaline high. Her limbs had started to quiver, followed by a violent shaking she couldn't stop. She pulled over to the curb and braked in front of a brown-brick house. Slipping the car into park, she lowered her head to the steering wheel and let the trembling run its course. She barely felt Bryce's hand on her back.

"Either I'm nuts," she said, "or he was there, Bryce."

"Who?"

"Abel's blond man." She glanced at them through the tangled web of her hair. "If it's him, he's tall. Looks like an athlete. Muscular, fit. His hair is short. He was just standing there, two doors down from Ben's office. Waiting. Watching."

"It's all right," Bryce told her. "You did fine."

She shook her head. "How did he know? God, Bryce, am I turning into a paranoid wreck, or what? I mean, what if he was just some guy? What if the police get there and he turns out to be some man waiting to see a doctor? People are going to think I'm a lunatic?"

"Then you're a lunatic. But you're a live loony-toon, rather than a dead—but incredibly brave—corpse."

"How did they find us?" She heard her voice waver. "Dear God, Bryce, what are they? Magical? They're always ahead of us. How?" She looked over at him, fighting tears, knowing how close they had just come to disaster. The sick feeling swelled in her gut. "I'm scared, Bryce."

He nodded, smiling at her in reassurance. "Yeah, I know. Want to trade places? You look like you'd rather have someone else drive. And, since Abel can't reach the pedals, I think maybe it better be me."

She nodded and opened the car door; cool morning air washed over her hot skin. Her muscles felt rubbery— barely compliant to her control—as she stood. She met Bryce halfway around the front of the car and walked into his arms, desperate to be held, to feel his strong arms around her.

"We'll be all right," he told her. "We'll make it. We have to."

She nodded against his shoulder, frantic to believe him. For long minutes they stood there, the dappled shadows of a tall elm falling over them. The Cadillac purred quietly, the chime ringing to remind them that the door had been left open. Abel peered anxiously at them through the windshield.

"Come on," Bryce finally said, his voice reassuring. "We've got to put some distance between us and them. The sooner, the better."

"I don't get it!" Elias roared as the van crept down Eighteenth Street, headed for downtown.

Paxton glanced at him from behind the wheel. Elias was knotting and unknotting his muscular hands. The tendons bunched and slid under his tanned skin.

"It happens," Paxton said smoothly, trying to ease the man's coiled rage before it unleashed itself inside the confines of the van. The anger had grown behind Elias' eyes, as if the nerves in his brain were pulsing. That look, coupled with Elias' growing intensity, sent a shiver down Paxton's back.

"How did they make me?" Elias demanded and

slammed the dash for emphasis. "How in my Lord's name did they know?"

Paxton bit his lip, unwilling to tell Elias what he'd monitored on the cell system. No, he'd tell Elias later, when the man had settled down. Spring it on the guy now, and he'd tear the van apart.

Damn it, it was the twenty-second of June. They should have been halfway down the list. Instead they were screwing around Denver trying to tie up this one loose end. What the hell had gone wrong?

"It's Satan," Elias whispered, and just as suddenly he slumped into the seat. Someone might have flipped a switch. Where an instant before, Elias had been powered by nervous anxiety, he now looked dull and spent, a vacancy in his eyes.

The guy's nuts! Paxton swallowed dryly, shifting in the seat. Was it worth the money? Did he dare try to run? The acid of doubt churned in his gut.

Jack Ramsey stepped out of the elevator and onto the fourth floor of the University Medical Center. The hallway bustled with people. Uniformed Denver police officers stood in blue clumps. Occasional doctors and nurses passed by in a hurry, casting uneasy glances at the clusters of cops and uneasy hospital security personnel.

Ramsey flipped out his ID as an officer stepped toward him. "FBI," he introduced. "Special Agent Jack Ramsey. Who's the officer in charge?"

"That'll be Lieutenant Sanchez. She's in Doctor Tremain's office. Just down the hall on the right, sir."

Ramsey said, "Thanks," and followed the hallway to an open door. Inside, two uniformed officers flanked a female detective wearing a gray skirt and white blouse. They crowded around a metal desk piled with papers, photos, and X-ray films. In an office chair behind the desk, a handsome man rocked on the chair's swivels. He had dressed in casual clothing: a powder-blue button-down shirt, loose brown tie, and tan slacks. A battery of expensive-looking pens protruded from his pocket. When he looked up, it was with serious brown eyes.

"I'm Jack Ramsey, Federal Bureau of Investigation." Ramsey opened his ID. "I'm looking for Lieutenant Sanchez."

"That's me." The woman turned to give him an inquiring appraisal. Hispanic, about five-four, with short black hair, she raised an eyebrow. "I'm glad you're here, Agent Ramsey. Perhaps you could shed some light on this situation."

"Why the Marines?" he asked, indicating the hallway. "That's a lot of response for a routine call."

"Not so routine." Sanchez studied him thoughtfully. "When security answered Dr. Tremain's call, they accosted a suspect outside the door. The suspect, a Caucasian male, about twenty-five to thirty, assaulted the security officer, broke his nose and arm, and fled the scene."

"You're sure he was that young? Not in his mid-thirties, dark haired . . ."

She was shaking her head. "Blond, close-cropped. Definitely young, and from the description, very fit. The guard's impression was that he was an athlete. Maybe a soldier. The guard said something else weird: that the man was muttering a prayer as he ran off."

"Where's Dr. Tremain?"

"That's me," the handsome man said from behind the desk.

Ramsey glanced at him. "I meant Veronica Tremain. Is she still in the building? Are Dr. Johnson and the boy with her?"

"No one has seen them," Sanchez replied. "We were just talking to Dr. Tremain here, trying to figure out what this is all about."

Ramsey turned his eyes on the doctor. "And?"

Ben Tremain shrugged his shoulders. "They came to see me yesterday, wanted me to run some tests on the boy. I did. The results were, well, interesting. I called Ronnie, uh, Veronica, this morning. She was supposed to meet me here and discuss the results."

"You never saw her?"

Tremain shook his head. "I just got a call from Bryce Johnson. He said I was in danger, to lock my door and call security. So I did. I waited here for about five minutes until I heard a commotion outside. When I opened the door, people were clustered around a man on the floor. He was bleeding from the nose, holding his arm."

"That's it?" Ramsey felt a sinking sensation in his gut. "Just a call?"

"Just a call." Tremain steepled his fingers. "But, I can tell you, Bryce Johnson sounded rather upset. He said he'd call the police. Evidently he did. They were on the way by the time the hospital called to report the assault on the guard."

Ramsey pulled out his notebook and began jotting

notes. Damn it, where had Johnson gotten off to? What had tipped their hand? Was this "blond man" the same that the boy had reported outside the safe house?

"Special Agent Ramsey," Sanchez asked, "what is this all about?"

"It's about a little boy," Ramsey said absently. "I'm going to guess that it's the same one that Dr. Tremain, here, conducted tests on yesterday." Ramsey looked up from his notebook. "He's not exactly normal, is he?"

Ben Tremain slowly shook his head. "No. He's different." He frowned. "Yesterday, Ronnie said he wasn't human. I thought it was joke."

"It's not?" Ramsey asked.

"That depends." Tremain picked up a pen, rolling it between his fingers. "Is he viable? I'd say so. Is he out of the norm for a four-year-old boy? Definitely. He has a disproportionate muscular and bone mass for his age and height. Is he human? Again, I'd say so. His blood is type A, positive. I mean, look." He pointed to the X-ray film. "He's got the right anatomy in the right places. How else can you define human?"

"Then, what's 'out of the norm,' as you say?" Ramsey glanced at the smoky X ray. The little boy's head seemed long and low, the nasal bones curving and protruding from the face.

"His head is shaped differently than what you would expect for a four-year-old boy. He talks with an impediment. Looking at the radiographs, I'd say that his difficulties with speech stem from differences in the shape of his mouth, particularly the tongue and mandible. They cause him to pronounce some vowels and consonants in a nasal, or slurred, fashion." Tremain frowned. "Yesterday, looking at the X rays and MRI, Ronnie was talking about midfacial prognathism, a superorbital torus, lack of a chin. And we ran a karyotype . . ." At Ramsey's blank look, Tremain said, "Uh, his face sticks out, especially that beak of a nose. He's got browridges over his eyes which normal little boys don't get until they turn eighteen. Feel your chin, Agent Ramsey. That point is missing on little Abel. And, for your information, a karyotype is a picture of his chromosomes. The boy has several haplotypes, gene combinations, that we don't have records for in the catalog. My genetics people are fascinated."

"I see."

Tremain's lips tightened into a smirk. "I'm not sure you do. The point is, none of these gene frequencies have been reported—anywhere—in the world. So, where did Abel come from? Now, I'm only an M.D., but Scott and Amanda were anthropologists. It doesn't take a genius to put one and one together to come up with two. Ronnie was into paleoanthropology when we were married, so I picked up a little knowledge of the field. My bet, ridiculous as it may sound, is that somewhere, Scott found some ancient DNA. That kid's a clone, isn't he? Some form of extinct human that Scott and Amanda brought back from the dead." He tapped the papers before him. "And I have the data to prove it."

"That's nuts!" one of the uniforms said. Sanchez waved him down.

"Yeah," Ramsey said, another of the pieces falling into place. So, the kid wasn't a *manufactured* human, but a recreated one? "Nuts, all right."

Sanchez, being a good cop, read his expression and said, "Son of a bitch."

"Not hardly," Tremain quipped, his pen clasped between his fingers. "I thought the name was funny. You know, Abel? Maybe, it turns out that Scott Ferris has raised Abel. As in raised from the dead? And now it's Cain's turn to be worried."

The terrible fear is fading. Abel's stomach slowly unties itself. The moment Veronica had burst into the men's room at the hospital, it had knotted itself into a painful ball. The blond man! Veronica says that she saw him. There, at the hospital.

Now Abel sits in his car seat and hugs Chaser to his chest. They are driving again. The big car is fast, the white leather seats comfortable, and it is so much quieter than Mother's car, or even Bryce's blue Dodge.

Nevertheless, Abel can't help but crane his head, looking back through the window at the lines of cars following them. They are on a highway, headed north. The white cement of the road makes soft thumping sounds. Behind them, the cars glitter as sunlight sparkles on windshields and fenders. If the blond man is back there, how can Abel see him?

The knot begins to tighten in his stomach again.

He cuddles Chaser closer, whispering, "We be all wight. Vewonica and Bwyce will keep us safe."

He watches farmland pass by. The fields are lush, and some have tractors in them towing big sprayers. Clumps of tall green trees dot the land. And in the distance, mountains rise against the sky. Here and there, high up in the peaks, white patches of snow can still be seen.

He can smell the tension in Veronica, fear cloying her familiar odor. Bryce is upset, too; he doesn't show it like Veronica, but his scent betrays it.

Abel leans his head close to Chaser's ear where it sticks out just below the velvet horn. "What is death like? Does it huwt?"

Chaser watches him with his shining button eye and doesn't tell him the answer.

Wyoming. The miles vanished under the Cadillac's wheels. I-25 led them northward through an endless sea of grass. To the left, ragged-looking mountains rose against the horizon. White-and-tan antelope, and occasional cattle, grazed beyond the right-of-way fences. Patchy white clouds spotted the incredibly blue sky.

Bryce rested his hand on the steering wheel and played with the levers that moved the seat up and down, back and forth, and tilted it this way and that. He wondered if maybe motorized seats had been designed specifically for places like Wyoming. Every time he drove across it, he decompressed. Driving through the West was relaxing. What a concept!

He glanced at Veronica, asleep in the passenger seat beside him. She had reclined the seat back, her head pillowed on a bundled shirt.

For the life of him, he couldn't understand Ben

Tremain. To have a woman like this, and treat her the way he had? The man must have been a complete fool.

A ranch appeared on the right, set back from the highway. A white frame house, corrals, a barn, tractors, and other equipment sat in a hollow behind a windbreak of trees. They were miles from the nearest town, gas pump, convenience store, and doctor. It amazed him that people lived like that.

Veronica jerked awake. For an instant, panic filled her sleep-dazed eyes; then she sat up and stretched, muttering, "Bad dream."

"Yeah," Bryce agreed. "I think they're going to be with us for a while." With Veronica awake, he looked into the backseat, where Abel sat strapped in his safety seat and watched the world passing through the side window. "You okay, kiddo?"

Abel just stared expressionlessly, his eyes hollow with a deep-seated fear.

Bryce lowered his voice. "The poor guy's living like a football. A different bed every night. Constant terror. Never feeling safe."

"We're all living like that."

"But we can understand what's happened to us."

"We can?" she asked in a small voice.

His lips curled into an ironic smile. "No. Maybe not."

She took a deep breath. "I wonder if Ben's all right."

He chanced a glance at her, aware of the troubled tone in her voice. "Want to talk?"

After a long silence, she said, "In the elevator, just before I saw him—that man—I was thinking about what a fool I was . . . walking right back into Ben's life and all of his bullshit. Charging headfirst into the lion's mouth.

What was I thinking by involving myself with him again?"

"That you needed the X rays and MRI images to prove what we suspected about Abel." In the mirror, he caught Abel's sudden attention.

Veronica was staring sightlessly out at the rolling grasslands. "It was just instinctive. I was in trouble, and I scurried right back to Ben like some kind of whipped puppy."

"Ronnie . . ."

"No, it's all right, Bryce. I'm just shaken by the fact that every instinct drove me to run smack back into his arms." She made a face. "What does it say about women that they do that? Are we some kind of perverted moths that we have to go back and burn ourselves on the same damn flame that scorched us the first time?"

"It says that you're scared and human."

The sunlight shot blue tints through her long black hair as she shook her head. "You're a liar, Bryce Johnson, but I appreciate the effort. No, it's something destructive in my personality. It goes way back. I've got rotten taste in men."

He said nothing.

"Is it integral to female genetics? A flaw on the X chromosome? That women just naturally gravitate toward shmucks?" She crossed her arms defensively over her full breasts. "I mean, damn! It's something twisted in my psyche."

"I'm not a psychologist," he said, "but if I were, I'd wonder why you thought you had to destroy yourself. These things usually stem from a bad self-image, Ronnie.

You don't think you're worth all the things a good man could give you."

She might have been stone, so he added, "Myself, I'd spend the rest of my life doing everything in my power to see you smile."

Idiot! he told himself. *You just went over the line.*

An apology might sound even more stupid, so he cursed himself silently and fixed his eyes on the road ahead.

She brought the seat back upright, her body tense, and finally looked at him. When he glanced her way, his heart sank. A tear had traced its way down her cheek, and her eyes were shining and wet.

"Did you mean that?"

"I meant it."

He hesitantly reached out, and she took his hand, clutching it as if it were a lifeline.

CHAPTER THIRTY-TWO

"Jack? What the hell is going on?" Peter Wirthing, the Washington Field Office SAC, asked over the telephone.

Ramsey sat behind a desk in the downtown Denver

Field Office. Dole had given him this office as a command center for the Denver branch of the investigation. The place was cluttered with file folders, a couple of chairs, and the impedimenta that went with a federal office. He plucked a paper clip from the magnetic holder and pushed it across the blotter with a finger. For the moment, he looked up at a flowchart they had put together. White butcher paper had been taped to the wall. Notes, names, and events now cluttered the once pristine surface.

"Peter, this investigation is growing like mold in a bachelor's refrigerator." Ramsey stared at the notation for June 19: SAFE HOUSE BOMBED had been scrawled in blocky letters.

"Look." Wirthing's voice sounded strained. "I just got a call from Judge Harthow. The director wants to know what the hell you're doing. He just gave me the third degree. Used lots of phrases like 'loose cannon,' 'run amok,' and 'out of control.' "

Ramsey made a face. "Loose cannon? Peter, we've got dead citizens, a dead agent, a couple of wounded agents, and illegal wiretaps by third parties. What the hell does he mean, 'run amok'? I faxed my report through to you."

"Uh-huh, and I faxed it on to the Bureau to update the case." Wirthing's voice tensed. "I got the impression that the director wasn't impressed."

"Wasn't impressed?" Ramsey bent the paper clip. "Jesus, Peter, they killed Joe, blew up one of our houses!"

"Who?"

"Ted Paxton."

"But you don't have any proof. Not that it's him, and not that Billy Barnes and his church are behind this."

"Excuse me, boss, but isn't the idea behind a criminal investigation to gather, analyze, and present the proof?"

After a silence, Wirthing said, "Yeah, I know. I'm sort of between a bonfire and a waterfall. The director told me, and I quote, 'Call off your bulldog.' He meant you, Jack."

Ramsey glared at the desk. "Boss, I think there's something really wrong with this. And, sure, maybe it's not Billy Brown and his church, but something nasty is happening."

"Yeah, what's wrong with this is political. The president is trying to reach out to the Right. They've got an election coming up, and candidates are looking to increase their voter base." A hesitation. "Look, I know it's bullshit, but I'm under a magnifying glass. The director is about to come down on me like a brick shithouse. I've got reporters crawling all over the outside of the building."

"So, what do you want me to do? Pull the plug, tell the guys in the field, 'Sorry, it's politically inconvenient to go after the guys that killed Ferris, Alexander, Rebecca Armely, Joe Hanson, and Elizabeth Carter?' Tell Agent Jones that she might have to forgo nailing the bastards that tried to blow her up? What's happening to us? The same thing that happened in the fifties? Are we becoming a political arm of the government? Is that what you're trying to tell me in that inimitable way of yours?"

After a silence, Wirthing said, "No, Jack." Then, "Look, I read your report. Is this for real? Scott Ferris cloned some sort of prehistoric human? That's what this is all about?"

"It's a threatening idea to some people, Peter. Enough of a threat that they're willing to kill to stop it."

"What about that doctor, uh, Tremain? The ex-husband? What have you done with him?"

"What can I do? I can't charge him with being an asshole and place him under protective custody. I think I got through to him that certain people would like to break his limbs, douse his body with gasoline, and torch him like they did Ferris. That sobered him, so I think he'll lay low."

"And Johnson, the woman, and the kid? Still on the run?" Wirthing sounded unhappy.

"Uh . . . yeah, but we've got feelers out. She'll call in soon, and we can find a place to pick her up. Peter, we're in a race. We have to get to them before Paxton does. Look, I know this is a weird case, but it falls right into our jurisdiction. They're willing to kill that little boy, and for what? I mean, he didn't ask to be here, but he is. Even if he is some kind of prehistoric person, I looked into his eyes. I saw a frightened little boy. I don't know what the hell Ferris thought he was doing, bringing back a kid like that, but I'm not going to let someone murder him just because he doesn't fit some fanatic's convictions."

"All right, I'm willing to go out on a limb for you. Just do me a real big favor, okay? Don't saw the thing off while I'm out there. Is that a deal?"

"Deal. But you might get on the horn to Tom Powell and Karen Sues. Have them see what they can do as far as a CYA is concerned. They were there when I briefed the director. I think they smell a big rodent in the woodpile. In fact, I'm considering d-CON as an aftershave."

"Do you want to elaborate on that?"

"I'm not convinced that Brown is at the bottom of this, but he's not clean, either. Suffice it to say that I don't think the director is suffering from complete objectivity in this matter. Look, the Bureau has done this before—stumbled onto something that might prove politically inconvenient, let alone downright embarrassing to the powers that be. I'm not suited as a political lackey at the best of times. More so when there's something nasty going on. At least, lackeyness wasn't in the job description when I signed on."

A sigh, then the SAC said, "I hate it when my guys tell me things that I already know. Understand, Jack, I'm not going to be happy when I get an order from the director to squash this. I'll delay, obfuscate, and buy you all the time I can, so don't blow it. If you do, there's going to be a ration to go around for all of us."

"Comes with the paycheck, boss." Ramsey smiled. "If worse comes to worst, you can always imagine yourself in front of a congressional committee, and think about how you want to answer any hard questions they throw at you."

"Thank you, Jack, you've just set my mind at peace," Wirthing said with dry sarcasm. "I'll remember that when I write your next performance evaluation. Meanwhile, you may not have much time. Use it wisely."

"Thanks, Peter. We've got a line on the doers. I intend to run them in."

"Then get to it!" A pause. "Oh, and in your favor, you might want to know that these reporters smell a rat, too. One guy, uh, Skip Manson, is putting the puzzle pieces together to make the same kind of picture that you are. Rather than you being right, that might do more toward saving your ass than anything."

"Great."

"Take care, Jack."

The line went dead.

Ramsey replaced the phone and looked up at the flow-chart. Damn it! He *needed* information. Needed a way to get a handle on Paxton. Where the hell were Tremain, Johnson, and the kid? And worse, why hadn't they called in?

Skip Manson nodded to Maureen Killdare, the CBS investigative reporter, as he entered the room. Maureen seemed to be the only other professional colleague besides the locals from the Denver affiliate stations.

Skip hadn't been surprised when his boss said no to Tremain's demand of five hundred grand. Skip had dutifully called and left the message "no" with Tremain's answering service. And, to his surprise, he'd taken a call on his pager announcing a Ben Tremain press conference at 5 P.M. in the University Hospital conference room. His curiosity had brought him here, and as Kahlid set up his camera, Skip took the chair beside Maureen. She wore a professional red dress trimmed in white. Her hair was perfect, as usual, not a blond hair out of place.

"How you doing?" Skip asked.

She shot him a narrow blue-eyed stare from the corner of her eye. "You're kidding, right? We're coming up on the campaign season with the House and Senate in jeopardy after two years of the president's muddled policy implementation, and I'm out here chasing *your* conspiracy story in Denver." She smiled bitterly. "I'm hoping this will be so bad I can go home."

"Yeah," Skip said through a sigh. "But I'll bet you dinner in the Old Ebbitt Grill that you're not going home anytime soon."

At the tone in his voice she shot him a hard, probing glance. "Would you like to elaborate on that?"

"Nope I—"

Ben Tremain stepped into the room and walked past the line of chairs. He wore a slick three-piece suit; he might have just stepped off the cover of *GQ*. A folder of papers was under his arm as he walked up to the podium, pausing long enough to flip a switch on an overhead projector. A white square of light glowed on the screen behind the podium.

He laid the folder to one side and grasped the podium, looking out at the audience through challenging dark eyes. "Good afternoon. Thank you for coming." He cleared his throat. "My name is Dr. Ben Tremain. Many of you already know that I am Veronica Tremain's exhusband. Veronica's late brother, Scott, has been in the news recently. I'm here to tell you why."

Skip looked around the room, noting the boredom and impatience of the audience. Most of them were here on assignment, already having figured it for a bust.

"What you don't know," Ben continued, "is that Veronica Tremain, Dr. Bryce Johnson, and Scott Tremain's creation were in my office yesterday."

Skip leaned forward, as someone said, "Excuse me? Creation?"

"A little boy," Tremain told them coolly. "His name is Abel. As in the biblical Abel. Developmentally he appears to be about four years old. He's the reason for all of these murders."

"You're telling me that a four-year-old boy is killing people?" one of the locals asked incredulously.

Tremain glared at the man. "I'm afraid, sir, that you are not a credit to your profession. No. What I said is that he's the *reason* behind all of this." Tremain lifted his eyes, fixing Skip. "This morning I was supposed to meet with Veronica, Dr. Johnson, and the boy. I received a warning call from Dr. Johnson that my life was in danger. Subsequent to that, a man was nearly apprehended outside of my office door. I believe him to be one of Scott Ferris' killers."

"What is the story on the boy?" Skip asked, sensing Tremain's divergence onto the grandstand. "You used the word 'creation.' I take it the little boy is a synthetically created person."

Tremain smiled thinly. "Evidently you've given it some thought since last night, Mr. Manson?"

Skip nodded. "Yeah, it's the only thing that makes sense." He could feel Maureen's burning stare. "Scott Ferris cloned a human, didn't he? What is the boy? Scott's clone? Was that what this was all about?"

"No. The boy, Abel, is a prehistoric human being." Ignoring the guffaws that broke out, Tremain reached forward and slipped a transparency from the folder and laid it on the projector. "This is an X ray of the boy's head and shoulders. Please take notice of the shape of the skull."

A dropped pin would have made a racket in the suddenly quiet room. All eyes had fixed on the overhead.

"And beside it," Tremain continued, "I am laying the X ray of a normal child. I'm sure you can see the gross differences in morphology."

"This could be just a case of birth deformity!" the skeptical reporter in the front row scoffed.

"It could," Tremain agreed. "But it isn't." He rapped his knuckle on the folder. "I've got plenty of evidence here, ladies and gentlemen. Copies will be made available to all of you at your request. Take it to your own experts, have them determine the correctness of my claims."

"Dr. Tremain?" Skip called, standing. "I don't understand. Last night you wanted to sell this story. Now you offer it up on a platter. Why?"

Tremain cracked a wry smile. "This morning my life was threatened. What good is a fortune if you're not around to enjoy it?"

"But what does this mean?" Maureen demanded.

"It means that somewhere," Tremain told her, "Scott Ferris and his colleagues found some ancient DNA and cloned a Neanderthal." He paused for effect. "That's right. I said a Neanderthal. For the first time in thirty thousand years, we are not the only species of human on the planet."

"Neanderthal?" the front-row skeptic asked in dismay. "No way!"

Ben Tremain fixed the man with a sober stare. "God, how I wish you were right. But, unfortunately, you're not. Veronica came to me to verify the child's race. She asked me to do the tests. The conclusions from the hard data are unmistakable. You will find that out for yourselves as you take the data to your own professionals. The DNA results themselves are conclusive. That little boy has haplotypes, um, patterns of DNA, that have not been recorded in any human populations anywhere."

"Wait a minute, didn't some scientists test Neanderthal

bones and claim that the DNA was different from ours?" Skip asked.

"They did," Tremain asserted. "I checked that information myself. The trouble is, they were only able to locate what we call mitochondrial DNA. It's only inherited from the mother, through the egg. What makes it somewhat unreliable is that when the children are produced from a mating, over half of them are boys. Males do not pass on mitochodrial DNA to their children, so, mathematically, about fifty percent is lost per generation. A man's son will only have his mother's mitochondrial DNA—not his father's. And Abel, I might add, has mitochondrial DNA different from anything currently available on this earth."

"I don't get it," the guy in the first row said. "What does that really mean?"

"It means that somewhere out there, a little Neanderthal is walking among us." Tremain crossed his arms. "And, are there any other questions?"

A flurry of shouts followed as people raised their hands.

Beside Skip, Maureen whispered, "So much for going home."

Veronica followed First Avenue North into Billings as she drove into the slanting light of a perfect Western sunset. Desultory evening traffic flowed toward the downtown area. The few tall buildings appeared modest, relaxed after the hustle and cavernous depths of Denver. To the north, the tawny rimrock that surrounded the city had taken on a golden glow. Pickups, SUVs, and cars idled down the wide streets.

Bryce craned his neck. "Uh, that's a Sheraton right there off to your left."

She grunted and, when the light changed, eased into the left lane and took Broadway. "And here's a Radisson. One's as good as another." She shrugged and pulled into the parking complex next to the hotel.

The attendant, a gray-haired man with a mustache, leaned out of the little white cubicle. "Checking in?"

"If they have a room," she told him.

"We're not that busy. Of course come the weekend, we've got a bunch of stock growers coming in for a conference. Have the desk validate a ticket for you. Parking's on the second level for the hotel. Need help with anything?"

"No, thank you." She grinned at him. "We're light on luggage."

She wheeled the Cadillac around the inside of the garage, wondering if this had been a mistake. The place looked at least fifty years old. The spaces were narrow, the turns on the ramp tight and close. From the scars on the concrete pillars, not everyone made them.

She eased them into a space, and sucked in her gut as she squeezed out of the Caddy's door.

"Come on, kiddo," Bryce said to Abel. "We're set for another adventure."

Abel emerged with his buffalo and his travel bag. They walked down the ramp to the sidewalk, and Bryce took a deep breath. "Air's better here," he said. "In Denver, I thought it would eat my lungs out."

They crossed the alley, Veronica noting that every

street corner seemed to have a casino on it. The lobby didn't have the flash of the Brown Palace or the modern opulence of the Denver Marriott. The place sported a dark fireplace at one end, and pictures of early Billings hung from the walls. She felt an air of history about the place, of cattlemen and miners, entrepreneurs and time. The Northern Hotel was "Western"—not the hokey Hollywood image, but authentic.

At the desk, she registered as "Dermain" again, and was thankful that the pleasant young woman didn't look too closely at the name on her platinum card.

"How long will you be staying?" the girl asked.

"A couple of days," Veronica decided. God knew, they needed the rest. "Do you have a suite?"

"The best in the city. Uh, it's a little more expensive. It'll cost you one hundred and six dollars instead of sixty-five."

After four and five-hundred-dollar rooms in Denver, that didn't sound so bad.

After they received the keys they took an antique elevator to the fifth floor. To Veronica's surprise, the suite surpassed her expectations. The rooms were large and airy, with a homey feel she didn't get from more modern hotels. Bryce and Abel immediately went to the window to stare down at the street. In the distance, the rimrock had turned purple in the evening.

"Nice city," Bryce observed. "The pace here is more civilized."

Veronica flopped her bag on the bed and lowered herself gratefully beside it. "Good. I'm ready for a little relaxation." She glanced at him. "Do you think they'll find us?"

Bryce shrugged, turning back from the window. "As long as we don't call anyone or announce our presence to the rest of the world, no. Not for a while." He frowned. "Unless they can access your credit card account. I would like to think an American Express Platinum card would buy you a little bit of security."

She pursed her lips, thinking back. A cold dread washed through her. "It had to be the phone call. They can monitor cell phones, can't they? I mean, that's why you're not supposed to use credit cards over them."

Bryce sobered. "You told Ben that you'd meet him at his office at nine-thirty."

Abel remained at the window, Chaser on the ledge in front of him. "We see caws," he told the little buffalo, holding it up so it could see. "Down thewe, look."

Veronica smiled, oddly reassured by the little boy's fascination with the street below. "I'm half starved, Bryce."

"I saw a restaurant across the way: Jake's. Looked like a nice place. Want to give it a try?"

"Take me, I'm yours." She offered her hand and let him pull her up off the bed.

"Don't make offers you're not about to keep," he warned, and held her hand for a moment longer than necessary when he pulled her up.

She stood there, close to him, feeling an unaccustomed warmth grow within her. His eyes had softened, and she had to force herself to step away. She felt an excited flush as she reached for her purse and opened the door.

In the hallway, waiting for the elevator, she glanced at him, aware of the way he was avoiding her gaze. He looked flustered and seemed to have trouble deciding what to do with his hands. Abel was watching them, having caught the undercurrents of the conversation. His nose was working, as if scenting the air.

A sudden notion brought her pause. She had already discovered that he could see better at night. Was his sense of smell superior as well? If it was, and she was physically responding to a man, what kind of pheromones were advertising themselves to young Abel?

Embarrassment coursed through her as she stepped into the elevator.

"You're looking abashed," Bryce noted as he pressed the knob in for the first floor.

"Abel," she asked, "do Bryce and I smell different?"

He looked up at her with big sober eyes. "Yess."

When the elevator opened to the lobby, they stepped out and she asked, "What do you smell here?"

He sniffed the air. "Food. People. I smell caws. Smell gwass and twees." He frowned. "Paint. Something musty." He looked at her again. "Smell you and Bwyce."

Something tightened at the base of her throat. "Well . . . I see."

Bryce lifted a curious eyebrow as they walked out the Broadway entrance and into the cool evening. "You mind telling me what that was all about?"

She chuckled nervously. "No. At least, not yet, but I suspect that there were no secrets among Neandertals." They walked along the sidewalk and around the corner to First. "The thing is, we have at least seven genes in the human nose that are nonfunctional. They've mutated over time, and selection hasn't worked to retain our sense of smell. With the coming of agriculture and civilization, we haven't needed to scent the breeze to locate predators or find a mate. It's the poorest of our senses. I'm starting to see advantages to that when people live in cities."

"I get your drift." Bryce dropped into a thoughtful mode, giving her curious glances as they walked. She chafed, aware of his presence, of the subtle change in his posture, of the excitement when they made eye contact.

At Jake's they were asked for reservations; having none they were told that it would be about thirty minutes.

Veronica led them to a table next to a window that looked out onto Twenty-seventh Street. She started to help Abel into one of the tall chairs, but to her surprise, he climbed up with remarkable agility and perched, his buffalo in the chair beside him. Immediately, he turned his attention to the street, watching with somber eyes as the cars and people passed.

Veronica took a chair opposite him, and Bryce settled in beside her. Cattlemen sat at the table next to them, discussing their perennial trouble with the Bureau of Land Management, trucks, and something called weaning weights. Across from them a table full of lawyers in three-piece suits moaned about the stock market and falling real estate prices.

"Quite a place," Bryce told her. "Cowboys, Indians, and lawyers." He grinned. "I could come to like this."

She shot him a fleeting smile. "Denver isn't the real West. Neither is Frisco, despite being in the mountains. It's all Yupped up. Me, I've never been to Montana before. Pretty place."

"Yeah," he agreed.

She reached out and took his hand. "Thanks. For everything, Bryce. I don't know how I could have done all this without you."

At the tone in her voice, his eyes seemed to expand. Their gazes locked for an eternal moment.

She started to bite off the next words, but relented. "I've got to tell you. I did a lot of thinking on the way up here. I mean, about Ben, about me." She swallowed. "About you."

He glanced uneasily at Abel, who watched the street with complete concentration. He seemed to be eternally alert. Why? Watching for the blond man? "And?"

She shrugged, uneasy at the vulnerable sensation that filled her. "I don't know. This is difficult." A shallow laugh. "It's a funny thing to say, but I've never really 'talked' to a man before. I mean, not about what's real. What I'm feeling. Maybe it's having been so close to death. Somehow, Bryce, I've missed life. Really living, I mean. Sure, I took chances as a kid. Did some wild things. But that was just taking risks . . . not living."

"Uh-huh." He tightened his grip on hers. "What have you discovered?"

She smiled wistfully. "That in all my life, I've never been intimate with anyone. By that, I mean I've never dared to share myself with anyone. I couldn't trust anyone. God, back in Denver, there I was, scared like I've never been before, and I wanted to run right back to Ben."

"Ronnie, don't blame yourself for—"

"No," she insisted, meeting his eyes, pleading with him. "I was all set to fool myself again. It's like the blinders came off and I could really see myself for what I am: a screwed up mess."

"I think you are the most marvelous woman in all the

world," he said gently. "I wouldn't want you any other way than you are: brave and resourceful."

At that her heart warmed and her lips curled into a wistful smile. "Thank you. You're the most charming man I've ever met."

He lifted an eyebrow. "You're very special to me, Ronnie. No matter what, I'm with you. All the way. No matter where it takes us."

The barmaid appeared: a young woman wearing a white blouse and black skirt. "Can I get you anything?"

Bryce squinted up at the chalkboard menu. "What on earth is 'Moose Drool'?"

"A locally made stout. It's really rich—"

"I'll take it. Anything with a name like 'Moose Drool' has got to be tried." He winked at Veronica. "Right now, I'm on top of the world."

"So, how's Matt doing?" Ramsey asked.

"Doing fine," Paula's voice told him over the phone. *"Matt made two goals last night. His team's in first place in the league. You'd have been so proud, Jack."*

"Tell him for me, will you?" Ramsey looked up at the clock. Almost 8 P.M. after a really long day. He still had to pick up the GSA vehicle and drive out to the Sheraton at the Federal Center. The choice had made such good sense when he expected to do a simple debriefing at the safe house and fly home a couple of days later. Now he had to deal with the morning commute on Sixth Avenue, into the sun in the morning, into the sun all the way back to the hotel at night. From the sounds in the Denver Field

Office, he wasn't the only one working late. That helped a little.

Paula said, *"I will."* A pause. *"When are you coming home?"*

"I don't know. This is a mess, Paula. But it can't go on forever."

"They never do, Jack." She sounded so sure of herself. *"If anyone can finish it, you can."*

"I love you. Did I ever tell you that? That you're the most wonderful woman in all the world?"

"Yes. A time or two. But I've got a good eye. That's why I love you, too."

The little yellow light on the phone blinked: a call coming in.

"I've got to go. Take care of yourself for me. I'll be counting the minutes until I get back to you."

"So will I. Love you, too." A short pause. *"Jack, be careful and come home to me."* She hung up, and Jack pushed the button for the second line.

"Ramsey, here."

"Agent Ramsey? This is Veronica Tremain."

He triggered the system that would start a trace.

"Are you all right? Is Dr. Johnson and the boy with you? Are they all right?"

"We're all fine."

"Where are you?"

"At a pay phone in someplace far away." She paused. *"Look. I don't feel comfortable talking. I think that they overheard my cell phone call to Ben. They were waiting at the hospital when we got there the other morning. The blond man . . . he didn't see me. At least, if I'm not crazy and that guy was who I think he was."*

"He was, Ms. Tremain."

"Is . . . is Ben all right?"

"He refused protective custody. He told me he could do better on his own." The number on the trace flashed. One with a 406 area code. That was Montana, wasn't it? "Dr. Tremain, your ex-husband told us some interesting things about the boy. He thinks that he's some kind of prehistoric human. Is that—"

"A Neandertal," she said. *"That's what I needed to find out."*

A Neanderthal? "That's not a joke, is it? You can't mean—"

"I sure do, Agent Ramsey. This is just a guess, mind you, but I think my brother and his team wanted to end the controversy over human evolution once and for all. Little Abel is exactly that. A Neandertal boy. Living proof that evolution did indeed happen, and that no amount of faith could make it any different. That's why Billy Barnes Brown, and his church, are so threatened."

For a moment, Ramsey could only stare across the office at the cubicle wall. A Neanderthal kid? That odd little blue-eyed boy? Somehow, when Ben had said a "prehistoric human" it hadn't had the same impact. They had to be joking! But, if they weren't. . . . "We've got to bring you in. Move you to—"

"The last time, they almost killed us!"

"Dr. Tremain, I'm serious. These men that we're dealing with are professionals. We need to put you someplace safe where—"

"Where what? Where they can really blow us up next time?"

"No. Listen, we know that they can monitor our com-

munications. We need some time to . . ." And, in that instant an idea came to him. A nutty idea. But then, success
on the street often hinged on nutty ideas. "Dr. Tremain,
you're coming in. And this time, we're doing things a little differently."

For the first time, he thought he saw light at the end of
the tunnel. "Here's what I want you to do."

"Why should we trust you?"

"For one thing, these people killed Joe Hanson. He
was one of mine. A member of my squad. A friend, as
well as a damn fine agent and human being. For another,
I may not agree with what your brother did, but I *do* dis-
agree with torture, murder, executions, and breaking the
law. I've got my own score to settle here." *No matter
where it leads us.*

*"All right, talk. Assuming that your phone isn't being
bugged by the blond man."*

And talk, he did.

CHAPTER THIRTY-THREE

❖

"HANK THE COWDOG" WAS IN REAL TROUBLE. VERON-
ICA glanced over to see Abel's eyes closed, his breathing
deepened, and his mouth open. The fingers of one hand
were woven into Chaser's curly hump fur.

She closed the book and looked across the bed to
where Bryce lay propped up on one elbow, the traces of
a smile on his lips.

The muted sounds of Billings could be heard below as
occasional traffic passed on the street. In the distance, a
train hooted its air horns.

"That's a cute book," Bryce said, and indicated Abel.
"He's out like a light." Bryce eased from the bed and
stepped into the other room. He stood at the window,
looking out at the night.

Veronica slipped off the side of the bed and stopped in
the doorway, studying him in the half-light. His hair was
slightly mussed, his muscular arms crossed on his chest.
She could see the rusty fur on his forearms. A pensive expression lay on his face. How handsome he looked: oddly
vulnerable, tired, and at the same time a pillar of strength.
Wasn't that what a man was supposed to be? Not the con-
niving braggarts she had always associated with, but a
real man, one who was comfortable with who he was,
what he was. In his presence, despite their precarious situation, she felt secure in a way she never had.

In all of her time with him, she had yet to hear a cross word, a bitter reply. Not once had he belittled her ideas or actions.

She met his eyes as she stepped into the room and closed the door behind her, blocking the bedroom light. A building excitement filled her as she snaked an arm around his waist. His warmth soothed her as she looked out at the night. The lights of Billings twinkled. Across the rimrock, white lightning flashed through a distant thunderhead.

"Peaceful, isn't it?" he asked.

"It is. Hard to believe there's an angry world out there."

"What do you think of Agent Ramsey's plan?"

She pursed her lips for a moment. "It's worth a try, Bryce. You said we couldn't live in a hotel forever."

"I could . . . with you." He made it sound so easy.

That half-forgotten tingle began in her loins. It would be so easy; all she had to do was raise her face, part her lips, and he would meet her halfway. If she did, was this what she wanted? This reliable, handsome man, with all his strength and . . .

It just seemed to happen. Her lips were meeting his, her other arm twining around him as he turned to her. At the first delicate touch, her pulse began to race. Electric sensations coursed along her spine, and her breathing deepened. Under her hands, he tensed. She could feel his muscles drawing into knots.

When his tongue parted her lips and slid along her teeth, she shuddered, responding, probing and exploring. He tightened his grip, her breasts against his chest. Reflexively, she arched against him.

"My God," she whispered when their lips parted. He was tracing the lines of her face, the tips of his fingers ever so gentle.

"I love you, Ronnie."

"Bryce? Are you sure?"

He nodded. "As sure as I've ever been." His fingers combed her long hair. "I thought you were beautiful the first moment I saw you."

Her body melted against his, her hands running down his sides, along his slim hips. The ache was building in her loins, warm and liquid. In the soft light, she unfastened the buttons on his shirt, exposing the curling hair on his chest.

"If we do this," she whispered, "nothing will ever be the same."

"I'm counting on that," he said hoarsely.

She sighed as his hands rose under her blouse. Unlike other men she had known, his touch was gentle as he explored the round swell of her breasts.

Any last hesitations eroded as her fingers slipped his belt from its buckle. Her blouse drifted off her shoulders, fluttering to the floor. His tender hands slid her jeans and panties over the curve of her hips. Deliberately, sensuously, she undressed him. The bedspread rested coolly under her skin. The weight of his body reassured her as he lowered himself beside her; she pulled him close.

Abel is haunted by the images of the dream: He is alone in a dark forest. Lurking in the shadows, the

blond man watches, waiting, unseen, but with a presence that raises the hair on Abel's head and prickles his skin with spider feet.

He scuttles from shadow to shadow, but unlike at the condo, the inky darkness doesn't hide him. Though he can't see him, he can sense the blond man smiling as he closes in. Abel tries to run, his small legs no match for the silent and swift pursuit of the blond man.

Then Death shoots out . . .

Abel bolts upright. That final moment of horror lingers as Abel looks around the darkened hotel room. The walls are illuminated by the red glow of the clock on the bedside stand. It says 1:38. His next realization is that he is alone. Only Chaser, lying on his side an arm's length away, remains. Abel flings himself onto his buffalo and chokes back sobs.

Where is everyone? He sniffs and looks around. The bed is empty, the door closed.

Anxiously, he clutches Chaser and slides off the bed. His muscles tremble. He stands for a moment, too scared to move. The distant sound of a train is heard. A car passes on the street below, and the vents whisper softly. Otherwise, the hotel is quiet. Too quiet. It presses down on him like a thick blanket.

Tears trickle down his cheeks as he fingers his buffalo. His first instinct is to crawl under the bed, but where a space should be, he only finds a wooden barrier. For a long time, he crouches down in the shadow next to the bed and cries into Chaser's fur.

What can he do? Where can he go? Why did they leave him here alone?

In a dark corner of his head, the blond man laughs.

Abel cries out. Tugging Chaser along behind him, he bolts for the door, flinging it open.

In the next room, he briefly sees Veronica and Bryce, their bodies outlined by a white sheet. Crying, he leaps onto the bed and burrows his body between theirs.

They are awake now, sitting up. Abel barely hears their worried questions as he huddles between them. All he can do is cry as relief washes through him.

To Bryce's surprise, the black plastic clock read 7:15. He normally woke up earlier. He shifted his leg, feeling a weight on it. Looking down he found Abel's compact body curled into the crook of his knee. The little boy's blond hair glistened against the floral-pattern spread. His right thumb was in his mouth, his left hand on the buffalo as though they were some sort of symbiotic life-forms.

Bryce settled his head back against the pillow and glanced at Veronica, sleeping soundly beside him. Her hair lay spilled in a black wreath around her. An artist would have draped the sheet like that; a molded shroud that accented the swell of her hip and dipped into the hollow of her waist. Where the fabric twisted around her, the round globe of her right breast, dotted by the brown nipple, lay exposed. In sleep, the fine features of her face had relaxed, her expression slack and vulnerable.

A warmth, like nectar, grew as he watched her and relived every glorious detail of their coupling the night before. Good sex was always a novelty, but a subtle difference had infused their lovemaking, as if here, finally, lay the reason of existence, the purpose behind the entire frustrating male-female dialectic. Words didn't express the harmony and contentment that had left him so giddy in the afterglow.

Good God, Bryce, you're finally, truly in love. Heart and soul. After all those years of fumbling experiments, he understood. Damn, he felt good! Epiphany. A giant piece of life had just clicked into place.

He smiled at himself, reaching out to finger her silken hair. The memory of her burned within him, how her hair had tumbled around her as she settled onto him and arched her back. Such images as those smacked of the mythic.

This woman was *his*. The soft length of hair twined around his fingers wasn't part of a lonely man's dream, but real.

He squirmed around, mindful of waking Abel, until he could press his lips against hers in a gentle kiss. She shifted, murmuring as her eyes blinked open, startled, to stare into his. He watched with amusement as she struggled to understand; then a dreamy acceptance grew and she extended a slim arm, smiling against his lips, drawing him close and returning the kiss with a sensual passion.

"Good morning," he said softly. "I love you."

"Good morning," she returned, voice husky with sleep. "Sleep well?"

"Better than anytime in my life. I made an effort to syncopate my heartbeat with yours. It's remarkably peaceful. Pretty cool, actually."

"Romantic." She smiled.

"Muvver?" Abel asked in a groggy voice.

"Hey, kid," Bryce called. "We're in Billings, remember?" He tactfully reached over to pull the sheet over Veronica's breast.

Abel sat up, eyes rheumy, and looked around. "Muvver's dead," he repeated, as if to remind himself.

"Yes," Veronica said gently. "But we're here." When she smiled, Bryce thought she looked radiant.

"Muvver and me. We went to the wiver." Abel looked down at his hands where his fingers absently wove together. "Thwew wocks."

Bryce nodded. "Yeah, and made big splashes, huh?"

Abel gave him a reserved look, as if trying to decide if a grown-up could really understand.

"I grew up on a lake," Bryce said. "I threw lots of rocks. The big ones will even splash on you." He grinned. "My mother never really liked it when I threw rocks like that." He glanced suspiciously at Ronnie. "I don't think girls understand."

Abel couldn't help but watch to see how Veronica would react.

"Oh, yeah?" she said. "Well, I happen to know that there's a big river, the Yellowstone, just outside of town. I'll bet there are a lot of rocks to throw into it. Not only that, but I'll bet that I can throw a bigger rock than either of you. And I don't care if I get wet or not!"

Bryce winked at Abel. "This sounds like a challenge. I don't think we can let this pass, do you?"

Nothing changed in Abel's expression. His eyes just drilled into Bryce's, as if waiting to see if they really did it.

The next blow came when Bryce stepped out of the

bathroom. He'd just taken his shower and was wearing one of the hotel's white terry-cloth robes. Veronica sat on the corner of the bed, her eyes fixed on the television.

Bryce said, "I was just—"

"Shhh!" She pointed as he settled himself next to her.

On the television, a newsman was saying, *". . . And if it's true, what does it really mean?"*

A woman that Bryce recognized as Maureen Killdare said, *"Then overnight our status has changed. If Dr. Ben Tremain's claims can be substantiated, and as of now it looks like they can, then Scott Ferris cloned a Neanderthal. Somewhere out there, crazy as it sounds, is a little Neanderthal boy."*

"Dear God," Veronica whispered. "The whole world knows."

Bryce pulled the June 24 edition of the *Billings Gazette* from under the door. NEANDERTALS AMONG US? was the prominent headline.

The CNN monitor at the DIA boarding area flashed a scene from Ben Tremain's press conference. Jackson Ramsey tuned it out as he watched the Boeing 757 nose into the gate. Around him passengers waited for the D.C. flight. The television showed a scene of reporters shouting questions at Judge Harthow, asking if the FBI was aware of the "Neanderthal" murders, and what the Bureau was doing about it.

"There have been no Neanderthal murders," Harthow insisted, waving his hands as if to put the crowd down. "This is all a cruel hoax."

Ramsey winced; then the report shifted to a woman identified as an anthropologist who insisted that cloning a Neanderthal was impossible. The feeding frenzy was on.

"Can you believe that crap?" a man seated behind him asked his wife. "Some clown cloned a Neanderthal? No wonder they killed him."

"Oh, come on," the woman retorted. "It's some kind of publicity thing."

"But what if it's true?" the man asked. "We could have cavemen walking in and taking a flight to L.A." And he laughed a corny laugh.

Ramsey stepped away, thoughts churning. He couldn't make himself think of that little boy as a troglodyte. Why had Scott Ferris done this? It was an act of lunacy from a man that no one who knew him had thought of as a lunatic.

What were you after, Ferris? How he wished he could have asked the man. Unfortunately, Scott Ferris had taken any answers to his grave.

Fully a third of the D.C. flight emerged from the jetway in Denver International Airport's Concourse B before Mitch Ensley stepped through the gate. He met Ramsey's eyes and turned in his direction. Behind him, a sallow-complected kid, fair-haired, with traces of acne, followed. A small aluminum case dangled from the skinny kid's arm. He wore a white shirt with a narrow black tie and gray slacks. The perfect "nerd": young, bright, socially maladapted, and the sort of brain child that kept the Bureau in a competitive position amidst the burgeoning age of computers and sophisticated technology.

"Hey, Jack." Ensley grasped Ramsey's hand, flashing

white teeth in his dark face. "I want you to meet Henry Van der Beek. From Hoboken. He'll tell you about it when he's not boring you half to death with frequency modulation, carrier waves, and all that other stuff that no one sane can understand."

Van der Beek was smiling uncomfortably. When Ramsey shook his hand the grip was weak. "Good to meet you. How are things down at Quantico?"

"The same." Van der Beek shrugged.

"That's the box?" Ramsey asked.

"Yeah." Van der Beek nodded. "Built it myself."

"And it's secure?"

Van der Beek gave him a reproving look.

"All right," Ramsey relented. "I'll take your word for it. But these guys we're up against, they're the best. Years of experience."

Van der Beek shrugged again.

"We got wheels?" Ensley asked.

"Yep. GSA all the way."

"Peachy. Just peachy." Ensley reached in his pocket for a toothpick. "Lead the way, boss man."

Ramsey nodded, turning toward the moving walkway, pushing through the crowd. He pulled his phone from his pocket and tapped in Bob Dole's number at the Denver Field Office. On the second ring, Dole answered in his laconic voice.

"We've got our package," Ramsey said. "We're on the way to the barn. See you soon." Then he punched "end."

"Yeah," Ensley muttered. "I want you to know that the SAC is sweating bullets about the budget. Wirthing's sure that Harthow is going to call him up on the carpet, audit the books, and chop his head right off his neck."

"What are all those multitudes of forms for if you can't cook the books on occasion?" Ramsey asked. "I mean, heck, accounting errors happen all the time."

"I'll pretend that was a joke," Mitch said with aplomb. Then he glanced at Van der Beek. "Life in the field is a little different. If you hear anything that burns your ears, forget it. Immediately. It never happened."

Van der Beek swallowed hard, and Mitch broke out in raucous laughter.

"Trust me," Ramsey said. "You'll get used to it." Then to Ensley, "What else do you have on Joe?"

"A lot." Mitch's humor evaporated as quickly as it had begun. "The lab thinks Joe was pumped up with sodium pentothal. At least that's the signature they found in some fat cells."

"Jeez." Ramsey made a face. "So, they took him, wrung him dry, and set him up. No wonder they know what we know."

"We think we got the place, too," Mitch added darkly. "A church, up in the hills. One of our friend Billy's congregations. The place has a big concrete bunker. Two rooms from the remote imaging that we took. The mustard seeds on Joe's cuffs and the bit of gravel from his shoe match those on the premises. It's nothing we can go to court with—at least, not without a warrant to go in and see if we can find fibers, hairs, prints, or skin cells in a thorough sweep—but I didn't think we wanted to go for a warrant yet. It might tip our hand."

"Yeah. Well, if they haven't already sanitized the place, they probably won't." Ramsey considered his options. "No, we're better off holding back. When . . . *if* we nab these guys, we can go back." Even if Joe's killers had wiped the place down, corners always held a little residual dust. He was betting the stuff that had splattered on Joe's pant legs would still be there. Concrete had little nooks and crannies that held residue. They wouldn't have shot the place down with a power washer, would they?

Ramsey led them to the escalators that descended the two levels to the electric trains and waited before the stainless steel doors. If this worked, it was time to reel in the bait and see what snapped at the worm.

The perfect scenario would have been to have the HRT come in, but that would flag Harthow at the Bureau. He would just have to hope that Dole's SWAT guys were up to the challenge. More than that, he had to do this quickly, and with a minimum of manpower. That added complexity tied his hands. Draw down the bank, and the Bureau would be on top of them like flies on shit.

If that happened, what would he do? Disobey a direct order from the very top? How could he keep his team together if that happened? He couldn't ask Dole and his people to go out on the wobbling limb where he now found himself.

Just what kind of a screwy way to make a living was this, anyway?

"So, what's the gig?" Mitch asked as they crowded into the train. "Have you got a handle on this thing yet? Everyone's talking about Neanderthals. It was all over the radio this morning."

"Yeah," Ramsey said, glancing nervously at the people around them. "I'll tell you in the car. You're not going to believe it."

"Satan-cursed bitch!" Elias stormed into the motel room. The complex was small, a two-story collection of rooms in a cut-rate place off of Sixth Avenue and Federal. Thin walls covered with wood paneling barely kept the occupant from sharing the next-door neighbor's most intimate of bodily functions. Two threadworn beds and a TV stand made up most of the furnishings. When a toilet was flushed anywhere in the complex, the hot water went away.

Elias thrust a wrinkled photo he clutched in his right hand forward for Paxton's inspection. The grainy image had been torn out of the morning's *Denver Post* article. "Ferris sister at bottom of 'Neanderthal Craze'?"

"She was there! Walked right past me. I'd know her anywhere. Foxy-looking bitch. I thought she was a little peculiar. You know. Like she saw me and froze up. Went down the hall a couple of doors and knocked on it. Then ducked out the stairwell."

"Yeah, well, she made you." Paxton frowned as he looked at the photo. He stepped across and opened his briefcase before removing the photo they'd taken from Ferris' house. There, Scott Ferris and a short-haired Veronica Tremain stared at the lens. In the years between, Ms. Tremain had grown her hair. Making an ID of an unknown person from a photo was hard enough. But with a change in hairstyle? He could forgive Elias for that mistake. But how in hell had the Tremain woman known? When he studied Elias, he could figure. Something about Elias put women off. He'd seen their reaction. At first glance, Ron Elias caught a woman's eye. His physique, the muscular butt and broad shoulders, made them notice. Then, all it took was one look from Elias' peculiar eyes and they froze up, went frigid as bats in winter.

"If Johnson and the kid had been with her, I'd have nailed them. Sent them off to judgment." Elias resumed his tiger pacing.

"Punching that security guard didn't help much." Paxton crossed his arms where he sat on the edge of his bed.

"Why didn't we have an accurate photo?" Elias stomped back and glared down. "You're the brains, the 'intelligence' officer. How come you didn't peg her for an ID? Huh? She's the guy's sister!"

Paxton kept his lip from twitching. "What do you mean, I 'didn't peg her'? I'm the one who thought to take the one photo we had from Ferris' house, remember? You were too busy . . . couldn't be distracted from piling books on top of the guy and dousing him with gas. And which one of us thought to lift her cell number from Hanson's notebook in the first place? But for me, buddy, you'd have squat on Ms. Tremain."

"Screwups," Elias said through gritted teeth. "I hate it when things unravel. It causes mistakes. Just like this one."

Paxton waved him down. "What's past is past. Stick with the 'now.' She saw you. Can describe you. She's another of these damned anthropologists. With her knowledge of bones and stuff, she'd probably be able to put together a pretty good composite sketch with the right forensic artist."

Elias cocked his head, considering. "We take her out first thing. It makes sense. God's will. She's with the spawn. Satan's infected her with his evil."

Paxton nodded, seeing Elias refocusing, planning. Then that weird glaze settled in his eyes; the lips parted in a vacant smile.

"I'm going back to the van." Paxton indicated the TV. "Keep track of the news. That damned Ben Tremain has everyone on earth talking about the spawn. For the most part, they don't believe it. If that changes, we've got a problem."

The expression on Elias' face didn't change. He only tightened his fist, crumpling the photo of Veronica Tremain until the tendons stood from his powerful forearms.

This is more than I signed on for. He's going over the edge. The notion filled Paxton's head as he shut the motel door behind him. *Find the kid, kill him, and collect the money.* He patted his back pocket where the passport snugged against his billfold. *And get the hell out while you still can.*

CHAPTER THIRTY-FOUR

GIANT GREEN COTTONWOODS DOMINATED THE PARK BEside the swirling Yellowstone. The leaves rattled in a lazy breeze that blew down from the west, causing the branches to sway. A thick mat of grass covered the ground, ripe and full of the early summer. Birdcalls over-head mixed with the sounds of water and the distant noises of humans: autos, high-flying aircraft, and the belly roar of a Caterpillar bulldozer working on a build-ing site just south of the shaded park.

Veronica leaned back on the grass overlooking the river and watched. Abel had been quiet at first, plucking round cobbles from the bank and slinging them out into the murky current. His attention fixed on each splash as if it were the most wonderful thing in the world.

Bryce had joined the fun with verve and enthusiasm, helping to lever bigger rocks from the ground, and adding his strength to sling them out into the water. Both males were dappled with wet spots on their clothing.

Only with the biggest rocks had Abel begun to giggle, and now, as each of the stones sailed through the air, he shouted gleefully. Bryce chimed in, whooping when the thud-splash was followed by a chimera of sparkling droplets.

Abel continued to surprise her. For his size, he picked up what she considered to be huge rocks, perching them on his shoulder for leverage, and jumping as he boosted them out into space. At four, he could cast as big a rock as she could. If that Neandertal musculature could do that at age four, just how strong was Abel going to be as an adult?

Veronica had done her share, casting a modest-sized boulder into the current. It hadn't carried more than a couple of feet beyond the bank, and had drenched her jeans. Bryce had winked at Abel and said, "We can beat that." They had, by quite a bit.

A curious happiness suffused her. She had never done anything faintly resembling this. In the first place, her father wouldn't have considered coming to a location like this, and in the second, Mary would never have allowed her participation in anything as absurd as throwing rocks into a river. It just wouldn't have been proper for a young woman of Veronica's station.

How much of life had she missed out on? A faint ache grew in her gut. This is what real people did, and watching the expressions on Bryce's face and the gleam in Abel's eyes, her soul lightened and soared.

Bryce might have been a boy again. This man who had loved her with such tender and consuming passion last night now leaped and crowed like a water sprite. When he looked at her, his grin split his face.

She found herself laughing, sharing his joy. Idly her fingers toyed with the grass, winding around the supple stems. Yellow sunlight glinted from the water. For this one moment, she experienced an unfamiliar freedom, a sense of well-being.

The damp T-shirt conformed to Bryce's muscular body. She could remember it, how her fingers had traced over his shoulders, along his back.

To her surprise, the anticipated awkwardness hadn't reared its head when she awoke to his kiss that morning and looked into his eyes. The difference hadn't just been in the lovemaking, but in the look that he'd given her, as though he were the keeper of a wonderful and intimate secret.

Their coupling had been different. She'd participated in gymnastics with Ben, rutting with Louie and her teenage partners, but Bryce had truly made love to her. Shared with her, cherished her as much as the act. The results left her with a delightful confusion, and an aching desire for more. Sex might always be pleasant, but who would have thought it could be cathartic?

Bryce launched a huge rock into the air, grunting with the effort. It seemed to travel slowly, tumbling in a lazy manner as it arced into the water with a mighty impact that drove spray as far as her perch on the bank. Bryce had ducked, turning his back to the shower while Abel screamed in shrill delight as the spray soaked his already plastered head. In the aftermath, Bryce beat his soggy chest, howled, and scooped Abel up, swinging him around; the little boy squealed as his body sailed out over the water, carried by momentum. Bryce swung him in circle after circle and then lowered him to the ground before collapsing beside Abel, one arm around the boy's stocky shoulders.

Abel was transformed, his face alight with sheer unadulterated glee. For the first time he looked alive, animated, and happy. Had any man ever truly played with Abel before? Or had the serious and sober Rebecca always treated the boy as a prized specimen? Something to be guarded rather than nourished? Abel's infectious giggle carried over the sounds of the morning.

She refused to think about the future, about what might happen between her and Bryce, about Abel's long-term prospects, or about the blond man who lay in wait for them. Sometimes, it was better to linger in the dream. If only for a little while.

Theo frowned and rubbed his cheek with the knuckles of his right hand. The rasp of stubble against his fingers reminded him of the hour. On the blotter before him lay the testimony of Warren Hardesty, his latest case. Hardesty fell into that category of client who had a great deal more money than sense. He had insisted on pleading innocent, willing to fight a losing case to the very last gasp. Despite Theo's adamant protest, the man had insisted on testifying in his own defense. The bluster he had shown in the office had crumbled once he took the stand. A client who refused to look the jury in the eyes, fumbled with his fingers, and stuttered his answers didn't inspire confidence. Damn it, he'd just looked guilty. Worse, tomorrow at nine, the prosecutor would begin his cross, and Warren was positioned to go into the meat grinder headfirst.

Theo couldn't concentrate. Mary's face kept intruding, her wounded look haunting him. He should be there, helping to ease her terrible worry and grief. Somehow it wasn't enough that he had only hired a security firm to keep the constant stream of journalists from Mary's front door as they sought an interview with the "Neanderthal grandmother." She kept blaming herself, as if it were her fault that Scott had placed them all in this mess.

The case, fool. Concentrate on the case.

The only good thing about the case was that Hardesty paid his bills. Assuming that he was convicted, and only an act of God or a fumble on the prosecution's part—the same thing, really—would save him. Hardesty would have had a better chance for either in the lottery. Thus the prospects were good that for a long time Hardesty would be writing big checks to the firm to cover appeals.

The phone rang.

"Bennet here."

"Theo?"

"Ronnie? My God, where are you? Are you all right?"

"Fine, Theo. We're all fine. We're coming in."

"Ronnie, I should warn you—"

"Tell Agent Ramsey that we'll be waiting to hear from him. We can't trust my cell phone, Theo. I think the blond man can monitor it. And we can't trust Ramsey's safe houses. You know how that ended up last time. We have to have some special assurances that Ramsey can keep us safe."

"Yes, yes, I know. Um, look, we're working on it. Ramsey's sure that they can monitor his communications, too. They have identified a man. A fellow named Ted Paxton. They call him 'Leopard.' He was an electronic intelligence officer. Into picking locks, planting bugs, that sort of thing. Ramsey has brought in a specialist, a man who can fix the communications so that this Paxton can't listen in." He swallowed hard, a fist tightening in his chest. "Ronnie, this is a very dangerous situation."

"I know, Theo, believe me."

"Where are you?"

"At a pay phone. That's all I'm going to tell you."

"All right. What do you want me to do?"

"How's Mary doing?"

"She's worried sick about you, grieving for Scott. Her house is surrounded by the press. I've been up there every night. I'd be there now, but I have a big case." He winced, guilt washing through him.

"Tell Mother that I'm fine. Call Dr. Johnson's family, and tell them that he is alive and well, working with the FBI to solve a special case."

"Ronnie, what's this all about? As your attorney, I

have visited with Agent Ramsey. He thinks this is about some sort of prehistoric human. That can't be right, can it?"

"The little boy, Theo; he's a Neandertal. Scott—"

"Then it's true, what the press is saying?"

"You heard right. Scott cloned him from some ancient tissue he obtained from somewhere. Probably, as best we can guess, from Russia, since one of his partners, a fellow named Ostienko, worked in Moscow."

"It still doesn't explain why, Ronnie. The Scott Ferris I knew wouldn't have done something like this just for the novelty. What possible purpose would bringing a Neanderthal back serve?"

"It's Scott's answer to the Creationists. He's telling them: 'So, you don't accept evolution as a fact? Well, here's the proof! A live Neandertal.' I'm sure he had a plan for all of this, but someone found out about it and killed him, Amanda, and Avi Raad. Bryce was on their list, as is little Abel. They want to destroy the evidence, Theo. That's why they cleaned out Scott's files, burned his books."

"In God's name." Theo blinked, the Hardesty testimony forgotten in front of him.

"I imagine so, Theo. This isn't the first time that people have justified murder, torture, and suppression in God's name."

"But this is the twenty-first century!"

"So? When it comes to heresy, they're just a little more sophisticated about it these days. Be they Christians, Muslims, Jews, or whoever. Ideas are dangerous to certain kinds of people. Threatening. Especially anthropol-

ogy. We study things that make a lot of people uncomfortable."

"I suppose."

"Theo?" Ronnie's voice lowered. *"I want you to do something for me. I want you to check into Rebecca Armely's claim on Abel. I mean, who he belongs to. Rebecca would have had family in Ohio. Assuming that we survive this, Abel would have to go back to them, wouldn't he?"*

"Yes, her parents would be next of kin."

"Bryce says they're dead. Rebecca is survived by an older sister. I want you to call her, tell her the whole story. Explain to her that Abel will be the center of the spotlight. That if she takes him, their lives will be dissected. That he is not *a regular human boy, but one recreated out of prehistoric DNA. Every kook in the world will be hounding them. If she wants the boy, fine; I can't fight her. But if . . . if when she understands the situation, she wants a way out, well, I'm it. I'm willing to adopt Abel."*

To keep his swimming thoughts from deserting him entirely, Theo began scrawling notes on a legal pad. "Ronnie, are you sure you want to—"

"Yes, Theo, I am. I may have to spend the rest of my life in a witness protection program. So might Rebecca's sister if she decides to keep the boy, but, Theo, right or wrong, Abel is here now. He needs a chance." A pause. *"Maybe, so do I."*

"I'll look into it." His voice sounded weary, bewildered.

"Thanks, Theo."

The connection clicked, leaving the futile dial tone sounding in his ear.

Mouth dry, Theo replaced the receiver and swallowed hard. Too many shocks: A Neanderthal? That little boy? And Ronnie wanted to keep him?

He rubbed his face, feeling hot as he stared at the phone. He had known the call was coming, dreaded it, but hadn't thought she'd lay a bombshell like that on him. Not when she knew Paxton would be listening.

"Oh, God, Ronnie, I hope you were just saying that." But deep inside, he knew better. If she survived this, she wanted to keep that little . . . what? Caveman?

For long minutes he stared emptily at the Hardesty file. With numb fingers he closed the folder and walked out into the hallway and then down to Dennis Appleby's plush office.

Without knocking, he walked into his partner's inner sanctum, saying, "Dennis, I hate to do this to you, but you're going to have to take over the Hardesty case. Immediately."

Appleby, balding, in his fifties, looked up from the journal he was reading with cadaverous eyes. "You're joking! That case is worth millions!"

Theo felt his face tighten. "I have more important things to deal with. Trust me on this." He couldn't shake the image of Veronica's body, scorched and blackened, the skull exploded from the brain boiling inside, a little boy's dead body lying beside her.

Ted Paxton removed the headset, staring blankly at the electronic gear that monitored the lawyer's office. So, they had figured out that he had compromised their communications. The task would be that much more difficult now. And this "expert"? One of the whiz kids from Quantico, no doubt.

"Something?" Elias asked from where he was reading a magazine.

"They have figured out that we're monitoring their communications. They're bringing in a counterintelligence specialist. That's the bad news. The good news is that Tremain, Johnson, and the spawn are coming in."

Elias' cold blue eyes fixed on him. "When? Where? Can you penetrate their net?"

Paxton shrugged. "I don't know. We'll just have to wait and see. I need a name. If I know who the expert is, maybe."

Elias pursed his lips. Did white cobras have blue eyes with that flat intensity? An unusual anxiety was building in Elias, one that Paxton had never seen before. And it came to him suddenly: Elias trusted him, or at least his talent with electronics.

Paxton gave him a sour look. "Oh, stop worrying. So they've got a bright kid? I can break anything he puts in place."

"In the name of the Lord, you'd better be right."

"Listen, I've been doing this for years. If I could penetrate Saddam Hussein's net, with all the security he had, I can break this. But I'll need some help." A pause. "It will be expensive."

Elias nodded, doubt hidden behind his eyes. "Better get on the horn, call the client."

Paxton flexed his fingers. "They'll try to scramble the signal. Probably changing frequencies as they go. It won't be as sophisticated as the military or intelligence services. The Bureau doesn't have the money, or, if we can believe the press, the backing from the Seventh Floor."

"So, what do we need?"

"A computer. The right software." He made a fist, studying it in the half-light that penetrated the back of the van. "The computer is easy. The software, well, I've got a number. FedEx can have it here within twenty-four hours."

"It'll work?" Elias cocked his head.

He smiled knowingly. "Trust me."

In the silken afterglow of lovemaking, Veronica pulled the sheets up and grasped Bryce's hand. Muted light from the city filled the hotel room, sneaking past the narrow slit where the drapes didn't close. The red digital glow from the bedside clock illuminated the pillow under her head.

"Worried?" Bryce asked, sensing her mood.

"I don't want to leave. I don't want to go back. What if it all goes wrong again?"

Bryce indicated the closed door leading to the other room. "It's got to be all right. For him." He tightened his grip on her hand. "For us."

She exhaled wearily. "He's the real target. We're just incidental."

"Yeah, well, for being incidental, I'm not about to end up blown into little pieces, or burned up in my house." She could barely see his crooked smile as he said, "I've never been this happy in my life." A pause. "I love you, Ronnie. Like I never knew I could love a woman."

"I love you, too, Bryce." To her surprise, her heart surged with the sudden awareness that she meant it. At the thought, a warmth suffused her chest. Not the electric excitement she had felt for Ben, but a deeper sense of contentment that emanated from within. With one hand, she reached out to trace her fingers along the line of his cheek. "I want to stay with you forever."

"I'll keep that bargain. Somehow, some way, I swear I will."

Would it work that way? Was Ramsey's word good? Could the FBI keep them safe this time? And, if they did, would they ever get a chance to live like normal people, or would they always have to look over their shoulders, fearful of those who wouldn't give Abel a chance?

As though he were sharing her thoughts, he said, "What is it about people that they can't accept what they can't understand? I mean, just because Abel's different, a Neanderthal, doesn't mean that he has to be destroyed, does it? Can't people just accept that he's a miracle, and appreciate him for what he is?"

She snuggled closer to his naked body, reveling in his warmth. "The majority will. But some people will see him as a threat. They're the same ones who gassed Jews in the camps, or killed their neighbors because they were Muslims, or Croats, or Serbs, or Tutsis, or Hutus."

He remained silent for a moment. "People are just plain nuts. Makes you wonder if we're really worth all the trouble."

She shifted, holding him closer. "Among anthropologists, we have a saying that humanity is an experiment that hasn't proven itself yet."

"How's that?"

"Well, from the standpoint of evolution, Bryce, the cockroach is one of the more successful experiments. Six hundred million years old, they haven't changed much; and they manage to survive just about everywhere in spite of our best efforts to exterminate them. Genus *Homo* has only been around for about two million years. What's that compared to six hundred million?"

"So, we're neophytes. Big deal. You've got to start somewhere."

"It's more complicated than that. We don't have a very good record. We wipe out our competition, overutilize our resource bases, and poison ourselves on our wastes. Intelligence may not be such a good idea."

He thought for a moment. "Maybe, but on the other hand, even though humans do dreadful things in the name of God and country, they also place themselves at risk to save stranded whales. We're not all evil."

"No." A sadness had driven the warmth from her.

"So, tell me, didn't humans and Neanderthals exist side by side for tens of thousands of years? I remember reading about the caves in Israel. One occupation was us—moderns, I mean—and the next was Neanderthal."

She nodded. "Skuhl and Qafzeh caves had moderns, while Tabun and Kebara had Neandertal occupations. From the dates of the levels and the environmental reconstruction, moderns occupied the area when it was warm, and Neandertals when it was cold. We're talking about tens of thousands of years, and lots of environmental fluctuation."

"So, it isn't like we're mutually exclusive." Bryce shifted, twining an arm around her.

"No." She kissed him lightly and drew back. "I was there in 1999, at the physical anthropology meetings in Ohio when Erik Trinkaus first reported the Lagar Velho skeleton. Half modern, half Neandertal. At the time, paleoanthropology was split over whether moderns and Neandertals intermixed, or whether moderns replaced the Neandertals. Trinkaus said, that from that one burial, he could state that 'Neandertals and moderns viewed each other as *people*.'" She traced a finger over the curve of his shoulder. "If we could do that twenty-five thousand years ago, is it too much to ask of us now?"

"Maybe not." He shrugged. "I would hope that in twenty-five thousand years, we've learned something."

"Scott and Amanda might not agree."

"No, but we can fight the cretins, Ronnie. Ignorance and bigotry can't always triumph. Someone has to stand up for the better angels of our nature. I'm willing."

"You're pretty wonderful, Bryce Johnson."

"So are you." He lifted his head to glance at Abel's room. "Tell me, do you think we've got time enough for seconds before he wakes up and figures out we're here? I mean, what's the point of all this evolution if a man and woman can't do what we've been programmed to do?"

"I think we have time."

He slid his hand down her side, over the swell of her hip, and kissed her with an unusual urgency. She sighed gratefully as she rolled onto her back and accepted his weight. She would take this moment, revel in it. Who knew how many more they'd have?

CHAPTER THIRTY-FIVE

❖

The place is called the Muzzle Loader. It is a bright restaurant, filled with men who smell of sweat, tobacco, and earth. They wear caps, cowboy hats, and overalls. Some have leather bags full of tools hung on their belts. The talk is loud, with much laughter.

Abel wrinkles his nose as he sits perched in a booster chair. He can smell the human odors, the food cooking in the kitchen, and the cigarette smoke. It barely masks the curious musk that clings to Veronica and Bryce. Abel wonders at the new odor, and the change that has settled over them like a blanket. They are seated in a booth next to the window that looks out over battered trucks—some dusty, others dented—with ladders, shovels, and equipment of kinds that Abel doesn't recognize.

Veronica laughs at something Bryce whispers into her ear. A gleam fills their eyes when they look at each other. Then Bryce sneaks a glance at Abel and winks, as if they share some secret.

This time, though, Abel isn't reassured. Something is different between them. He just doesn't know what. That worries him, making the tingle in his stomach grow. This isn't fear, but an uneasiness that he can't quite grasp. He glances surreptitiously at Chaser, who is perched on the cushion beside the booster chair, and *wonders what this means for him. Veronica and Bryce don't seem to pay as much attention to him now.*

Abel bites his lip, picks up his fork, and throws it angrily. It flips through the air, clattering across a table across from them. The men sitting there, smoking and drinking coffee, jerk back with surprise.

One cries out, "What the hell!"

Bryce leaps from his seat. "Abel? Why did you do that?" To the men he says, "I'm so sorry."

Abel is suddenly stricken with fear as he sees the look on Veronica's and Bryce's faces. They are horrified.

Veronica slides out of the booth and steps over to kneel beside him. He looks into her eyes and sees anger brewing. It frightens him, and he bursts into tears. He is barely aware of Bryce talking to the men at the next table. Hears him say, "I don't know what got into him. He's never like this."

"It's okay," one of the men says, "We was just about done anyway."

Veronica grasps Abel's arm with one hand. She turns his head with the other, forcing him to look at her. He hates this, but is too scared to look away. "We do not throw things, Abel. It's dangerous. Do you understand?"

Looking into her eyes is the most terrible thing he can imagine. He blubbers and can't seem to get his breath.

"Abel, stop crying. Right now."

He has never heard her speak like this to him. A hard knot forms at the base of his throat.

"That's better," Veronica soothes. "Now, crawl down and go apologize to those men." She points a finger like a knife.

Abel chokes on the tears, frozen.

"Now," Veronica says, "or face the consequences."

He wonders what "consequences" means and decides that he doesn't want to find out. Half blinded by tears, he reaches for Chaser.

On wobbling legs, Abel climbs down, head bowed, and mutters, "Sowwy."

Bryce's hand rests lightly on his shoulder.

"It's okay," one of the men says. Abel can't make himself look up to see which one. He stares at the floor through a silver haze of tears.

"You should'a seen my kid," another of the men says. "Used to throw anything in sight."

"Well, we're sure sorry," Bryce tells the man. "It won't happen again, will it, Abel?"

He shakes his head, wanting to melt right through the floor like the wicked witch of the west.

He whimpers, "I want Muvver."

Bryce lifts Abel and hugs him for a long moment, then sits him back down in his booster chair and pats his hair.

Abel tries to imagine himself back in Salt Lake, in their apartment, with Mother and all his things. He wants to be there, now, away from this terrible place. He wishes, as hard as he can, squeezing his eyes shut with the effort. Hot tears drip down his cheeks, making them wet and cool until the next tear trickles on its hot path.

"Abel?" Veronica says. "Why did you do that?"

She has to repeat the question several times until he finally says, "I don' know."

Bryce says, "Abel, look at me. I need to tell you something very important."

It takes Abel several tries to finally meet and hold Bryce's eyes.

Bryce says, "Veronica and I love you. We're going to take care of you."

He clamps his lips between his teeth and nods. The miserable feeling is eating his stomach, making the bottom of his tongue hurt. He whispers, "Muvver . . ."

The food arrives. Abel just stares down at his pants as the plates are set on the table. The smell of the French toast doesn't even tickle his hunger.

Bryce leans toward Veronica. "The wonder is that he hasn't blown up before this." To Abel, Bryce says, "Hey, little buddy, you want to try a bite of this chicken-fried steak? I can tell you, they didn't lie. This is the best chicken-fried steak I've had in years."

"What does someone from New Hampshire know about chicken-fried steak?" Veronica asks.

"Hush, woman. When you cook like I do, you know good food when you find it."

Able looks up and sees a morsel stuck on the end of a fork before him. He shakes his head and looks down again.

Bryce says, "How about if I just put it here on the edge of your plate and you can try it later?"

Abel nods, but he feels miserable. They are going back to Denver, and in his heart he knows someone is going to die. How can he tell them? Why is this happening to him?

Ramsey stood at the head of the table in the "operations room" in the Denver Field Office. Bob Dole sat to his right, Van der Beek to the left, with other members of Dole's squad seated around the table. One wall was covered with white butcher paper, a crude plan of the operation sketched out there. A plan view of the building had also been drawn. For the last two hours, he had outlined the operation. Now he racked his brain, trying to anticipate problems, to solve them before they fouled up the operation in the field.

"Okay, people," Ramsey said as he looked at the faces. "Can any of you think of anything we missed? If there are any flaws in this, we have to find them now, anticipate screwups, and be able to implement an alternate plan at a moment's notice."

"No assumptions," Dole repeated. "If it can happen, we need a plan for it."

"We're sure Henry's machine will work?" Dan Dern, head of the Denver SWAT, asked.

"As sure as we can ever be." Ramsey shrugged. "Look, any communications system can be compromised with the right equipment and software."

Van der Beek had been doodling on a legal pad. Now he looked up. "I've studied Paxton's file. He's good. I'm aware of just how good. We can't use the usual system." He was referring to the standard scramblers that the Bureau used to block eavesdroppers—like the ones the media used to monitor FM band transmissions. "I've got something better here. It uses a random distribution of wave frequencies. I based it on a fractal program used to protect computer systems. But I made a few modifications that adapt it to our special needs. Given time and the right equipment Paxton could probably crack it. I don't think he's got that kind of computational power at his disposal."

"But that's an assumption, isn't it?" Dern asked.

"It is," Ramsey replied. "But that's the best we can do. It isn't a perfect world, and we don't have all the support from the Bureau that we should given the current political situation and the media buzz around this thing."

"Politics," muttered Dole. "I remember the good old days when we were supposed to be apolitical."

"Times change," Ramsey told him. "Maybe if we break this case it'll shake up the bureaucracy. But that underscores the point that we can't screw this up. We need a good solid collar and the evidence to take it to the source."

"And then?" Dole asked.

"Then the chips fall where they will." Ramsey shrugged. "In the meantime, let's get to work. I want each of you to put yourself in Ted Paxton's head. Look at the operation as I've laid it out. What would you do to get around us and kill the witnesses?"

It would be a long night.

Billy Barnes Brown straightened his tie, looked at Eunice Campbell, and nodded. She was standing, arms crossed, beside the rack of lights on the side of the stage. What a handsome woman she was. Today she had dressed in an immaculately cut tangerine-colored suit that accented her slim body in a professional way. She'd pinned her hair up; it caught the light, shimmering in blond radiance. Her blue eyes were filled with a curious intensity. She ignored the bustling technicians wearing headsets and microphones who scurried around the stage on smudged tennis shoes.

She hadn't been herself since the flight up from Atlanta. When she had slipped through the door adjoining his suite last night, she had been preoccupied. Nor had she responded to his lovemaking with her usual passion. In the midst of their intercourse, he had looked down to find her eyes focused on some distant point beyond the ceiling. Was it just him, or the pressure of the job, of knowing the FBI was nosing around at the edges of his life, no matter what Judge Harthow might have decreed?

"Reverend?" a voice called. "We're ready."

This was his moment. He stepped out and crossed the stage to the chair. After seating himself, a technician helped him to snake a clip-on microphone under his suit jacket. In the chair beside him, Dr. William DeVries was undergoing the same treatment. DeVries was a professor of anthropology who had written several books on Neanderthals. He was a portly man in his late fifties, balding, with a round face that reflected a bad case of nerves.

Good. A nervous opponent was bound to misspeak, to fumble, being more worried about the cameras than he was about his facts. Even the keenest brains could freeze under the lens—a fact Brown counted on.

The show's host, Skip Manson, walked out in a gray suit, shook hands all the way around, and took his seat under the glare of the lights. The set behind them displayed an image of the Washington city skyline.

"Ready?" Manson asked, glancing at each of them.

"Ready." Brown smiled and shot a challenging glare at DeVries. The anthropologist nodded and reached for a glass of water.

Brown assumed a relaxed pose as the technician gave them the countdown.

"Good evening," Manson said as he smiled into the camera, "and welcome to the June twenty-fifth edition of 'Impact on Washington,' where we discuss the hottest topics in the nation's capital. Tonight we take on the current Neanderthal craze. Is it real, and if it is, what does it mean to all of us? This morning, Senator Dallas introduced legislation making the creation of cloned organisms based on human DNA illegal. We will discuss the impact of this legislation with two guests, both renowned in their respective fields. Joining me are the Reverend Billy Barnes Brown, of the Apostolic Evangelical Church of the Salvation, and Dr. William DeVries, professor of anthropology and author of three books about human evolution and Neanderthals in particular. Welcome, both of you."

"It is my pleasure," Brown said easily, taking the initiative. DeVries just nodded.

"I'll start with you, Reverend: This notion that someone has created a Neanderthal . . . Outside of the fact that a murder investigation is involved, I'd like to get your initial reaction just to the very idea that someone, allegedly Dr. Scott Ferris, created a prehistoric human. How does that affect you as a man of God, and what does it mean for your ministry?"

Brown smiled wearily and laced his fingers together. "I have yet to see this so-called Neanderthal. Skip, in all fairness, all we have is this Denver physician's claim that one exists. And to be honest, the experts I have talked to tell me that the X rays and MRIs the doctor produced are those of a four-year-old boy—probably a child with developmental problems and not a mythical Neanderthal at all. In answer to your question, I'm entirely unaffected by this. The Bible tells us how the world and humanity was created. Anything else will undoubtedly turn out to be a sham perpetrated by misguided scientists attempting to use genetics to prove their own faith: secular humanism."

"A hoax?" Skip asserted.

"They have nothing else," Brown returned easily. "Evolution is only a theory."

"Doctor DeVries?" Manson asked.

"It's a theory that has stood the test of time." DeVries straightened uncomfortably. "Look, this argument goes back over one hundred and fifty years. The theory of evolution just doesn't go away. We keep finding more and more fossils. And yes, we've had our hoaxes. Anthropology is tailor-made for hoaxes. The evidence for human evolution is scanty and covers millions of years. Simply because the time span of evolution disagrees with a two-thousand-year-old holy book's doesn't mean it doesn't exist." DeVries frowned. "It boils down to this. What do you believe? Fact or faith? If you choose faith, there is no point in discussing this."

"But what about this claim, Professor? Could this alleged Neanderthal exist?" Manson leaned forward.

Brown lifted an eyebrow, a skeptical smile on his lips as he watched DeVries squirm.

"It could," DeVries said soberly, his eyes focused on something off stage. "I knew Scott Ferris. Assuming he found a bit of tissue—and that is problematical. It would have had to have been over thirty thousand years old—"

"Why problematical?" Manson asked.

DeVries shifted, one arm propped on the chair. "DNA is in many ways a delicate molecule. Potassium forty is a problem. It has a long half-life and damages DNA. So does an acidic environment . . . or one that is subjected to gamma radiation. The tissue source would have to have come from a protected circumstance where none of the above could have denatured the molecule. As I told you, I knew Scott, Amanda, and Avi Raad. Given modern advances in biotechnology and provided they had a viable sample, yes, it lies within the realm of possibility that they could have reproduced a living specimen."

"Could have?" Brown interjected. "Skip, that's my problem with all of this. The answer you get is always 'could have,' 'might have,' or 'it is possible.' You never get a straight 'here it is' answer out of any of these people. Never in a way that is irrevocable 'fact' as the professor is so fond of quoting. In the Bible we have it, written down in black and white . . . the Holy Word of our Lord God!"

Manson asked, "Professor?"

DeVries had begun to perspire under the hot lights. "The debate over evolution aside, the only way we can know about this Neanderthal is to read Scott's notes or to examine the child."

"But Dr. Ferris is dead, and according to my sources"—Manson shuffled his notes—"his research has either been destroyed or is missing. You, however, have seen the data presented by Ben Tremain in Denver. What do you think of his X rays and MRIs?"

DeVries squinted up at the lights. "As a scholar, I can tell only that they are similar to what we would expect from a Neanderthal child of that age. The cranial morphology, uh, the shape of the skull, the lack of a protruding chin, are all the hallmarks indicative of—"

"Or someone with a developmental problem," Brown chimed in. "Professor, as I recall, people in your profession are fond of referring to something called 'the range of human variation,' a phrase relating to the miracle of God's Creation of all living things. Part of that miracle is that none of us are exactly the same, that He made all of us as unique individuals. Now, tell me truthfully, is it entirely out of the realm of possibility that such a unique little boy was the source of those X rays?"

"No," DeVries said uncertainly. "Not out of the 'realm of possibility.'"

"Thank you, Doctor." Brown sat back smugly.

Manson then asked, "The Neanderthals, Dr. DeVries, what really happened to them? Were they just an evolutionary dead end?"

"Not at all," DeVries replied. "They were a highly successful regional adaptation of human beings. They thrived for nearly two hundred and fifty thousand years across Europe and western Asia. They had different body morphology than we do—muscular, big-boned. Their brains were larger than ours. I'd call them very well adapted given the length of time they span and the numerous environments they inhabited."

"Then why did they disappear?" Manson asked.

"That is the subject of some heated debate among anthropologists," DeVries began.

"Yes," Brown agreed, "if you have nothing else, hot debate at least makes it sound like you are dealing with substantial issues." He smiled at the camera. "In my reading of the good doctor's own material I have discovered that he and his colleagues believe these mythological beings to be slow, stupid, technologically inferior, without religion or ornament. To me, it seems that they have created Neanderthals to fulfill the role of trolls and troglodytes. In their mythology, they become the dark side of the human condition."

"The best *science* that we have"—DeVries didn't fall for the bait—"indicates that modern humans replaced them, either through competition for resources, or moderns simply were more successful in hunting and fishing and the exploitation of plant resources. Myself, I lean toward the latter hypothesis based on changes we see in Neanderthal culture . . . um, the Chatelperronian archaeological remains we see during the period around thirty thousand years ago."

"But not a dull-witted dead end like the Reverend would have us believe?" Manson insisted.

DeVries rubbed his hands together as he hunched forward. "Had modern humans not migrated northwards from Africa about a hundred thousand years ago, Neanderthals would still be living in Europe."

"Then it was modern humanity—through warfare, interbreeding, or whatever—that ended the Neanderthals?"

"Correct."

"But," Brown asked thoughtfully, "were I to play 'Devil's advocate' I would have to ask, were they human?

Did they believe in God? Did they believe in anything? Where is their art? Their sculpture? What did they create?"

"Well, they didn't." DeVries committed a cardinal sin on television: He wiped his face. "We only have the rudest of stone tools, and as to art, we don't know—"

"Of course you don't. They never existed. What you have are the remains of those whom God destroyed when he cleansed the world. We have a word for that: catastrophism."

DeVries stopped short, gaping at him.

To keep the interview on track, Manson asked, "Professor, tell us a little about the Neanderthal life. What was it like?"

"Well"—DeVries seemed to catch himself—"they lived in a terribly harsh environment and were good at it. At least we are led to think so. They were excellent hunters, and although their stone tools, of a sort we call Mousterian, were rather primitive, we can't really know the extent of their abilities. They did a great deal of woodworking, made credible spears, and were capable of hunting and killing the largest of the Pleistocene animals. They seemed to worship the great cave bear."

"Now, that sounds satanic at best," Brown interjected.

DeVries ignored him. "They cared for each other. The old man of La Chapelle could only have survived through the charity of others of his kind. They buried their dead—"

"Or at least covered them up in rude pits," Brown chided. "None of the burials show the interment of grave goods."

"Quite the contrary," DeVries said indignantly. "At La Ferrassie we have the oldest cemetery in the world, where at least seven people were interred, one child under a sort of tomb."

"But," Skip Manson pointed out, "in my research, I've found that we have no real indication of a belief system, or ornamentation that would point to a well-developed sense of 'self.' Even their stone tools, as has been said here, were most rudimentary. And even experts, like Olga Soffer, note that they didn't have the kind of tools to indicate tailored clothing."

DeVries waved his hand. "I would not count on that. True, we can't *prove* that they had tailored clothing, but as Dr. Soffer herself points out, the bone needles that we find in later, more modern sites, were most likely used to tailor fabric clothing. To tailor hides all you need is a sharp point, as could have been done with Mousterian tools. And, if you wish to draw comparisons, the Mousterian tool kit might look primitive, but it is more advanced that that possessed by the historical Australian aborigine. Despite the aborigine's limited technology, they have a most beautiful and intricate culture with a rich heritage. Rudimentary technology doesn't mean that it wasn't *effective* technology when it came to putting food on the table. What we do suspect is that Neanderthals were extremely good at exploiting all the resources in a limited area. They were specialists rather than generalists like later peoples."

"Getting back to the real subject at hand, I have a question." Brown raised his hand, anxious to derail DeVries' momentum. "This child, this alleged Neanderthal . . ."

"Yes?" Manson asked.

"Assuming it really is a Neanderthal . . . a thing that Scott Ferris and his team raised from the dead. If it were from a species that God destroyed, and if, as is asserted, it were created through genetic manipulation, would it have a soul?"

Manson paused for a moment. "A soul?"

Brown nodded. "We believe that human beings have souls. I'm sure even the good professor here, despite his other failings"—Brown smiled kindly to lessen the impact—"believes he has a soul. Don't you, Professor?"

"Of course I do." DeVries nodded.

"Well," Brown continued, "if we hold that God imbued Adam with soul in that moment after having fashioned him from clay, can we assume that this alleged Neanderthal boy, if he exists, has a soul?"

Manson seemed off stride, "Well, I . . . er . . ."

"Neanderthals were human." DeVries grunted angrily. "Of course they had souls."

"Or," Brown countered, "was that why God destroyed them and gave ascendancy to humanity? Was it because the soulless couldn't inherit the earth?"

"I'm not sure we can answer that here on this program," Manson said warily. "I'm sure that if the Neanderthal exists, we'll be revisiting this topic more than once."

"But it does matter!" Brown said decisively. "It goes right to the heart of things! For one, I support Senator Dallas' legislation. We—humanity—have no business in the creation business."

"Elaborate on that." Manson gestured with one hand.

"If this being exists, and that's a big if, it was created in a laboratory, correct?"

At Manson's nod, Brown stated, "Not conceived, Skip. That's the key here. This being would not have been born of man and woman in a holy state of union, but put together, molecule by molecule, in a laboratory. In a creation like that there is no Divine spark, no essence of the soul imparted from God to his creations. It is a sterile thing, bereft of God."

"I thought you didn't believe there was a Neanderthal out there?" DeVries asked.

"I don't," Brown replied. "I doubt that Scott Ferris brought back a Neanderthal. I don't believe in Neanderthals. I think they are figments of people's imagination based on antediluvian remains left from when our Lord cleansed the earth. The Holy Bible tells us how God created the heavens and the earth. I don't know what Dr. Ferris thought he was doing, or what he concocted by stringing bits of DNA together in his laboratory. I don't even know if his murder is part of some bizarre conspiracy on the part of some misguided anthropologists to lend credence to an unprovable theory, but it serves as a warning to the rest of us. *We should not meddle in the making of soulless synthetic beings!*"

"And on that note, we will be right back." Manson leaned back as the red light on the camera flicked off. "Good work, gentlemen. Fascinating stuff."

The crew stood back from their cameras, listening to their headsets.

"You're wrong, you know." DeVries gave Brown a sober look.

"Am I?" Brown glanced at Eunice and basked in her supportive smile. She was nodding, a light of vindication in her eyes.

"The problem with science," DeVries said, "is that it won't go away. Even if you could stop the teaching of evolution, burn the books and ban genetic studies. If you could take us back a thousand years to complete theocracy, someone will find a new fossil or build a new microscope and the whole thing will start again."

"Are you a Christian, Doctor?" Manson asked as he shuffled his notes.

"No," DeVries answered, "but I do sincerely believe in God."

"Indeed?" Brown asked wryly.

"Just not as limited a God as yours appears to be," DeVries answered.

At the countdown, Manson leaned forward. When the camera light went live, he said, "For those of you who missed the last segment, we are dealing with the Neanderthal craze sweeping the nation. Reverend Brown assures me he doesn't believe the boy is real, and points out that indeed, no one has produced the actual child."

Manson turned to Brown. "But let's assume hypothetically for the moment that this child exists. If he does, what would it mean for the rest of us?"

Brown took the initiative. "Very well, for the sake of argument I would have to say from the perspective of a Christian that if Neanderthals existed, they were God's creation. Those of us who read and study the Word of God know that God once destroyed the earth by flood. If they were destroyed, it was God's will."

"And, taking that to its theological conclusion," DeVries said unexpectedly, "it would provide a rationale for someone to murder Scott, Amanda, and Avi . . . for daring to violate God's law!" The anthropologist sat up straight, animated. "That's it! I have been agonizing over why Scott, Amanda, and Avi would have been killed like this. For the first time, I think I know why."

Brown felt a cold surge run down his spine. In clipped tones, he stated, "That would *not* be a Christian thing to do."

"Indeed?" DeVries asked, sinking back in his chair, a bitter smile on his lips. "I'm so reassured."

When Brown glanced at Eunice, he could see a cold rage in her eyes. She had fixed her angry stare on DeVries, and it promised pure fury.

"Excuse me." Brown shifted, looking straight into the camera. "It was part of my agreement with the producers of this show that we would not mention the Elizabeth Carter murder. As many of you know, she was killed several miles from this very studio. The method of her murder was similar to that of the Ferris and Alexander murders. I have been working in cooperation with the FBI, providing them with any information to help them solve this case. Ms. Carter was a member of our church, a devoted woman whose loss grieves us all. However, I cannot comment on an ongoing police investigation, and for others to do so would be the utmost in irresponsibility."

"Did Elizabeth Carter have any ties to Scott Ferris?" Manson asked, taking his opportunity.

"None that I'm aware of. She worked to defuse the insidious propaganda of people like Scott Ferris before it corrupted innocent young minds." He paused for emphasis, "And perhaps there lies the true motive for her murder."

"How long was she—"

Brown held up his hand, stopping Manson's question.

"That's all I'm going to say, Skip. I just couldn't let the professor here make a mockery of, or misdirect, a serious criminal investigation."

"But you yourself brought it up. Why do you think Elizabeth Carter—"

"I will not say more on that subject." He looked into the camera again. "As to this alleged Neanderthal, well, until the child ever really appears it remains all academic, doesn't it?" He smiled at the camera. "My challenge to those who have climbed on the Neanderthal bandwagon is this: If you're so sure that your soulless caveman exists, produce him. Let the world see. And, until then, the most logical explanation for the Ferris deaths is that they are some sort of suicide pact."

"What?" DeVries leaned forward.

"Oh, I think it makes a great deal more sense than lost Neanderthals, don't you? After all, Scott Ferris, Avi Raad, and the rest of the team had run-ins with religion before. I think, at a minimum, it behooves us to at least consider the fact that this whole Neanderthal thing was Scott Ferris' last desperate hope for notoriety."

This time when he looked, Eunice graced him with a triumphant smile. Good, it would make for a much more pleasant evening when they got back to the privacy of their hotel room.

Bryce stopped Veronica from throwing the hotel's TV remote control against the wall. He caught her wrist and carefully removed the slim plastic box from her hand and laid it carefully on the stand beside the bed.

"Asshole!" Veronica hissed as she hugged Abel where he rested under her arm. "How dare he insist that Scott committed suicide, for God's sake!" She literally trembled. "Him! Brown! And he's right in the middle of this! Probably Scott's murderer!"

Abel glanced back and forth between them, his expression tense, ready to turn and run.

"Relax," Bryce told her easily. "Trust me. That was smoke screen. Look, crime scene investigators—especially on high-profile cases—know the difference between suicide and murder. And, if Billy Barnes Brown doesn't know that, he's dumber than I thought he was."

Veronica considered that. "I suppose."

"The more troubling thing, and potentially more damaging in the long term, is Brown's question about Abel's soul."

Veronica took a deep breath, obviously stilling her anger. Then she reached over and ruffled Abel's wispy hair with her other hand. "Oh, you've got a soul, Abel. I see it every time I look into your eyes."

"Souw," he said uncertainly, that wary expression on his wedge-shaped face.

"The very one God put there when your chromosomes came together," Bryce insisted. "And to hell with what anybody else in the world says."

But deep down, Brown's assertion worried him. Was that the rationale for an entirely new kind of pogrom? The way that humans would keep other humans in bondage in the future? Dear God, if the narrow of mind could be convinced that genetically altered people were soulless, what kind of atrocities could be justified? Who could impose the limits? Would the excesses of the past be a feeble model for those of the future?

As if in answer, Billy Barnes Brown's smooth smile lingered in his memory.

Ramsey paced, his mind fuzzy from too many hours of coffee, adrenaline, and worry. No way around it, they were understaffed. He would have liked to have the entire Denver Field Office for this case, but Dole had more on his plate than just Jack Ramsey's somewhat "shady" operation. While Ramsey might have had approval from his supervisor, he was still acting in opposition to the director's wishes, and if this all went sour, Harthow could fall on him, Pete Wirthing, and Bob Dole like a ton of proverbial shit.

The problem was, Ramsey couldn't let it go. Dole had a stake in it, too. It was his safe house that was blown up, his agent who had landed in Intensive Care with a chunk of wood sticking in her chest. Denver wanted a piece of Paxton and his accomplice just like the WMFO did.

Mitch had been champing at the bit, but Ramsey had reluctantly sent him back to Washington. Someone had to supervise the investigation of that church bunker in Virginia. Van der Beek had picked up the tension, plunging into his job, fiddling with the radios, testing his equipment with meters, and mumbling in some arcane language about signals and carrier waves.

Now it was a matter of waiting, of hoping, and playing all the cards right. If he snapped up Paxton and the blond man, he'd have his perps. Assuming that their equipment was portable, that it was in the white van described by Johnson and Tremain, he'd have his evidence. Especially if the Thompson Center Contender that ERT suspected had been used to shoot Rebecca Armely was there. They had identified the bullet as a .308, 168-grain Sierra Match King, which, from the penetration and lack of a report, was most likely a 300 Whisper, a sniper's specialty cartridge. Find that weapon in association with Paxton, and, for the first time, he had a case. With it, he could tie the lighter, the thiopental sodium molecules found in Hanson's body, and the ligature marks to Paxton. Even Amanda Alexander's answering machine made sense. Paxton had been rigorously trained to evade security systems. What better way to make sure Alexander couldn't retrieve a message from her machine than to take it? Like the other operations, no evidence of entry had been left.

He glanced at the clock. Forty-five minutes until the start of the operation. He took one last look at the flowchart on the wall, carefully running each aspect of the plan through his mind one last time. What had they failed to anticipate? What could go wrong?

He picked his coat off the back of a chair and slipped it over his shoulders. Then he paused, punched in his home phone number on his cell, and waited for the answering machine.

When the familiar message had run its course, he said, "Hi, Paula. I just wanted to call and tell you that you're the most wonderful thing that ever happened to me. I wish I was there just to see you, to look at you. I love you more than ever, sweetheart. I'll be calling soon. Bye."

He slipped the phone into his pocket and took a deep

breath. If this went rotten, if people ended up dead, Wirthing would cover his own bases first, which was all right. Ramsey understood the position he was in. That meant that ax would fall right on S.A. Jack Ramsey's neck. After that, well, Paula would have to be a saint, because it wouldn't be pretty.

He stepped out the door and walked down the hall, a nervous energy in his legs. It was a fifteen-minute walk to Theo Bennet's office. He didn't want to be late.

"Soul." The word rolls around in Abel's head as he lies in his hotel bed. The world has gone quiet with the night, only the distant sound of traffic and the vents intruding on his thoughts. What is a "soul"? How does he prove he has one when he isn't really sure what it means?

He hugs Chaser close to his chest, reassured by the buffalo's warm fur.

Veronica says that she sees it in his eyes, but when he looks in a mirror, all he sees is himself. No secrets lie behind his big blue eyes, only his fear and worry that everything will not be all right.

No, he does not know if he has a soul. If he had one, would Daa have called him a monster before he left? Would Aunt Eu have liked him? Would any of the horrible things that have happened, have happened?

He thinks about the man on TV, about the things he said about God. Looking up at the dark ceiling, he says, "God? If I have a soul, I will give it back if you will

*keep Bwyce and Vewonica and Chasuw safe. If you
will bwing Muvver back, I will die in her pwace."* He
swallows hard, trying to be brave. *"Pwease, God."*

In the silence that follows, he wonders if God hears.

CHAPTER THIRTY-SIX

THEY SPENT THE NIGHT OF THE TWENTY-SIXTH IN THE
"Phonograph Jones" room in the Irma Hotel. The room
was quaint, furnished in 1890s decor. The faucets on the
antique porcelain sink looked original. A skylight in the
middle of the room cast a homey glow on the patterned
blue wallpaper. Pictures of historical Cody, Wyoming,
lined the walls. Veronica might have stepped back in time
to when Buffalo Bill Cody still owned and operated the
hotel he'd built and named for his daughter.

"Phonograph Jones," it turned out, had been one of
Buffalo Bill's cronies—one of the eternal spongers who
had helped to exhaust the famous star of the Wild West
Show's fortune. After all, how could Cody charge one of
his best friends for room and board? Unfortunately, Bill
Cody had lots and lots of friends, all of them broke, all
living on his largess until he died in poverty.

Tension had begun to build in Veronica earlier in the day. Beartooth Pass had been all that it promised, a spectacular road across the roof of the world with vistas of several hundred miles. She thought it more beautiful than Trailridge Road in Colorado. They had stopped for coffee and ice cream in Cooke City, and Abel had started to come out of his funk.

Yellowstone had been packed, and while winding through the coagulated two-lane roads, plugged solid here and there with motorhomes, SUVs, and minivans, Abel had seen buffalo. He had stared, rapt and speechless. His complete fascination stirred Veronica's wonder. Did some genetic sense tie him to this animal that had roamed the Neandertal world? Or was it simply the living manifestation of Chaser that gave him such a thrill?

Those thoughts had subsided as they drove down the North Fork of the Shoshone River, coming ever closer to Cody, and the phone call she would have to make.

Through dinner in the historic dining room downstairs, she had hardly noticed the famous cherry-wood bar that Queen Victoria had sent to Bill Cody, or the million-dollar silver saddle in its window in the bar. Rather, she had stared at the pressed-tin roof and fought the butterflies pirouetting in her gut. When her eyes weren't casting uneasy glances at the restaurant clock, she was preoccupied with her wristwatch.

Bryce told her the buffalo prime rib was wonderful, but her stomach might have filled with sawdust for all she remembered.

"Bryce," she had said, "how can I sound normal knowing that this 'Leopard' Paxton and the blond man are listening to me?"

He had given her a smile. "It's okay, Ronnie. You did fine the first time you called. You'll do fine this time, too. Just think of it as being wild. What was it you said? Anything and everything?"

Now, locked safely away in the hotel room, she had to nerve herself. The telephone looked ominous where it sat on the small antique table. Malignant in its very nature.

"Time," Bryce said evenly. He sat on the corner of the bed and gave her an encouraging smile.

She nodded, stared sightlessly at the TV, the sound off. One of the talking heads on Headline News recounted the day's events, showing pictures of a disastrous flood somewhere in Asia. For the moment, the Neanderthal story seemed to be cooling off.

Rubbing her hands on her Levi's she steeled herself against the eerie knowledge that the people who had tortured and murdered her brother, and shot Rebecca Armely down in front of her, would listen as she spoke to Theo.

She lifted the handset, the plastic cool in her hot hand. One by one, she pressed the numbers, each tone like a gunshot in her ear.

The phone rang once, twice: *"Theodor Bennet here."*

"Theo? It's Veronica. I've just talked to Agent Ramsey." She took a deep breath. "Theo, listen. We're scared." Hell, she didn't need to act to sound convincing. "We can't spend the rest of our lives running. Agent Ramsey wanted us to come in, just drive up to the Federal Building in Denver. He said he'd have people there. All we need to do is drive up to the front door, get out of the car, and he'll take care of everything."

"I don't think that's a wise idea, Ronnie. I think you should—"

"No, Theo, the deal's already made. Bryce, the boy and I, we're tired . . . and we're running out of money."

"All right, Ronnie. I'll have everything ready." He cleared his throat. *"I have placed calls to Ms. Armely's sister. So far, all I've gotten is the answering machine."*

"Thanks, Theo. When we're in Denver, I'll call you. I imagine you'll want to be informed. Ramsey is talking about a witness protection program. I just don't know what to think anymore."

"All right, Ronnie. When are you meeting Ramsey?"

"As soon as we can get there. Ramsey will be waiting."

"Be careful. I'll hope to hear from you soon."

"Right, Theo. If this doesn't work out, thank you for everything. Please tell Mother I love her."

"You'll be able to tell her yourself. Agent Ramsey is a very capable man."

"Bye, Theo." She hung up the phone and exhaled the tension from deep inside. "How'd I do?"

"Great. Didn't she, Abel?"

From where he sat on his bed, he nodded with reservation.

So, that's how you hope a lie will keep you alive. Every muscle in her body had tightened to the point of vibrating. Bryce reached out and hugged her. "It will be all right. I promise."

Abel began to cry again. Veronica disentangled herself from Bryce and crossed to the boy.

"Scared?"

He nodded.

Veronica sat down and wrapped her arms around him. "It's all right, Abel. We'll get through this. The most important thing is to sucker these evil men into a place where Agent Ramsey can catch them. Then we can relax a little and figure out what to do with the rest of our lives, okay?"

He had his head buried against her chest. Bryce lowered himself beside her and patted Abel tenderly. "It's all right, little buddy. We're going to make sure that nothing happens to you or Chaser. My word on it."

"Scawed," Abel said miserably.

"It's all right to be scared," Veronica told him. "Being scared is part of life. We just have to deal with it, Abel, and do whatever we have to to make things better. Right now that means we have to help Agent Ramsey catch the bad men who have hurt us and put them away where they can't hurt anyone else."

His chin trembled. "I want Muvver."

Veronica smoothed his mussed blond hair. "I'd bring her back if I could, Abel. But death only works one way. The best thing you can do right now is help us to get the men who killed her. Can you do that? Keep your eyes open? Just like you did at the FBI house?"

"Chaser will help you," Bryce said. "Just like the buffalo you saw today, he's big and brave, and he loves you just like Veronica and I do."

Abel remained cuddled against Veronica's chest, his face averted.

"Hey, Abel," Bryce insisted, gripping him by the shoulder. "We've made it this far, haven't we? They've tried to get us three different times, and we've escaped. This time, we're going to trap them. It's our turn now."

Something about the positive tone in Bryce's voice

caused Abel to look up, to meet those reassuring hazel eyes.

Bryce smiled and winked. "We'll get the bad men this time. You just watch and see."

Veronica could feel the tension draining from Abel's body. After a moment, his eyes still locked on Bryce's, Abel said, "Okay."

Bryce reached out and ruffled Abel's hair. "Now I want you to crawl under those covers, and I'll read you another couple of chapters in your book. Then tomorrow we'll go set our trap for the bad guys."

Abel released Veronica and followed her into the bathroom; she made him wash his hands and brush his teeth. Then she got Abel undressed and into bed.

By the time she had taken her turn, Bryce was reading, his voice doing the high squeaky sounds for some characters and deeper ones for others. She used the remote to turn off the soundless television and slid her tired body under the covers.

The phone rang.

Abel bolted up in bed.

Veronica met Bryce's worried look. He reached for the black handle of his pistol where it was snugged under his belt.

She picked up the receiver. "Hello?"

"Dr. Tremain?" Ramsey's familiar voice asked.

She exhaled explosively, demanding, "Good God, you just scared me half to death! How did you find us?"

"American Express, Dr. Tremain. We've followed you from the Denver Marriott to Casper, Wyoming, where you bought gas and food at the Flying J; and then to Sheridan, Wyoming; to Billings, and the Northern Hotel.

You ate at a couple of restaurants and bought a shoulder holster at Scheel's sporting goods. Interesting—we didn't know that you had a pistol. Now you're staying at the Irma Hotel, in Cody. Credit cards can tell you quite a bit about a person."

"Jesus, we didn't think American Express would let us down."

He laughed. "It's all right. No one else can use it to trace you. I've taken precautions."

"Did you have a reason for calling us . . . other than to tell us we've been idiots?"

"You haven't been. You've done great. I just wanted to let you know that you did a tremendous job on the phone. Hopefully, Paxton and company were caught off balance. If they've snapped at the bait, we'll set the hook first thing tomorrow. Other than that, everything is proceeding according to plan. When will you be in?"

She guessed at the mileage. "Tomorrow night, I'd say."

"Fine. Follow the plan and everything will work out."

"Ah, bedtime stories." She smiled wryly.

"What's that?"

"Nothing. Private joke." She glanced meaningfully at Bryce. "Anything else?"

"No. Get a good night's sleep. God willing, we'll have this all wrapped up by this time tomorrow."

"Good hunting."

"Have a safe trip, Dr. Tremain." The line clicked.

Veronica replaced the receiver and flopped back, a hand over her eyes.

Bryce chuckled. "Just be happy he's on our side." He closed Abel's book, tucked the covers up around the boy's chin, and gave him a reassuring pat. "You sleep now. Everything's happening just the way it should."

"G'night, Bwyce," Abel said.

From under the shadow of her hand, she watched Bryce cross to the bathroom and close the door.

Of all the stupid things, of course they'd trace her card usage. This was the government, after all; they did that sort of thing all the time. She shook her head. In the panic after the safe house explosion, they had thought of someone calling around, asking for names, but an American Express *Platinum* card, for Pete's sake, should have some kind of special security. Maybe it did—from anyone but the FBI.

She was still kicking herself when Bryce opened the bathroom door and turned off the room lights. She heard the rustle of fabric as he undressed and slid into the bed beside her. A reassuring arm slipped around her, his cool skin against hers.

"You okay?" he asked.

"Feeling dumb."

"I do that a lot." He nuzzled her ear. The gentle nibbling, the warm breath, shot a tingle through her.

"I'm sure he's not asleep yet."

"Probably not," he agreed, his hand tracing patterns across her belly until it ended up massaging her left breast.

"Bryce."

He whispered, "I'm betting he'll be out like a light in five minutes."

"I'll be melted by then."

"Good."

Their relationship was at that stage where sexual satiation seemed impossible. Waiting for Abel to fall asleep seemed to take forever.

By the time Bryce shifted to cover her, every nerve in her body burned with tingling anticipation. She wrapped her arms around his shoulders and locked her legs around his hips, desperate for his entry.

Hanging in that eternal instant was like . . .

The impact shook the bed. Bryce went rigid in her arms. The mattress sunk as Abel crawled up beside them and plopped his weight on the sheet that covered them.

"Bad dweams," he said plaintively. "Can you tell me a stowy?"

Bryce slumped limply on top of her. "Yeah, bad dreams, all right."

The roar of traffic on Sixth Avenue penetrated the thin walls of the motel room off Federal Boulevard. Denver had cooked all day under a late June sun, the air hazy, sizzling with pollution and humidity. Now, with the clock nearing midnight, the oppressive day should have been over; but the heat pressed down.

Leopard Paxton paced back and forth between the two threadbare beds. At the rickety desk in the corner, Elias busied himself with the finishing touches on his masterpiece: a satchel bomb containing five pounds of C-4 explosive, a remote detonator, and a parallel-wired mercury switch. A black nylon tool kit lay open beside the backpack that held the blocks of explosive.

"I don't like this," Paxton muttered, stopping short to narrow his eyes. "When that goes off in a federal building, we're gonna have more shit falling on us than fell on Afghanistan."

"It's cool, Pax." Elias didn't even break a sweat as he worked with enough explosive to flatten the building. "It's the only way."

"You're sure this will work?"

"God told me." Elias looked up, his blue eyes curiously serene. "I leave this just inside the door. As soon as the spawn drives up, I tap the remote trigger. The explosion tags the kid and Johnson, and we blow these digs in the confusion."

"The escape route is ready?"

"Ready." Elias smiled again. "God wouldn't let me down here. It's His war we're fighting."

Yeah, you and your God. I don't know which one of you I trust the least. "I still don't like the bomb. It's too random. It puts us on the same level as Osama bin Laden."

Irritated, Elias looked up. "How else are we gonna make the hit? In the middle of downtown? We can't park anywhere close. The meters down there are for short-term only. Anyone feeding that many quarters would be instantly under suspicion. The last thing we need is traffic control knocking on the van while I'm setting up for a shot. Pax, they're not expecting a bomb."

"If we only knew what time they were coming in. We could cover it. This"—Paxton indicated the bomb—"makes me nervous. There's too much chance that something could go wrong. Someone could pick it up. A bum or . . . or a kid." He winced.

Elias shot him a sidelong glance. "We're fighting a holy war, Brother. If—and I say if—some innocent is killed, the Lord will see to him." He paused, frowning. "That's why a person can't take chances. Each day has to be lived as if it's your last. You never know when your soul is going to be delivered to our Lord. Keep yourself in a state of grace, your thoughts and actions pure. I do."

Paxton frowned. "So, you sit there, building a bomb, and you're pure? What if, say, a minister of your 'Lord' happens to be passing when that thing goes off? You're going to kill a good man . . . take his life and cause his family suffering. How pure will you feel then?"

Elias' expression didn't change as he used the screwdriver to connect a piece of eighteen-gauge wire to the battery. "Then it is my Lord's will that he die, Brother. If he's a good man, our Lord will reward him as is his due. If not, then he will pay the price for his sins. My concern is the state of my own soul . . . my own grace. When I kill, it's not motivated by hatred, or anger, but by the fulfillment of my duty to my Lord. It is a job which must be done, without the failings of pride, wrath, hatred, or arrogance."

"It's that easy for you?"

"I'm a Christian soldier. That's my calling. You weren't there, locked up in that place. God came to me, Pax, and gave me back my soul. God owns me, you understand?" He turned his lunatic eyes on Paxton. "And I would warn you, Brother: Emotion leads to sin. It is inevitable."

Paxton rapped his fingers on the television's plastic top. "You mean you don't hate the spawn?"

Elias said simply, "I cannot allow myself to hate. I only send them back to my Lord. It's a constant battle. I have to be pure at the moment when my soul is sent to stand before our Lord. Anything else is sinful."

Paxton imagined Elias as he must have been in the institution: in a white room, bound up in a straitjacket. "Yeah, except when you're waiting for something to happen. I see it in you then, Ron. You start to go stir crazy." Was that the result of his years locked away in little rooms? "What if they catch us? I'd like to know how you'd handle that. Just like the asylum, man. Years upon years of sitting in a box. Nothing but a toilet, a cot, and four walls. Day after day. And you sit there rotting away, talking to yourself. I've heard of guys scratching the concrete until the skin on their fingertips, their nails, even the meat is gone. Then they wear away the bone. That night, a guy comes in, suited, and hoses the blood off the walls. Then you start all over again, just scratching to see the blood, to have something other than endless white."

A flicker betrayed the hard blue in Elias' eyes, the screwdriver forgotten in his hand. "My Lord wouldn't do that to me. Not if I'm pure, not if I do his work. And if Satan tricks me, I *won't* let them." His eyes were unfocused. "I won't do that again, Pax. Even if you got to do me."

"Yeah," Paxton said, "just like Job. He was pure, too. Without sin. A good man." He shook a finger at Elias. "Problem is, Ron, you never know when God's gonna find out just what you're made of."

Elias stared in silence, swallowed, and seemed to shake his shoulders. He turned back to his bomb. After several minutes, he said, "You're sure that they're going to the field office? You're sure it will be the front door?"

"That's what Tremain said: the front door. That Ramsey would take care of the rest. So, we get the package close, say just inside the door. They'll be expecting a sniper, or maybe someone to pull a pistol and take a shot at the kid. They won't be expecting a bomb. Not on this short a notice."

"If what you're getting from the lawyer's phone is correct."

"The chatter on the radios is routine. Nothing about Tremain. It's as if they've stopped talking about it." Paxton cocked an eyebrow. "That's suspicious in its own right."

"What about this expert they're bringing in?" Elias looked up from his work.

"It could be that they're expecting Tremain and Johnson to drive up, walk the spawn in the front door, and figure out what to do with him after that. I'll bet that's when the works start. They've got to find a place to stash Tremain, Johnson, and the spawn until they can process the paperwork for the witness protection program. That's when they'll need secure communications. But if we do this right, it will all be too late."

"What if you're wrong?" Elias straightened, slipping a small screwdriver into an elastic strap in the tool kit. "If your computer and its program can't penetrate their communications?"

"It can and it will." Paxton indicated the satchel charge. "Just make sure that that thing works the way it's supposed to."

"There's a newspaper dispenser inside the building. It's the perfect place. The spawn steps through the door, and we count. One-thousand-one, one-thousand-two, and bang! Given the containment in that lobby, we've got 'em. No one inside of one hundred feet will survive the detonation."

Paxton nodded. For Elias it might be holy war, but for him, it was the last straw. Sure, the bomb would kill Johnson and the kid, but if Elias thought he knew about the wrath of God, this would bring the whole federal government—FBI, BATF, Treasury, maybe even CIA and NSA, not to mention the press—down on top of them. And by the time that happened, "the Leopard" was going to be sunning his spots on the foredeck of a yacht in the Caribbean. All he needed was confirmation of the spawn's death, and an electronic money transfer from the client to his Swiss account. After that, Elias could fend for himself.

And God help him!

CHAPTER THIRTY-SEVEN

THIS WAS THE PART OF AN INVESTIGATION THAT RAMSEY lived for. From here on out, the plan, a hypothetical equation on paper, would be tested against reality on the street. Generally he put these operations together with his squad in D.C., but this time, Joe Hanson was dead, and only Mitch had been there for the planning phase, his toothpick shifting from side to side in his mouth. Now Mitch was on his way to D.C., to handle his end there. The rest of the squad that would take Paxton down were Dole's people, technically on loan.

Of course, the Denver squad had a stake in this. Paxton had struck in their territory. Motivating the recruits wasn't a problem. But, what about zeal? Would the Denver agents find that moment of restraint if the situation degenerated?

"They're professionals," Dole had insisted laconically. "They're *my* professionals."

"Yeah, buddy," Ramsey had responded, "just make sure that they understand that a dead Paxton and John Doe Blond, leave us without any way to trace this back to the source. Paxton and his pal aren't doing this on their own. I want the mastermind. If it is Billy Boy, and his Crusade against evolution, I want that son of a bitch."

Now Ramsey would wait. He would pace the halls of the DFO as the long night passed. Van der Beek had rewired the communications equipment. As of eight in the morning, FBI communications would sound sappily boring to any listeners. The real communications would sound like static as Van der Beek's scrambler did its thing.

The practice wasn't new. As far back as the eighties, the Bureau had used scramblers to secure operation communications in sensitive situations. Anyone with an FM band scanner and a little sophistication could monitor field communications. The day of changing crystals had now given way to computer scramblers, and on this, Ramsey had bet the farm. While the rest of the operation was straight up-front police work—the usual steps to set up and collar an armed and dangerous perp—he had to bet on Paxton's skill. If the operation failed, it would be because of Paxton. Communications security was the key.

He walked to the end of the hall and turned, pacing back the way he had come. Again and again, he ran the plan through his head. What could he have forgotten? What detail would trip them up? What contingency hadn't they foreseen?

The key—and the tricky part—was to keep Paxton off balance. In juggling the unknowns of Paxton's competence and poise, Ramsey had an element of control unusual in investigations. Here, he had the ability to dangle the bait. Paxton wanted the boy. As long as Ramsey controlled him, he had a handle on Paxton. Lose the kid, and all bets were off.

So, what did you miss, Jack? What didn't you foresee? He walked back into the office and stared at the drawings on the butcher paper that covered the walls.

In one, the layout of the streets around the Federal Building were sketched. Each street-level business was labeled. Every vantage point that a sniper could use was marked and would be placed under observation at first light. Police barricades had been erected across the parking meters on the street; two Denver police officers were detailed to patrol that section of sidewalk.

Ballistics suspected, based on the rifling engraved on the recovered bullet, that the weapon that had taken out Rebecca Armely was a Thompson Center Contender. Given penetration, and trajectory, the shots had come from the parking lot. If Paxton still carried the pistol, it would complicate matters a little.

The Thompson Center Contender, a break-action, single-shot pistol, didn't function as a long-distance weapon. A good marksman could place shots reliably out to about 250 yards with a high-power cartridge. The .300 Whisper cartridge was designed to leave the barrel at less than the speed of sound, thereby avoiding the supersonic crack of a high-speed bullet. That meant a curving trajectory something like a rainbow at longer distances. But the Contender pistol's ingenious design allowed a shooter to switch barrels and cartridge chamberings. The sniper could switch to, say, a .223, or one of the JDJ wildcat cartridges, and obtain rifle ballistics out of the long-barreled Contender.

Then again a pistol might not be their only weapon. Paxton might have a rifle, something like the Robar system, which folded in half for easy carrying. That would extend their range out to eight hundred yards—an advantage muted by the downtown terrain. Tall buildings shortened line-of-sight, and that fact argued for the pistol.

As he stared at the diagram of the street, he tried to imagine Paxton's thoughts. The Tremain car would pull up at the curb, and Paxton would have between eight and fifteen seconds, depending on how fast the witnesses could move, to take the boy out. One shot at a small moving target. Where would Paxton set up? It made for an interesting intellectual exercise.

Ramsey looked up at the clock: 3:42 A.M. He should be back in his hotel room, getting some sleep instead of prowling the halls. But then he should do a lot of things that he didn't. He padded down to the room with the coffeepot and drew another cup. Then he walked back to the operations room and studied the diagram on the opposite wall. He had examined the photographs, read the reports, and taken a trip to study the terrain.

All he needed was a couple of breaks and he could wrap this whole thing up. Neat, clean. If it broke the other way . . .

Don't even think it.

But he had to. That was his job.

Blue letters proclaiming ANDERSON NEWS COMPANY, marked the side of the white van that pulled up in front of the Federal Building. Elias turned on the emergency blinkers and checked his watch, seeing 6:42 flash on the quartz display. He blew a pink bubble from the gum he chewed, and popped it. Across the street, wooden sawhorse barricades had been erected to block off the parking. Even at this early hour the streets were filling with commuters on their way to work.

Elias spotted the two Denver police officers walking a beat up and down the sidewalk opposite him. One had lifted a radio, calling in his truck, no doubt.

Elias reached back into the supply of newspapers, magazines, and books for a bound stack of today's edition. He tucked them under his arm and eased the backpack over his other shoulder. Taking a deep breath, he stepped out onto the sidewalk. The blue uniform shirt he wore proclaimed him to be "Kent." His freshly darkened hair and cheeks should exclude him from recognition based on any sketch made by the hospital guard or the Tremain woman.

Feeling the penetrating scrutiny of hidden eyes, Elias

sauntered into the lobby and stepped over to the newspaper dispenser. He used a key on the ring he'd taken from "Kent" that morning when he had ambushed the route driver at the stop sign outside of the ANC warehouse. He fiddled with the key, inserted it into the dispenser, and opened the steel case. Retrieving the two papers remaindered from yesterday, he shrugged the backpack off his shoulder. His fingers pushed the nylon bag snugly into the box. Unzipping the top, he attached a wire to the mercury switch. If the backpack were moved now, it would be lethal.

Elias pulled the old front paper from the clips that held it against the glass and inserted that morning's June 27 edition. He emptied the change box and pocketed the quarters. Then he coughed, hacking loudly, and spit the gum into his palm. Surreptitiously, he used a fingertip to jam it into the coin slot, plugging the hole. The spring-loaded lid clanked shut reassuringly. Shouldering the load of papers under his other arm, he calmly walked back into the morning, crossed the sidewalk, and chucked the bundled papers into the rear of the van, where Kent lay bound, gagged, and drugged.

Elias had the truck in gear and moving, signaling as he merged back into traffic. Casting wary glances, he could see no indication of a tail, of any reaction at all.

A grim smile crossed his lips. His Lord was watching over him. The display on his watch flashed 6:47. Now, all he needed was a blanket and a wheelchair.

Ramsey's phone rang. He plucked it from his pocket and flipped the cover open. "Ramsey here."

"Hi, boss. It's Mitch. I've got good news. We've been showing Paxton's picture around Rappahannock County. We've got two hits on Paxton and John Doe. One was at a motel where they spent the night. Paxton signed the register. He called himself Richard McClure. Paid in cash. Stayed there the same night that Joe did his swan dive."

"Good work. Take it to the judge. Get a warrant for that church. Clear it with Wirthing first. Try and keep a low profile about it. Five will get you ten that the moment you serve that warrant Harthow will issue a direct order pulling us off the case. In the meantime, Mitch, we've got to have enough evidence out of that place to save our skins, and Peter's, too. As the SAC, he'll take a hit if we screw up." He paused. "Are we that sure that Joe was held there?"

"You tell me, boss. You're the squad supervisor. Me, myself, I'm willing to bet my ass on it."

"Go for it."

"You got it. I'll be in touch."

Ramsey killed the call and flipped the cover shut. He took a deep breath. The fat was in the fire now. So, what if Paxton and John Doe didn't show for the bait? What if he'd misread the situation in Denver? What if they'd missed something, hadn't read Paxton's personality right? What if . . . what if . . . It could drive him crazy. This wasn't an ordinary investigation. If this didn't turn out right a lot of good men and women were going to get the ax. Letters of reprimand at the least, requested letters of resignation at the mid level, or outright dismissal at worst.

And for what? The unbelievable story that Scott Ferris

and his crew had brought back a Neanderthal? Was that worth destroying careers?

They're killing people, you fool. After all, that's why he joined the Bureau in the first place, and got into Domestic Terrorism in the second. Of all the dangers to a civilized society, hate crimes fit his bill for the most insidious. Like acid they ate at the social fabric. Thugs with a self-righteous sense of "truth" had a habit of growing out of control. He had studied the rise of Hitler, unthinkable before the social confusion, depression, and bitter legacy of the Armistice toppled the Weimar Republic. The last century had been filled with examples in Iraq, Cambodia, Serbia, and the Soviet Union.

America was supposed to be better, and to keep it that way, the bigoted thugs had to be hunted down before they could be turned into messiahs by social, economic, or political events. If they escaped the caldron, grew out of control, and swayed the masses with their propaganda, rights would be subverted, and foul corruption, once loosed and legitimized, would run rampant.

Ideology aside—he'd do it for Joe. And because, damn it, it just wasn't right for people, no matter what they'd done, to be tortured and burned in their houses. Not in his America.

He resumed his pacing, listening to his earpiece as the agents checked in. He moved to the window and looked down at the pavement below. The cars parked there seemed oblivious to the drama he hoped would be played out soon.

Come on, Leopard Paxton. I want to pull your spots off one by one.

Ted Paxton sat in the rear of the van with his back hunched, ears buried under the headset. He cocked his head, uneasy with the traffic on the FBI bands that morning. The agents he had come to know over the past couple of days sounded stilted, as if they were talking from scripts instead of in the easy banter he was used to.

Swiveling in his little chair he slowly ran the scanner through the bands, picking up a plumbing company, two construction outfits, the Denver police, then a surveyor talking to his rod man. Leaving the commercial bands, he listened in on the FAA and several military wavelengths.

He glanced at the computer, its power adapter clipped to the posts on a deep-cell battery. On a hunch, he turned it on, initiated the program, and set it to scanning function.

He retuned his receiver to the FBI band and listened to the sporadic chatter again. No jokes. None of the clever inflection that expressed an agent's feelings in the field. Instead, it sounded wooden. No mention of the spawn coming in.

He glanced uneasily at the computer, humming away as it analyzed frequencies, studying the static. The client had paid out twenty thousand for that program. It had cursed-sure better work, or if it didn't, and Paxton found out about it, he'd pay a visit to certain parties in their secret lab in Florida and read to them from the Good Book.

Black coffee steamed as he poured it from the Thermos. Solar radiation had started to warm the van's sides, and he could hear someone in the parking lot cursing in Spanish as he got into a car and slammed the door. The engine squealed as the starter ground before roaring to life. He could hear a clank as the transmission was put into gear; then the car backed away to drown in the morning sounds of traffic choking Federal Boulevard.

His headset crackled as Elias' voice overrode the system. *"Anything yet?"*

"No. But something's not right. They haven't said a word about the spawn."

"They're coming. Cops are everywhere. Every place I'd set up for a shot has someone in it, or watching it."

"You okay?"

"Yeah, man. Made sixty cents already. I got a sign says, 'Paralyzed Gulf War Vet. Please help.' Come midday I can retire."

"Cops been by?"

"Of course. All they see is a beggar in a wheelchair with a Walkman on his head, a blanket, and a sign. No weap—" A pause. *"Thanks, pal. God keep you."* Another pause. *"Make that ninety-five cents."*

"Where are you?"

"Far corner where I can look down the sidewalk."

"Keep in touch."

"Yeah." Silence.

Paxton sipped his coffee and checked the clock: 8:45. He shouldn't expect them in too early. The Bureau would want everything covered, people in place, no chance for a slipup.

He pressed the button on the machine that stored calls from the lawyer's phone lines. Using the fast forward, he skipped through two calls about the Hardesty case, neither of them containing Tremain's voice. The cellular scanner remained quiet, nothing coming from or going to Tremain's or Johnson's cell numbers.

God, he hated the idea of using a bomb. It was a red flag for trouble like nothing else. Elias had been right, though. They sure wouldn't be expecting it. After the detonation, Paxton was through. Finished.

From his vest pocket he withdrew his passport and the airline tickets. Flipping the Australian passport open, he looked at the picture of himself. He was staring soberly at the camera. Underneath was written the name: Richard Albert McClure. His tickets had him booked out of Albuquerque for Mexico City on an 8 A.M. flight tomorrow morning. Quantas would take him from there to Brisbane. After that he had a cross-continental hop to Perth, and the rest of his life relaxing in a winery just north of Augusta.

All he needed was Elias' confirmation that the kid was dead. By the time Elias figured out that he'd been ditched, Paxton would be southbound on I-25. He'd be in Albuquerque tomorrow morning if he had to drive all night.

The hard disk began whirring on the computer behind him, the little green light glowing evilly. Something had caught its attention. The speakers hissed softly, and then a familiar voice could be heard. One of Dole's Denver agents. *"Flashlight Three, I'm on the roof. Nothing here."*

"Roger that, Flashlight Three. Hold your position."

"Roger."

Paxton smiled thinly. He'd just been saved a nasty trip to Florida.

Veronica fought the queasy feeling in her stomach as she lifted the receiver from the cradle and began dropping coins into the slot. A hot Wyoming sun burned into her shoulders, the dry air tugging playfully at her T-shirt as a breeze blew in across the western steppe. The time had come for the next step in the desperate gamble.

She heard the ring—once, twice, three times—and then Theo's voice. *"Bennet."*

"Theo? It's Veronica. There's been a change of plans."

"Ronnie? What change of plans? What's happening?"

"We're not going to Denver." She took a deep breath. "Bryce and I have talked it over. If we just walk in, what guarantees do we have that we'll be taken care of? I mean, if they can't catch these people, what then? Do we live in fear for the rest of our lives?"

"Ronnie, what are you going to do? Where are you going to go? Listen, you've got to trust someone. If the government can't keep you safe, who can?"

"Us. I mean, Bryce and I can. We've done all right since we left the safe house. If we go in, we'll feel like sitting targets."

She could imagine Theo wincing at the fear in her voice. *"Ronnie, listen, as your attorney, I must advise you—"*

"Theo, I can't give up control of my life. Do you understand? I can't trust the government to keep me safe. Not until they catch these men. Then I'll come in. Then I can take up my life. . . . No, I mean I can build a new life. Bryce, the boy, and I. For the first time ever, I see a purpose. Does that make sense? I've got a chance now, and I want to take it."

"Ronnie, I . . . all right. I'll call Ramsey. Where are you going to be? Where can I reach you?"

"We'll be at the condo, Theo."

"My God! Where Rebecca was shot? How could you go back there?"

"I told you we were smart. They'd never think to look for us there. It'll be pretty tough on Abel, but we'll figure out a way of keeping his mind off of what happened."

"How's my car?"

"Fine. Not a scratch."

"Call me when you get in." She heard Theo clear his throat. *"Ramsey isn't going to be happy about this. Not at all!"*

"Tough," she said absently. "Life's like that, isn't it? Full of little surprises."

She carefully placed the handset on the cradle and slumped against the side of the aluminum weather casing. Every bone in her body felt pulled from place. She knotted her fists and looked across the gravel parking lot to the Cadillac. Bryce sat behind the wheel, watching her pensively. Abel was standing on the backseat, an ice cream cone dripping in his right fist.

She hadn't exactly lied to Theo. They hadn't scratched the Cadillac yet, but she wasn't sure what long-term effect ice cream and pizza stains would have on the upholstery. Of course, not everyone could say that a genuine living Neandertal had soiled their pristine white leather.

Lifting the phone again, she punched in her home phone. When the answering machine clicked on, she tapped in her code. She listened to six calls from friends and faculty concerned about her, wanting to know if the Neanderthal rumors were true. The seventh call shocked her. *"Ms. Tremain,"* the accented voice began, *"my name is Pietor Ostienko. I am colleague of your brother's. He told me if anything ever happened, I should contact you. Call me back. We should talk."* He gave a number, and the machine clicked off.

Swallowing hard, Veronica punched in the 303 area code number. After the fourth ring, the receptionist at a Boulder area motel answered. Veronica asked for Ostienko's room, and moments later the accented voice answered, *"Da!"*

"Dr. Ostienko? This is Veronica Tremain. Scott's sister."

"Da! Yes. I wait to hear from you. This thing with Scott and Amanda. It is terrible, yes? It is all over newspapers and television. A mess. Not the way we planned at all. I am so sorry."

"Why, Professor? Why did you do it?"

"We meet, yes? Talk? You have place that is safe?"

She told him, a curious mixture of excitement and anxiety let loose inside her. And at that, he hung up.

She felt loose-jointed as she walked back to the car, gravel crunching under her feet. The hot wind sucked her dry. It whipped her long black braid back and forth, tapping it against her butt.

"How'd it go?" Bryce asked.

She tried to order her thoughts. "Theo said that Ramsey would scream."

Bryce's lips went crooked. "I would if I were him. I got this buggy gassed up. Did you know that Owen Wister wrote *The Virginian* about this little town?"

She looked up and down the dusty main street. Medicine Bow, Wyoming, was dominated by a four-story, stone-block hotel with a gabled roof. Several bars, a gas station, and a convenience store composed the business district. Across the highway, sunlight shot gleaming lances down the railroad tracks. Huge windmills could be seen to the south, their giant blades turning slowly.

"I'm glad something happened here." She opened the passenger door and slid into the seat.

"Dynosaws hewe," Abel said. He pointed to the east. "Bwyce saw the sign in the stowe."

She looked at the map and shrugged. "All right, east it is. On the map, here, it says that we'll go right past the Como Bluffs dinosaur digs."

As Bryce started the car, Veronica bent over the back-seat and buckled Abel into his car seat. She took a moment, patting him on the shoulder. "It's okay. We'll come back someday to see the dinosaurs, all right?"

He nodded and gave her a frail smile.

She turned back and fastened her own seat belt. Bryce accelerated out onto the two-lane blacktop and turned east, into the empty distance.

"Ostienko called, Bryce. He's alive."

Bryce turned to gape at her, almost running off the road. "Ostienko? *The* Ostienko?"

"We're meeting him tonight. And finally, Bryce, we're going to find out why Scott and Amanda did this."

"Stinking God-damned bitch!" Paxton slammed a fist into the back of the driver's seat. The van had become an oven, and he hadn't started the air-conditioning. Sweat had begun to bead and trickle down his face. Now he glared at the electronic equipment that had just replayed Tremain's call to the lawyer.

Within ten seconds, the lawyer's phone was activated again. Paxton listened as Theodor Bennet outlined the Tremain woman's conversation.

Ramsey exploded. *"She's what?"*

Bennet went on to state that Veronica Tremain had changed her mind. That she would not come in until the FBI had wrapped up the case and could guarantee her safety.

Paxton could sympathize with the anger in Ramsey's voice. He knew that feeling. All the planning, all the investment in man-hours to set up an operation, and at the last minute, some flake blows the whole thing on a whim.

"Sorry, Special Agent Ramsey. But you've been screwed, buddy."

"You tell her she's playing with fire!" Ramsey thundered over the phone line.

"I'll relay your concerns to my client. Until then, Agent Ramsey, she is a frightened woman, alone in a hostile world, and I suggest that you remember that." Bennet hung up.

Paxton chewed his lip for a moment, and then the cipher program that had broken into the FBI's scrambled band filled with Ramsey's voice, under control now: *"All right, people, the operation's off. She's not coming in. Pack up and pull your stakes, guys. It's a bust."*

Paxton calculated the time needed to pick up Elias, to make the trip to Frisco, and to set up for Tremain's arrival. They could be ready for her in two and a half hours, minimum. If she got there early enough, he still had time to make that Albuquerque flight tomorrow. If not, he'd cancel and go a day later.

He keyed his mike. "Ron? We've got a problem."

"Yeah, so what's up, man?"

"She's not coming in. She just called the lawyer. She's headed back to the condo in Frisco. Says she doesn't trust the Fibbies . . . and that we'd never look for her back there."

"This is not good," Elias replied woodenly.

"Maybe, maybe not. As of this moment, only you, me, and the lawyer know where the spawn is headed. Abort the bomb. You can pick it up tomorrow morning, and no one will ever be the wiser. I'm on my way to the pickup."

He initiated the programs to shut down his equipment, then secured it. Within minutes, he had the van started and took the turn onto Federal that would lead him to Sixth Avenue and downtown. If they could get to the condo first, or even just behind the spawn, it would all be over within hours. When Elias went after the bomb, "the Leopard" would disappear, leaving his maniac partner, three corpses in Frisco, and shadows for the FBI to chase.

CHAPTER THIRTY-EIGHT

Abel *worries as he watches the familiar scenery passing. Through the side window he can see the tall mountains. The car hums along, heedless of the fear growing in Abel's breast. How is it that cars can't fear? Mother always talked to her car, but the day she was killed, they left it at the condo. Did it, too, have a soul? Did Mother's car ever feel sad to have been left like that? Did it cry for Mother the way he did?*

Abel pulls his Sam Weller's bag close and rests a hand on Chaser's furry head. They are going back, back to the place where the blond man lurks. That knowledge winds around in his stomach like a big worm and makes him feel like throwing up.

He doesn't want to go back, but when he says so, Veronica and Bryce smile and tell him that he'll be safe, that they'll keep him that way.

He has tried to tell them that he doesn't believe them, but he can't quite seem to say the right words that would convince them of the growing fear in his belly.

He remembers the big white skull with the huge spikey horns that stared at him from above the doorway at the condo. He should have known that any place guarded by a monster like that couldn't have been a good place. Nothing but death had come there. He hoped that Mother's soul was prowling the rooms, driving back the evil, maybe hanging around the fascinating bronze buffalo that sat on the shelf.

He tries to imagine the condo and recalls with perfect detail how the rooms are laid out. In his mind, he can see them clearly: the texture and colors of the carpeting, the stairs along the wall, the knots and grain of the wood. He can smell wood, carpet, and dust. The odors of a place little used by people. It's all clear in his mind, just like the memory of the kitchen, and how the stove, refrigerator, and table looked.

Until he dies, he will remember that place. He will remember: Mother died in that place. She left him. It isn't as if she'd willed it, but sometimes he can't help but think it was her fault. Now Bryce and Veronica are taking him back to the place where the blond man prowls. Will they end up dead, too?

Who will he stay with then?

He thinks of Agent Jones, but Bryce told him that she was in the hospital. He doesn't know where the hospital is, or how he could find it. Even if he did find Agent Jones, would she take him? And, if she did, where would they live? Her house has been blown up.

Maybe she would take him and run away in a car again.

Turning his head, he watches the mountains. The peaks seem to shine in the afternoon sun. They look cool, and that makes him remember the Wasatch Mountains on that last day in Salt Lake with Mother. When he looks at these mountains, his chest feels like something heavy lays on it. It hurts.

I don't want to go back. I don't. I don't. . . .

But the big smooth car just keeps motoring along, closer and closer to the blond man.

Abel absently curls his fingers in Chaser's fur and wishes they were back in Montana where, for a little while, he'd almost forgotten.

Peter Wirthing wasn't thinking about Jack Ramsey when the phone rang at his desk in the Washington Metro Field Office. His attention for the moment had fixed itself on the middle section of the quarterly report that dealt with narcotic pipelines into the city. The agent in charge of writing that section had a sixth sense when it came to breaking drug rings, she liaisoned well with the DEA and ran dynamite field operations, but her abilities as a writer would have scarcely challenged a dyslexic third-grader. How did it happen that someone so competent in one arena couldn't spell "cat" or string a subject and predicate together with any regularity?

Wirthing grimaced as the phone continued to bleat by his elbow and finally picked it up. "Wirthing here," he mumbled absently, and penciled a verb into a sentence.

"One moment please, for the director," the nasal secretary said on the other end. That was one of the perks of power. You had subordinates place your calls so that you didn't have to waste your precious time punching numbers or listening to ringing, busy signals, or answering machines.

Wirthing took a deep breath, calming himself. Before

Harthow's harsh voice said, *"Hello,"* he knew what was coming.

"Good day, Director." Wirthing winced.

"Just what the hell is going on down there?" Harthow's Tennessee drawl thickened with each word.

"Sir?"

"Don't 'sir' me, Wirthing. I thought I was clear the other day. I said hands off Billy Barnes Brown. I just got a phone call from my old friend informing me that my Bureau is harassing him. He says that your boys just raided one of his churches. Tell me it isn't true?"

Wirthing stiffened. "We didn't 'raid' it, sir. We served a search warrant for the premises."

A moment of silence was followed by an explosive venting of breath. *"You get your butt over here, Mr. Wirthing. I want you in my office, pronto. I've known Billy Barnes Brown for years. Years, you hear me? I know him for a decent and God-fearing man. I've seen him and his people working for the poor, alleviating suffering, and pitching in to help after tornadoes and floods. And now, just because you might not agree with his politics, you and your people are badgering him and his. Well, I won't stand for it."*

"Sir, we've had a break in the case. Special Agent Ramsey has—"

"Been placed on administrative leave! Now. As of this minute. You have him clean out his desk, because he's going to be looking for other employment. In fact, you better tell him to amend his 171 Form, because if he ever gets a job with this Bureau again, it's going to be emptying trash cans as a GS-3!"

"Sir, I don't think that dismissing Special Agent Ramsey is either prudent, or wise. We've just about—"

"*What is the matter with your hearing? Since none of your staff can take orders, maybe you can't either, Mr. Wirthing. Either you're the SAC in your office or I'll find someone who can do the job. I want this thing tied up and finished. As of this call. Now, you call Ramsey and have him shag his bottom over here so I can personally ream his butt. This operation against Billy Barnes Brown and his church is over. Terminated. Finished. Closed. As of this very instant, you got that?*"

"Yes, sir." Wirthing winced. "But Special Agent Ramsey isn't in the city. . . . he's in Denver, sir."

"*Denver? What the hell is he doing there? Who authorized his travel to Denver?*"

"I did. If you will recall your briefing, it was S.A. Hanson's witnesses who were being protected in the Denver safe house. They had turned themselves into the DFO and were—"

"*Then Dole's in on this, too?*"

"You will have to take it up with Bob, sir. He is pursuing an active investigation—"

"*You bet your ass I'll take it up with Dole. I might just clean house over this.*" An angry pause. "*You get your butt over here. I want everything you've got on Billy Barnes Brown. Each scrap and shred of paper. And I want it here now. You and I will go over it together, and if it doesn't add up to a real case you're going to follow Ramsey out the door so fast that it'll knock you spinning.*"

His secretary leaned in the door. She wore a grim expression and waved for his attention. Uncharacteristically, she blurted, "Excuse me, sir, but someone just bombed the Denver Federal Building. The DFO is head-quartered there. Since John Ramsey was there, I thought you should know."

"Jesus." Wirthing froze, the phone to his ear. He swallowed hard.

"Wirthing?" Harthow's voice grated. *"Did you hear a single word I said? Don't you ignore me."*

"Sir, I've just been informed—"

"What's that?" Harthow said to someone out of earshot. *"Just a minute, Wirthing."* A pause as someone talked in the director's office. *"What happened? Where? Denver?"* Then, *"Wirthing? Get over here.* Now!*"*

"It's a bomb." Bob Dole's harried voice carried through the headset. Ramsey was sitting in the front seat of his GSA ride, putting the last of his gear into a bag. "We've had an explosion in the lobby of the Federal Building downtown. There's no estimate on casualties or damage yet. Jack, I'm sorry, but—"

"Yeah, yeah, you need people. Take everyone. I'll fold the operation. We'll just have to start over anyway."

"Thanks, Jack." Dole sounded like he'd been wound past his stem. "Who on earth would have thought someone would bomb the Federal Building? We didn't get any warning—not a clue through local channels that something was about to happen. It's as if—"

"Jesus!" Ramsey's gut twisted. "God, Bob, you don't think it was them? What better way to take out Ferris,

Johnson, and the kid? According to the plan, they were supposed to walk right in the front door."

"And if they had, it wouldn't have taken a sharp-shooter, or a guy with a gun stepping out of a phone booth."

Ramsey chewed on his lip, thoughts running parallel in their minds. "They've bumped the game up, Bob. The stakes just got a little higher."

"That, or they're ahead of us. No, wait, we don't have the facts yet." Dole was thinking hard. "We can't assume, Jack. Not until we've got a fix on this blast. Look, I've got people stacking up around here. I'm going to be pretty busy for the next couple of days. Take my five best. Just in case we're not wrong about this."

"Thanks, Bob." Ramsey closed his eyes, a sudden welling of futility rising inside him. "You're the best. Go deal with your problem; I'll deal with mine."

Dole didn't even say good-bye. He just canceled the connection.

A bomb! So, had it been Paxton and his blond crony, or was this just a fortuitous strike by some demented Bubba who picked this instant to screw up Jackson Ramsey's life? And, if it was Paxton, did it mean that Van der Beek's machine hadn't worked, and worse, that the killers were way ahead of him?

"So?" Dan Dern asked. He stood to one side, dressed in a black tactical suit that covered his Kevlar; a Mossberg shotgun hung in its sling from his shoulder. His head was covered with a riot helmet, the clear Plexiglas visor raised.

"So, I'm keeping five of you. The rest are detailed to the Denver Federal Building. Right now. Move like you've got a purpose. Someone bombed the place, and Dole's going to need all the bodies he's got for evidence recovery, crowd control, communications, and coordination."

"Then . . . the operation's folded?" Dern's expression turned bitter.

"Sort of. That's why I'm keeping five of you—and we stick to the plan. Just in case our bombers are Paxton and the blond unsub. If it's them, we'll know by tonight."

"It's a violation of Bureau policy," Dern replied. "You know the drill, Jack. Overwhelming force with no chance for the operation going to shit. All bases covered. That doesn't mean continuing an operation understaffed. And, with only five us, we're understaffed."

"Yeah, I know," Ramsey said as he shoved the last of his gear into a black nylon bag. He could see Dern's desperate desire to be present at the Federal Building. Hell, it was the Denver squad's home that had just been violated. "But what if that's just what Paxton and his blond chum are counting on?"

Paxton ground his teeth, hands clenching the wheel as he parked the van in a pull-off a quarter mile below the Eagle Condo sign on Colorado Highway 9. Summer traffic whooshed past, vacationers enjoying the late June weather as they drove to or from Breckenridge, Alma, or Fairplay. To the west, fluffy masses of cumulus clouds obscured the peaks, threatening an afternoon shower.

As he shut off the engine, he glared hard at Elias. The

lunatic seemed completely oblivious. Even now, despite the reaming Paxton had given him, he didn't understand the consequences of what he'd done. The bomb changed everything. Now, no matter what, Paxton's time was running out. If they hadn't killed the kid by eight o'clock that night, "the Leopard" was running. Tomorrow morning, in the midst of heightened security, Richard McClure was flying to Mexico. Elias would be on his own.

Elias swung the door open and stepped down before slinging a full pack over his shoulder. His close-cropped hair was still dyed black from the morning's operation. He looked trim, fit, every inch a soldier. A set of coveralls with the name "Kent" stenciled on the breast was partially unbuttoned to expose his black T-shirt—and allow quick access to the Sig Sauer 220 resting in the shoulder holster.

Paxton wore a canvas bush jacket that concealed his own pistol, a Walther 99 in .40 S&W. He carried a battered toolbox in his right hand and clapped a white plastic construction hard hat onto his head. Turning, he locked the door, gave Elias a curt nod, and started down the slope through the trees.

They walked single file, each wary, eyes on the forest around them. Duff crackled underfoot for want of rain. The smell of conifers filled Paxton's nose. The single burning question was whether they'd beaten the spawn to the condo. Where had the Tremain woman been when she called the lawyer? How far away? The answer would be worth a million dollars to him. Money enough to make the rest of his life in exile a little more pleasing.

Knowing the layout, they would approach openly, climb the steps, and knock on the door. If anyone answered, they were contractors looking for Mrs. Ferris. The people next door had reported an infestation of carpenter ants. Had Mrs. Ferris seen any in her section of the building? They would push their way in, overcome any resistance, and finish the job.

If no one answered, he'd slip his lock picks out of the pocket in his bush jacket and be inside within fifteen seconds. Then when the spawn arrived, no one would be the wiser. Either way it ended here.

He could see the wood-sided wall of one of the condos through a gap in the trees; the sound of a motorboat moaned its muted call from the lake below. Overhead, a squirrel chattered at him, leaping from branch to branch. Someone had left an old Coors can on the ground. Impulsively, Paxton picked it up and crushed it in one hand before placing it in one of his pockets. People could be such pigs.

"How do you want to do this?" Paxton glanced at Elias.

The younger man frowned, studying the layout of the condos. "Split up," he declared. "You go in." He pointed to a tarped trailer sitting by itself at the side of the parking lot. "I'll set up there. If anything goes wrong, if one of them gets out, I can tag him before he gets back in the car. If they've beaten us here, I'll follow along as soon as the door's open." He shot Paxton a cold-eyed look. "I'm tired of loose ends."

Then maybe you shouldn't have blown up that building, Brother. Talk about a loose end.

Paxton waited while Elias circled and walked nonchalantly to the trailer. With a stroke of his knife, Elias severed the white cord holding the tarp down, glanced inside, and then wiggled into the back of the trailer like a fish.

Paxton took a deep breath and stepped out from the screen of fir and lodgepole pine. As he walked down past the second building, he studied the vehicles. Rebecca Armely's Honda sat beside a BMW Z3. Both were grimy, covered with a layer of rain-spattered dust and the yellow tinge of pine pollen. The Oldsmobile that belonged to the unit on the far left sat in its stall. None of the other spaces were filled.

He smiled grimly. It looked like they'd come in time. He read the name on the unit next to the Ferris'. It read SCHOTT. That was the name he'd use if anyone was home in the Ferris unit.

His heart began to pump with the familiar adrenaline high as his boots thumped on the wooden steps. He had watched Rebecca Armely climb these very steps in that last instant before Elias had severed her spine with a bullet and sent her tumbling face first into the doorway. He glanced up at the elk skull over the door, gazing at the big rack, sun-bleached and flaking.

Someone had ripped the yellow crime scene tape off the front door, leaving a ripple of plastic stuck in the jamb.

Paxton cocked an eyebrow. If their luck held, no one had been here since the ERT had combed the place. He raised a hand and knocked loudly. For fifteen long seconds he waited, each counted by the anxious beat of his heart. He rapped again, louder this time.

No answer.

The lock was a Yale, a standard, if ornate, pattern. Paxton slipped his picks out, knowing from long practice which profile fit this design. The tumblers turned easily under his manipulation; then he pulled on a glove and grasped the knob to open the door.

"Hello?" he called as he stepped inside. "Anyone home?" The Walther rested easily in his hand, the square muzzle following the path of his eyes.

He moved off to the right, circling the room. In his slight crouch, he looked like a hunting cat, an ultimate predator.

"We've got 'em," Paxton said, the calmness of a sure thing rising in his gut. First the spawn and whoever accompanied him, and then Elias. After that, he could disappear. No loose ends.

Something, the faintest of sounds, tipped him off. He raised the pistol, safety off, as a faint movement caught his eye.

CHAPTER THIRTY-NINE

"Stop! FBI! You are under arrest! Lower your weapon!" Mike Hammond's voice roared in the stillness of the condominium.

Jackson Ramsey stepped out of the closet just in time to see Ted Paxton freeze, his pistol half raised.

"Lower your weapon," Dan Dern ordered, only the corner of his helmet and the ugly barrel of the twelve-gauge Mossberg exposed beyond the doorjamb.

Ramsey saw it: the sudden look of futility in Paxton's eyes. The thought barely had time to form in Ramsey's mind: *Dear God, no. He's going to*—Paxton's pistol blasted in the confines of the condominium. The sound was deafening. Two agents, helmeted, wearing FBI jackets over Kevlar, returned fire from behind the protection of the breakfast bar.

Ted Paxton's body jerked under the impact of .40-caliber bullets. Then Dern's shotgun loosed its thunder. Ramsey would remember Paxton's expression, the mouth opening as the man's eyes widened with surprise and the incomprehensibility of death. The Walther discharged again, the action reflexive, the shot going into the floor as Paxton stepped back on wobbly legs. Then his left knee gave way, and he pitched backward in a half roll. The Walther clattered across the floor, and the white hard hat rolled in a half circle.

"Heads up!" Dern called. "Keep an eye on him. Mike! Check the door. Find his partner."

Ramsey watched as the team followed procedure, closing on Paxton's bleeding body, taking no chances. Mike Hammond cut sideways for the door, his Heckler & Koch MP5 at the ready. There, he ducked low, glanced quickly out, and shouted, "Clear!"

Paxton, eyes bugged, gave off a gurgling sound and coughed bright red blood from his mouth. The holes in his chest made rude sucking sounds.

"Alpha One to Zoo." Dern used his collar mike. "We have a suspect down. Request an ambulance."

"Roger, Alpha One," the FM unit responded.

"Alpha Two, move in and secure the compound. At least one unsub is still at large."

"Roger Alpha One."

Ramsey watched wearily as Paxton's body convulsed and relaxed. The man's pupils began to dilate with the emptiness of death. Blood continued to spread from his riddled body.

"He's going," Ramsey said softly. "Damn."

"He's gone," Dern said, and looked up helplessly.

"We needed him alive," Ramsey reminded pointlessly.

"He didn't give us a choice, sir." Dern straightened.

Ramsey's earpiece reported, "Summit County Sheriff's Office reports they have a white van under surveillance. We have an ambulance on the way. Alpha Two is in the process of clearing the area. No sightings of unsub two."

Ramsey bit his lip, looking down at Paxton's dead body. As it turned out, "the Leopard" had kept his spots in the end—and the blond man was still out there. But where?

Veronica hesitated as she scanned the ornate lobby in the Brown Palace Hotel. Behind her, Bryce and Abel waited warily. Abel clutched Chaser in one arm, his other hand interlaced with Bryce's. In that moment she spotted him: a white-haired man with a fleshy and slightly florid face. He was seated beside one of the glass-topped tables amidst a cluster of chairs and a small couch. His recessed blue eyes met hers, and he nodded, reaching for a shining black cane as he struggled to rise from the overstuffed Victorian chair.

Veronica led the way, offering her hand. "Dr. Ostienko?"

"*Da!* Yes. And you must be Scott's sister, Veronica." The syllables rolled off his tongue in a musical Russian staccato.

"Doctor, may I present Dr. Bryce Johnson, and this is Abel Armely. Scott and Amanda's son."

Ostienko looked down at the little boy, a huge smile spreading across his face. Despite his cane and bad leg, he squatted down in a crackling of joints, excitement in his aged blue eyes. "Yes. Abel. I am Pietor." He seemed somewhat at a loss for words as Abel tried to wedge himself behind Veronica's legs, mistrust welling in his eyes.

"Say hello, Abel," Veronica insisted. "It's just good manners."

"Hewo," came the softly whispered response. Ostienko's gaze had taken on the wonder of a pilgrim at the end of a holy quest.

"You are miracle brought to life, Abel." Ostienko made the sign of the Orthodox cross and added, "God bless you. You are more than we hoped you would be."

Abel tried to pull Bryce's arm out of joint as he retreated around Veronica. She extended a hand to help Ostienko to his feet. The old man grimaced at the grinding in his knee.

"The students, when I am dead, they will love to look

at my knees. The pathology must be marvelous. Exostosis and eburnation is all over joints."

"They can replace those, you know," Bryce said.

"Bah! I have no time for that. I can die fullfilled, yes?" Ostienko continued to beam down at Abel. "Look . . . look at him. Scott sent pictures, but to see the miracle fulfilled? That, my friends, is reason enough for the price we pay."

"Professor, what's this all about?" Veronica asked, and indicated Abel. "Why on earth did you, Scott, Avi, and Amanda do this?"

Ostienko seemed not to hear for the moment, then barely glanced at her. "Scott did not tell?"

"No. They killed him before he could." Bryce straightened, physically dragging Abel out from behind Veronica. "I was part of the research, Dr. Ostienko, and I didn't even know. Oh, sure, I was fascinated by the data and wondered where the hell Scott and Amanda were getting it, but I had no idea."

"No, you did not." Ostienko continued to watch Abel and smile, half of his mind on the boy. "It was best, yes? The fewer who knew the more time we have." He smiled down at Abel like a doting grandfather. "Is difficult, this thing."

"Why?" Veronica insisted. "Surely you knew that bringing back a Neandertal was going to cause a great deal of trouble."

Ostienko nodded, a sadness replacing his joy as he looked Veronica in the eyes. "I have sorrow over Avi, Scott, and Amanda. I have sorrow for you, Veronica. But, for this boy, I have only joy."

"Tell that to his mother." Veronica crossed her arms angrily.

Ostienko read her posture and smiled warily. With his cane, he gestured. "Please. Sit. We talk."

Ostienko lowered himself into the chair. Veronica took the chair beside his while Bryce and Abel settled themselves on the couch. He studied them, one by one, the gravity of his expression belying the sparkle in his eyes. "I was born in a ruined country." He fingered the polished silver top of his cane. "It was ruined by political ignorance and greed, yes? Stalin was greatest monster of twentieth century, and I grow up in his intellectual shadow." He thumped his bad knee. "Soviet science was political science, yes?"

"Trofim Lysenko," Bryce whispered. "Science had to reflect political reality."

"*Da!* You understand, Dr. Johnson. Lysenko was monster, just like Stalin. Set true Soviet biological science back one hundred years. Even now, is hard in Russia to teach scientific method instead of old truth."

"I don't see what Abel has to do with Lysenko." Veronica leaned forward as if to insist on an answer.

"Everything." Ostienko leaned forward himself, his grin widening. "You think Lysenko is only Russian problem?" He waved his finger back and forth. "*Nyet!* Lysenko is dead, yes! But his shadow lives on as metaphor. Is fight of all humanity. Problem comes when ignorance is given political power. Here, in this country, I see president inviting this Reverend Brown to White House. Is not good. Politics and religion and science *must* be separate. Put them together, and after time you get a Lysenko."

"That still doesn't explain Abel," Bryce reminded. "How does he fit in?"

"What is biggest opposition to science in world?" Ostienko asked calmly. "Does anyone stand up to say, 'Chemistry is only theory!' Does anyone stand up to say, 'Physics is only theory!' No, is only evolution that is attacked. And why? Is because it is 'science of man.' Is all right for atoms, rocks, and stars to be studied, but not people. Why? Because people would rather believe old stories handed down from Dark Ages than know facts of human origins. Is much better"—he reached up, as if grasping a truth from the air—"to believe we are created from touch of God as 'Chosen People.' Makes committing crimes against other humans okay. We are 'chosen'; they are not. So, who cares if we kill Chechens by thousands? Is okay to kill Serbs. Is okay to kill Red Indians. Is okay to kill Catholics or Jews. They are not blessed like us."

"We can agree on that," Bryce said with a nod.

"So, if we can 'prove' evolution, prove study of man . . . ?" Ostienko raised his bushy white eyebrows.

". . . Then you remove the most insidious argument against science," Veronica finished.

"Has great implications for humanity," Ostienko replied sagaciously. "Is lesson for all of us. Humans are same . . . related. All from same ancestor." The finger shook again. "We are not created special by different gods. Jews are not God's chosen. Christians are not God's chosen. Muslims are not God's chosen. White, black, yellow . . . all people same. We are one. Brothers and sisters." Ostienko smiled then. "This boy, this miraculous little boy, he is future for mankind, yes? He is proof that we are all from same family. That is why some people fear him. Avi, Scott, and Amanda have changed future of humanity. Is reason enough to kill, yes?"

Veronica shook her head. "But you had to know the risks."

"*Da!* We had plan. Slow and gradual. Release information slowly. Allow people to get used to idea, yes? Do so in academic journals first. Then release data on Neandertals in press. Put on program like *Nova*. Is truth about people that they can get used to anything. Slowly develop curiosity and educate, then show them Neandertal, yes? Is not shock to them. Do not have wild speeches on television like I see in motel room." He shook his head. "Was good plan. But someone found out." His expression fell. "I call Scott and Amanda. To warn them, yes? Scott, he is American and does not believe it. You do not have tradition of extreme measures like we do."

Veronica looked at Bryce, reading his thoughtful eyes. "What do you think?"

Bryce nodded slowly, his mind working over the things Ostienko had said. "It matches my own thoughts over the last couple of days. Look at the furor over Ben's news conference. It isn't just that Abel's a Neanderthal, Ronnie. It's the implications. It's one thing to *think* evolution is true. It's another to *know* beyond any doubt. Abel's presence on earth means that we all, even you and I, have to deal with a different mental template. Scott, Avi, and Amanda have changed our perception of ourselves forever. That's going to take time to sink in."

Veronica turned to Ostienko. "What makes you so sure

that it's a good thing? You referred to Stalin. What about Hitler? What makes you think that Abel isn't being set up as a target for extermination just like Hitler did with Jews, Slavs, and Gypsies? Isn't that just as much a part of who we are as a species? As it is, a great many people are going to look at him like some sort of freak."

Ostienko nodded in slow agreement. "Veronica, no one, not one of us, thought this would be easy or perfect. Human capacity for evil and intolerance is only rivaled by capacity for good. Since we cannot break news gently, task will be more difficult."

"Where on earth did you find the DNA?" Bryce asked. "Which specimen did you use?"

"Specimen, called Tadjik I, is in freezer in CSU laboratory. Is part of Neandertal head." Ostienko smiled at Abel. "Is your true father. Is young man, perhaps twenty given his teeth. Fell into crack in glacier. Date from tooth enamel is sixty thousand years. Was protected from radiation and deleterious effects of freeze thaw. Three weeks later, we find part of arm. Is female Neandertal. So have two sets of genes."

Abel squirmed around on the couch and whispered, "I'm hungwy."

Veronica was staring into space, her mind racing. "My God, the questions that that data can answer. It provides us a complete genetic marker that we can compare to the human genome."

"Point five percent difference," Bryce said laconically. "That's the work I was doing. Neanderthals and moderns, according to the data sets Scott sent me, were a half a percent different."

"But why make a child? He's being set up as a freak!

How did you expect him to live his life out as the only one? Didn't you take into consideration the loneliness? The cruelty?"

Ostienko gave her a curious look. "You do not have Scott's notes? You have not read research?"

She shook her head. "No. Everything in his house was burned."

"Fascists," Ostienko whispered. "I thought Scott would hide research somewhere where you could find."

Veronica straightened, her fists knotting. "We're not sure that he had time before they killed him."

Bryce arched an eyebrow.

Ostienko was grinning again, his attention focused on Abel. "You are part of future of all humanity, my hungry little friend. What makes these people think you are alone?"

"Oh, he's not," Veronica said wearily. "Somehow or another, he wheedled his way into my heart. I'll always be there for him."

"I mean why you think he is only one of his kind? You think we are monsters? That we make only one?" Ostienko had a gleam of satisfaction in his deep-set eyes.

"There are more?" Bryce asked, stunned.

"*Da!* As of last count, nineteen! Ten boys. Ten girls. You did not know? World soon be full of Neandertals!"

It took until the night of the twenty-ninth before John Ramsey finished the last of his reports, checked in his equipment, was debriefed by Dole, and made his way to the Brown Palace Hotel. He gazed at the stained-glass skylight above; his steps were muffled by the thick carpeting as he crossed the lobby. Rows of ornate brass railings rose one after another to the opulent ceiling. In the corner a pianist stroked a delicately classical piece that might have been Beethoven—but Ramsey had no ear for such things.

The woman at the front desk had told him that his party was in the dining room. Grand hotels worked that way. They always knew where the guests were. He shook his head. Life wasn't the same when you rented rooms in places like the Econo Lodge.

At the dining room entrance a man in a tuxedo stood behind a podium upon which was spread a large leather-bound reservation folio. He glanced Ramsey up and down, as if measuring him. "Welcome to the Palace Arms, sir. How may I help you?"

Ramsey cocked an eyebrow. "The desk sent me over. I'm looking for the Findley party. I guess they're eating in here."

The guy in the tux carefully checked his register. Imagine that: a register for a restaurant. Ramsey couldn't help but smile. He could imagine Paula's expression, that hidden trace of delight creasing the corner of her mouth.

"They have a reservation for three, sir." The tux looked up. "Might I tell them who wishes to see them?"

Ramsey gave the man his best evil grin. "Tell them Special Agent Jack Ramsey of the Federal Bureau of Investigation would like a word with them." He widened his grin. "Would you like to see identification?"

To Ramsey's surprise the tux never batted an eye. "If

you would be so kind as to wait for a moment, I'll go and check with the party."

"Sure." Ramsey bit off a strained chuckle. Damn, there was professional, and then there was *professional*.

Within a minute Tux had returned, a graceful smile on his face. "This way, please, Mr. Ramsey."

Ramsey followed Tux into a dark cavern of restaurant. The decor was based on European nobility, with suits of armor, flags, and big shields with colorful coats of arms. The stained wooden walls looked appropriately old and venerable. The tables and booths were packed with expensive silverware. More staff than customers hustled about, each in an immaculate black coat, ruffled white shirt, and black tie.

Even as Tux led him to the booth, two waiters were rapidly and efficiently setting another place. By the time that Tux pulled out the chair and held it for Ramsey, the job was done.

"Have a nice meal, Mr. Ramsey," Tux said. "If I can be of any other service, please let me know. My name is James."

"Yeah, thanks, James." He turned, aware of the expression on Veronica's face as she watched him across the yellow candle flame. Bryce Johnson sat beside her—close beside her, one of his hands intertwined with hers. The kid was to Veronica's right, snugged in the curve of her arm.

Ramsey squinted at the boy, seeing the low forehead, the way the bridge of the nose jutted out like a beak. He'd thought it a northern European face at first, something Germanic, or Nordic. Those big blue eyes had fastened on his, as if seeing into his very soul. This was a Neanderthal? That notion seemed to stick in his thoughts, overwhelming everything else. Sure, the kid had a big, bulbous nose, *but a Neanderthal?*

"Agent Ramsey?" Johnson said dryly. "Did you want to see us about something?"

Ramsey blinked against the weary fatigue that had settled over him, took a deep breath, and cleared his throat. He shot them an apologetic look and shrugged. "Yeah, sorry. I just . . . Well, it's been a long, tough couple of days, and to tell the truth, I've never sat around with a Neanderthal before." He could feel them stiffening, so he forced himself to relax and stuck out his hand, saying, "Hello, Abel. I'm Special Agent Jack Ramsey . . . of the FBI. I didn't really get to meet you last time. You've been very important to me during the last couple of days."

"Hewwo Mistuh Wamsey," Abel said in an awkwardly nasal voice, offering his hand, uncertainty still lingering in his encompassing blue gaze.

Ramsey shook, surprised at the strength behind those small fingers. Taking the boy's measure, he added, "Do you play soccer? My boy, Matt, does. He's good at it, and I'd bet you'd be, too."

"Soccew," Abel said. "Pway kick." He reflexively swung his leg in a kicking motion that rumpled the white linen tablecloth.

"That's the game." Ramsey nodded, then glanced at Tremain and Johnson. "I take it you didn't have any trouble getting here?"

Tremain arched a slim eyebrow. Tonight her hair was down, brushed to a sheen and gleaming in the candlelight.

"No, although the news about the bomb scared us. Was that . . . I mean . . ."

"For us?" Johnson asked, leaning forward, tension in his hazel eyes. He had hardened in the past few days.

"It's not conclusive yet, but yeah, we're pretty sure." Ramsey studied them, aware of the sexual tension between them. He hadn't pegged them for lovers the first time they'd met. "Mr. and Mrs. Findley?"

"Theo's idea," Tremain told him. "He thought another name would be prudent when he booked the room."

"Yeah, and a sight further from Dermain, or whatever you called yourselves before."

"You saw through that?"

"Give me some credit, Dr. Tremain."

A waiter arrived, standing politely to the side until Ramsey finished before he asked, "Would you care for something to drink, sir?" He handed Ramsey the menu, then explained the special for the evening: a buffalo hump roast, cooked "Wellington style." Whatever that was.

"Uh, that'll be fine," Ramsey said. "Medium rare." Then he made a choice on the vegetables. "And whatever Dr. Johnson here is drinking." He squinted, seeing something red that looked like beer in Johnson's glass.

"Thank you, sir." The waiter gracefully vanished.

Ramsey stifled a yawn. "God, I'm tired. It's been forty-eight hours since I've had any kind of real sleep. I choked down a hamburger at about noon today." He grinned wearily. "In short, I'm beat."

"What about Paxton and the blond man?" Tremain asked warily. "Any sign of them?"

"Yeah." Ramsey sat back, lips thinned. "I've got good

news and bad news. But, first you should know, I'm off the case."

"What?" Johnson leaned forward, eyes narrowing. Abel was watching Ramsey like some hunted animal, aware that he might have to run or duck on a moment's notice.

Ramsey rubbed his face; it felt like a latex mask. "Yeah, well, the director himself, Judge Harthow, has placed me on suspension. It seems he didn't like the way I was doing the job. He thought I exceeded my authority." He held up a hand, stifling the outburst before it came. "Which I did. So, the thing is, my good friend, Special Agent in Charge Bob Dole, is handling affairs now. That includes the bombing of the Denver Federal Building."

"What about you?" Tremain asked, her smooth brow lining with worry. "What about us? Should we think about moving again? Can Paxton find us here?"

Ramsey's smile lacked humor. "Oh, I doubt that." He leaned back, frustration spreading through him and mixing with the warm sensation of fatigue. "At this very moment he's on ice at the Summit County coroner's pending transport to Denver. The bad news is that I didn't get him alive. The really bad news . . . well, his partner got away."

"How?"

"Lack of manpower. Look, they'd bombed the Federal Building. Up to that point everything had gone according to plan. Dole pulled all but five of his people for the bombing. We got the drop on Paxton, but he started shooting. The Summit County S.O. covered the highway, where we picked up their van. We know the guy arrived with Paxton, but he didn't enter the condo. My one agent covering the outside said he saw the guy slip into a covered utility trailer that was parked at the edge of the lot. When shots were fired, he lost track for a moment. When we got around to the trailer, our unsub was long gone. We initiated the usual procedures—search, public announcements, and law enforcement alert—but we didn't get him in the net."

Ramsey straightened in an earnest manner. "ERT is going over the van as we speak, checking out the communications gear. We've got his prints, hair, fibers, DNA—for practical purposes, everything but his address. They've even recovered a remote detonator that we're betting dollars to donuts is going to match the pieces that the BATF guys are picking out of the walls of the Federal Building down the street."

As he spoke he watched Tremain and Johnson deflate with partial relief. "In short, people, we did it. You, me, Mr. Bennet, and old Leopard Paxton and his fancy eavesdropping equipment. Dr. Tremain, you were sensational. He never had a clue that you were anything but a frightened fugitive. When you made that last call to Bennet, Paxton dropped everything and ran for the bait. We were there, waiting, when he picked the lock on the front door and walked in."

"But the blond man got away," Johnson reminded.

Ramsey nodded soberly. "FBI doctrine is to use massive overwhelming force on an operation. The purpose is to remove the opportunity and will to resist. Don't give a desperate man a chance. Make resistance absolutely futile. Unfortunately I didn't have full support for this investigation to start with. Second, Paxton caught us all by surprise when he planted a bomb in the Federal Building. After the explosion I was ready to bag the whole operation." He shrugged. "My first thought was that Paxton had truly outsmarted me. Seen through the layers of deception. My second thought was that he was using the bombing as a diversion. So I gambled—and Paxton walked into the condo." He frowned. "Problem was, I think he was in so deep he couldn't see a way out. Maybe, if I'd had a full team, we could have taken him alive."

At that moment, the waiter brought him a giant bottle and carefully poured a glass of crystal red ale. "What is this?"

"Chimay," Johnson told him. "It's a Trappist ale, brewed in Belgium by real monks in a monastery."

Ramsey stared at the big bottle with trepidation. A glass of that and he might just fall asleep on the spot. He caught Abel looking at him and shot the kid a wink. Then he sipped, and tasted. By God, that was good stuff.

Veronica Tremain leaned back, body slack, eyes closed. "So, the blond man's still out there."

"We'll get him. The noose is drawing tight. Mitch cleaned out a church storage unit in Virginia earlier today. He thinks it's the place where Joe Hanson was held before he was killed. The forensics will tell us within the next day or so. They've got fibers, hairs, residue, all the stuff they retrieve with sticky-tape. Quantico will give us a complete rundown on who, what, where, and how."

"So, Brown is definitely involved?" Tremain asked.

"Maybe. Look, they bombed a federal building. Nothing, and I mean nothing, brings down a full-scale investigation like a terrorist bombing of a federal building. If Brown is involved we'll find a tie. Phone records, credit cards, weapons purchases, something. These guys can't operate like they've been doing without financial and technical support. Mitch seems to think they've been using church personnel. Having them do legwork, basic reconnaissance, that sort of thing. Brown's a charismatic kind of guy. His type can generate fanaticism in his followers. We'll start showing pictures around in Fort Collins; Athens, Ohio; and Manchester. Someone in the church will know something. We will just follow the evidence where it leads."

Ramsey reached into his pocket. "Speaking of which, I need you to look at this. I think Joe Hanson mentioned the infamous list. Do you know any of these names?" He handed them a photocopy.

Tremain nodded as she and Johnson studied the names.

"They found that in the van. It starts with Avi Raad, lists Ostienko, your brother, Dr. Alexander, Dr. Johnson, Rebecca Armely, and then another nineteen women in various cities. Do you know any of them?"

Tremain and Johnson both looked as if the obvious had just hit them with a bat.

Bryce met Ramsey's eyes and said, "Sally Mayfield? Celia Smith, and the rest? They're the other women."

"What other women?" Ramsey took the list back, knowing he was about to have a major revelation.

"Ten boys, ten girls," Tremain said, satisfaction in the set of her lips. "We had a meeting with Dr. Pietor Ostienko today. The Russian on your list. He's alive. He's here, in Denver. Because of his background—call it

Russian paranoia—he recognized when Paxton and the blond man began following him. He immediately left Russia."

"The way it worked," Bryce continued, "was that Amanda bore the first child. Someone had to see if the procedure was safe, if they could produce a viable embryo. After that, women who were referred to Avi's clinic were discreetly asked if they would be interested in a 'special' child. If they were, and if they passed a stringent set of psychological exams, they were allowed into the Neanderthal program."

"What? You mean women actually *agreed* to carry Neanderthals?" Ramsey sat back, shocked.

"Fertility clinics are expensive," Veronica reminded. "Most procedures start at thirty thousand and go up. Those accepted into the Neanderthal program were not only impregnated for free, but cared for, and given financial assistance with the child." She raised an eyebrow. "As Bryce mentioned, the screening was pretty comprehensive. Take Rebecca Armely. Amanda had known her for years, understood that she had come from an abused childhood."

"Sexual abuse can cause several long-term psychological problems." Bryce steepled his fingers. "In some people it can drive them to social pathology. Your forensic profilers at Quantico can tell you more about that. In other people, like Rebecca, it can make them desperate to ensure that a child will *never* be subjected to harm. They become super nurturers."

"If they're like Armely, they probably went to ground, too. That explains some of the phone calls made the night of Scott Ferris' death. He was activating some form of

Neanderthal phone tree." Ramsey paused, staring at the list. *Twenty of them! Twenty Neanderthal children!* How on earth did you deal with that? He couldn't keep from staring at little Abel.

"You look stunned," Bryce said. "It's going to take a while for this to sink in. We're only beginning to glimpse what Scott and Amanda had in mind. They were changing our world, and our opinion of ourselves. You'll never view humanity through the same eyes again."

"No," he murmured, still trying to get his mind around it. *Twenty!* That number stuck in his head as he looked at the list of names and tried to decide why twenty women would bear Neanderthal children. And then, his mind locked on women, and how they differed from men, something hit him. "Odd thing, it doesn't look like the Reverend's handwriting. If it was me, I'd say a woman wrote that. The circle instead of dot on the *i*. The loops look feminine. Just a hunch. One the guys at Quantico can sort it out."

Johnson and Tremain and young Abel hung on his every word. Johnson asked, "So, what does this mean? Is the case closed? Are you close to finding the blond guy? No Federal Witness Protection Program?"

Ramsey stifled a yawn. "That will depend on how long it takes us to collar the blond unsub. After that, you tell me. What's the risk? Are you comfortable that other crazies out there won't come gunning for little Abel here?"

Tremain and Johnson looked at each other, tension in their eyes.

Abel sank down in his seat, his eyes just visible over the tabletop.

"We'll have to think this over," Veronica said. "In the meantime, are we safe here?"

Ramsey nodded. "Unless you've told someone, only Bennet, me, and the two of you know where you're staying. But we're not taking chances. Dole detailed three agents to keep an eye on the hotel."

"We met Pietor Ostienko here today," Johnson said. "He's the only one, and since he knows his name's on the list, he's not telling. We told him that you might want to talk to him."

"That's mild understatement if I ever heard it."

One of the waiters pushed up a cart and began building a Caesar salad. Ramsey watched, hearing his stomach rumble. When the plates had been distributed, he pitched into the best Caesar he'd ever eaten.

Balancing his fork, Ramsey said, "Have you given any thought to the fact that when this is wrapped up, the whole world is going to be crowding through your front door?"

"Not mine," Johnson said deadpan. "Paxton and his buddy burned it."

"Good point."

"We'll deal with it," Veronica said. "I don't know how, but Abel and the children need a chance to just be kids."

Abel stared down at Chaser. The little fingers looked vulnerable against the mat of curly brown hair. Just how did Veronica Tremain think she was going to do that?

"I still can't believe they suspended you." Johnson shook his head in disbelief. "You were doing a great job."

"Politics." Ramsey finished his salad. "But like I said: They bombed a building. Two innocent people are dead and twenty others are hurting. It'll blow wide open. The good judge is an old friend of the Reverend's. By placing me on suspension, curtailing my investigation, the judge might have just cut his own throat." Ramsey considered that. "*If* it's Brown. And, damn it, I'm still not convinced he's the joker in this deck. Something about him . . ."

"What?" Veronica asked.

"I don't know. Sure, the battle against evolution makes him millions. And having met the man, yeah, I can believe that he has it in his personality to kill—maybe over self-preservation—but not over cloned Neanderthals. Somehow the willingness to murder, torture, and bomb doesn't fit the man I met outside of Atlanta."

"What about you?" Johnson sipped his ale.

"I'll survive." Ramsey cocked an eyebrow. "I got the collar. Tagged one of the bad guys. Would have got them both—alive—and probably could have stopped the bombing if I hadn't been cut off at the knees on manpower. In short, it's pretty tough to can the guy that brings in the bacon." He winced. "You know, if this goes to a congressional, I'll have to tell them everything, and the press is going to be all over it like flies on honey."

Veronica sagged, reaching out to take Abel's hand. "I just wanted a life. Was that too much to ask?"

"Sometimes," Ramsey said, thinking about how this was going to affect Paula and Matt, "it is."

Bryce held Veronica's naked body, her head pillowed on his chest. A sheet draped them, conforming to the sensual swell of her hips. He breathed deeply, every muscle and nerve relaxed in the aftereffects of sexual release. He traced his fingers down the concave smoothness of her slim waist, her warm skin damp under his fingertips.

She tightened her arms around him. Black twists of hair fanned out over the rumpled pillows.

They had returned to the room in time to catch the Denver news at ten. Each station led with the shooting of a suspect in the Denver bombing that had killed two people. That it had occurred in the Ferris condo tied Paxton to the Scott Ferris and Rebecca Armely murders. A cautious Bob Dole had stood before the cameras trying to deflect the barrage of questions. After that, Headline News had picked it up, and they reran it every fifteen minutes. The file footage of Mary's house on Lookout Mountain ran over and over as reporters speculated on the biggest story since the nine-eleven attack.

"Judge Harthow?" one reporter shouted at the white-haired FBI Director as he scurried from his black Lincoln to his family home in Georgetown, "is it true that the special agent in charge of the operation has been suspended? And if so, why?"

"No comment!" Harthow had shouted over his shoulder, smiling limply as he bolted for the door.

By that time Abel had fallen asleep. Bryce had carried him to his own bed, and had returned to Veronica's arms, and to the desperation that had seized their lovemaking.

Bryce extended his hand over her round rump. "Until talking with Ostienko this morning I didn't understand the long-term implications of this. Pietor is right. They have changed the way humanity thinks about itself. The rest of the species just hasn't realized that yet." He frowned. "The problem is, did Paxton and his goon destroy it all? It makes it a little difficult to explain just how Abel was created. If he was just mixed up in the laboratory like a batch of biscuits, it lends credence to that damn Brown's notion that he's a soulless creation."

"I don't know, Bryce." She shifted to look at him. In the dim light, her eyes appeared as dark pits framed by the black wealth of her hair. "I haven't told you this, but Scott called and left a message on my machine before he was killed. He told me he left me a packet, hidden someplace in the condo. I looked for it that first night. It wasn't where I thought it was supposed to be."

He propped himself on an elbow. "You're kidding."

"No." She shivered. "Eerie, hearing his voice like that when I'd seen his dead body. That's why I drove up there that day . . . to get those papers. I checked that night, unscrewed the kickboard under the counter where I used to hide drugs. All I got out of it was dust."

Bryce leaned back onto the pillows and exhaled. "And Scott knew you hid stuff there? The Scott I knew would have checked it periodically. As much as he hated drugs, he'd have flushed whatever you had down the toilet."

"He did," she said sourly. "I could have killed him. The—" She started, bolting upright. "Damn! Of course!"

"Of course, what?"

She was shaking her head slowly, as if disappointed in herself. "God, the assumptions we make."

"Would you like to explain that?"

"I *know* where they're at!"

"Great. Where? And what does that have to do with assumptions?"

"Because Scott knew, because he found that one stash of pot, I moved my location. I just naturally assumed Scott knew. I was more careful, didn't leave stuff up there where he might look for it. So, anytime I knew Scott was going to be coming, I made sure he couldn't find anything."

"Which means?"

She was beaming. "That just this once, I outsmarted him. I didn't think of the trash chute because I hadn't used it in years. Not since junior high."

"The trash chute?" Bryce made a face. "The one we slid down?"

"Tomorrow," she promised, "we're going up there to see. And if we don't find it in the chute, we'll tear the place apart."

Bryce rubbed the angle of her shoulder as she resettled her head on his breast. "You're Scott's sister. The Ferris murder is now tied to a Neanderthal and the bombing of a federal building. The media is going to be insatiable in their attempts to find you, looking for an angle on the story. If they don't have the condo staked out, they will."

"Yeah, so we're going to have to hurry."

"Lucky us." He kissed the top of her head. If having Ronnie to love was the price of the coming hell, it was well worth it.

CHAPTER FORTY

❖

"*I SUSPECT THAT IT'S SOME SORT OF ELABORATE HOAX,*" THE voice on the radio stated matter-of-factly. "*Assuming that Dr. Ferris did recreate a Neandertal, where would he have come up with the genetic material? All of the known Neandertal remains are fossils . . . in most of them the bone has been replaced by minerals. To obtain the raw DNA from existing specimens would be impossible.*"

"Little does he know, huh?" Veronica looked into the Durango's backseat, where Abel rode in his car seat. His eyes were filled with uncertainty. They were climbing the steep grade of I-70 just past Georgetown. She rode in the passenger seat, Bryce frowning from behind sunglasses as the high Rocky Mountain sun beat down on them.

The Durango looked like new, Theo having sent it to a body shop for repairs while they were in Montana. The lawyer had scowled, not really buying Veronica's explanation that not just everybody had ice cream and pizza stains on the leather interior of his Cadillac that had been left there by a real breathing Neandertal.

Veronica said, "I think the good Dr. Adam Smyth is in for a real shock."

Bryce laughed. "Life's tough when you're the president of the American Association of Physical Anthropologists and the rug has just been pulled out from under you. The good Dr. Smyth is about to take one on the chin."

She stared thoughtfully at the road. "The whole profession is."

Bryce asked, "Abel, how does it make you feel to know the entire world is talking about you?"

He twined his fingers in Chaser's fur. "Whass a Neandewtal?"

Bryce shot an inquisitive look at Veronica. Finally she said, "It means you're special, Abel. Kind of like Chaser: one of a kind. But we already knew that, didn't we?"

She found another radio channel. Reception was good on this side of the Eisenhower Tunnel.

The female voice on the radio said: *"ABC News has learned that Elizabeth Carter, the woman nailed to her floor and burned to death in her Alexandria, Virginia, home, had just returned from a trip to Atlanta where she is suspected to have spent the weekend with Reverend Brown in a 'love tryst.' Jonas Wade, a spokesman for the Apostolic Evangelical Church of the Salvation Crusade for Ultimate Truth had the following response."*

"That's just ludicrous. Ms. Carter spent her weekend in Atlanta working on church business."

The woman's voice continued. *"The Reverend Brown is unavailable for comment, as is his wife of twenty-six years, Bobby Sue. Spokesmen for the church report that the Reverend, who has been questioned in regard to the Ferris murders, is in retreat, meditating and praying. Mr. Wade had the following comment."*

"The allegations that have been made that the church was involved in the Ferris-Alexander murders and the

bombing of the Denver Federal Building are patently false."

"Yeah, right," Bryce muttered. "I'm sure the Bible says something about bald-faced lying."

Veronica glanced up at the sheer mountain rising beside the road. A herd of buff-colored mountain sheep were grazing just beyond the right-of-way. "You can lie in the name of God, you know. They don't consider that a sin."

"Apparently they don't think of torture and murder as sins, either."

"People have been doing it for centuries," she replied.

Her cell phone rang. Veronica flipped it open and said, "Hello." She frowned at the static, making out Theo's voice. "*Ronnie? I've been trying to reach you all morning. There's a complication. . . . Campbell, Rebecca Armely's sister . . .*" Static obscured his voice. "*. . . this morning. I told her you were going up to the . . .*" More static. "*. . . will talk. She was adamant about taking the boy . . .*" A loud burst of static killed the connection.

"Damn it!" Veronica pushed in Theo's number. The *beep beep* of the "no service" indicator left her fuming.

"What?" Bryce asked.

"Something about Rebecca's sister wanting to take Abel."

"Maybe we should go back?" Bryce cast her a sidelong glance. "Do you still think this a good idea?" He jerked a nod toward the backseat. "How's he going to handle it?"

"You two stay in the car. I'll just run in, check for the packet, and run right back out."

"Promise me you won't have to go out the trash chute. I won't be there to catch you."

She smiled at him and reached over to hold his hand. Yes, just in and out, and she'd never have to see the place again. Never have to relive that moment of terror as she stared at Rebecca's dying body. Even as she thought it, a knot of fear tingled in her gut.

Rebecca's sister, the crazy one, wanted Abel? No, don't even think about it.

Abel watches the town of Frisco passing beyond the passenger window. He doesn't remember pulling Chaser into his lap. He sees the Safeway store where he and Mother shopped for groceries. Each of the familiar scenes brings her back, stronger, as if she still walks these streets.

Abel can sense the growing tension as Bryce and Veronica stare steadfastly ahead. He doesn't want to be here, in this place, where bad men changed his life.

He makes himself look, trying to see Mother. Maybe she is still alive? Maybe that was all a bad dream? Maybe the blond man didn't really shoot her?

He tells himself that is what happened. They will drive up to the condo, with its terrible white-skull monster, and Mother will open the door, and he will run into her arms.

But another voice in his head tells him that it won't be so. That the white-skull monster has killed Mother. Eaten her soul. What if it tries to eat his, too?

They make the gentle curve out of town, and Abel can feel his heart hammering in his chest. The car seat straps that hold him are too tight. He strains against them, kicking his feet.

"You okay?" Veronica asks from the front.

He can't speak, is ashamed of his fear, and looks away. His hands clutch futilely at the straps over his chest.

He doesn't look as Bryce signals and makes the left turn into the condo complex.

"We shouldn't have brought him," Bryce says in the front seat.

"Where could we have left him? With whom? Ostienko? He'd have the kid atop an alabaster pedestal."

Tears flood down Abel's face. He can feel Mother's presence. Images of her smiling at him, reaching down to comfort him, keep forming in his mind.

They pull to a stop, parking in a space beside Veronica's dusty BMW.

"I've got an idea," Veronica tells Abel brightly. "On the way back, you can ride with me in the sports car. We'll put the top down and feel the wind in our hair."

Words won't come. Abel is barely aware of Bryce and Veronica staring at him over the seats. His vision is blurred by silver tears. He wants to go away from here. To be back in Billings, beside the river, throwing rocks into the water. He wants to let Bryce swing him around and around and let him go to fly up into the sky and disappear.

He tightens his grip on the buffalo, unable to stop the sudden trembling in his limbs.

A warm wet rush seeps out of his pants, wetting the car seat.

"Oh, Abel," Veronica whispers.

He can't stop the terrified sobs.

"Come on," Bryce says. "We'll take him inside and clean him up. Poor little guy."

"No!" Abel screams.

"All right," Bryce relents. "It's all right, Abel. We'll do it later." To Veronica. "You go. Be quick."

Abel hears the door open and cringes; the last protection from the white-skull monster is opening. In desperation, he hugs Chaser to his chest, squeezing the soft fabric to kill the fear.

Veronica hurried up the steps, hearing the wood echo hollowly under her heels as she fished her keys from her purse. She barely glanced up at the elk skull, then shoved the key into the slot and turned it.

Her heartbeat might have been a drum in her chest as she turned the knob and swung the door open. She ducked the yellow crime scene tape left by the FBI and stepped inside.

Rebecca's body was gone, of course. As was Paxton's. Someone had cleaned up the blood, the square of white vinyl flooring spotless. The rug had been steam-cleaned. A pattern of tracks marked where the FBI had entered to lay their trap for Paxton.

She passed the breakfast bar into the kitchen and opened the trash chute. Setting her butt on the ledge, she twisted her body into the space. There, in the darkness, perched over the long fall, her fingers found the section of plywood and pushed it back.

Come on, Scott, tell me it's here.

What if it wasn't? What if this place, too, was empty? Her fingers slid along the edge of the cardboard box. Withdrawing it, she snugged it to her breast and sighed with relief. Only ghosts lingered in this place now—Rebecca's ghost, watching her from the shadows. Paxton's hovering in the room like a vulture. She almost dropped the plywood as she fit it back into its space.

She extricated herself from the narrow confines of the shaft and straightened. With one hand, she closed the door and studied the heavy box with its reams of typewritten pages. Scott's data, there was no doubt about it as she quickly thumbed through the stacks of paper. Washed by a sense of relief, she opened a drawer and took out a white plastic grocery bag from Safeway. The heavy box just fit, stretching the plastic.

She'd made three steps across the kitchen when she heard the footsteps.

He emerged from the hallway under the stairs; a blocky-looking steel pistol with a protruding cylindrical tube centered on her stomach.

"I was curious," he said in a slow Southern drawl. "Now, what would Dr. Tremain want? Why would she rush to the trash chute and climb into it." He pointed to the breakfast bar. "Put it there, Doctor. And step back." He tapped the pistol with his left index finger. "Yes, I will shoot you. It might just as well be now as later."

Her shocked mind slipped, then caught, recognizing

the close-cropped blond hair, the muscular body, that cold-eyed stare. "Are you—"

"A soldier of God," the blond said. "Ma'am?"

A woman stepped out from the hallway, narrow-faced, dressed attractively in beige slacks and wearing a suit jacket over a form-fitting white blouse. She appeared to be in her mid-thirties, with a sensual mouth and probing blue eyes. Wavy blond hair had been pulled back in a ponytail. For a split instant, Veronica had a vision of Rebecca Armely, only older, and with a sharply edged intensity.

"Ms. Tremain?" the woman said. "I missed you at the lawyer's office. I am Eunice Campbell. Rebecca's sister. I want the child."

Veronica glanced back and forth between the woman and the alert blond man. "You're Rebecca's sister?"

"Unfortunately."

"Why are you doing this?"

A laconic smile bent her lips. "Keeping the world safe from the soulless spawn of Satan, Dr. Tremain. Or haven't you listened to the Reverend's sermons?"

CHAPTER FORTY-ONE

❖

VERONICA FELT SUDDENLY FAINT AND GRABBED FOR THE stove. Every muscle in her body went weak.

"I was a lost soul," Eunice said calmly. "I didn't understand God's plan. All the things that happened to me as a child, at first I thought it was my fault. I didn't understand that for everything there is a reason. Even my volunteering in the institution where they were torturing Ron Elias. God brought him to me, and prepared me for this most sacred Crusade."

"And Billy Barnes Brown?" Veronica tried to make herself think.

"He gave me back my life . . . returned my very soul. Under his guidance, I found my way back to God and salvation." She smiled as she said that, her eyes shining. "And now, I've found a way to repay my Lord and my church."

"You?" Veronica fought to understand. "Your sister was *killed* in this very room. By him!" She pointed at the blond man. He smiled grimly, the silenced pistol unwavering in his hand.

Eunice's expression intensified. "Yes. She tried to have me committed, you know? Ron Elias and I met in the asylum. Funny how God works, preparing me, and all because of Becky's satanic possession. She had become an instrument of his evil. It was God's will that she pay for her sin. Her immortal soul will be judged accordingly." A pause. "As will yours."

How could she say it so calmly?

"He's out in the car?" Elias tilted his head to indicate the parking lot.

"Who?"

"The satanic spawn that your brother and his minions conjured from Lucifer's pit." Elias cocked his head.

Eunice sighed, as though under a terrible load. "God destroyed them once, you know. Banished them from the face of the earth. Your brother's terrible sin of pride brought them back."

"He didn't bring them back. They've always been part of us. Modern humans and Neandertals interbred—"

"Ms. Tremain, our Lord found the Neanderthals wanting, their souls corrupt and impure, so he smote them like he did the Amalachites."

"They're just like us. Human beings."

"You poor misguided woman," she said evenly. "Genesis tells us that we are made in God's image. Not them. They were abominations."

Play for time. Bryce has got to know this is taking too long. . . .

"Did you know Elizabeth Carter?"

Her face stiffened. "She betrayed us. Betrayed the church and her Lord. I was there the night she took my list." Then she smiled again. "I'd left it on the desk. The Reverend actually tried to talk me out of this. He's such a good man. Poor Elizabeth. If she had remained obedient, like a good wife should, she wouldn't have ended like she did."

"Wife? From what I heard, she was your reverend's whore."

She smiled coldly. "And, since I share his bed, am I his whore, too?" At Veronica's hesitation, Eunice stepped forward, pointing a finger. "Reverend Brown is a prophet. Like the prophets of old, God has given him dispensation to take as many wives as he wishes. I am like Ruth; his people are mine. His work is my work."

"And your work is to kill? Is that what Billy Barnes Brown preaches? Come off it, Eunice. The FBI is about to descend on you and your precious reverend like an anvil. It's over, they're—"

"They have nothing on the church," she said simply. "I've done this on my own. Used my money the way your brother used his. And no matter what I might have told William, any confidence is protected. If I fall, I accept the consequences. My soul is redeemed."

"But to kill your sister—"

"She was *Satan's*! Any regard I had for my sister died the day she filed papers to have me committed. She lost her soul the day she accepted that Satan-spawned child! She had to *pay*!"

Elias raised the pistol. "I think I've heard enough. Good-bye, Dr. Tremain."

"*Ronnie?*" Bryce called from outside and she heard his steps on the wooden stairs.

"Bryce, *run!*" Veronica shouted, fists clenching at her sides.

Elias called, "Come in, Dr. Johnson. If you don't, I'll shoot Veronica Tremain low down, through the crotch where the bullet breaks bone and bladder and colon."

Bryce stepped into the room, face tense. He shot a

look at Elias and then at the woman. "What a surprise. It's Eunice, isn't it?"

"Where's the child?" Eunice demanded.

"He's safe. We left him in Denver."

"Let me handle this," Elias said evenly. "Dr. Johnson, step over here, please. In front of the couch . . . and leave the door open." Elias smiled coldly as Bryce walked into the room. "The lawyer told Mrs. Campbell he was with you. And I think he's in your car. He'll be here soon."

"Don't be so sure," Bryce answered. "You goons killed his mother right in this room."

With certainty, Elias said, "He'll come. He won't want to be by himself."

"This won't get you anywhere," Veronica said, watching the door, waiting for Abel's little form to tentatively step into the room. He *would* come, driven by the terror of being alone.

"How'd you know about all this?" Bryce studied Eunice thoughtfully, stopping short beside the couch. "I mean, I didn't know and I was part of the team."

Eunice lifted her chin. "Becky told me she'd adopted a child. I can't have children. So I had to see for myself. God, what a sham . . . to act as if I were truly sorry that we'd grown apart. I was good. She never knew how much I hated her. When I saw the spawn, I knew it was some sort of monster. So, I bided my time. She wouldn't tell me anything about the child. I was there when she and the spawn went out for groceries. Avi Raad, from Tel Aviv, called. When I said I was her sister, he told me he just wanted to check on the boy. And then I knew he was the Antichrist."

"So you sent your goons to Israel," Bryce supplied.

Eunice smiled. "I was there with Reverend Brown for the international conference on religion. Ron and Ted worked under my instructions. They found Avi Raad and obtained the confession of his sins. Everything was there in the files. Everything."

"Jesus!" Veronica cried. "What kind of cold-blooded bitch are you?"

"I am a soldier of God." She nodded at Elias. "Shoot them both. Then we'll deal with the spawn."

From the corner of her eye, Veronica caught movement at the door. "Abel, no! *Run!*"

Abel tightens his stranglehold on Chaser. The world grows silent. Fear builds, filling him until he can taste it, penny like, in his mouth.

All he can hear is distant traffic, and the soft shishing of the wind in the trees.

He cries. It is so hot, and the smell of urine clogs his nose. Blubbering, he fingers the release for the car seat and climbs into the front. His wet pants cling to his legs. Chaser is safely clutched in one hand.

"They awe coming back, Chasaw," he whispers.

The white-skull monster is staring at him through the windshield, watching and waiting, the empty eyes fixed on him.

Abel can't swallow. Every muscle is tight as he reaches for the door latch and hears it click open. He eases down to the ground, dragging Chaser with him.

Abel doesn't close the door behind him because he might need to run back quick. He lingers by the front fender and kneads Chaser's fur. "It will be all wight. Don't wowwy."

He takes a step, eyes pinning the skull that shines so brightly white in the sunlight. Like a cartoon, it seems to be grinning at him, daring him and laughing.

At the foot of the stairs, he hesitates. Where is Bryce? Where is Veronica? What if the blond man is inside? What if he's killed them?

Step by step, Abel creeps up the stairs. He can hear voices now. Veronica's, Bryce's, and two strangers'— a man and woman. Something about the woman's voice is familiar.

Abel stands paralyzed, wanting to turn and run for the trees, to climb up where the squirrels live and spend the rest of his life there.

He eases around the railing, sidestepping to stay as far from the giant skull as he can. It looms over the doorway like some malevolent guardian. He can hear the fear in Veronica's voice as she talks to the stranger.

Abel chokes on a sob and edges to the doorway. The blond man is pointing his gun at Bryce. He sees Aunt Eu, arms crossed, looking angry like she did that last night in Salt Lake when she fought with Mother and said terrible words.

"Abel, no! Run!" Veronica shouts.

The room explodes.

Bryce dives behind the couch, and the pistol bucks in the blond man's hands: phuut! phuut! Bryce is down, clawing at the back of his shirt above the belt. Shot! Bryce is shot!

Abel shrieks and pitches himself headlong into the room, stumbling, scrambling behind the overstuffed chair next to the bookcase.

Veronica screams, "Abel, get out of here!" as she throws a kitchen chair at Aunt Eu. The blond man turns, pivoting on his heel, the pistol swinging toward Veronica where she is tearing a big knife from the kitchen drawer.

The blond man smiles, and aims the pistol at Veronica's face. She is about to die. In that frozen moment, Abel hears the song sung by the bronze buffalo. It rings so clearly in his head that he understands.

Abel drops Chaser and grabs the bronze buffalo statue from the bookcase. With both hands, he lifts it, shrieks at the top of his lungs, and throws it. The heavy bronze buffalo wheels in the air. It strikes the blond man full in the back, knocking him sideways. The pistol phuuts, and splinters fly from the wall beside Veronica.

Bryce leaps to his feet; his familiar black pistol thunders: Bam! Bam! The blond man jerks with each concussion, and gasps. He drops to his knees, choking, grabbing his chest.

Bryce shouts, "Drop it!" A faint curl of smoke rises from the barrel of his black pistol. His shirt is torn loose in the back, the pistol holster barely visible.

The blond man sags against the refrigerator. His eyes are wide as he slides down the sleek front of the appliance. A smear of crimson streaks the gleaming white enamel.

In that moment Aunt Eunice sprints for the door and bursts out into the sunlight. Her feet hammer the stairs as she runs.

Veronica is crying, the sounds like a kitten's.

"Call the sheriff," Bryce orders gently. "Call nine-one-one, Ronnie."

Abel's knees buckle, and he sags to the carpet. All he can do is clutch himself and cry. "Chasaw?" he calls. "I want Chasaw!"

The small white room mirrored Bryce's soul: empty.

He sat on the metal cot where it was bolted into the cement floor. A "holding" cell, they had told him. He wore his pants and a shirt, his boots and socks. They had taken everything else.

He could do nothing but sit there, his hands clasped in front of him, and stare at the featureless cement floor. Muted sounds could be heard through the door.

I shot a man. The words went round and round in his head.

Every single instant of it replayed: over, and over, and over. His frantic clumsy haste as he pawed at his shirt for the pistol. The fumbling panic as he tried to rise.

He'd seen Ron Elias steady his aim, Veronica frozen in the man's sights like a stunned deer. The terror in her eyes would haunt him forever.

In that instant as he'd lifted the pistol, he'd known her for dead; he was too slow, unable to save the woman he loved.

Then he'd glimpsed the incomprehensible image of a bronze buffalo cartwheeling through the air like slow motion, knocking the man and the shot sideways.

He didn't remember the sight picture, the squeeze, or even the sounds of the shots, although the deputy told him he'd fired twice.

All he remembered was the way Elias' body jerked at the impact of the bullets. How he'd looked so surprised and dazed as he slumped against the refrigerator. How his blood smeared such bright crimson down the smooth white surface as Elias sagged to the floor. Then the moment of realization that he'd killed a man.

Somehow he'd made it, hung on to that last thread of sanity until the wail of a siren pierced the room. He'd stood there, the pistol pointed at the gurgling and gasping Elias, while Veronica ran past him to Abel. She'd gathered the boy in her arms and rocked him back and forth on the floor, crying.

"Police! Put the pistol down! Now!" The harsh order had come from the door. Some instinct had kept him from turning, gun in hand, and had probably saved his life.

From there, it became a blur. He remembered the shakes, the need to vomit.

I killed a man! How in God's name had he come to this?

He had been a shooter all of his life. Fought against the people who wanted to confiscate and register guns. In all that time, he'd believed that rights entailed responsibility. That that one great golden rule underlined civilization.

And he had shot a man.

He looked down at his hands and the handcuffs that encircled his wrists.

He couldn't even remember being arrested, or the ride in the patrol car to the little jail in Frisco. They'd asked him questions, but he couldn't remember what he'd said, or even what he'd been asked.

He was trying to kill us. The little voice struggled to be heard over the horror of the shooting.

So what? It was so different when you pulled the trigger. So terribly different.

He fought the growing nausea, seeing Elias under the impact of the slugs, seeing how incredibly fragile the body was when a bullet tore through it.

Dear God, we are terrible creatures.

CHAPTER FORTY-TWO

THE ROOM MEASURED THREE PACES BY FOUR. VERONICA had been up and back so many times that she couldn't stand it any longer.

"It's all wight," Abel said where he huddled in a plastic chair, his buffalo in his lap.

"Yes, I know." She looked up at the clock on the wall. Two and a half hours now. What the hell was keeping Theo? A calendar, a picture of the Copper Mountain Ski Area, a mirror, and a table with three more chairs were the only other adornments. The mirror was no doubt one-way so that other people could watch interrogations.

"Whewe's Bwyce?"

"He's here somewhere." She winced at the way he'd looked: so pale and upset. She'd seen him struggle with the shakes, watched him wipe his mouth after he'd thrown up, and knew just how sick he'd felt. She'd been the same way, desperate to hold Abel and wish the world would go away.

Poor Bryce. The whole load had fallen on him.

"Come on, Theo!"

"Whass gonna happen?"

She looked at Abel. "Nothing. Theo will get us out of this. He always does. And, for once, it wasn't our fault." Our fault? Since when had she started thinking like that?

"They take me away?" Abel's huge eyes had gone glassy.

"No way, Abel. Not while I'm still drawing breath." With grim humor she remembered when the deputies had tried to separate them. The soul-searing screech that had come from Abel's throat had touched something feral in her paleocortex, and she would have fought like a banshee to keep him. In the end, they wisely figured that the two of them were better off in the same room.

"Why is Bwyce gone?" Abel stroked Chaser's fur.

"Because Bryce shot that bad man, honey." She studied him soberly. "It's only on TV that someone gets shot and there aren't a lot of hard questions."

He nodded, and a frown lined his little Neandertal forehead.

"Is the buffawo all wight?" Abel murmured.

She'd barely looked at the Jackson bronze. "Maybe a dent or two, but buffalo are tough." She paused, stepped over, and lifted his short chin with her finger. "You saved my life, Abel. Did you know that? Not even G'Kar could have done better."

His miserable expression didn't change.

"I love you, Abel. You're the bravest little boy in the whole world. I'll never let anything happen to you. I promise."

He blinked hard and swallowed.

"Muvver said that."

Veronica lowered herself in front of the chair. "I'm sure she did. And she was right. She brought you to us. To make sure that we'd be there if she wasn't. She was a wonderful person, Abel. Just like you."

The frown lines deepened as he lowered his gaze to Chaser and repeated, "Just wike me."

She heard the steps and was rising when the door opened. Theo, harried, his expensive suit rumpled, raised an eyebrow as he barreled into the room, a deputy hot behind him.

"Hi, Theo."

He shook his head. "Why is it that when there's trouble you're at the bottom of it, Ronnie?"

"Call it job security. Theo, it was Eunice Campbell, Rebecca's sister. She and Elias were waiting for us in the condo. They came there to kill us."

Theo waved her down, saying, "Wait, will you? I know this is a simple case of self-defense, but could you wait until the deputy is out of the room before you give me the details?"

She smiled, crossed her arms, and shot a questioning look at the deputy. A young man in his twenties, he seemed completely oblivious, attention fixed on Abel. "Is he really a Neanderthal?"

"I'll be out when I'm finished," Theo growled, and literally pushed the officer out before he closed the door. He turned to Ronnie. "First, Ron Elias, the man Bryce shot, is still alive. They've air-lifted him to Denver. He's critical, and they don't know if he's going to make it. Second, the FBI Evidence Response Team was hot on my heels. Agent Dole is really fired up about this." He paused. "Do I have anything to worry about? Will they find anything that won't indicate self-defense?"

She shook her head.

Theo slumped with relief. "Good. Dole has already been on the phone to the sheriff. They'll need a deposition from Bryce and you, but no charges are going to be filed. My God, when I told that woman this morning that you'd planned to drive up to the condo, how could I know that she was behind it all?"

"You couldn't, Theo. Everyone thought it was Brown."

"I tried to call your cell. All morning. I couldn't get through." He sighed. "If anything had happened . . . and it had been my fault . . . Well, no matter. It worked out. What on earth possessed you to go back to the condo? I thought you never wanted to see it again."

She pointed to the plastic Safeway sack, and the thick reams of paper that stuck out of the top. "Scott left it for me. It's probably all of his data. The reason he started this harebrained project."

Theo glanced at the stacks of paper. "One thing at a time, Ronnie. Now start at the beginning and tell me everything that happened. If Elias lives, there are going to be two sides to this, you know. It could get ugly."

"It always does, Theo. It always does."

The afternoon couldn't have been better for late June in northern Virginia. Instead of swelter, a balmy seventy-five degrees and low humidity made reclining in the lounge chair on the little cement porch a sheer delight. Ramsey reached over to the glass-topped garden table and sipped at his ice-filled glass of lemonade. Beside him, Paula reclined in the other lawn chair, her own glass of lemonade in her hands. She wore a straw hat, sunglasses that followed the form of her perfect cheeks, a halter top, and shorts.

Ramsey enjoyed the moment, admiring her long legs and the flat abdomen exposed between waistline and halter bottom. Her blond hair was tied in a ponytail. She looked pensive as she stared out at the yard, her yard, the one he'd worked so hard to provide for her. The big beech trees shaded most of it, and a pair of redstarts had nested in the oak.

"It's going to work out, Jack." She reached out to set her lemonade on the table and shook the condensation from her slim fingers. The diamonds in her wedding ring glittered in the sunlight. "They're scrambling like rats, and the press smells something funny."

Inside, just through the sliding glass doors, the phone rang again. After the second ring, the answering machine did its thing. Then a voice said, "Agent Ramsey? This is Michael Douglas from the *Washington Post*. It's come to our attention that you masterminded the operation that ran Leopard Paxton to ground, but despite that, you've been placed on suspension by the director of the FBI. If you could give me a call, I'd appreciate it. I'd really like to hear your side of the story." A pause. "Please, give me a call. My number is . . ."

Ramsey ignored the rest. Behind the sunglasses he could see one of Paula's arched eyebrows.

"What's that?" she asked. "Number twenty this morning?"

"Twenty-one, I believe." He crossed his hands on his belly, leaning his head back and exposing his face to the sun. "I'm sorry I did this to you. It's going to be a zoo for a couple of weeks."

She smiled that knowing smile that he had fallen in love with so many years ago. "Yeah, I know," she told him dryly. "Next you're going to remind me about what rotten taste I've got in men."

"You do. You could have married well. You know, someone responsible and reliable."

"It would be nice if they kept you on suspension for a couple of weeks. I think the garage needs painting. The garden's a mess. Weeds are coming up. The sink in the basement is dripping."

"Yeah, well, all right. I'll crawl back to Harthow and beg for my job. You've made your point. I'll be good next time and follow orders like a real *soldat* should."

She considered him—a sphinx behind a forbidding

wall of Ray-bans. "Crawl if you want, but judging from the frenzy on the morning news, Harthow's pretty hard to find. Billy Barnes Brown's new little redheaded spokeslady says that he's shocked to discover that a 'minor' functionary used church resources to run her own personal witch-hunt." Paula returned her gaze to her lawn. "She's a sharp-looking piece for a secretary. Why do I wonder if she can type?"

Ramsey recalled Hanson's report on his meeting with Elizabeth Carter. "I think she has other attributes."

"Really? You mean outside of too much eye makeup and a size forty D cup that defies gravity?"

"She needs them to compensate for rounded heels."

"Ah, what a world." He got the cocked eyebrow look again. "Maybe you should have been a reverend instead of a cop?"

"Naw, I got more than enough trouble at home as it is."

Paula shifted, crossing a slim knee. Ramsey took note of the shapely calf and wondered how she kept in such good shape for just hitting forty.

"And the little boy is really a Neanderthal?" Paula shook her head. "I mean . . . what? Like stoop shouldered and hairy and ugly? What was he like?"

"None of the above. Timid, scared, and insecure. He didn't talk much, but then after what he'd been through, you wouldn't expect that he would. I got the feeling, wife, that he's a really good little guy. Smart, too. But, well, different. It was funny, when I was around, he was always sniffing, not making a big thing about it, but testing the air. And his eyes are unusual, big, like they can see into your soul. He wasn't anything like I thought a Neanderthal should be."

"I never really thought it was real, Jack. Evolution, I mean. Knowing that a real Neanderthal exists, well, it changes things. I mean, wow, it's real."

"Not just *a* Neanderthal, but twenty of them! God, what some women will do to have children. But, yeah. Good, bad, or indifferent, we'll never think of ourselves the same again. That poor little boy is going to be in the spotlight forever. For that, I could really bust Scott Ferris one."

Paula's lips pressed into a thin line. "I wish your Veronica good luck."

"Yeah, she's going to need it."

The doorbell rang.

"What do you think?" Paula shot him a wary glance.

"I think nobody's at home." Ramsey reached for his lemonade. "If it's the press, they'll go away . . . or wait in their car. If it's the neighbors, they can borrow the sugar later. Me, I've barely caught up on my sleep, and damn it, this is the first and only time I've ever been suspended for being bad, and I'm going to enjoy every last minute of it."

The doorbell rang again.

"After they go away you could hit it with a hammer," Paula said frankly. "Hey, this is good. Matt's got a game this afternoon. He'll keel over from shock. You've never seen the opening play in your life."

"I have, too. Lots of times, and I can push the 'rewind' button and see it all over again." He replaced his glass. "Of course, the picture always jiggles, and I get lots of shots of the backs of other parents' heads, but until now, I've never complained."

"Fascist film critic."

"Life's tough, but . . ." The words died as Judge Harthow and two of his suited staff walked around the corner of the house, striding purposefully across the lawn.

"Shit," Paula muttered under her breath.

"Yeah, and wearing a two-thousand-dollar suit, too." Ramsey sat up, propping his elbows on his knees.

"I suppose you'll want to talk," Paula said, rising gracefully. "Call me when it's over."

He turned to watch her step into the house, and couldn't help but marvel at her slim body. Hard to believe, even after all these years, that a woman like that would love a man like him.

"Jack?" Harthow greeted gruffly. "We need to talk." He stopped short of the cement slab, hands hanging limply at his side.

Jack, was it? Ramsey cocked his head, squinting in the bright sunlight. "Mr. Director. Have a seat." He indicated the garden recliner Paula had just vacated. He wondered if any of the sunscreen would stain Harthow's silk suit.

"No, uh, thanks." Harthow finally stepped up on the concrete. "I've, um, read your report. Mitch Ensley's, too. It appears that we have a problem."

Ramsey fought the urge to smile. "Yes, sir. I wasn't left on it long enough to get Ron Elias. Poor Bryce Johnson had to do that. A bookworm anthropologist. Who'd have thought? What's the news about Joe's murder?"

"Special Agent Hanson was apparently held at one of Reverend Brown's churches by Elias and Paxton. Apparently this was done under the auspices of Eunice Campbell and without the Reverend's knowledge. Forensics ties them to the place by fibers and hairs. I've talked to Reverend Brown, and he assures me that he had no knowledge of these events." Harthow peered at him, as if to stress the point. "You know, sometimes people can take matters into their own hands. People like Campbell, Elias, and Paxton, who, in the zeal of the moment, involve themselves in activities which—"

"Do you want us to cover up Brown's participation in conspiracy?" Ramsey asked bluntly, still tired enough to speak without thinking.

"Now, you have no proof that Reverend Brown was involved in this, Jack." The tone was reproving, like a father to an errant son.

"No, sir. Nothing that will stand up as of this moment. Ron Elias died on the operating table in Denver, so we'll never be able to sweat the truth out of him. Damned inconvenient of him if you ask me." Ramsey glanced at the two suited agents who stood behind the judge. Both looked uneasy, their hands clasped before them.

"That's just the point." Harthow took a deep breath before launching into the topic.

Ramsey interjected, "But we'll find it." When Harthow missed his beat, Ramsey continued, "You see, Elizabeth Carter took a hit list with twenty-five names on it from Brown's office. Someone had her tortured and killed for it. Did you read the report, Mr. Director? They nailed her to the floor, just like a crucifixion, and poured gasoline over her and burned her alive for having the temerity to compromise the church. She was one of Brown's lovers."

Harthow stiffened. "You can't prove that."

Ramsey rubbed his hands together. "Maybe not, but Elizabeth Carter said it was a threesome that night. I got it straight from Veronica Tremain that just before the condo shooting Eunice Campbell admitted to being Brown's 'wife.' My sources tell me that Eunice hasn't been back to Atlanta. That she's disappeared. My sources also tell me that ERT has lifted her fingerprints from the Ferris condo and that it's her writing on the 'hit list' we got from the van. So she's out there, somewhere . . . unless the good Reverend charred her well-done to ensure her silence. Meanwhile, we'll link Brown to Elias and Paxton. I'm betting Karen Sues and her people can dig up some kind of a tie. Paxton and Elias couldn't afford the kind of equipment that they had in that van. We're talking about several hundred thousand dollars of sophisticated monitoring equipment. And the way they traveled around? Moscow, in an attempt to kill Ostienko, Tel Aviv for Dr. Raad, and then a different city a day in the U.S.? All of it booked under assumed names and identities on charter aircraft."

"That's speculation." Harthow looked panicked.

"No, sir. They went to all of those places. They were trying to stop Ferris and his team from cloning a Neanderthal. Eunice Campbell might have bankrolled them, but Brown knew; and even if we take his word that he didn't condone her activity, he could have stopped it."

"Why would he do a thing like that?" Harthow seemed genuinely baffled.

"Barnes made millions off of his Christian Creationist Crusade. Fighting evolution was a lucrative business, a real golden goose. But having a live Neanderthal, a real, intelligent, sensitive being so much like us, well that would have strangled his goose. Millions of dollars in donations would have dried up overnight. Evolution wouldn't have just been a theory anymore, but fact."

Ramsey shook his head. "What a poor fool Scott Ferris was. He thought he was proving a simple scientific fact. It would never have occurred to him that this whole battle was over power and money." He cocked his head. "You know—and this is a real guess—I don't know if Brown cares a hoot whether evolution is real or not. I'll bet he only cares because it makes him money."

Harthow tried his good-old-boy smile. "Agent Ramsey, I can see how you could construe the facts that way, but you must understand that in a huge organization like the church—"

"Sir?" Ramsey glanced at the two agents. "Could I have a word alone with you?"

At Harthow's gesture, the two agents turned and walked back around the corner of the house. "Now, Jack," Harthow began, "how can we solve this so that the agency and the good Reverend don't get a black eye out of it?"

"Sir? Why are you protecting him?"

Harthow took a moment, solemn thought reflected from his face. "Let's just say that I wouldn't be where I am today were it not for the influence of the good Reverend."

"Cut him loose, sir. He's an accessory to murder."

Harthow's bulldog face had a haunted look. "Jack, I can make things easy or hard for you."

"Yes, sir, you can do that." Muscles began to tighten, Ramsey's nerves prickling. "But that won't kill the facts. Barnes was involved, desperate to protect his power and prestige. Maybe he didn't call the shots; I'll give you that. But he knew, Director, and at the most generous of doubt, he didn't try to stop it."

"I'd like your resignation." Harthow turned on his heel and strode away.

"Yes, sir!" Ramsey called. "That's what I'll tell the reporters."

Harthow spun. "*Agent* Ramsey, you're under obligation not to discuss a case with the press."

He shook his head. "The media is going to want to know why I was placed under suspension, sir. They already smell a cover-up. How long do you think you can last if they start digging into your connection with Brown and his church?"

Harthow's face reddened in rage. "Do you want to bet on how this turns out? Reverend Brown will prove that Eunice Campbell acted alone, without his knowledge. He's a survivor, Jack. Are you?"

"I don't know, sir. You'd better start thinking about your own situation. Too many people in the Bureau know about this. It's going to come out. If it isn't spilled when I appeal my suspension internally, the media will dig it out. One way or another."

"We'll see who's smarter in the end, Jack." Harthow had turned. "You, or me."

CHAPTER FORTY-THREE

THE MAN WATCHED AS THE LONE WOMAN WALKED HURriedly down the weathered wooden planks of the dock. He read the last of the story in the *Picayune*. The headline read: FBI DIRECTOR RESIGNS UNDER CLOUD. Folding the paper under his arm, he checked his watch and then looked out to the west. The sun hung like a red orb just over the Gulf; the Louisiana shore was an evening silhouette, nothing more than a dark embroidery of trees rising above the marsh grass. Low swells rose and fell, the surface of the water unusually glassy. Behind him, the shrimp boat seemed to tug at the brine-encrusted lines that tethered it.

The woman's heels rapped on the gray salt-whitened wood in a hollow cadence as she approached. A scarf covered her head, and large dark glasses obscured most of her face. She wore a light blue tank dress that accented her full figure. Rays of red light caught her blond hair where it escaped the scarf, giving it a golden hue.

Nice figure, damned nice. No one had told him she'd be a hot number like this. He rubbed his jaw and considered the implications of her arrival. Right on time. Just like he'd been told to expect.

"God," she said breathlessly as she stopped before him and stared uncertainly at the grimy shrimp boat behind him. "I thought I'd never make it. They've got my picture everywhere, on TV, the papers. You'd think I was some kind of common criminal!"

"Yeah, I know. The important thing is that you made it. Step aboard."

"This? But it's . . ."

"Not a yacht? I know. Where did you leave the car?"

"Like I was told. Behind the bait stand."

She was a beautiful woman. He could see that through the makeup and the dark glasses. And with tits like those, who cared if she was a little thin-faced? "I'll make sure the car's taken care of. You didn't tell anyone where you were going?"

"No." She gave a nervous laugh. "Are you kidding?" She glanced again at the shrimp boat. "I was expecting something . . ."

"A little flashier?" He smiled. "Yeah, I know. But no one will notice another shrimp boat headed out into the Gulf. Think of it like that scarf and those sunglasses you're wearing. You know, camouflage." He held her hand while she climbed aboard.

One by one, he cast off the lines before he climbed nimbly up the ladder to the pilot house. He eased the throttles forward; the diesels hummed and the boat moved out onto the water.

He took one last look back at the dock, happy to find

it still deserted. The sun had dropped below the horizon, leaving a mauve sky to reflect on the limpid swells.

She climbed up to stand beside him and stare through the glass at the calm sea. He noted her slim fingers when she placed her hand on the console. The nails were long and polished.

"Nice night, huh?" he asked.

"You're sure this boat will get me to Jamaica?"

He glanced back at the large folded canvas sack that lay aft on the deck beside a coil of heavy chain. "Missus Campbell, this boat will take you for as far as you need to go. Reverend's orders."

Right below their feet was a small cabin. He'd send her down there as soon as it was dark and they were beyond the twelve-mile limit. In his mind, he was already unzipping that tight-fitting dress. It was a crying shame he'd only have her for a couple of hours, but the boat had to be back the following morning.

"What do I call you?" she asked, brightening.

"Just another soldier of God."

EPILOGUE

VERONICA SAT AT THE DESK IN HER SMALL OFFICE, A COLD cup of tea by her elbow. On the wall were the photos of her and Scott on Trailridge Road, the clipping of him with blood running down the side of his head outside the Harvard lab, and the AP photo of Special Agent Jackson Ramsey, now Acting Special Agent in Charge of the Washington Metro Field Office—his new assignment, after his congressional testimony regarding the FBI's handling of the "Neanderthal Murders," as they were now called. His boss, Peter Wirthing, had been sent to the Hoover Building, creating a vacancy.

This morning, she studied the notes Scott had left for her. Editing the sheer volume of the work for publication was going to take years. For the moment, however, she had two months to finish a monograph that would be acceptable to the New York publisher who had just advanced the Institute a cool million. If the continuing Neandertal craze was any indication, the royalties could support a great deal of future research.

For the moment, her attention was captured by the first

draft of an article that Scott had authored. In it, she read a section stating:

> From the Tadjik I specimen we have recovered the intact nuclear DNA from a twenty-year-old adult male. After sequencing the base pairs (see Ferris; 1999), we have determined that of the point five percent difference observed between modern humans and Neandertals, several haplotypes unique to Neandertals still appear in the nuclear DNA of modern Northern European populations (See Johnson; 2001).
>
> As a result of this observation, we can finally lay the notion of "replacement" to rest. While some observers have speculated that Neanderthal traits were still present in Northern European populations, we can now state that skin color, hair and eye color, and some cranial morphology are the modern Neanderthal legacy.
>
> As best we can determine, the influx of modern *Homo sapiens sapiens* entering Europe from Africa and the Middle East in the period beginning sixty thousand years ago found themselves in direct competition with less numerous and locally adapted Neandertal populations. That the assimilation of Neanderthals by modern humans took over thirty thousand years is indicative that Neanderthals were more than capable competitors, not the slow-witted unimaginative dolts that many investigators have perceived.
>
> Whether the interactions between moderns and Neanderthals were amicable or hostile—though probably both—Tadjik I proves that miscegenation and gene flow did take place between the populations. It leads this investigator to speculate that the blossoming of Late Paleolithic culture that led to the cave paintings at Chauvet and Lascaux were the result of a sort of hybrid vigor, the

result of biological and cultural stimulation between these two peoples.

In the end, Neanderthals, due to their smaller population and restricted geographic distribution, were doomed to be absorbed into the larger modern gene pool spreading out of Africa and across Eurasia. As our recovered Neanderthals age, we will be able to test these hypotheses. Perhaps, as they did in the past, Neandertals will once again lead us to a new cultural tumescence. Through their eyes, we will be able to view a much different future for all humanity.

Veronica considered the information. In the end, all Scott's team had done was bring back a long-lost relative. Was that such a sin? And, coming from the cells of another human being—albeit, one dead for sixty thousand years—did that mean that Abel didn't have a soul, as the hounded Reverend Brown was so wont to say?

She could look out the window and see Abel and the reporter, Skip Manson, where they talked at the edge of the grove of fir trees. That little boy, his eyes alight with wonder as he pointed at a squirrel up in the trees, had a soul, all right. Veronica saw it reflected in his eyes every night when she read him one of his stories.

"Ronnie? They're coming." Mary stopped in the office door. She had sold her big house after the wedding and the finalization of the adoption. Part of her fortune had gone to found the Institute, and she had come here, to live on the edge of the wilderness with the only family she had left.

"Coming, Mom." Veronica rose and walked to the front door. A white Suburban traveled the gravel road where it wound down the side of the mountain. Above the road, scalloped layers of forested ridges gave way to the weather-sculpted basalt formations known as the Pinnacles. Their snowcapped summits caught the afternoon sun. Splashes of aspen burned yellow in the afternoon. An eagle cut lazy circles in the blue Wyoming sky, and a coolness had settled on the Absaroka Mountains. Those who listened carefully could hear elk bugle up on the flanks of Togwotee Pass.

"Bryce? She's coming!" She straightened her sweater as she followed Mary out onto the porch that hung on the log building like a low brow. The white Suburban threaded its way down through the lodgepole pine and stands of aspen. It rattled across the cattle guard, slowing as it passed the little herd of bison yearlings that grazed in the grass-filled meadow.

In locating the North American Neanderthal Institute, they had chosen this place high in the Rockies just west of Dubois, Wyoming, for its cool climate and the added benefit of three hundred acres to run bison on. Be it some sort of genetic memory or simply an accident of chance, Abel had a real connection with the buffalo. He could stare at them by the hour. In the adjoining national forest he and Bryce stalked elk, moose, and deer through the shadowed black timber. Was it that Abel was closer to his roots? He seemed to have a natural affinity for the woods. He moved through them with an uncanny silence, sniffing, his eyes better attuned to the living world around him. As he grew he would teach them so much about Neandertals, and in a manner Rebecca Armely and the rest couldn't have hoped for given their dispersed locations and scattered resources.

The white Suburban had stopped even with the bison, and over the distance, Veronica could see the window rolled partially down as the occupants stared at the animals.

Bryce's boots rasped on the wooden porch as he came to stand behind her. His arm snaked around her waist, pulling her close. Into her ear, he whispered, "Are you ready for this?"

"I'm not sure. I didn't think I'd be this excited. When we set up the Institute, we didn't know if any of them would be coming."

Bryce looked across at the newly completed dormitory, resplendent with its gleaming coat of red paint. "Well, we've certainly got the room. Ostienko is going to be overjoyed. He's bringing in a busload of scholars next week."

"Only if this works out," she cautioned. "We're all going to have to do a lot of adapting. I want Sarah to settle in before she's harassed by Ostienko's team."

"Yeah, well, we've got a stack of requests a foot high from scholars and media and theologians, and just about anybody you could think of. I just got off the phone with CNN; they want to do an in depth 'day in the life' kind of thing. I told them we'd consider it. Dan Rather said he and his team could be here within twenty-four hours of our approval to do an interview."

"Wonderful," she said glumly.

Abel rounded the side of the building, calling, "Caw coming." Skip Manson followed, a television camera hung from one hand. Abel wore a light wool coat despite the chill in the autumn air. His blue eyes fixed on the Suburban, and he stopped, a frown lining his head. "Is that huw?"

"It's her." Veronica crossed her arms against the chill as the Suburban slowly accelerated away from the bison and rounded the final curve to pull up in front of them. Veronica noticed that Skip had his camera up. "You ready for history, Mr. Manson? Here it is."

"Dr. Ferris, am I ever. Thanks again for letting me be here for this."

"Just so you stay out of the way," Bryce insisted. "Let them be children."

"Oh, I will. You can bet on it." Manson was filming as the driver's door opened and a young brunette woman emerged. She was attractive, in her early twenties, wearing jeans, boots, and a Filson coat. She stopped short at the sight of the camera, indecision in her eyes.

Veronica called, "It's all right. It's only for the archives." She and Bryce stepped down from the porch. Side by side they walked up to the woman, Veronica offering her hand. "Good afternoon. We're so glad you made it. Welcome to the Neandertal Institute. I'm Veronica Ferris and this is my husband, Bryce Johnson. On the porch is my mother, Mary Ferris, and the reporter is Skip Manson. I imagine you've seen some of his Neandertal reports on TV."

"Sally Mayfield," the woman introduced, taking Veronica's hand and studying her with searching brown eyes. "I was one of your brother's students." Her gaze shifted to Abel, her eyes widening. "Dear God," she whispered. "Are you Abel?"

Abel nodded, his frown deepening. "Yess. Gwad to meet you."

Sally smiled then and turned. "Sarah? It's okay, sweetie. Come meet these people. They're our new friends."

Veronica turned her anxious gaze to the Suburban. A little girl clambered down from the vehicle, a spotted stuffed horse clutched in one hand; she rushed to Sally's side, her large blue eyes shifting from person to person. Sarah's face was wedgelike; her jutting nose and long low skull looked classically Neandertal. Wispy silver-blond hair covered her head. She stopped short, gaze widening in surprise as she met Abel's eyes.

Sally bent down, an arm around the little girl's shoulder. "Sarah, this is Abel."

"Hi," Abel said, the slightest smile on his face. "Aw you a Neanduwtal?"

Sarah shot a nervous glance at Sally, who said, "Tell him yes, sweetie. You're a Neandertal, just like Abel. You're going to be great friends."

"Hewwo," Sarah said in a nasal voice. She lifted the stuffed horse. "This is Magic. She's a hawse."

"Say it right," Sally corrected.

"Horrrse," Sarah said, a look of hard concentration on her face. Then she stepped forward, lifting her horse for Abel to see.

"Quite a place you have here," Sally said as she straightened and looked around at the snowcapped mountains.

"It is." Bryce spread his arms. "When Theo, our lawyer, set up the Institute we were able to purchase the land. We will hold it in trust for the children until such time as they reach their majority and they can take over the administration of the trust." Bryce paused, his eyes on Abel and Sarah, who were talking quietly, still unsure of themselves. Sarah was showing Abel the stuffed horse, pointing out each of the black spots on the animal's furry hide.

"Do you think the rest will come?" Veronica asked.

Sally crossed her arms, speculative eyes on Sarah and Abel. Then she studied Skip Manson, busy filming the children from the side. "I can't speak for the other eighteen. They'll have to make their own decisions. No matter what, it won't be easy for any of them, will it?"

Veronica shook her head. "No, it won't, but it might be a little easier here. We have a school planned, and if the other children are like Abel, they'll be delighted with the forest."

"That's why Sarah and I are here. But what about the future?" Sally asked. "When they grow up? There's only twenty of them."

"They can do whatever they want." Bryce shoved his hands into his pockets. "They can marry each other, or anyone else. Scott and Amanda didn't do this just to breed Neanderthals like cattle. They're fully functional and fertile. Just people . . . like anyone else."

"How do you know that?" Sally demanded. "Scott and Amanda only had two donors. Won't the genetics prohibit that?"

Bryce shook his head. "Nope. Remember, I did the computations on gene frequencies. I've been checking Scott's notes. Each of the children is a genetically unique individual. Scott tagged and Avi removed the deleterious genes."

"Want to come see Chasuw?" Abel asked Sarah. "He's a buffawo."

"Like those?" she asked, pointing to the herd.

"No, he's mine. Come on."

Veronica watched as Abel led Sarah to the door and inside the house.

"Ms. Mayfield," Mary asked, "could I provide a cup of coffee? You must have had a long hard drive, and goodness, these last months, they must have been terrifying."

Mary laced her arm in Sally's and led her into the house.

"Having a perfect hostess in the family isn't so bad," Bryce whispered in Veronica's ear and gave her a conspiratorial wink.

Skip had lowered his camera, eyes reflecting a pensive mood. "So, there it is . . . humanity's past. Meeting face-to-face."

"I don't think so, Skip," Veronica replied. "If it were up to me, I'd call it the future."

About the Authors

W. MICHAEL GEAR holds a master's degree in physical anthropology, is a member of the American Association of Physical Anthropology, and has conducted studies in the areas of human osteology, paleoanthropology, forensics and primate evolution.

KATHLEEN O'NEAL GEAR is the former state historian and archaeologist for the U.S. Department of the Interior. She has twice received the federal government's Special Achievement Award for outstanding management of the country's "cultural resources" and is a specialist in preliterate cultures and religions.

DARK INHERITANCE

by W. Michael Gear and Kathleen O'Neal Gear

"Once again, first-rate storytelling from this immensely prolific team."
—*Kirkus Reviews*

For thirteen years—since he became one of several scientists chosen to raise apes bred by the pharmaceutical giant SAC—Dr. Jim Dutton, his young daughter Brett, and the bonobo ape Umber have been a family. For Umber is far more than a subject or pet. She types, reads, speaks sign language, favors psychedelic clothes, and even contemplates the nature of God.

Umber and the other SAC apes are too intelligent to be pure bonobos—they are "augmented" apes, more similar to early hominids than to anthropoids. When SAC abruptly demands Umber's immediate return, it becomes vital for Jim to discover why the corporation created this new species.

The quest for answers will take Jim and his family to Africa, to a SAC facility whose grounds also hide a covert genetics lab, a missing band of blue-eyed apes, crude buildings decorated with skulls, and, deep in the shadows, human corpses savagely hacked to pieces. . . .

Now the struggle to uncover SAC's secrets becomes a fight for survival. Suddenly Umber, Brett, and Jim find themselves hunted by beings who are fiercely territorial, brutally aggressive, brilliantly inventive, and far stronger than any human.

And like humans they can be utterly, and murderously, psychotic...

Available in mass market from Warner

ISBN: 0-446-61096-8